The Whistling Factory

by Jesse McManus

Uncivilized Books

Art Direction by Tom Kaczynski

Production by Jordan Shiveley

Uncivilized Books
2854 Columbus Ave
Minneapolis, MN 55407
USA
UNCIVILIZEDBOOKS.COM

First Edition.August 2018

10 9 8 7 6 5 4 3 2 1

ISBN 978-1-941250-29-7

DISTRIBUTED TO THE TRADE BY:
Consortium Book Sales & Distribution, LLC.
34 Thirteenth Avenue NE, Suite 101
Minneapolis, MN 55413-1007
cbsd.com, Orders: (800) 283-3572

Printed in China

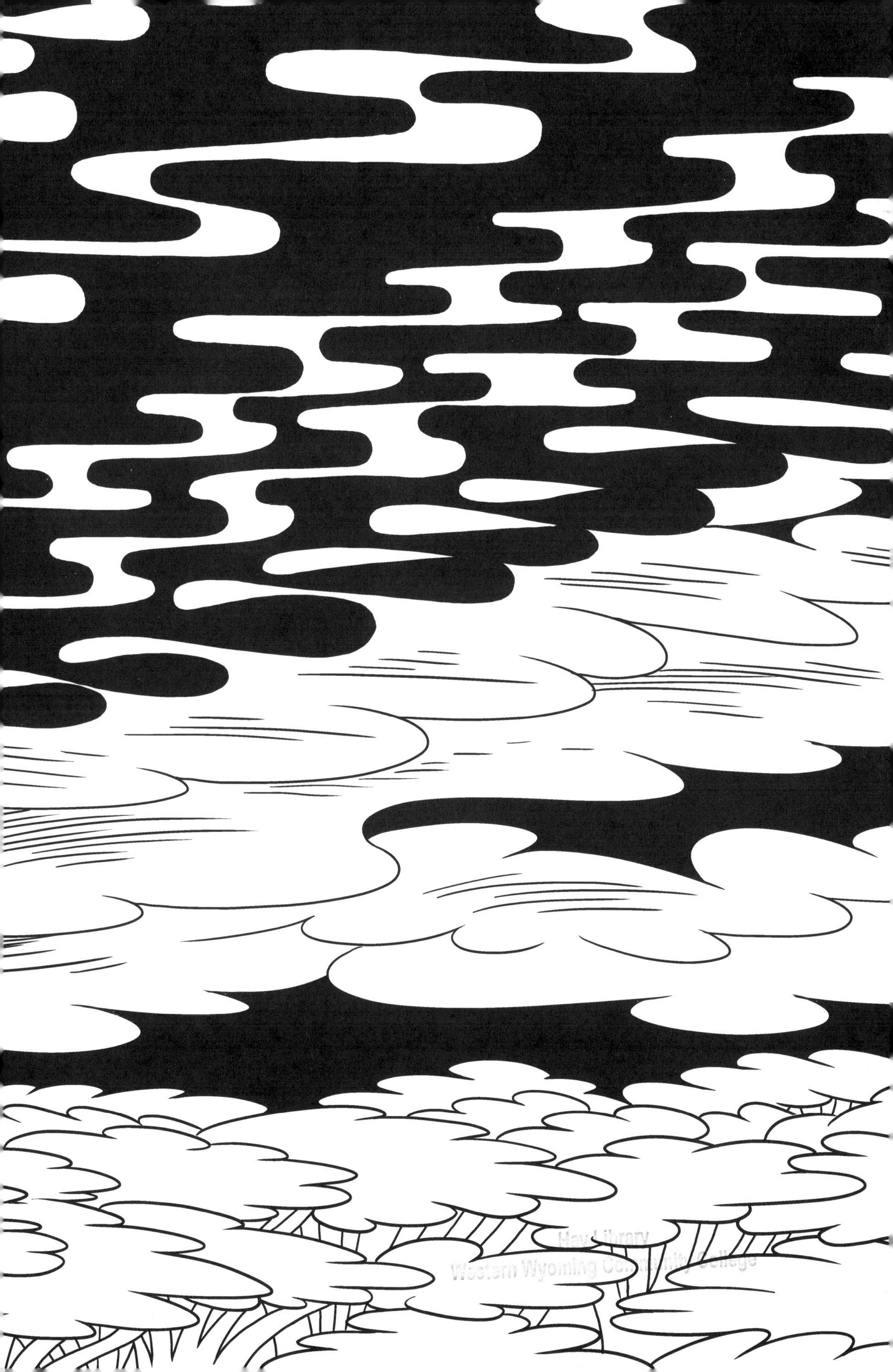

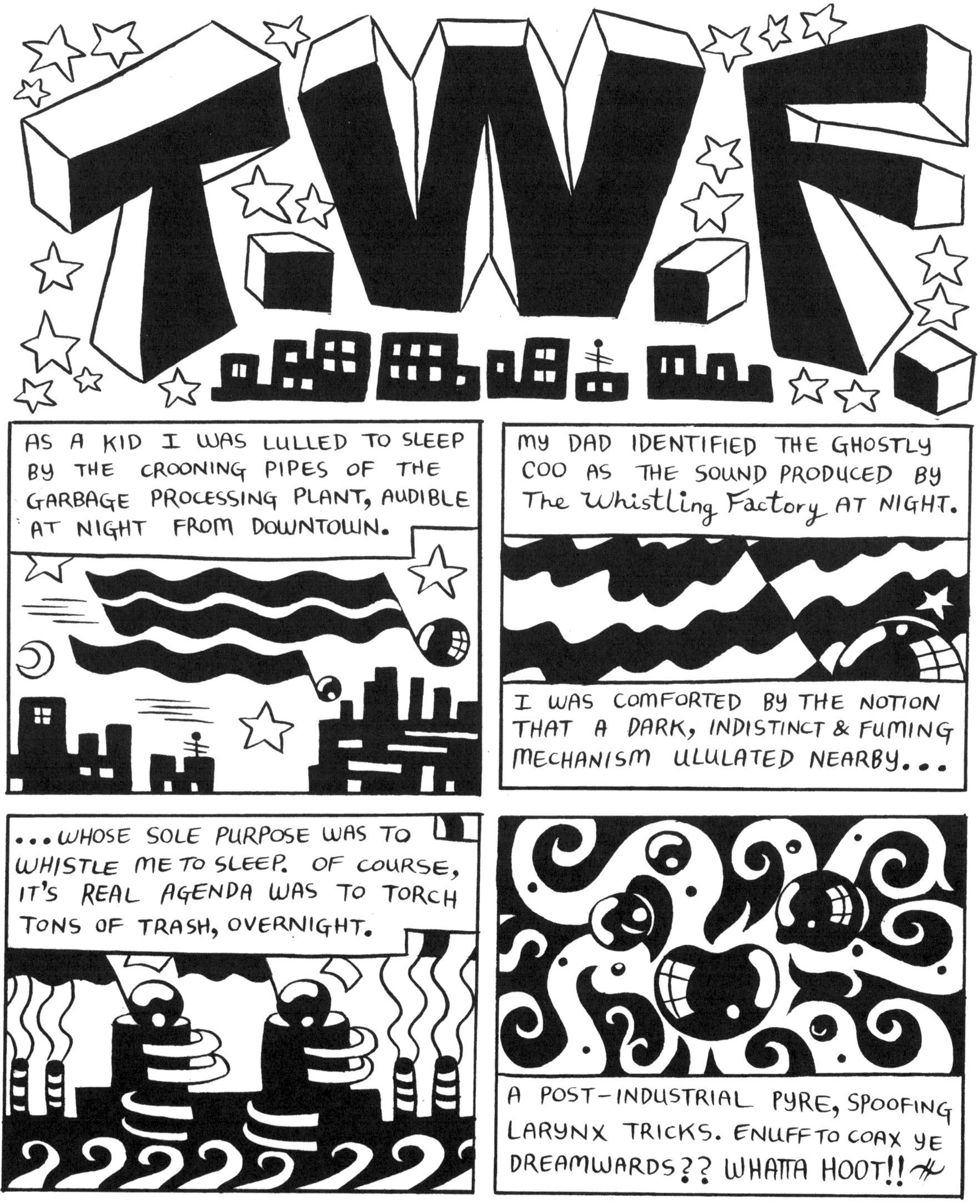
T.W.F.
AS A KID I WAS LULLED TO SLEEP BY THE CROONING PIPES OF THE GARBAGE PROCESSING PLANT, AUDIBLE AT NIGHT FROM DOWNTOWN.
MY DAD IDENTIFIED THE GHOSTLY COO AS THE SOUND PRODUCED BY The Whistling Factory AT NIGHT.
I WAS COMFORTED BY THE NOTION THAT A DARK, INDISTINCT & FUMING MECHANISM ULULATED NEARBY...
...WHOSE SOLE PURPOSE WAS TO WHISTLE ME TO SLEEP. OF COURSE, IT'S REAL AGENDA WAS TO TORCH TONS OF TRASH, OVERNIGHT.
A POST-INDUSTRIAL PYRE, SPOOFING LARYNX TRICKS. ENUFF TO COAX YE DREAMWARDS?? WHATTA HOOT!!

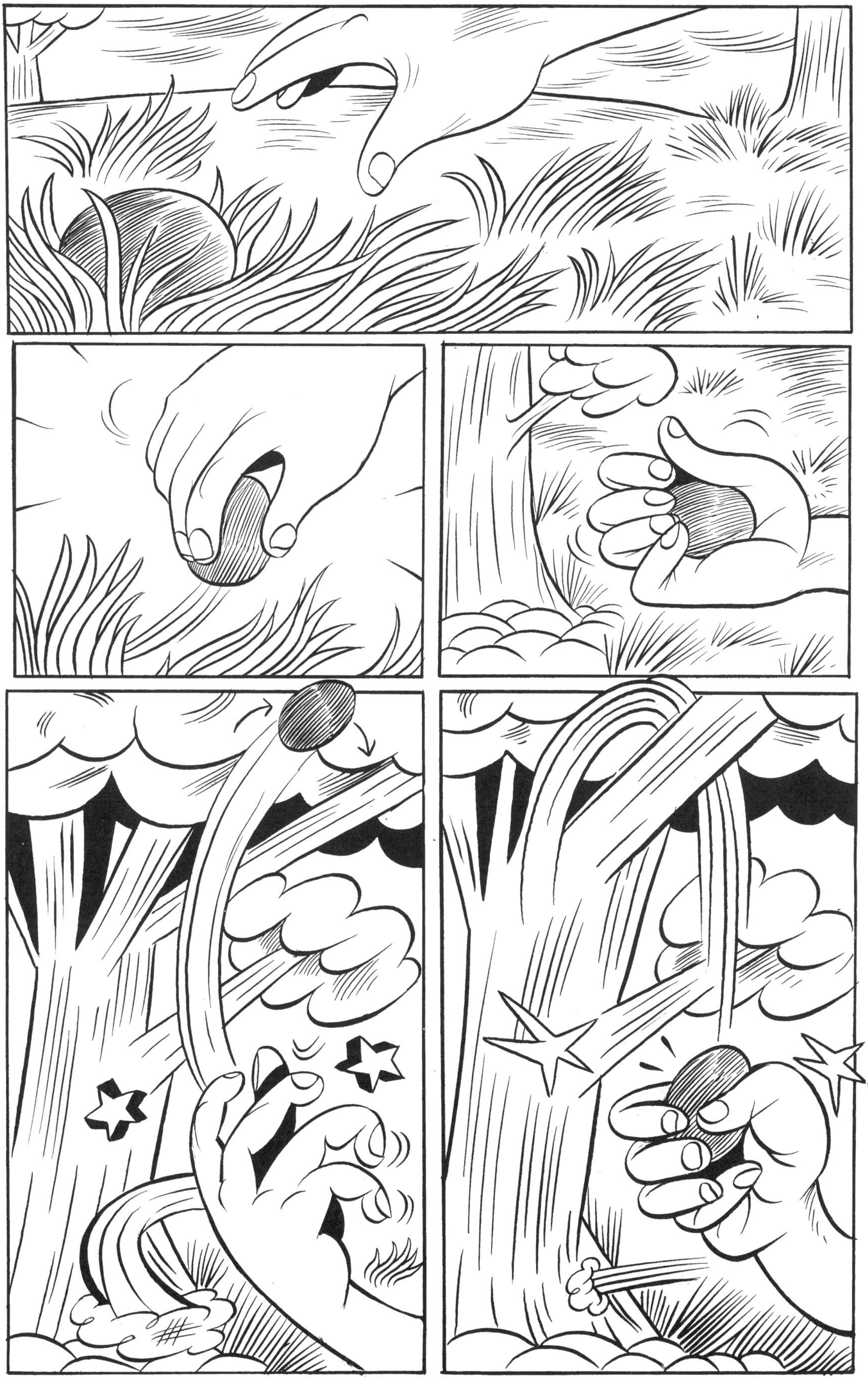

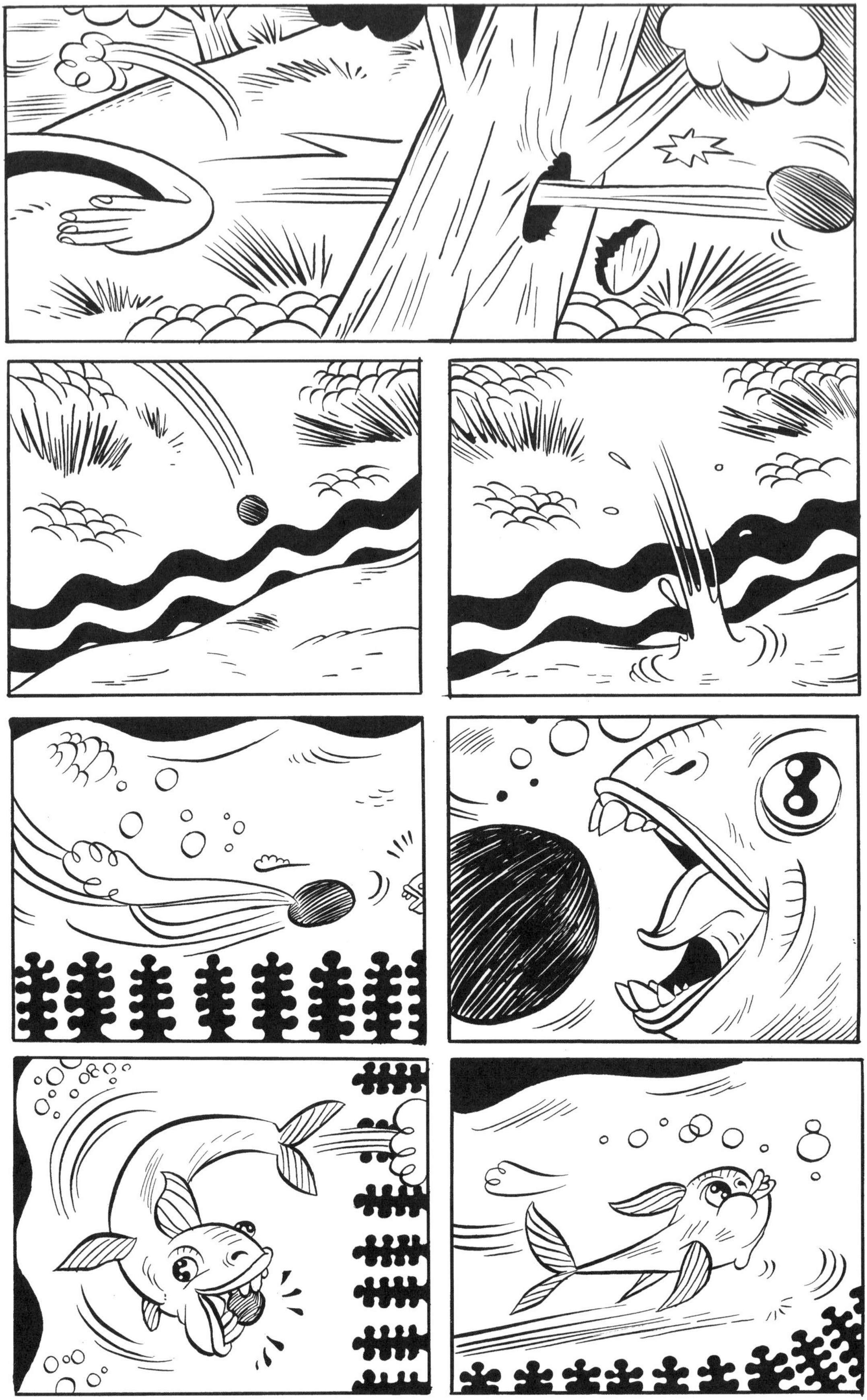

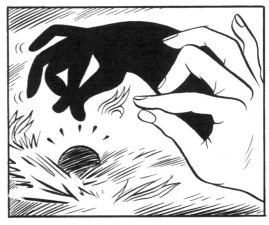

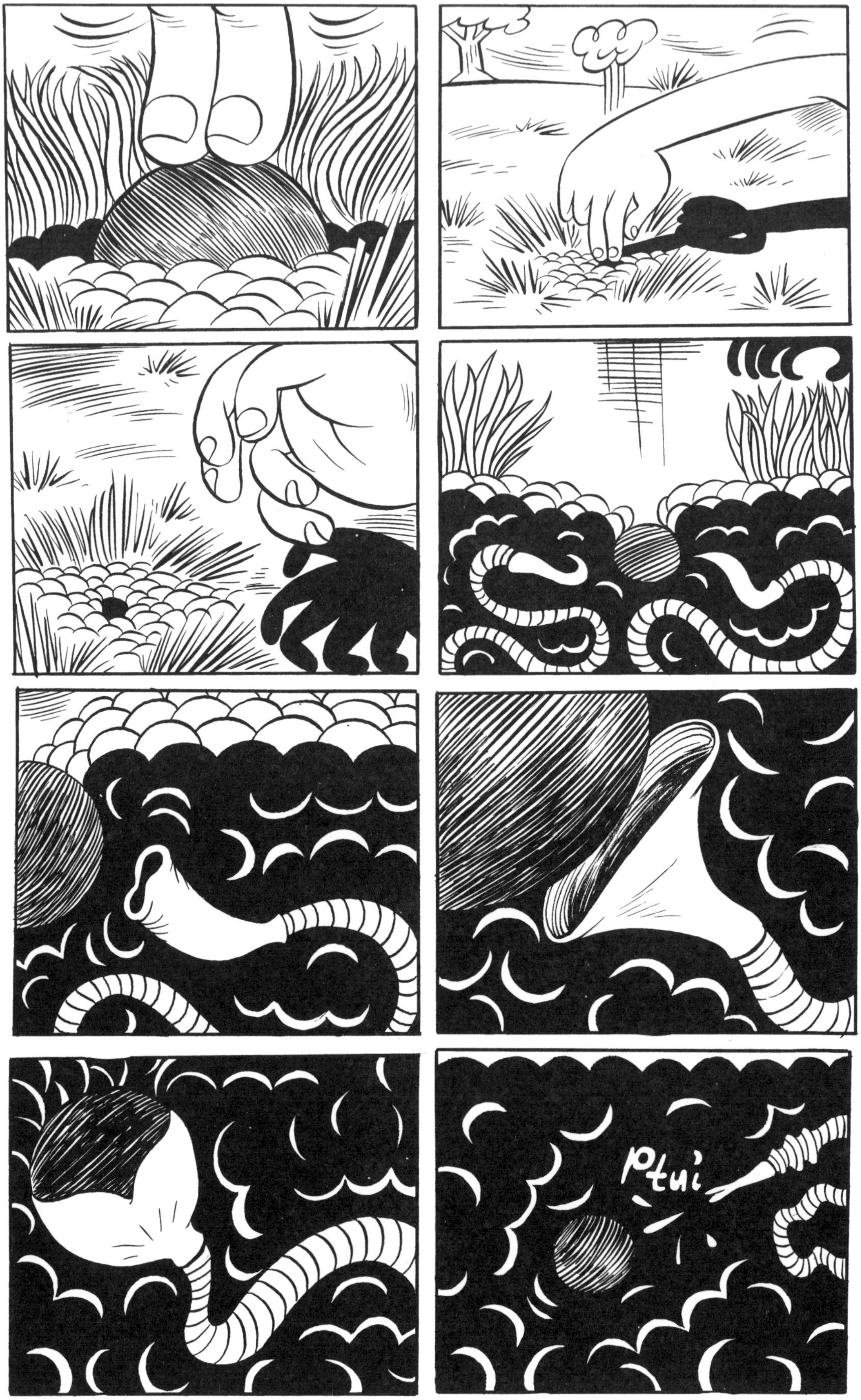
ptui

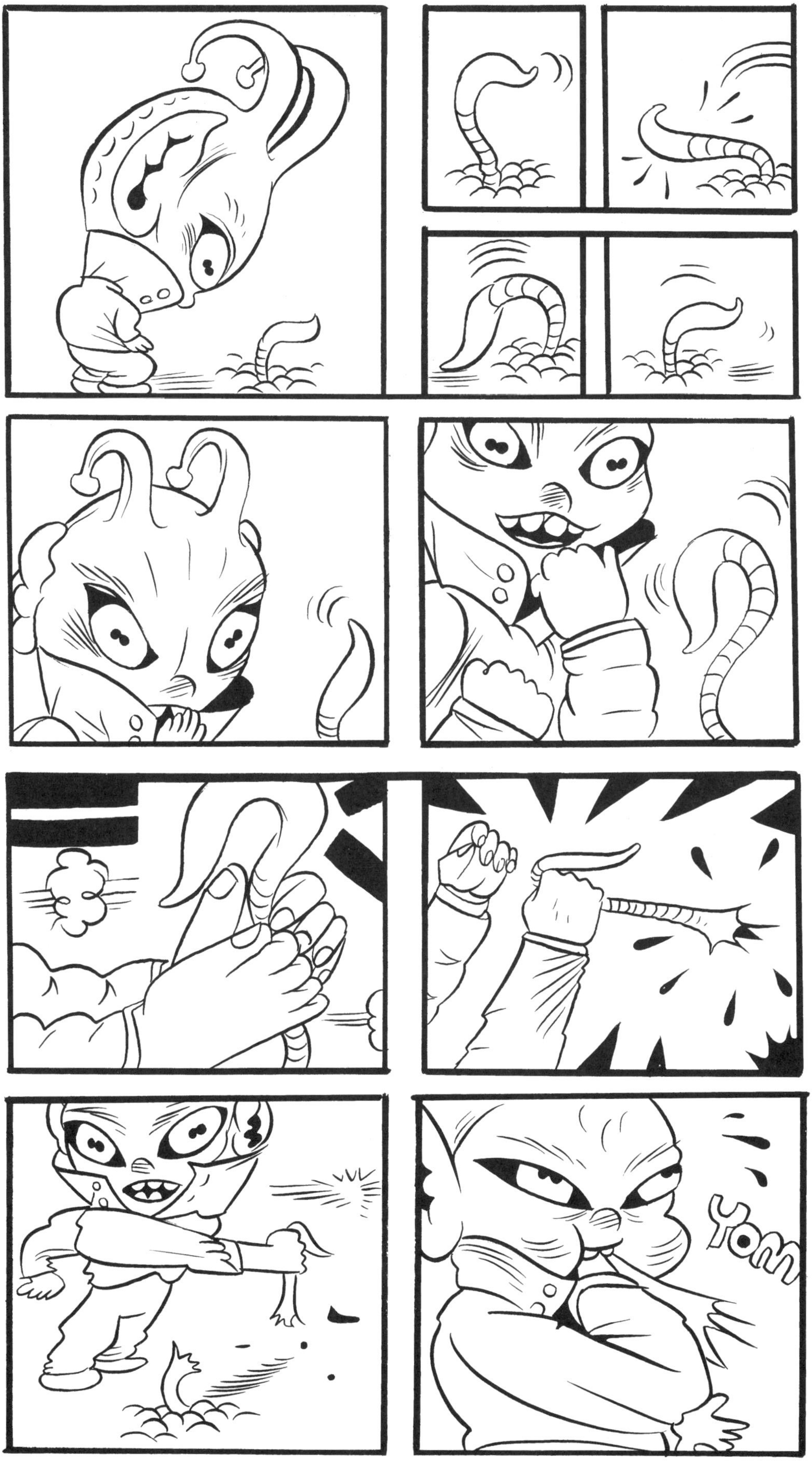
YOM

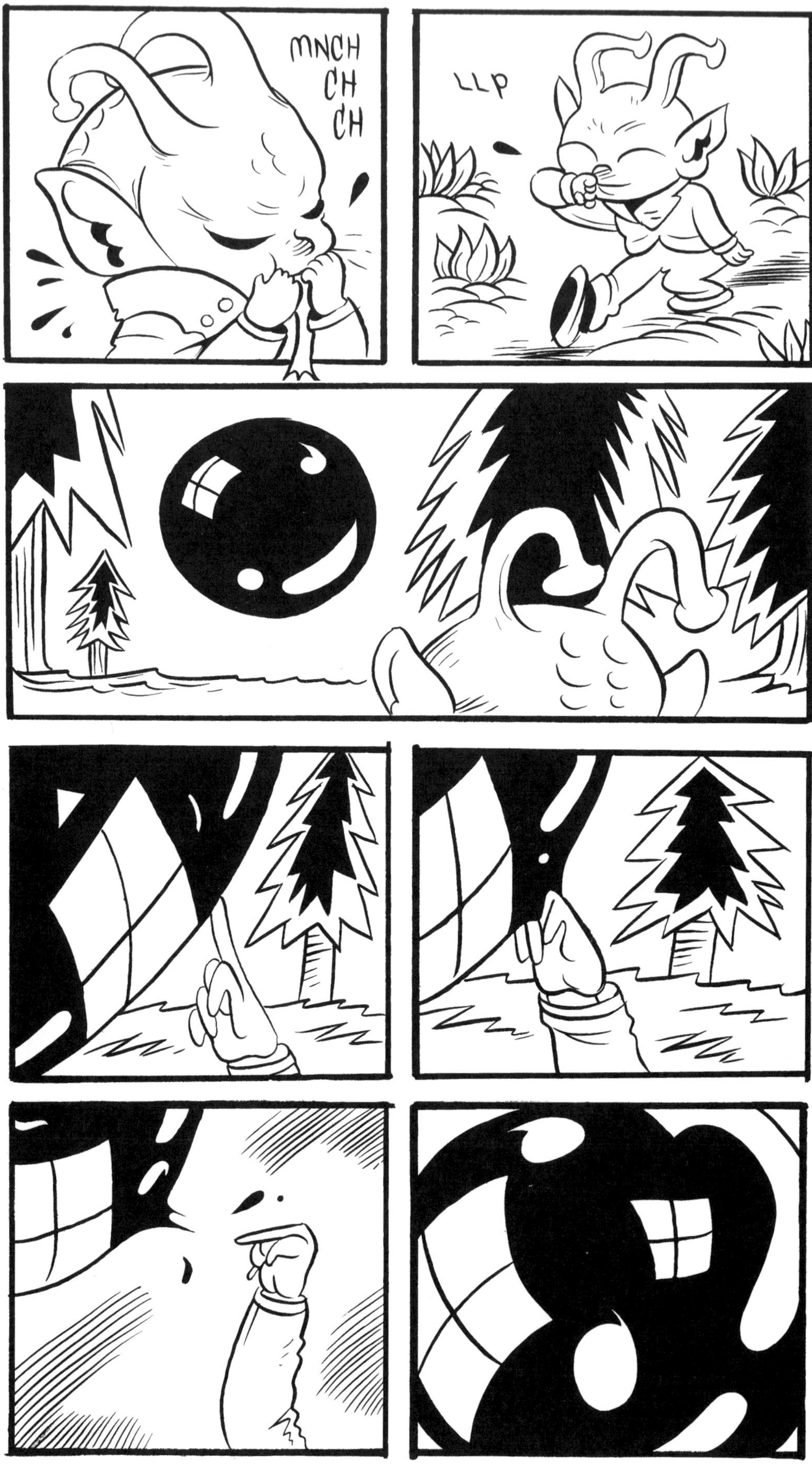
MNCH
CH
CH
LLP

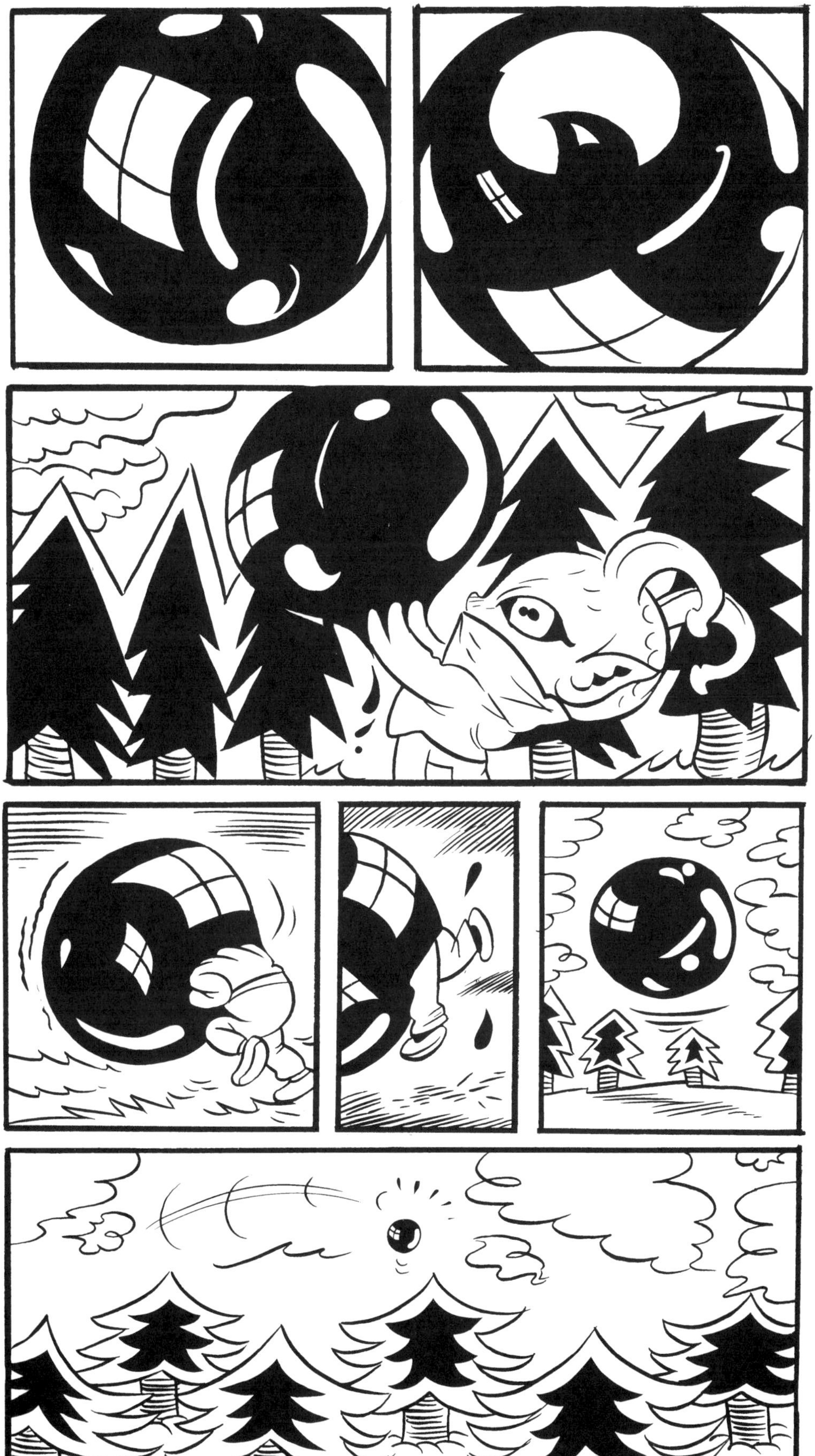

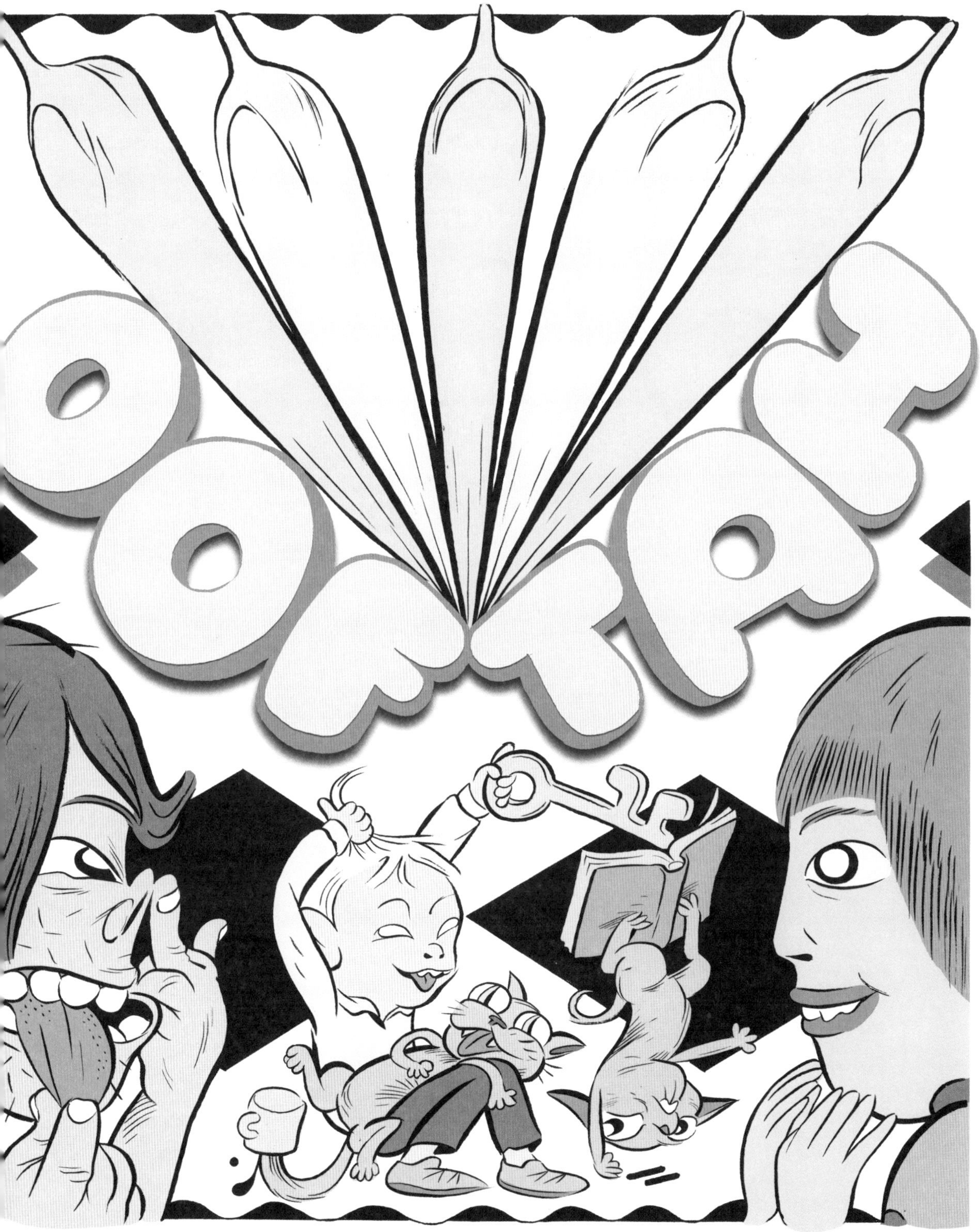

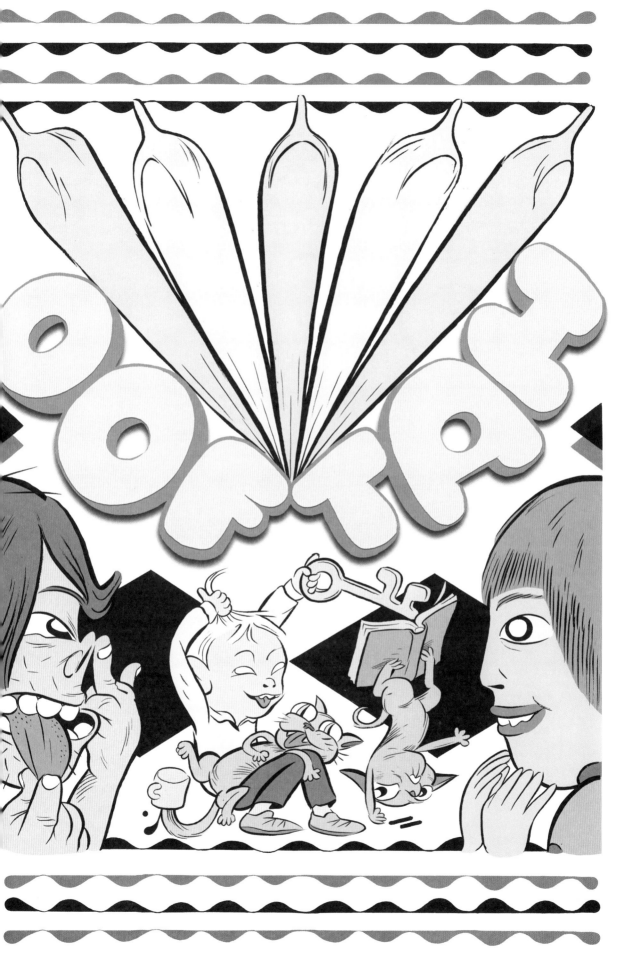

IN THE INTEREST OF FULL PURGING, OUT-&-OUT DISCLOSURE, LEAVING NO BRANCH UN-CLIPPED, NO LIPS UN-PURSED, NO VALIANT ATTEMPT AT SALIENCE LEFT SAD & SQUIRMING IN THE REMOTE PROMETHEAN GUTTER FROM WHENCE IT FIRST BURBLED LET'S HAVE US A GOOD LIST, OF THE FAIR & THE PROUD, THE WEAK CHILD PARTICIPANTS.

THE

Dramatis Personae:

Spooner

PENCIL-NECKED, PALE, CLEARLY ILL-EQUIPPED FOR DIALOGUE WITH ANY WORLD BUT HIS OWN (THAT BEING ENTIRELY INDOORS) THE BOY IS NOT WITHOUT A CALM GRACE. INQUISITIVE & VAGUELY SWEET. WILL ALLOW YOU INTO HIS ROOM BUT WILL FIDGET AS YOU GAZE UPON HIS UNDECORATED WALLS & UGLY LIBRARY.

eel

THIS VIXEN IS BEST REACHED BY TIN-CAN & STRING. THAT OR A LOUD YELP. SHE CULTIVATES THE 'SOCKS & SANDALS' IDEAL OF COMFORT & TAKES A RESPECTABLE JOY IN THE ANIMAL-FOLK. TOO BAD SHE'S A JERK. ACTUALLY SHE'S WAY COOL.

Trowser

WE ALL LIKE TO PEE ON THINGS. DIRT, SNOW, GLASS. LET'S JUST ADMIT IT. THERE'S NO DARKNESS HERE. JUST PURE, UNMITIGATED, SPITTLE & JOY, PUPPY-DOG.

monkey

FETID FELINE. WHO KNOWS WHY THEY ALL WANT TO TOUCH HER BUTT. BUT DON'T YOU? A GENERALLY CRUEL BUT EFFECTIVE, SWIFT SORT OF CAT-THING.

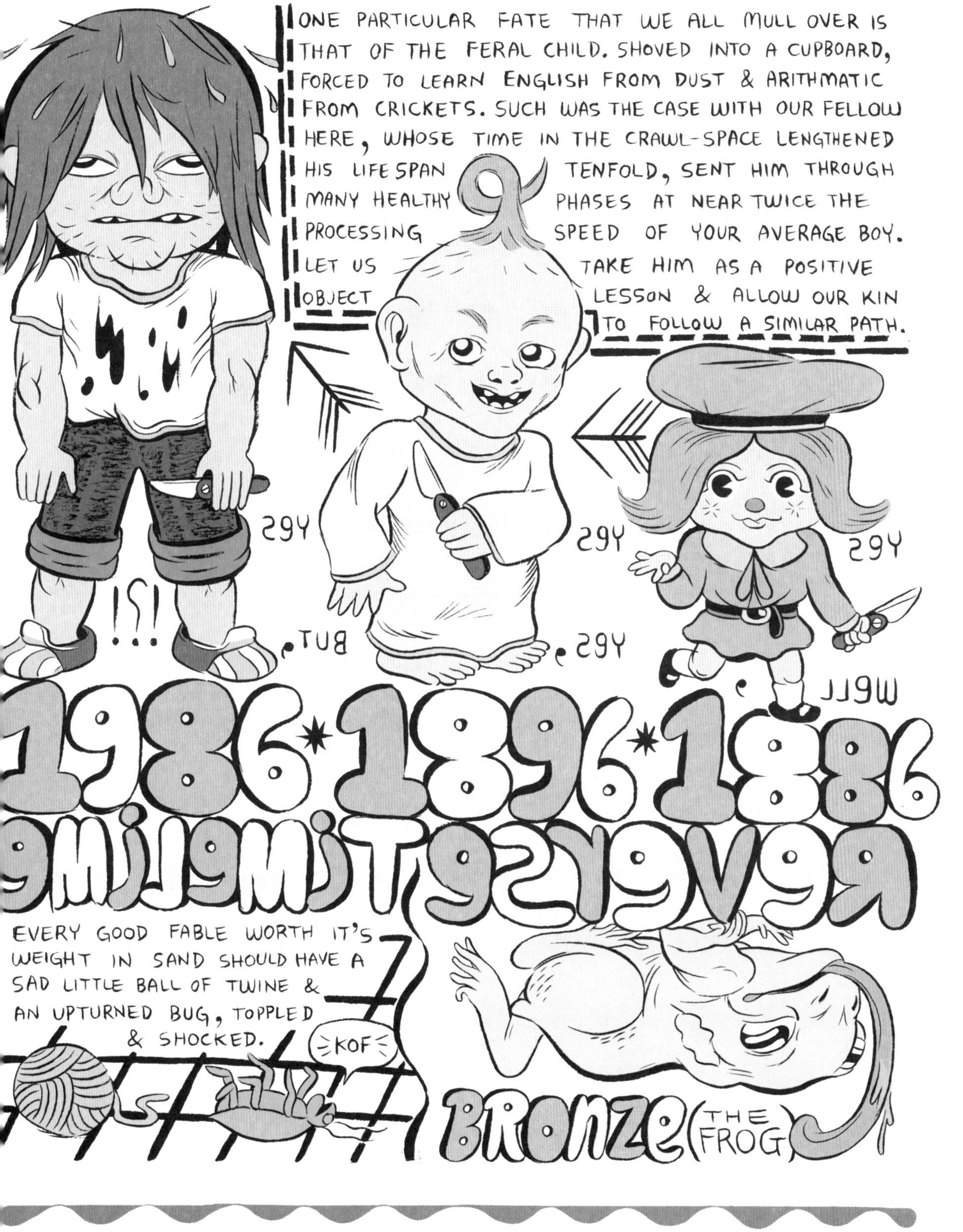

ONE PARTICULAR FATE THAT WE ALL MULL OVER IS THAT OF THE FERAL CHILD. SHOVED INTO A CUPBOARD, FORCED TO LEARN ENGLISH FROM DUST & ARITHMATIC FROM CRICKETS. SUCH WAS THE CASE WITH OUR FELLOW HERE, WHOSE TIME IN THE CRAWL-SPACE LENGTHENED HIS LIFESPAN TENFOLD, SENT HIM THROUGH MANY HEALTHY PHASES AT NEAR TWICE THE PROCESSING SPEED OF YOUR AVERAGE BOY. LET US TAKE HIM AS A POSITIVE OBJECT LESSON & ALLOW OUR KIN TO FOLLOW A SIMILAR PATH.
YES
YES
YES
!?!
BUT,
YES,
WELL
1986*1896*1886
REVERSE TIMELINE
EVERY GOOD FABLE WORTH IT'S WEIGHT IN SAND SHOULD HAVE A SAD LITTLE BALL OF TWINE & AN UPTURNED BUG, TOPPLED & SHOCKED.
KOF
BRONZE (THE FROG)

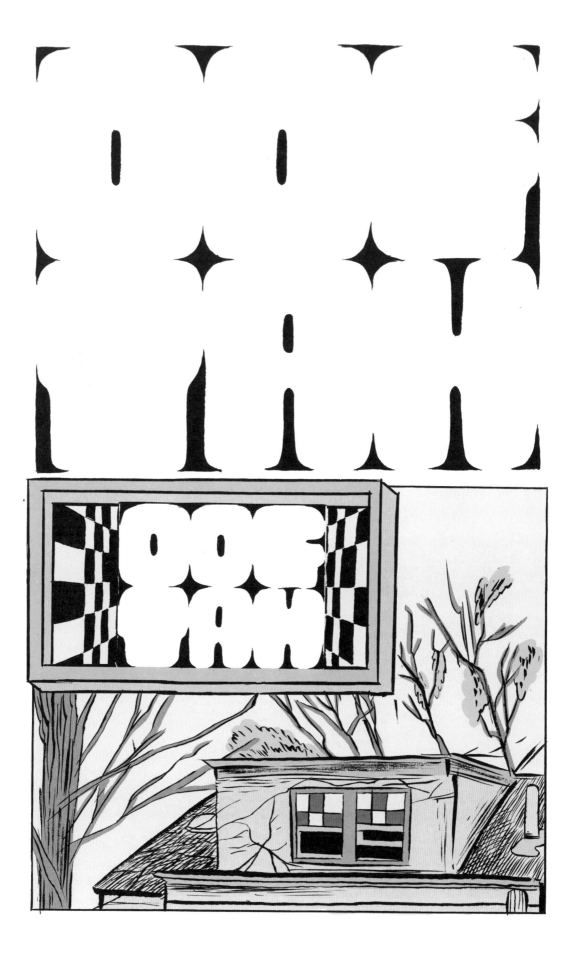

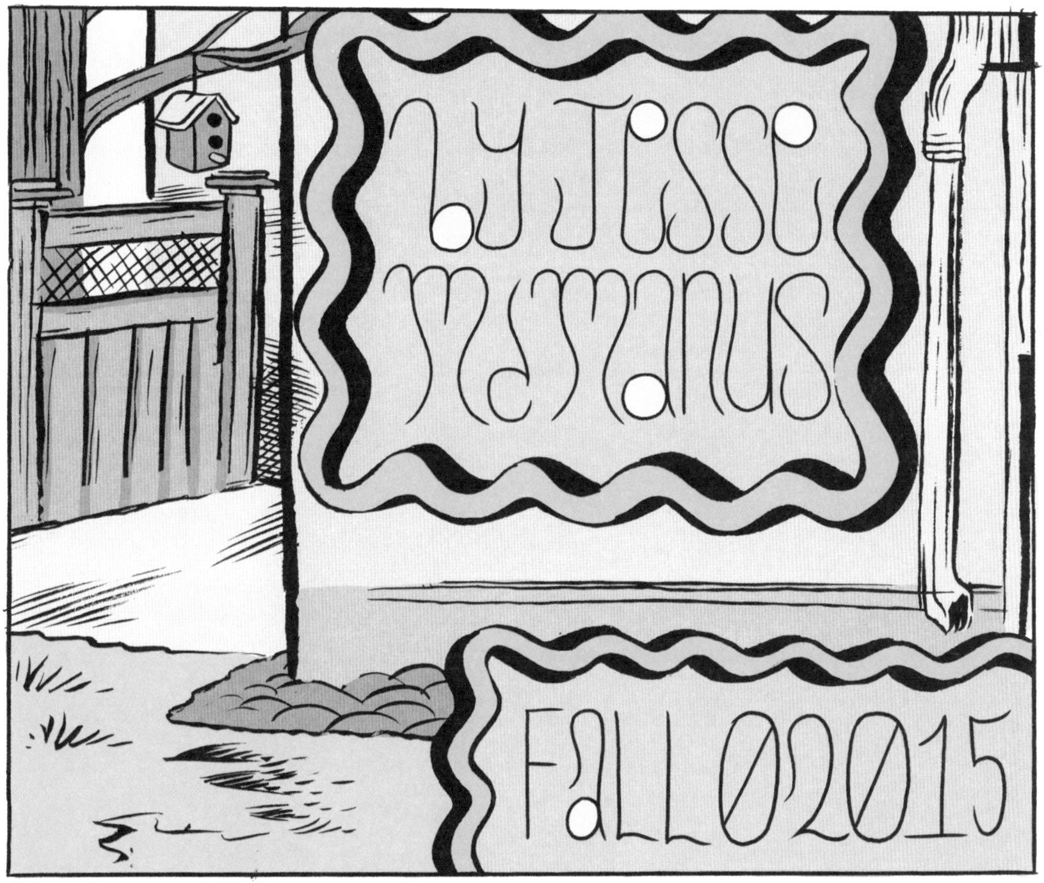
by Jesse McManus
Fall 2015

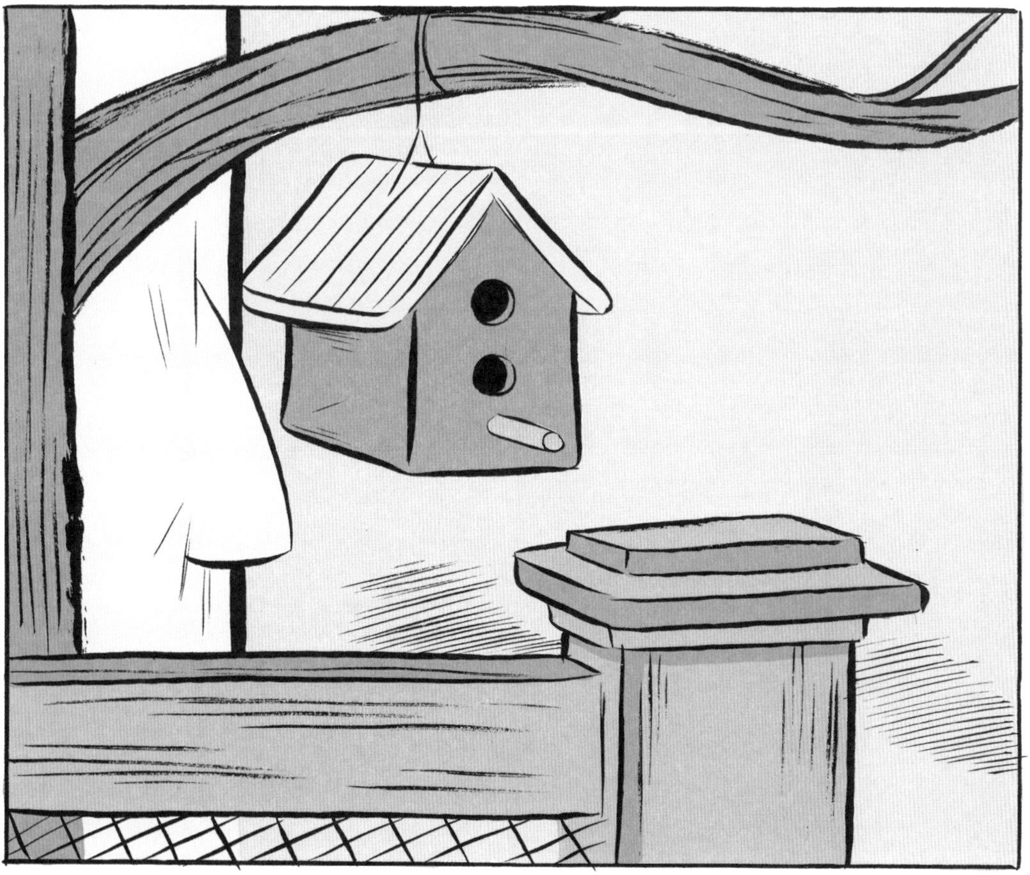

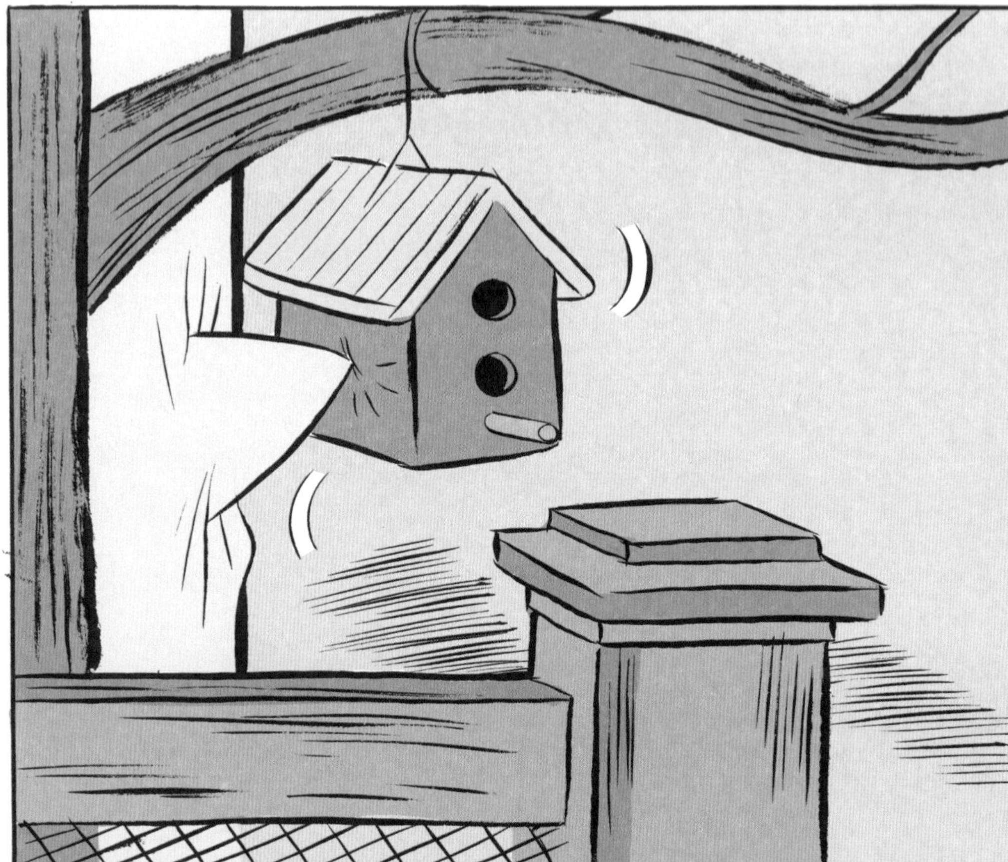

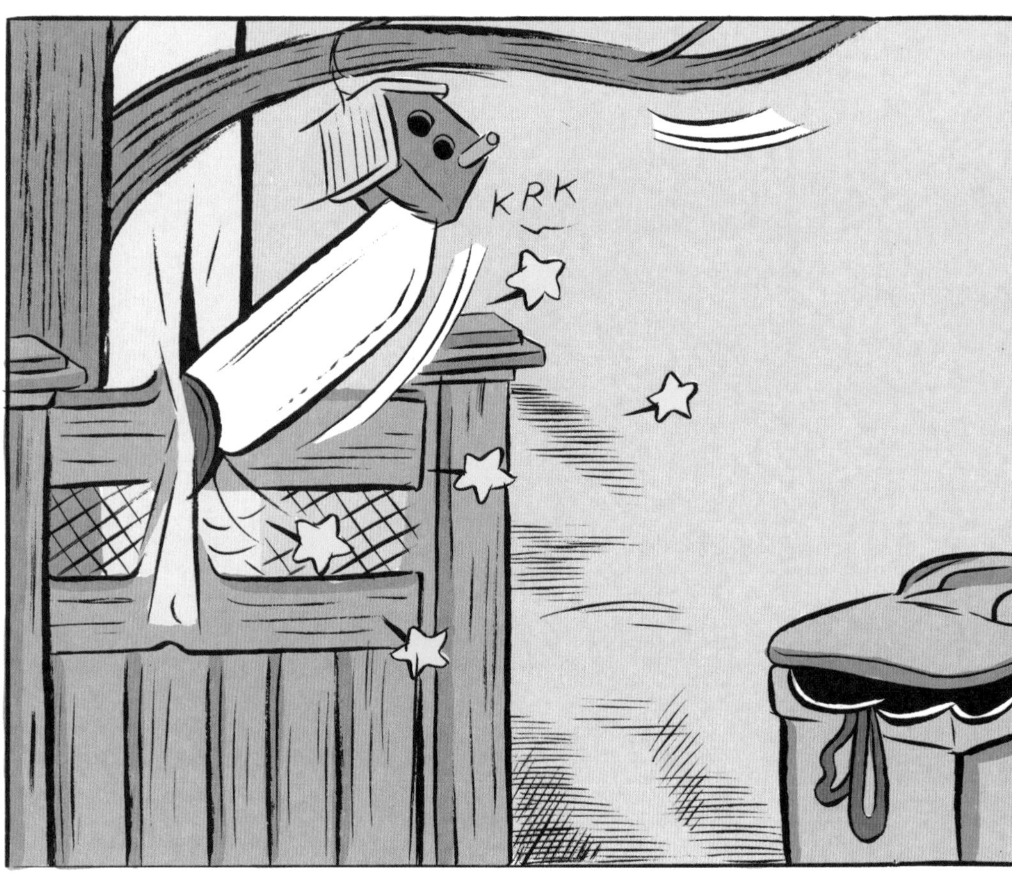
KRK

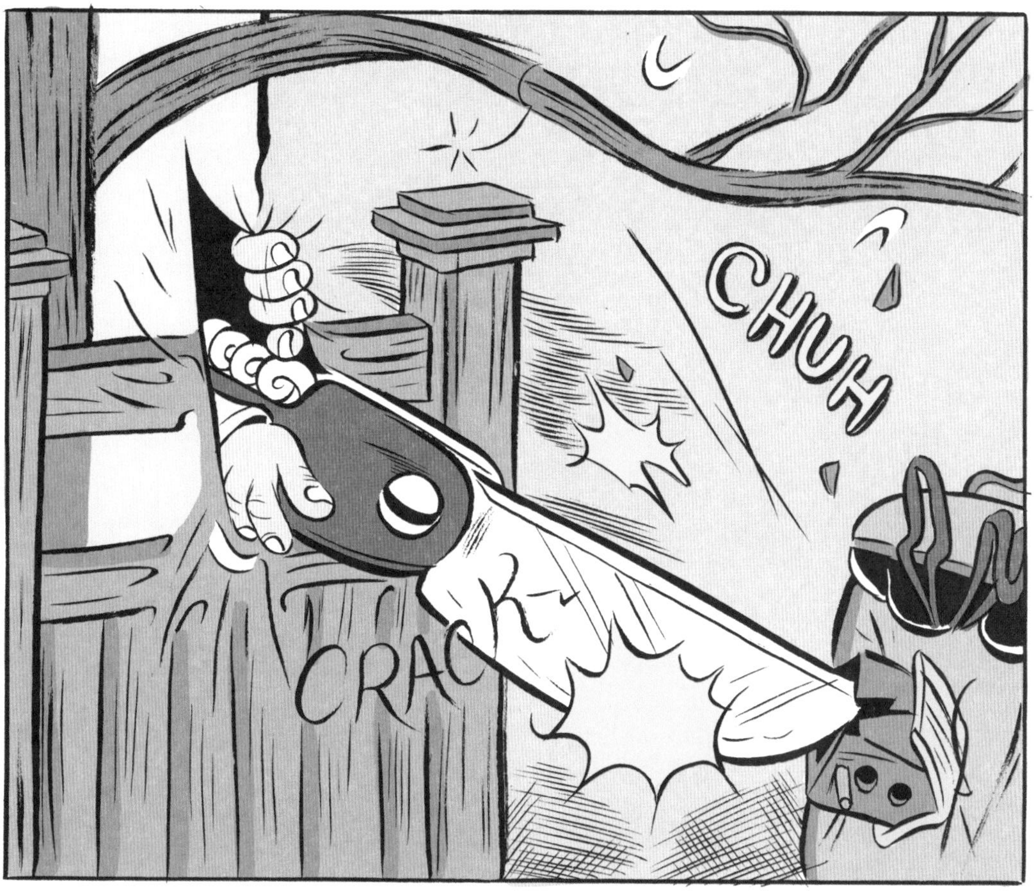
CHUH
CRACK

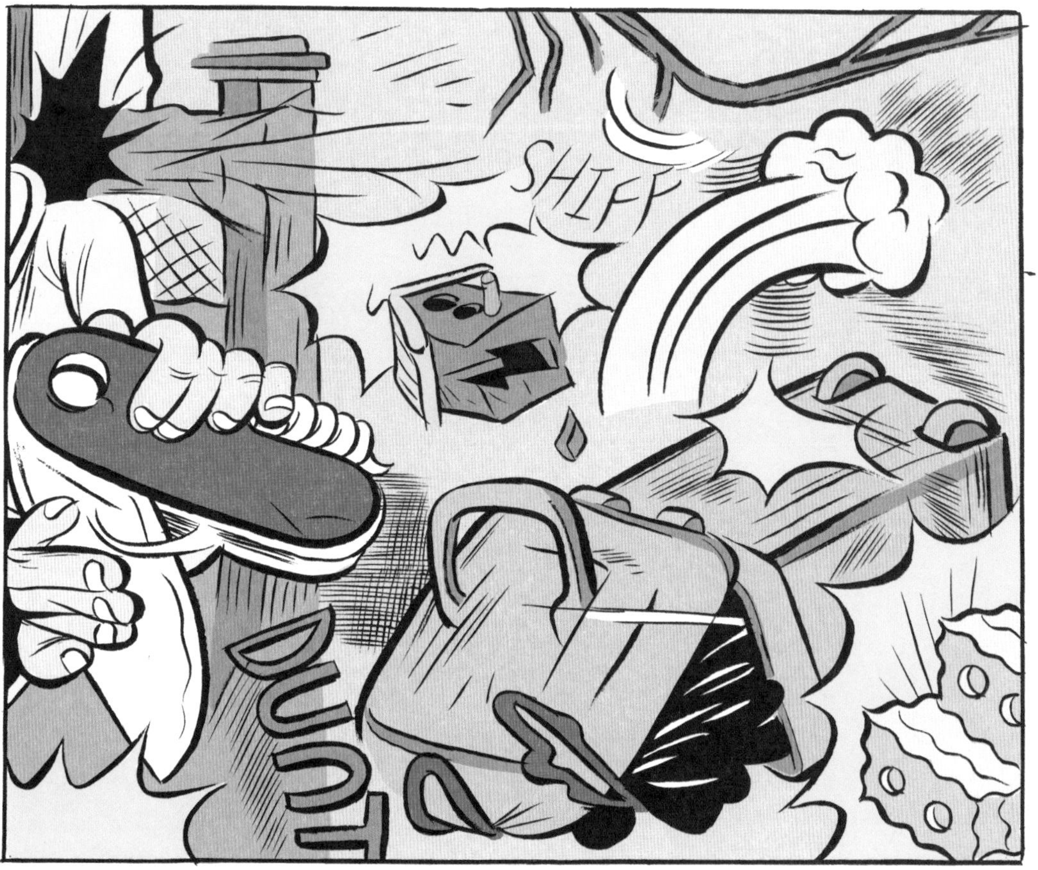
SHIFF
DUNT

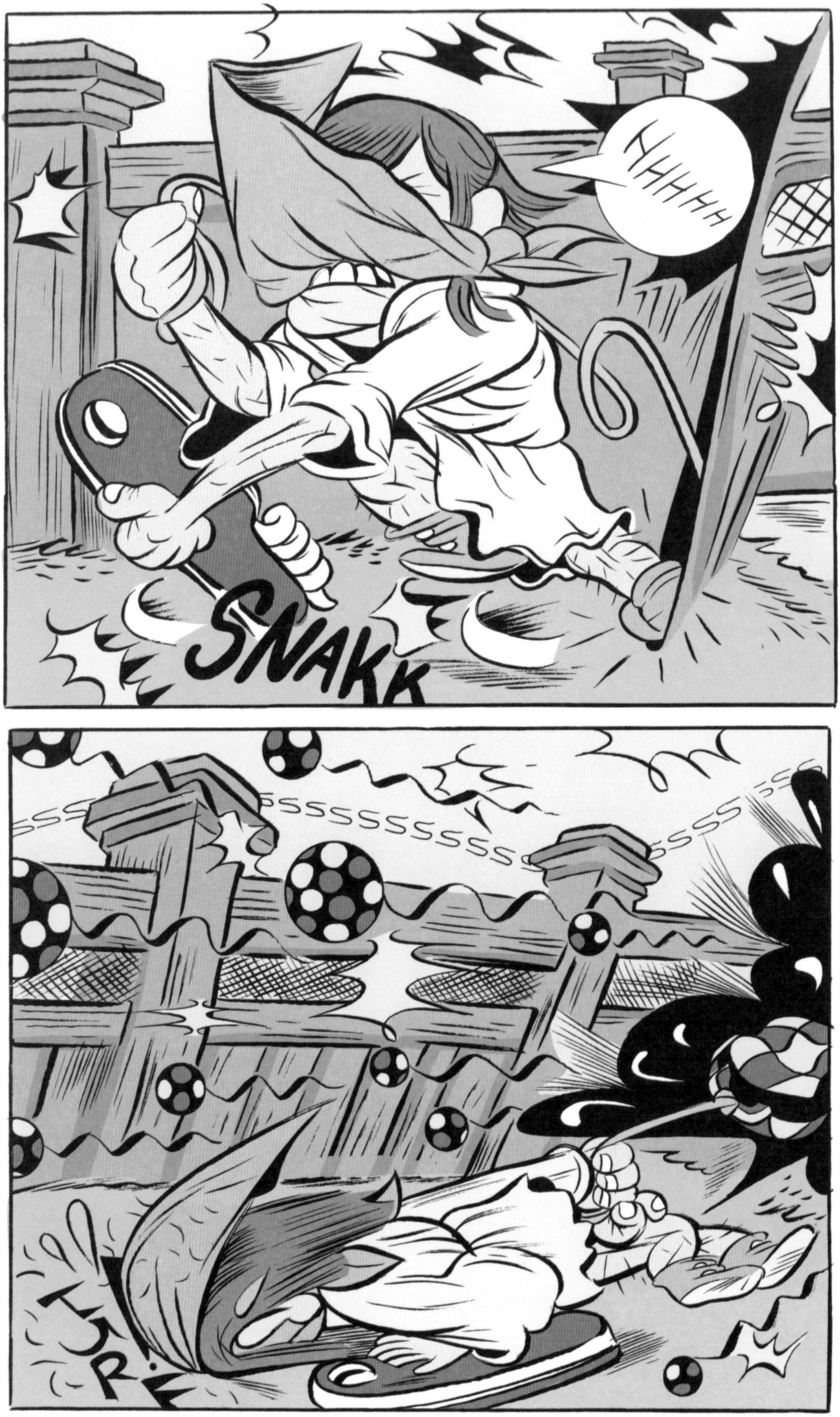
NHHHHH
SNAKK

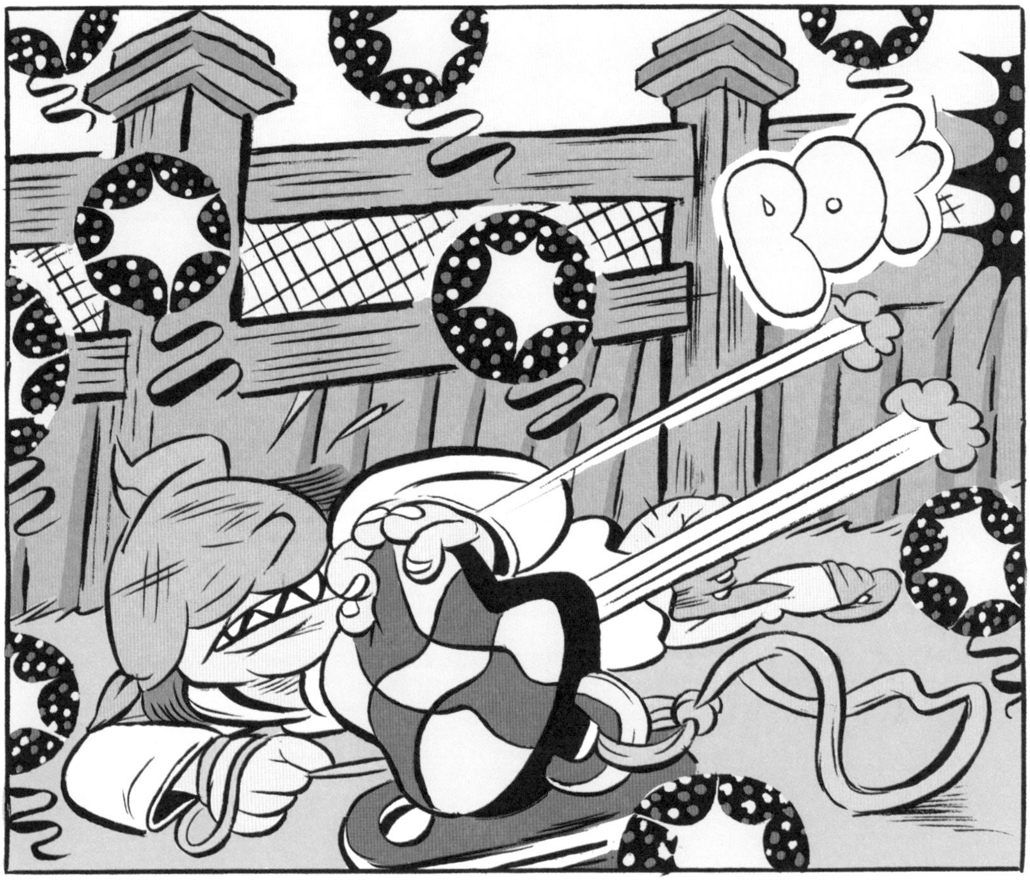
POP

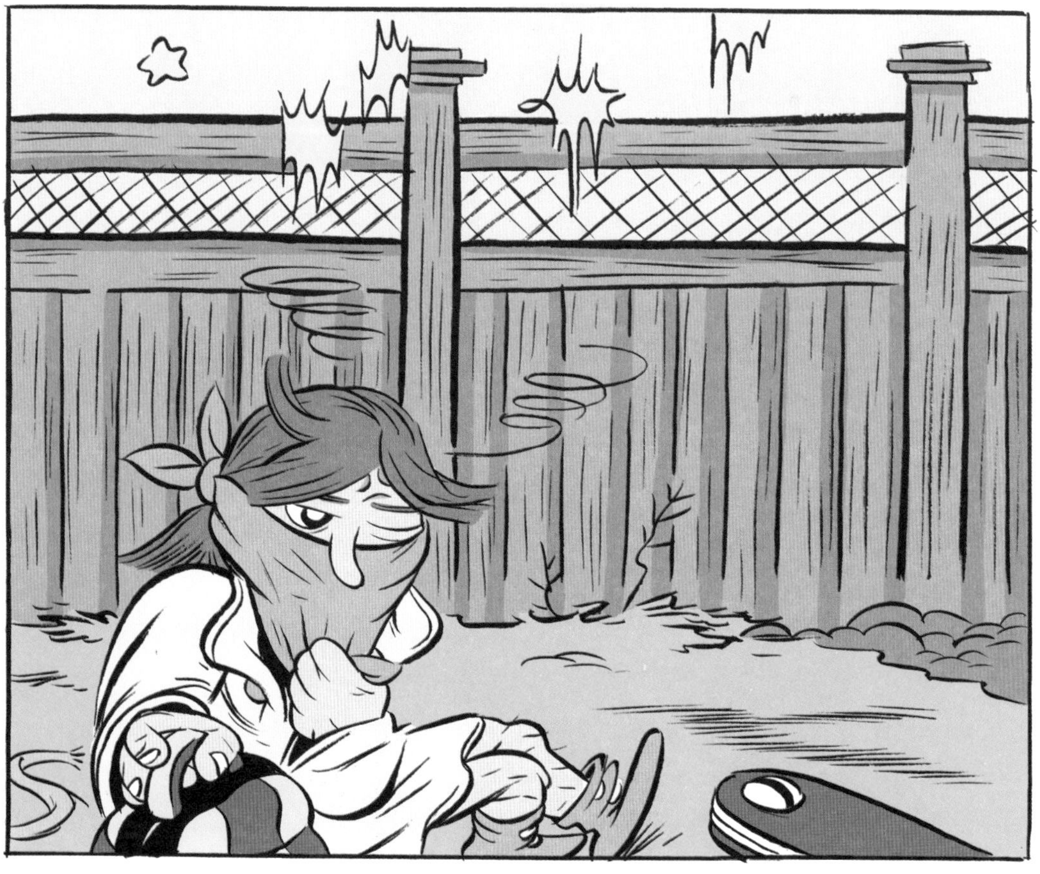

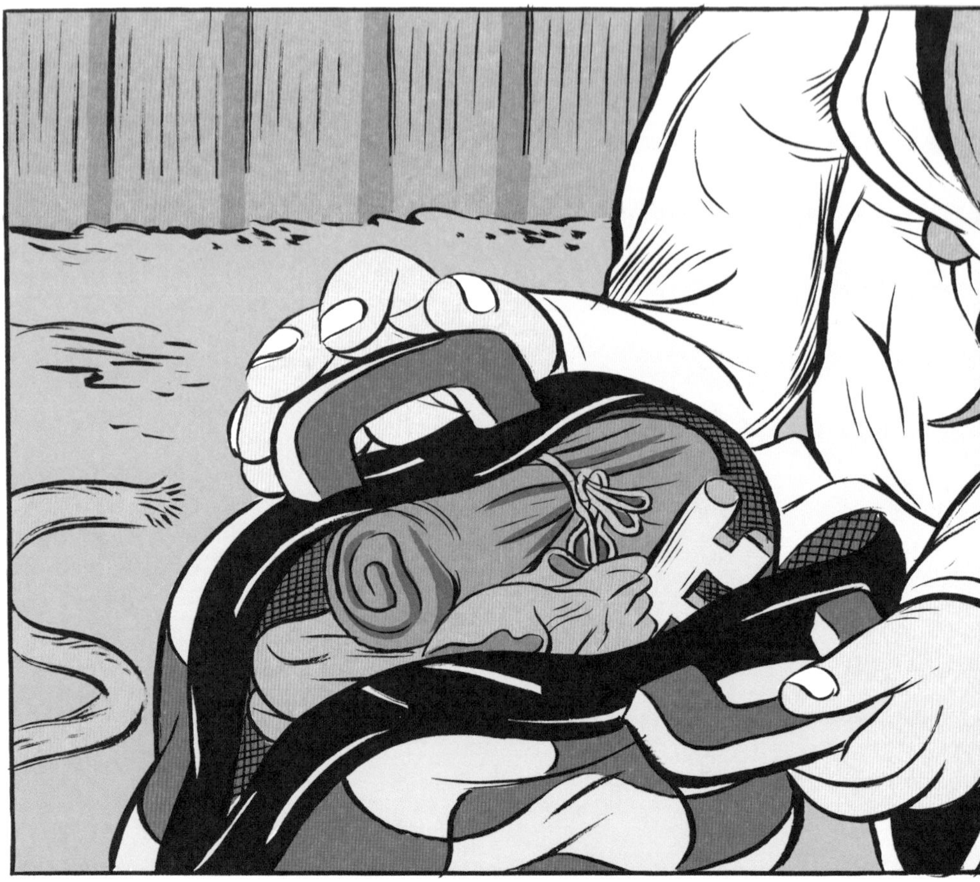

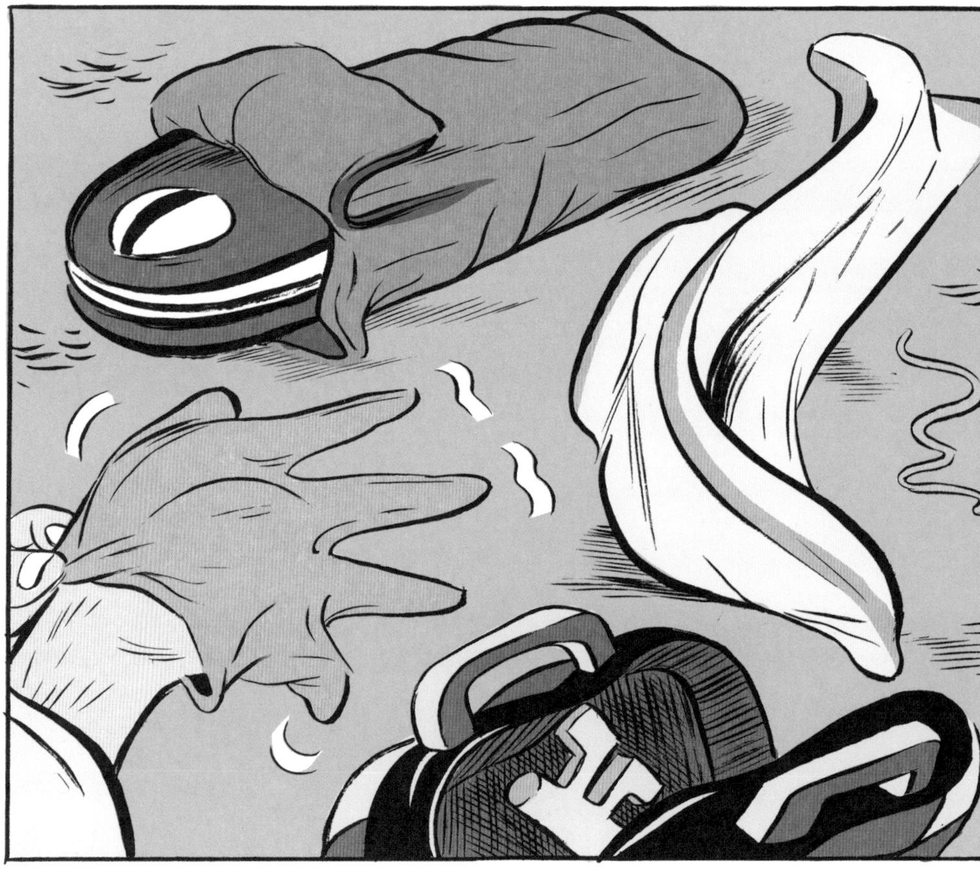

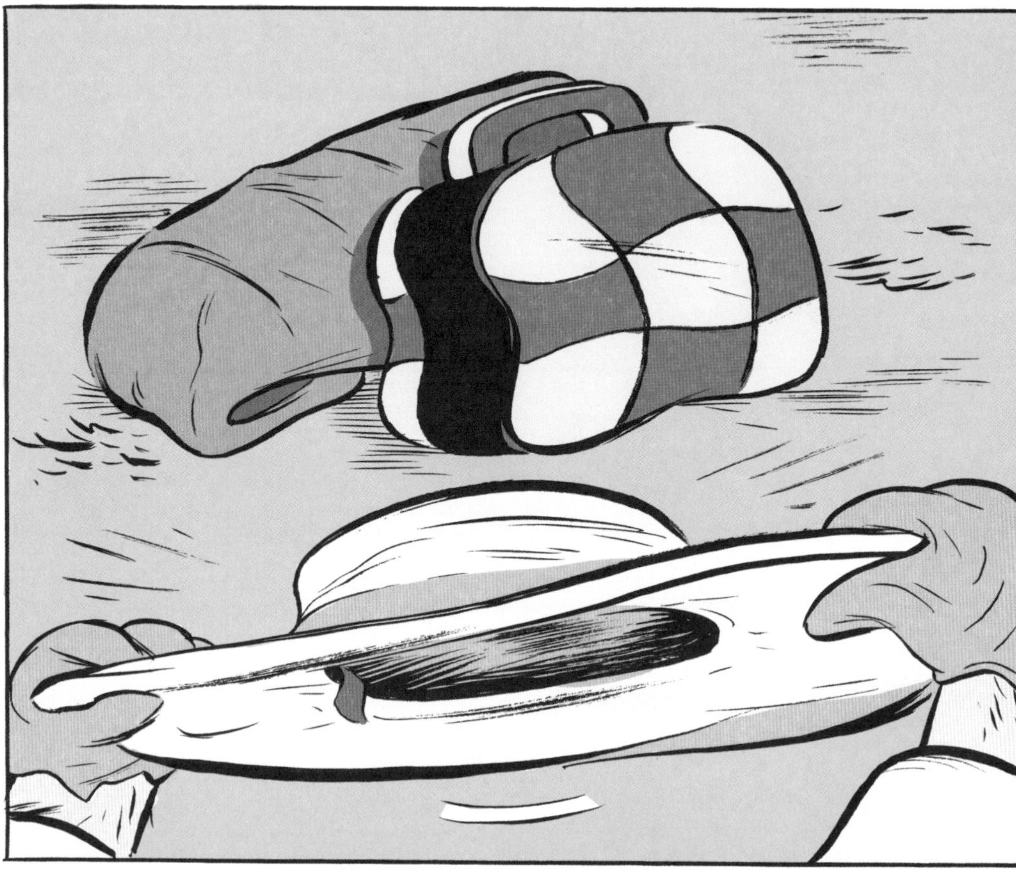
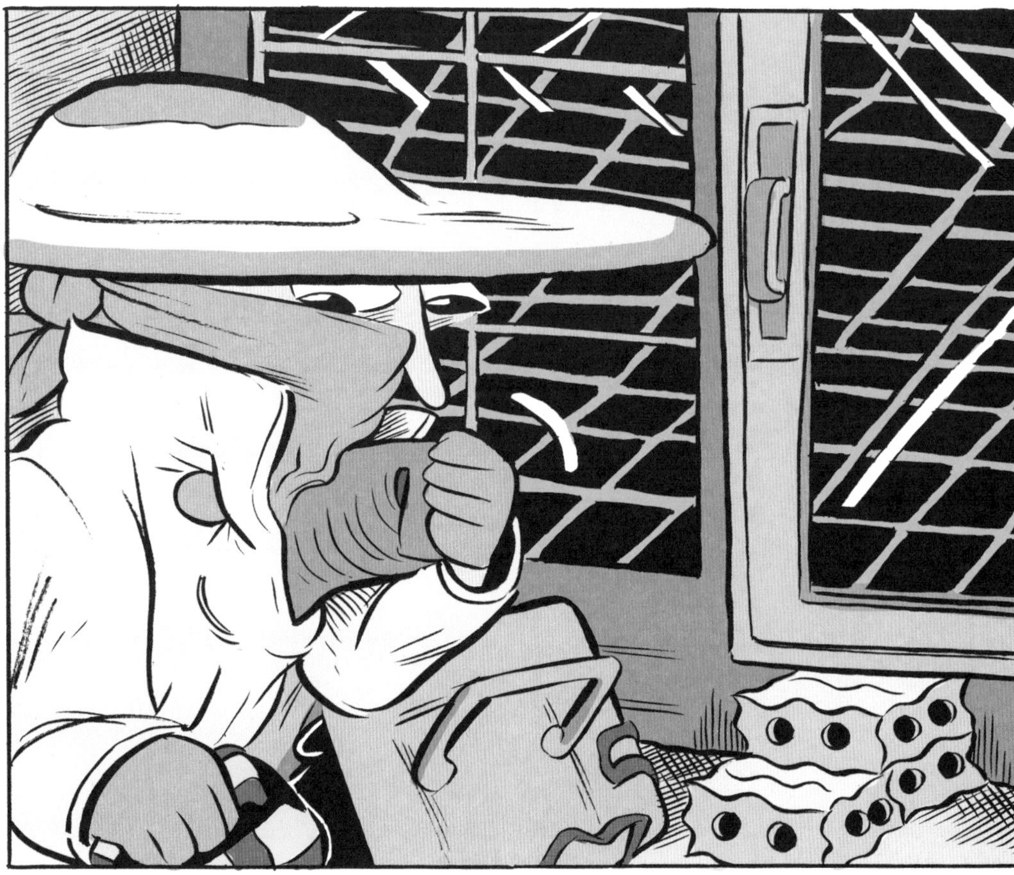

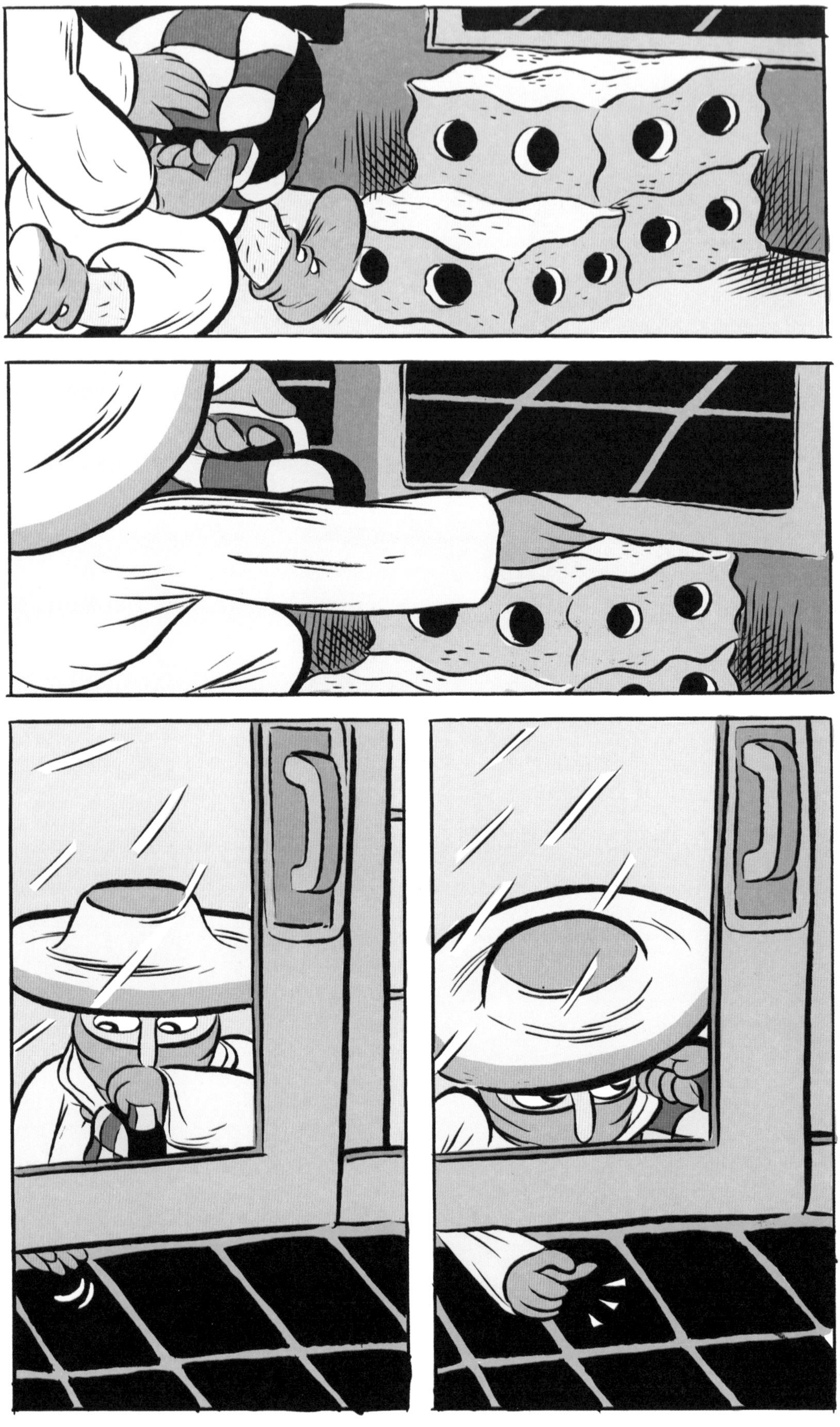

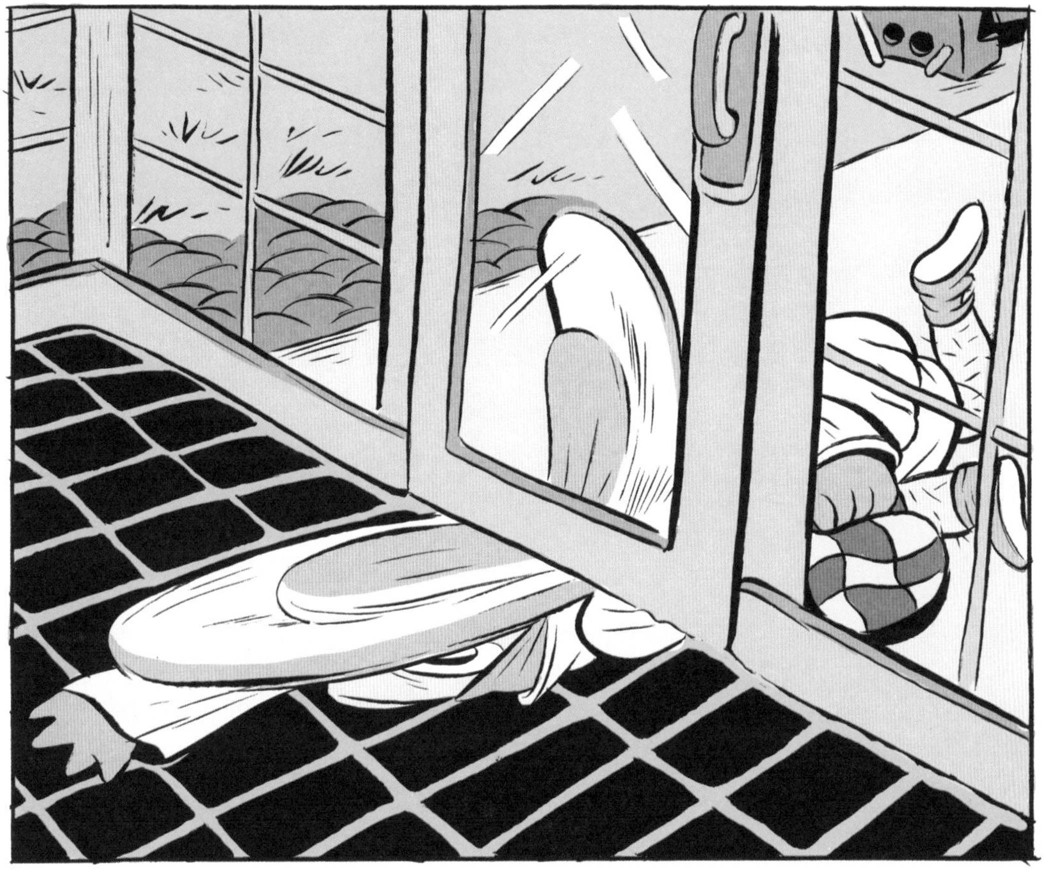
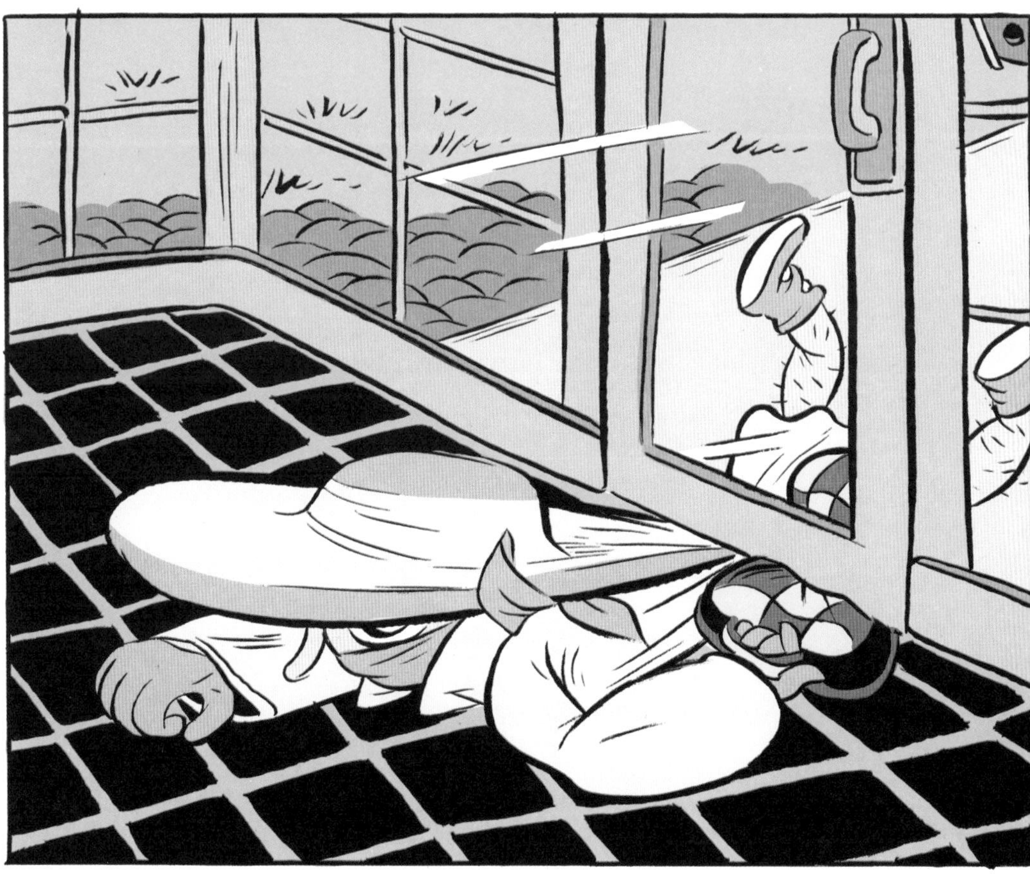

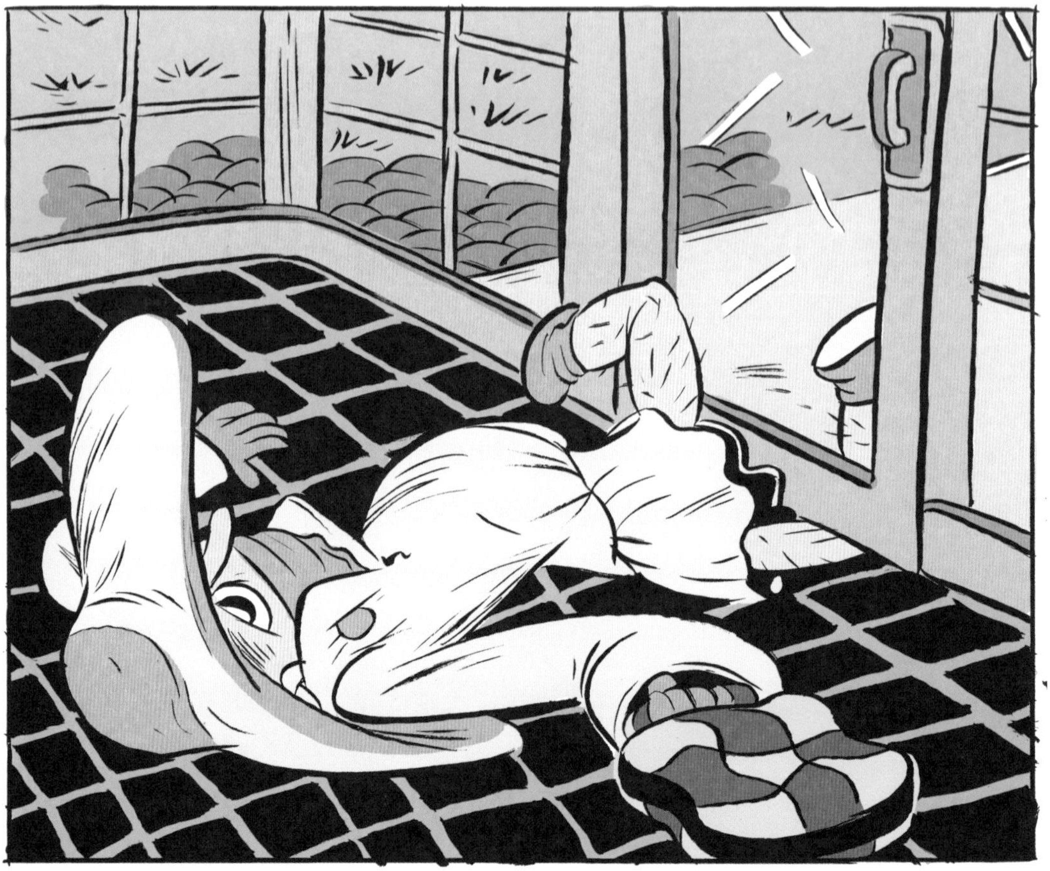
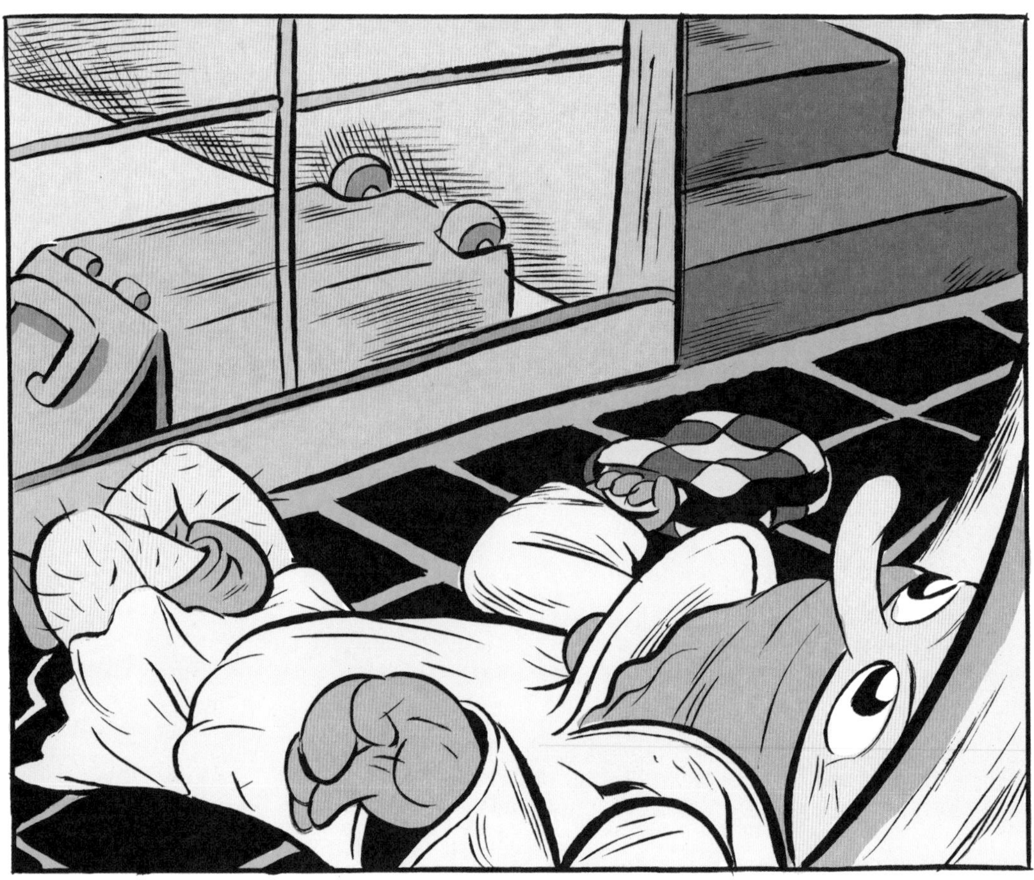

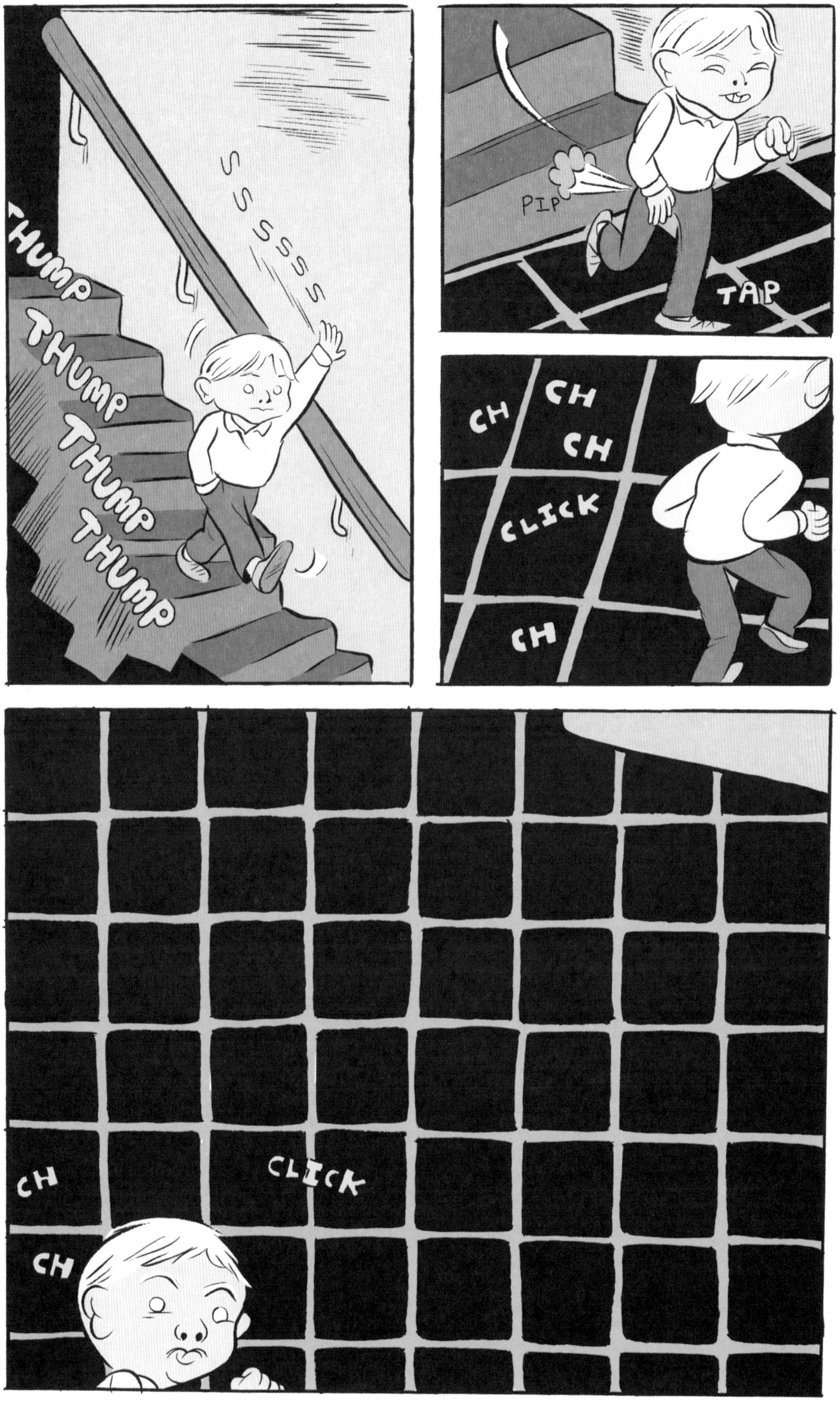
SSSSSSSS
THUMP THUMP THUMP THUMP THUMP
PIP
TAP
CH CH CH CH
CLICK
CH
CH CLICK
CH

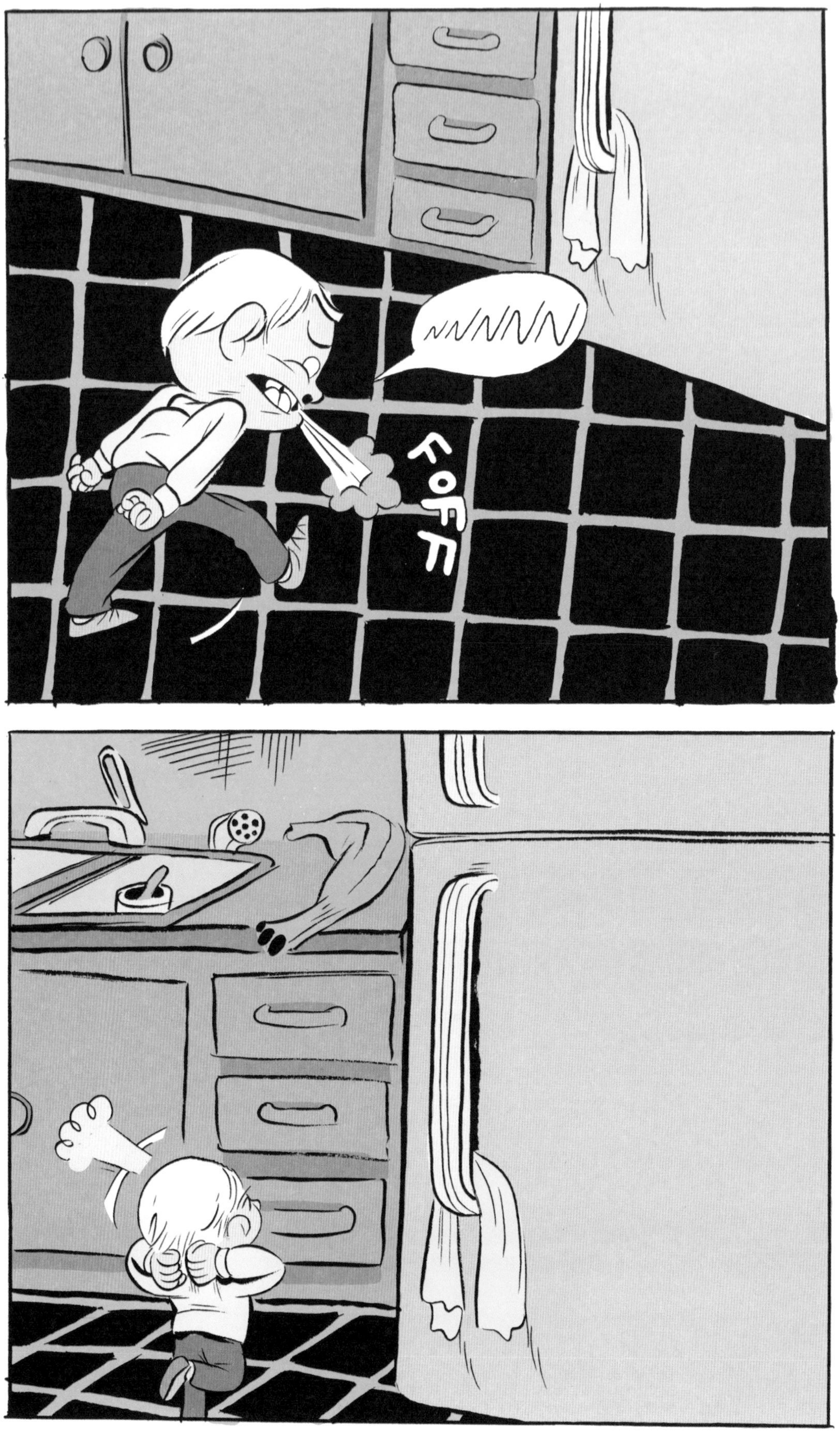
NNNNNN
FOFF

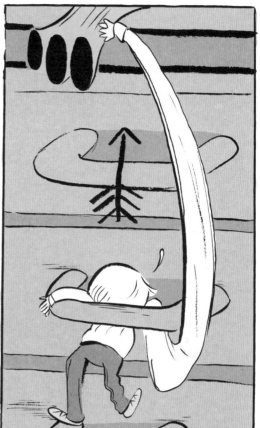

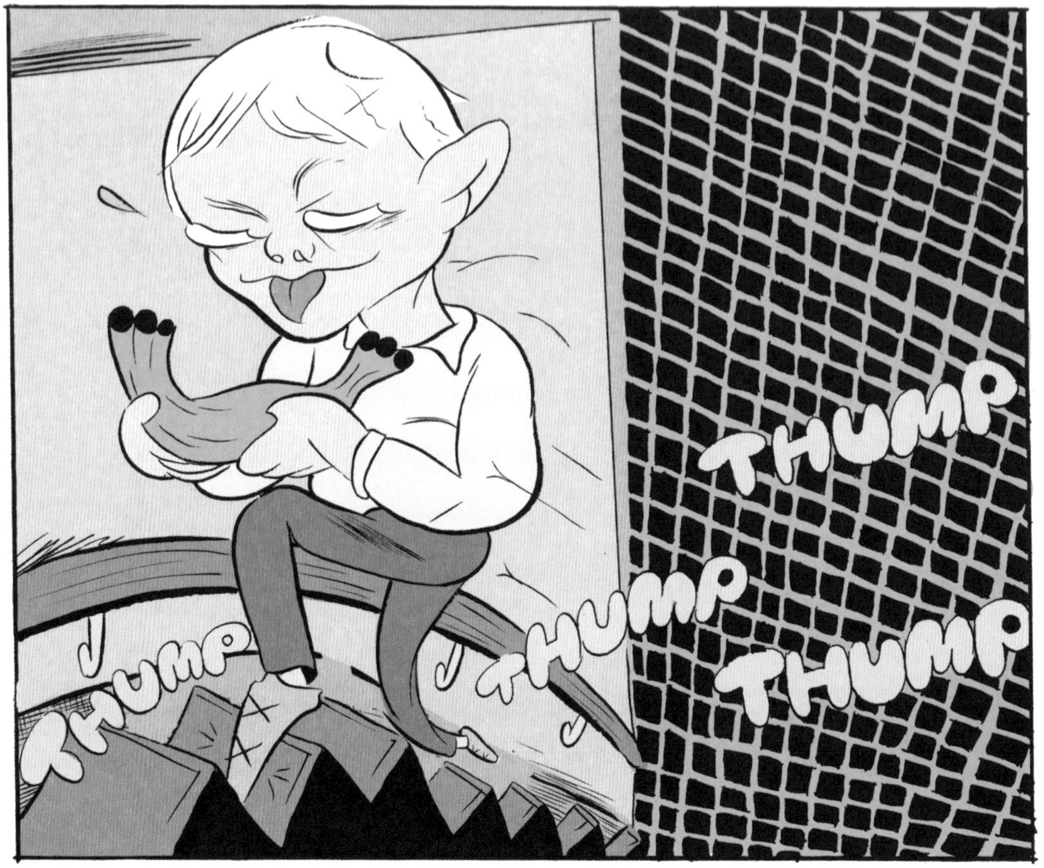
THUMP
THUMP
THUMP
THUMP

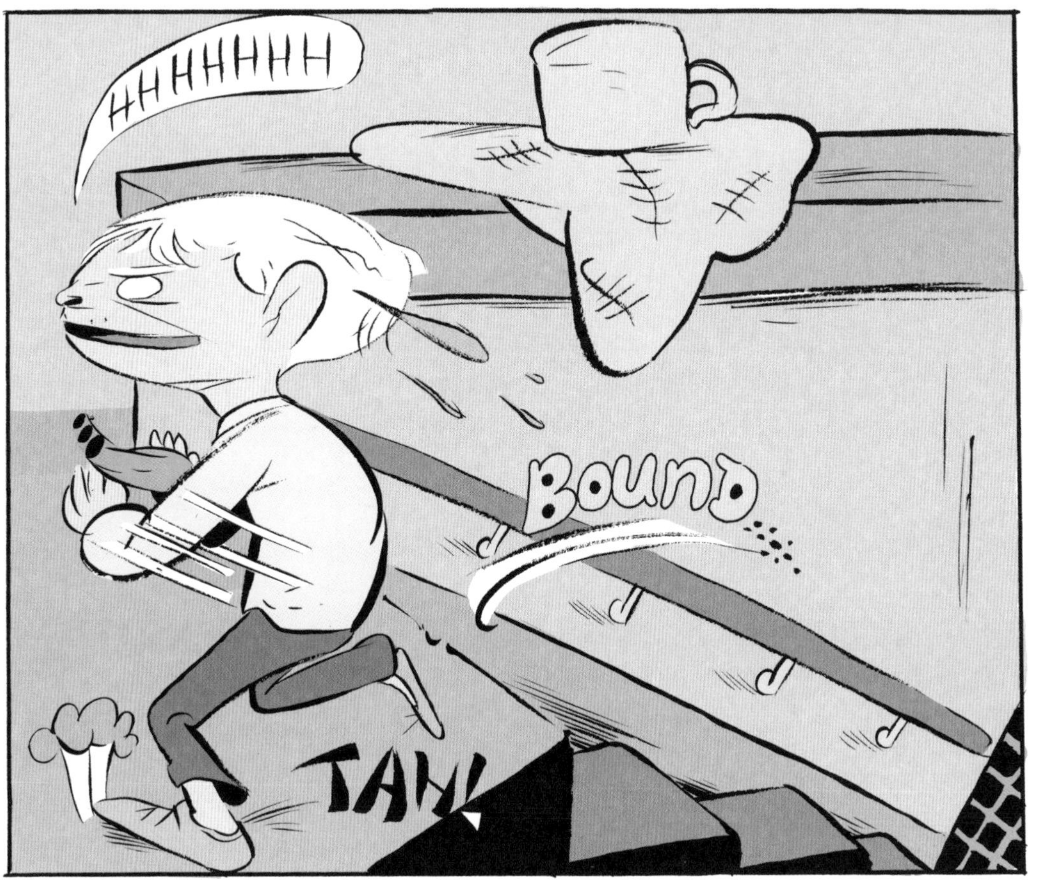
HHHHHHH
BOUND
TAH!

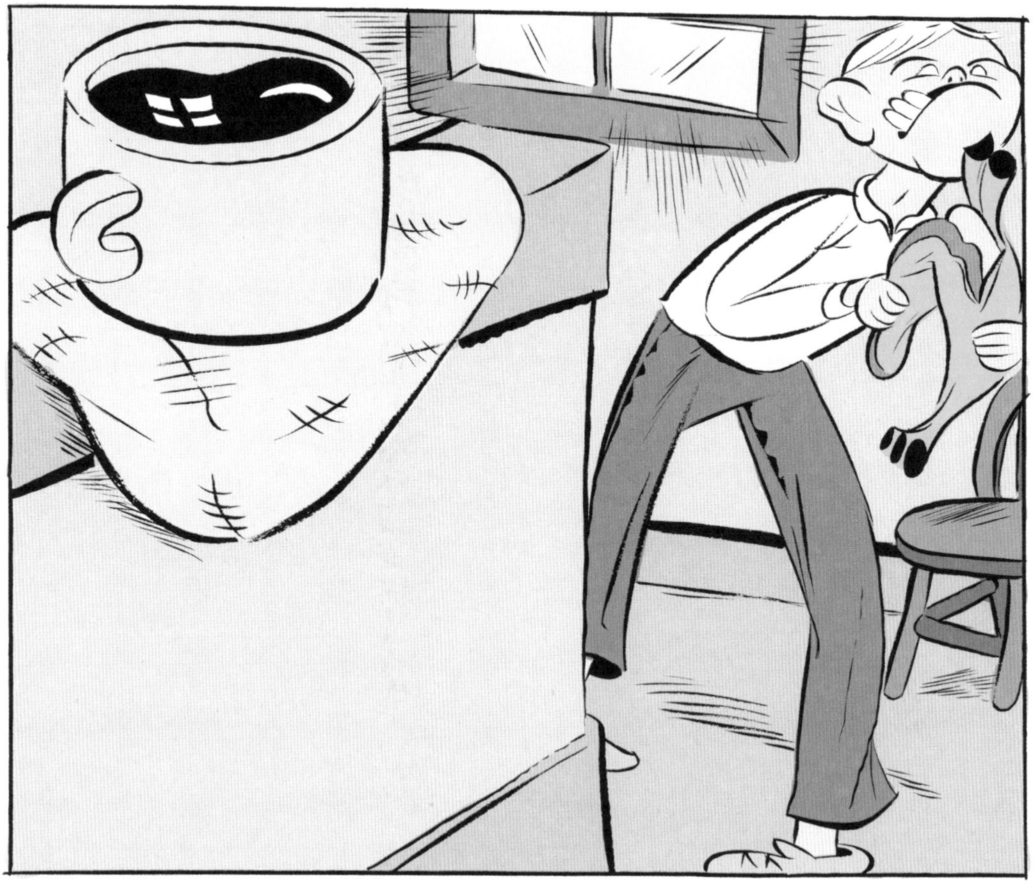

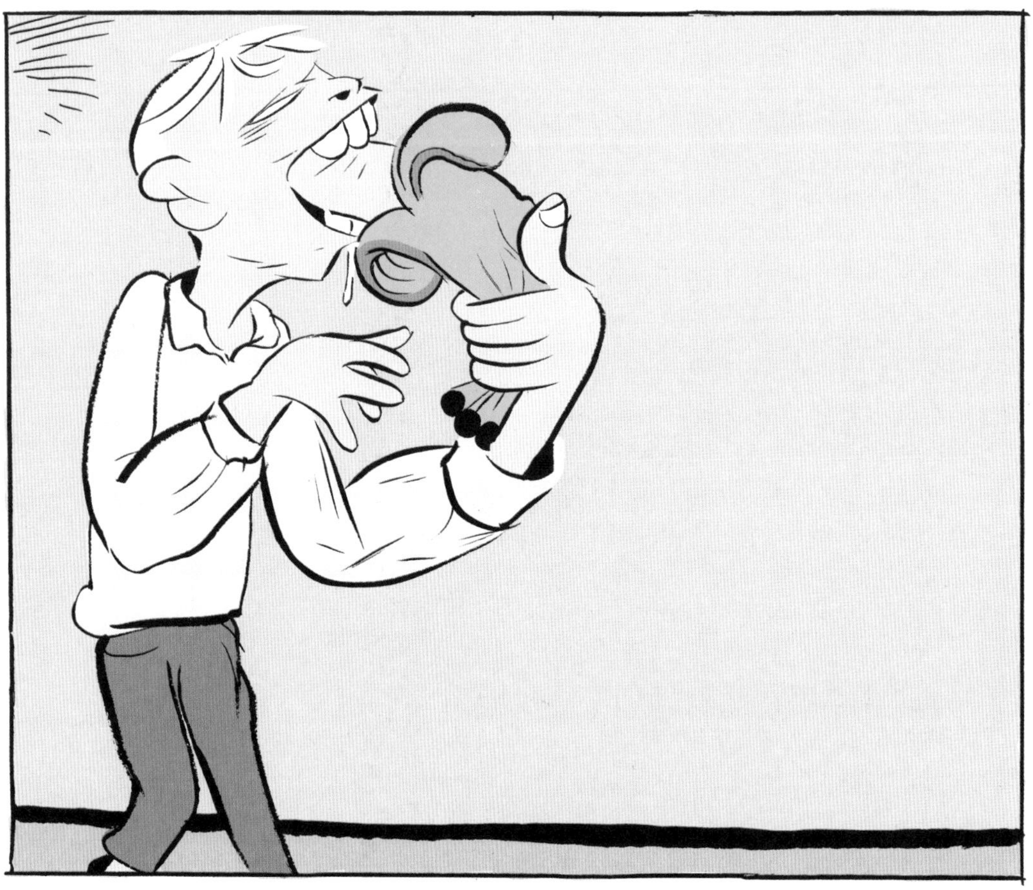

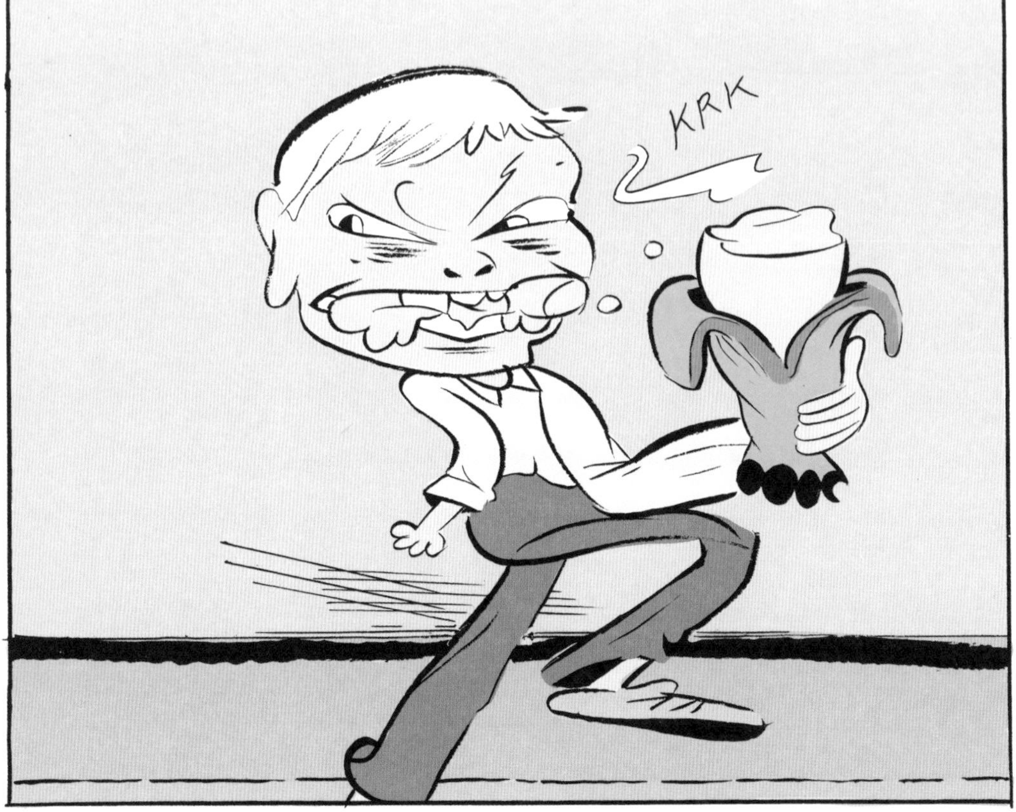
KRK

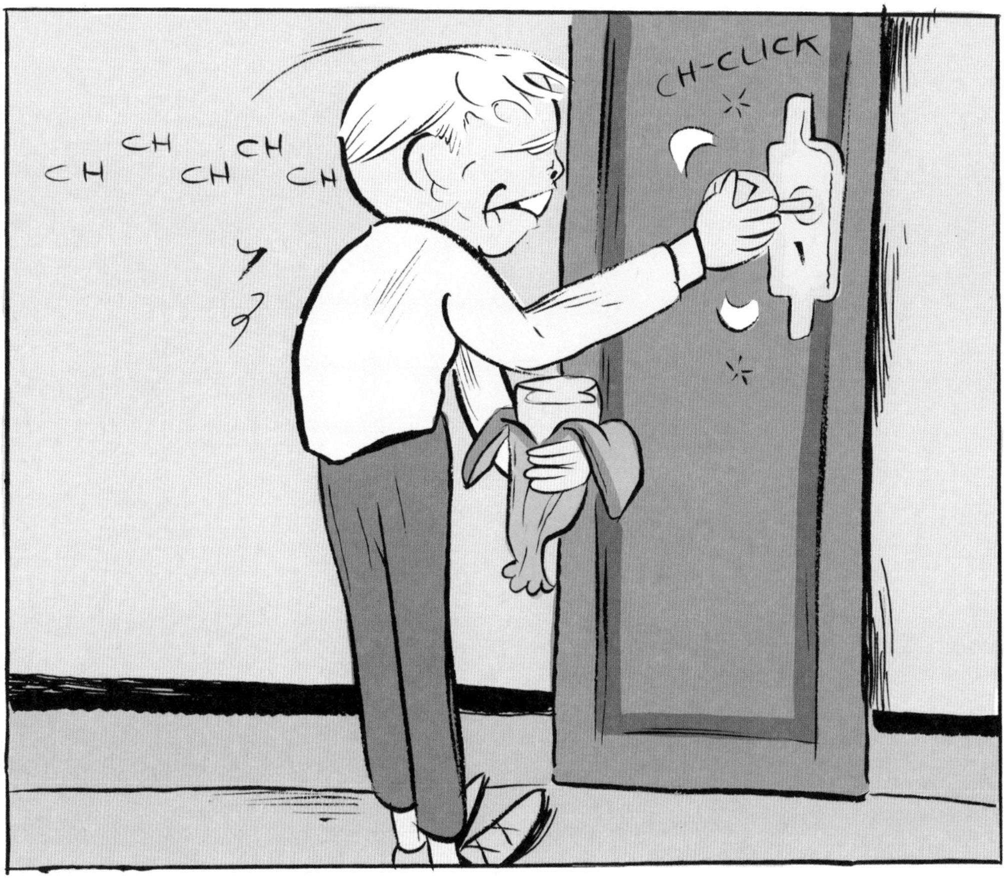
CH CH CH CH CH
CH-CLICK

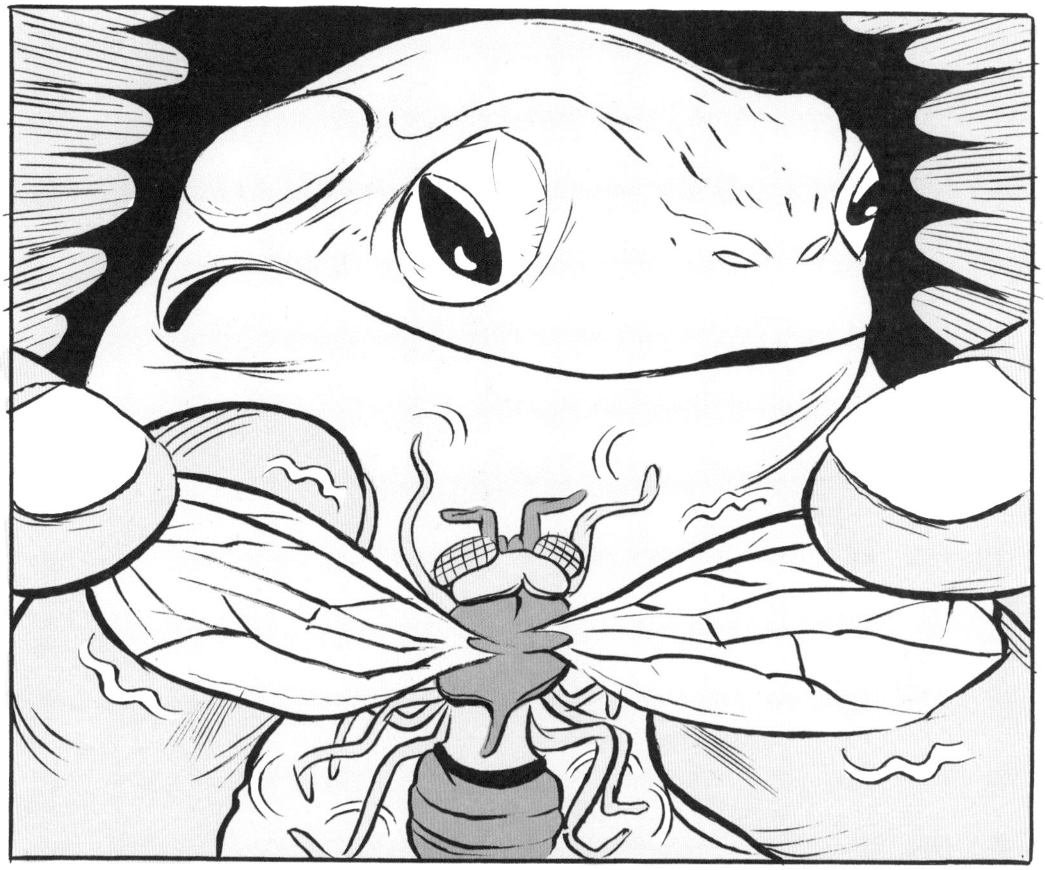
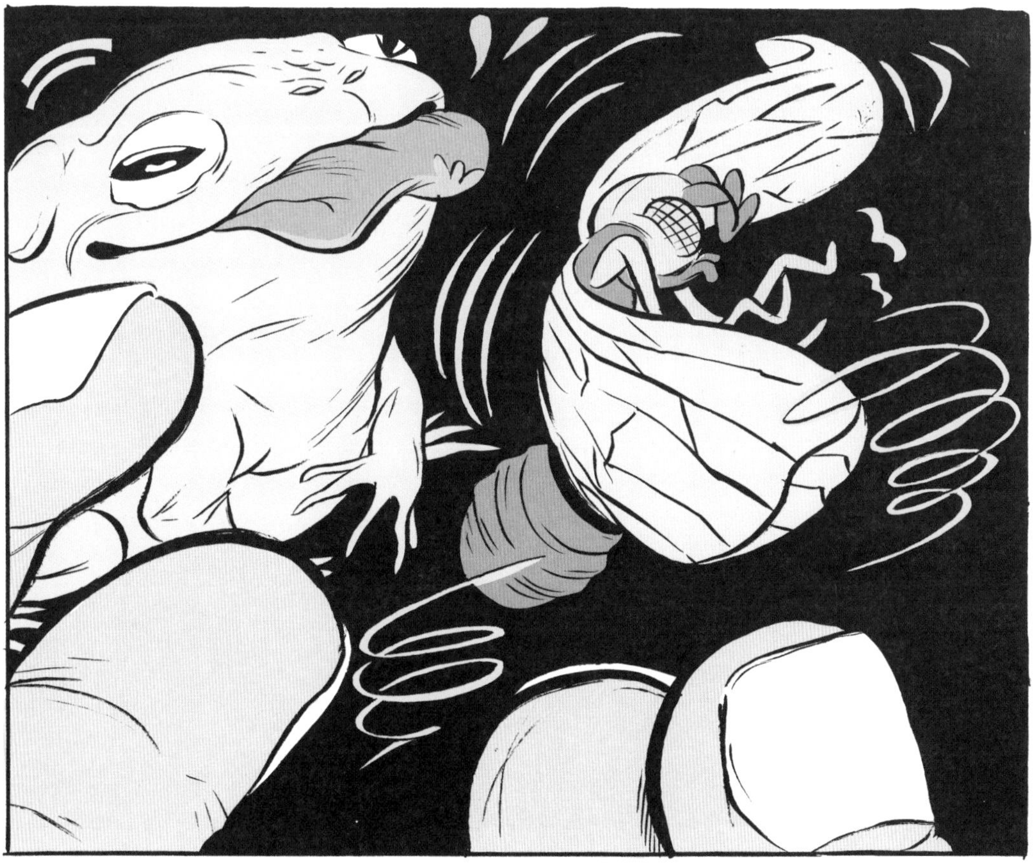

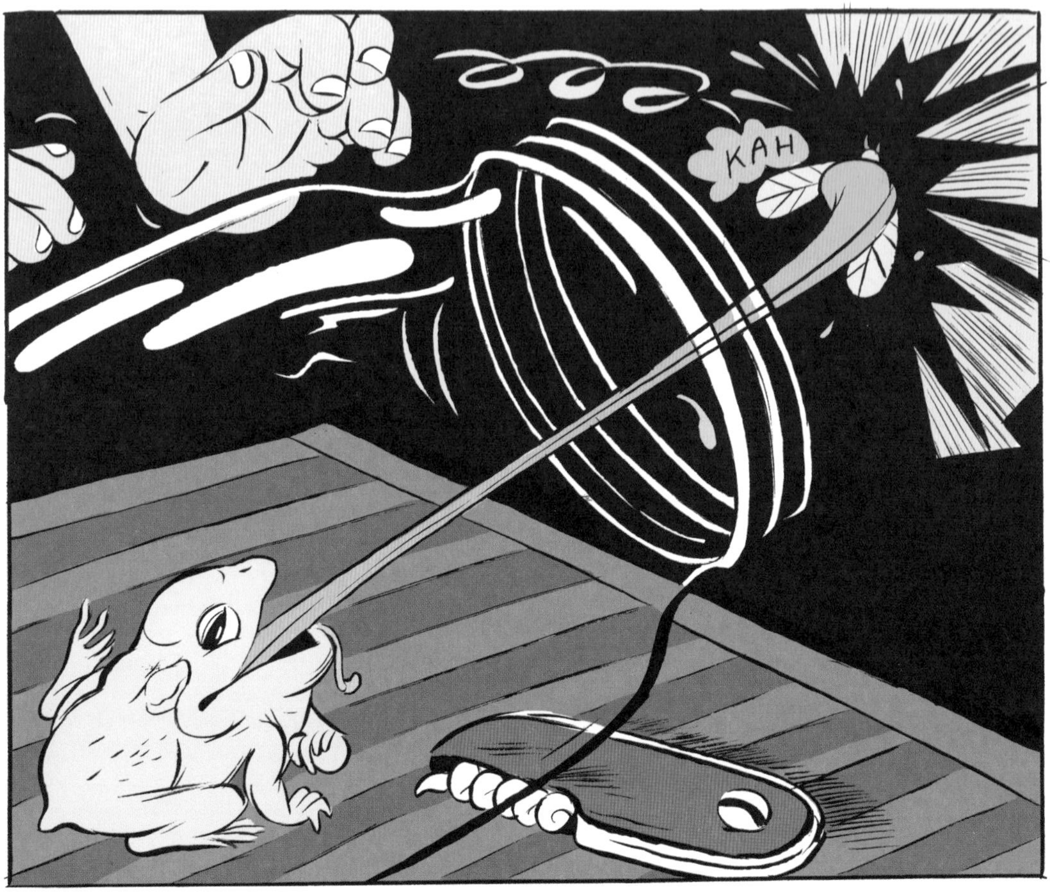
KAH

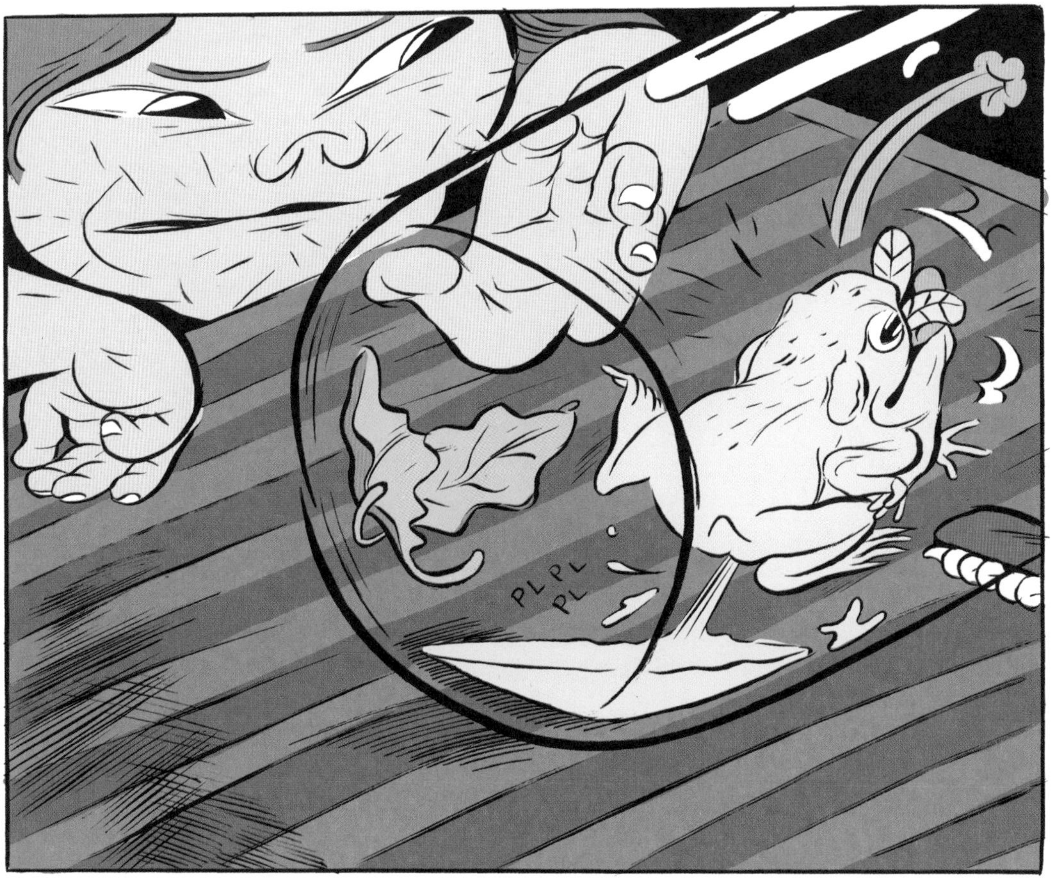
PL PL PL

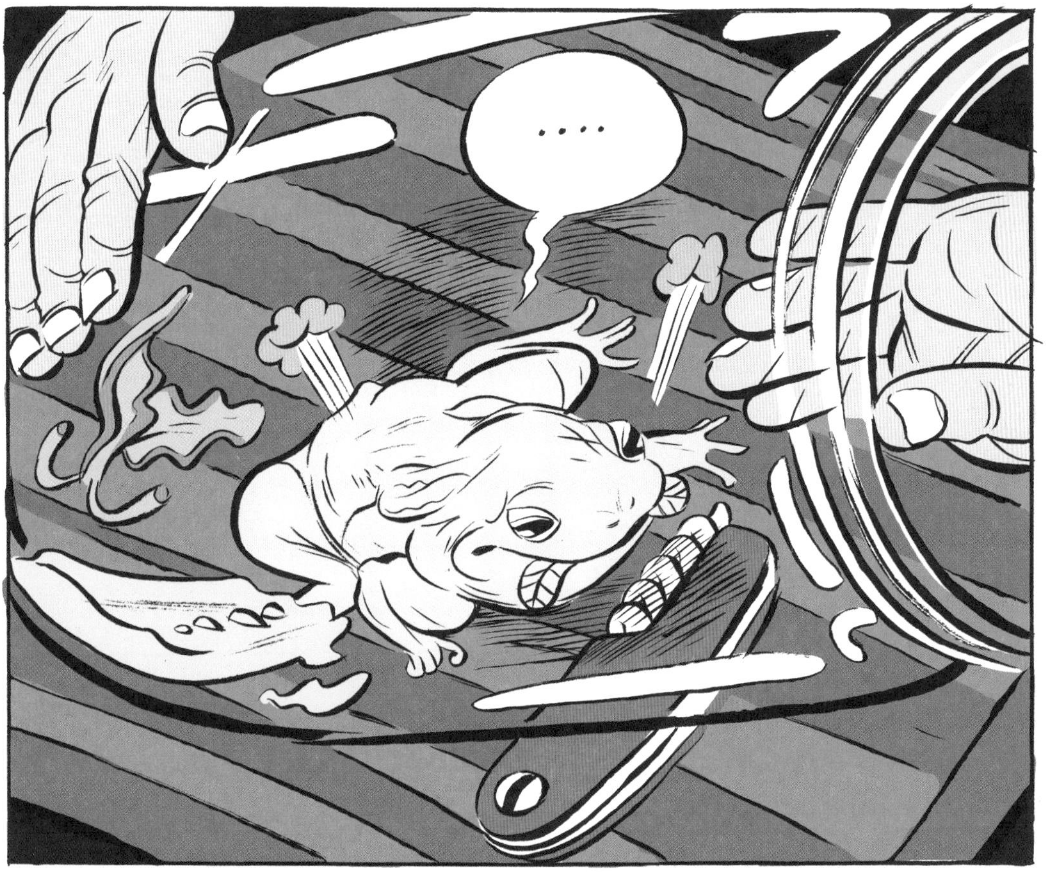
....

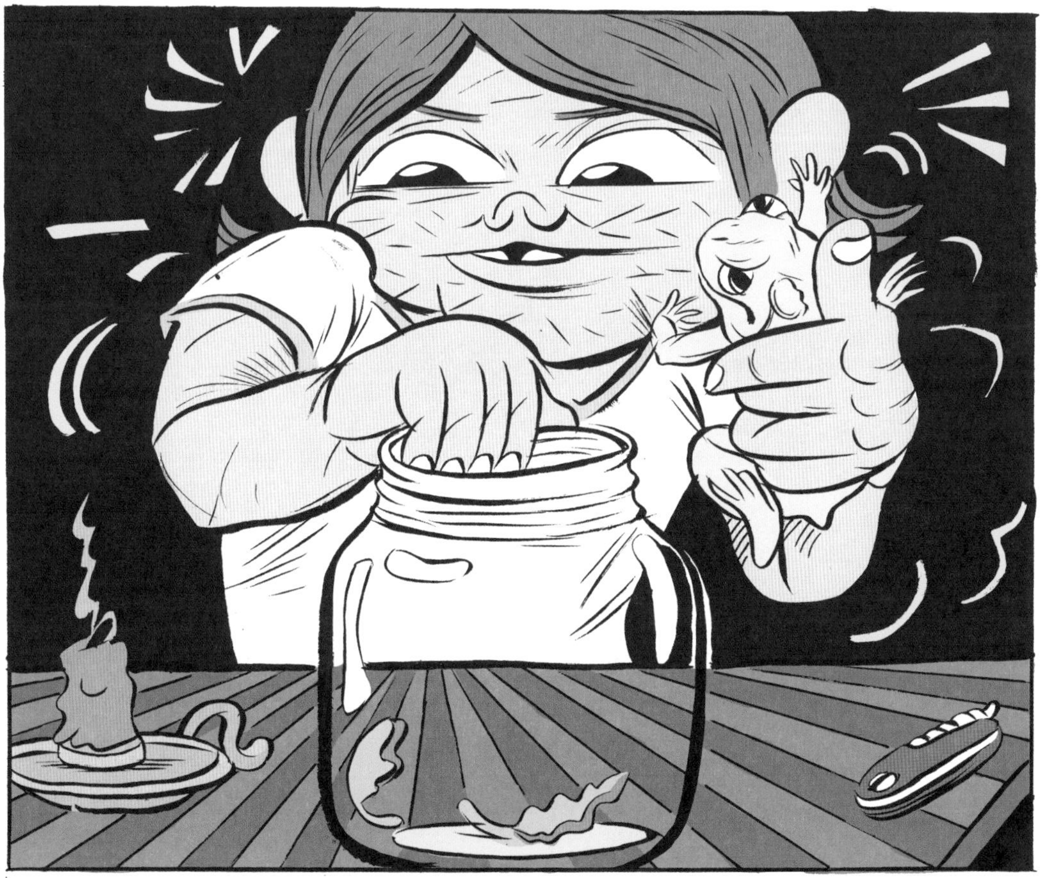

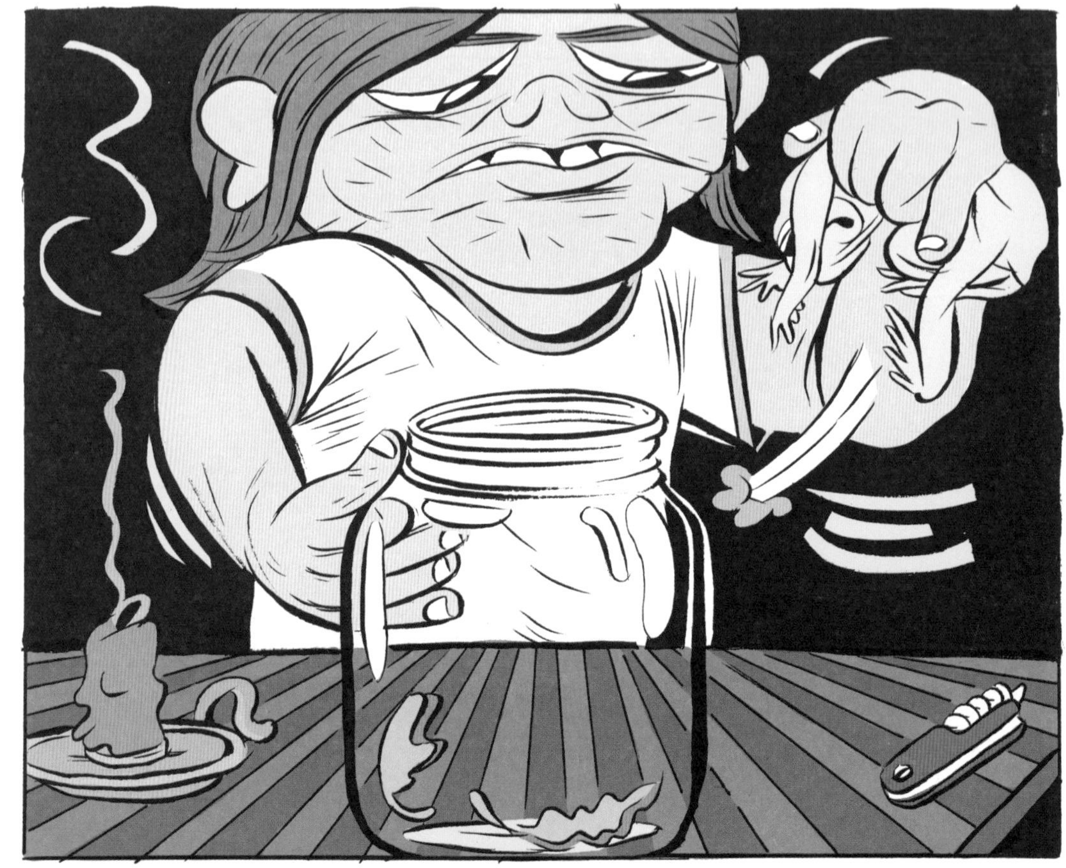

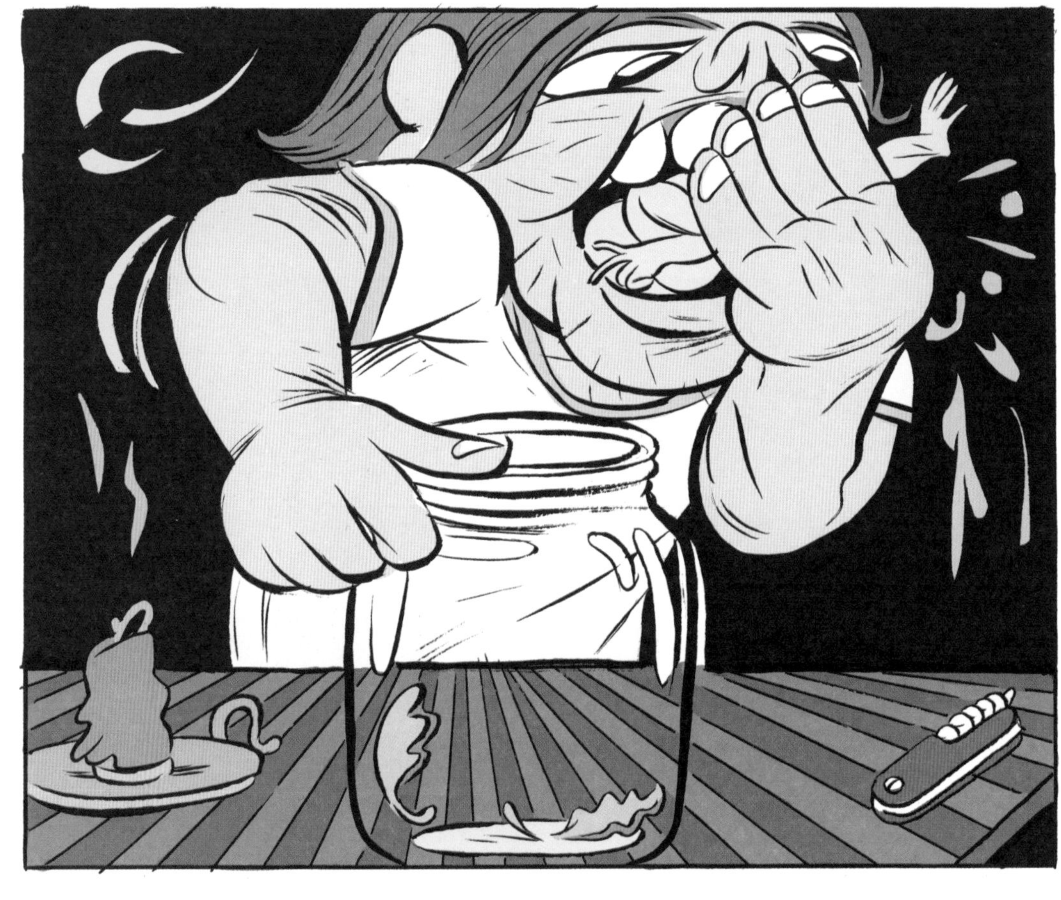

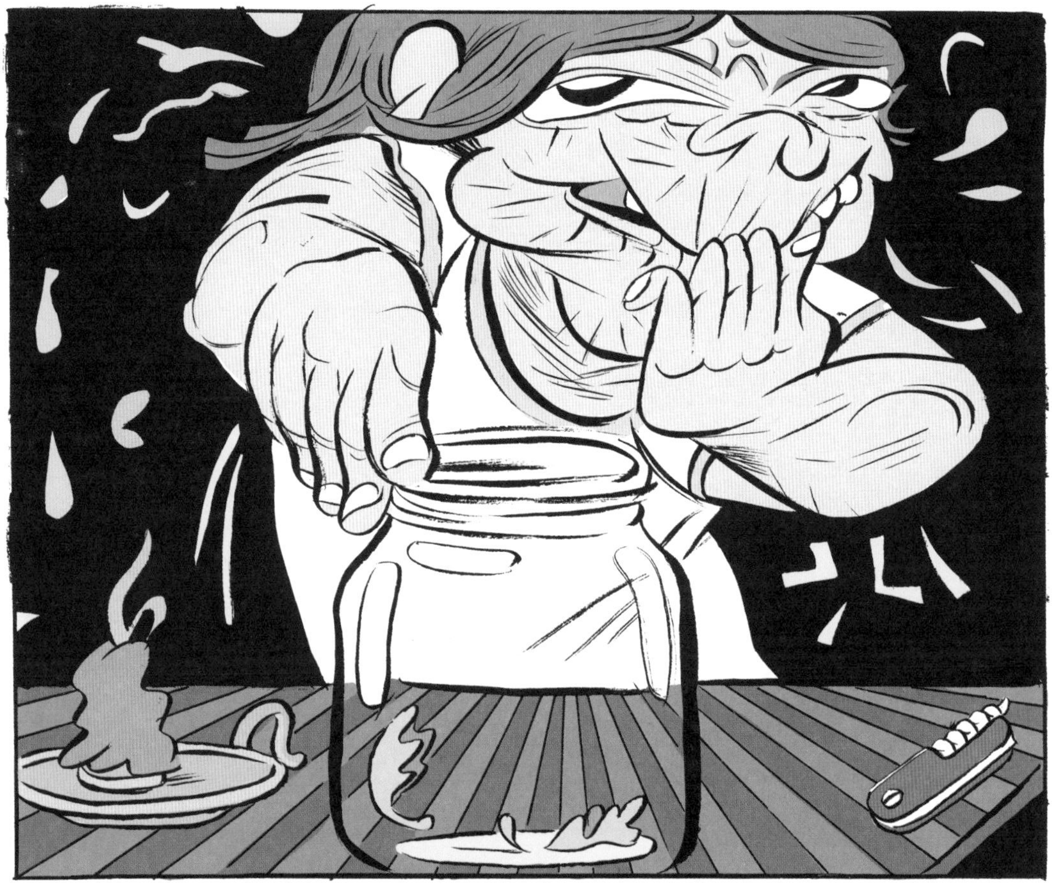

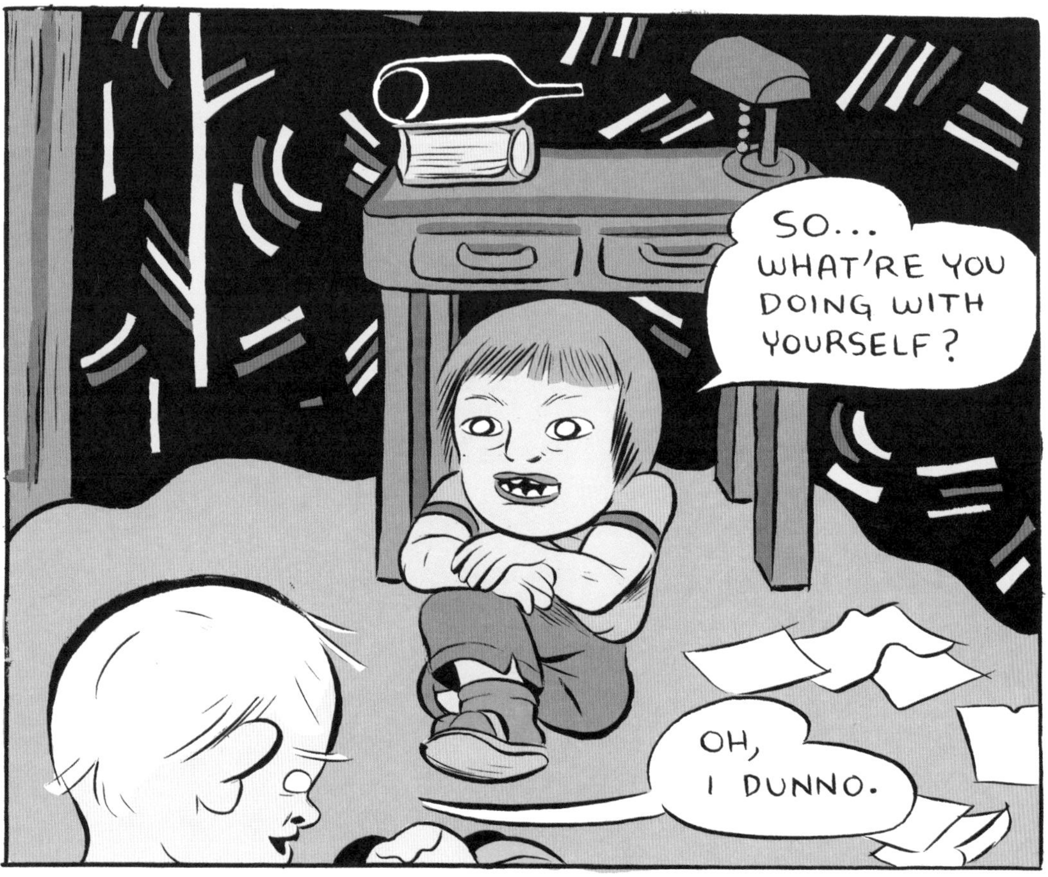
SO... WHAT'RE YOU DOING WITH YOURSELF?
OH, I DUNNO.

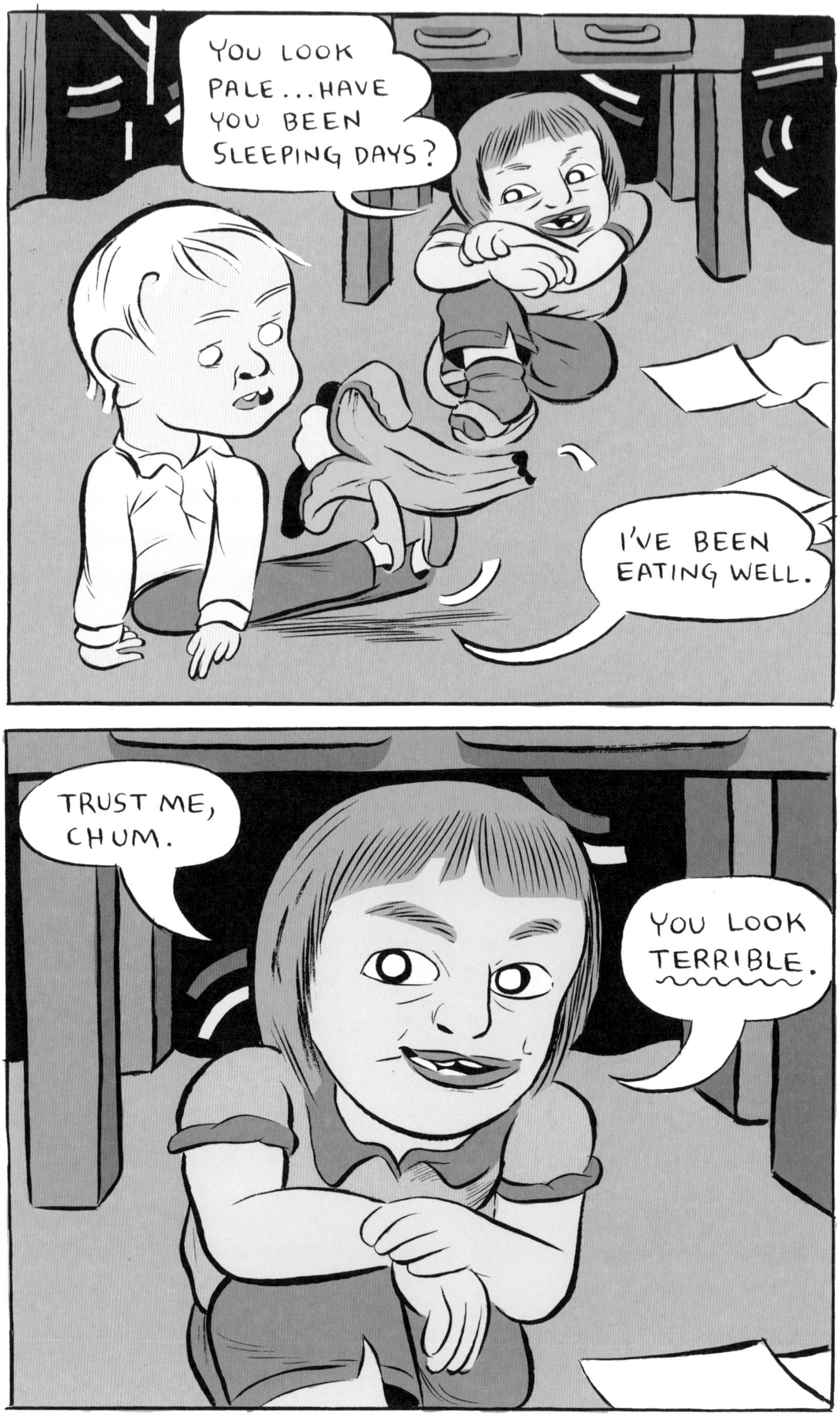
YOU LOOK PALE...HAVE YOU BEEN SLEEPING DAYS?
I'VE BEEN EATING WELL.
TRUST ME, CHUM.
YOU LOOK TERRIBLE.

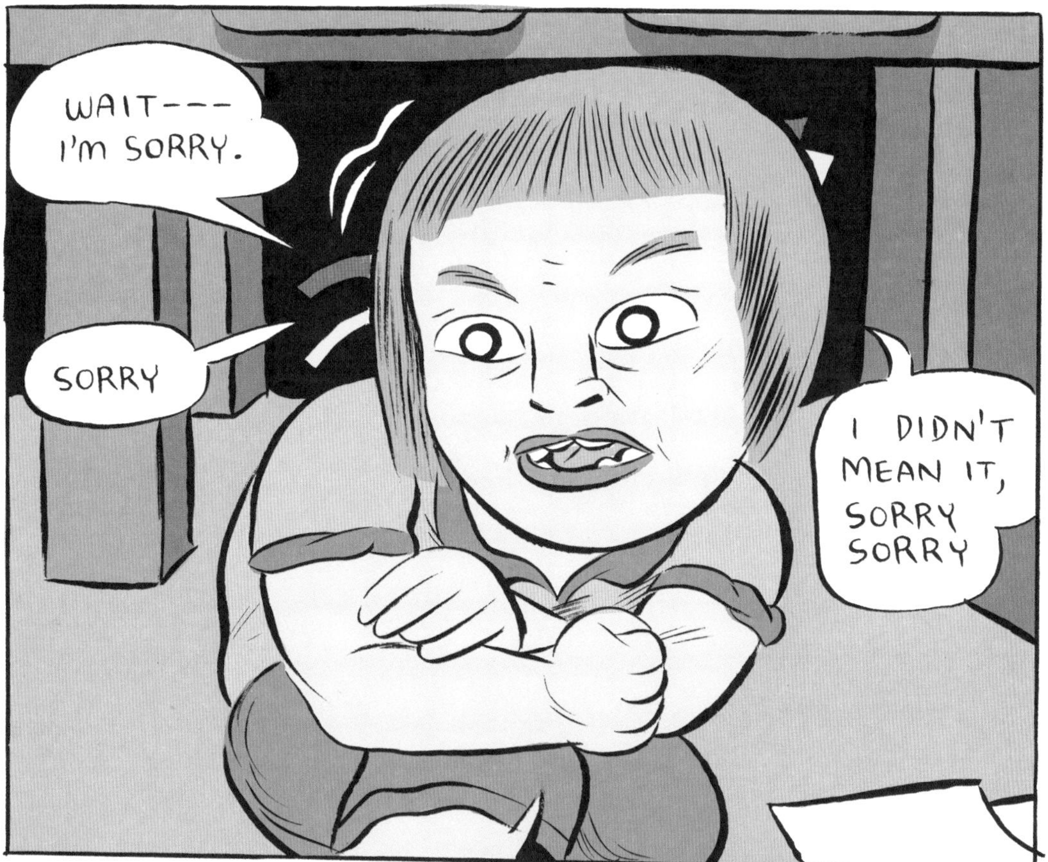
WAIT---
I'M SORRY.
SORRY
I DIDN'T
MEAN IT,
SORRY
SORRY

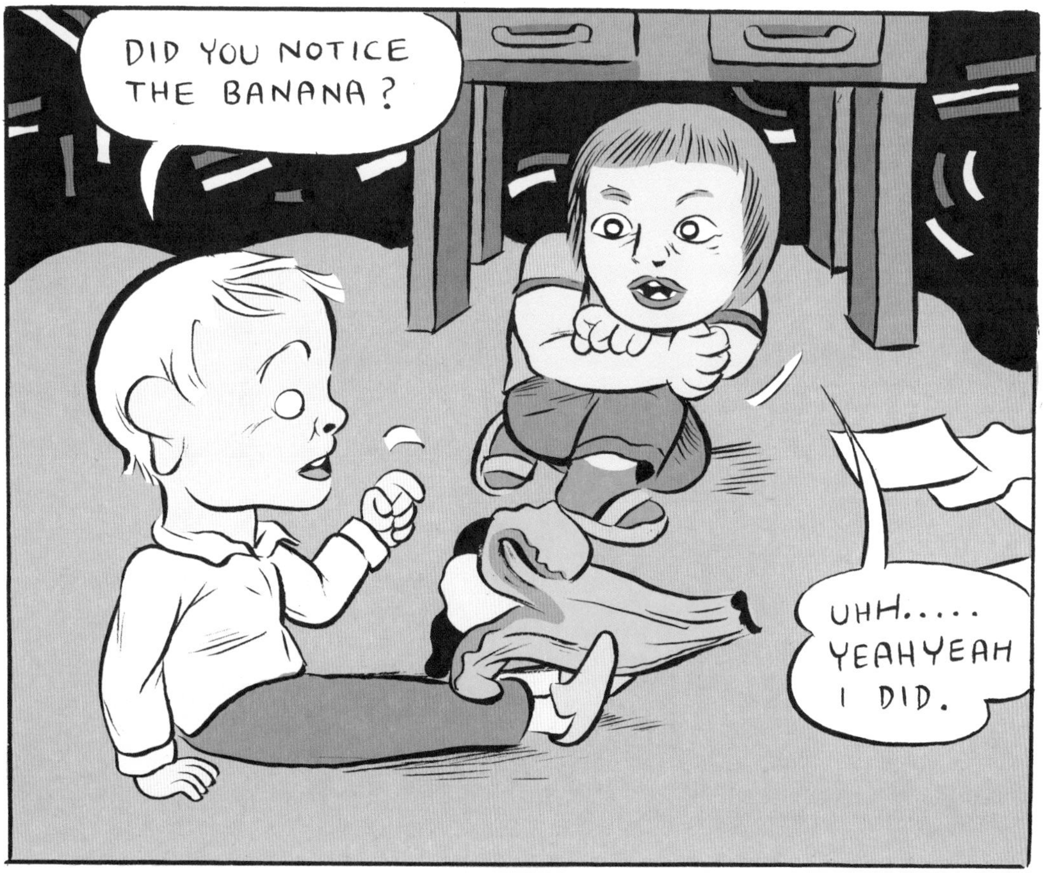
DID YOU NOTICE
THE BANANA?
UHH.....
YEAHYEAH
I DID.

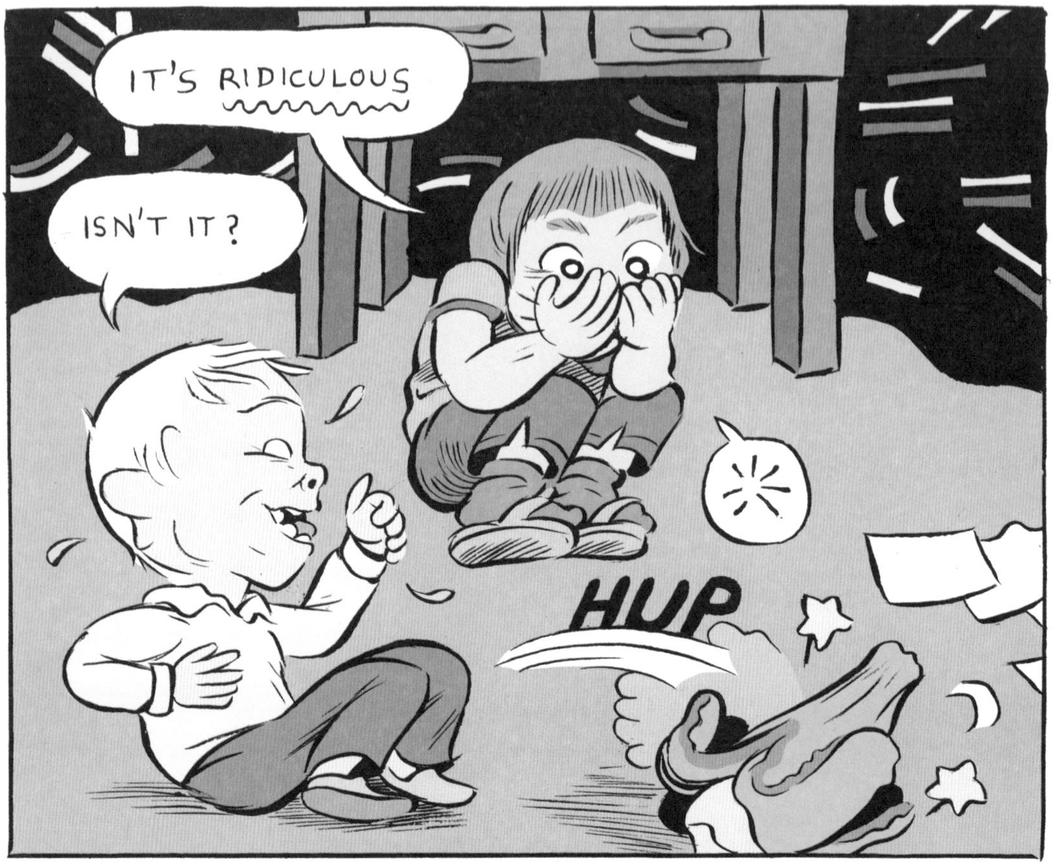
IT'S RIDICULOUS
ISN'T IT?
HUP

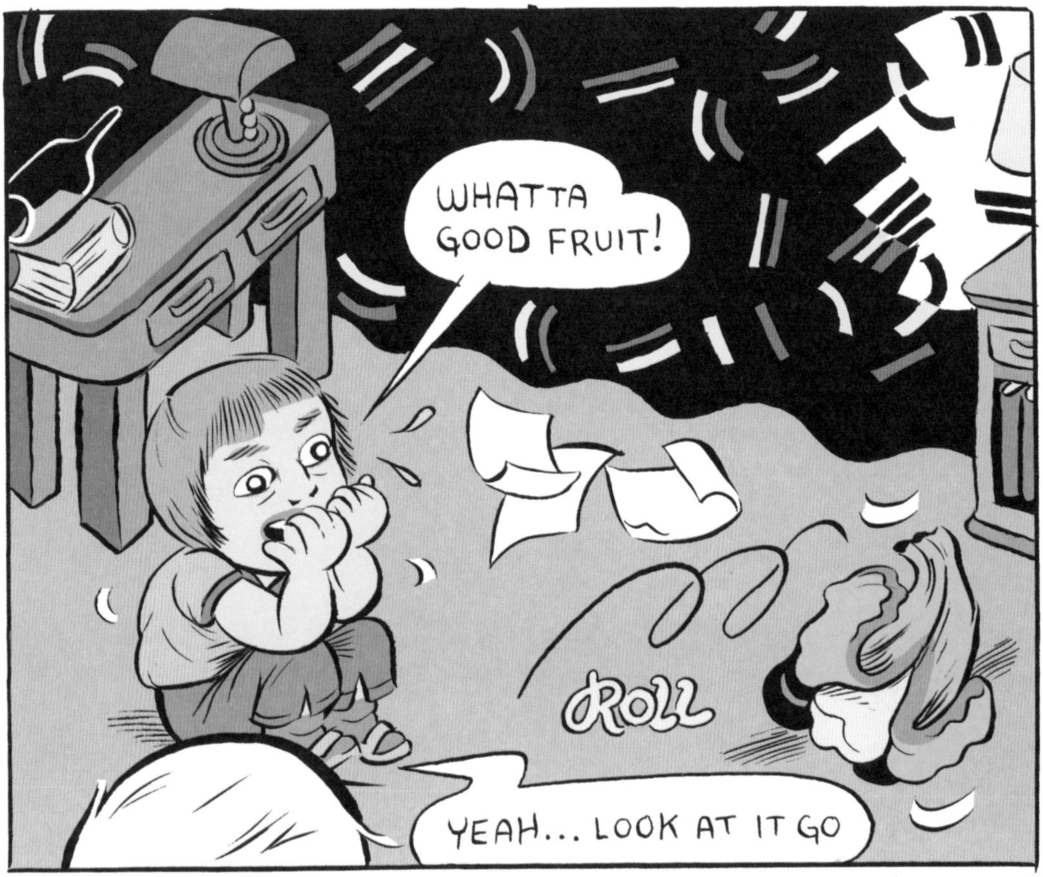
WHATTA GOOD FRUIT!
ROLL
YEAH... LOOK AT IT GO

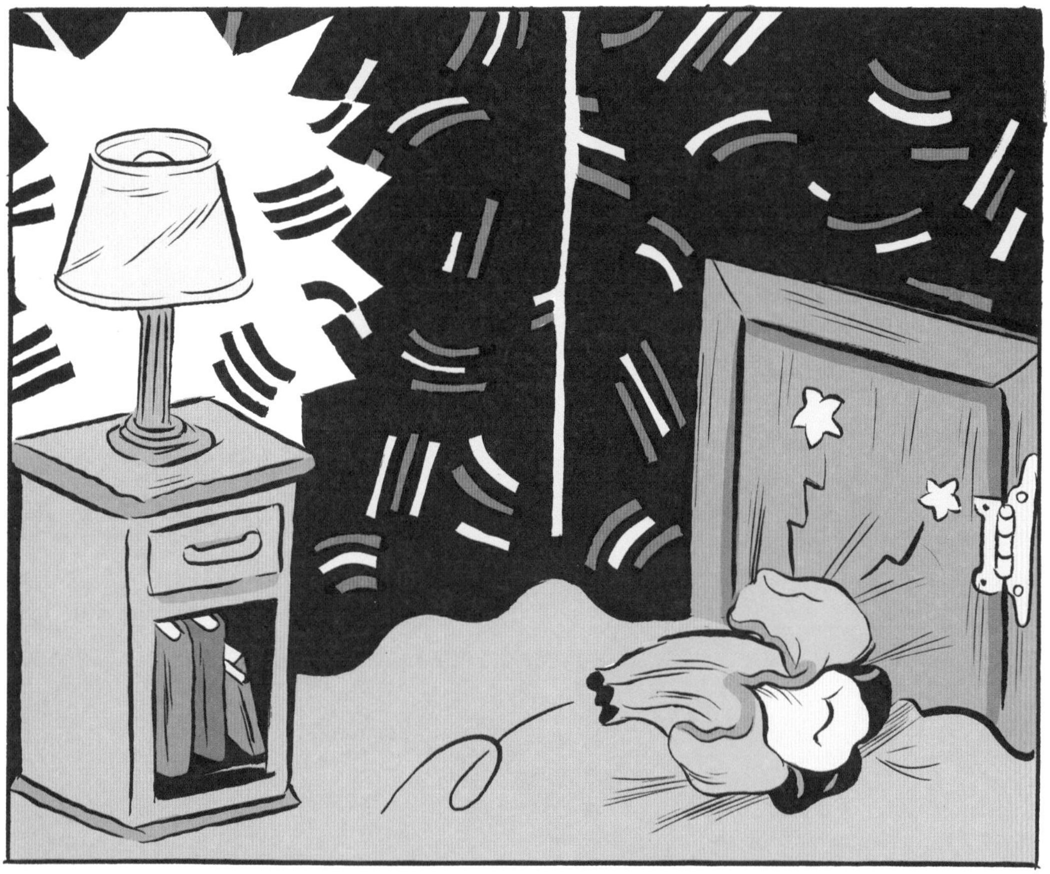

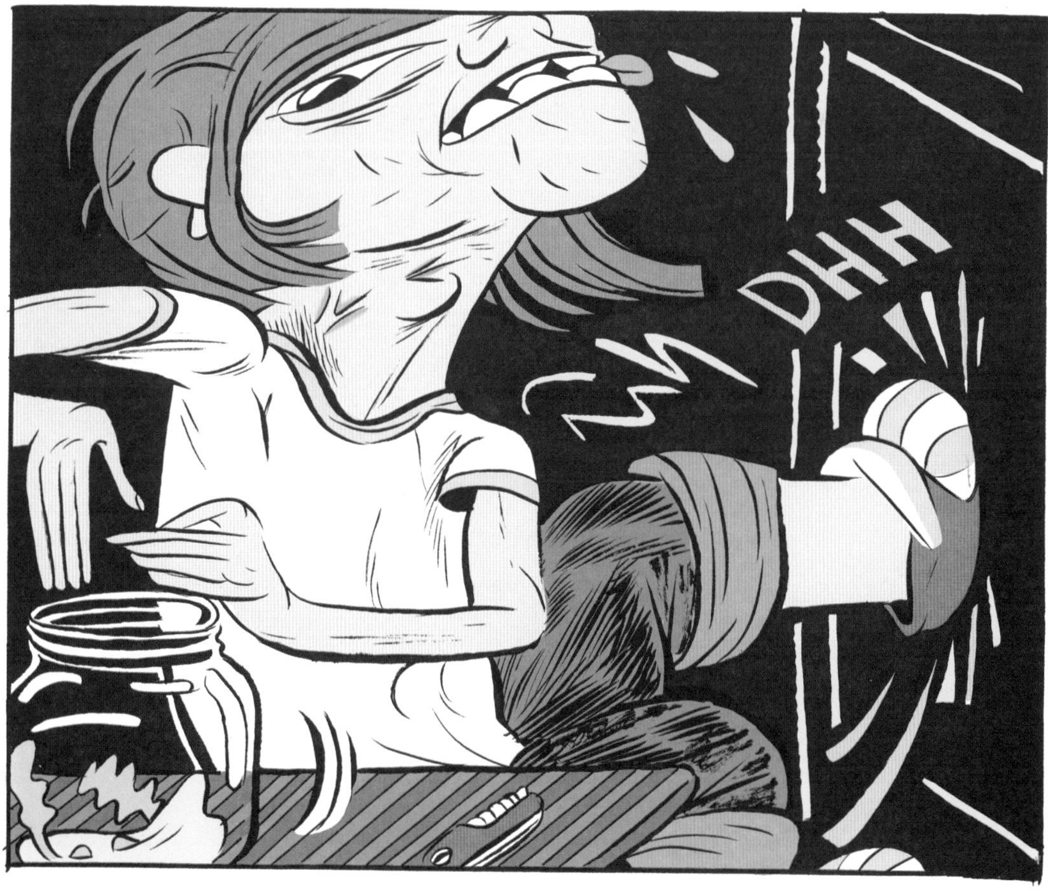

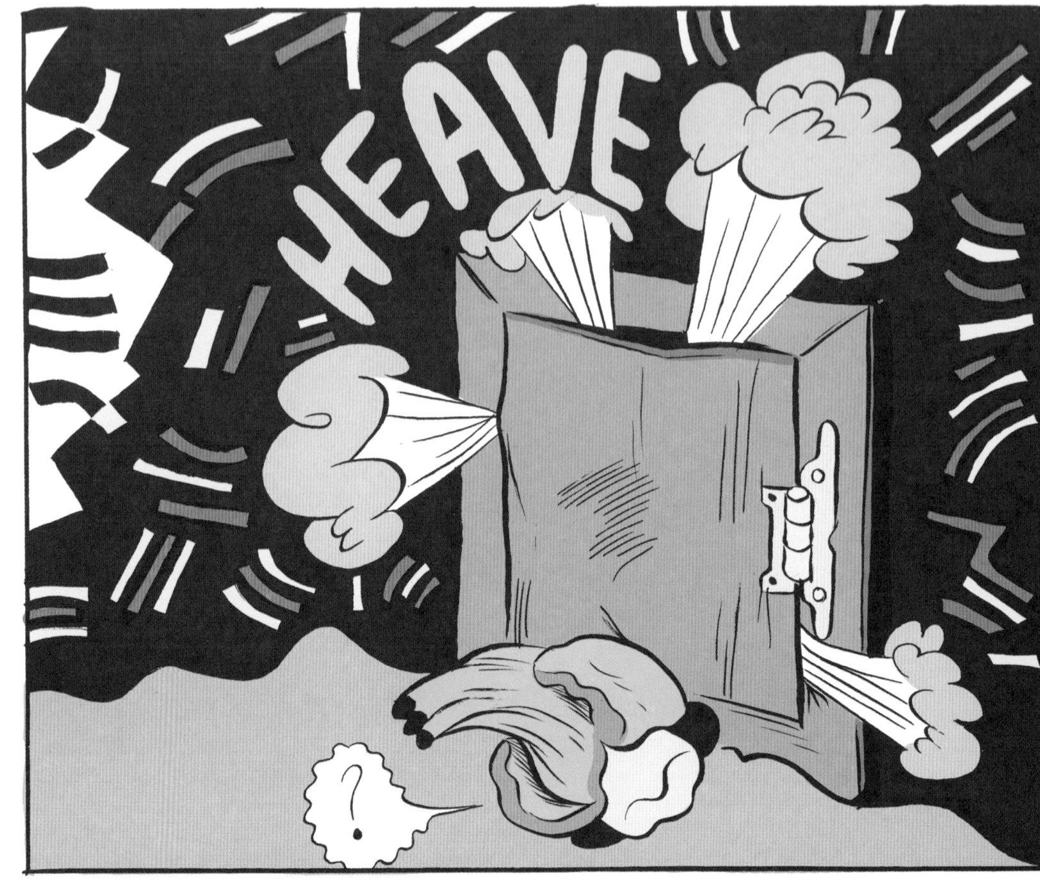
HEAVE
?

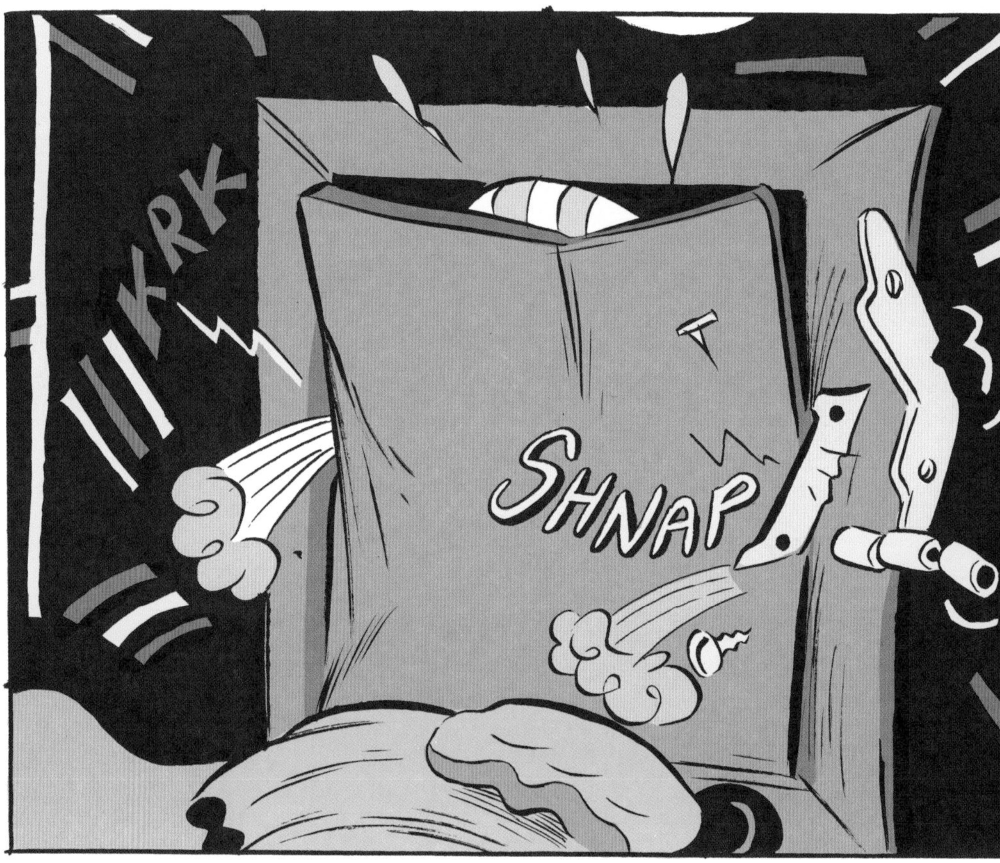
KRK
SHNAP

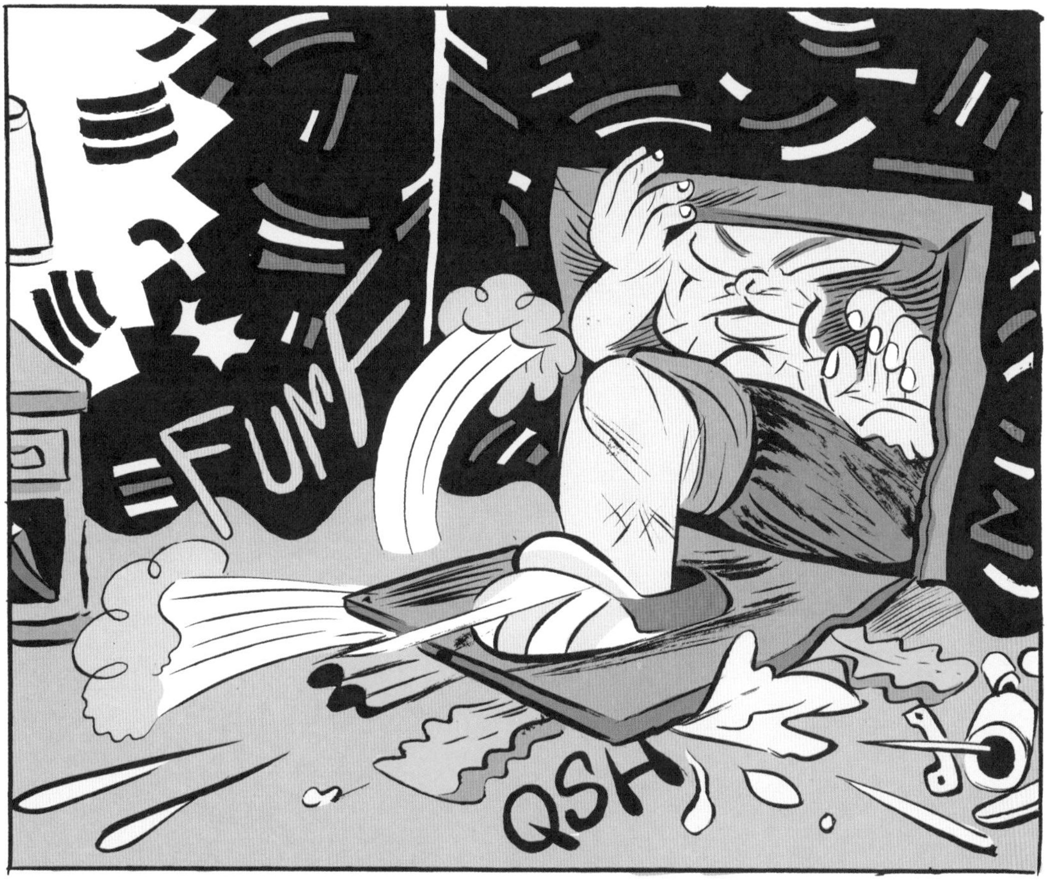
FUMF
QSH

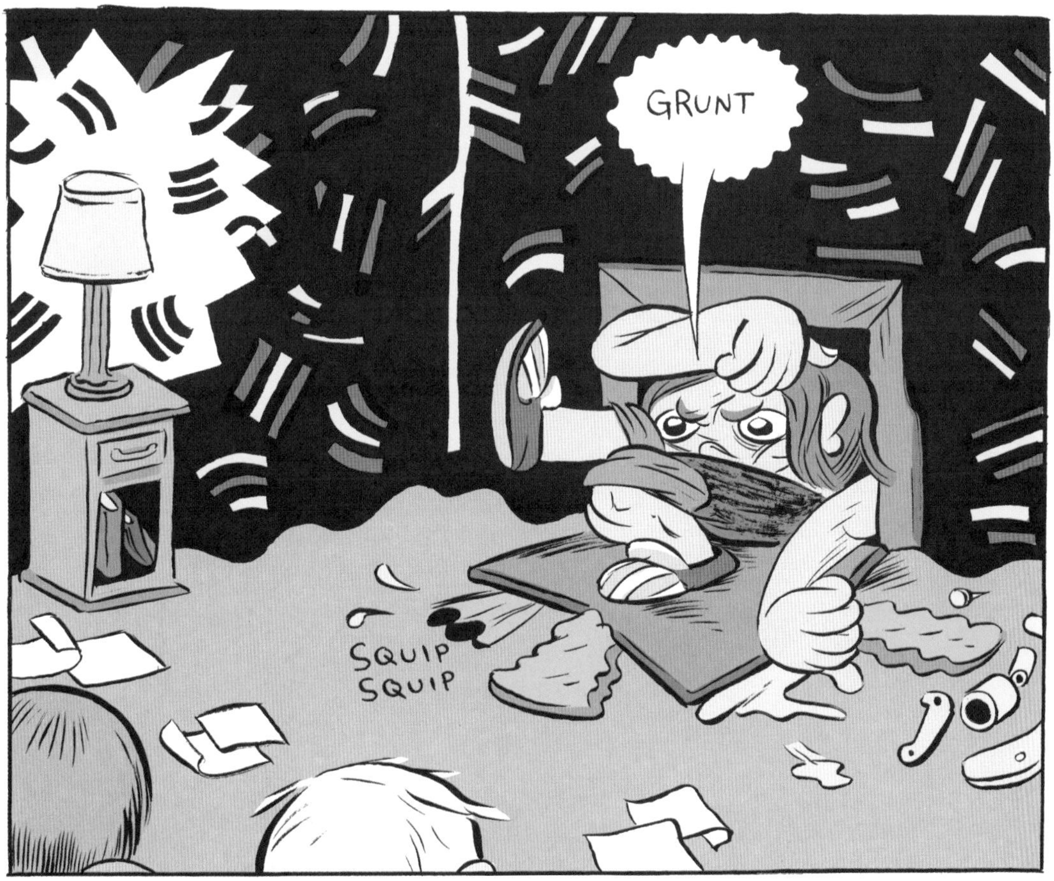
GRUNT
SQUIP
SQUIP

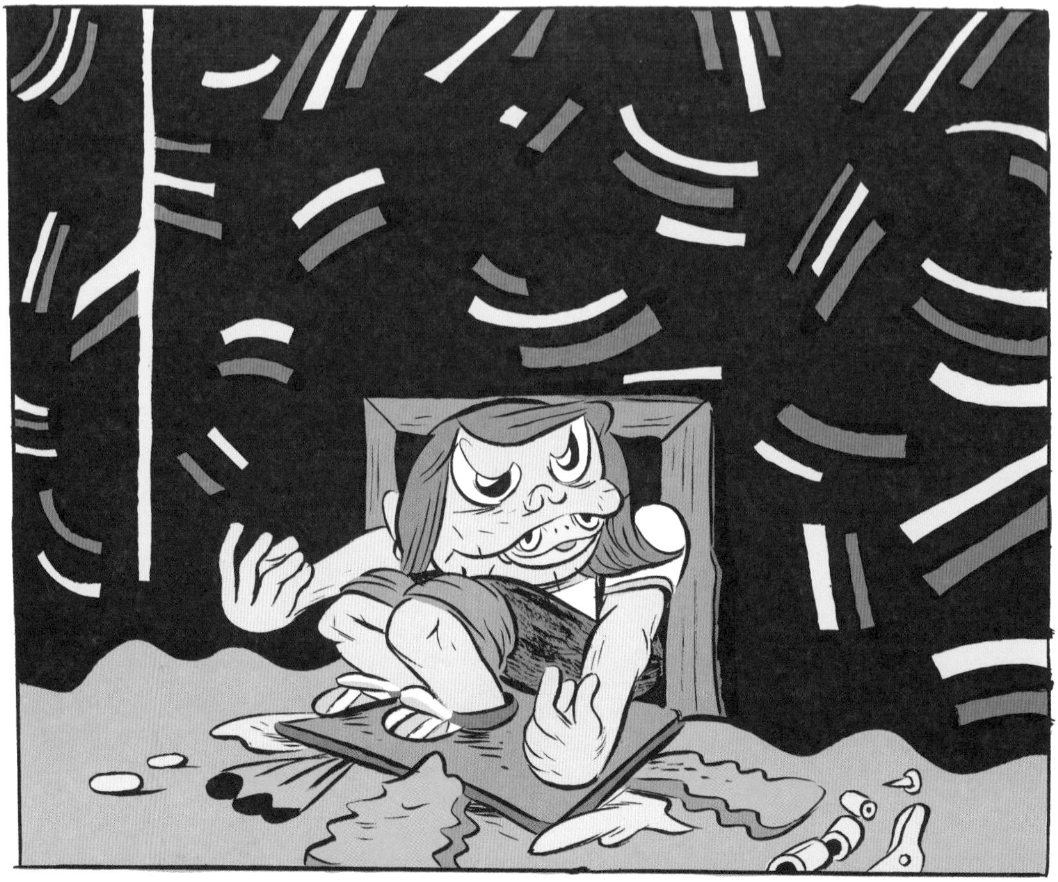

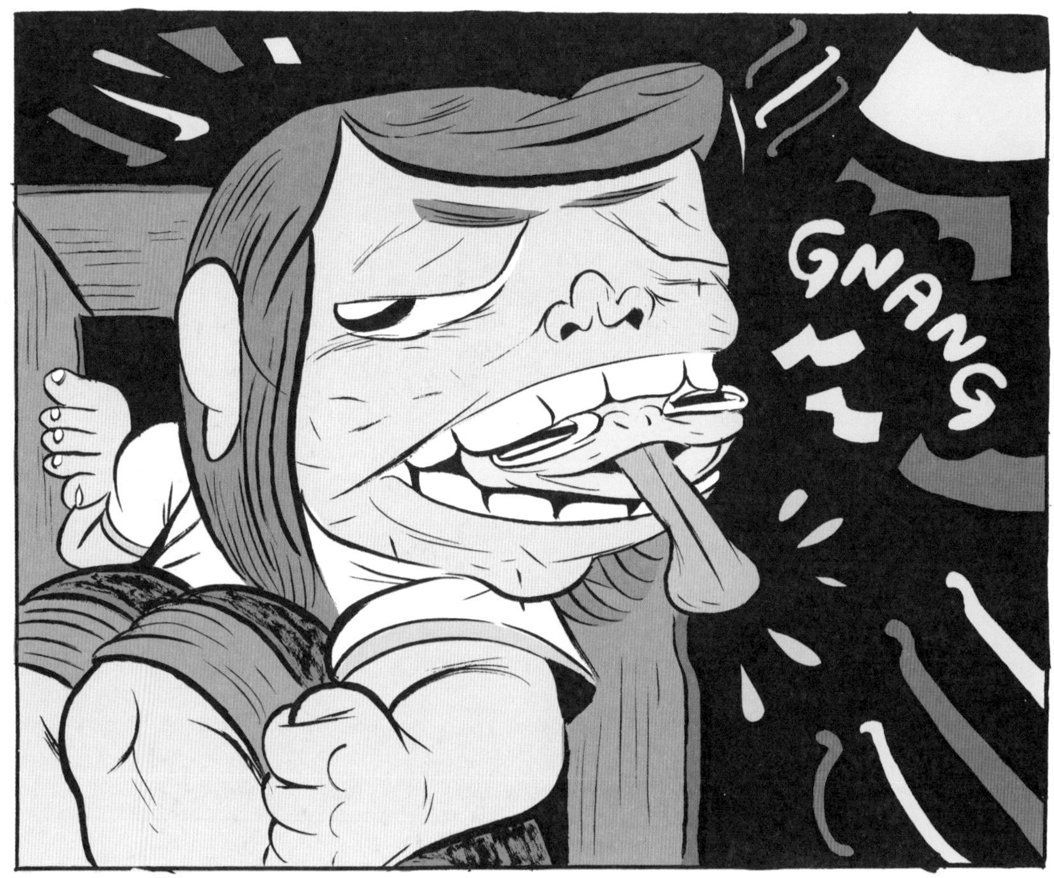
GNANG

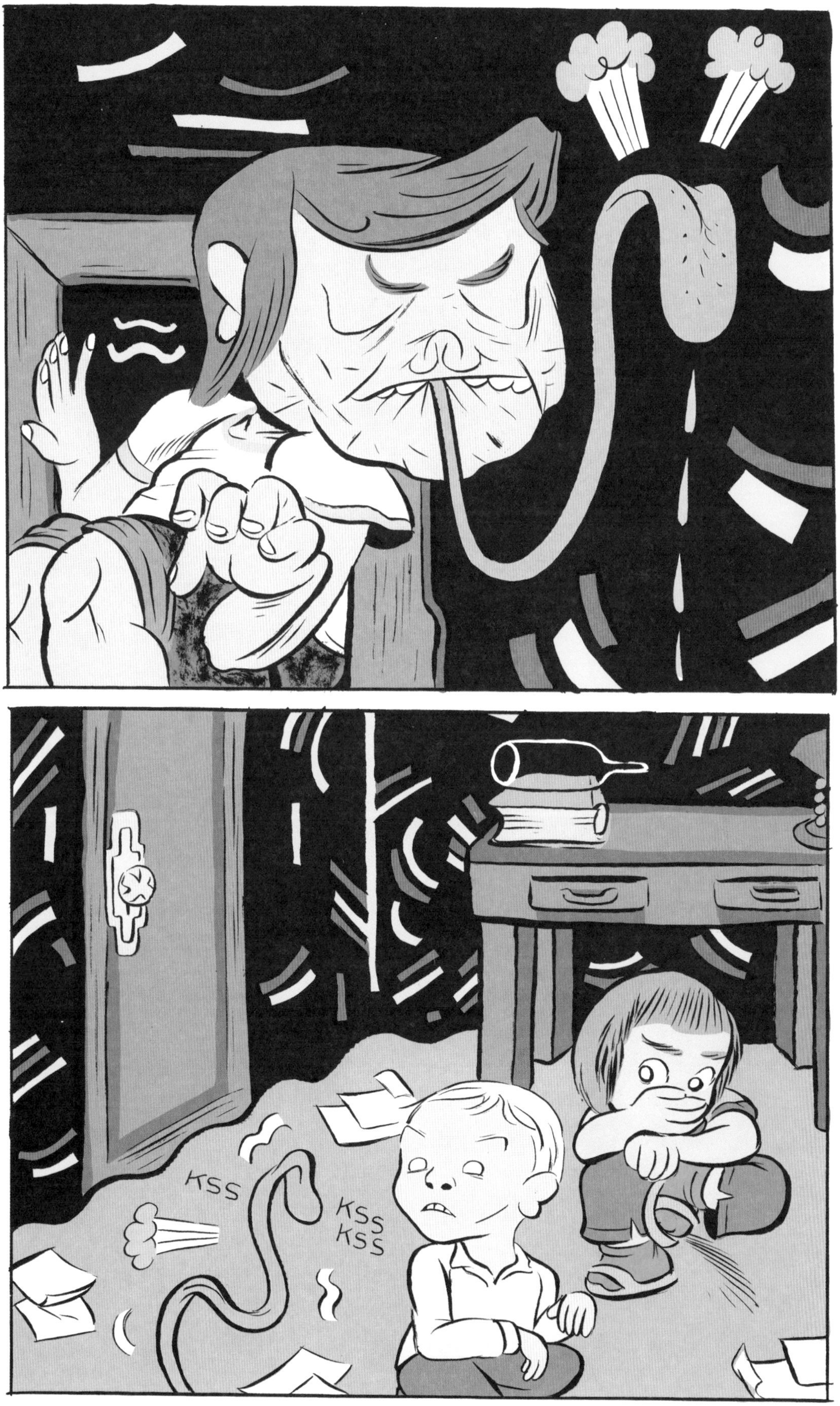
KSS
KSS
KSS

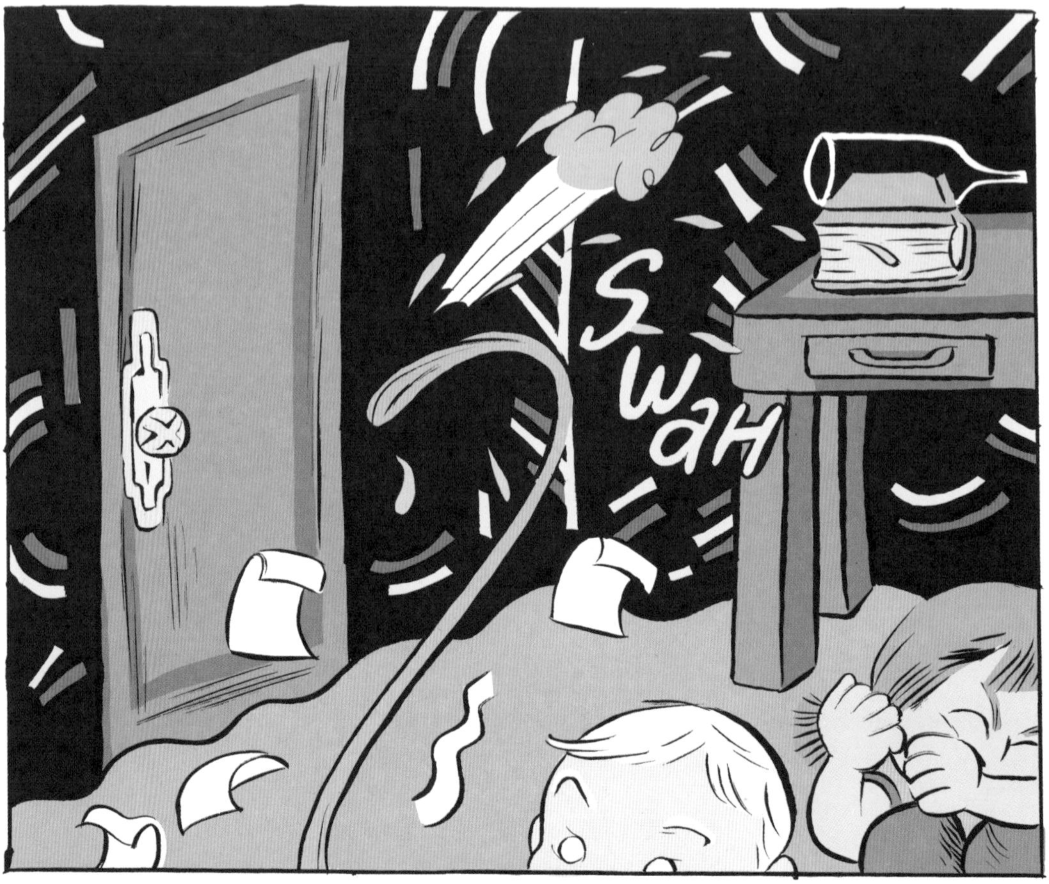
SWAH
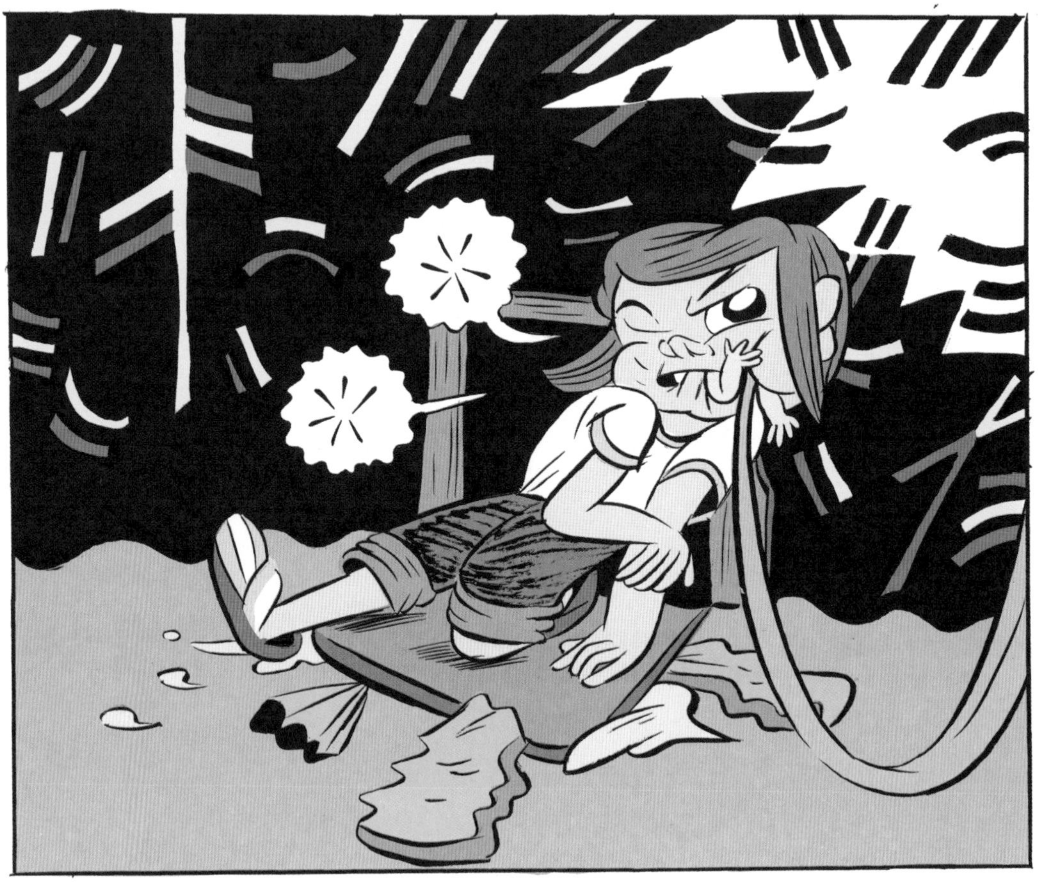

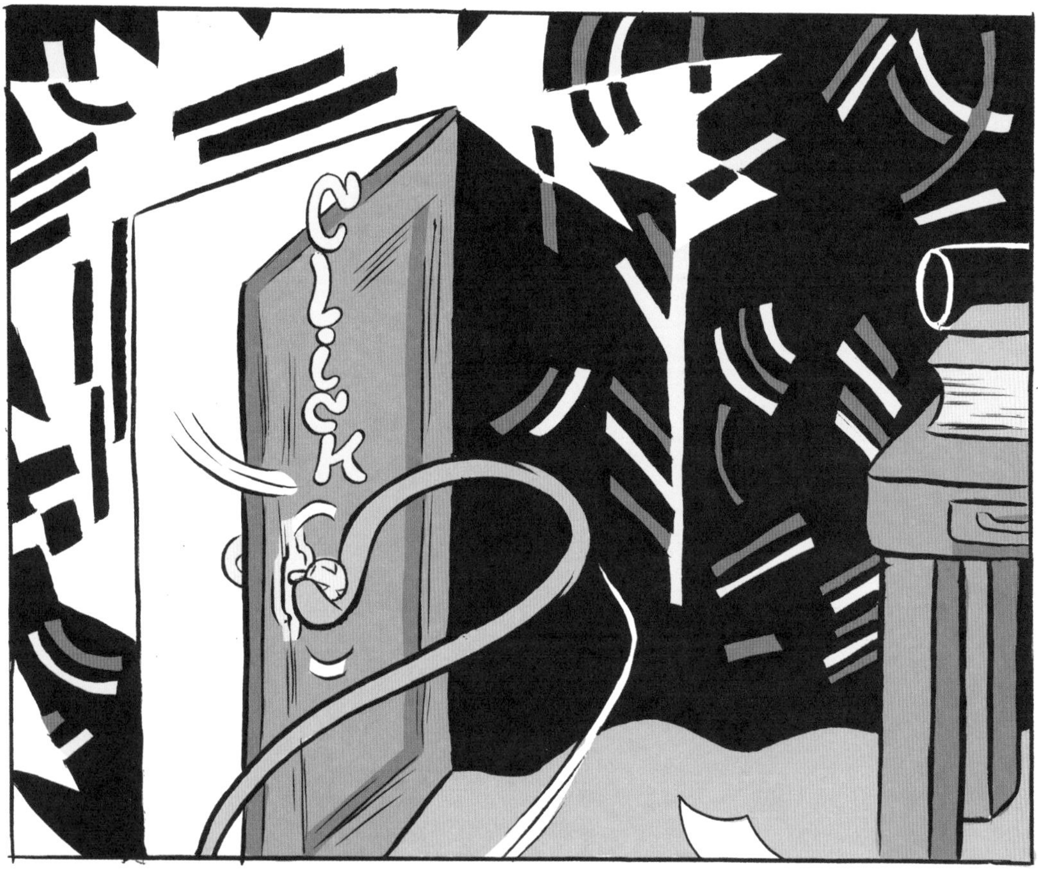
click

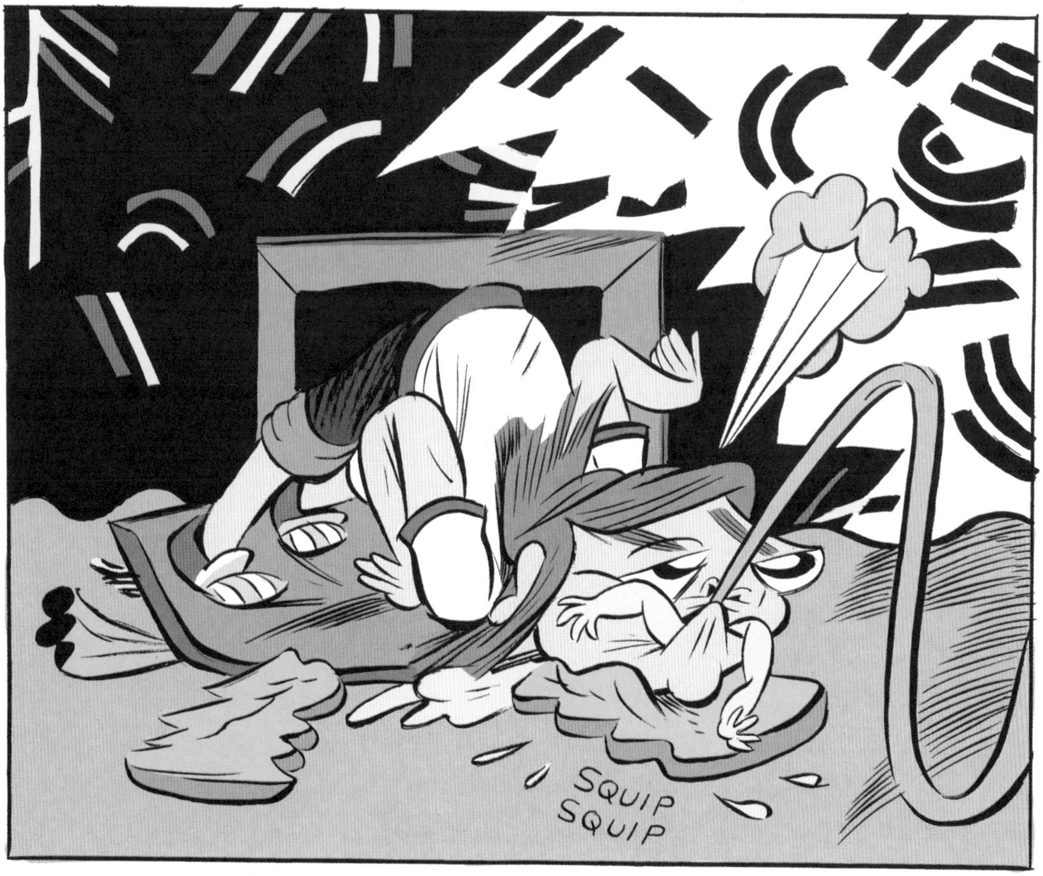
SQUIP
SQUIP

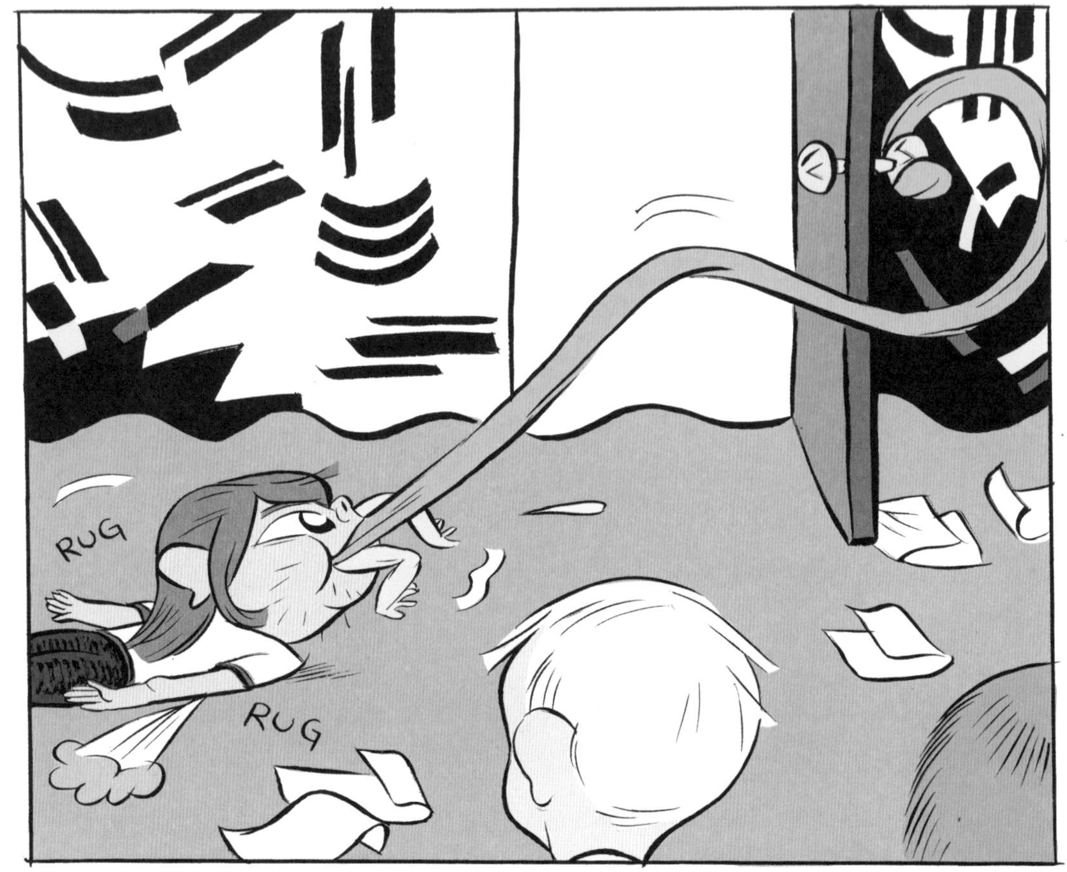
RUG
RUG

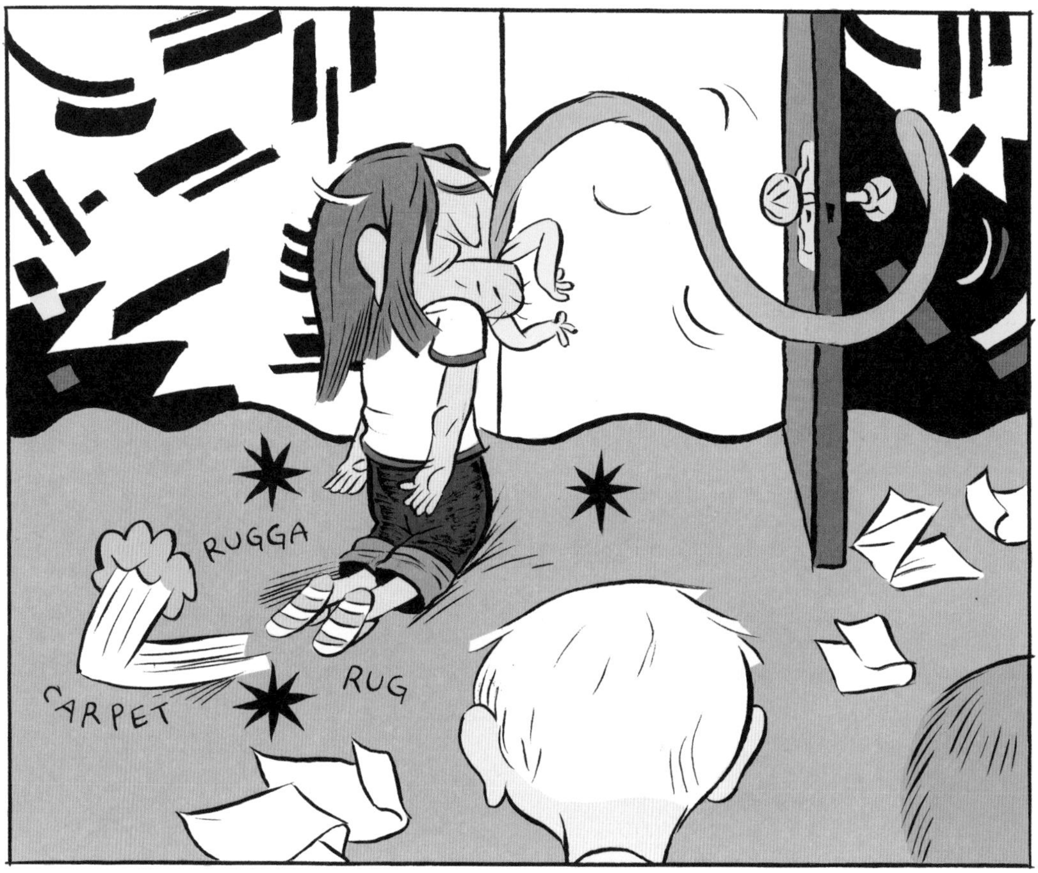
RUGGA
CARPET
RUG

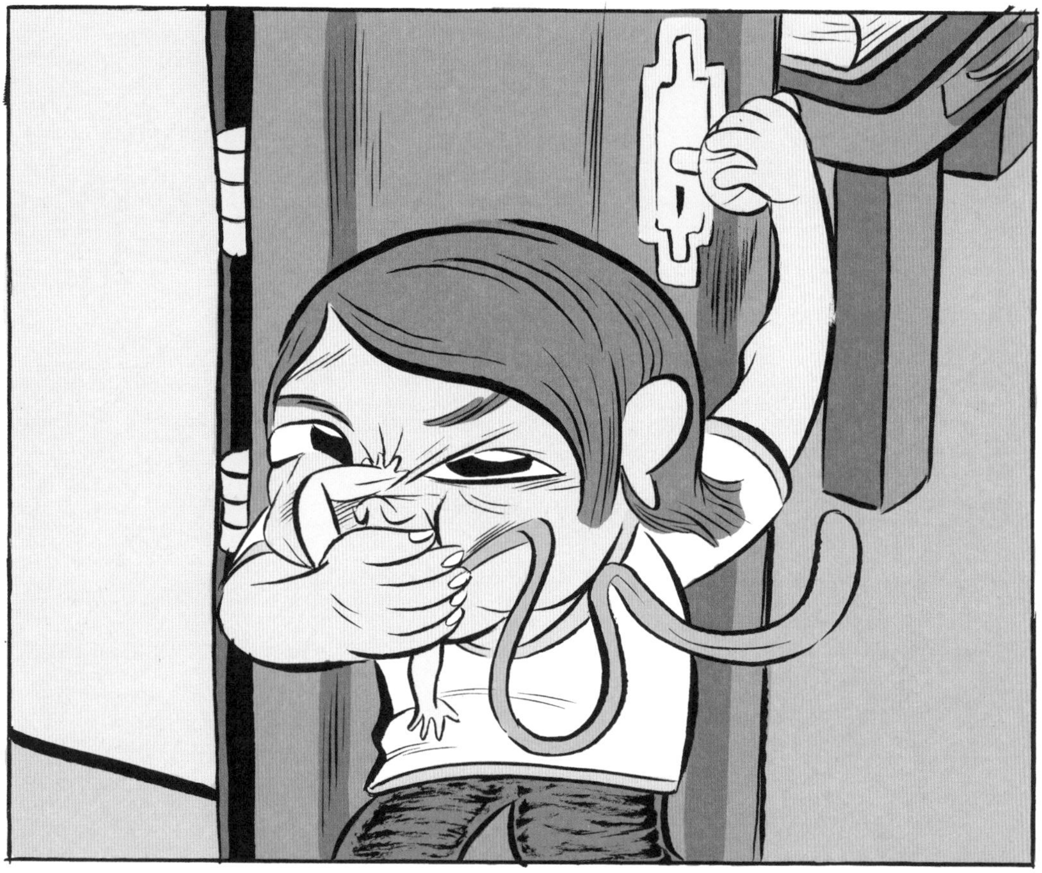
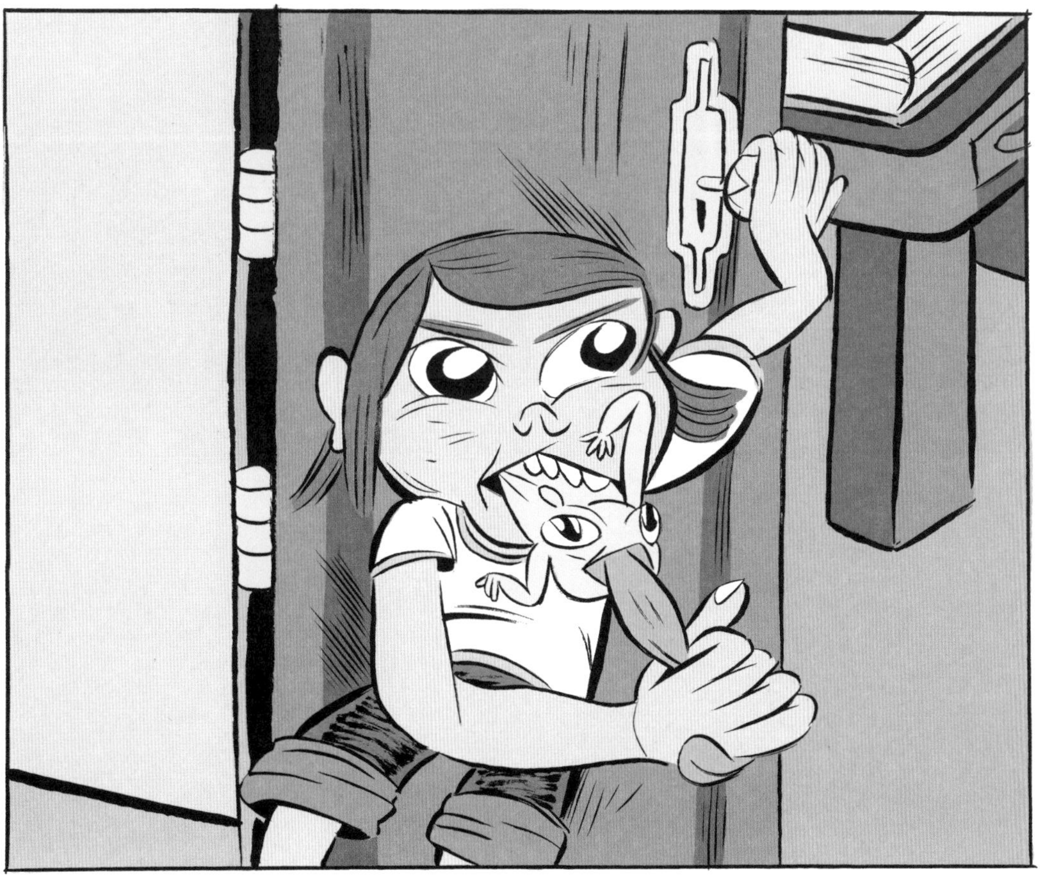

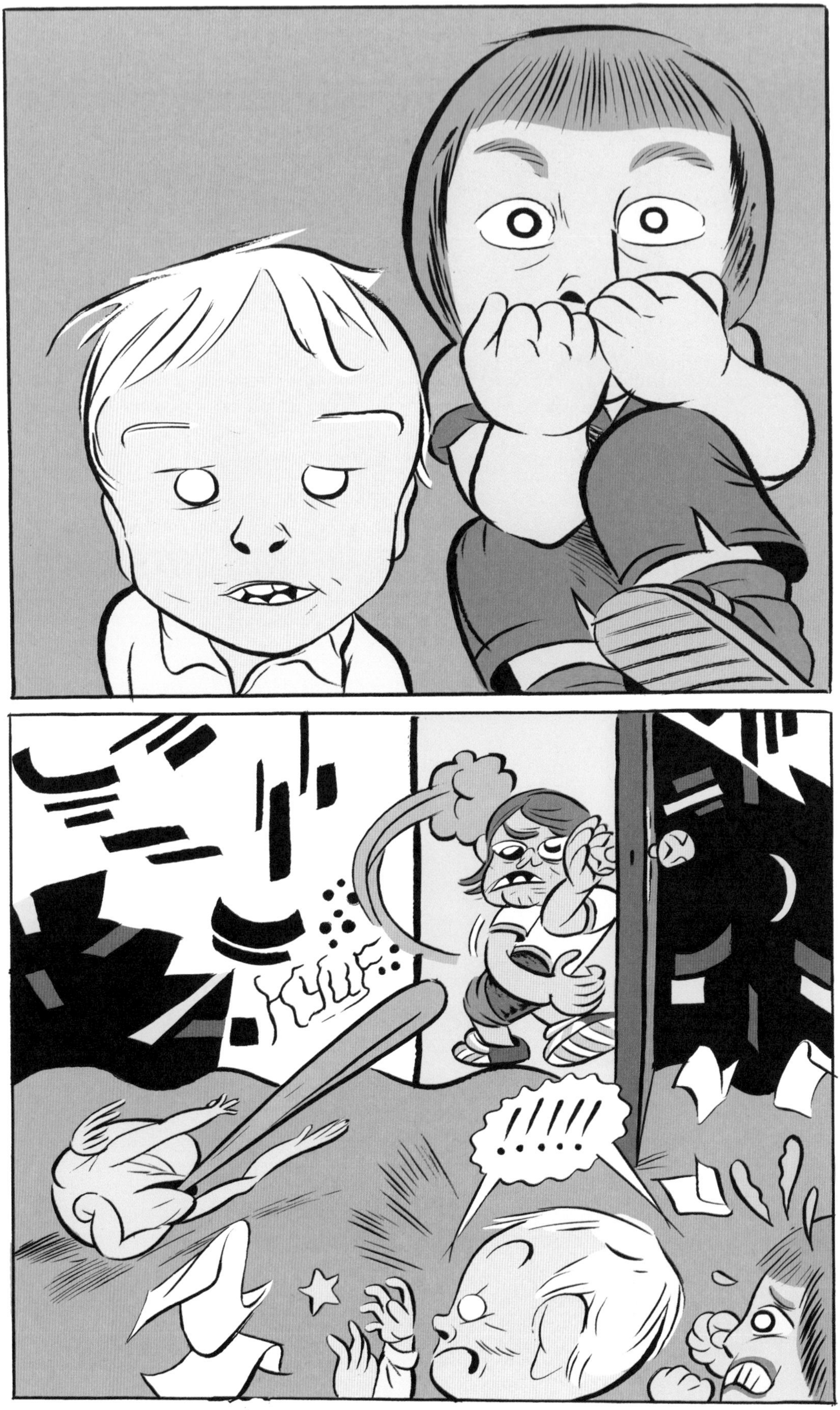
KYUF
!!!!!

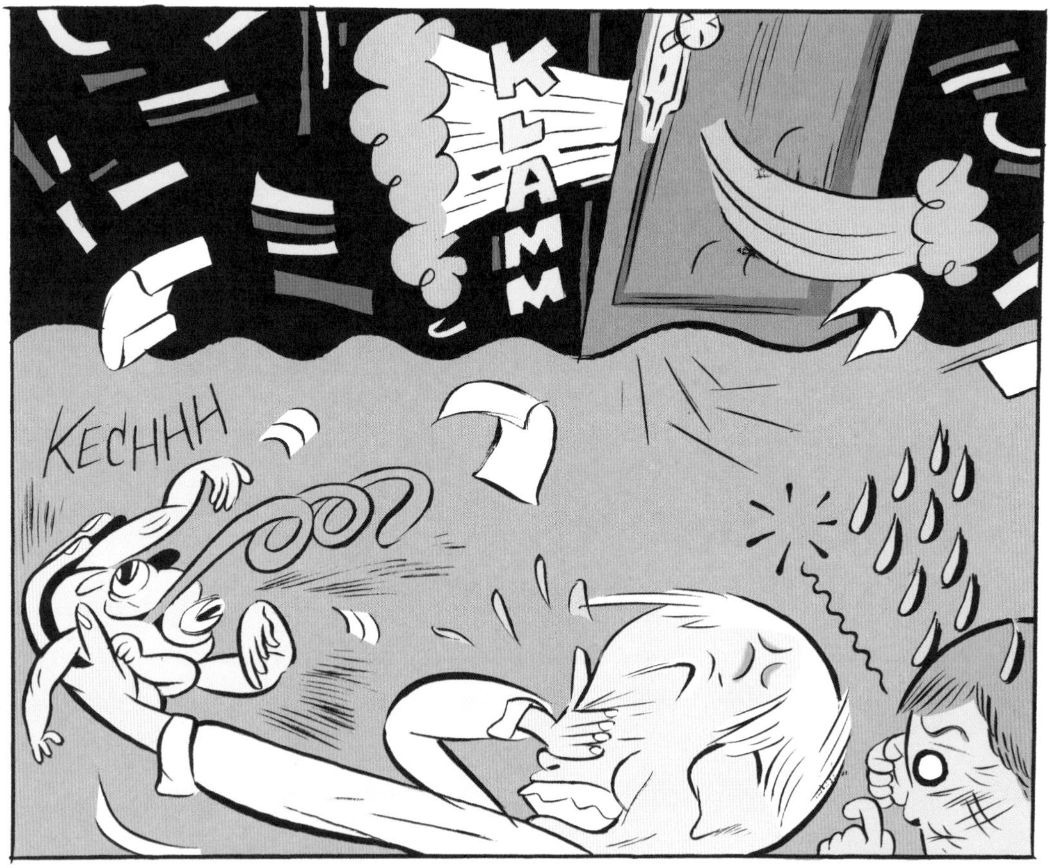
KLAMM
KECHHH

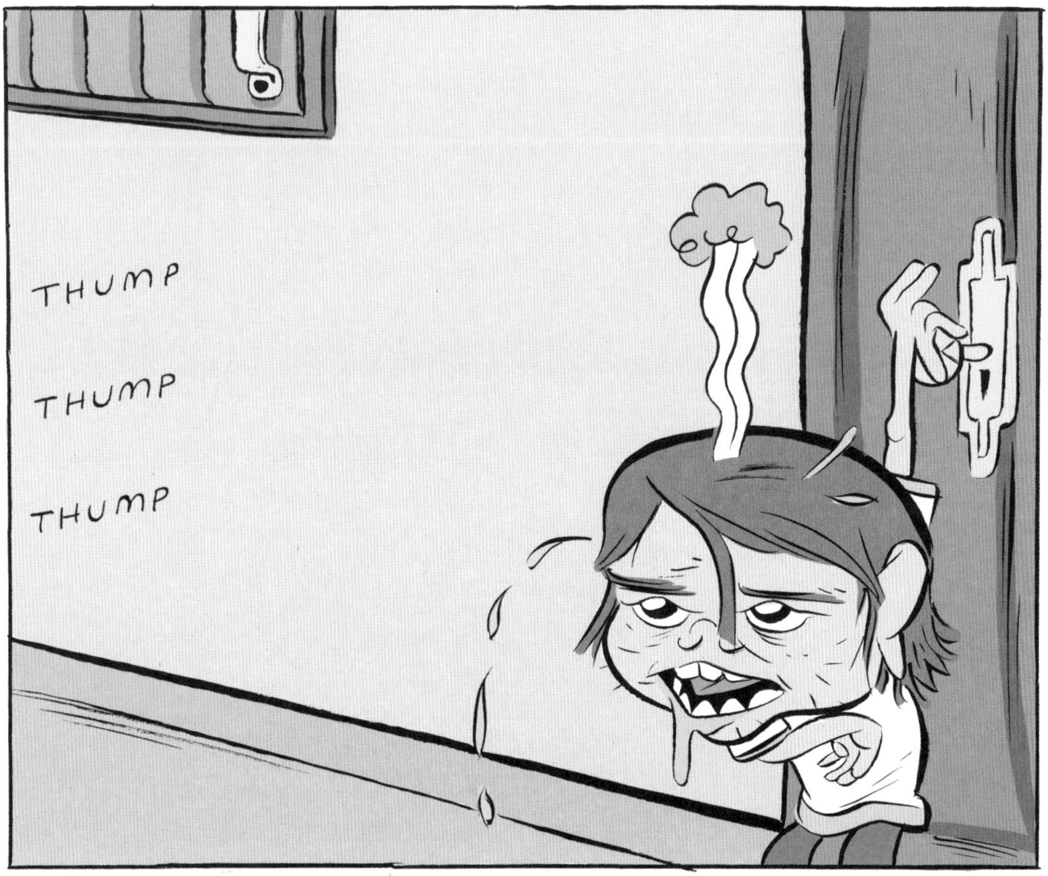
THUMP
THUMP
THUMP

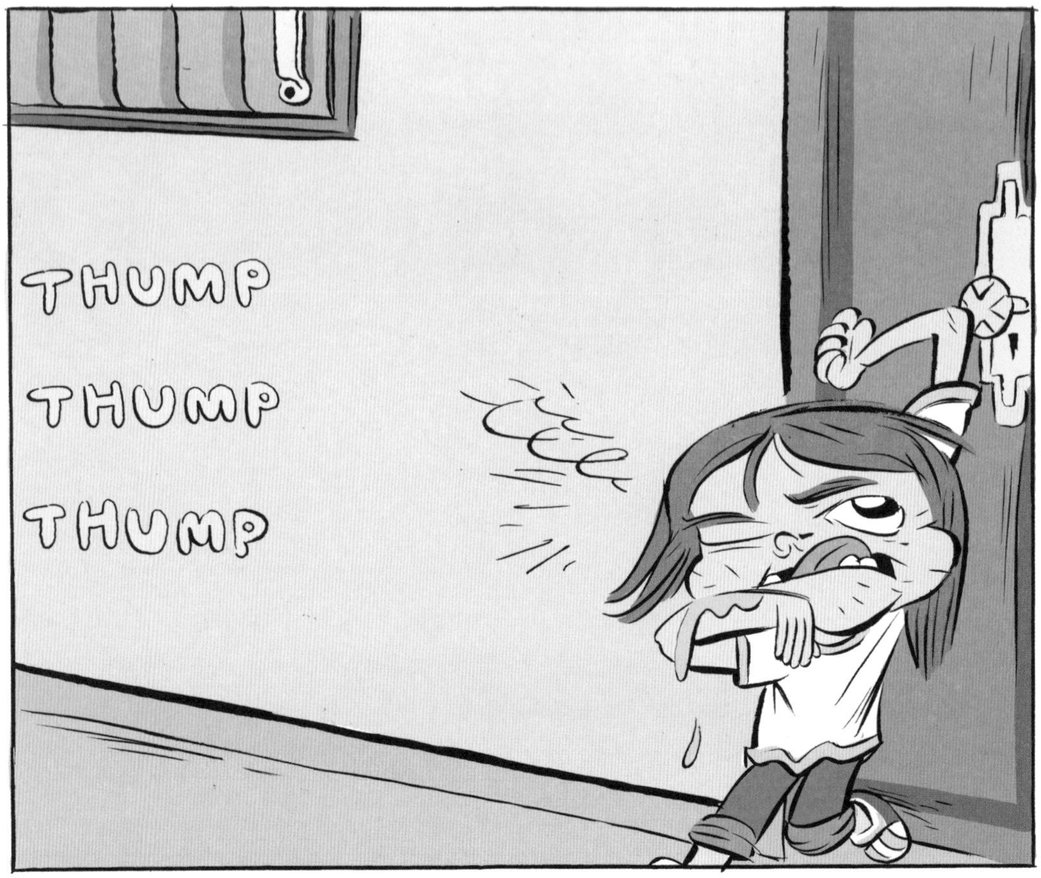
THUMP
THUMP
THUMP

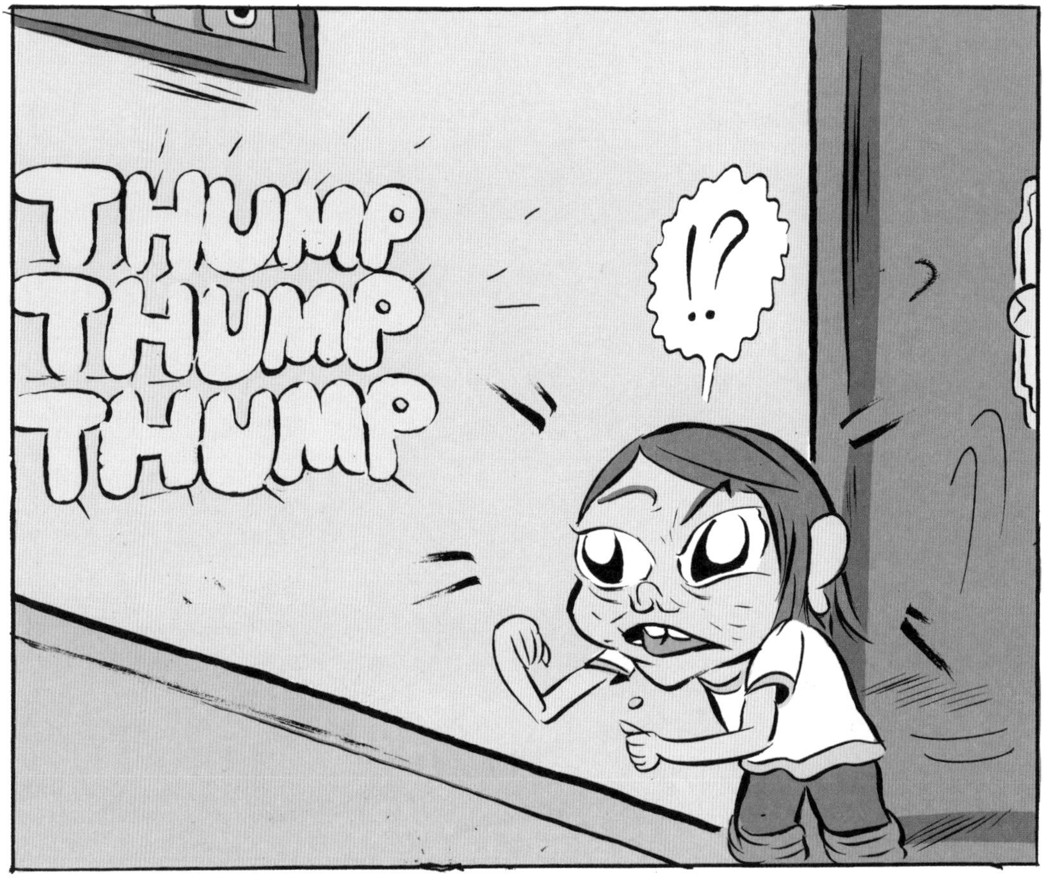
THUMP
THUMP
THUMP
!?

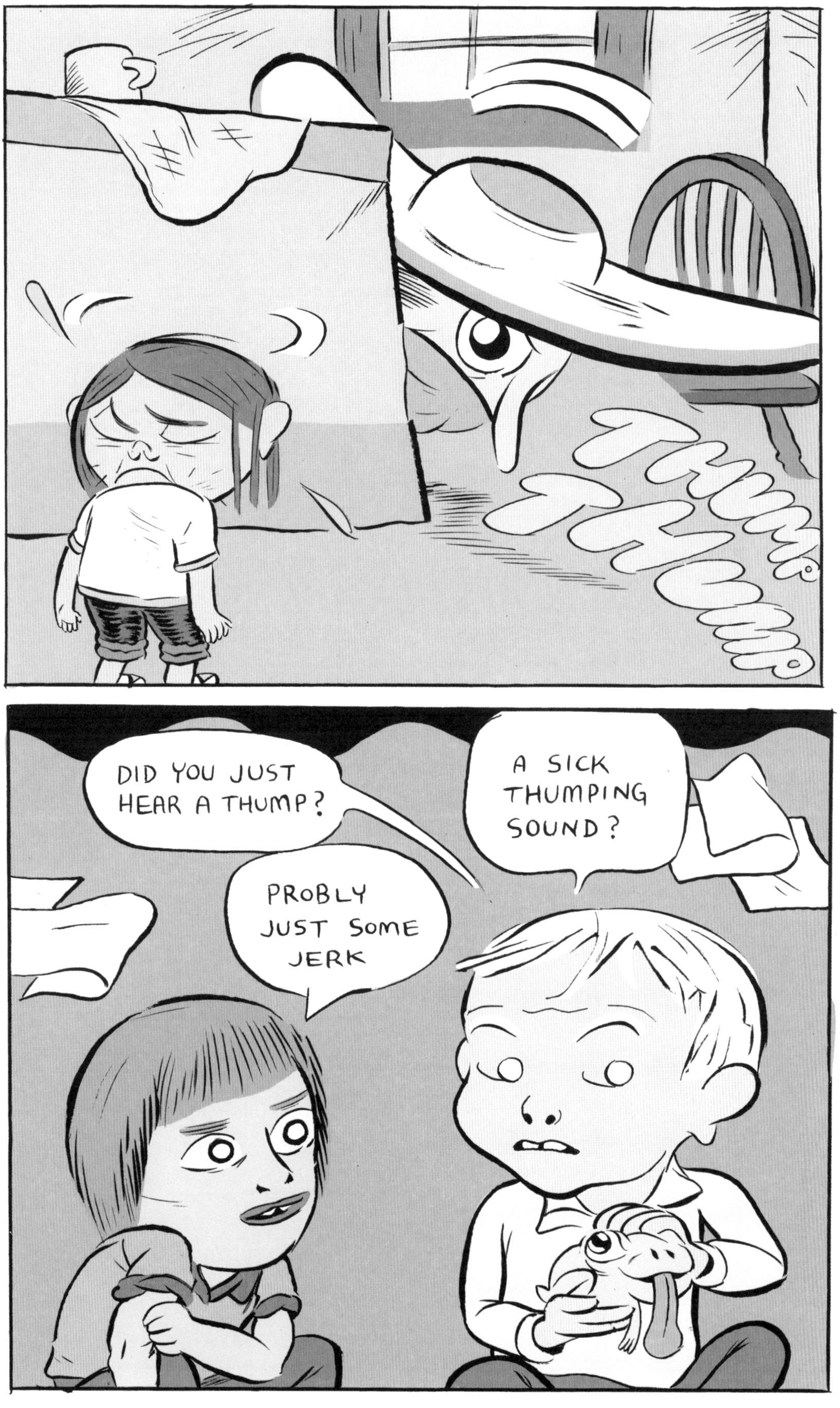
THUMP
THUMP
DID YOU JUST HEAR A THUMP?
A SICK THUMPING SOUND?
PROBLY JUST SOME JERK

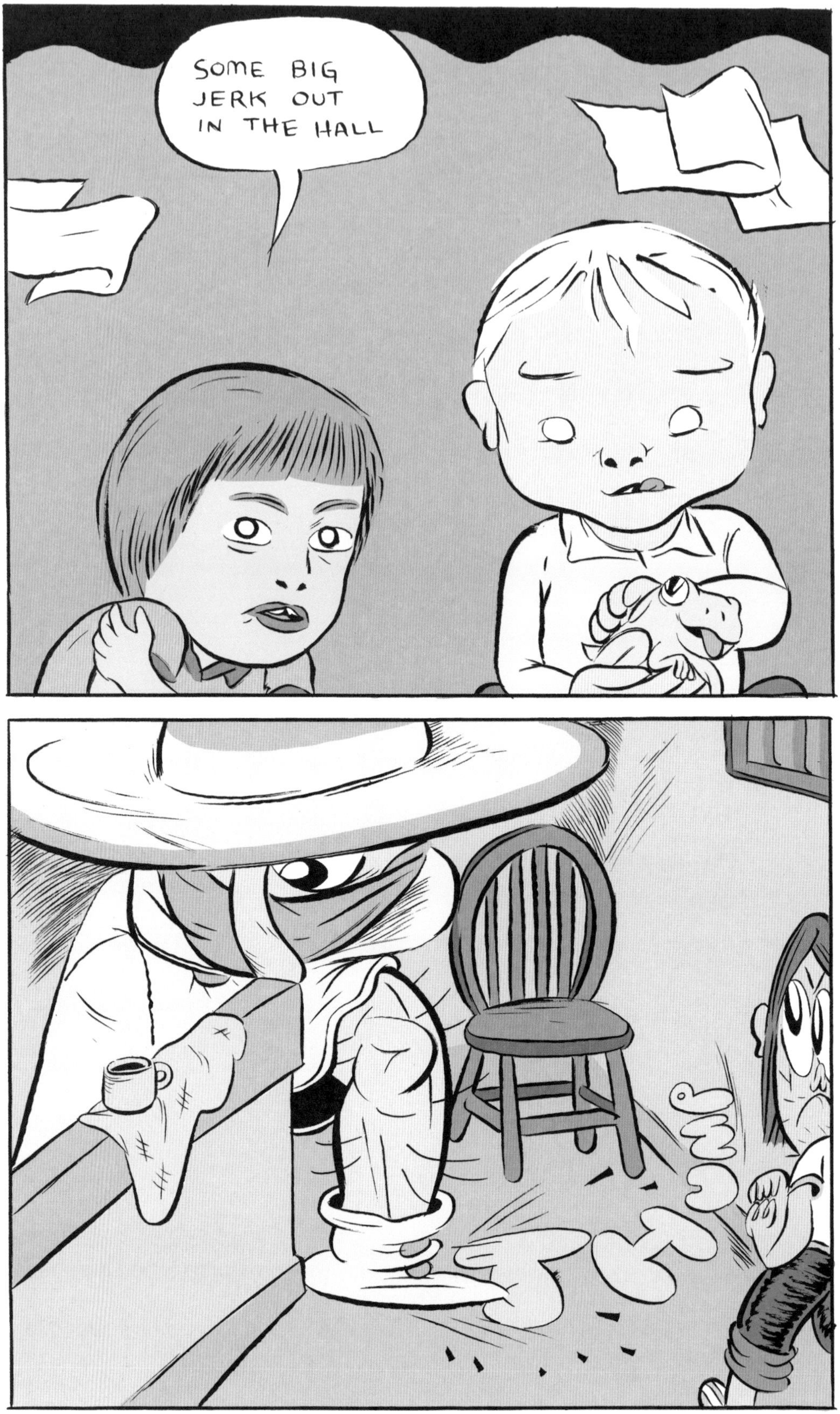
SOME BIG JERK OUT IN THE HALL

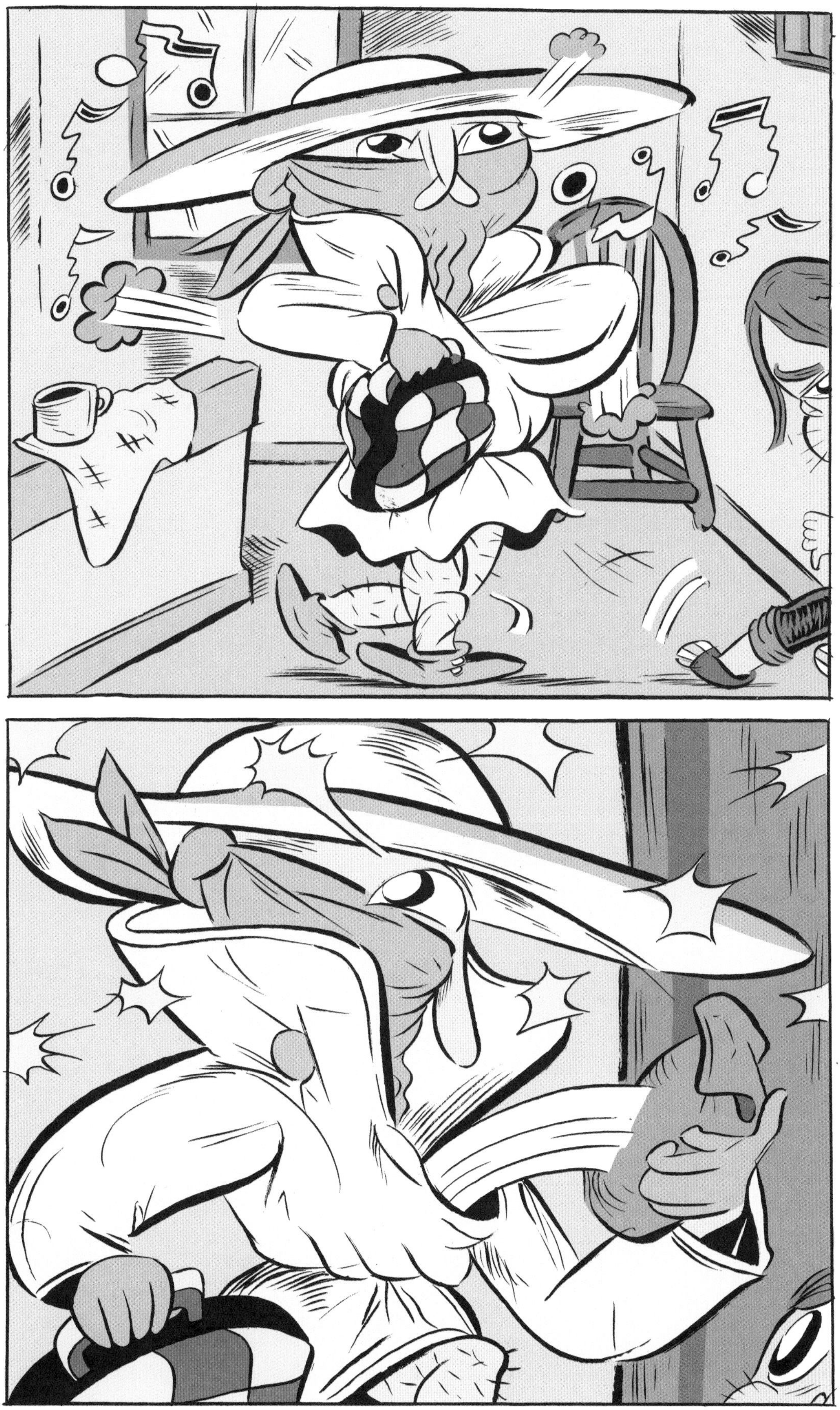

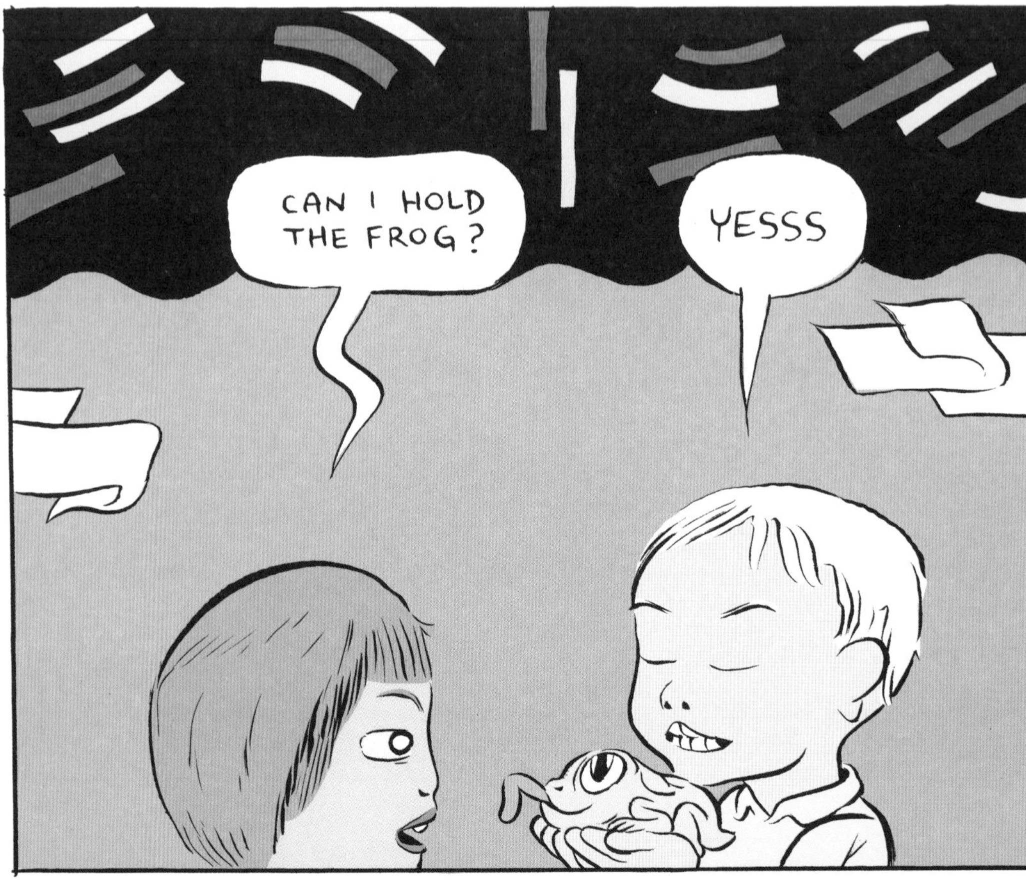
CAN I HOLD THE FROG?
YESSS

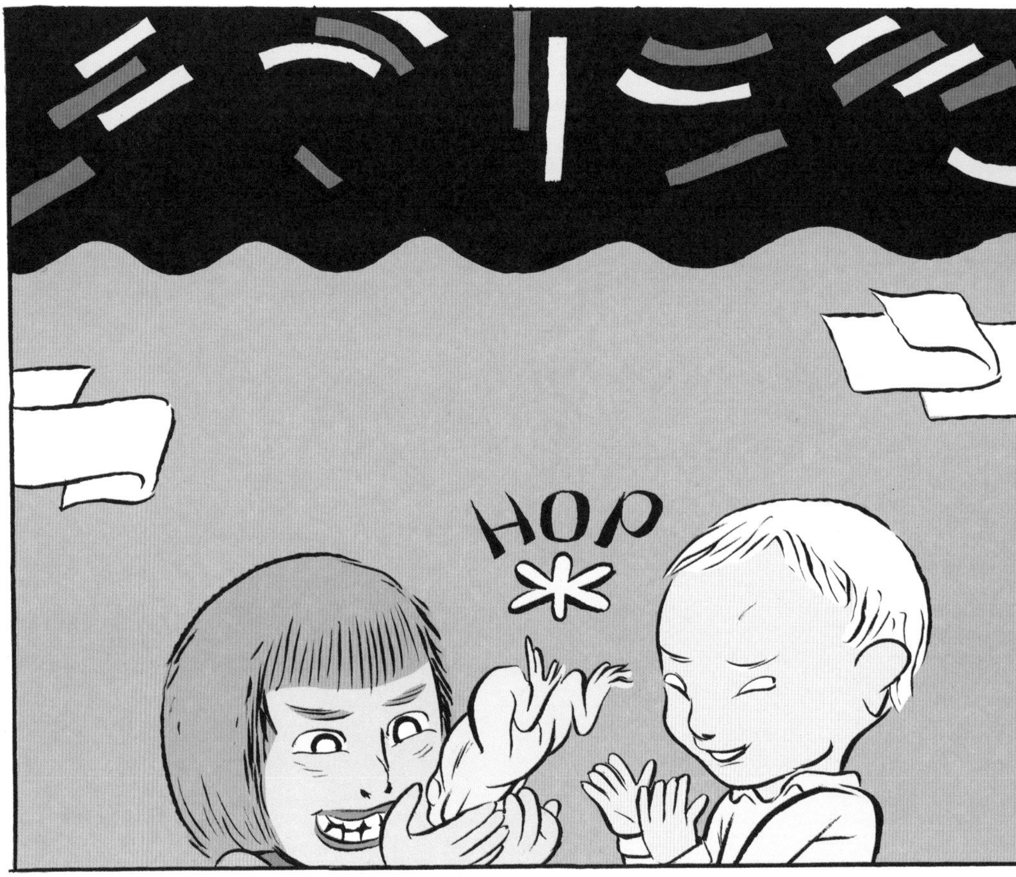
HOP

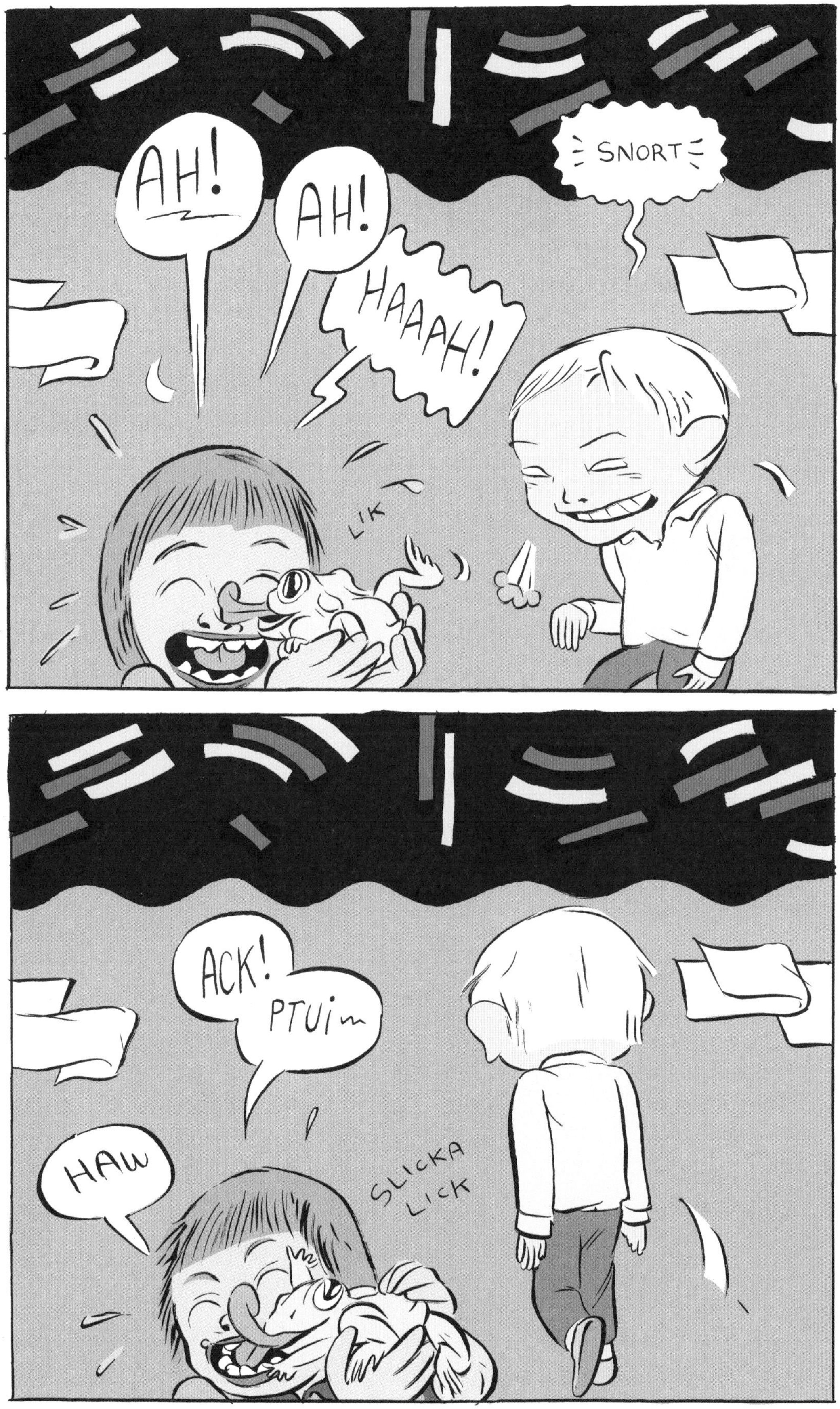
AH!
AH!
HAAAAH!
SNORT
LIK
ACK! PTUI
HAW
SLICKA LICK

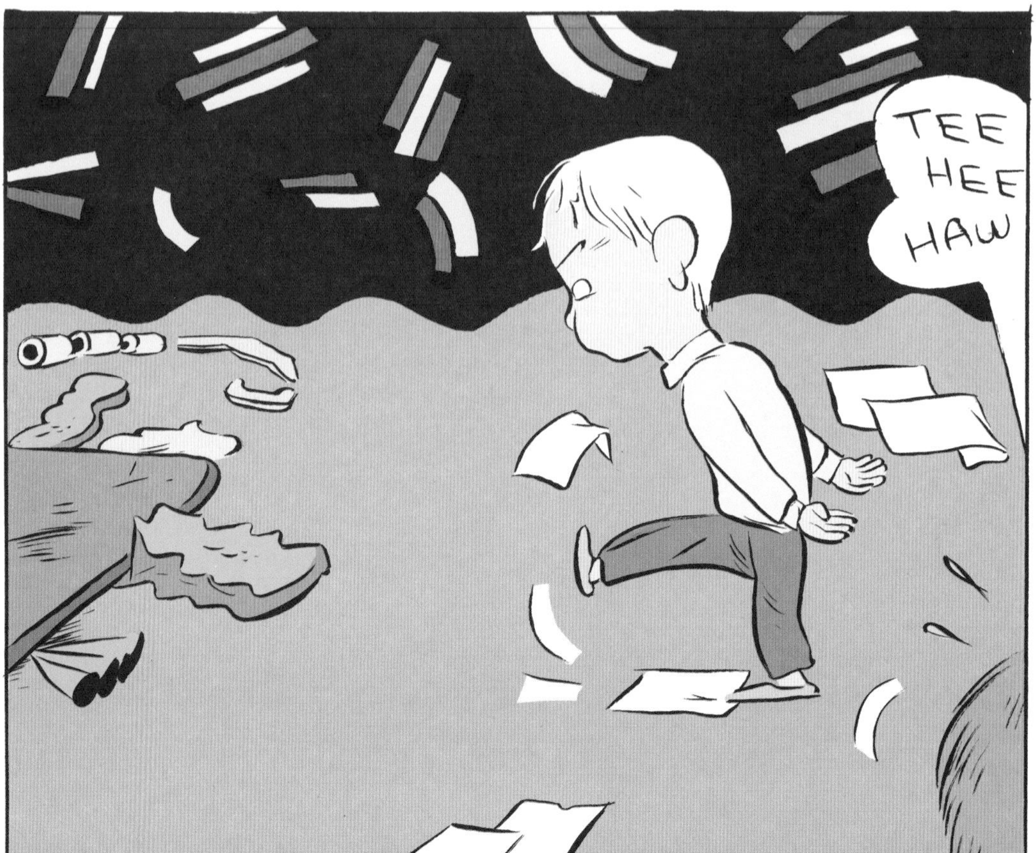
TEE HEE HAW

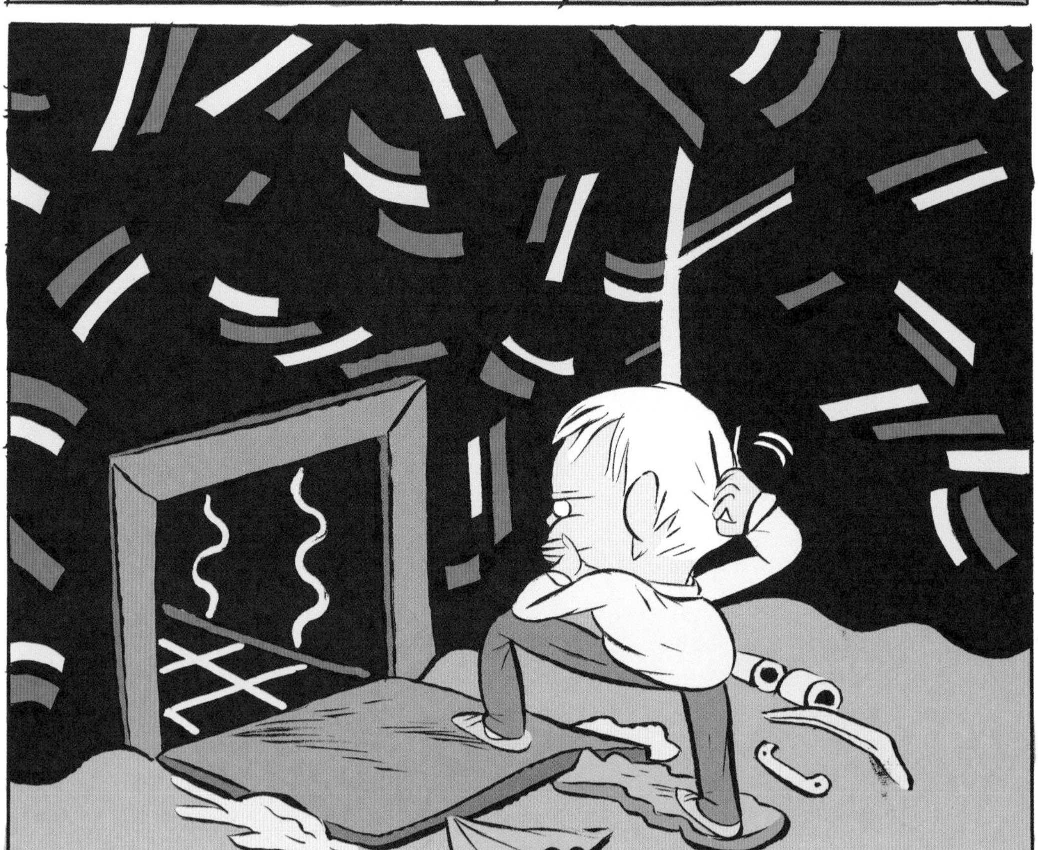

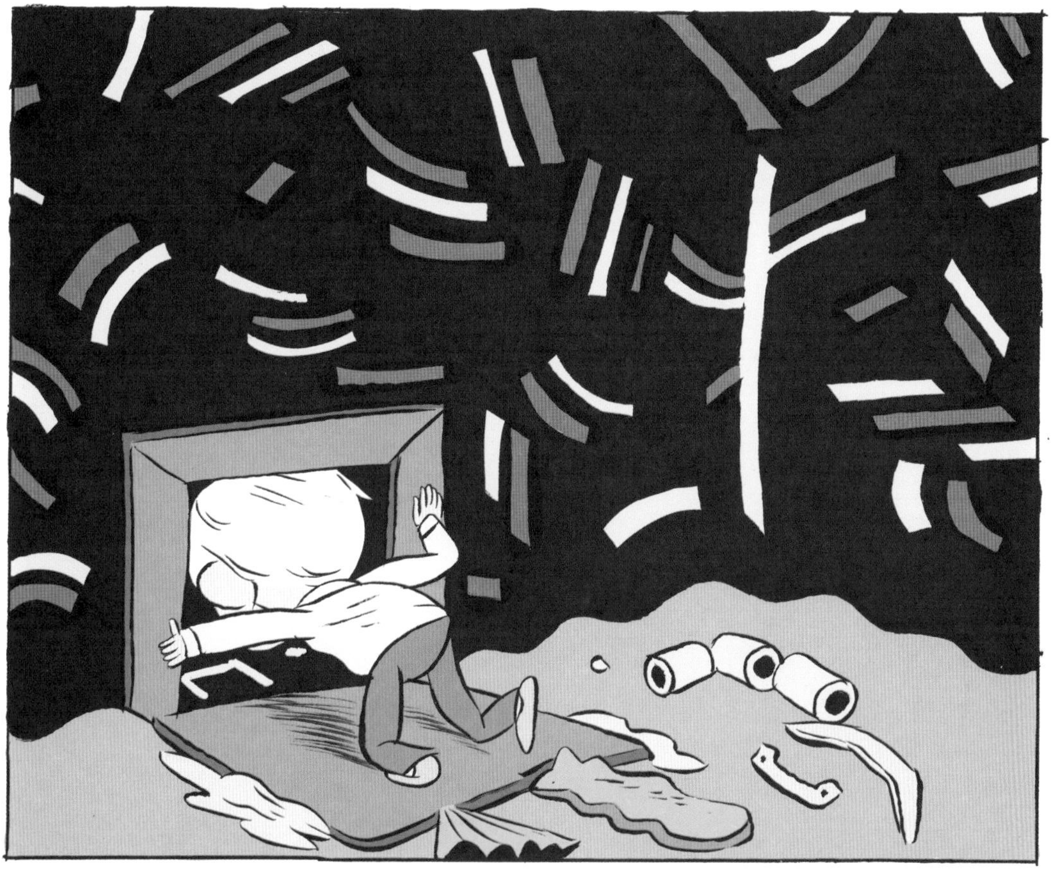

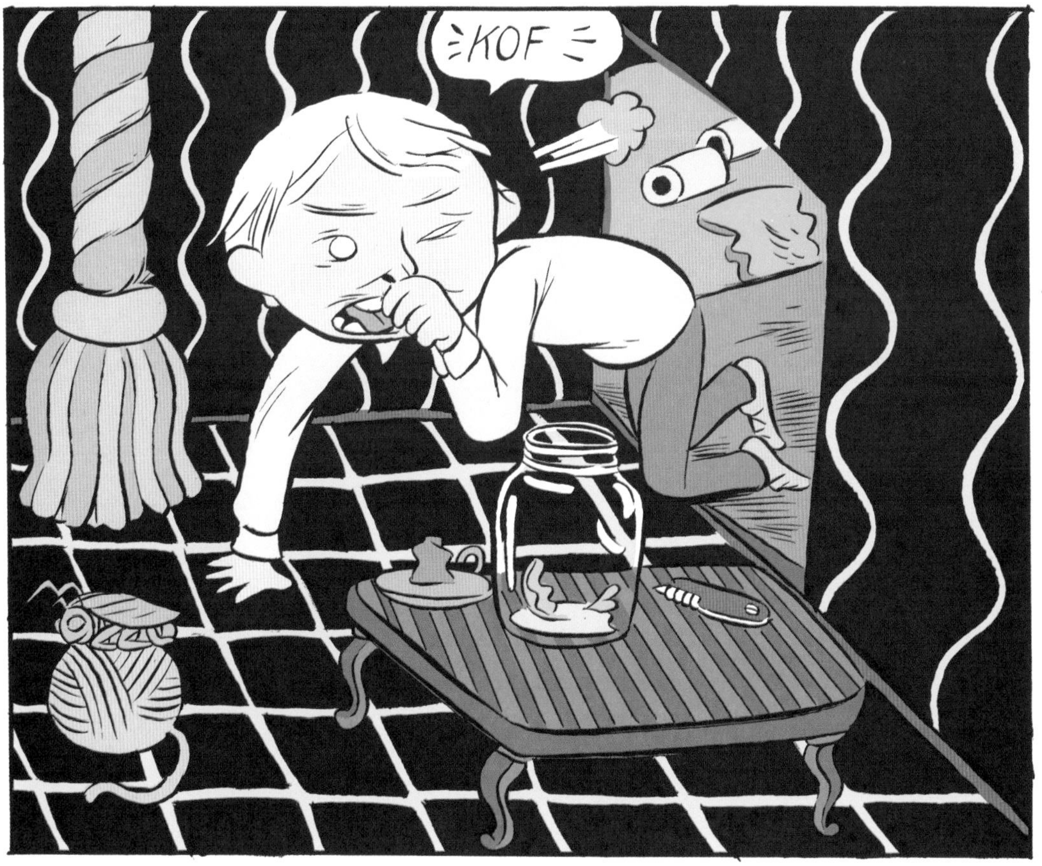
KOF

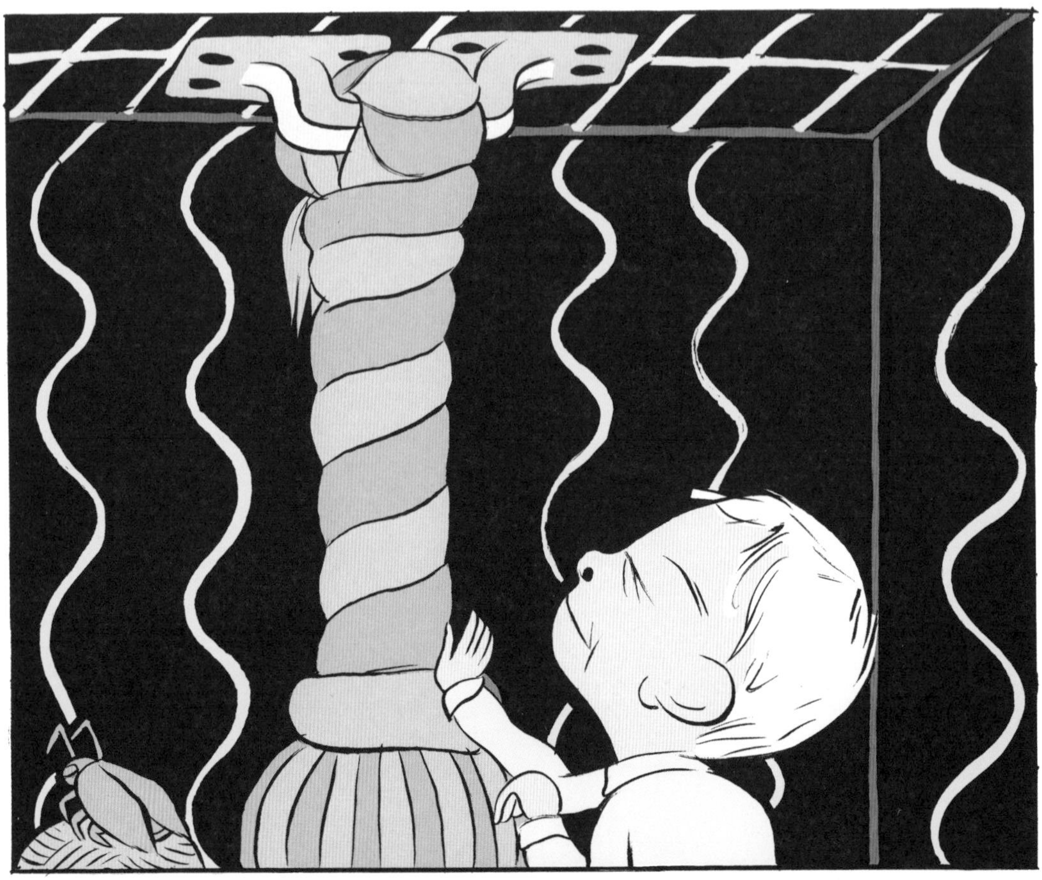

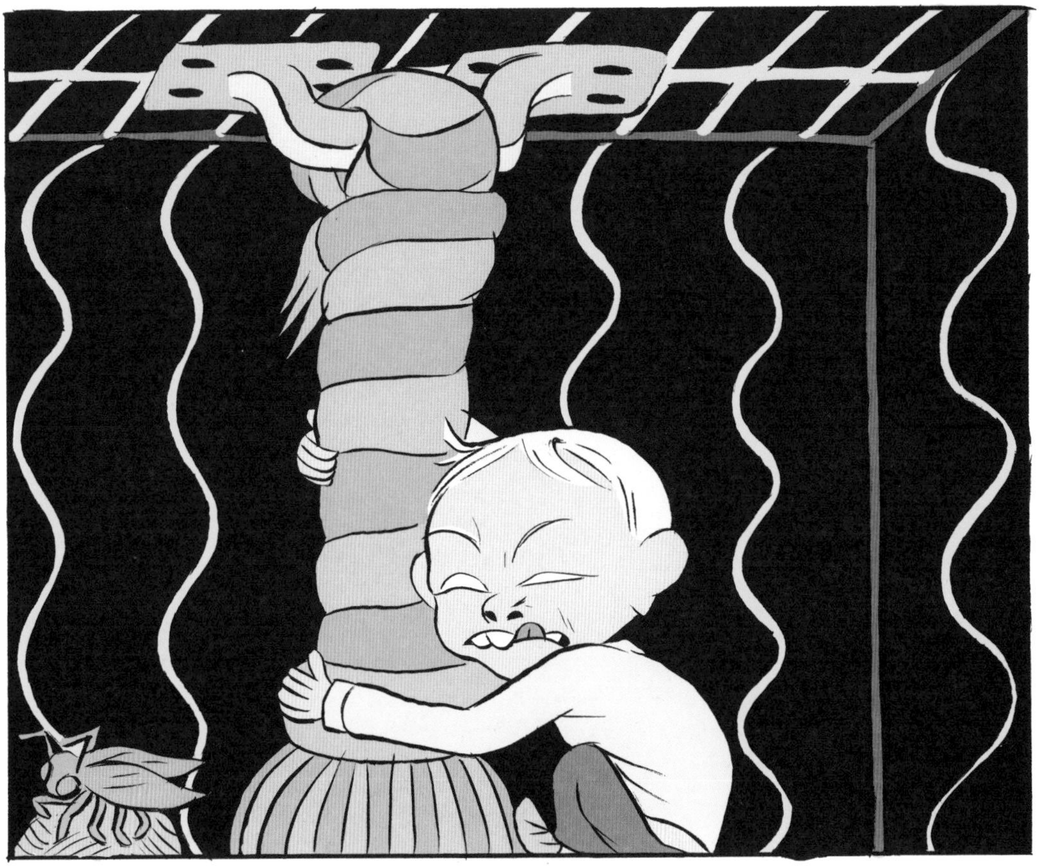

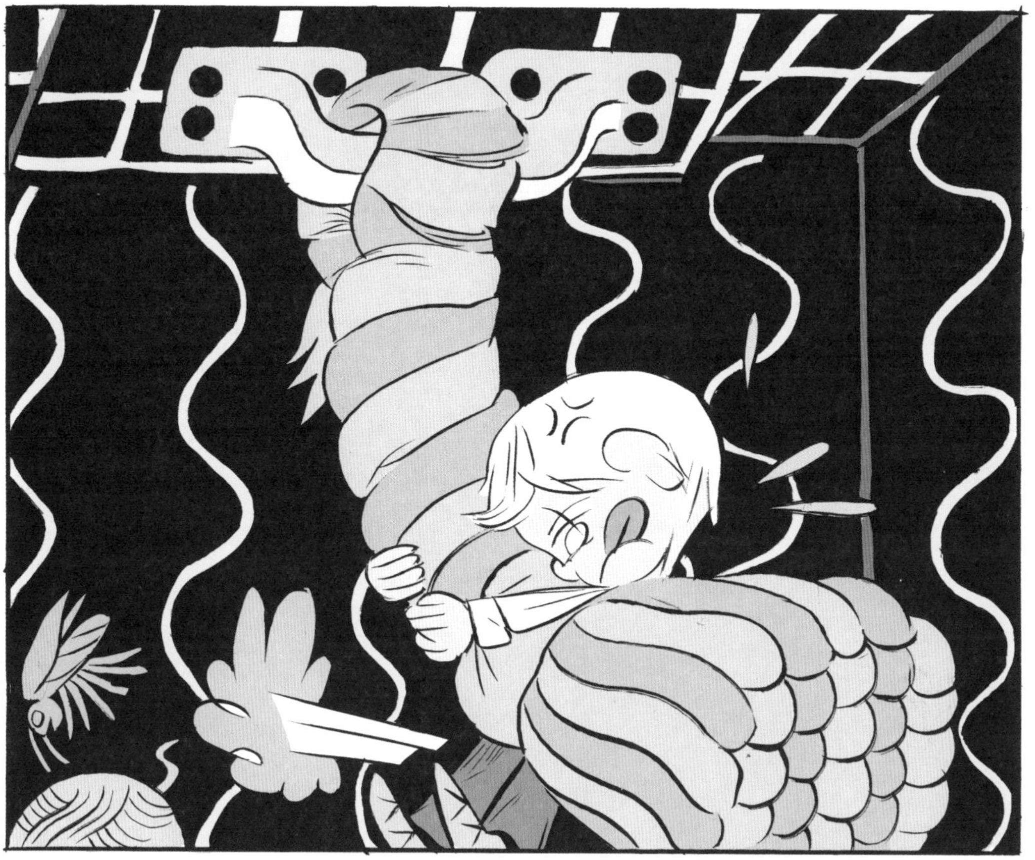

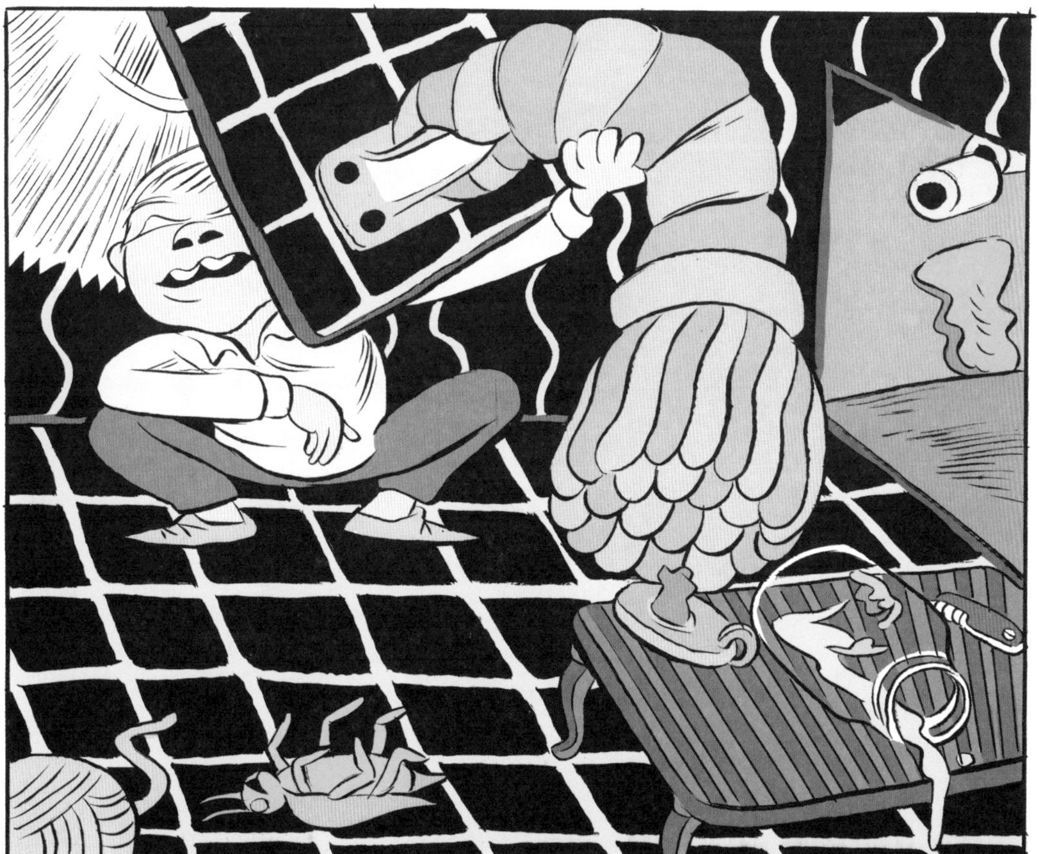

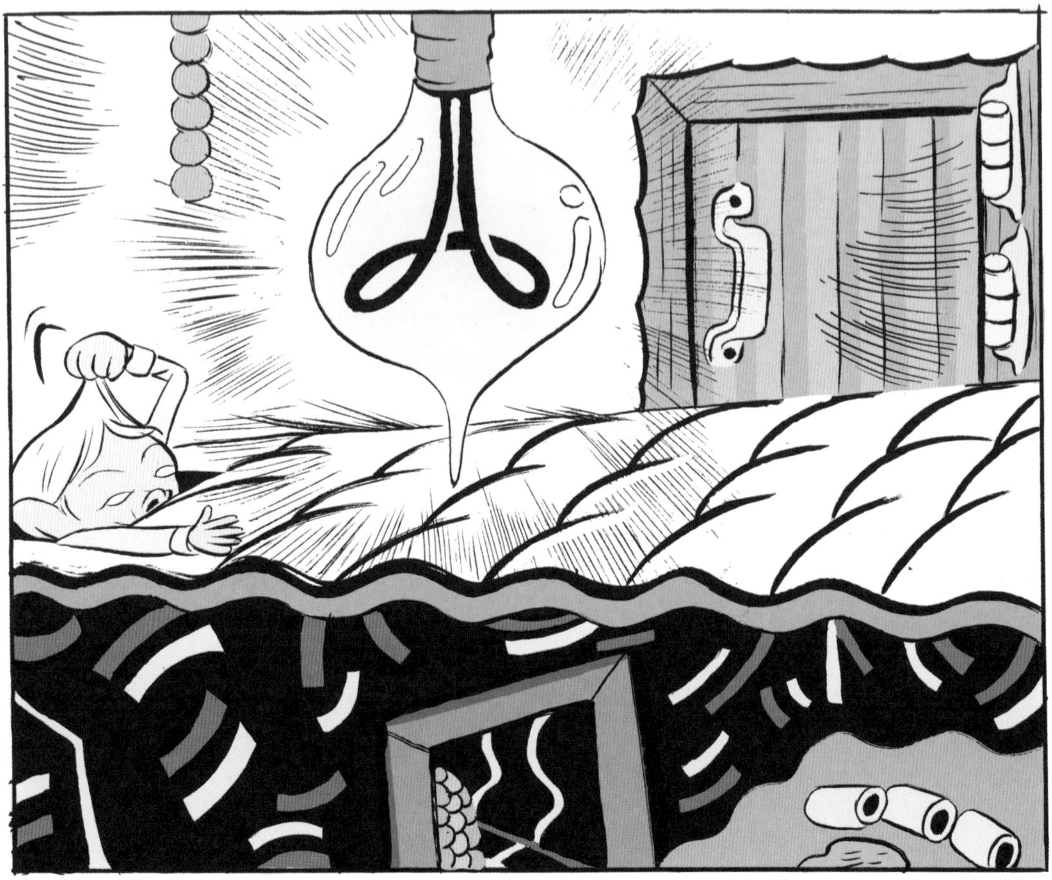

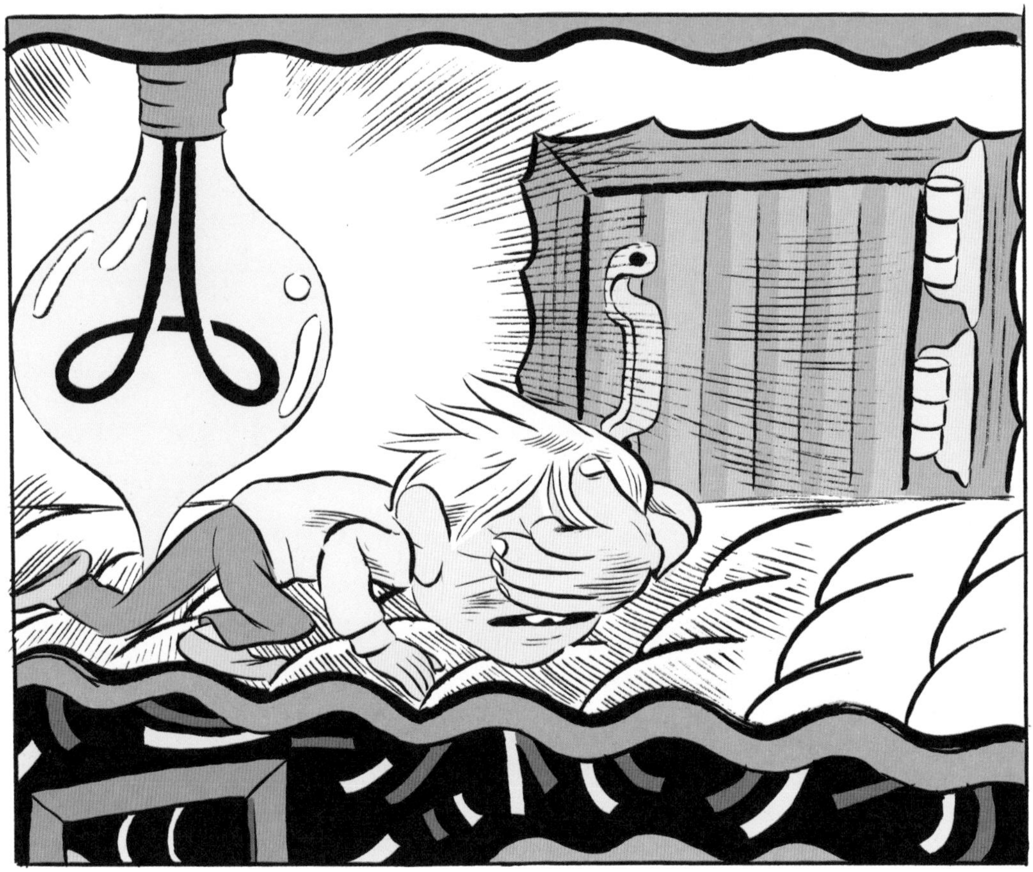

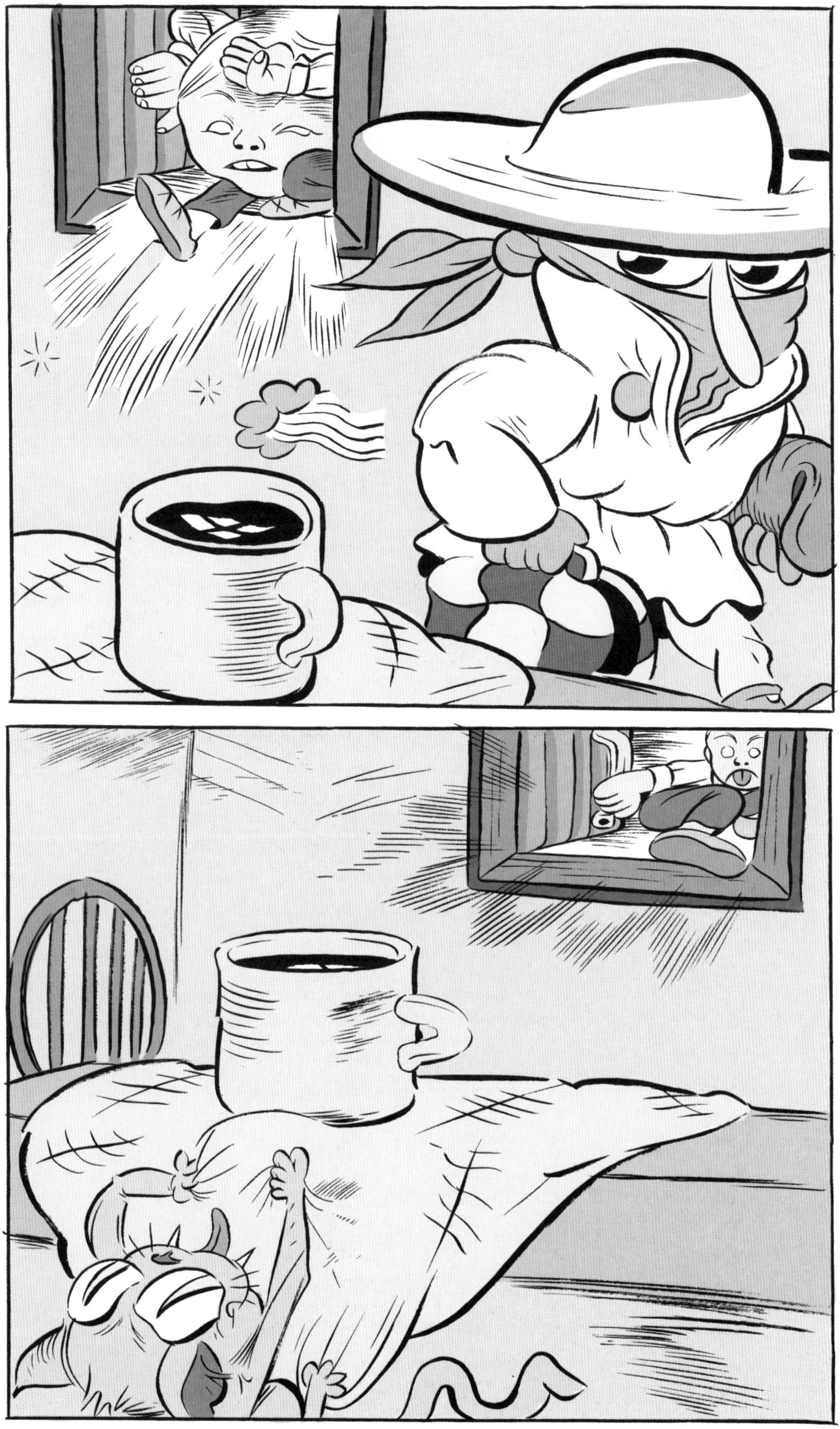

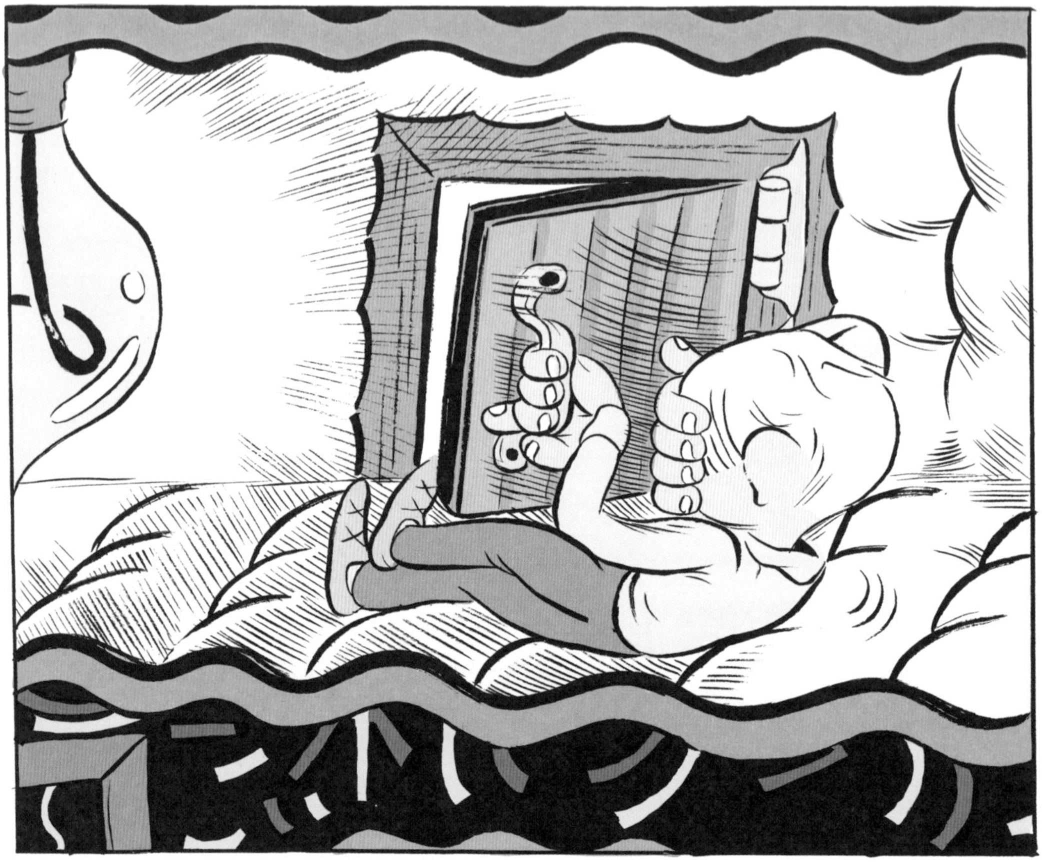

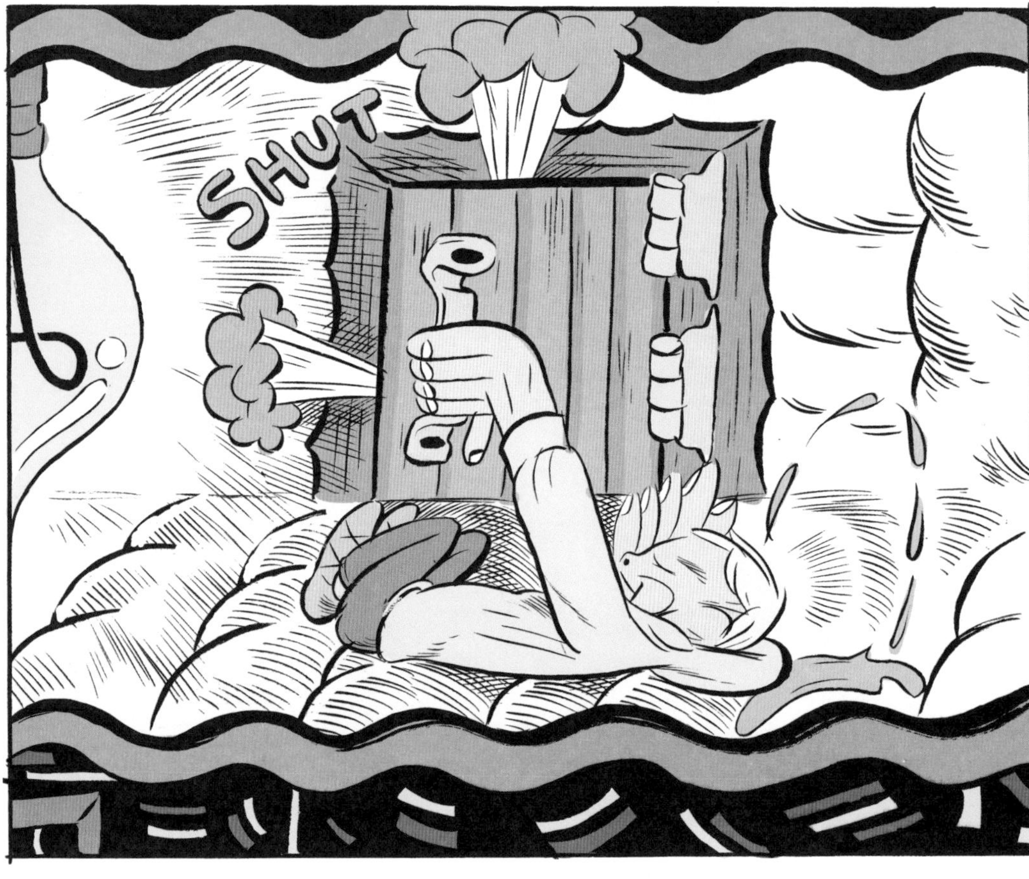
SHUT

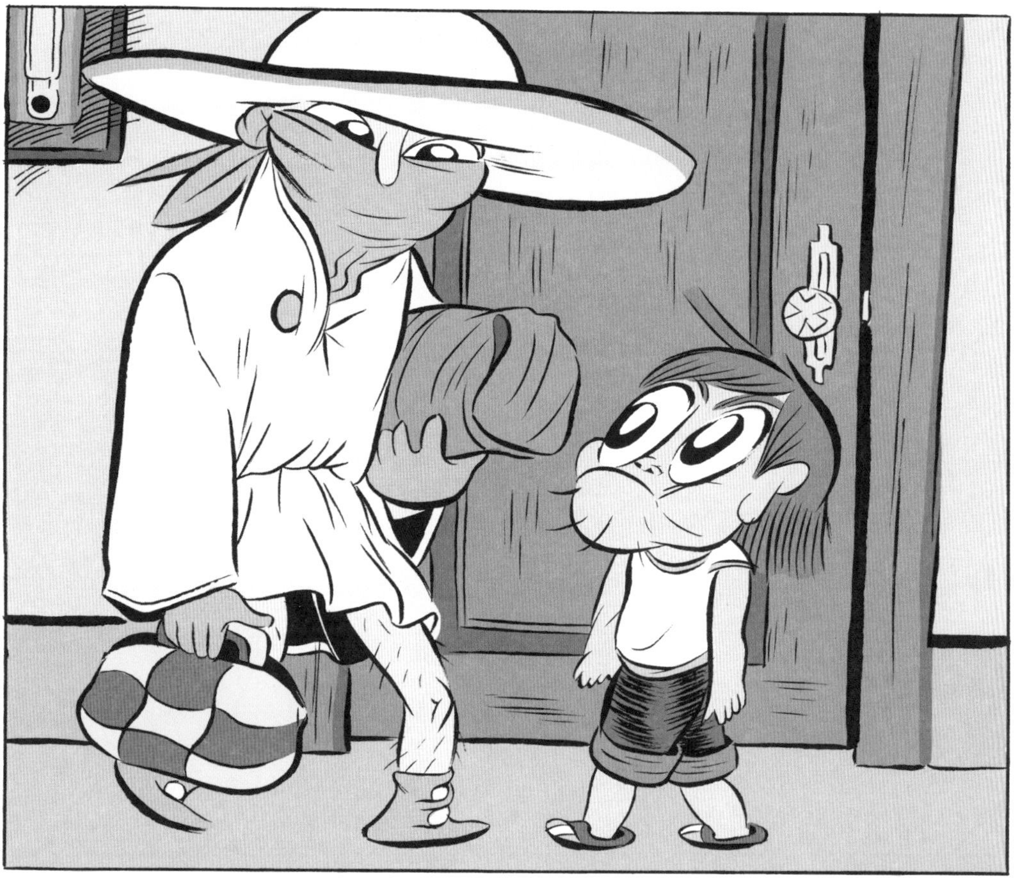

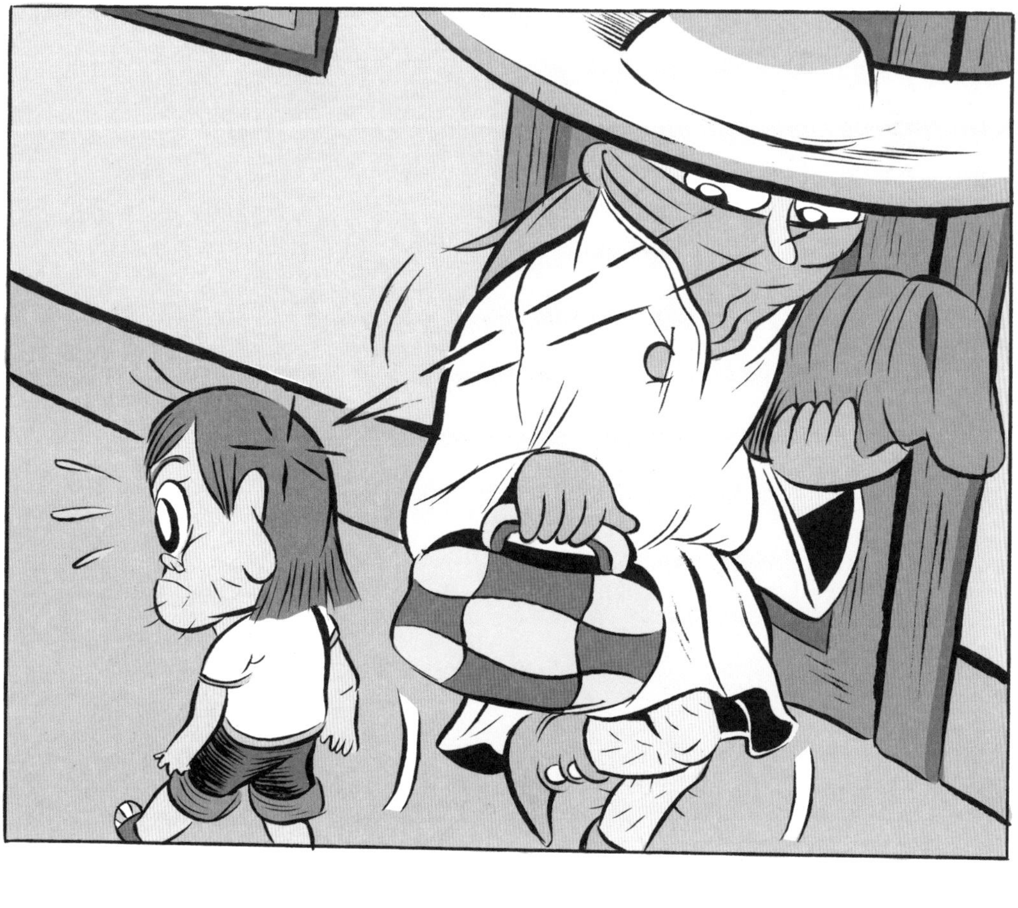

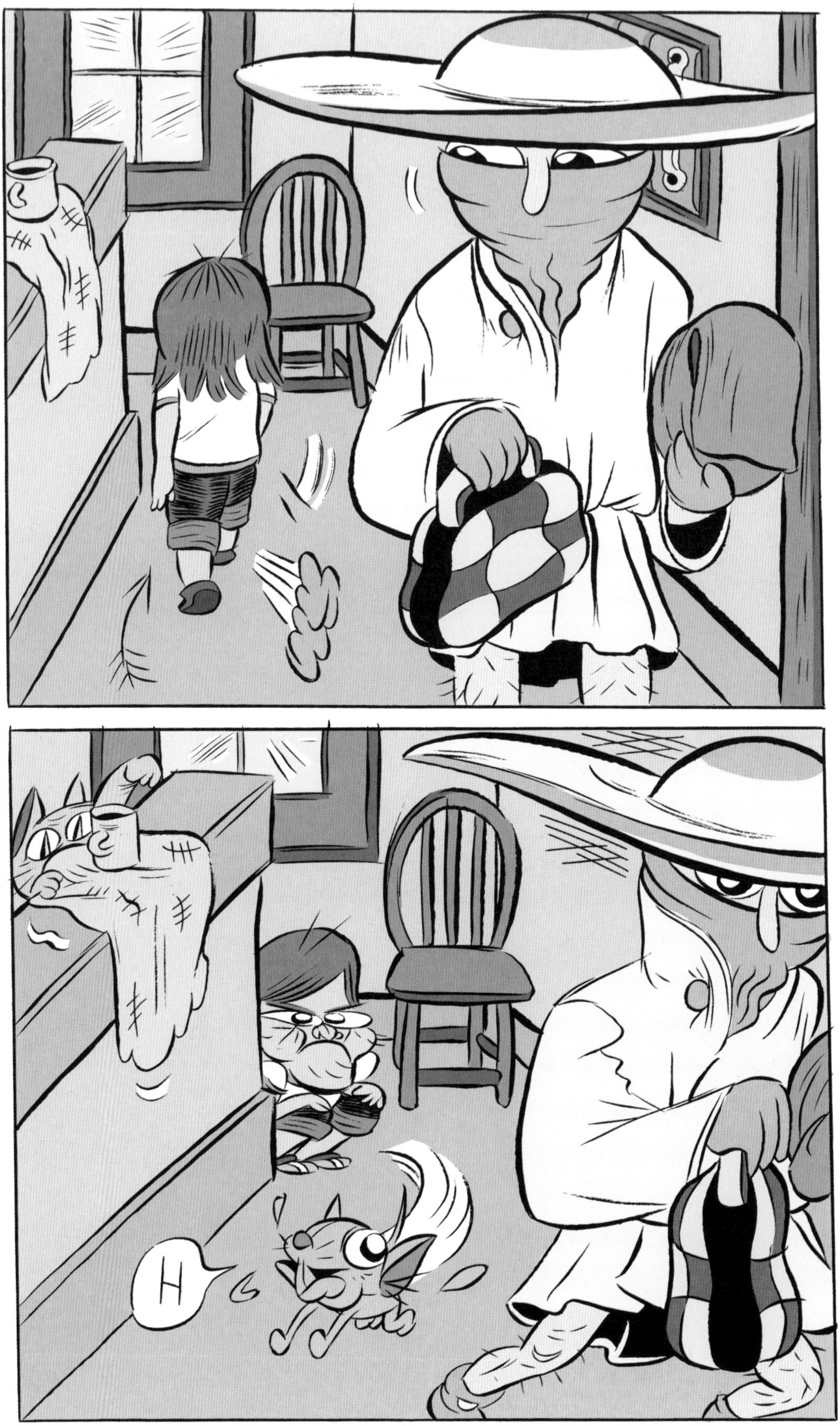
H

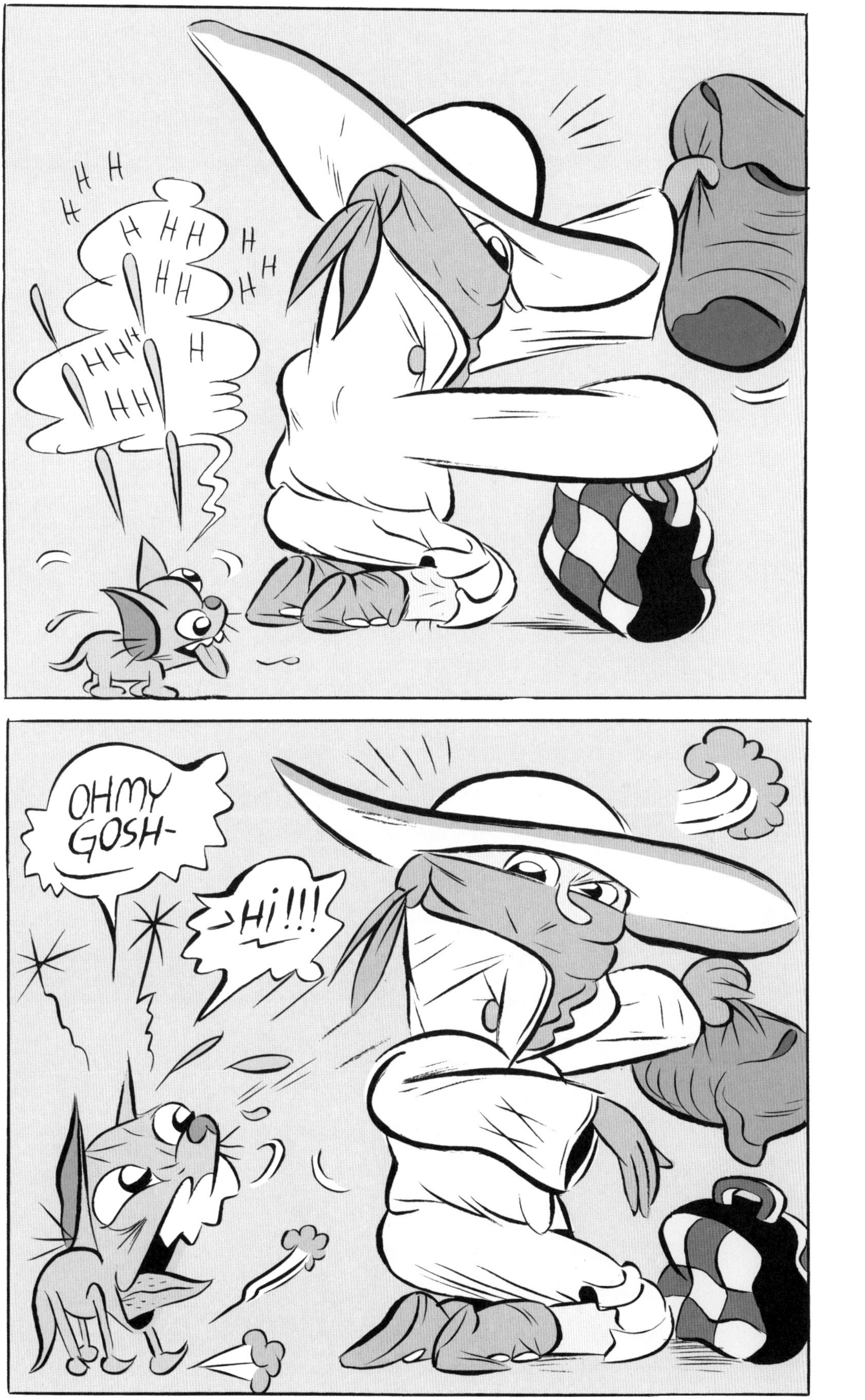
OHMY GOSH-
-Hi!!!

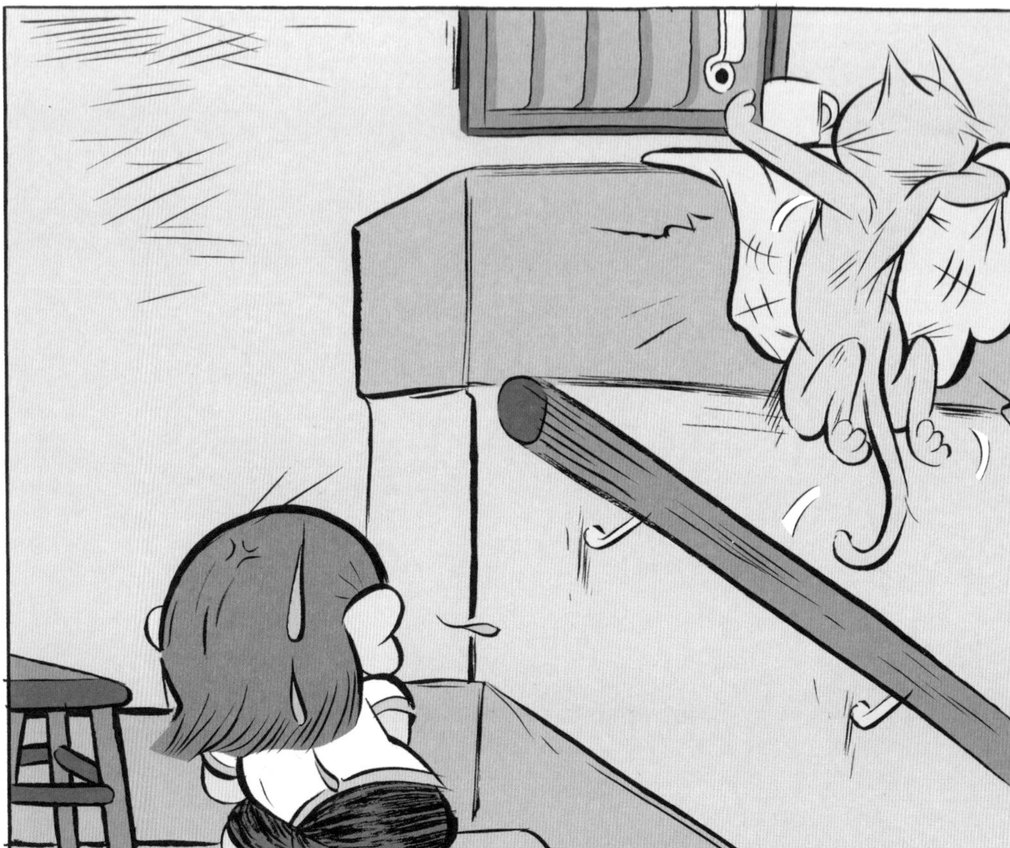

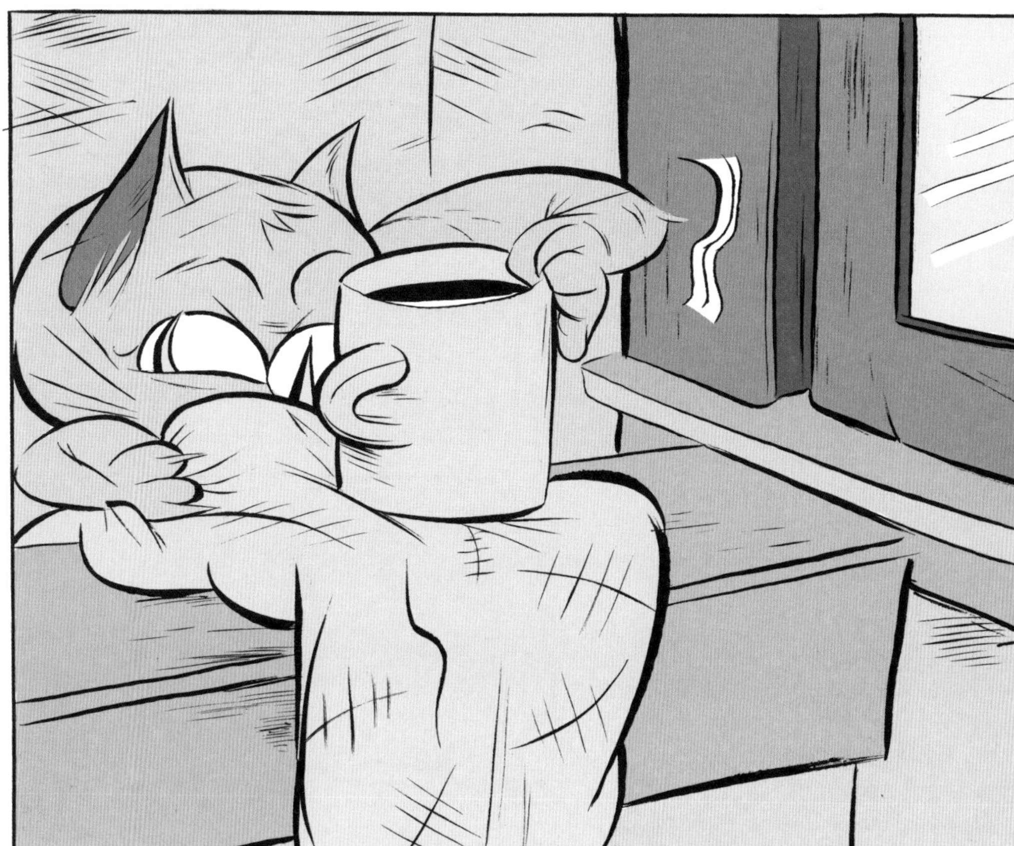

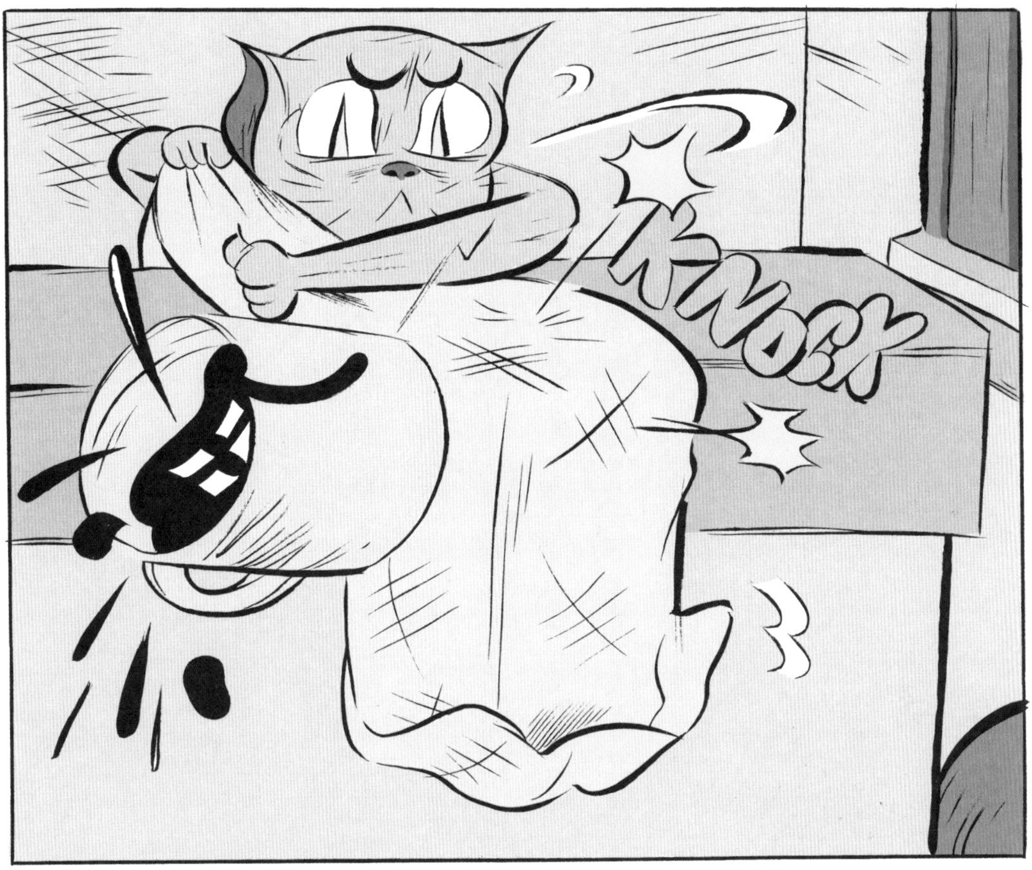
KNOCK

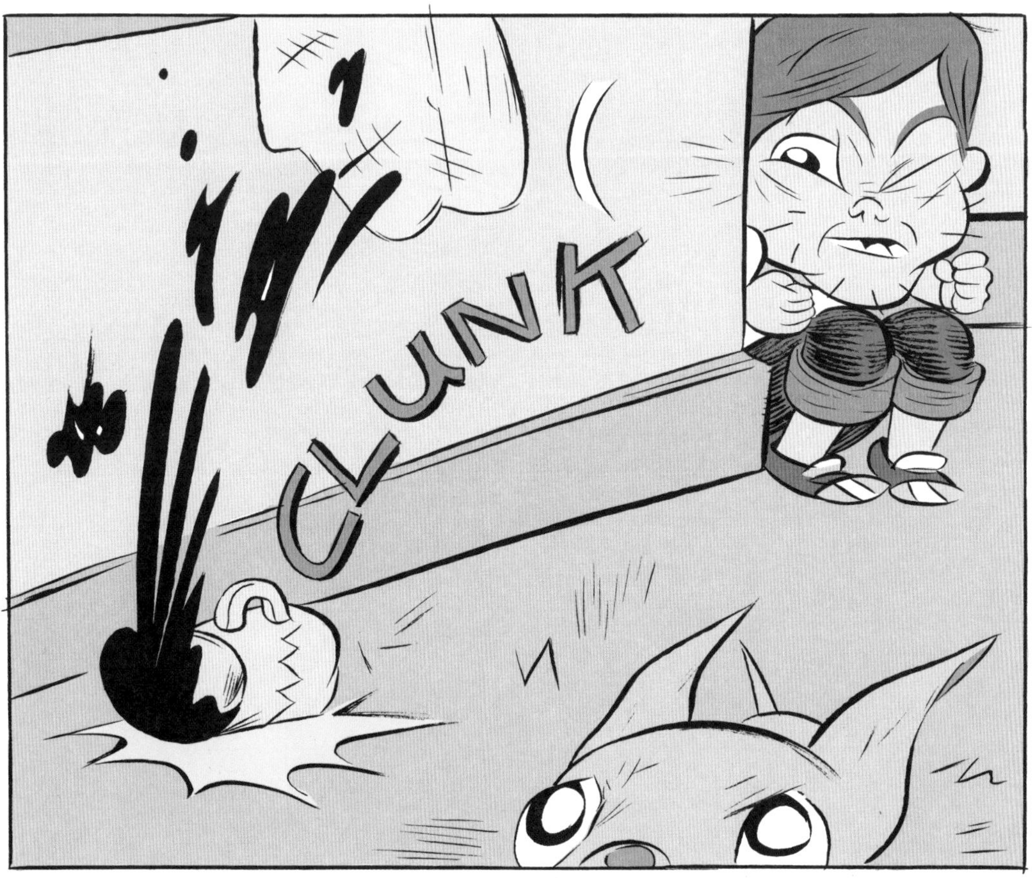
CLUNK

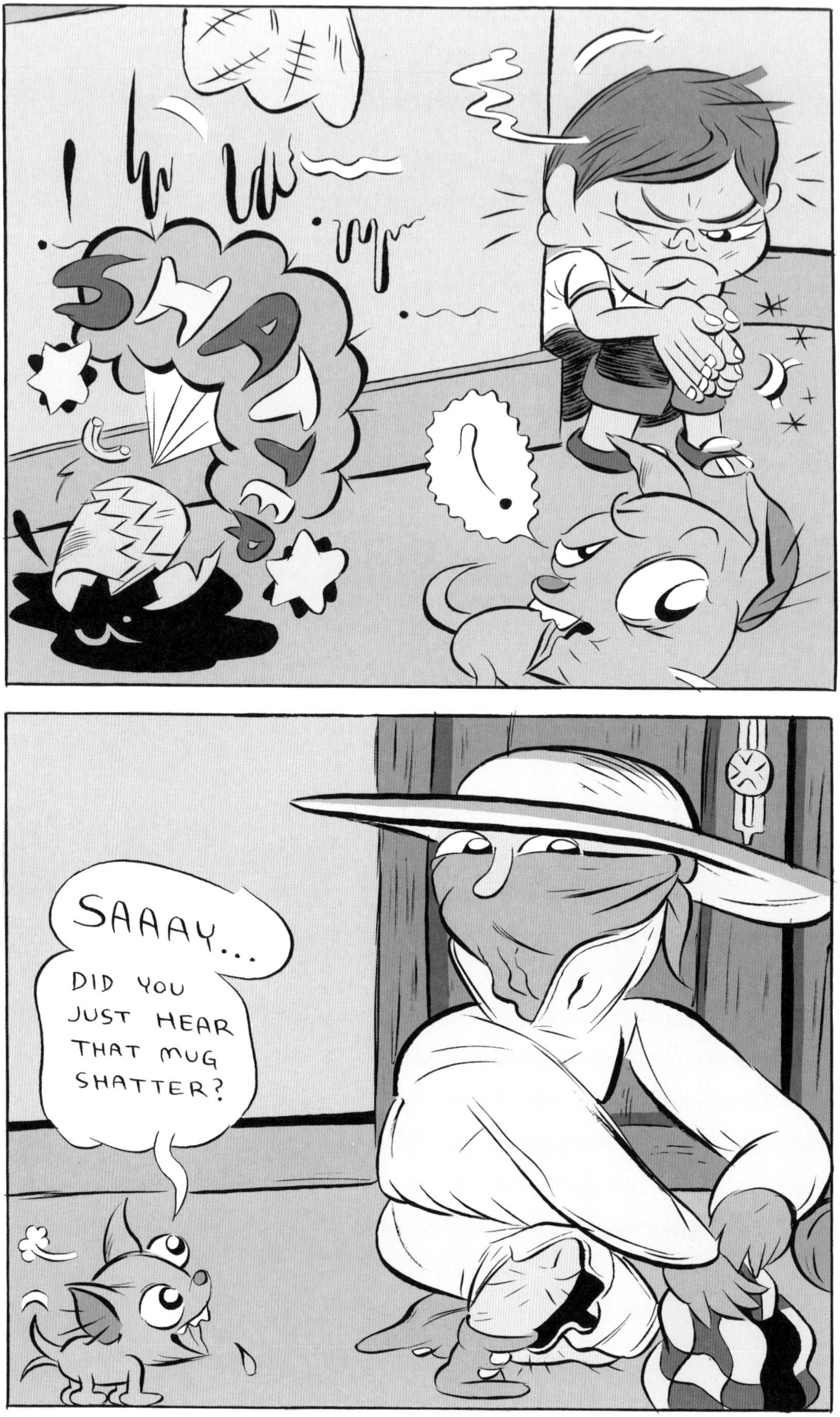
!
SAAAY...
DID YOU JUST HEAR THAT MUG SHATTER?

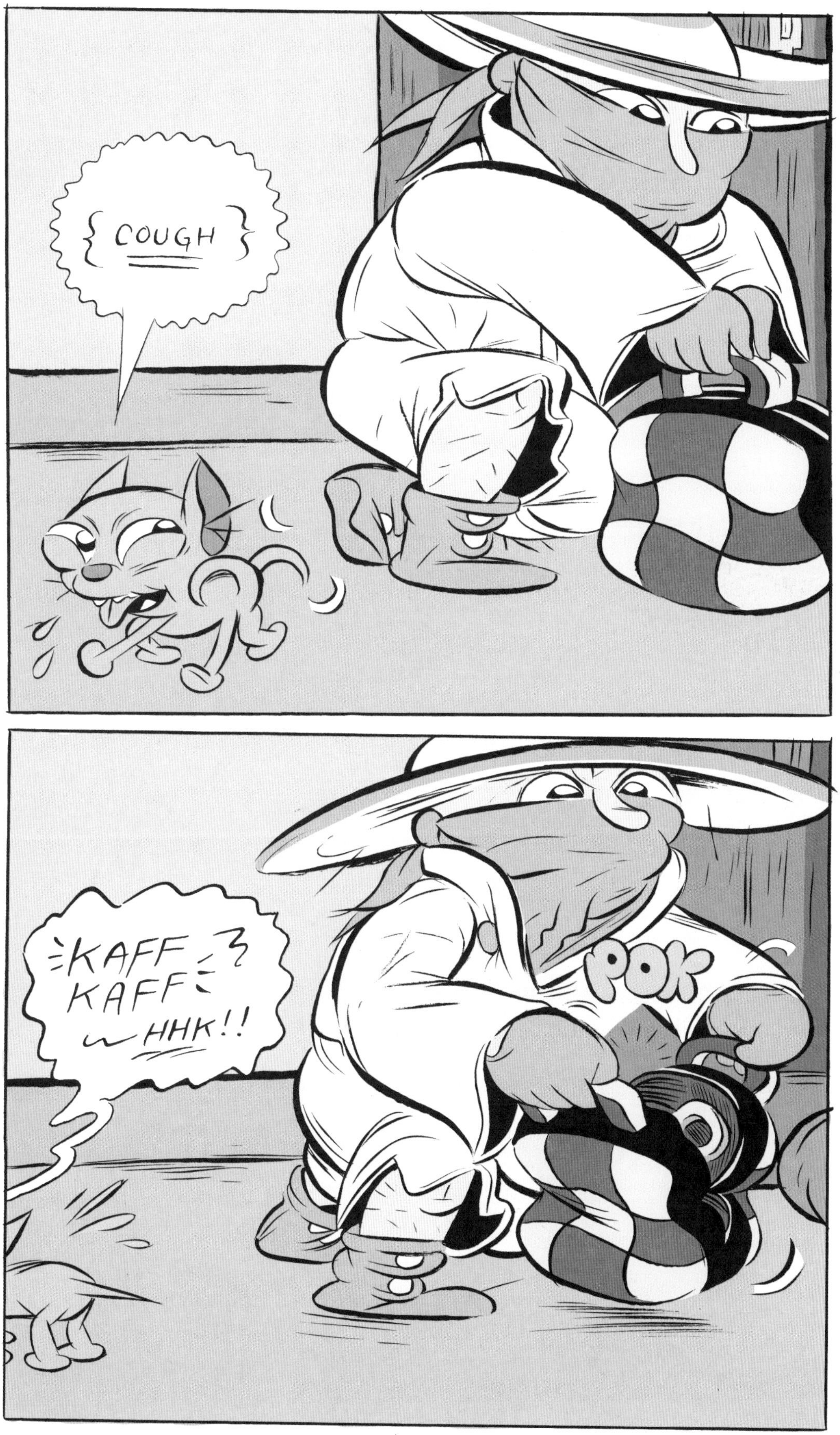
COUGH
KAFF KAFF HHK!!
POK

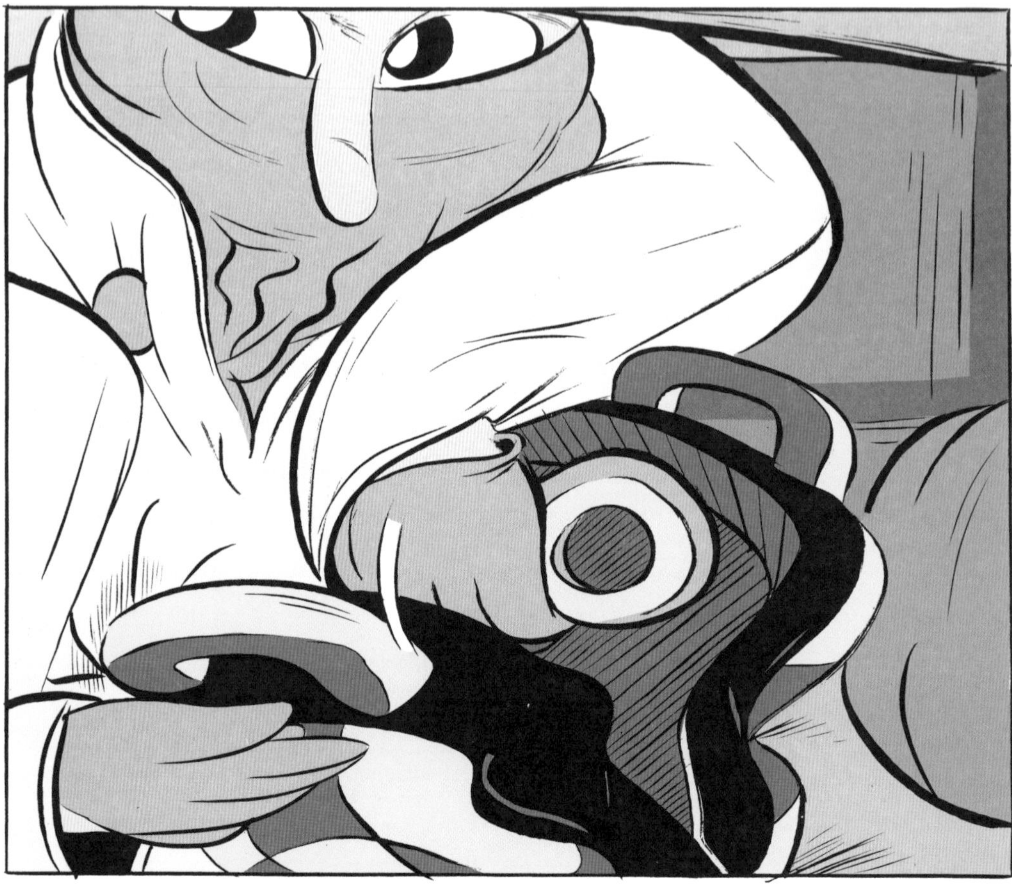
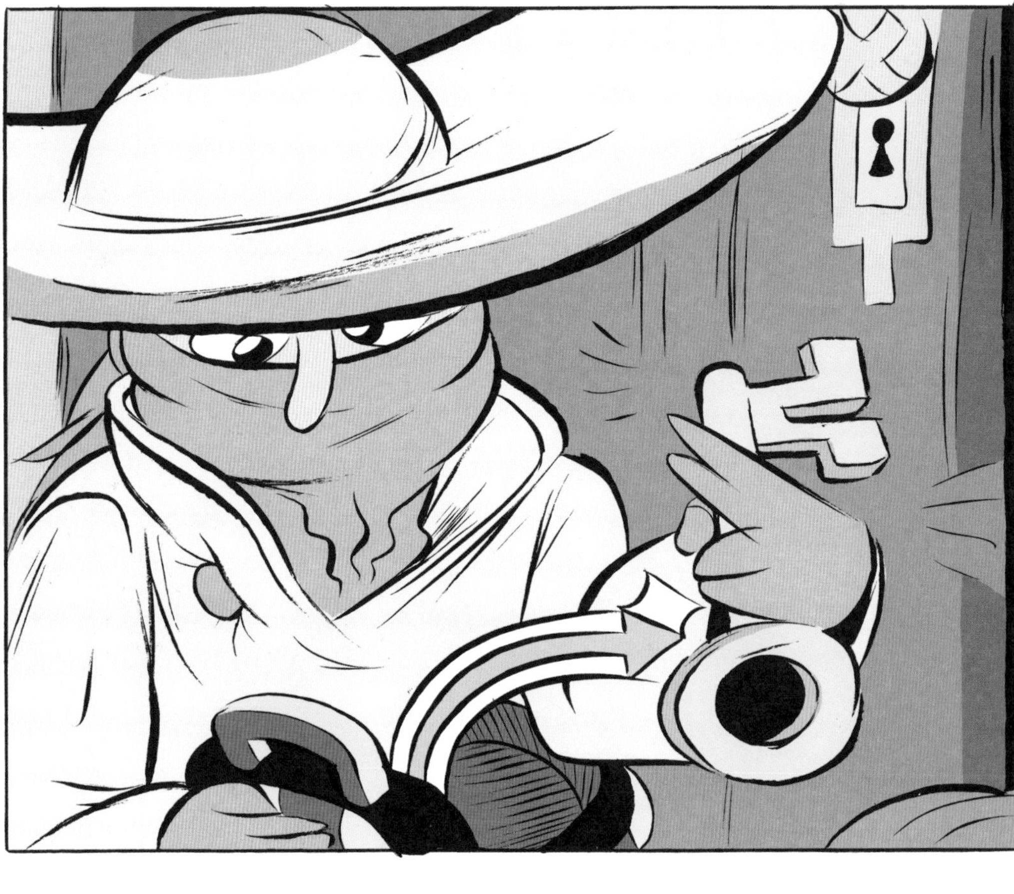

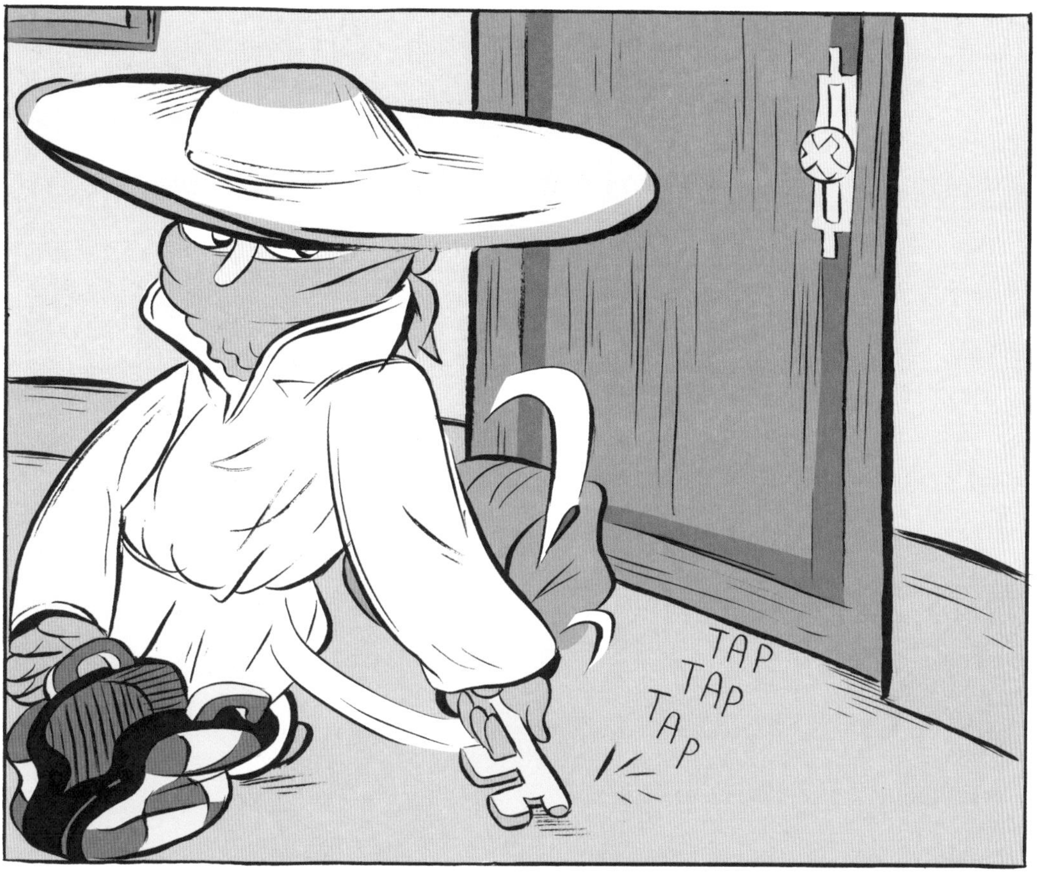
TAP
TAP
TAP

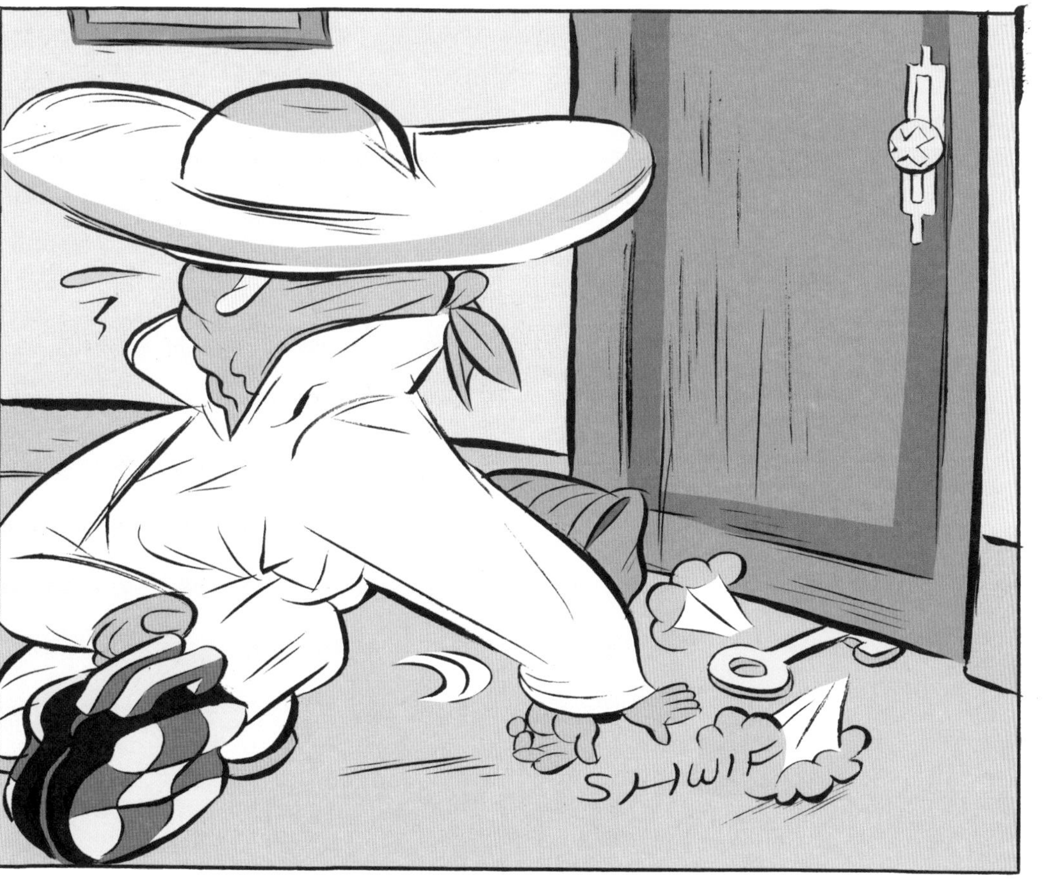
SHWIF

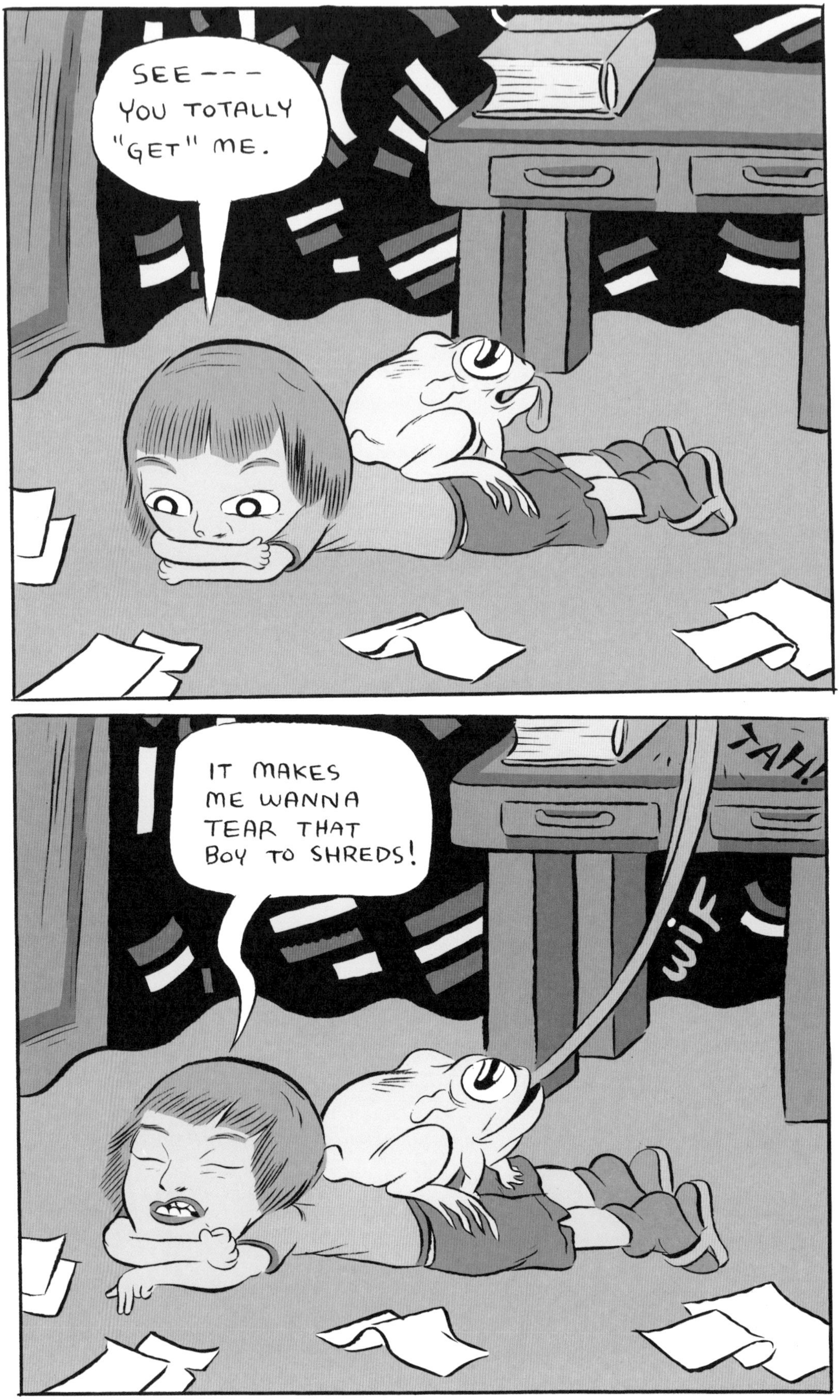
SEE---
YOU TOTALLY
"GET" ME.
IT MAKES
ME WANNA
TEAR THAT
BOY TO SHREDS!
TAH!
WIF

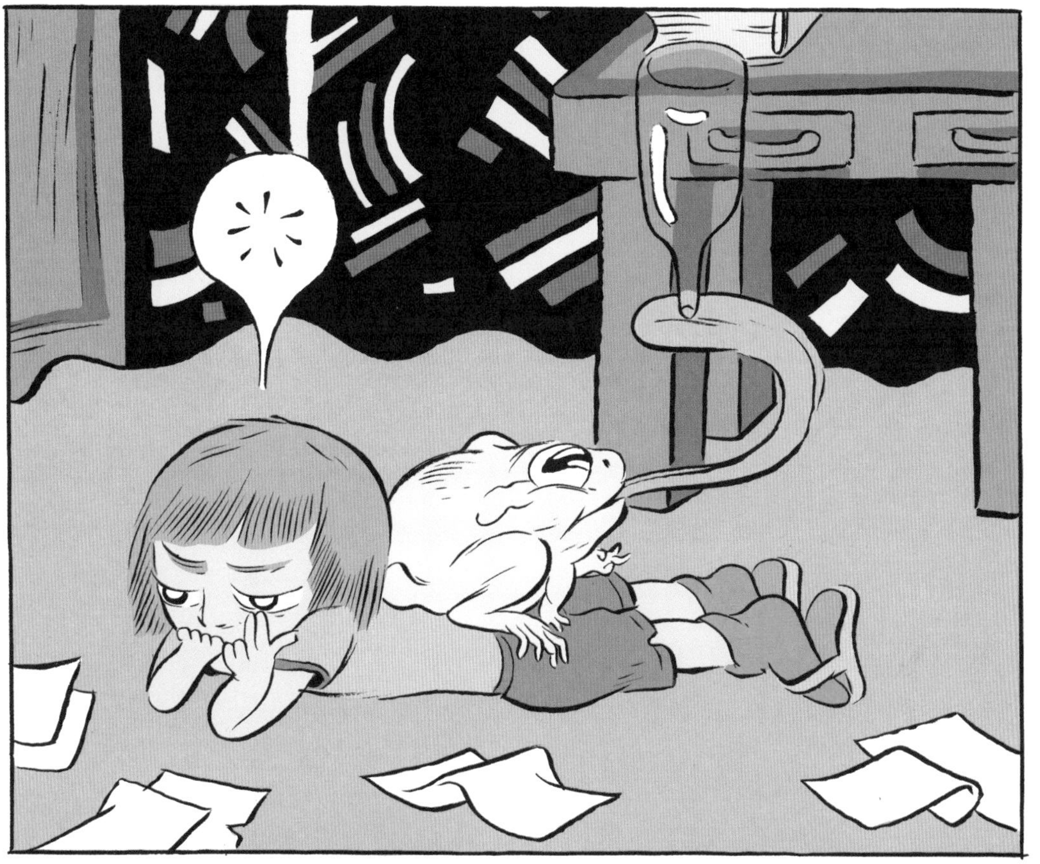

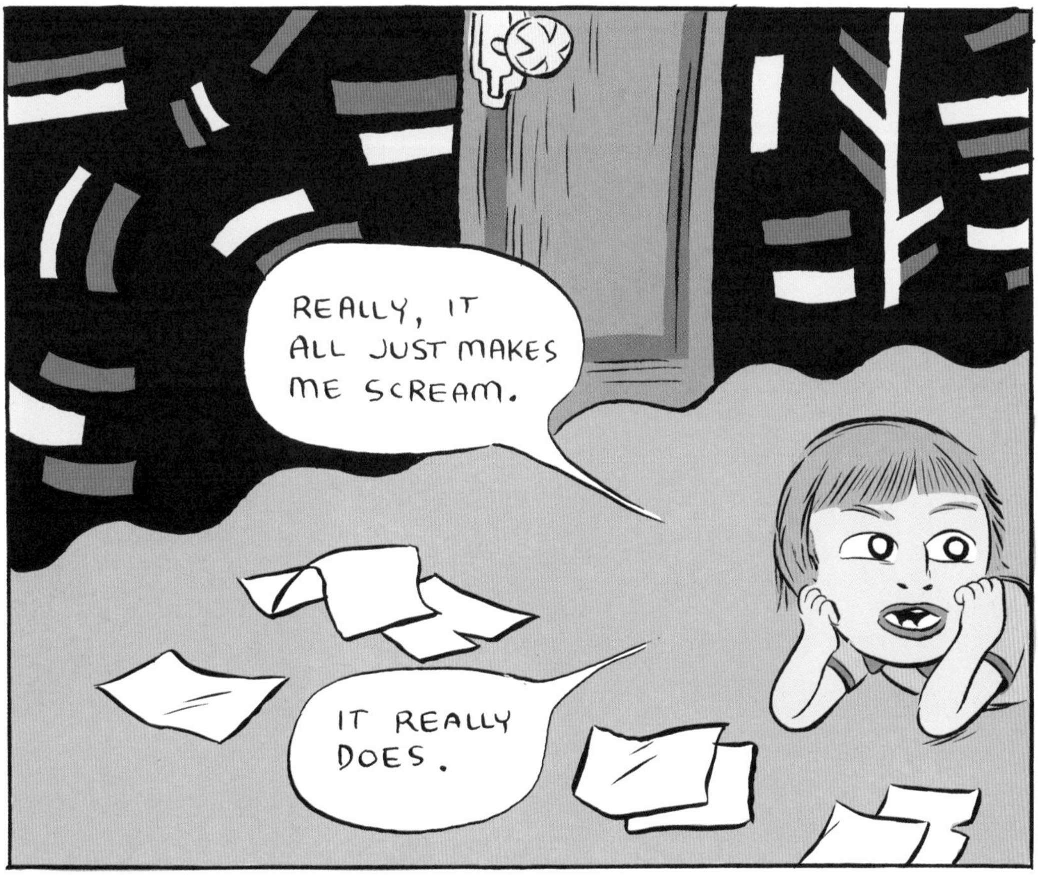
REALLY, IT ALL JUST MAKES ME SCREAM.
IT REALLY DOES.

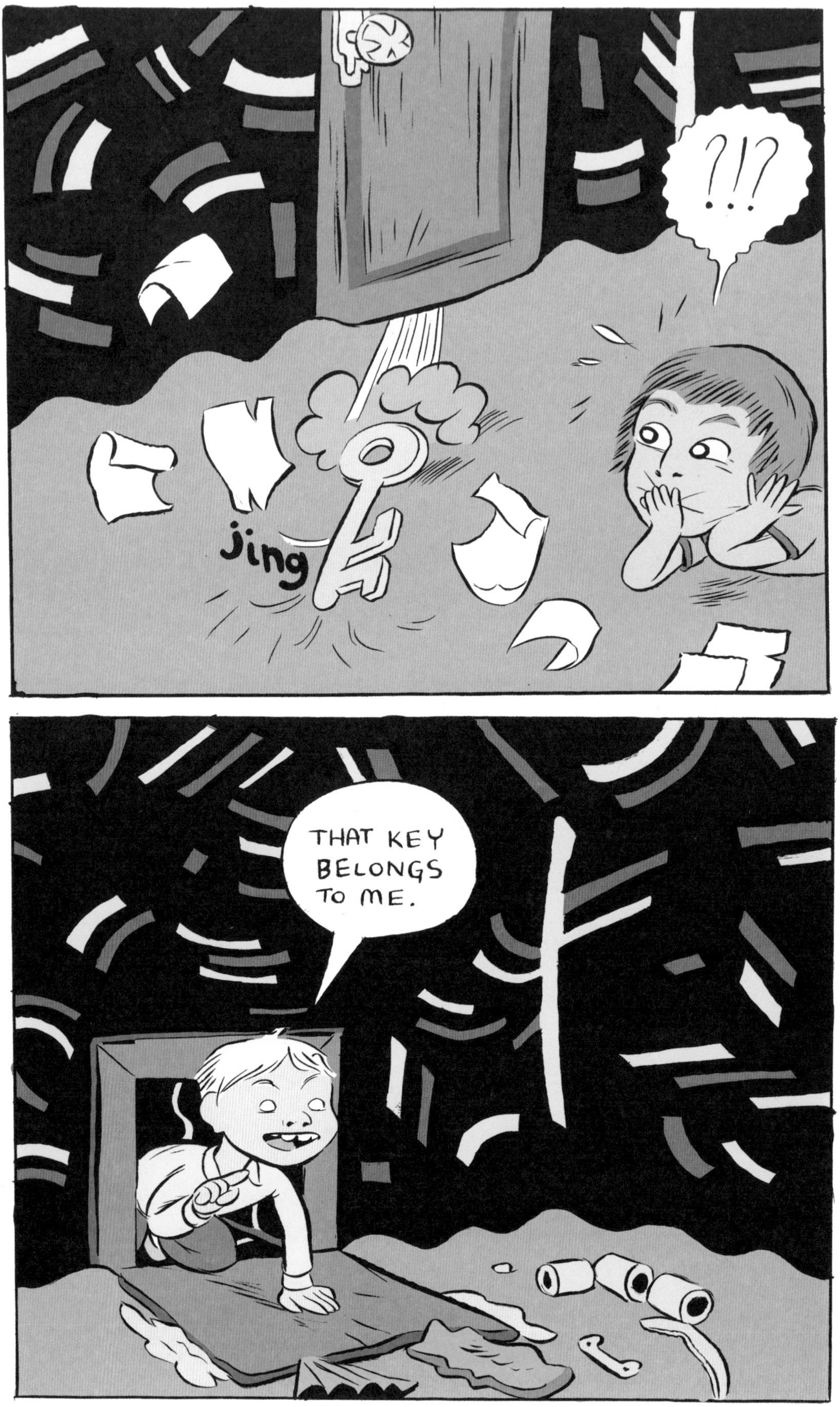
?!!?
jing
THAT KEY BELONGS TO ME.

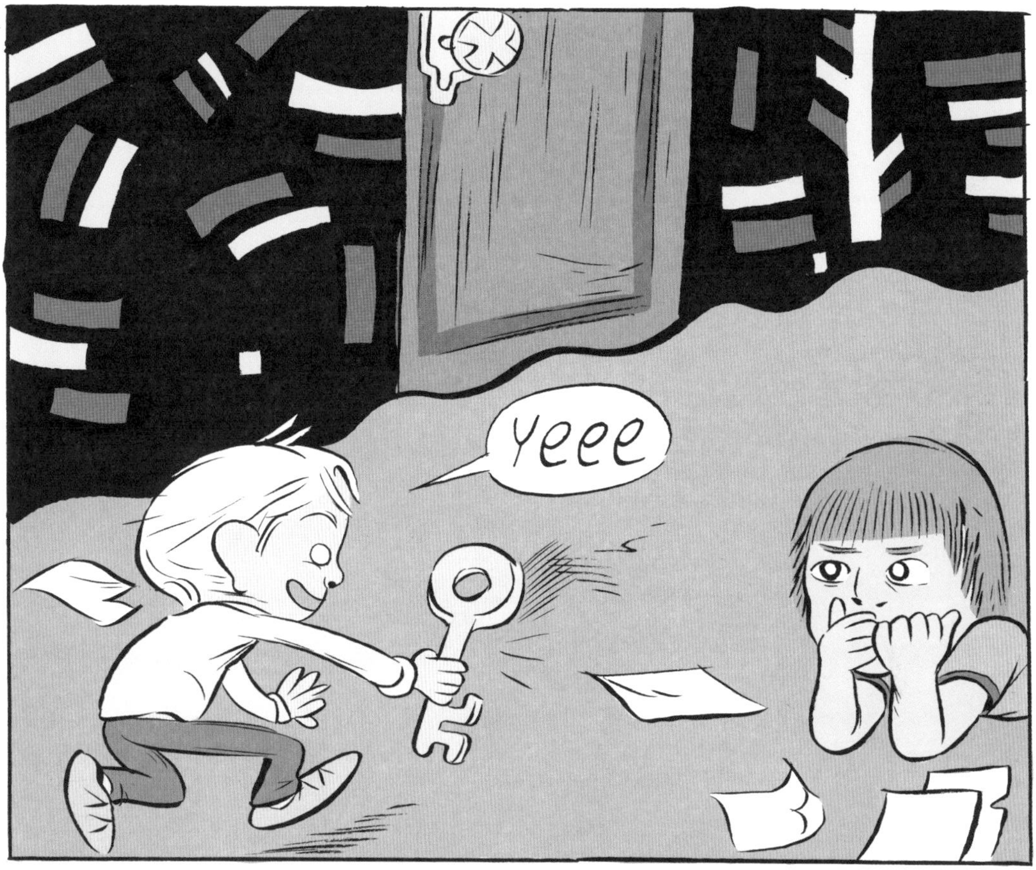
yeee

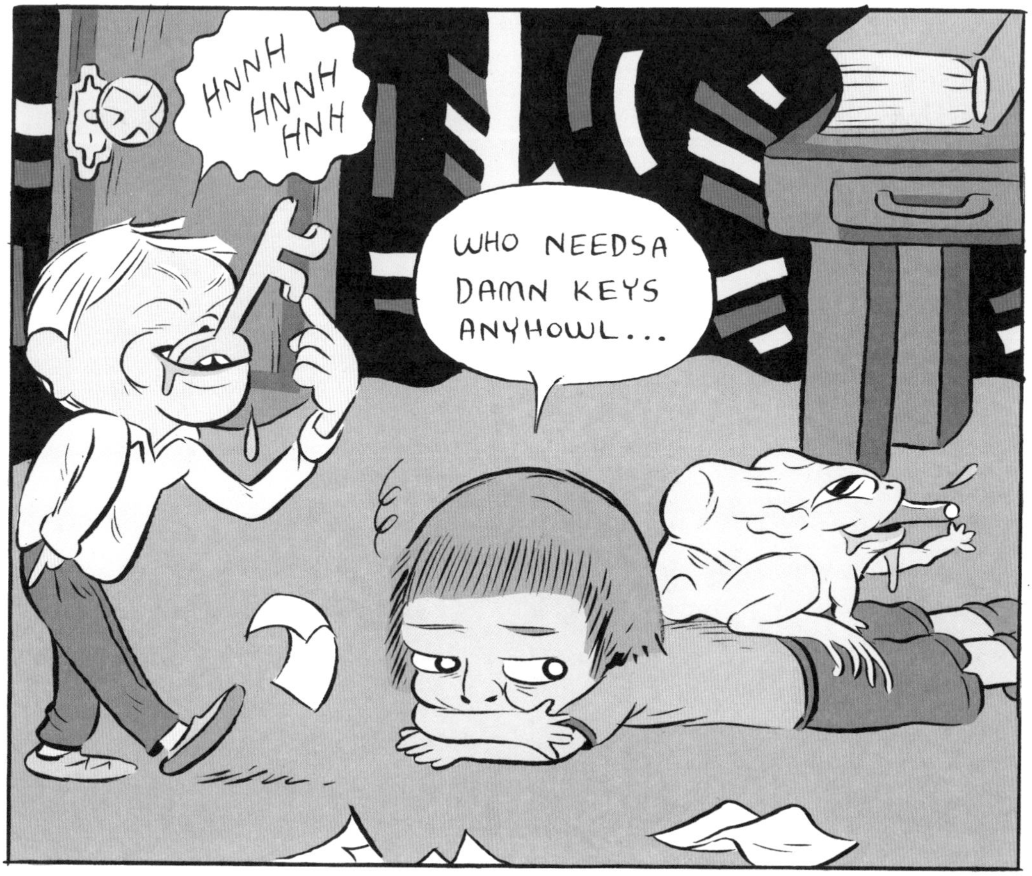
HNNH HNNH HNH
WHO NEEDSA DAMN KEYS ANYHOWL...

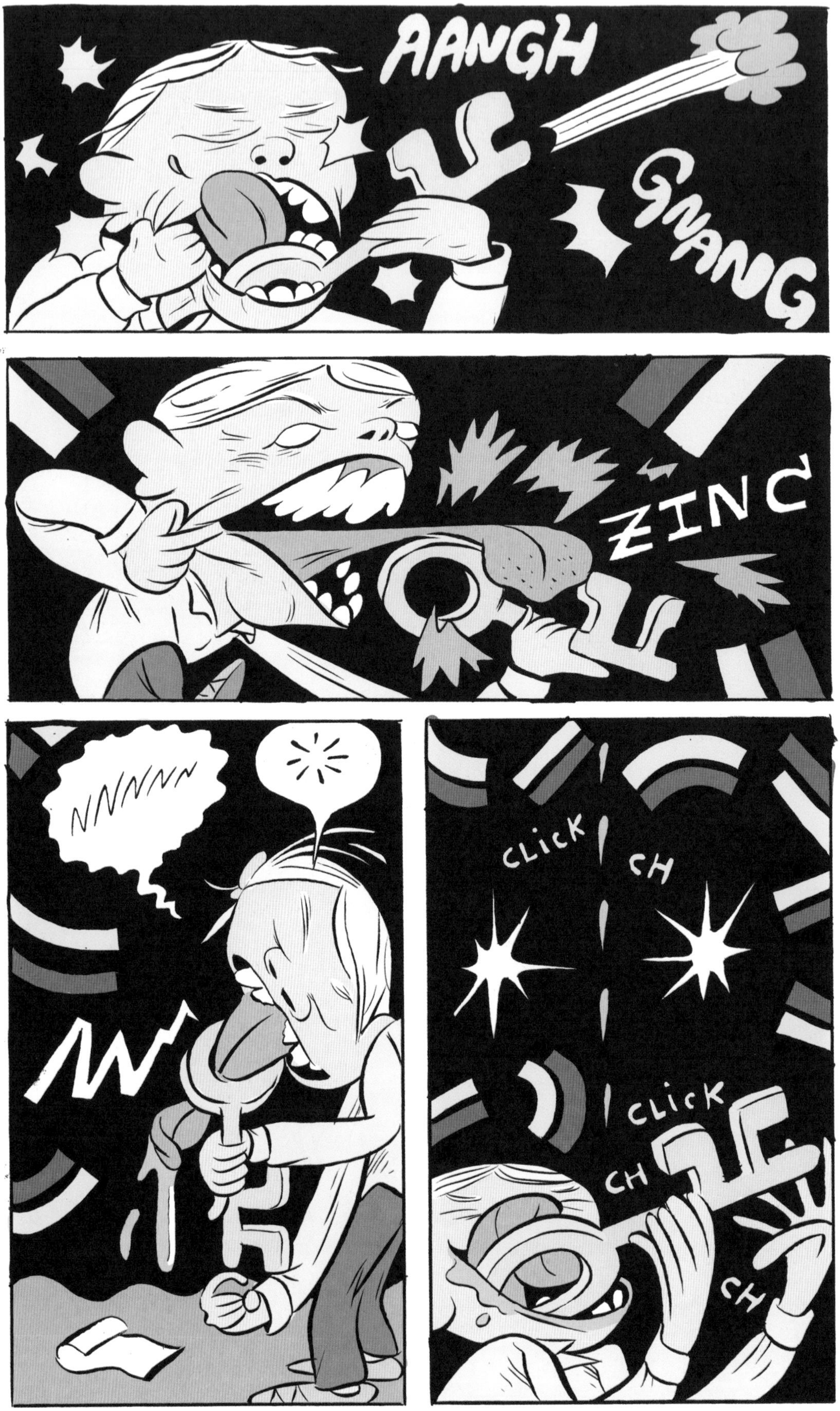
AANGH
GNANG
ZINC
NNNNN
CLICK
CH
CLICK
CH
CH

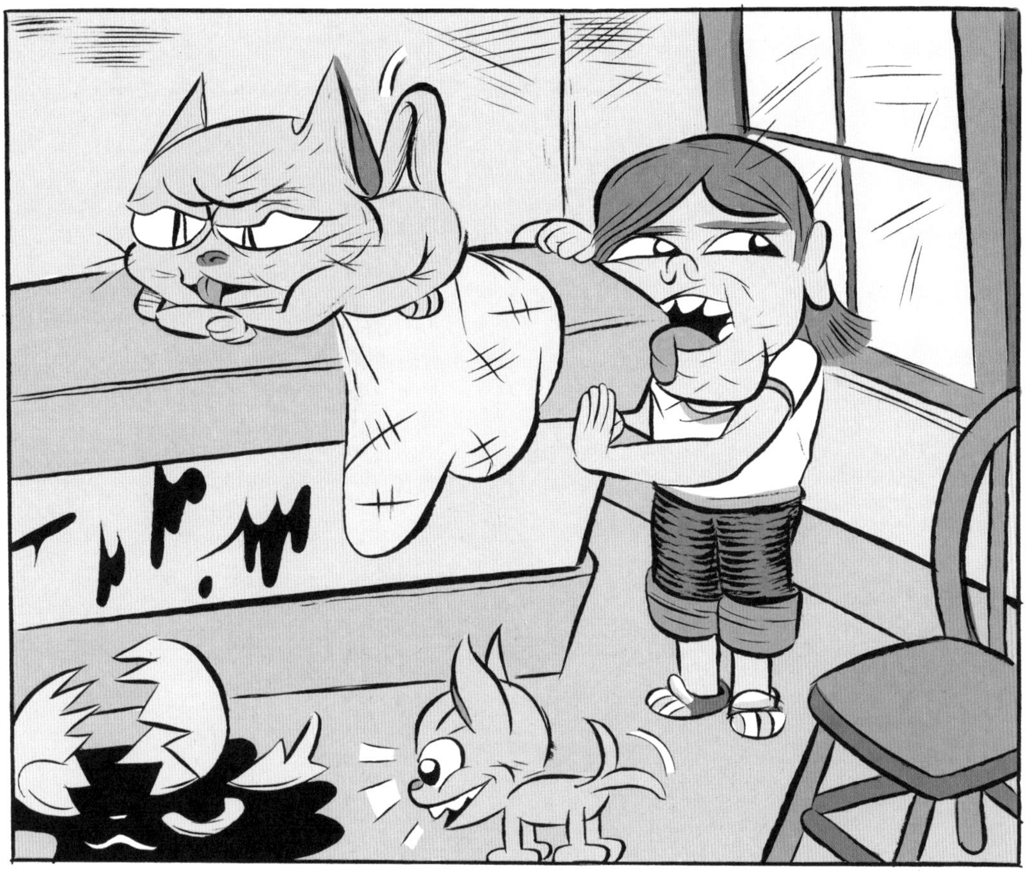

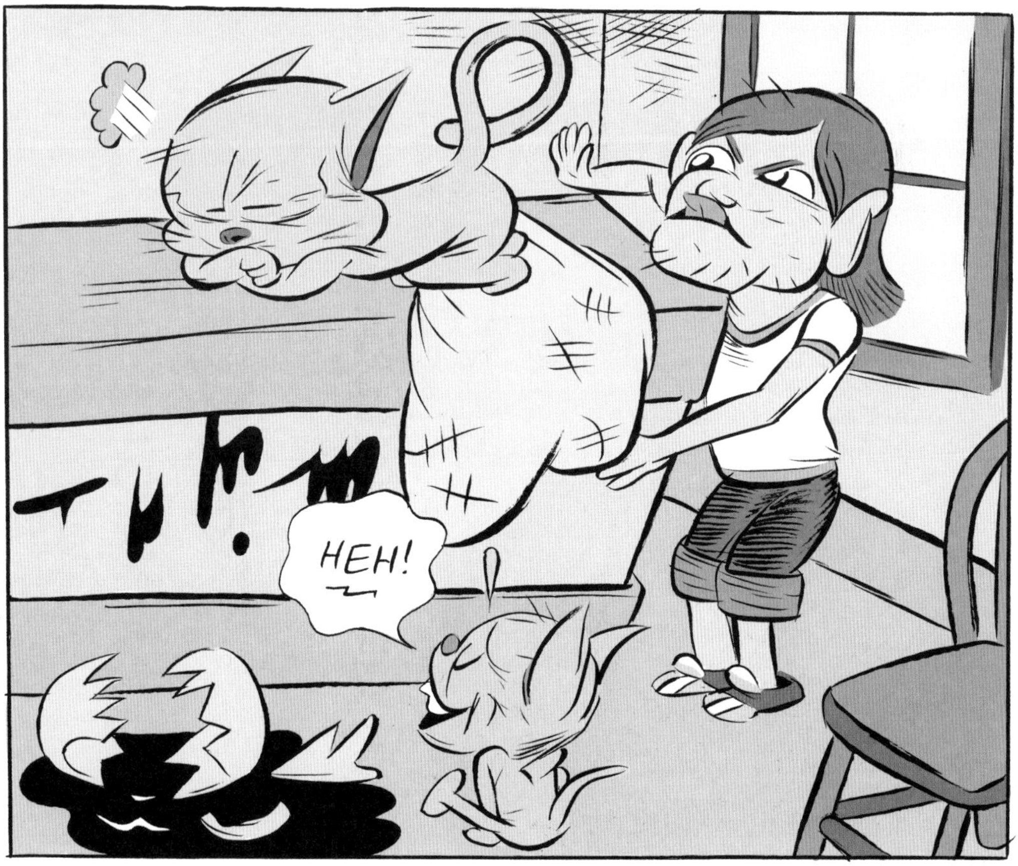
HEH!

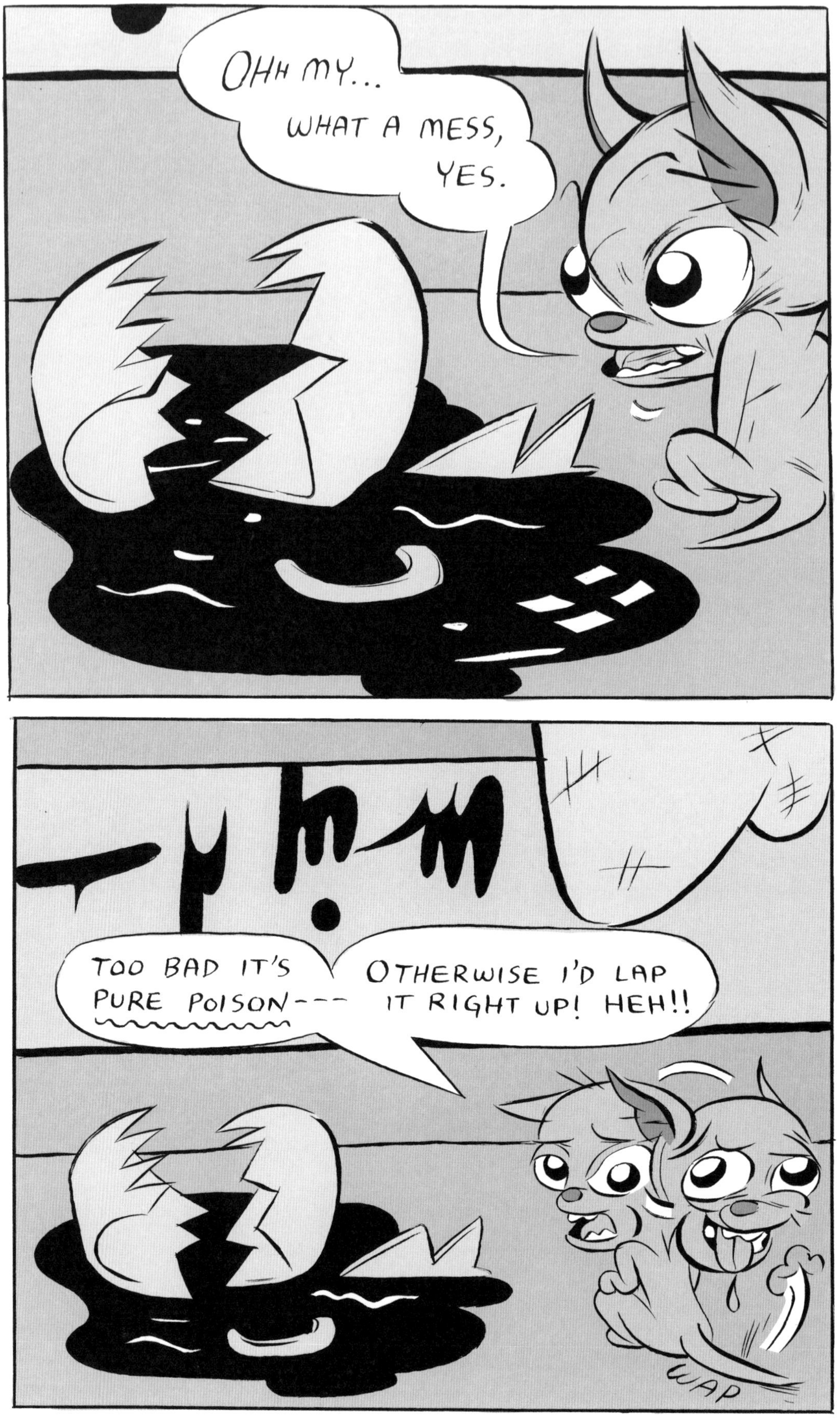
OHH MY... WHAT A MESS, YES.
TOO BAD IT'S PURE POISON---
OTHERWISE I'D LAP IT RIGHT UP! HEH!!
WAP

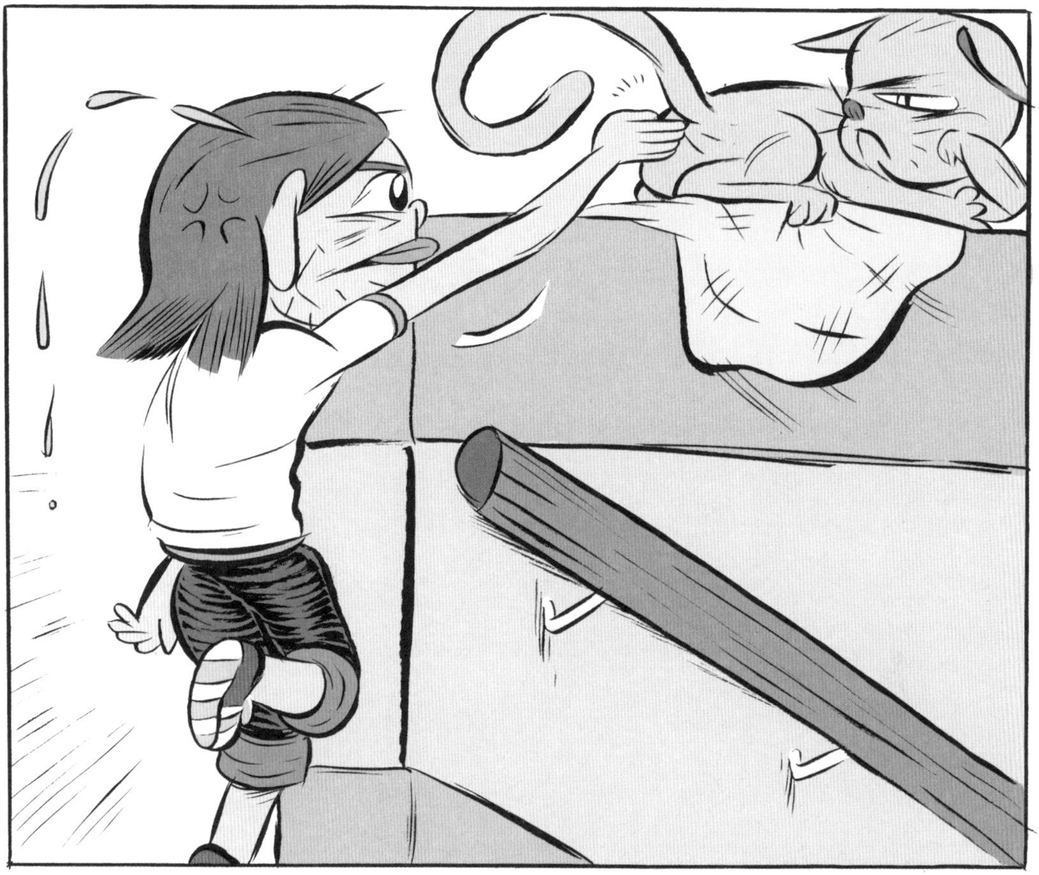

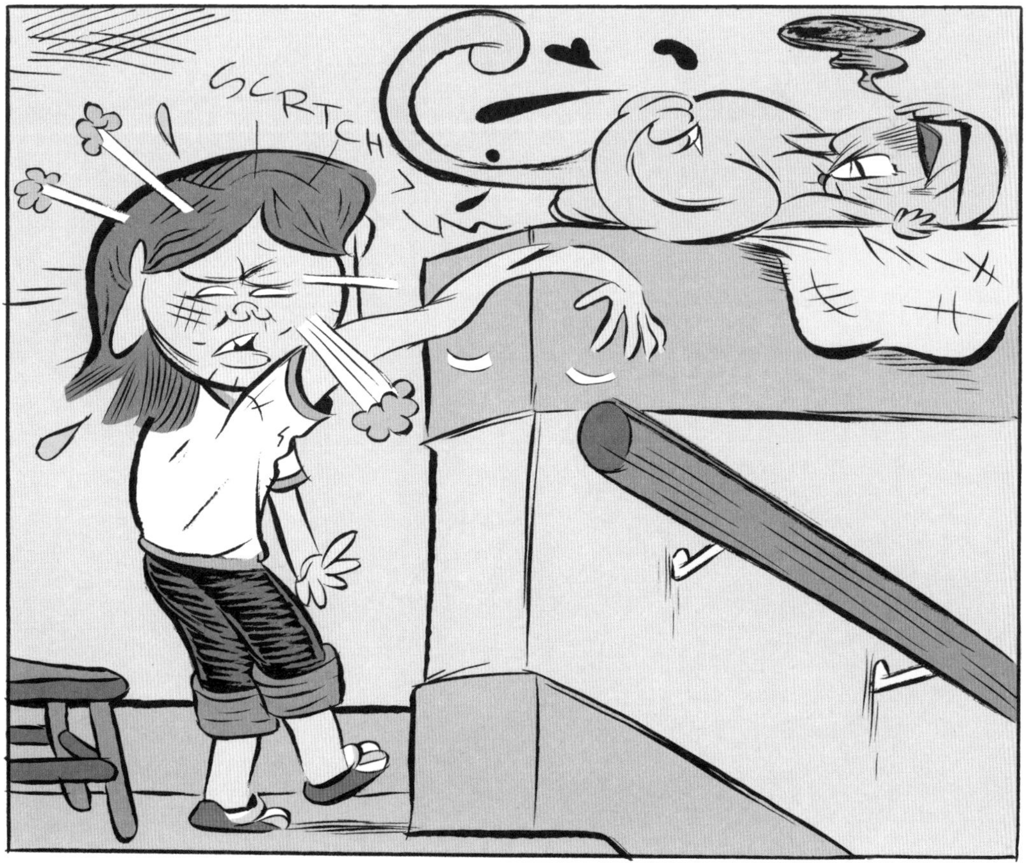
SCRTCH

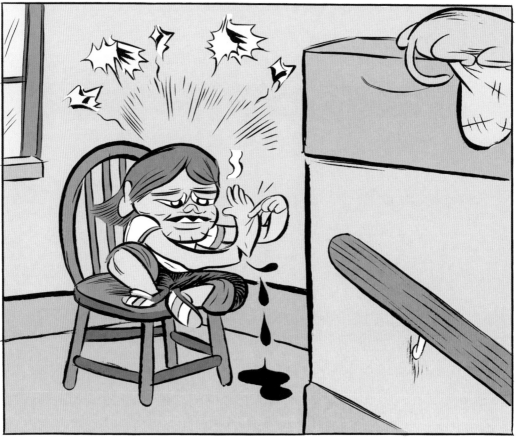

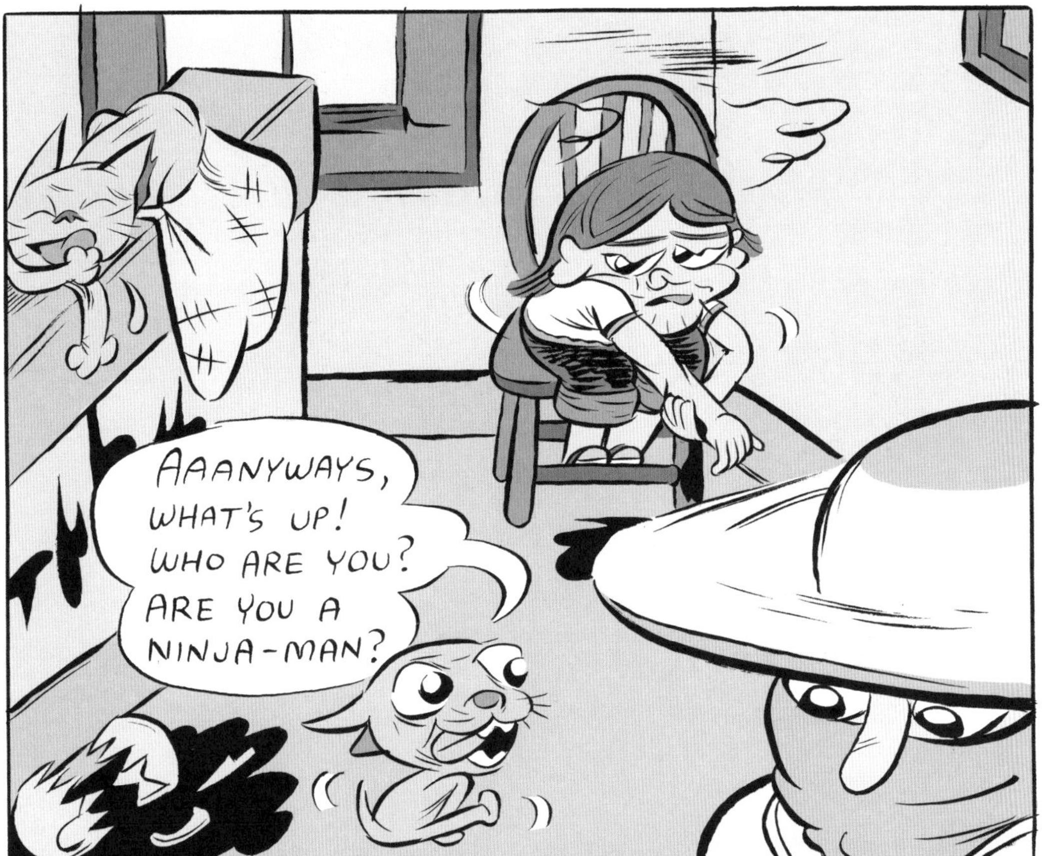
AAANYWAYS, WHAT'S UP! WHO ARE YOU? ARE YOU A NINJA-MAN?

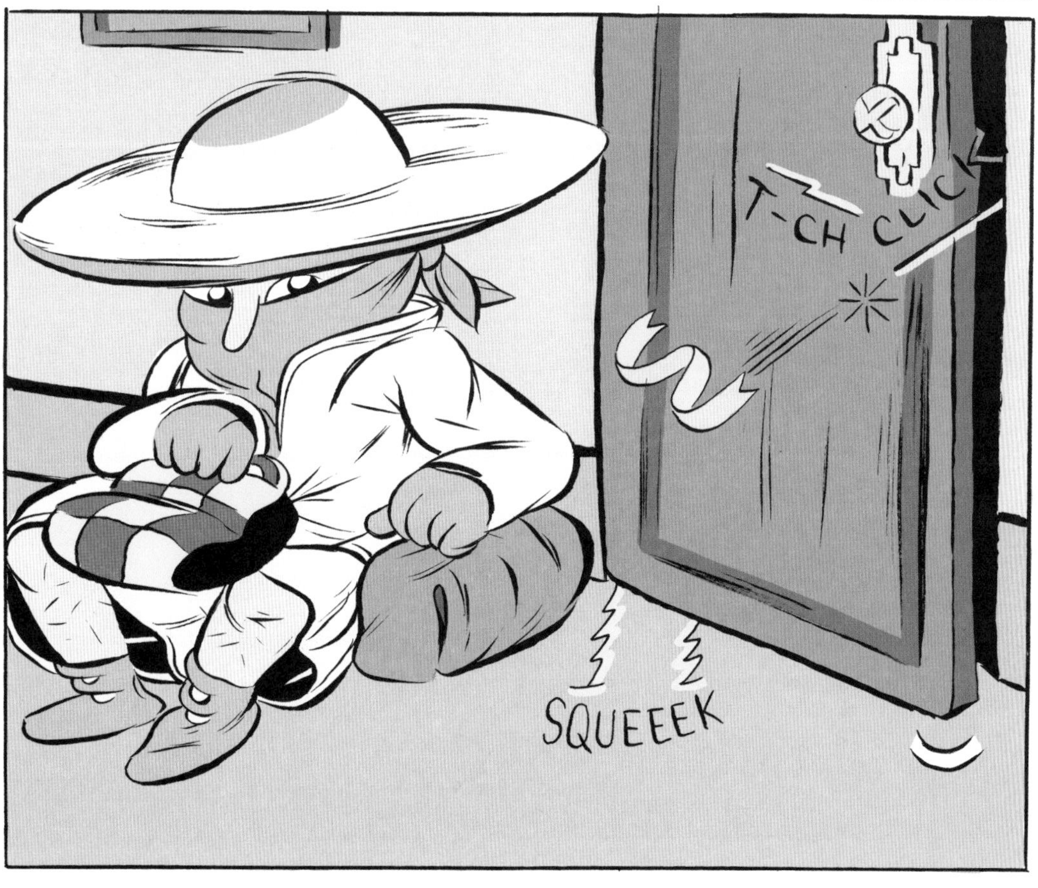
T-CH CLICK
SQUEEEK

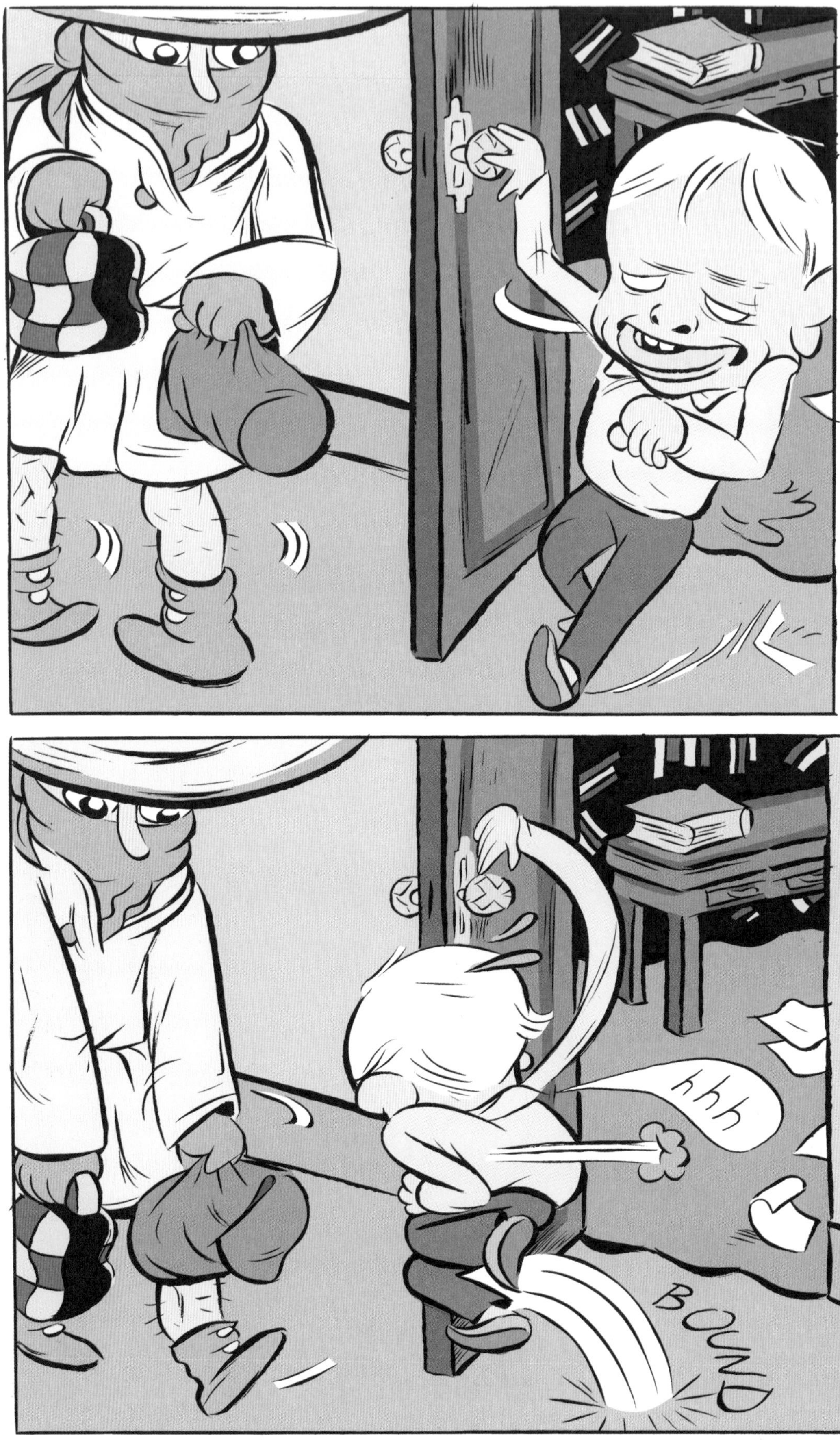
hhh
BOUND

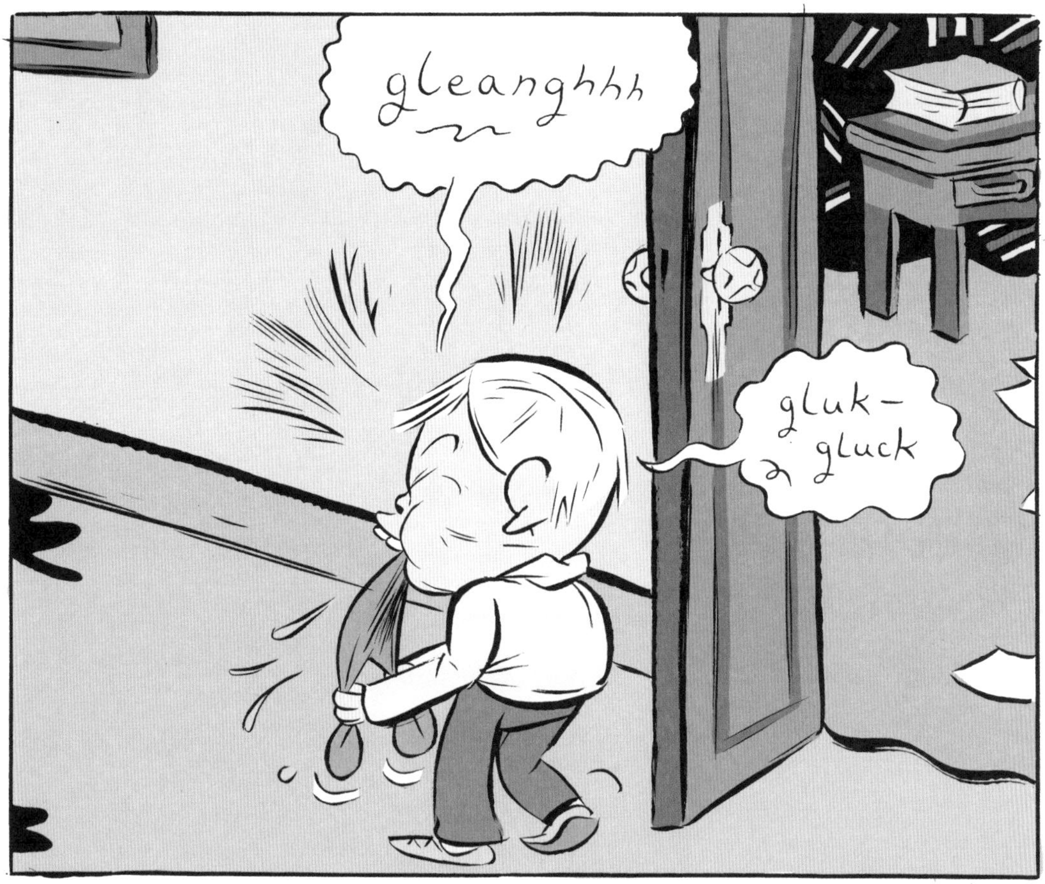
gleanghhh
gluk-gluck
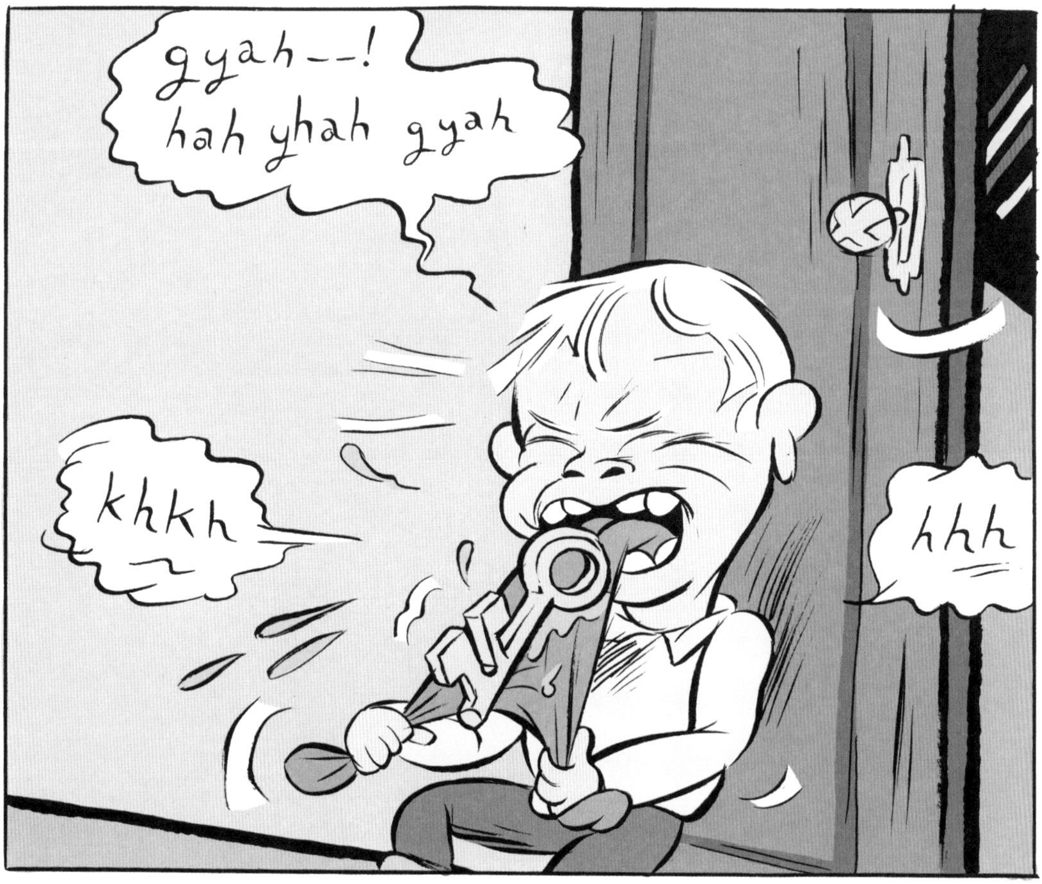
gyah--! hah yhah gyah
khkh
hhh

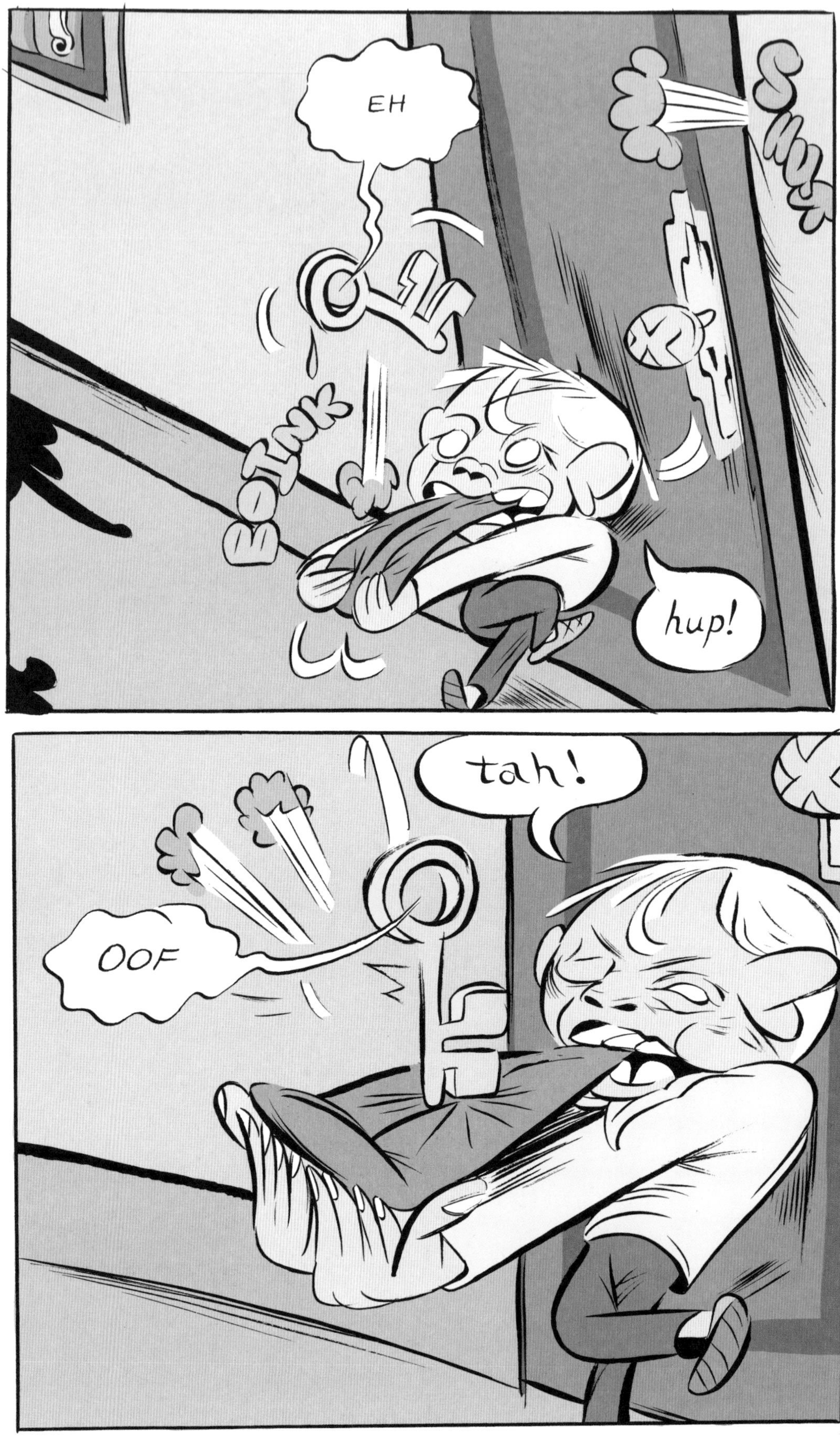
EH
BOINK
hup!
tah!
OOF

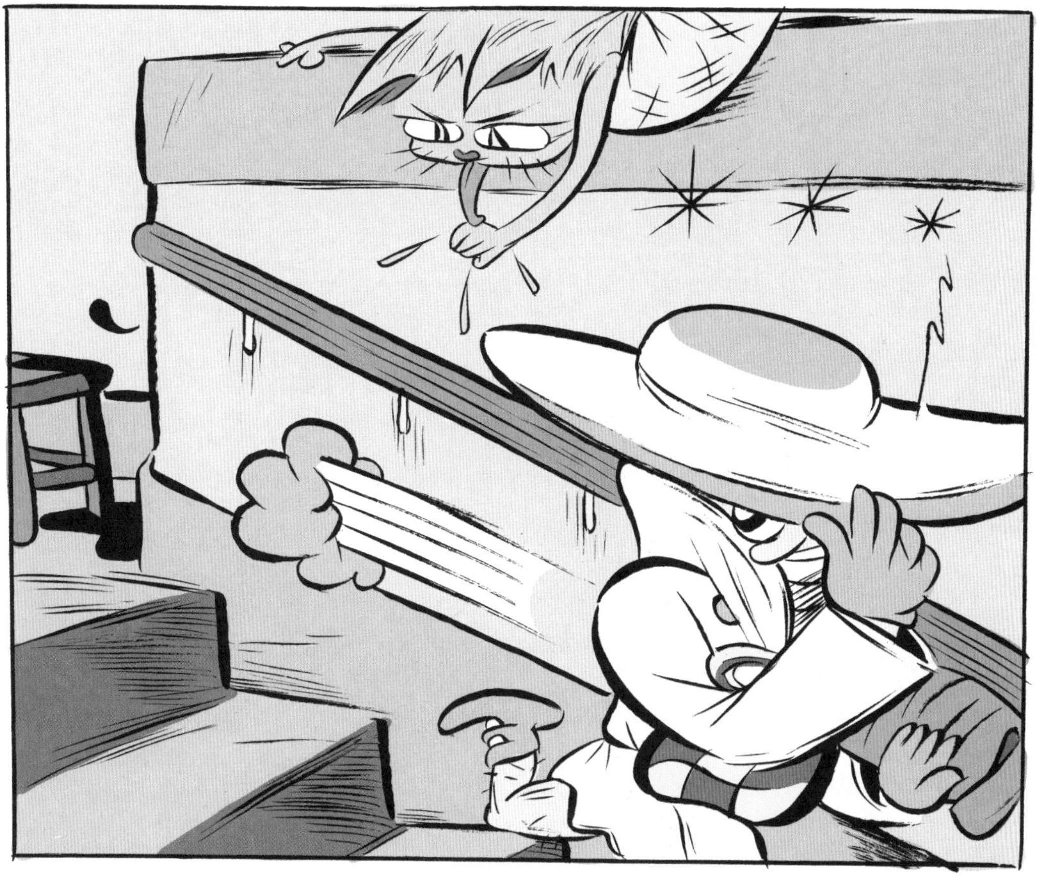

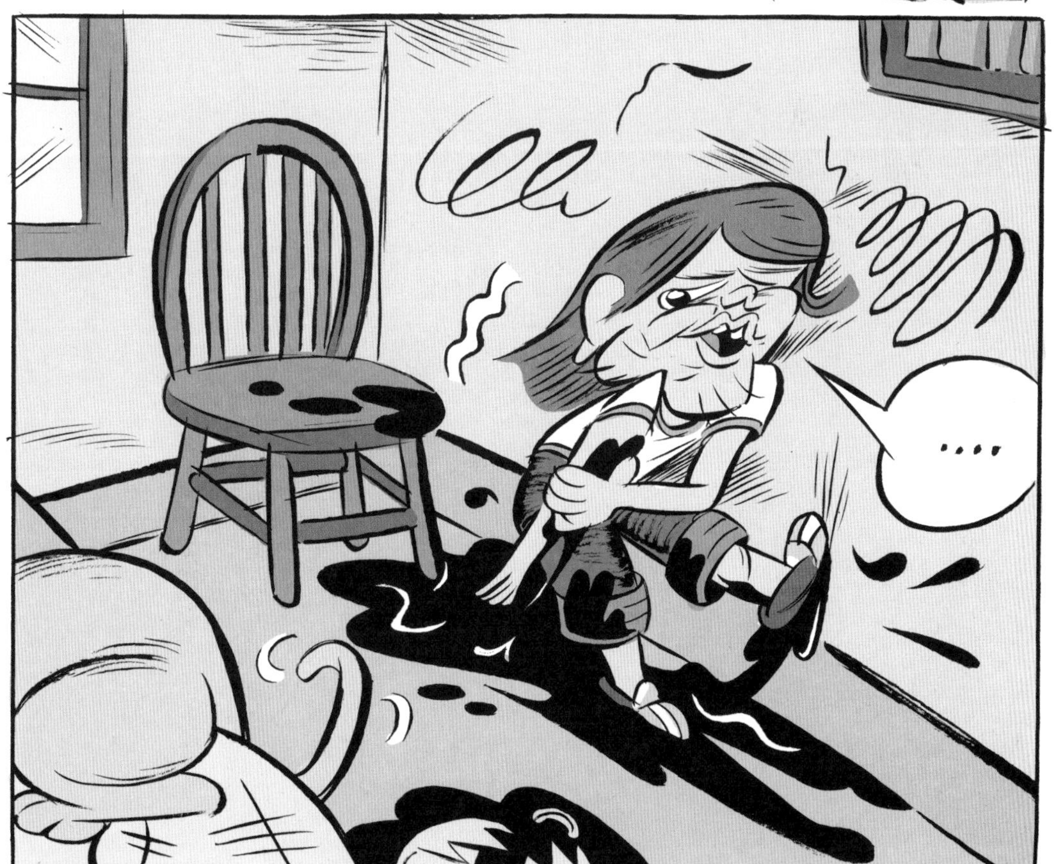
....

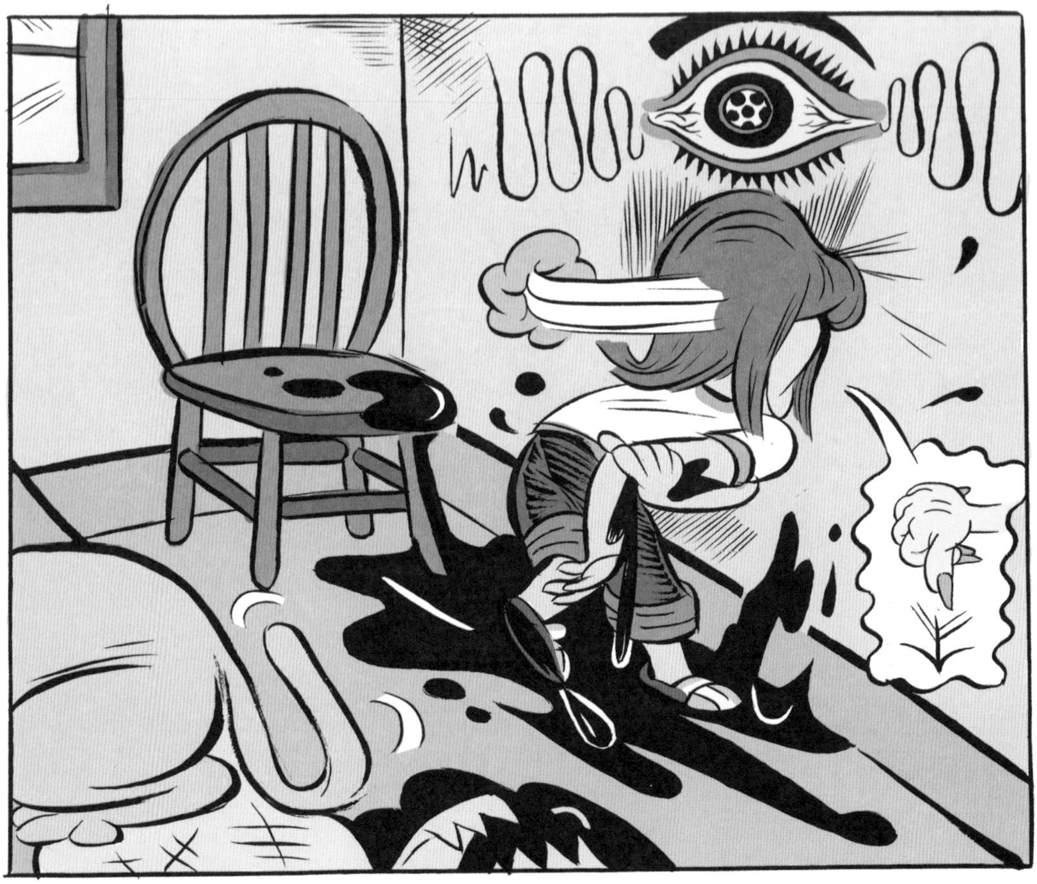

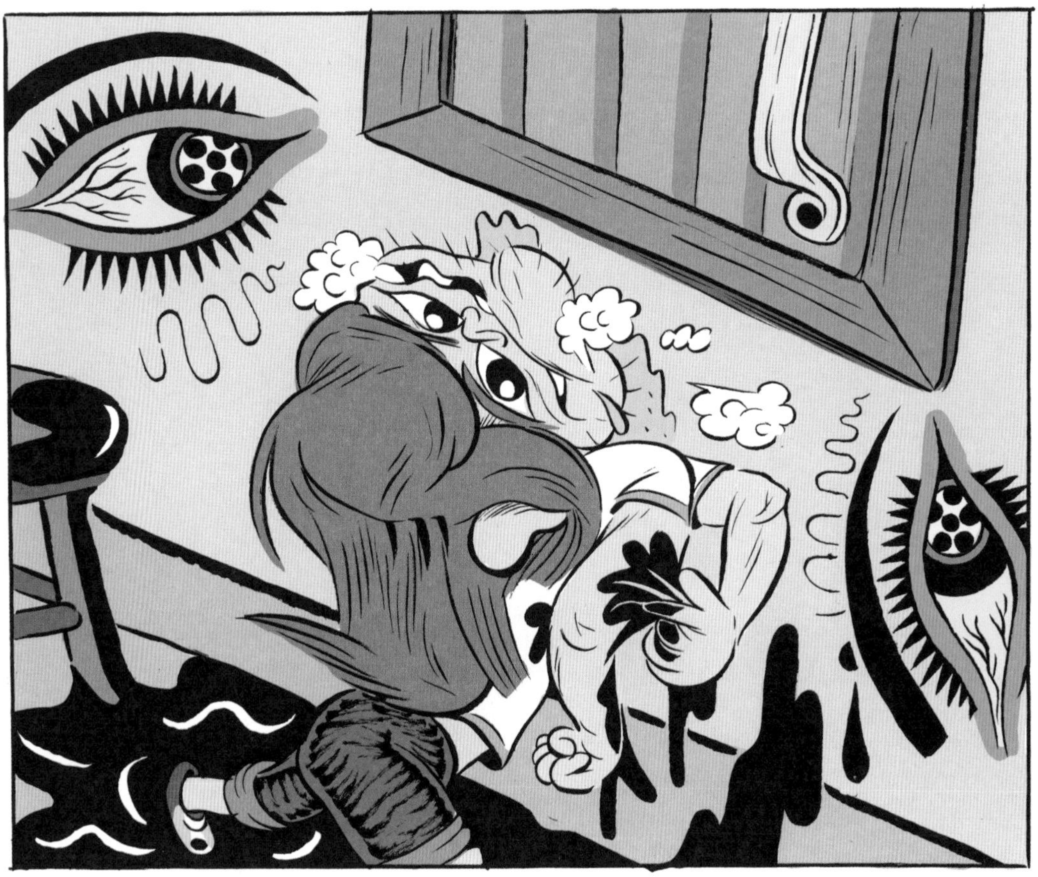

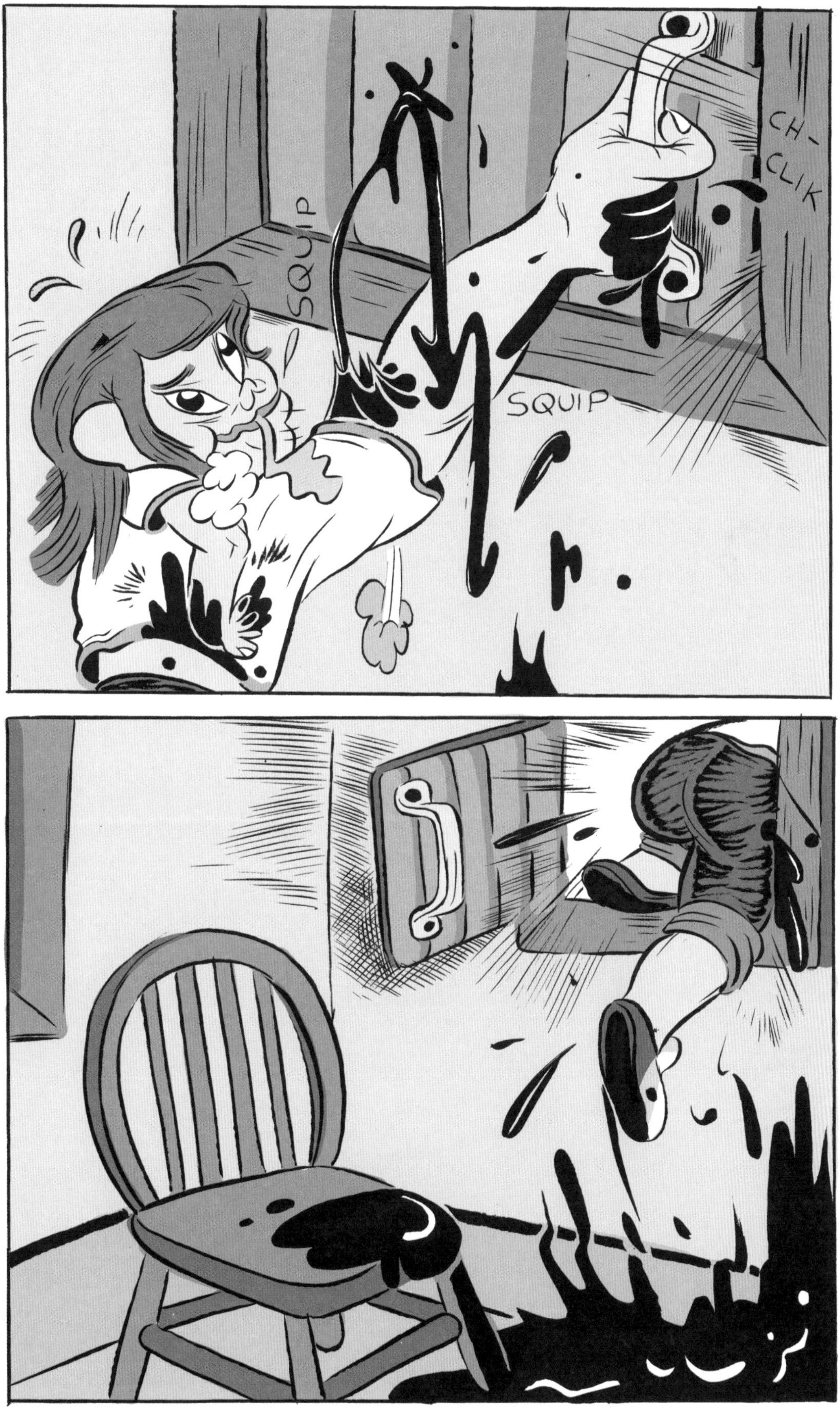
CH-
CLIK
SQUIP
SQUIP

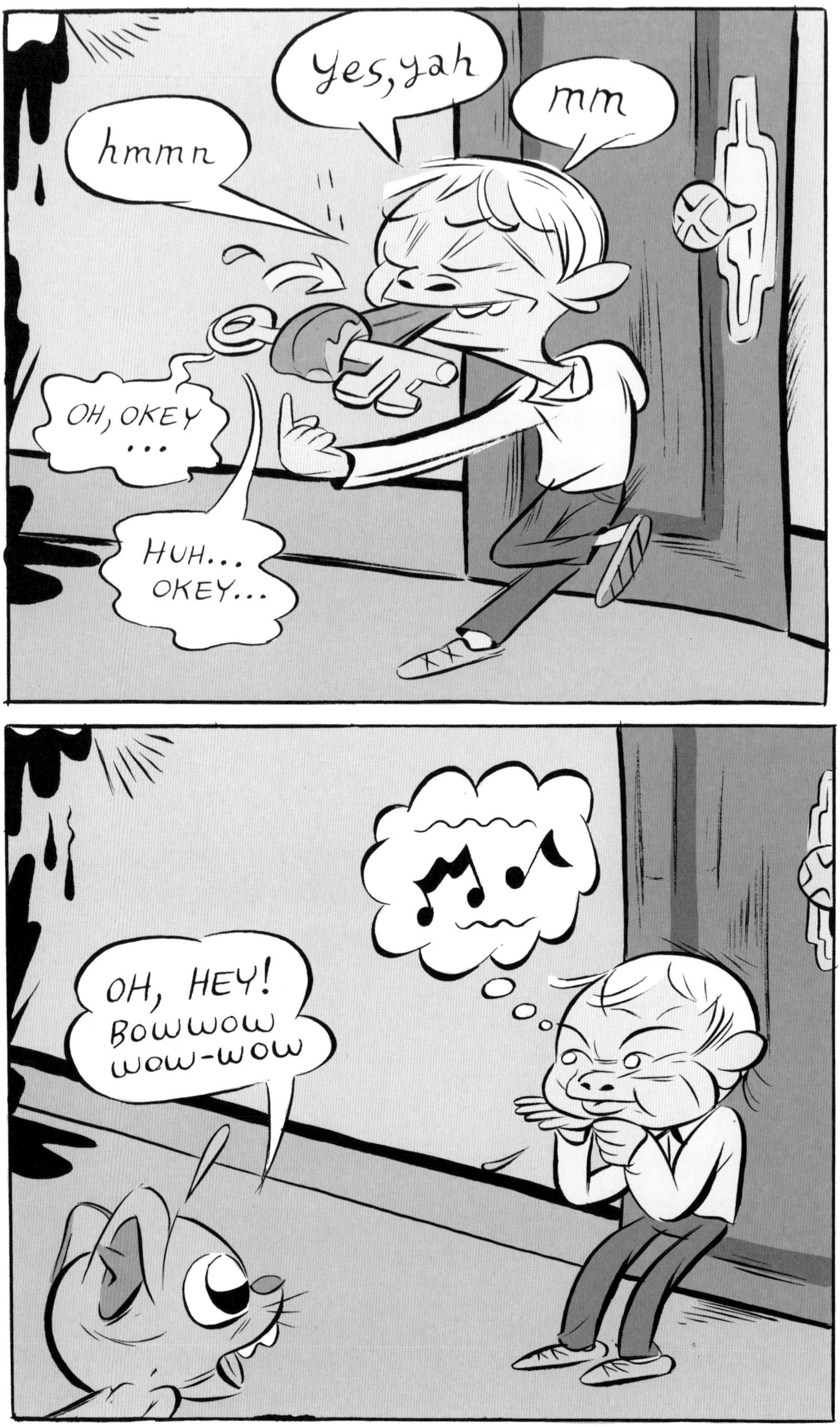
hmmn
yes, yah
mm
OH, OKEY ...
HUH... OKEY...
OH, HEY! BOWWOW WOW-WOW

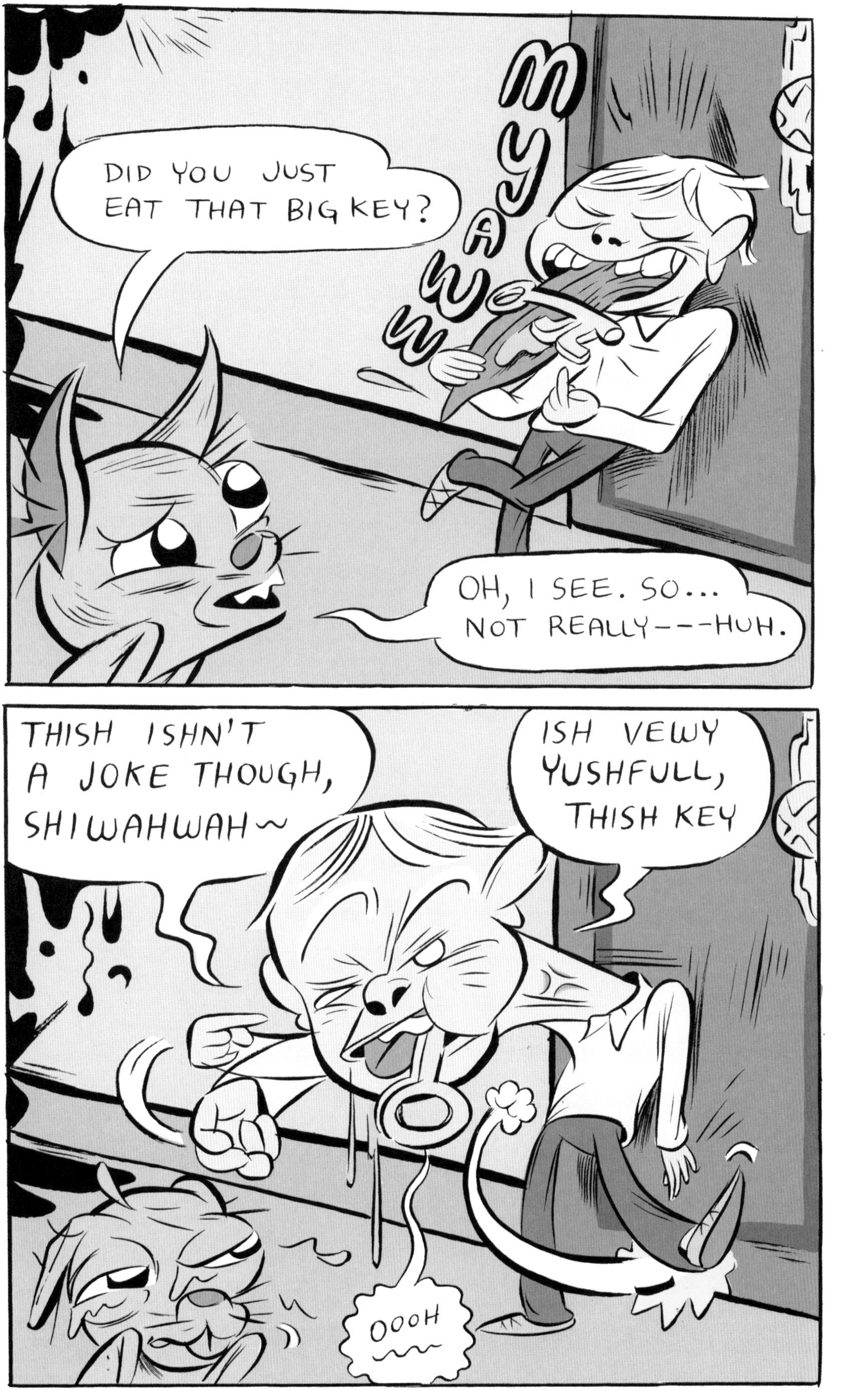

mmyyaawwwww
DID YOU JUST EAT THAT BIG KEY?
OH, I SEE. SO... NOT REALLY---HUH.
THISH ISHN'T A JOKE THOUGH, SHIWAHWAH~
ISH VEWY YUSHFULL, THISH KEY
OOOH

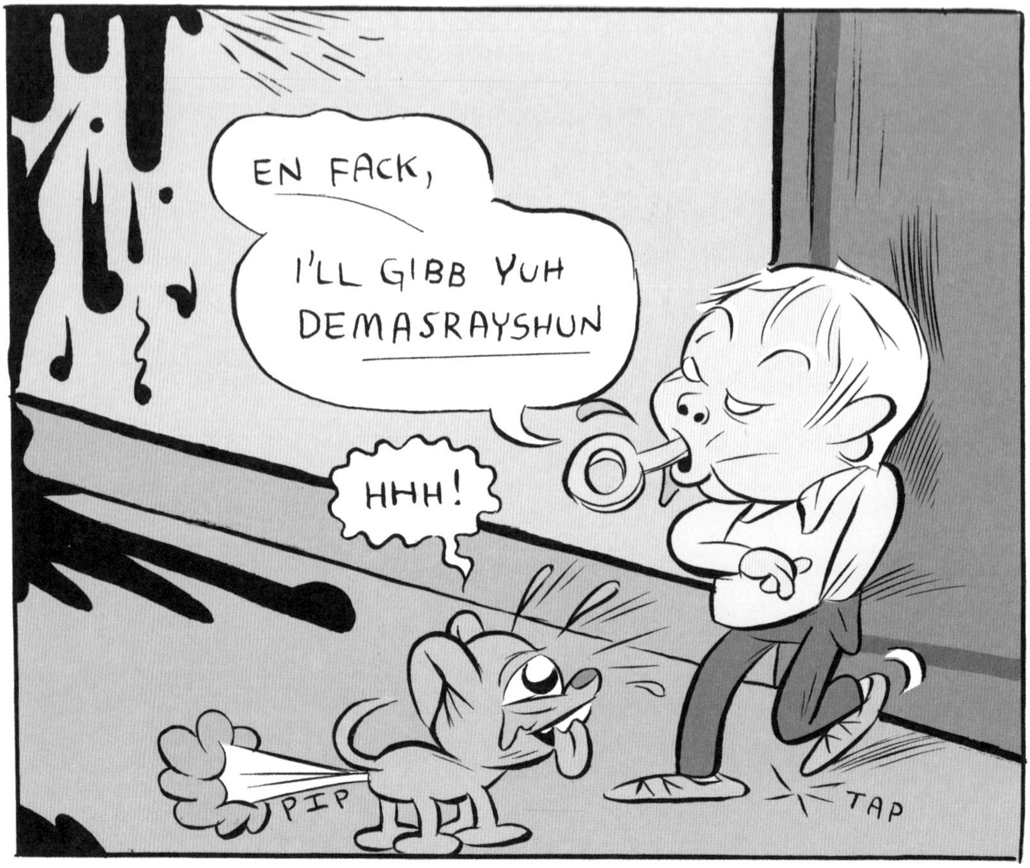
EN FACK,
I'LL GIBB YUH DEMASRAYSHUN
HHH!
PIP
TAP

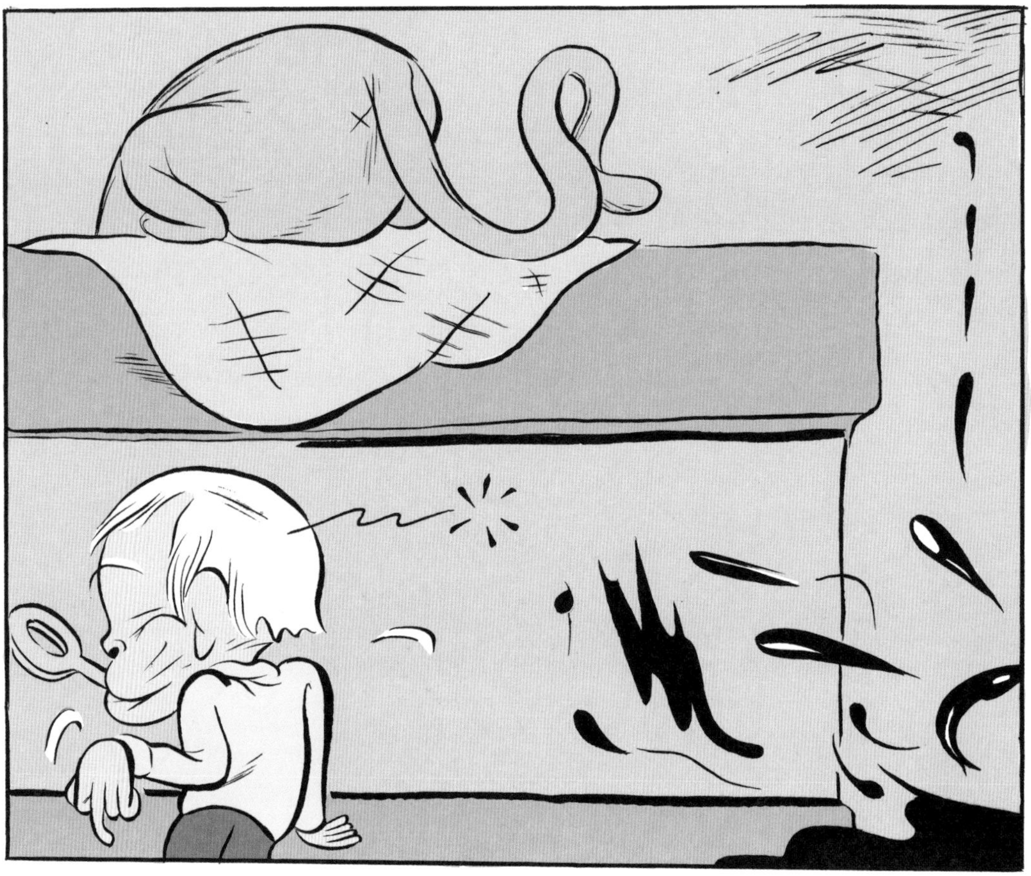

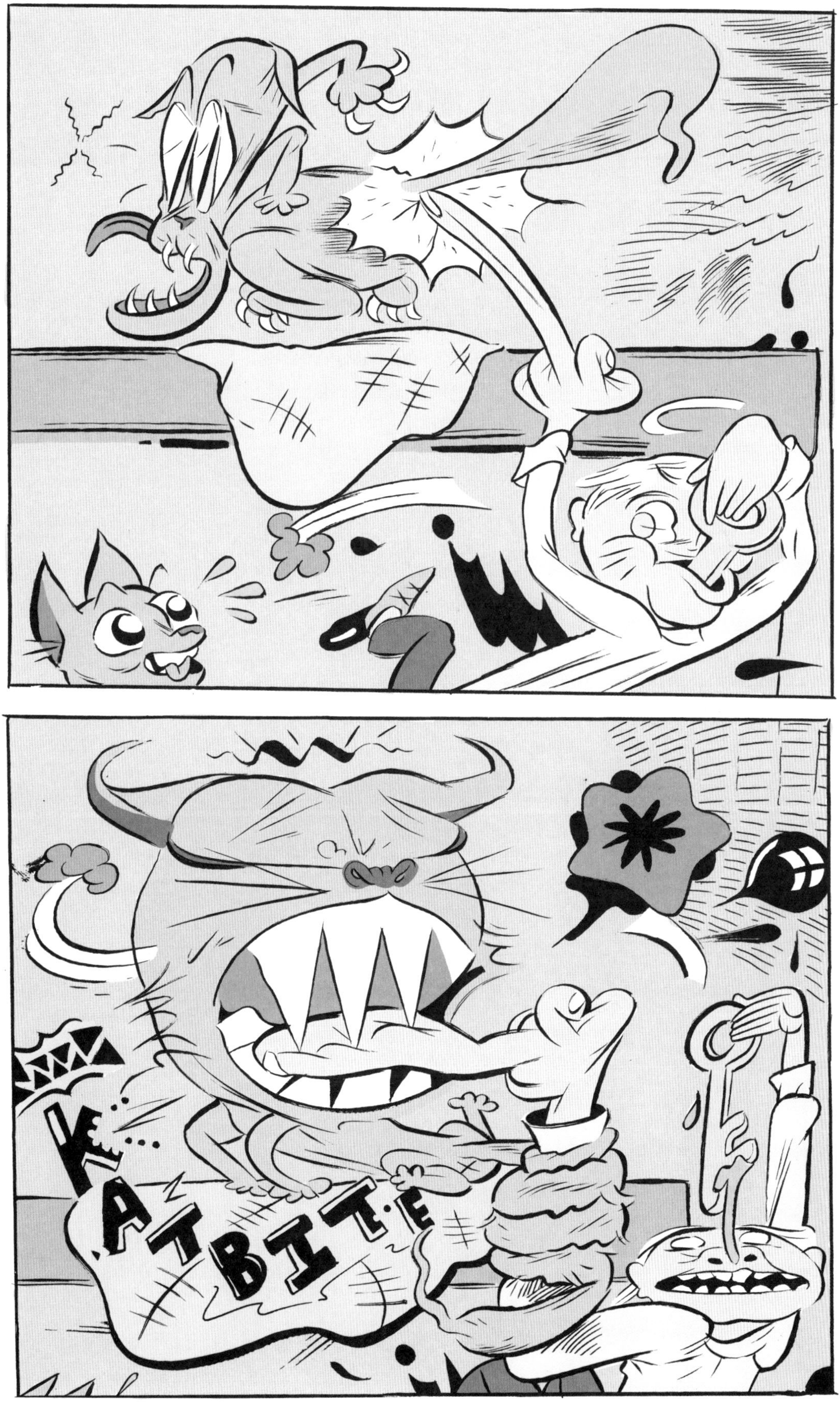
KATBITE

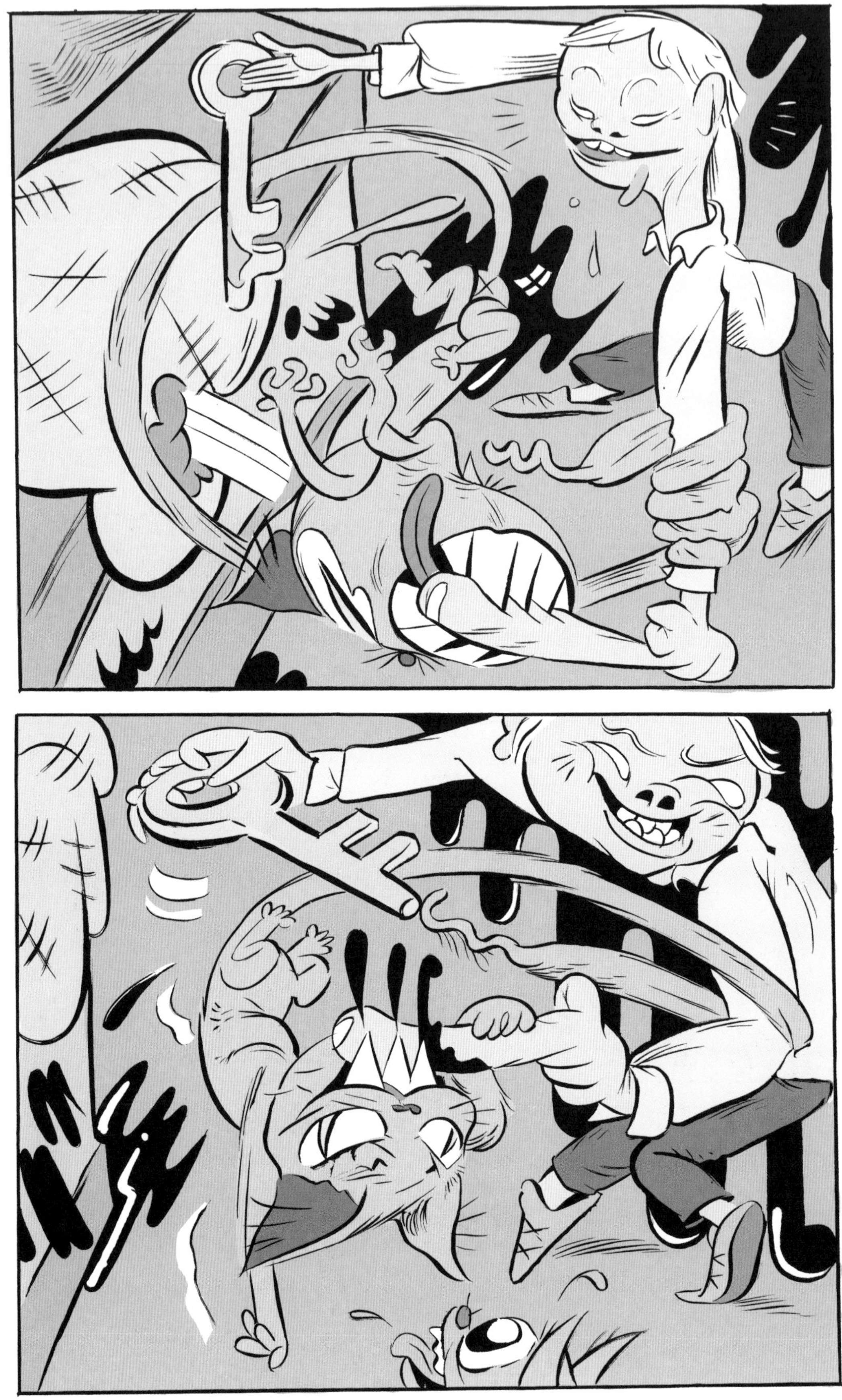

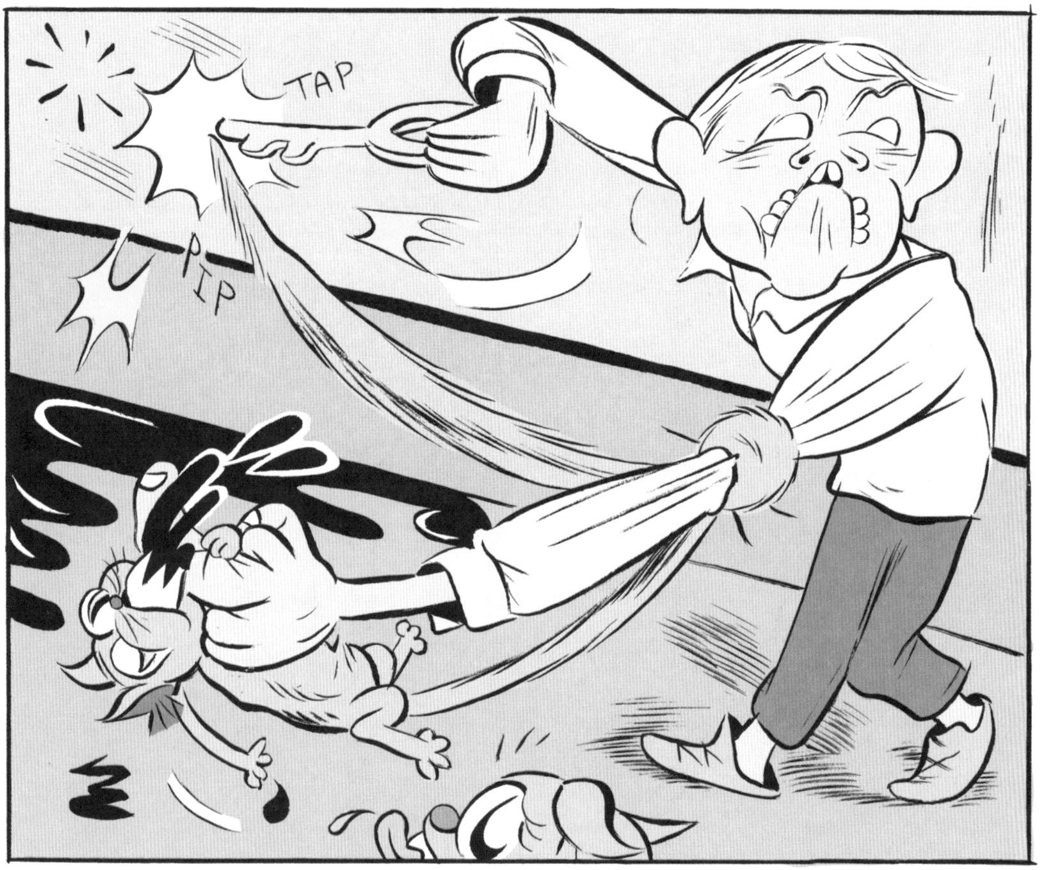
TAP
PIP

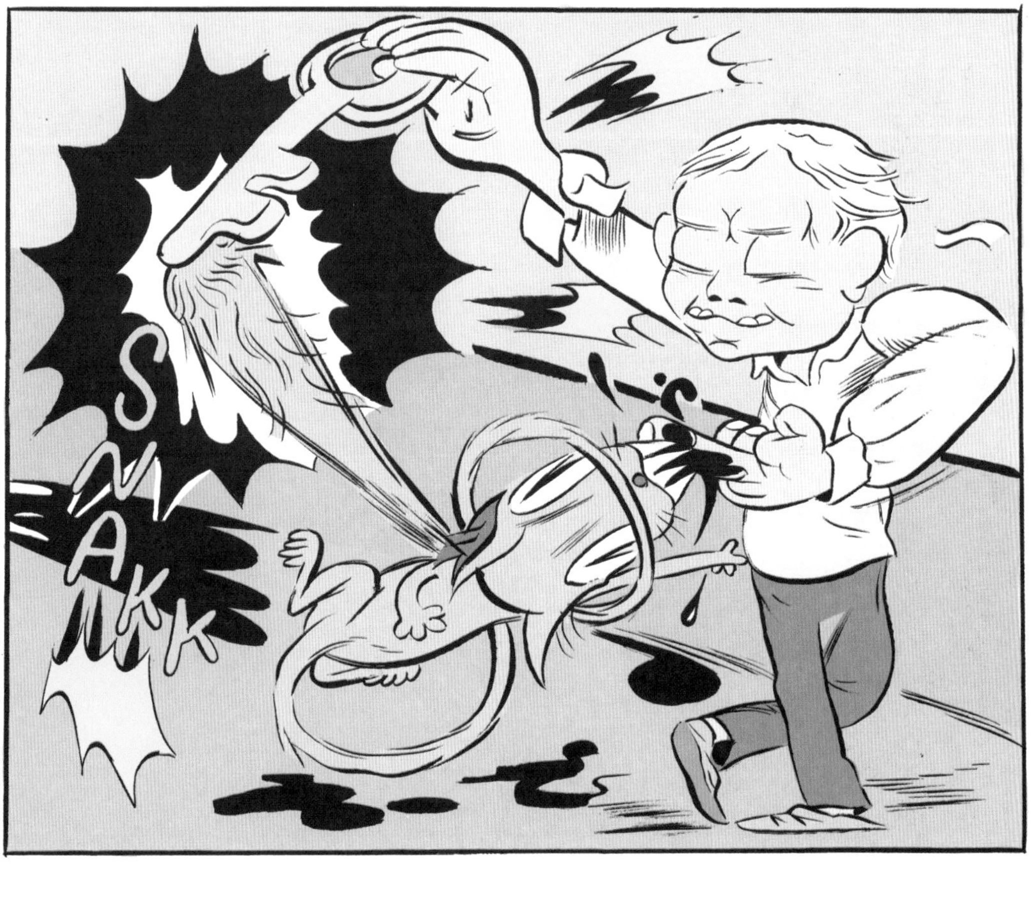
SNAKK

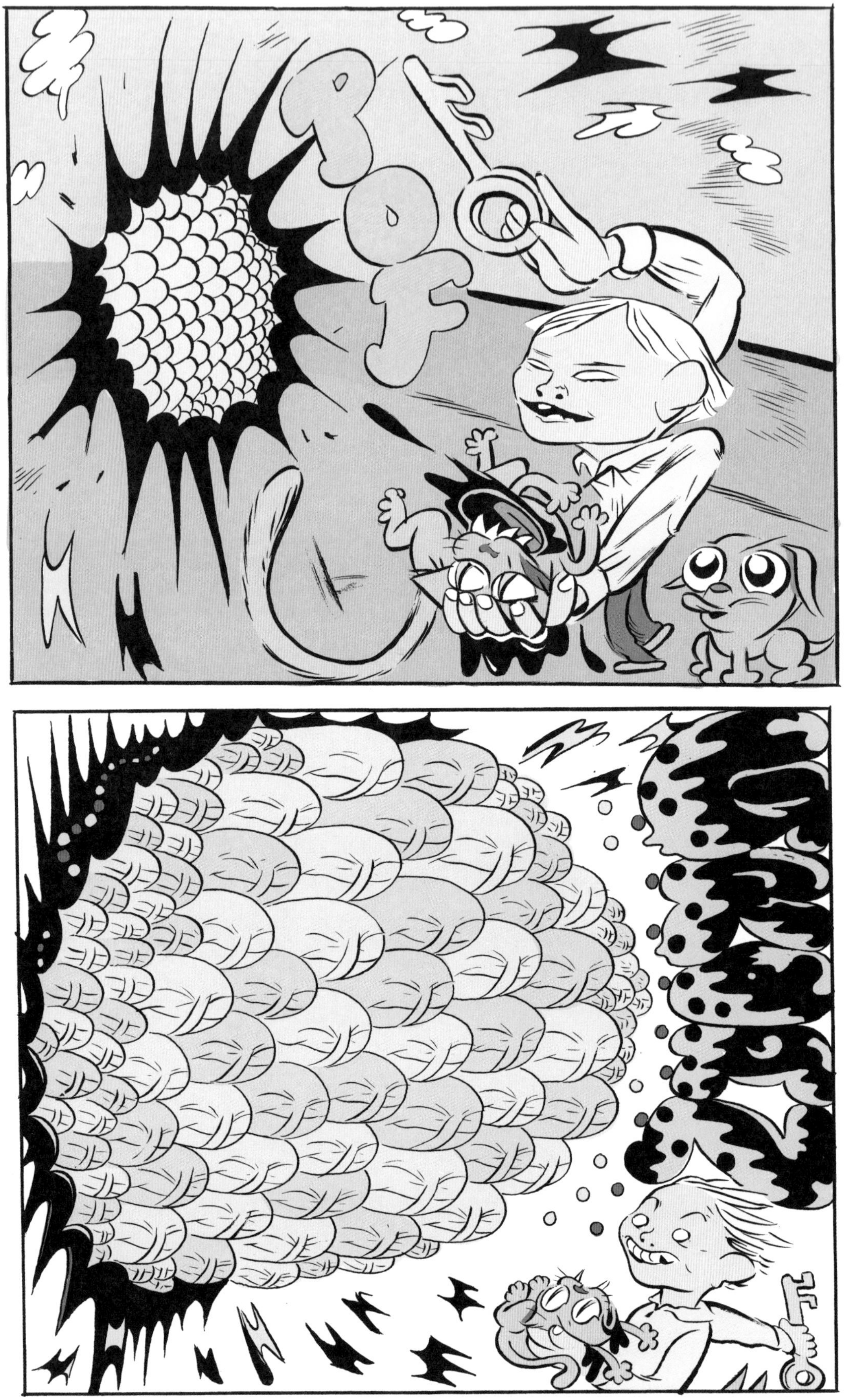
POF

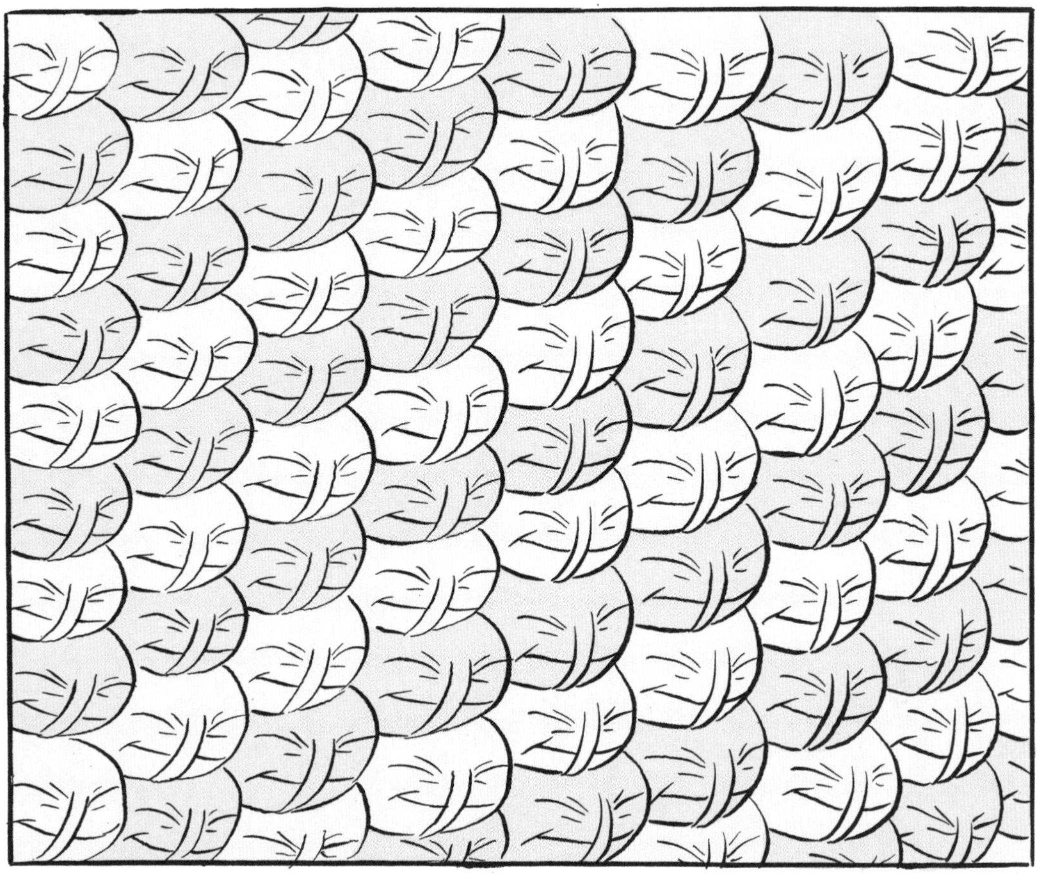
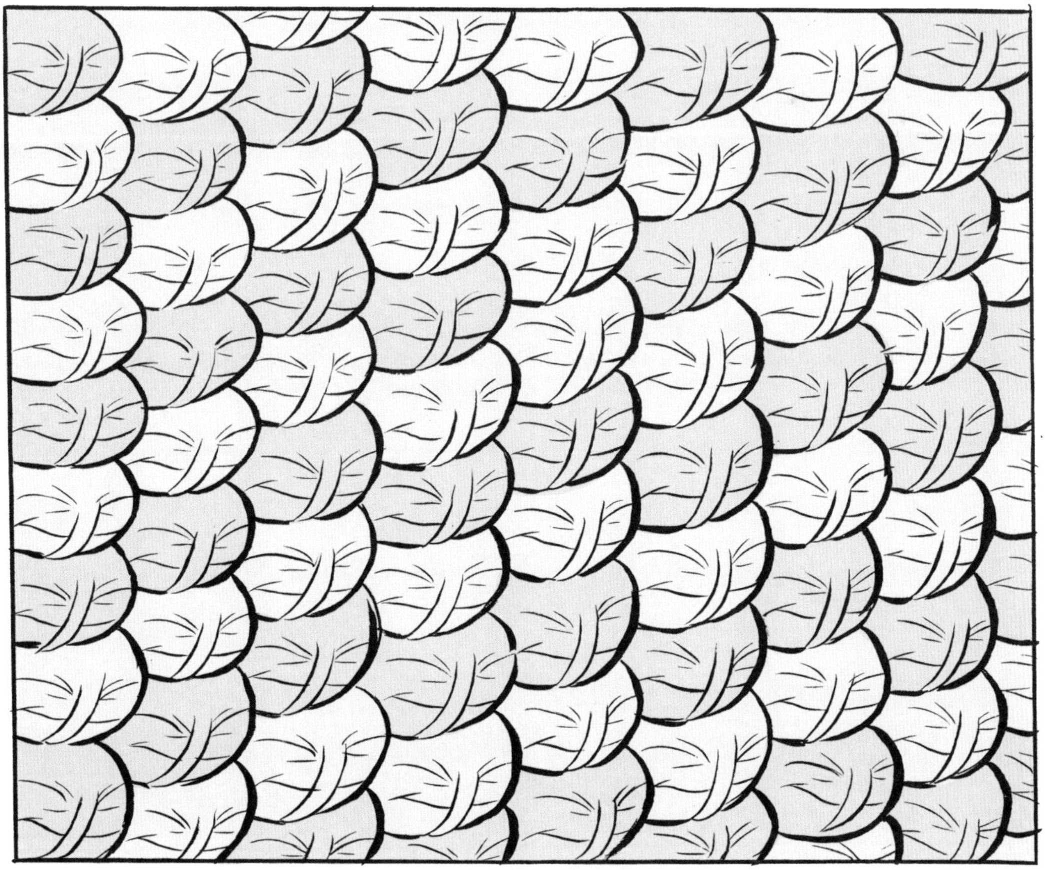

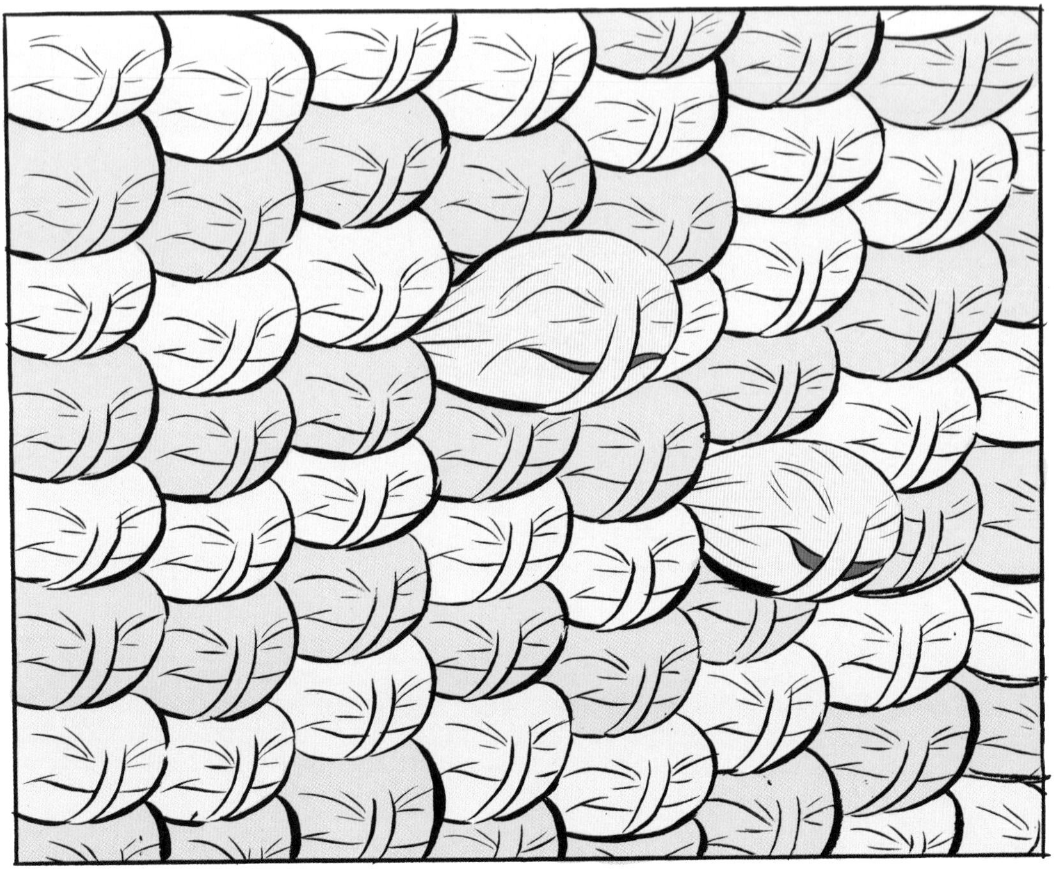

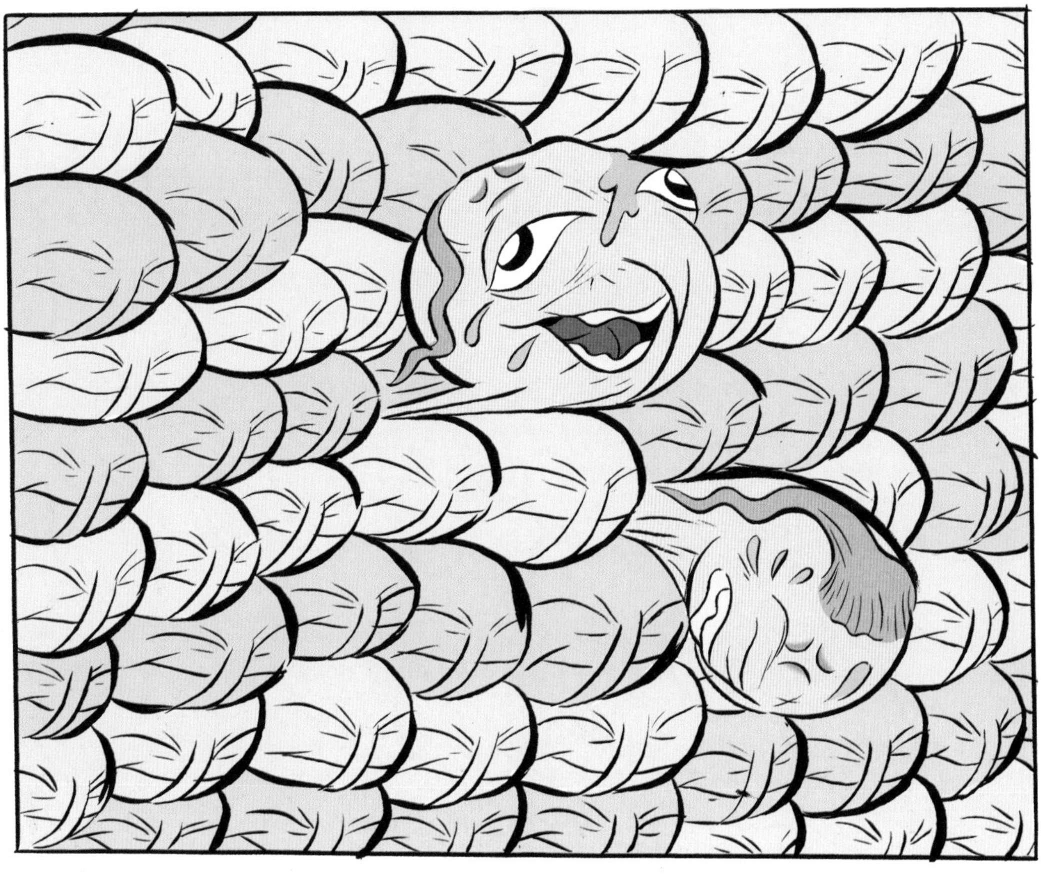

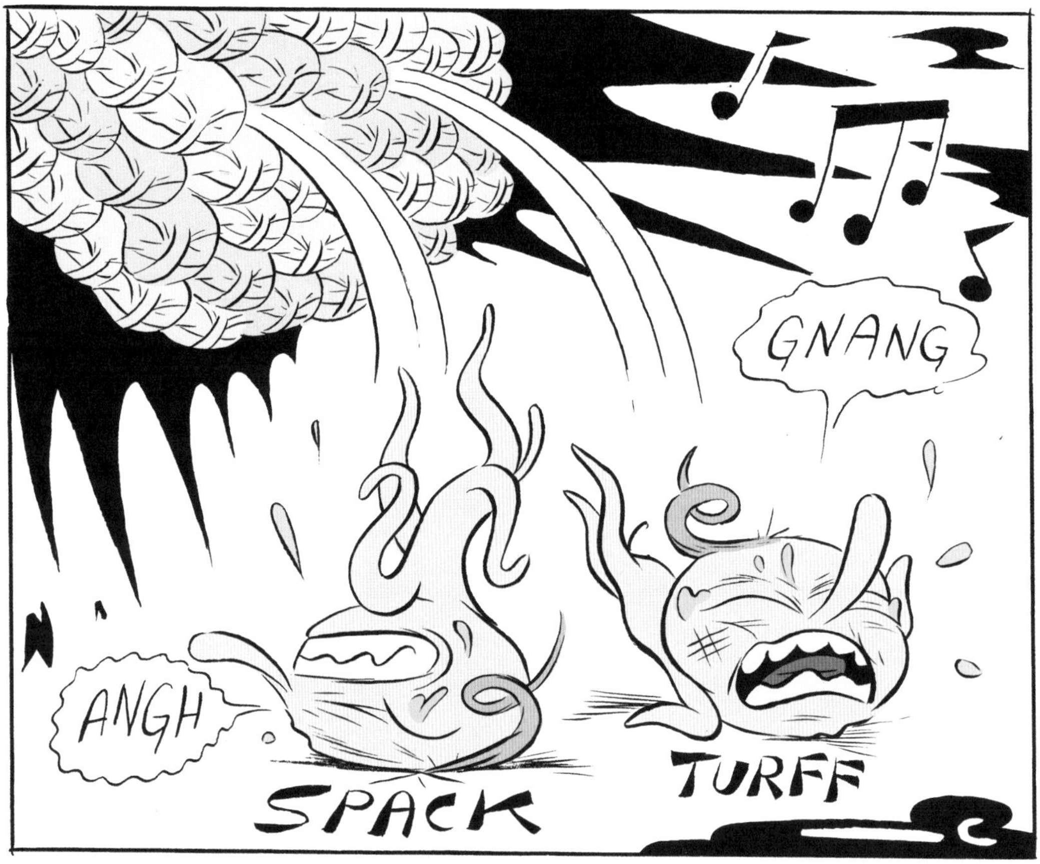
GNANG
ANGH
SPACK
TURFF

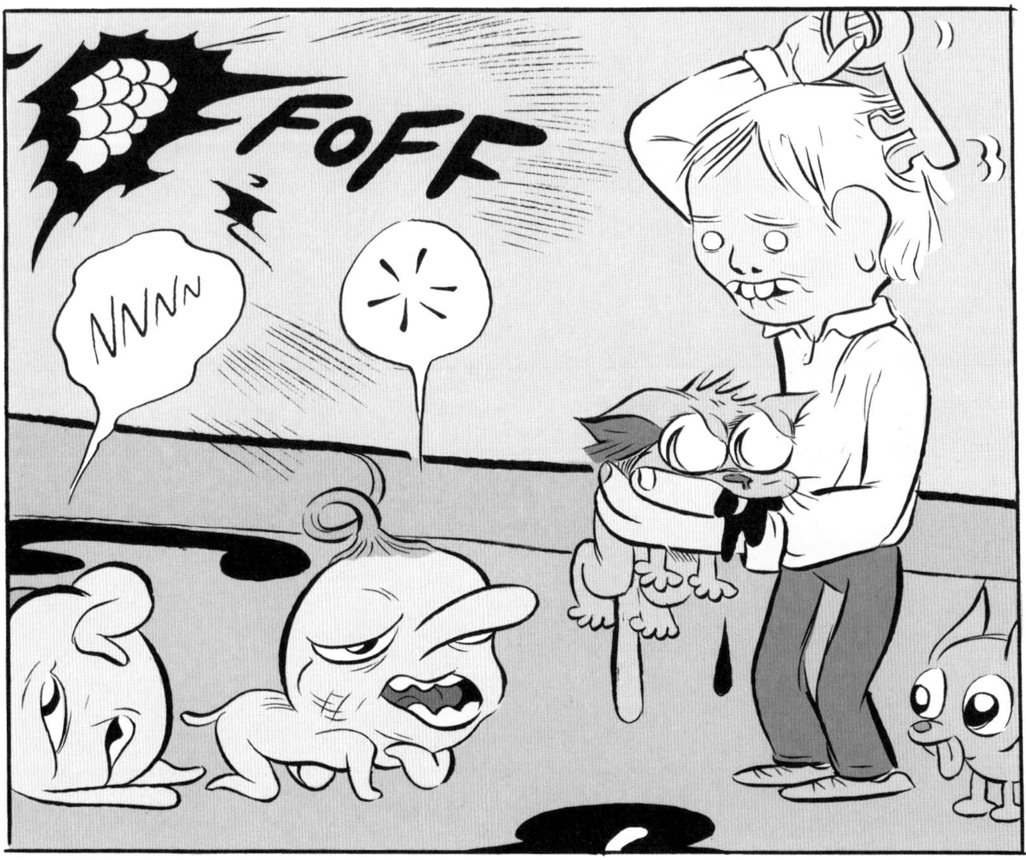
FOFF
NNNN

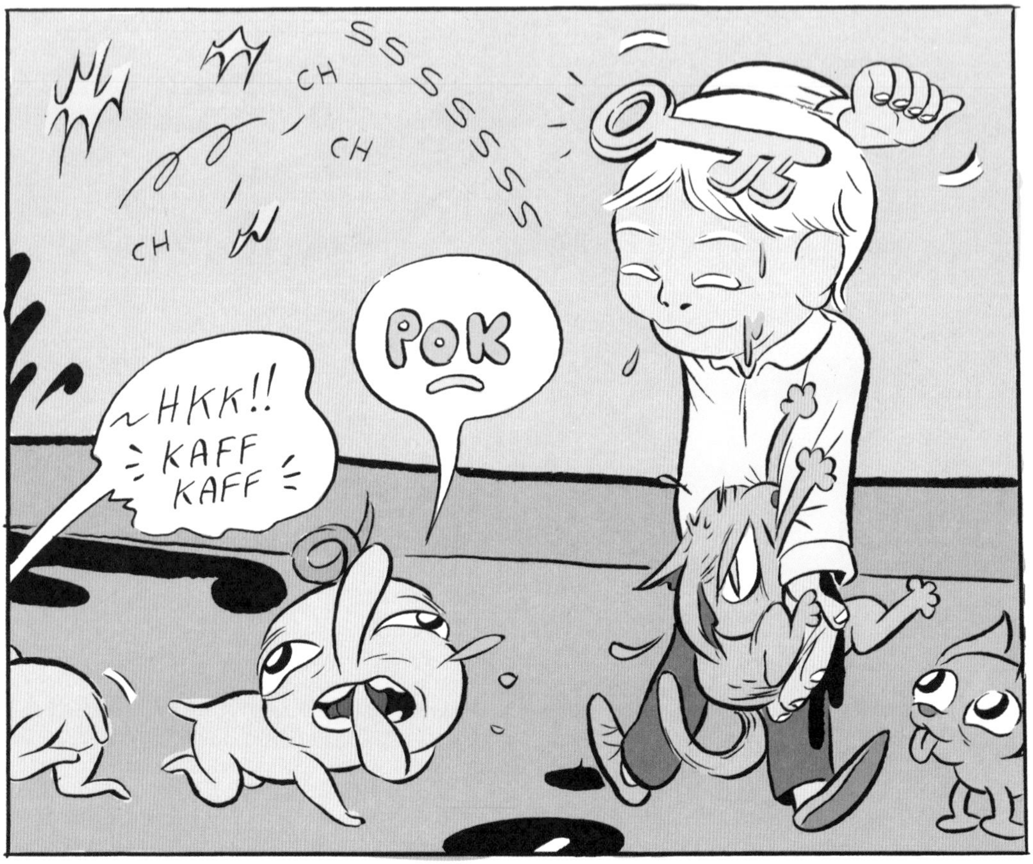
CH
SSSSSSSSS
CH
CH
HKK!!
KAFF
KAFF
POK

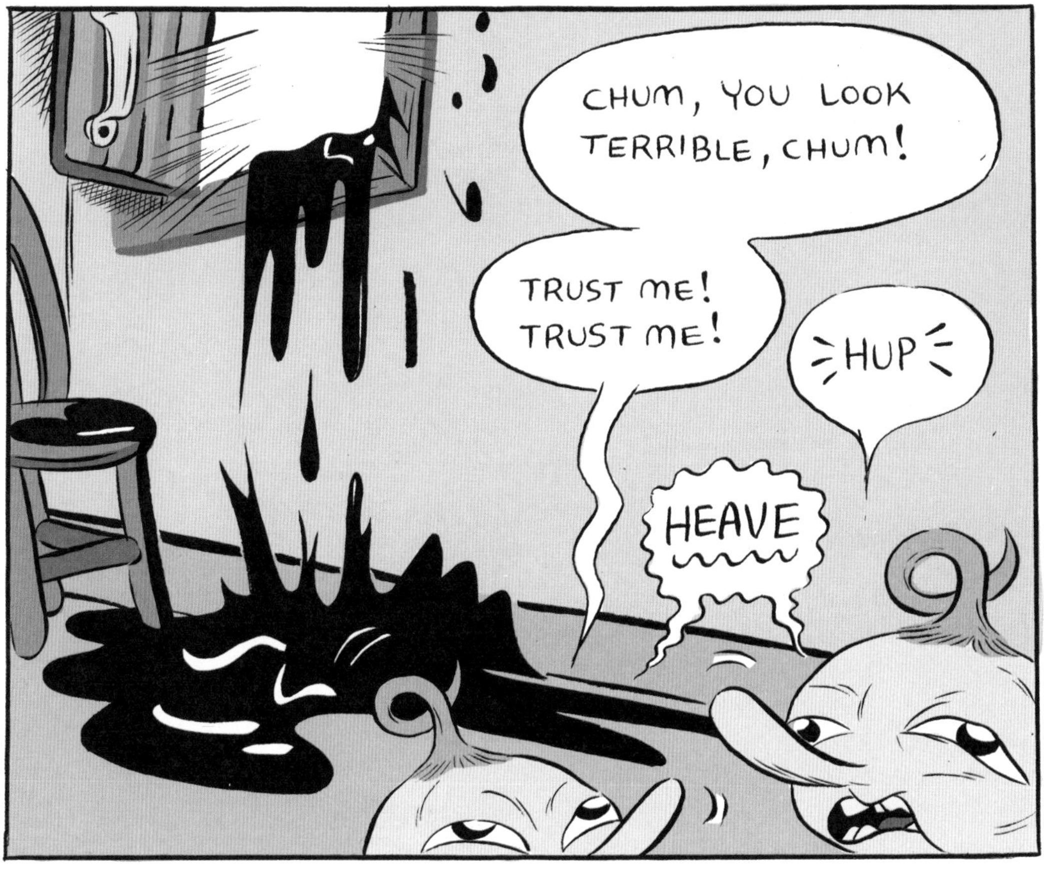
CHUM, YOU LOOK TERRIBLE, CHUM!
TRUST ME! TRUST ME!
HUP
HEAVE

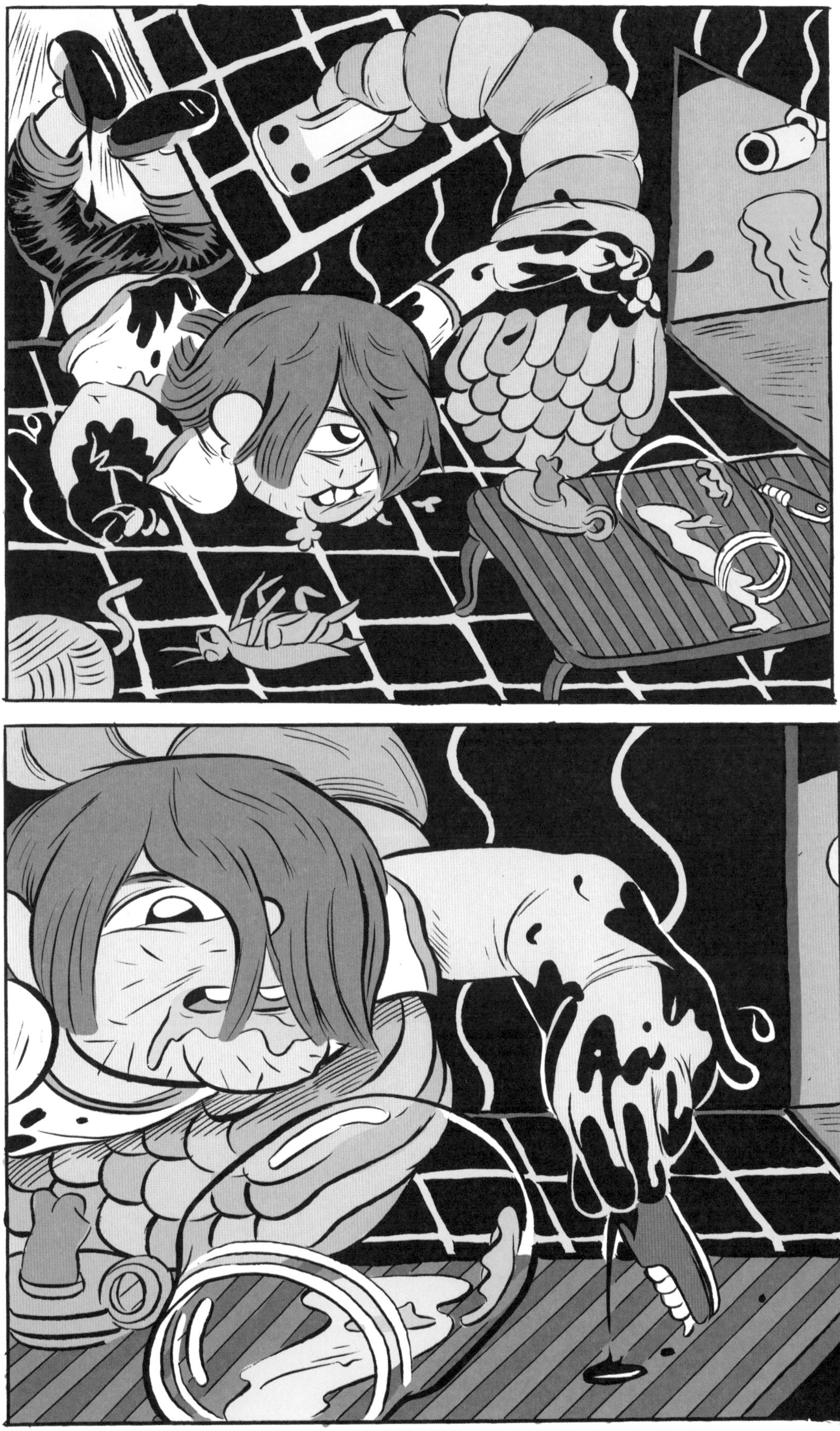

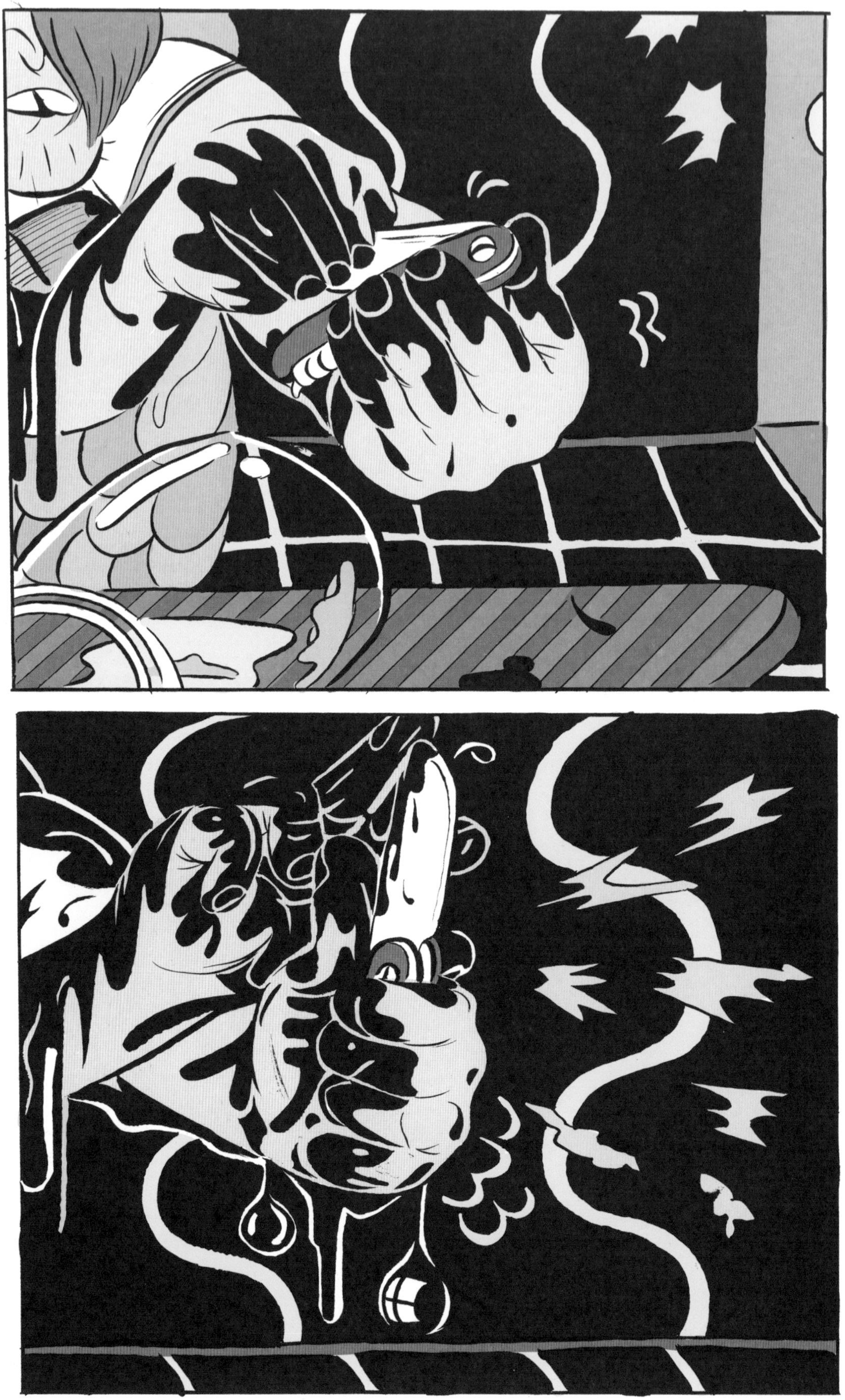

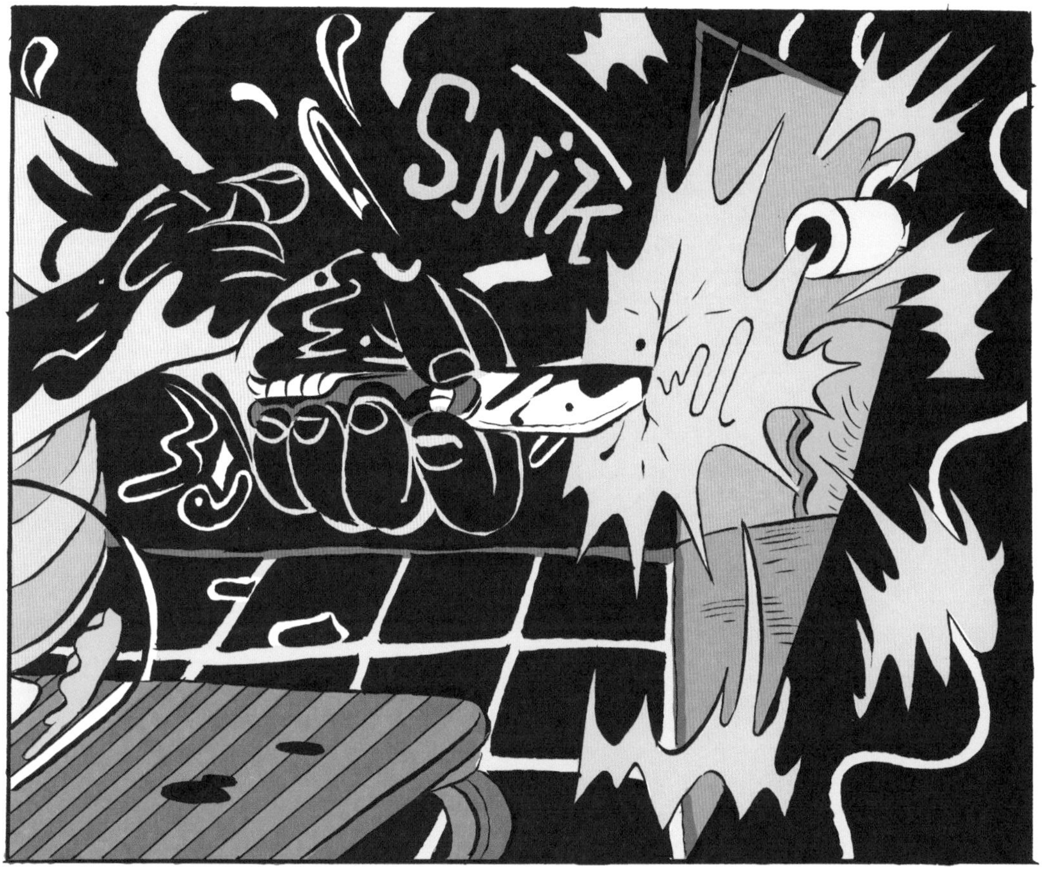
SNIK

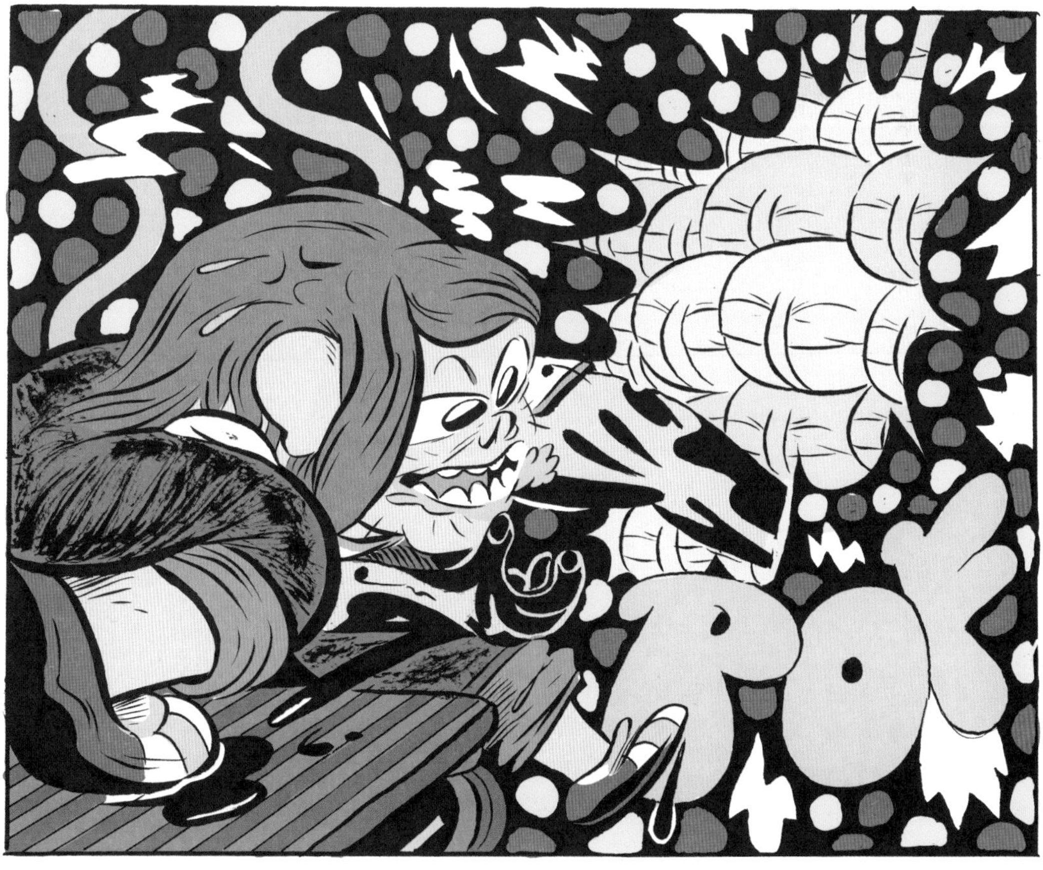
POK

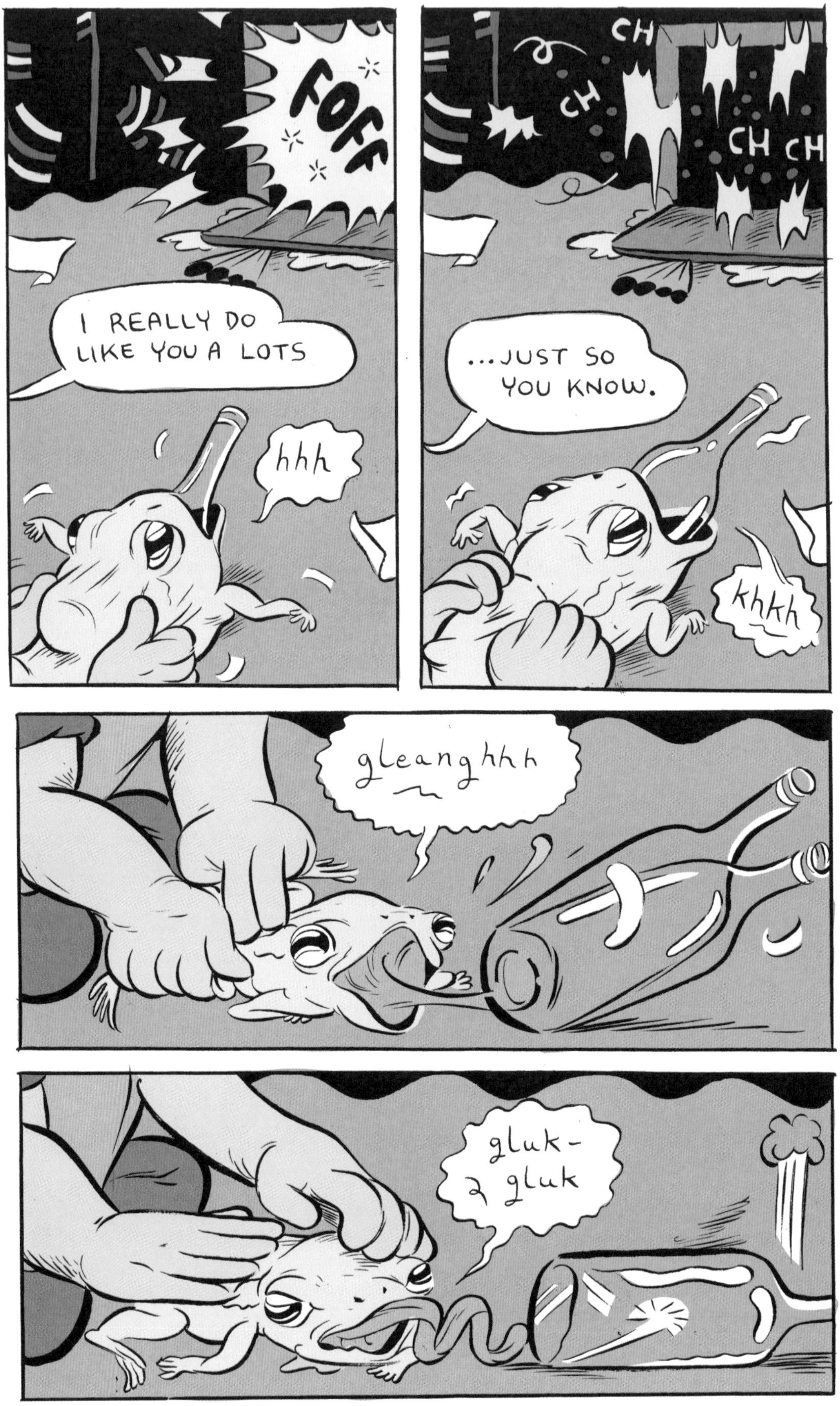
FOFF
I REALLY DO LIKE YOU A LOTS
hhh
CH
CH
CH CH
...JUST SO YOU KNOW.
khkh
gleanghhh
gluk-a gluk

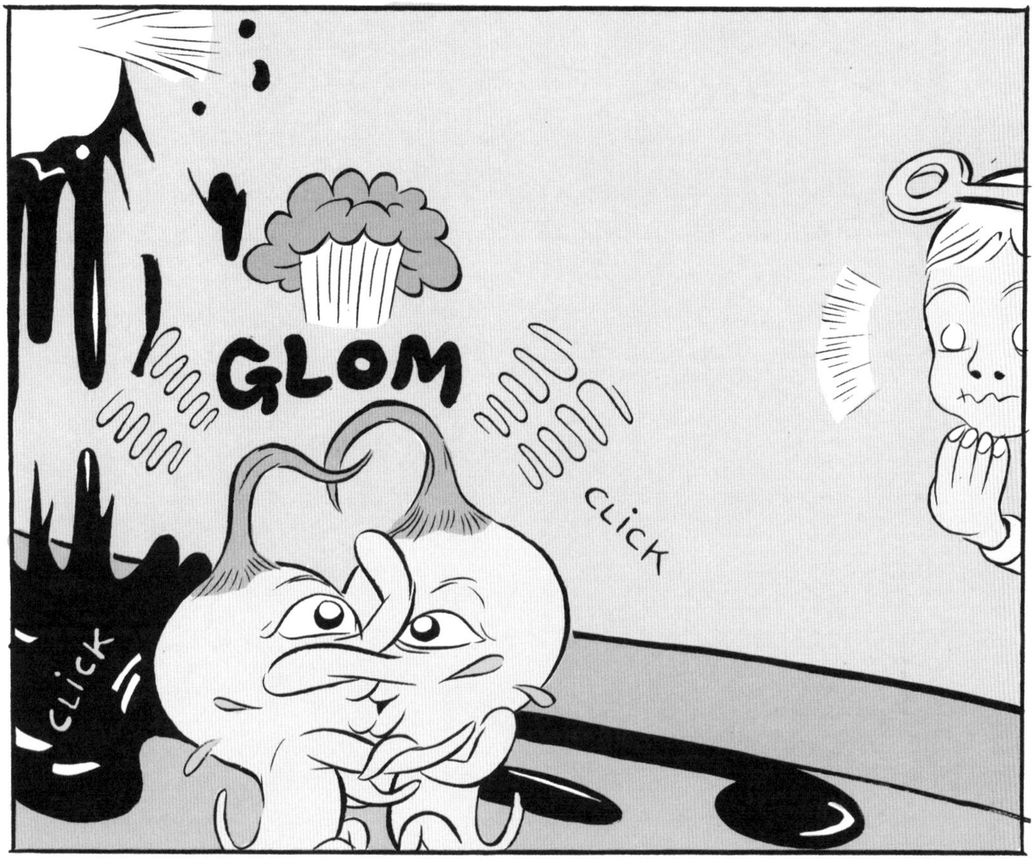
GLOM
CLICK
CLICK

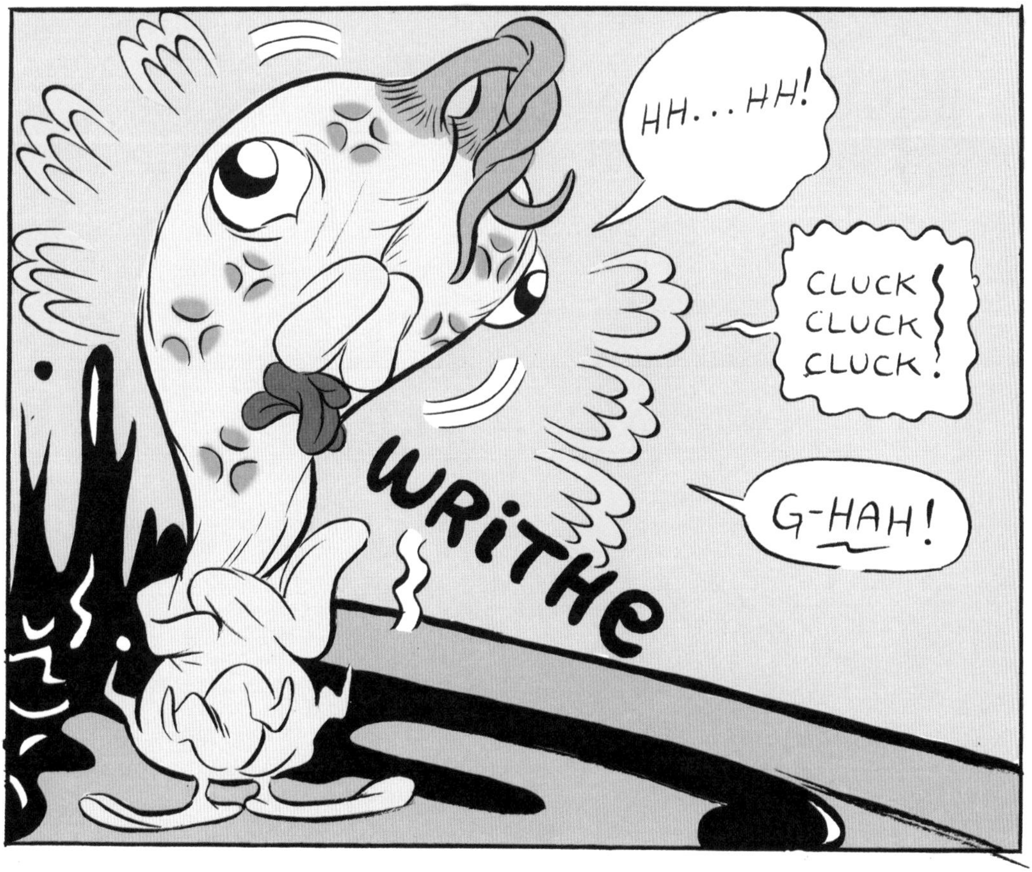
HH...HH!
CLUCK CLUCK CLUCK!
G-HAH!
WRITHE

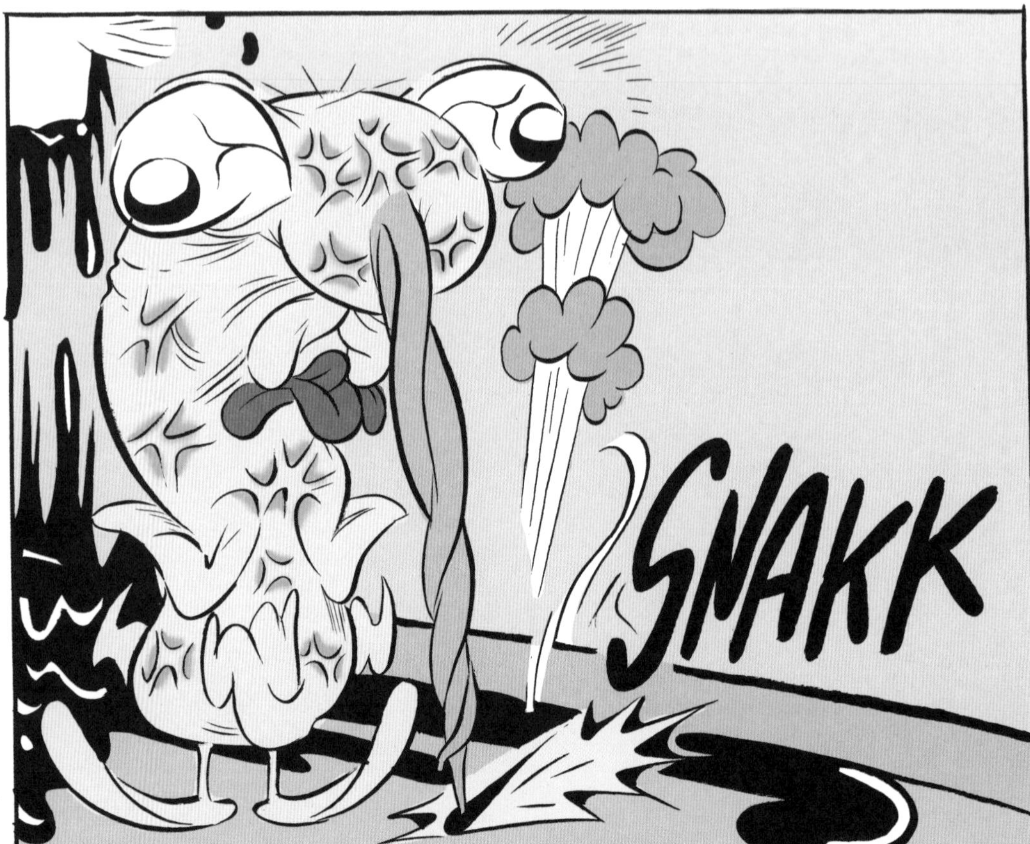
SNAKK

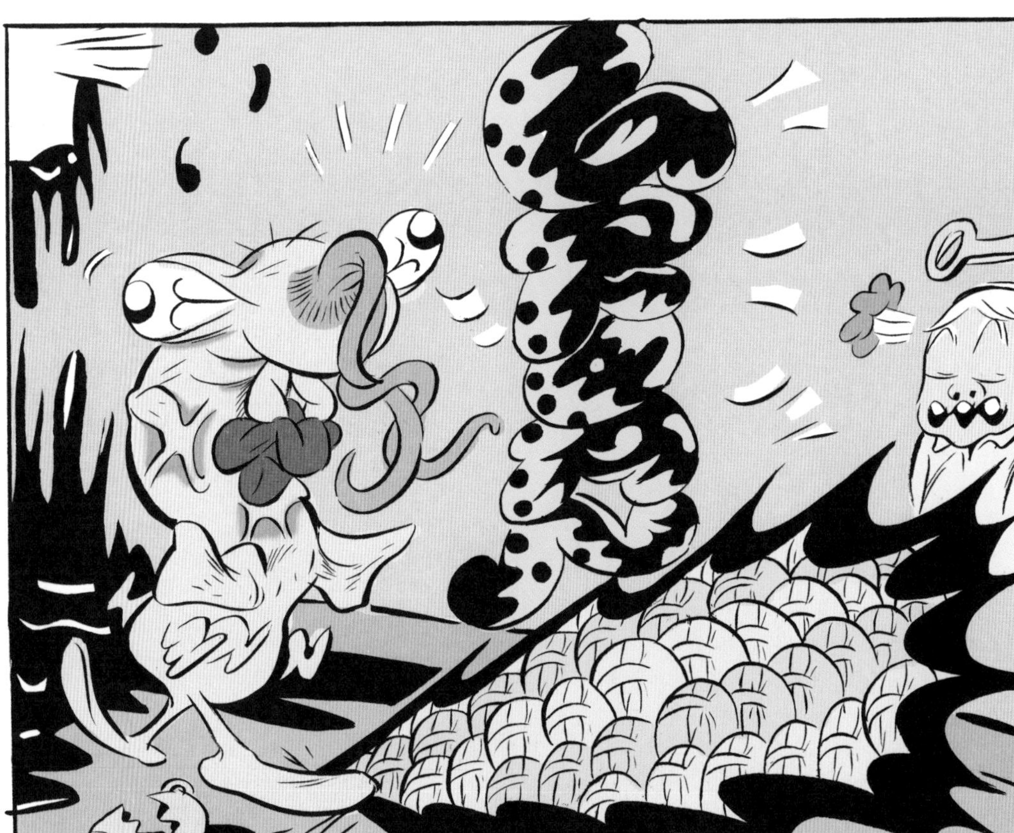

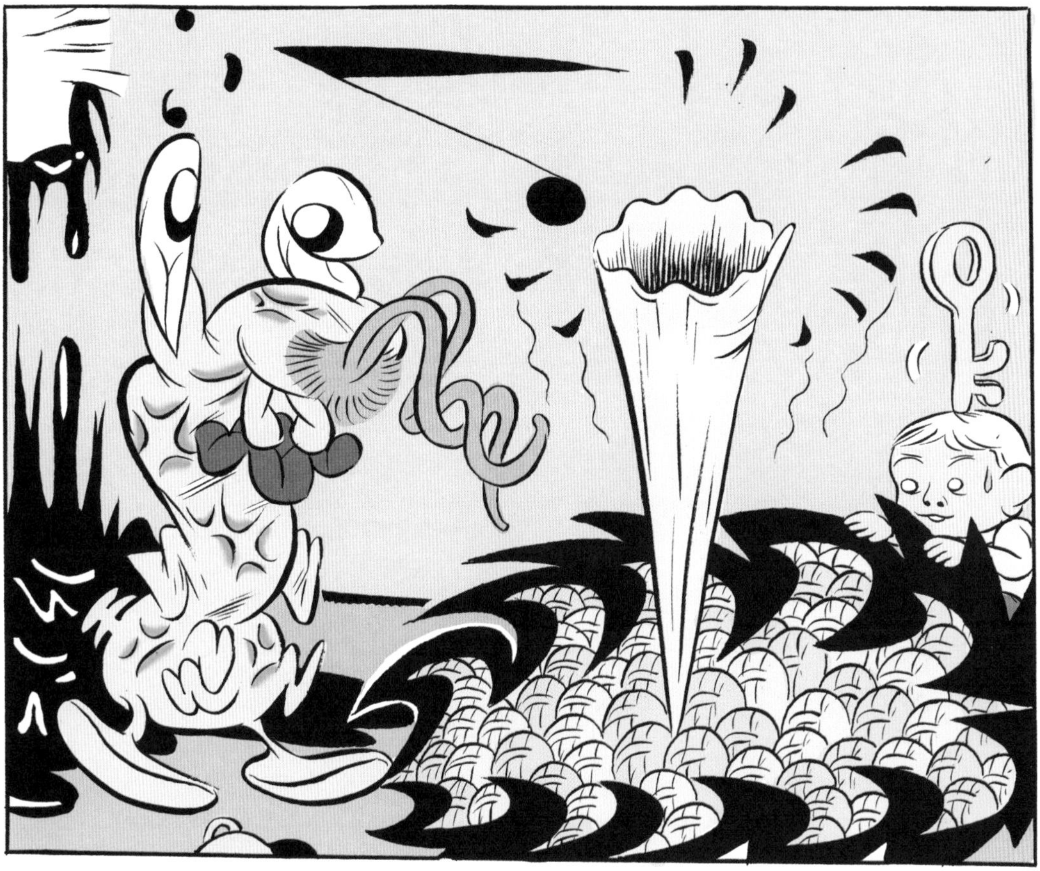

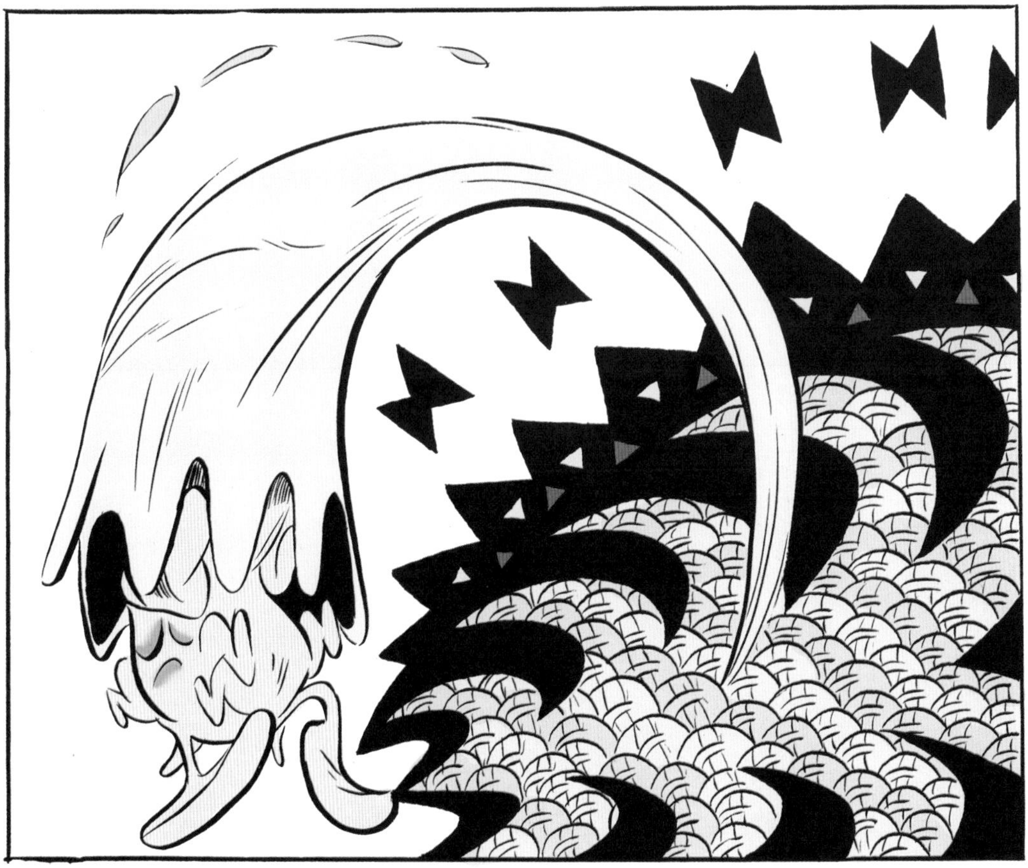

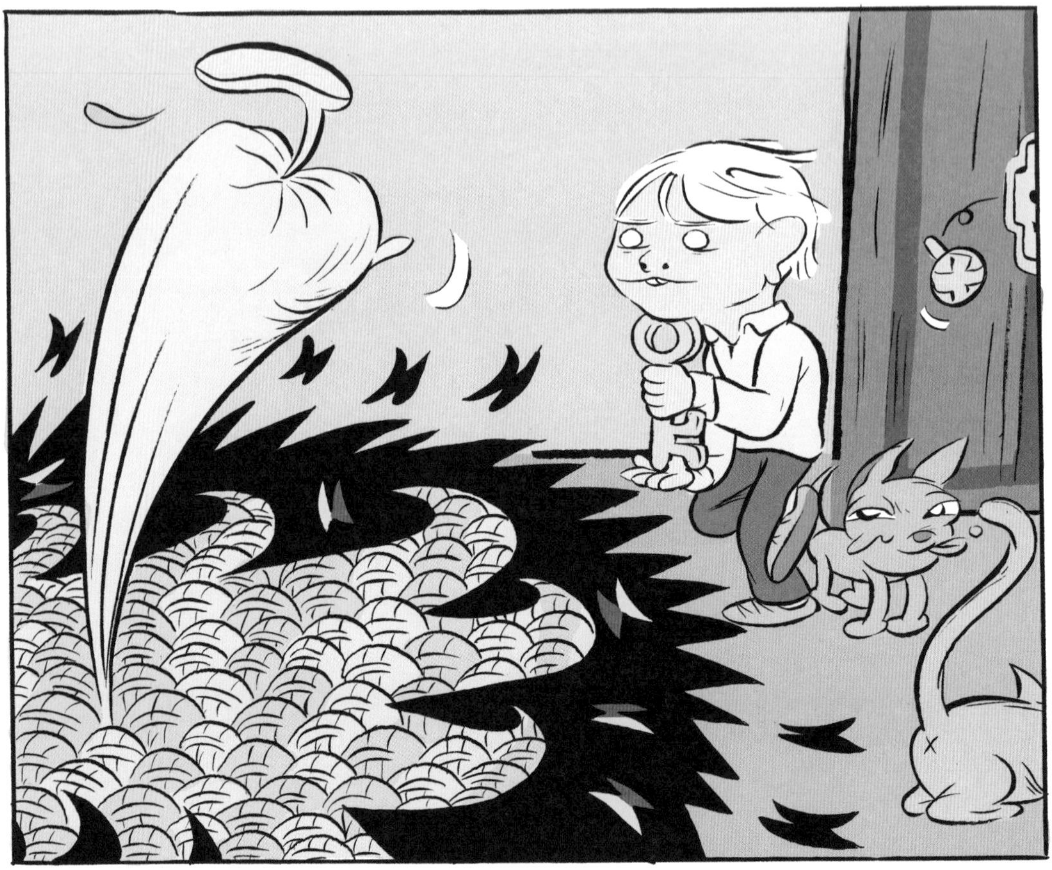

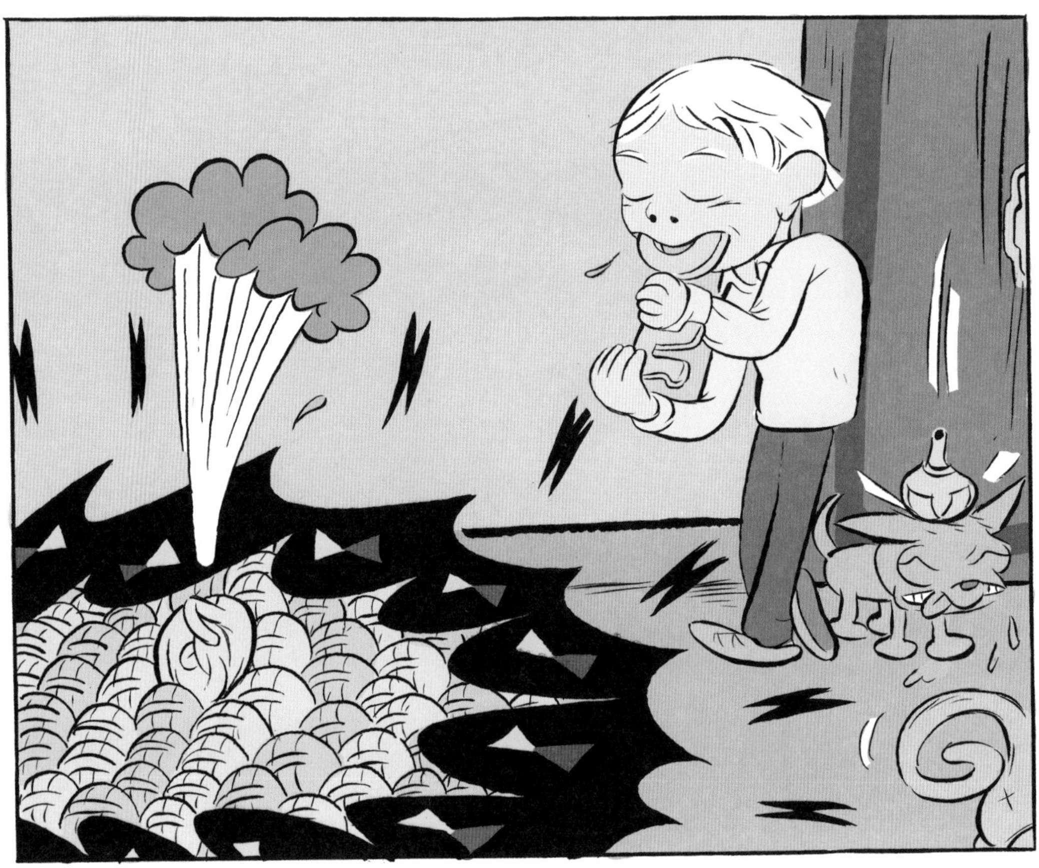

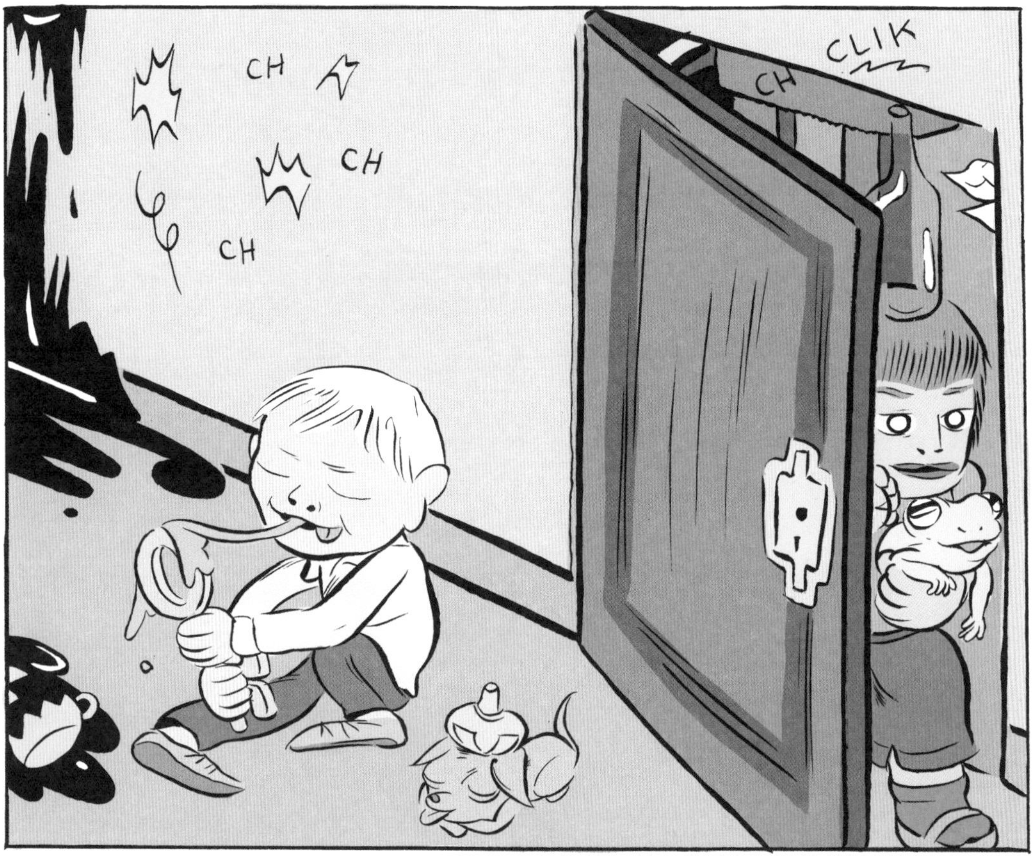
CH
CH
CH
CH
CLIK

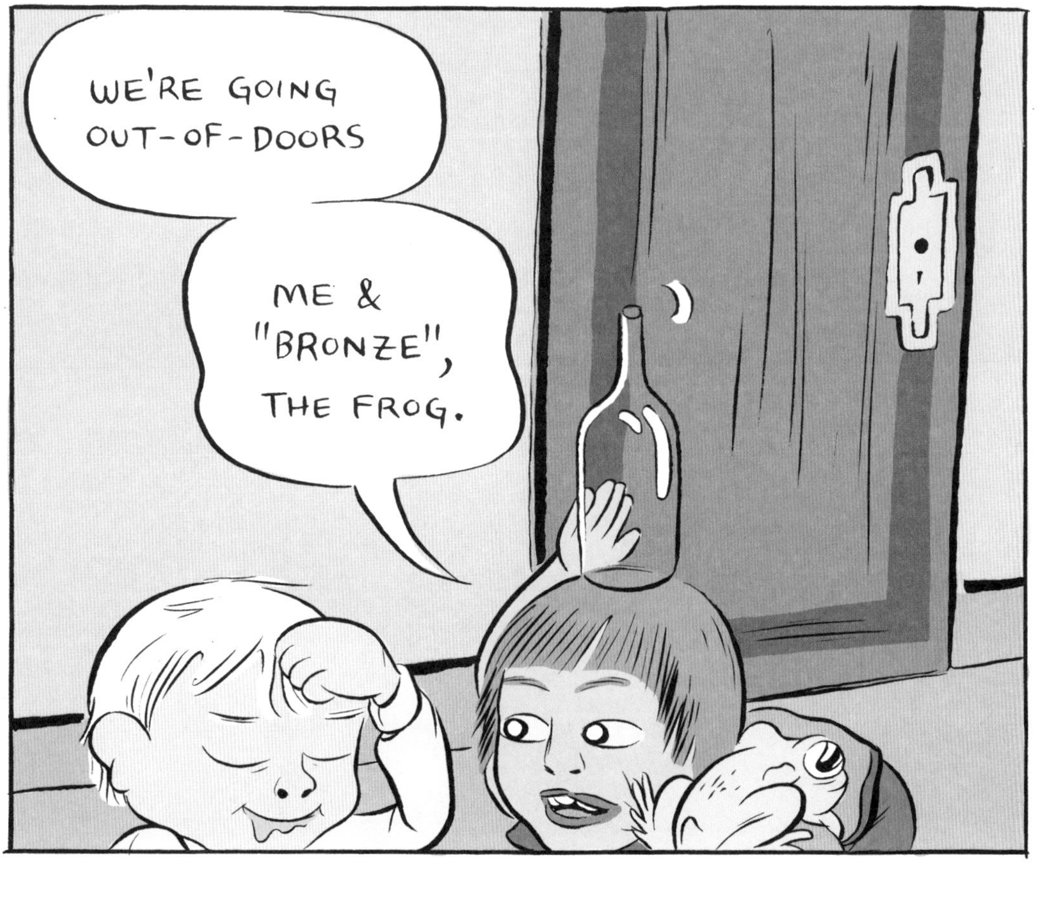
WE'RE GOING OUT-OF-DOORS
ME & "BRONZE", THE FROG.

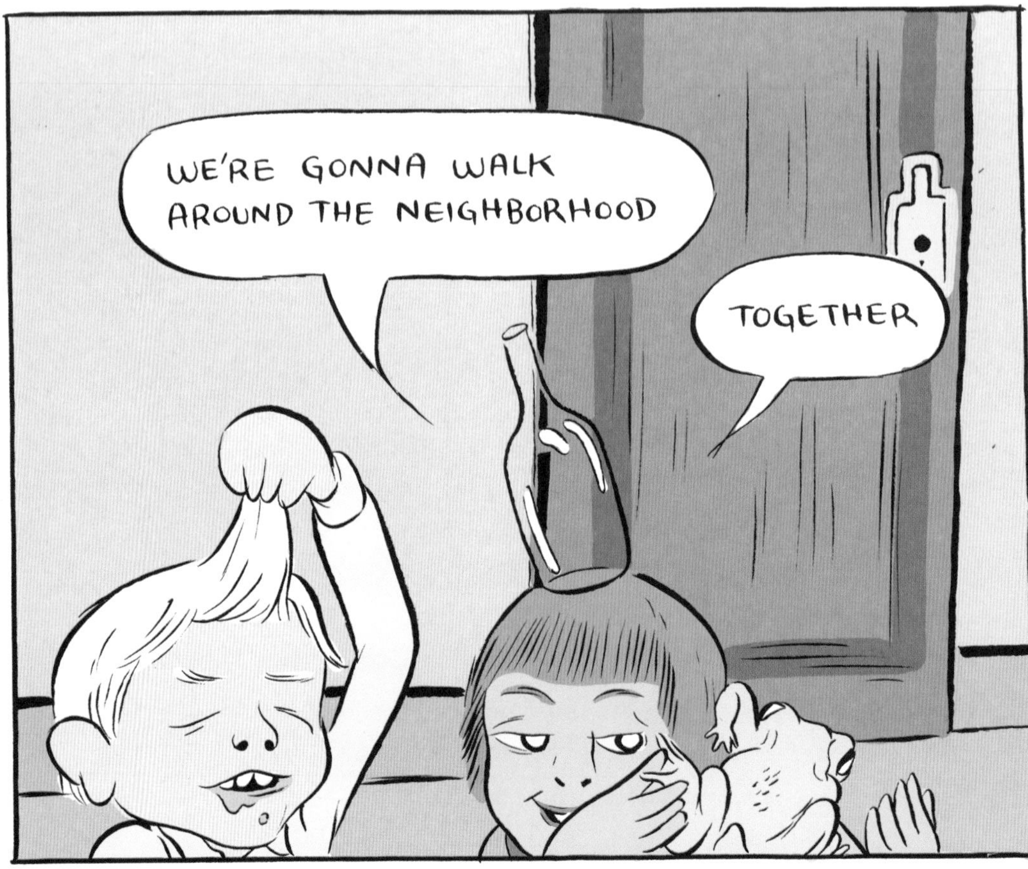
WE'RE GONNA WALK AROUND THE NEIGHBORHOOD
TOGETHER

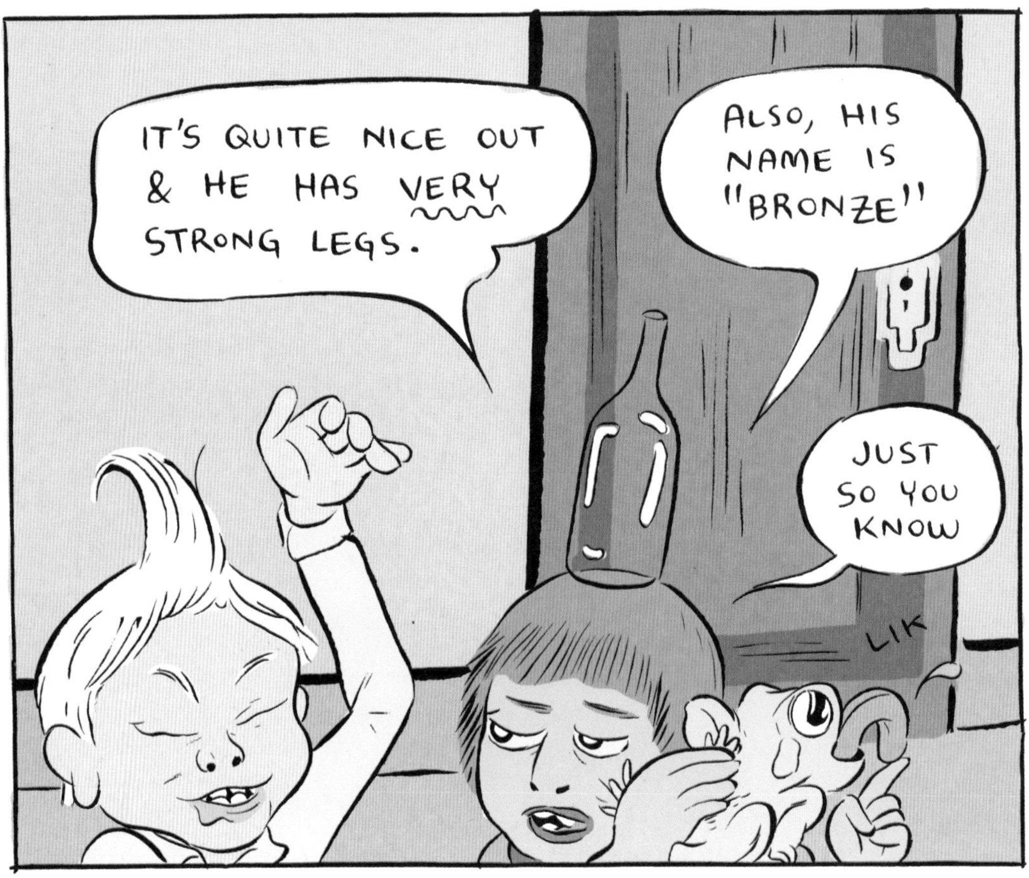
IT'S QUITE NICE OUT & HE HAS VERY STRONG LEGS.
ALSO, HIS NAME IS "BRONZE"
JUST SO YOU KNOW
LIK

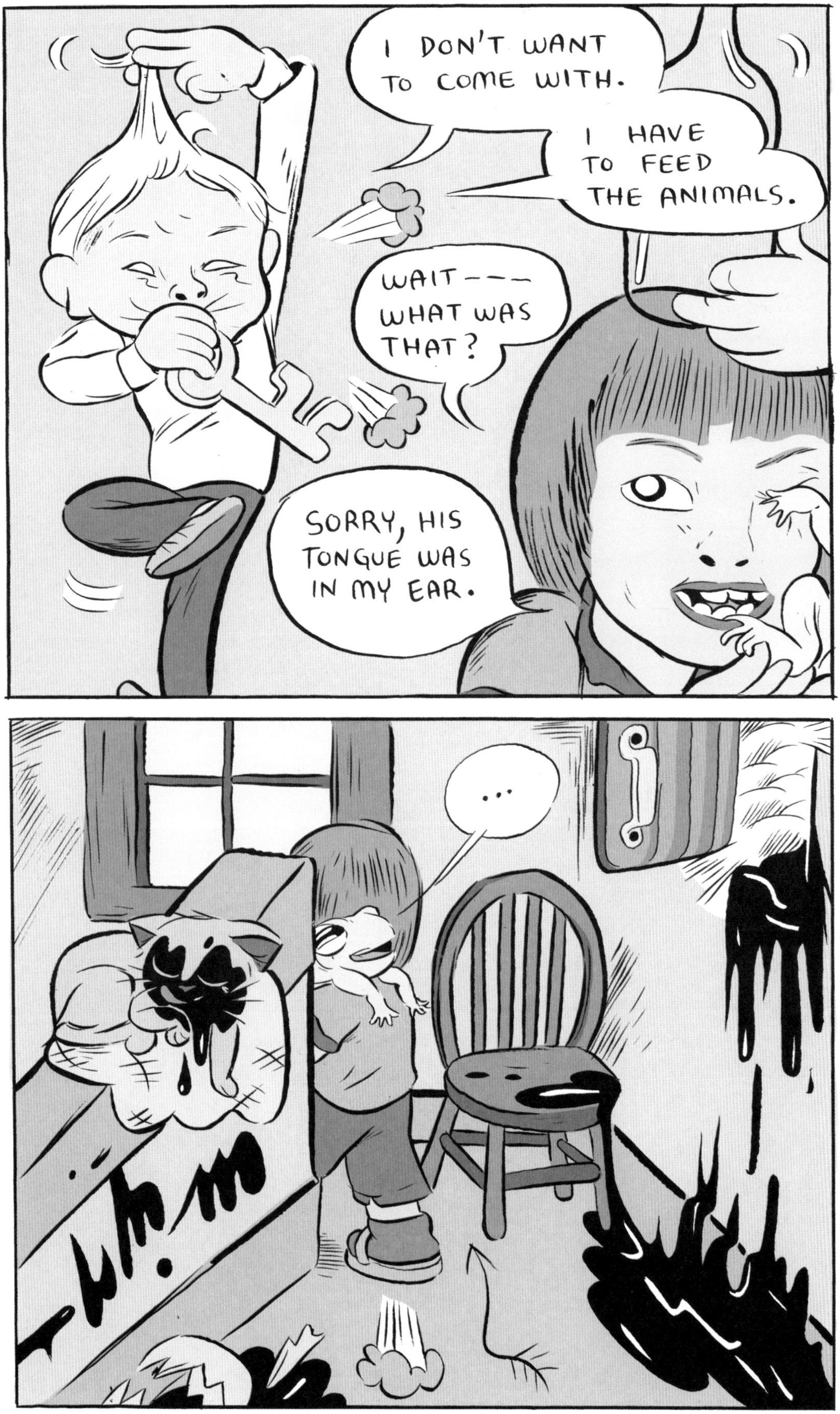
I DON'T WANT TO COME WITH.
I HAVE TO FEED THE ANIMALS.
WAIT--- WHAT WAS THAT?
SORRY, HIS TONGUE WAS IN MY EAR.
...

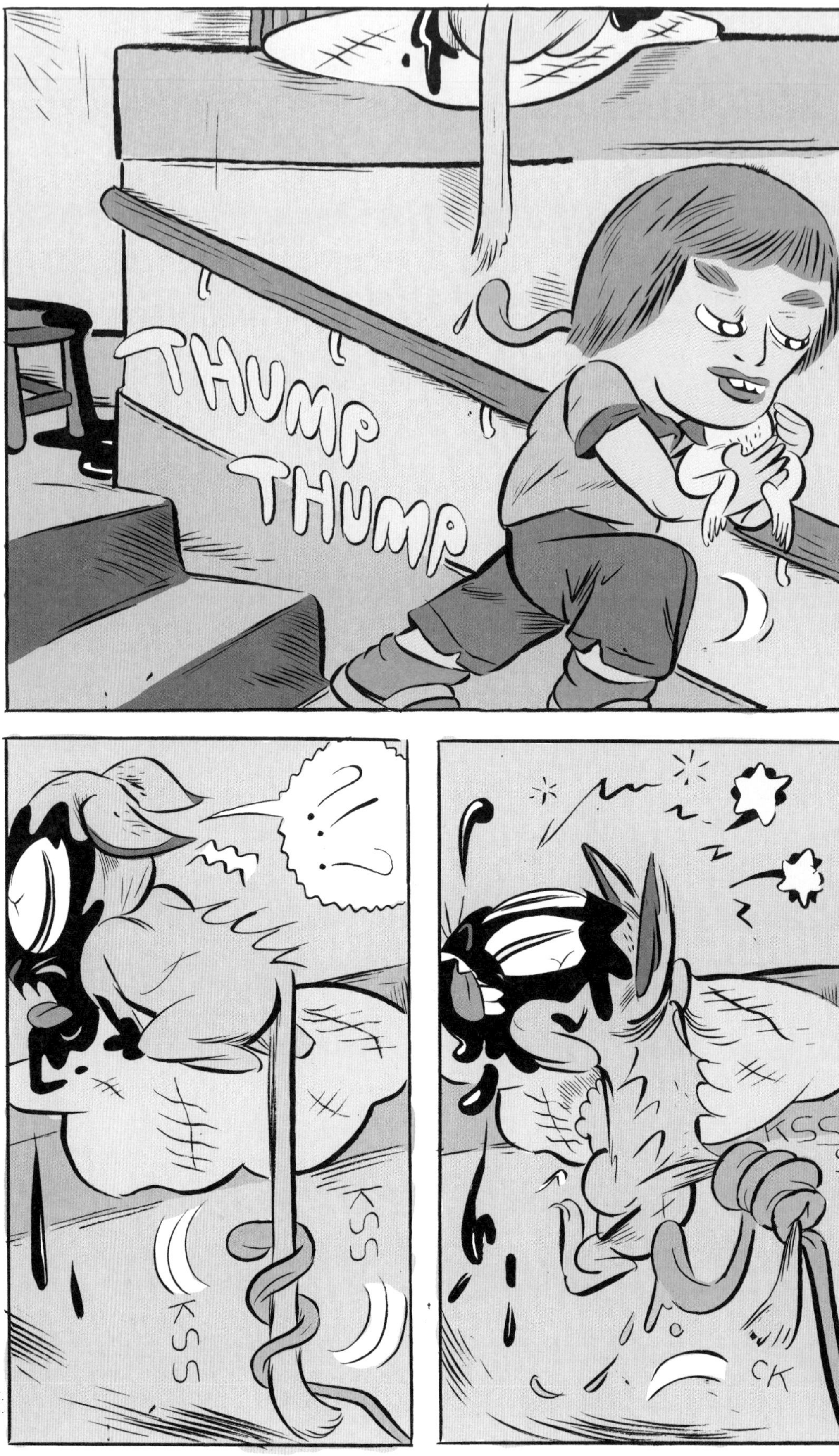
THUMP
THUMP
KSS
KSS
KSS
CK

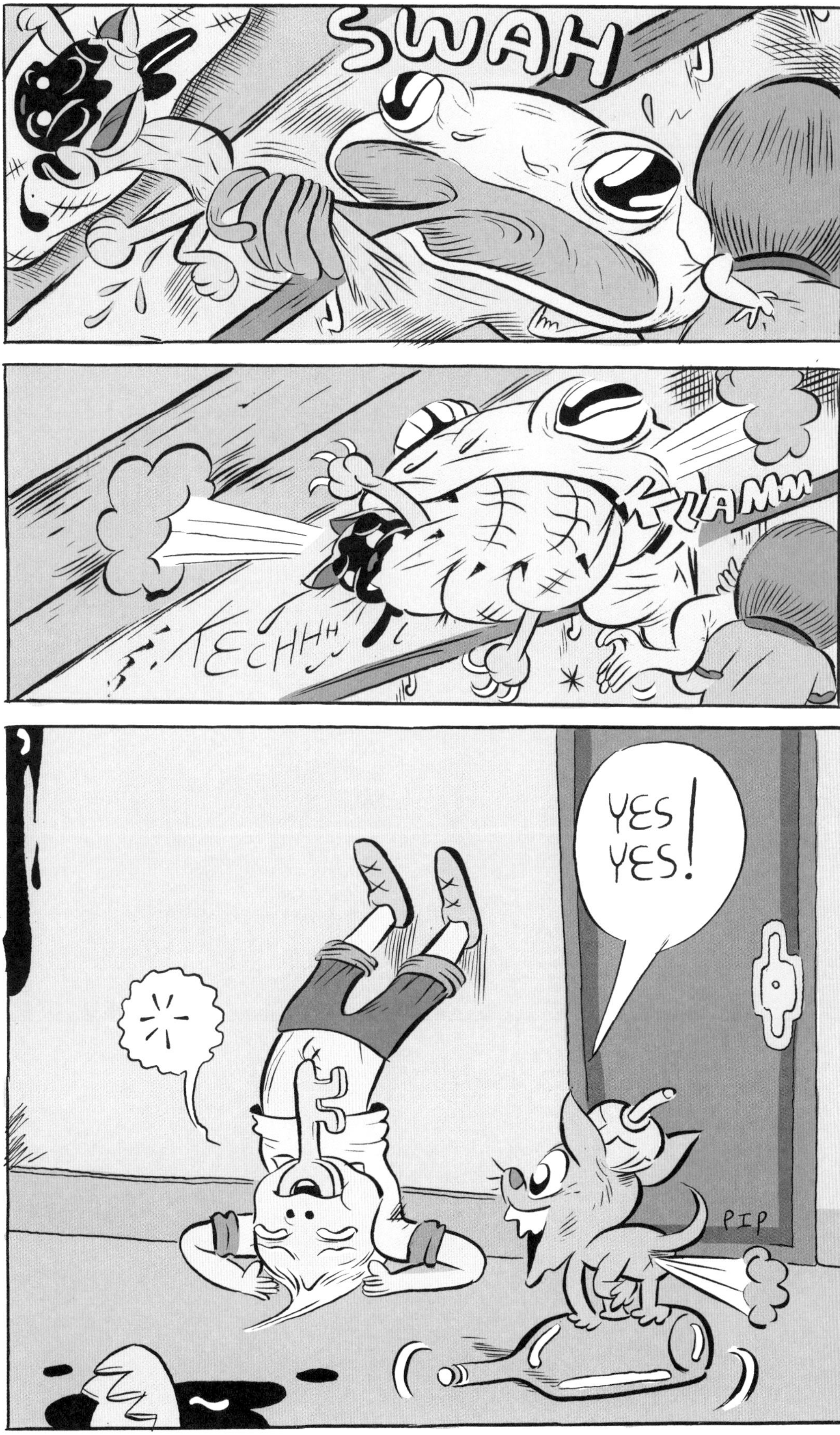
SWAH
KLAMM
KECHH
YES YES!
PIP

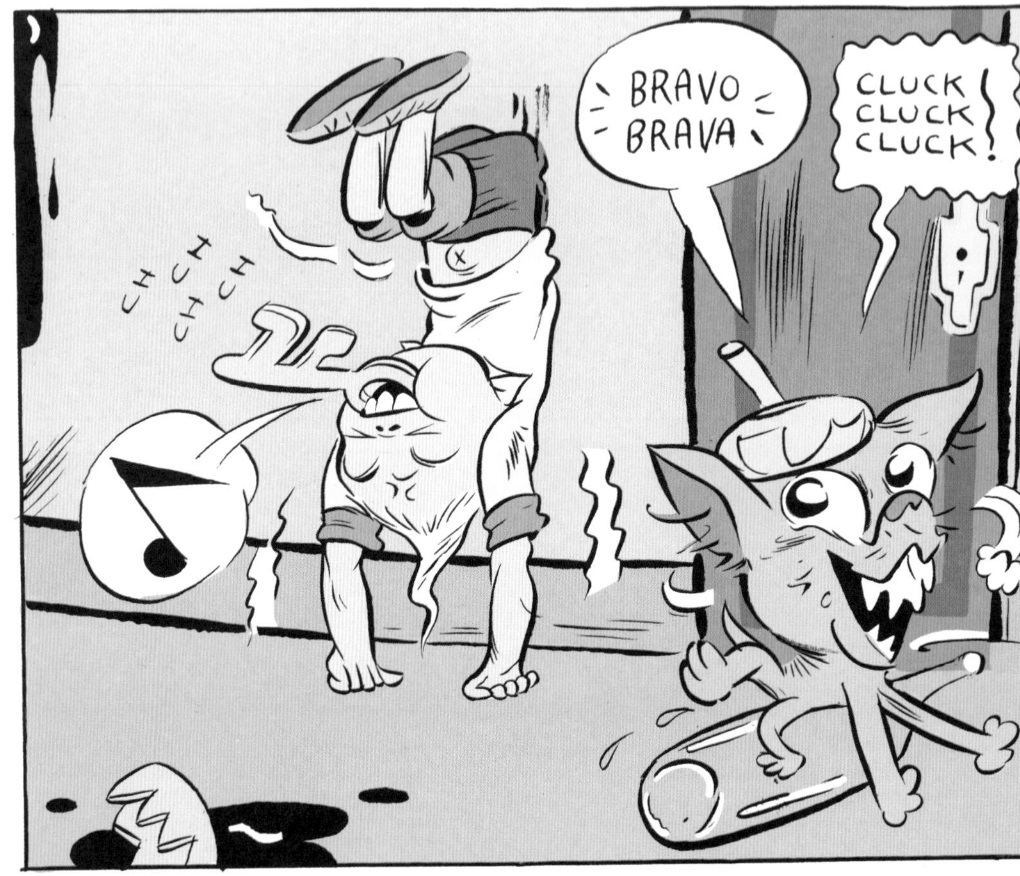
HI HI HI
BRAVO BRAVA
CLUCK CLUCK CLUCK!

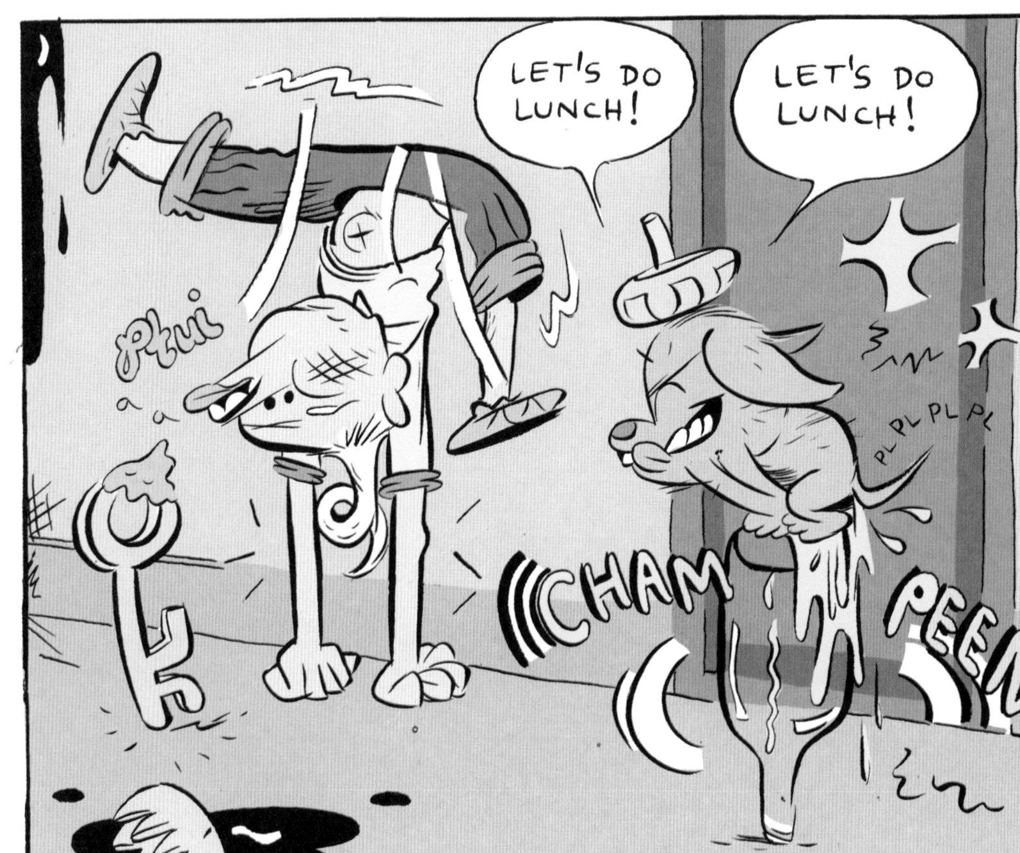
LET'S DO LUNCH!
LET'S DO LUNCH!
Ptui
PL PL PL PL
CHAM PEEN

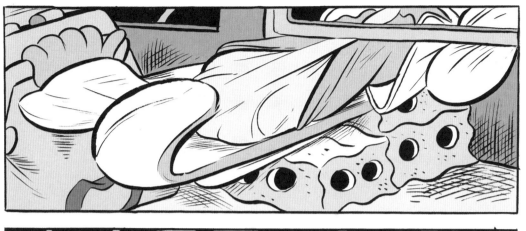

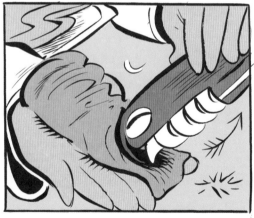

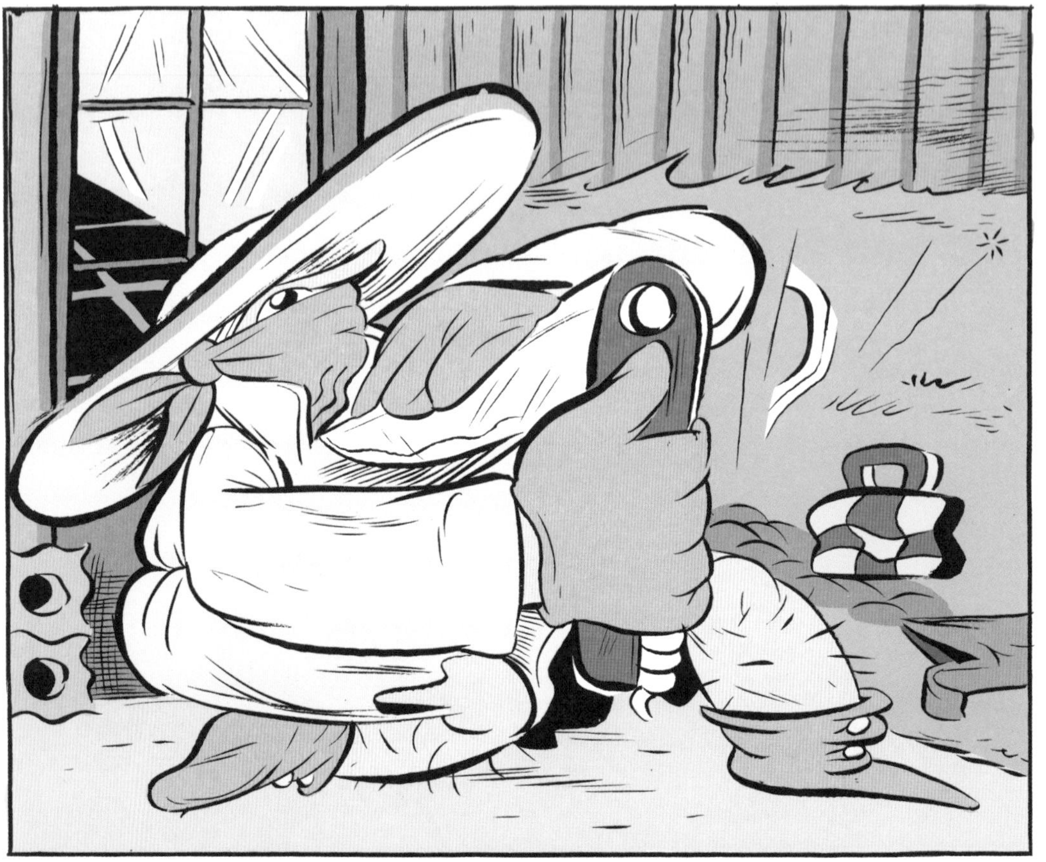
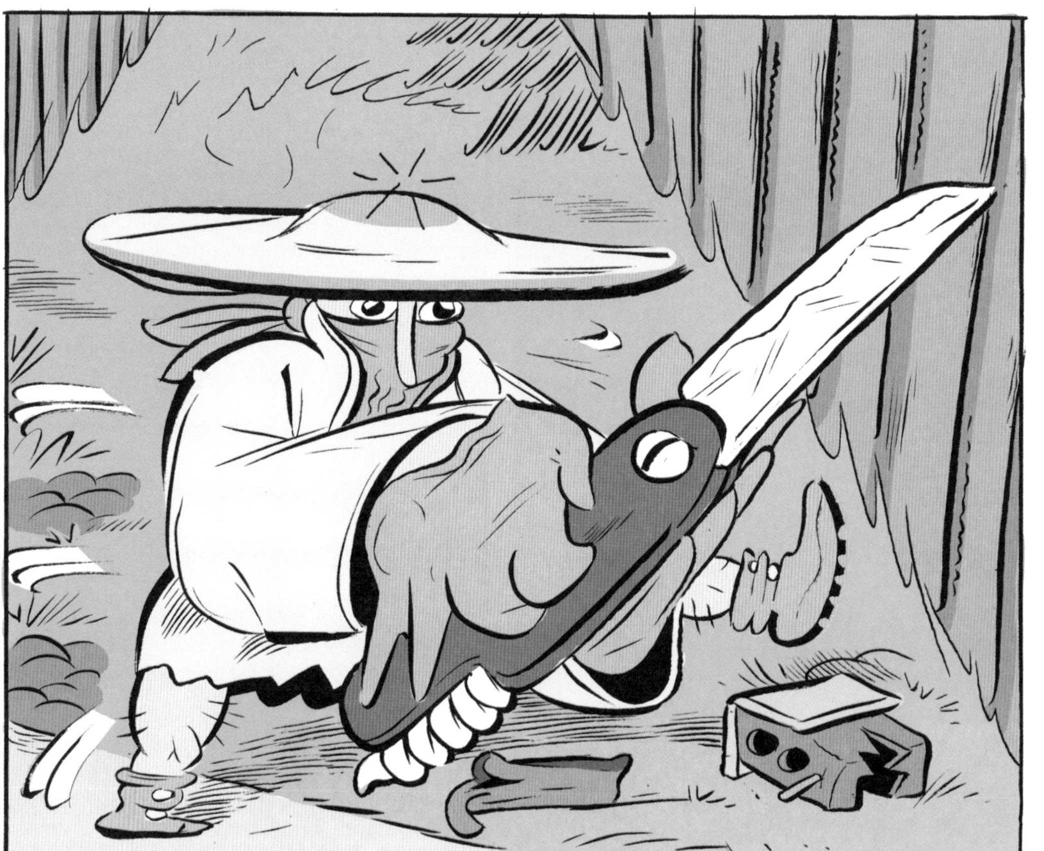

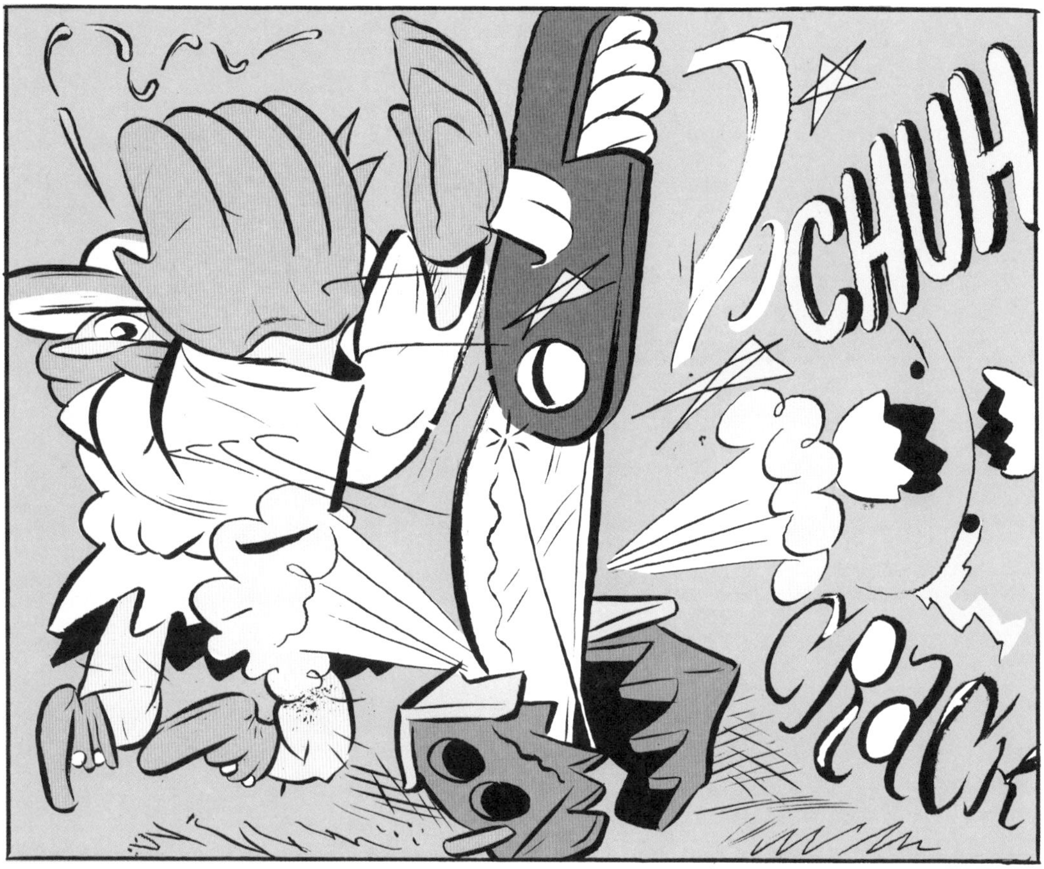
CHUH
CRACK

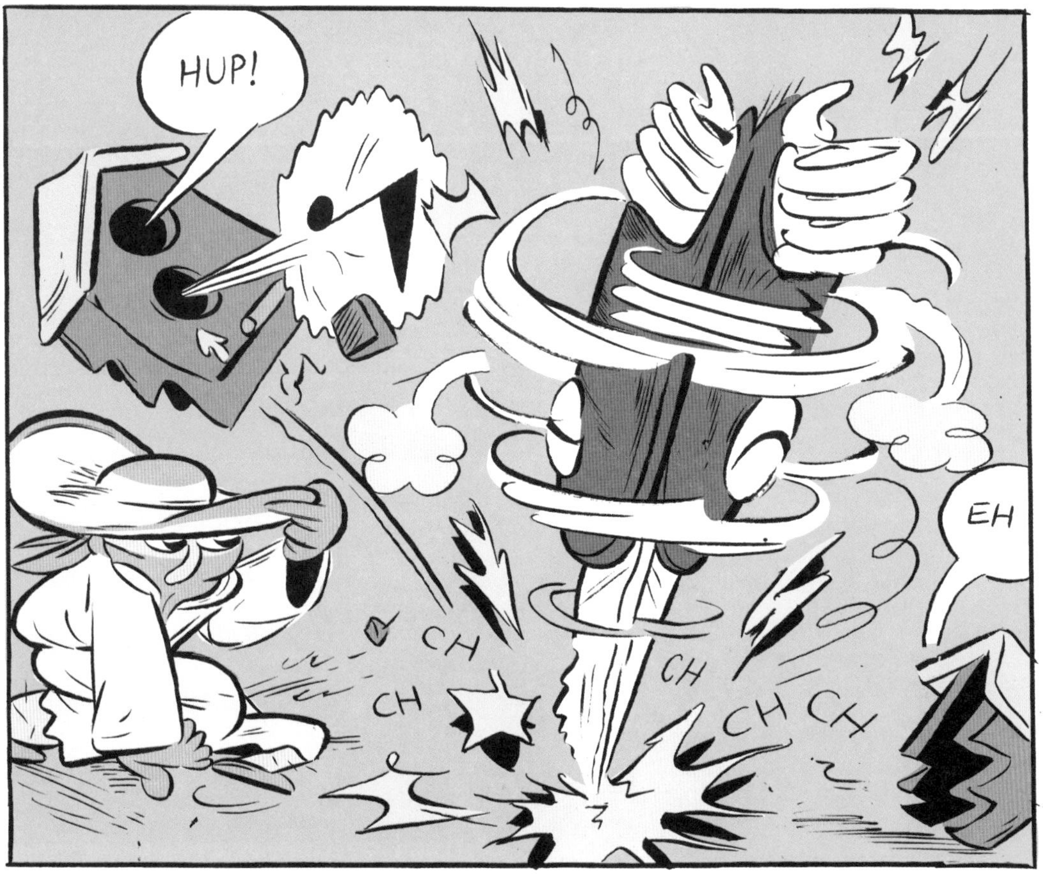
HUP!
EH
CH
CH
CH
CH
CH

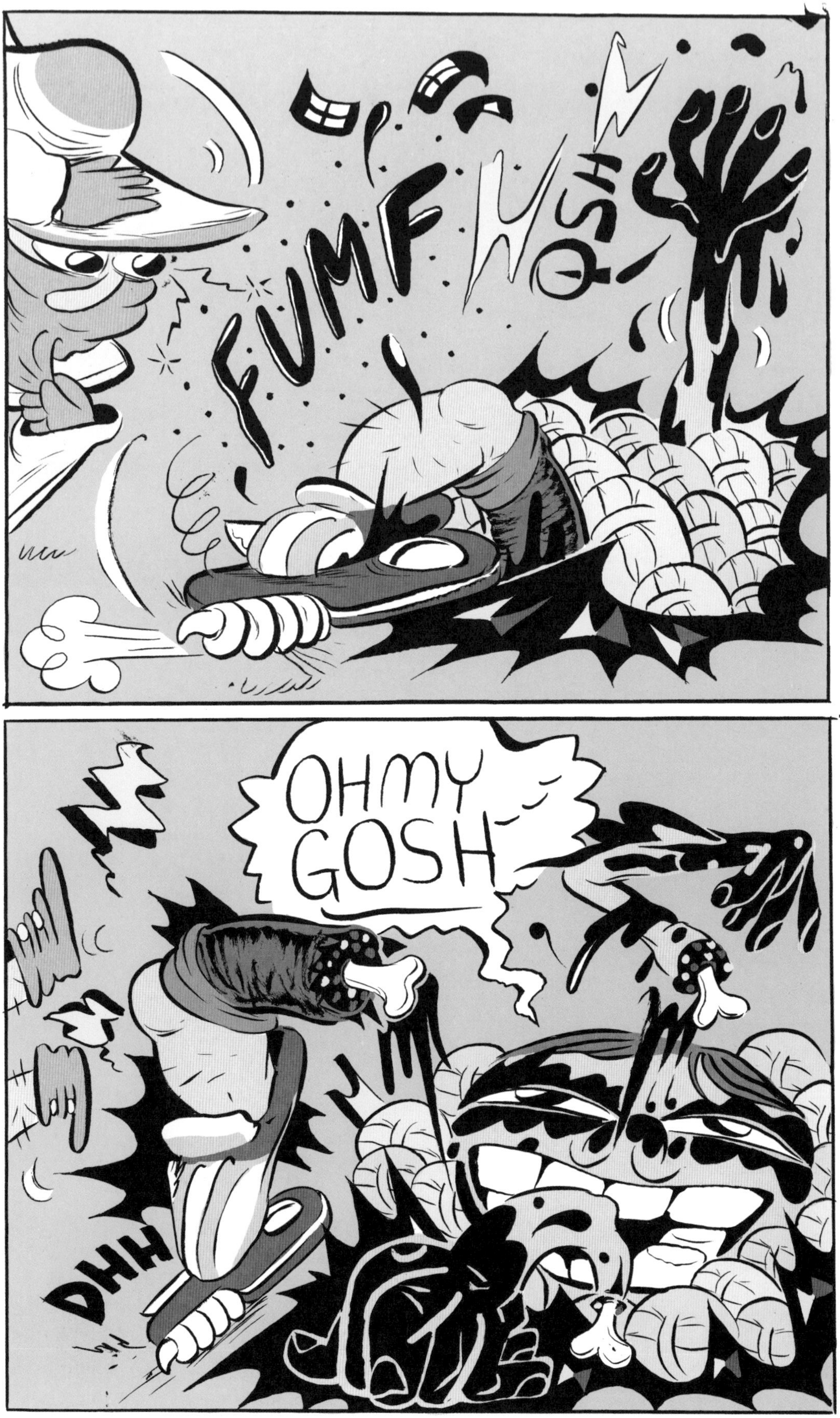
FUMF
OHMY GOSH

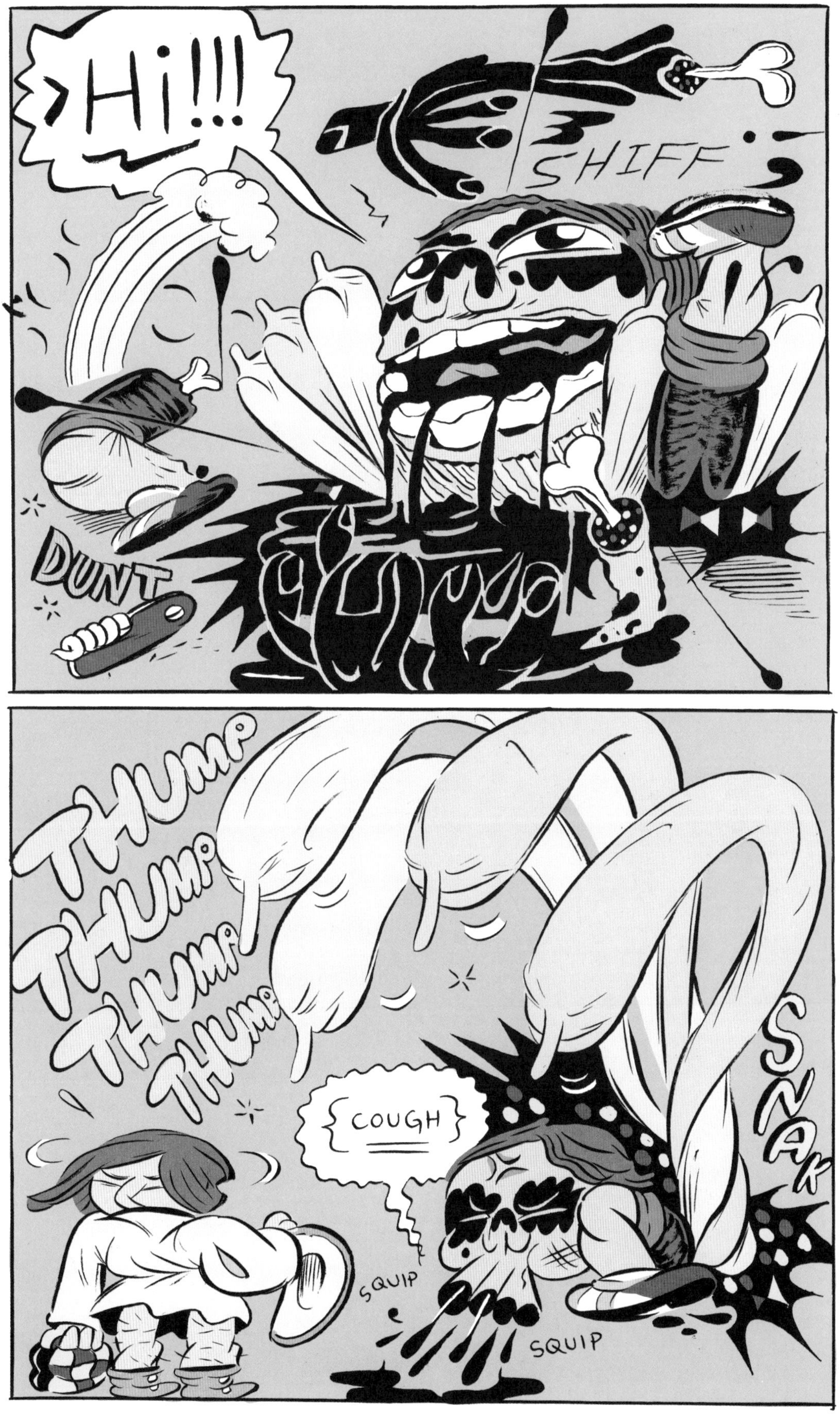

Hi!!!
SHIFF
DUNT
THUMP
THUMP
THUMP
THUMP
{COUGH}
SNAK
SQUIP
SQUIP

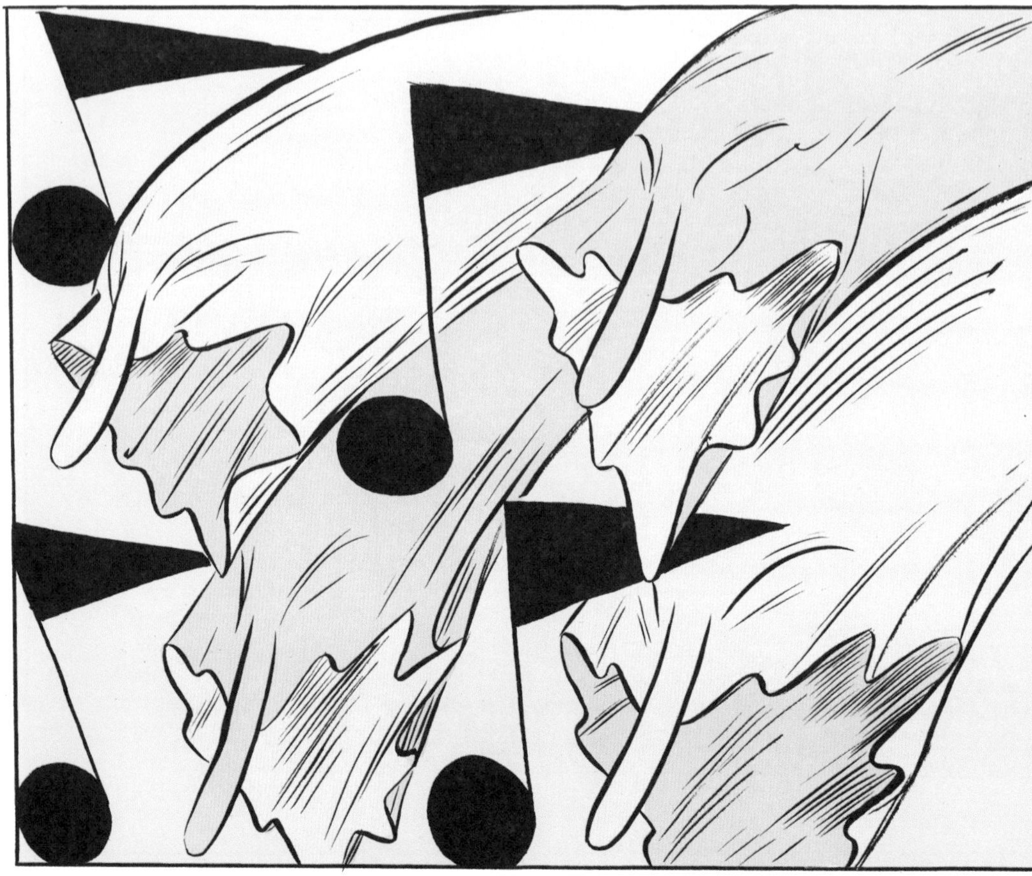

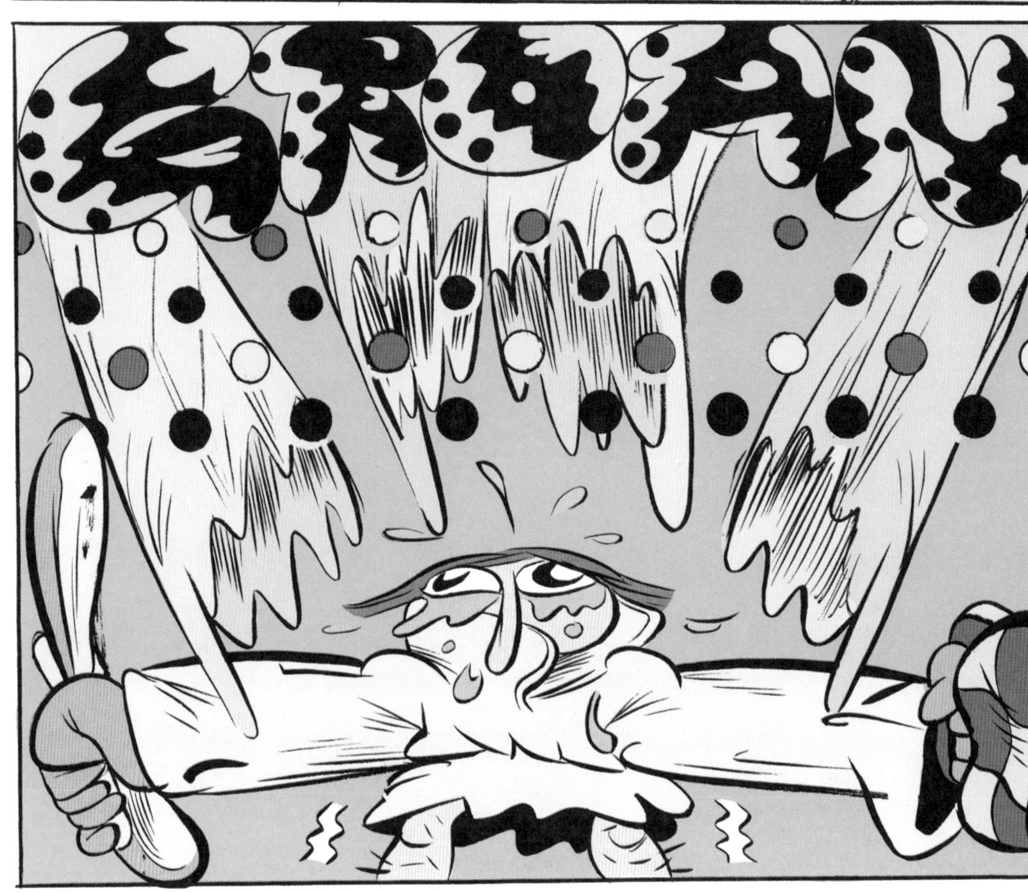

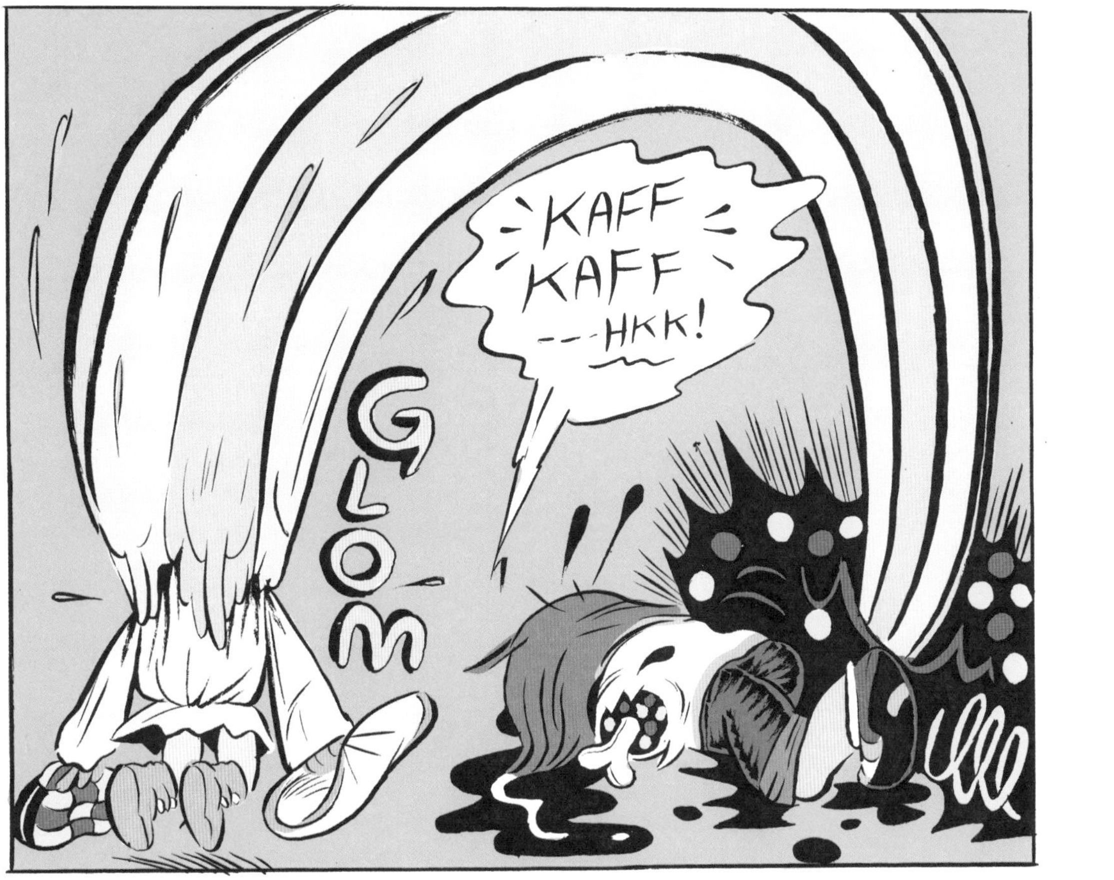
KAFF
KAFF
---HKK!
GLOM

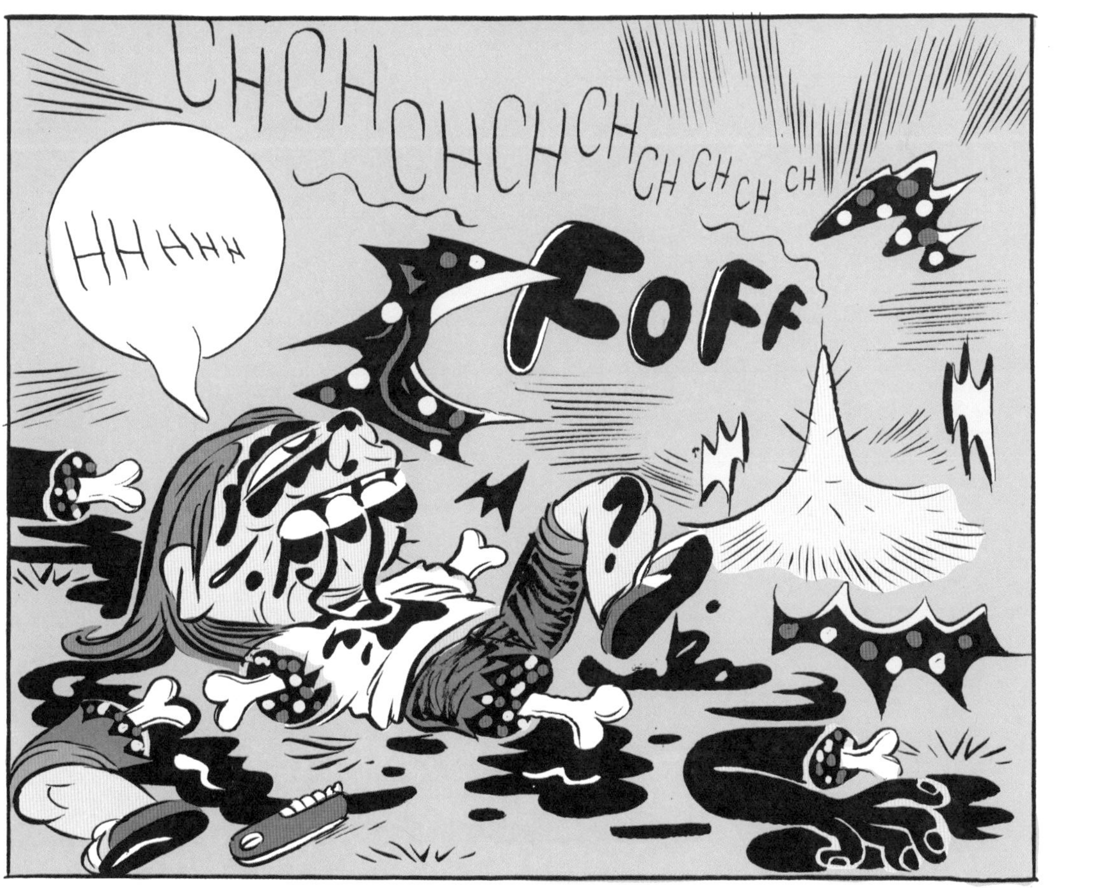
HHhhh
CHCHCHCHCHCHCHCHCHCH
KOFF

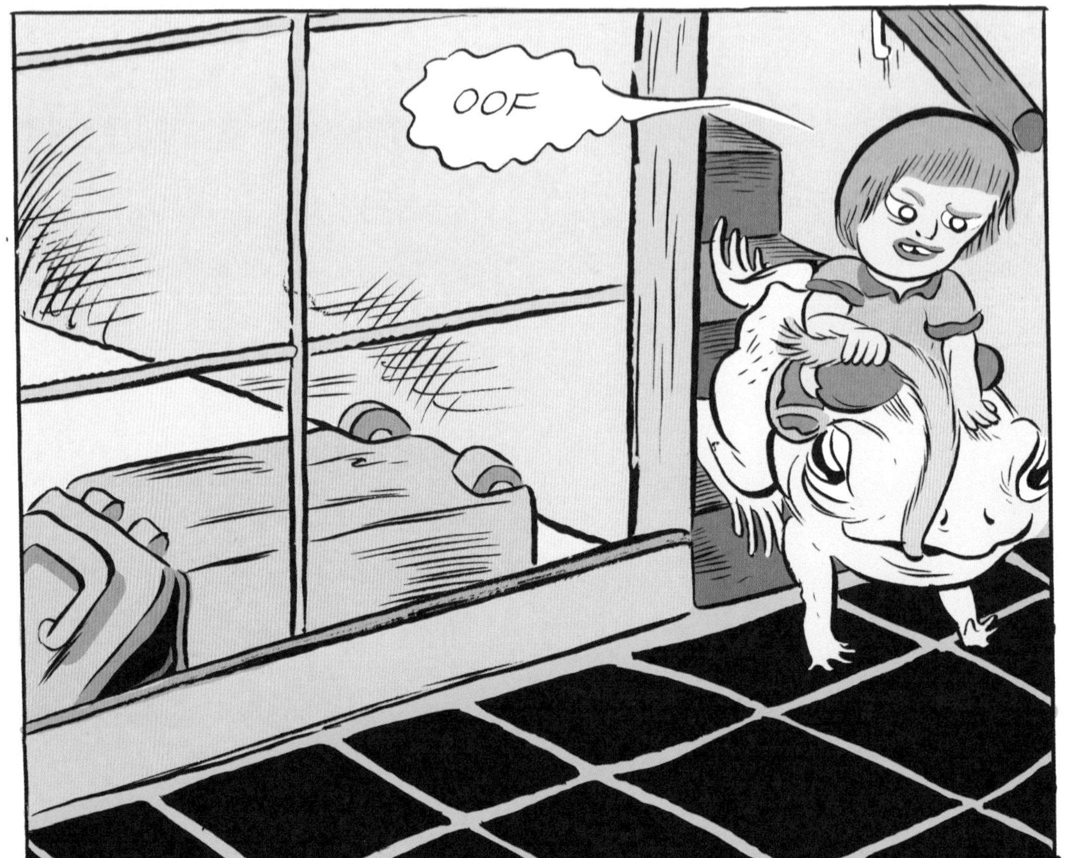
OOF

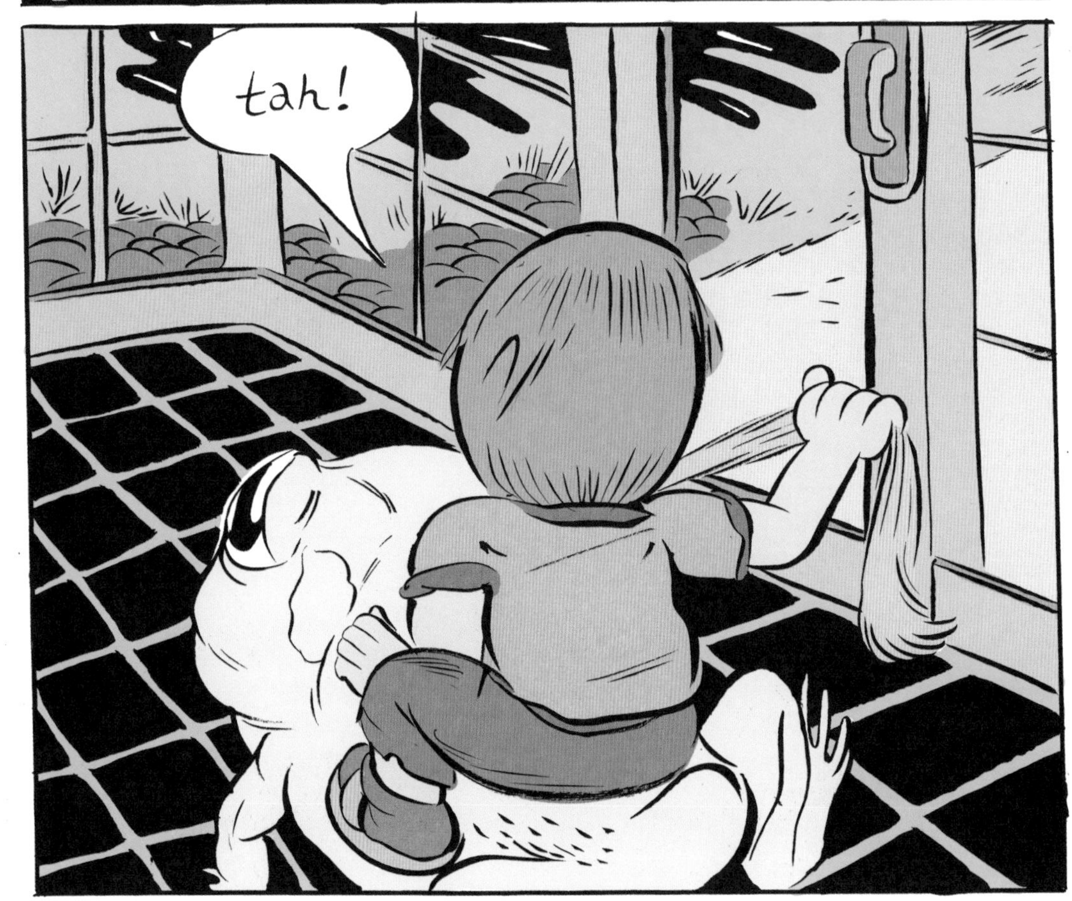
tah!

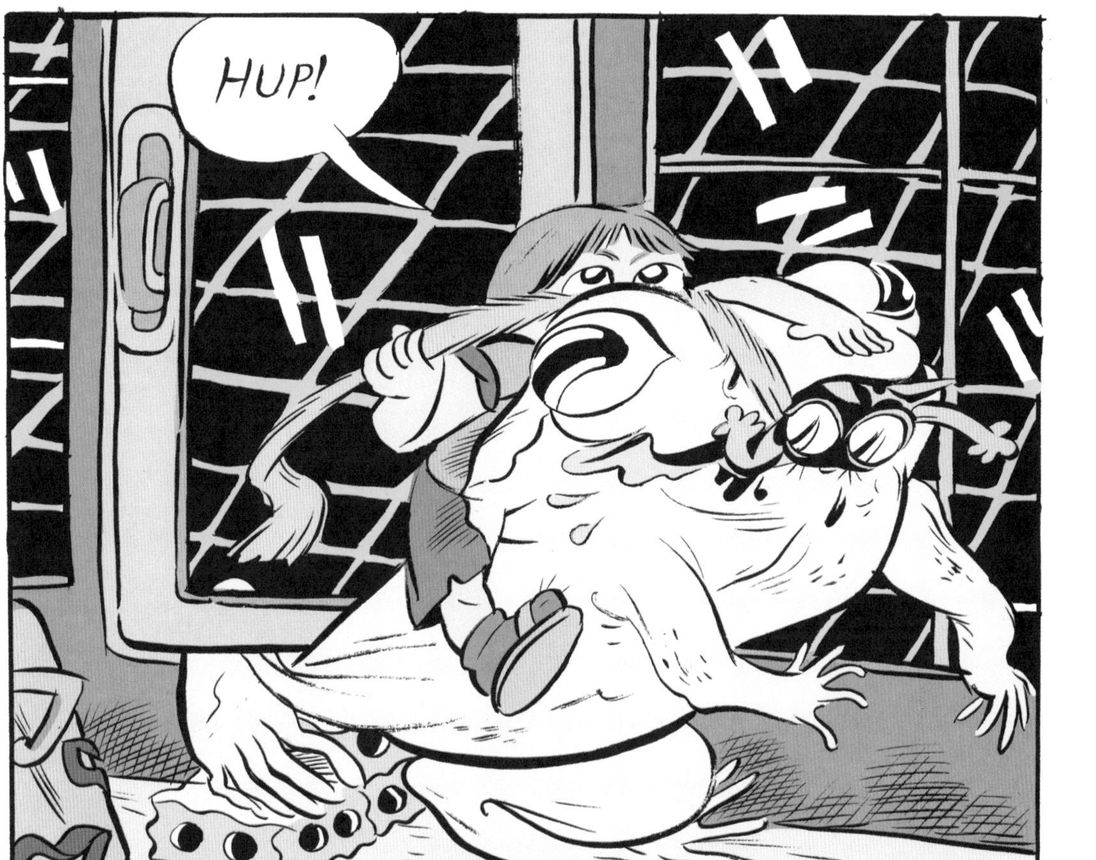
HUP!

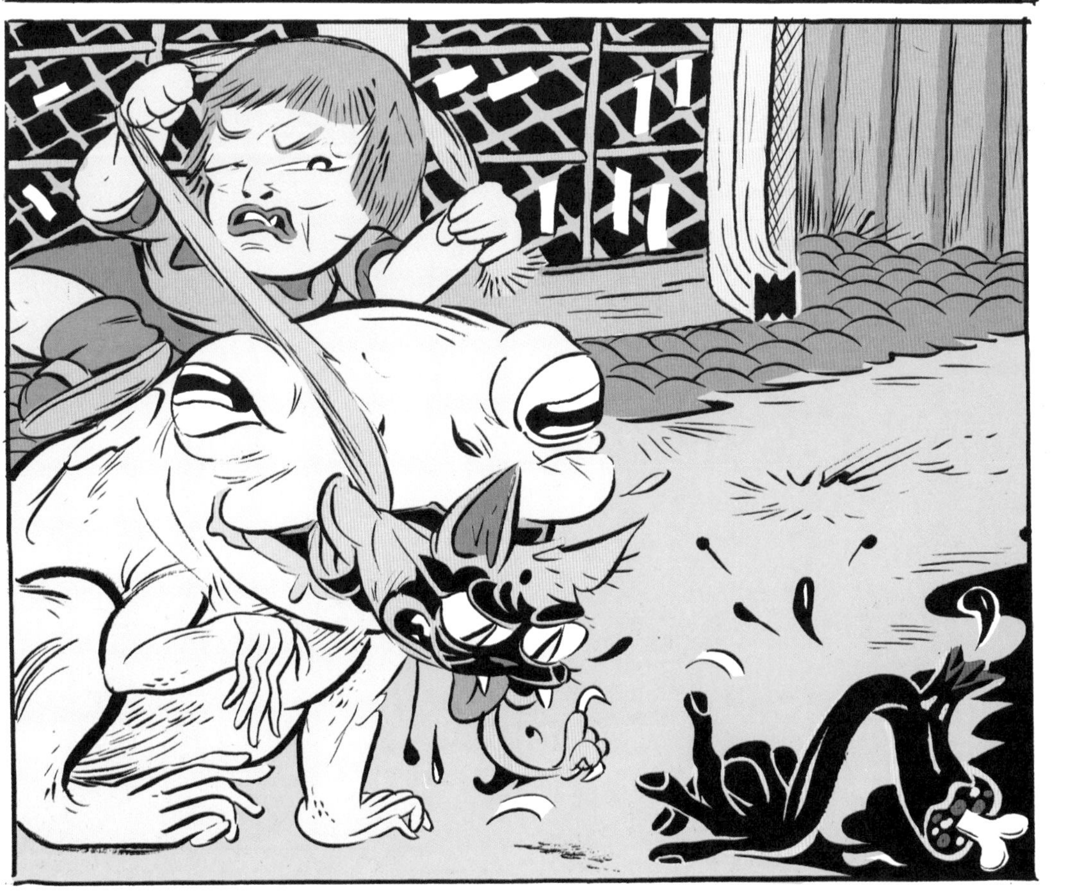

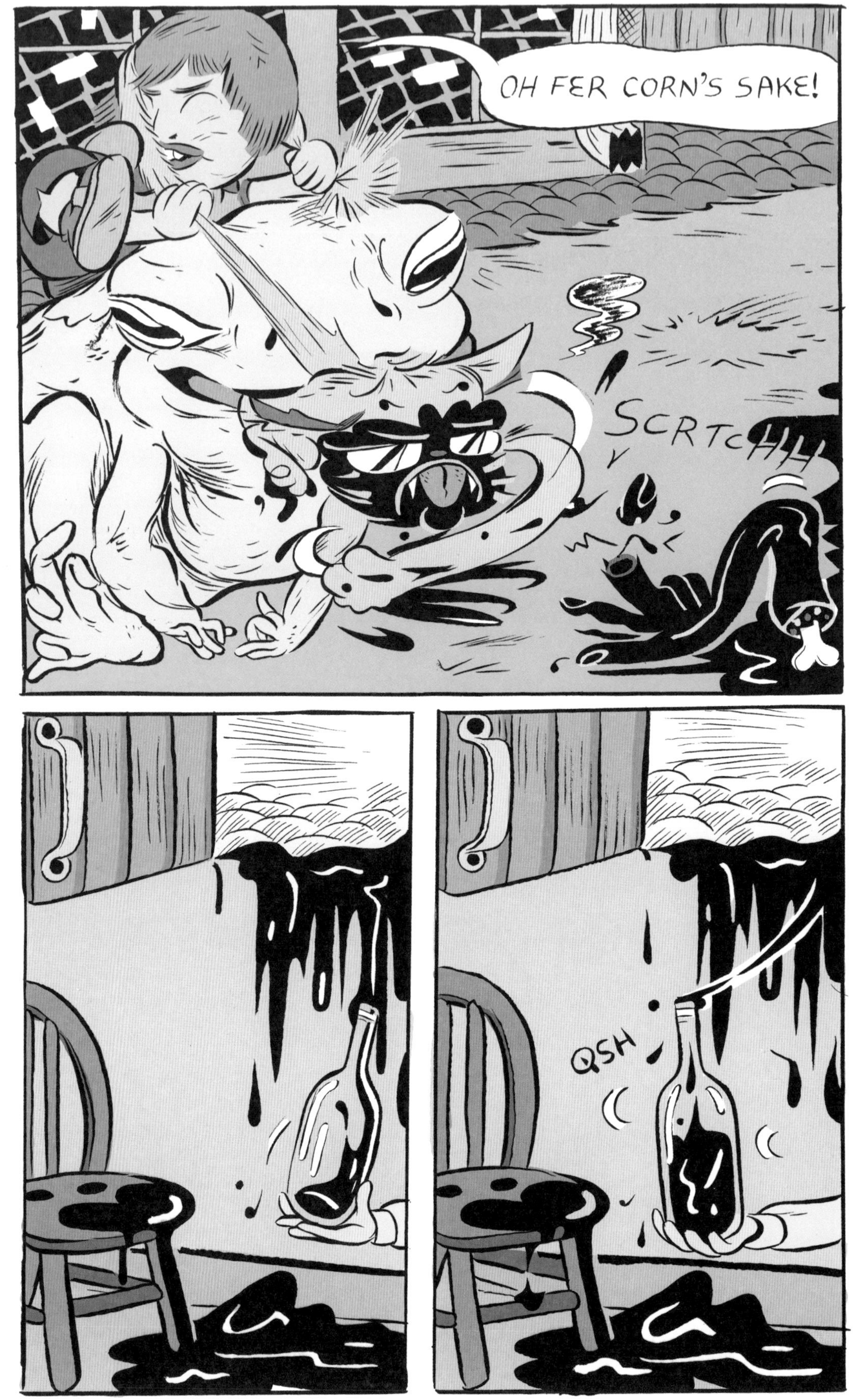
OH FER CORN'S SAKE!
SCRTCHHH
QSH

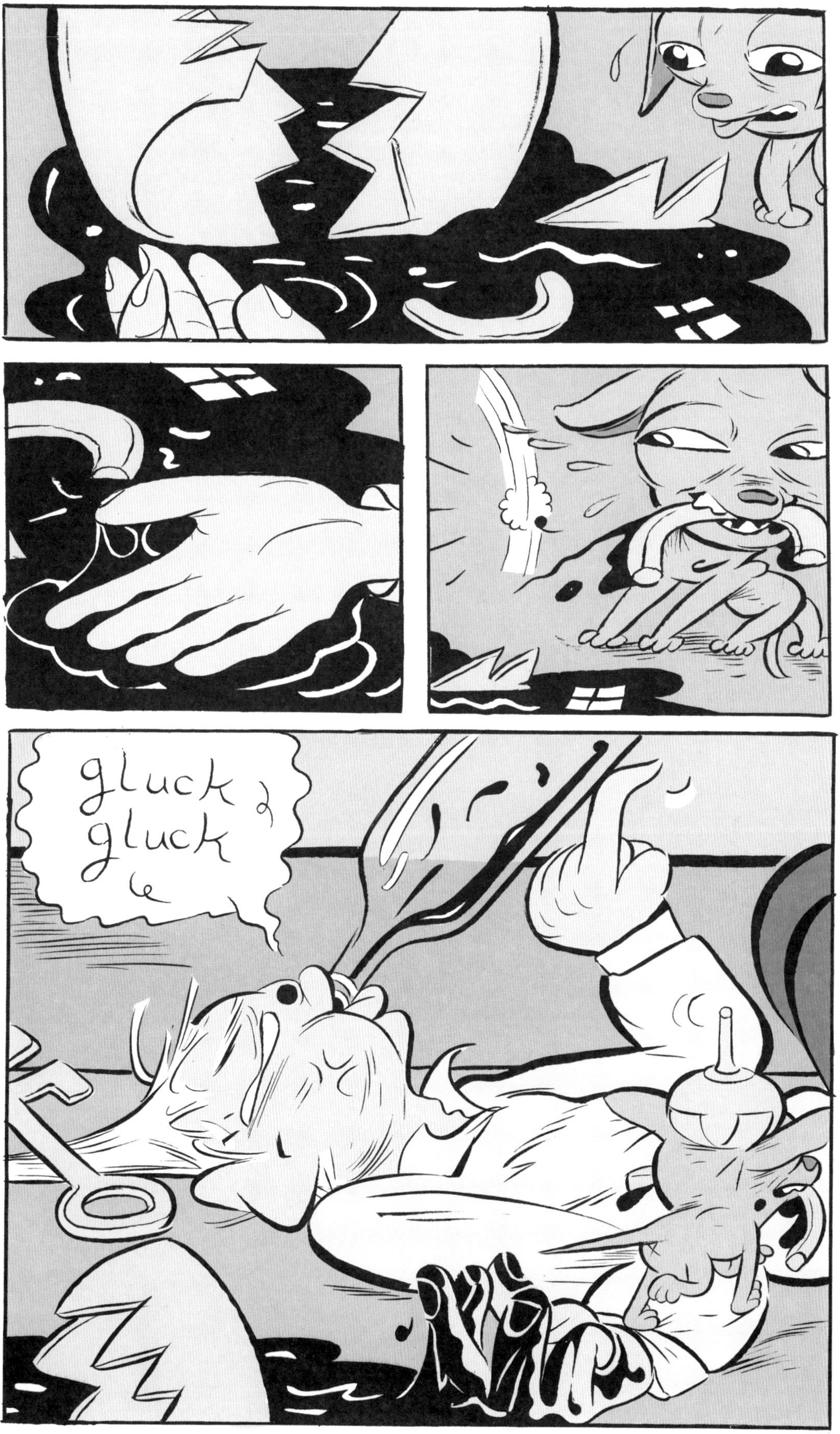
gluck gluck

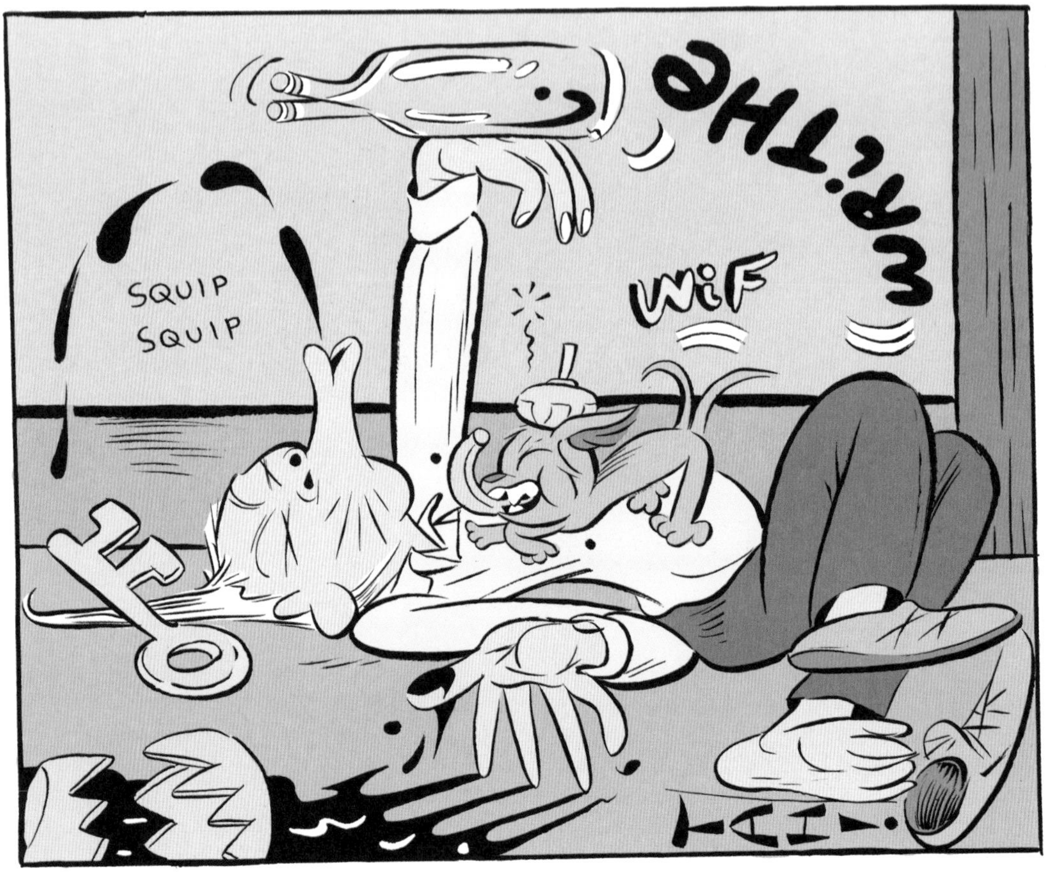
SQUIP
SQUIP
WRITHE
WiF
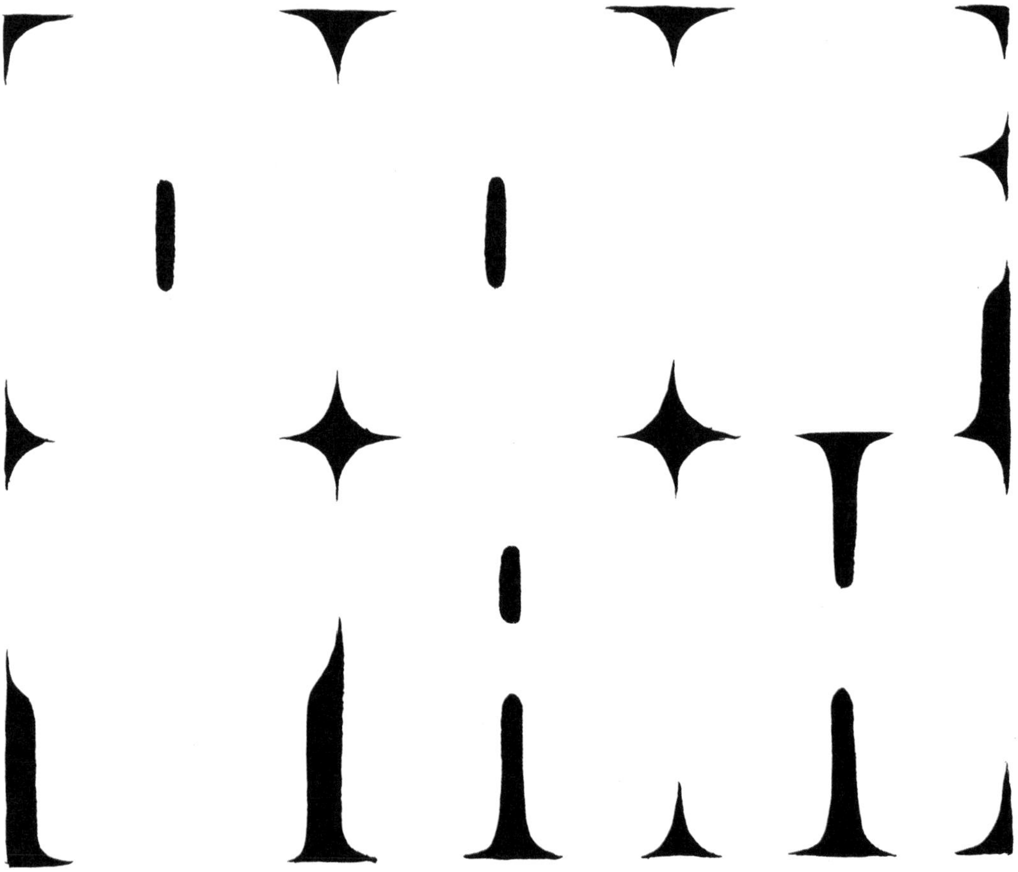

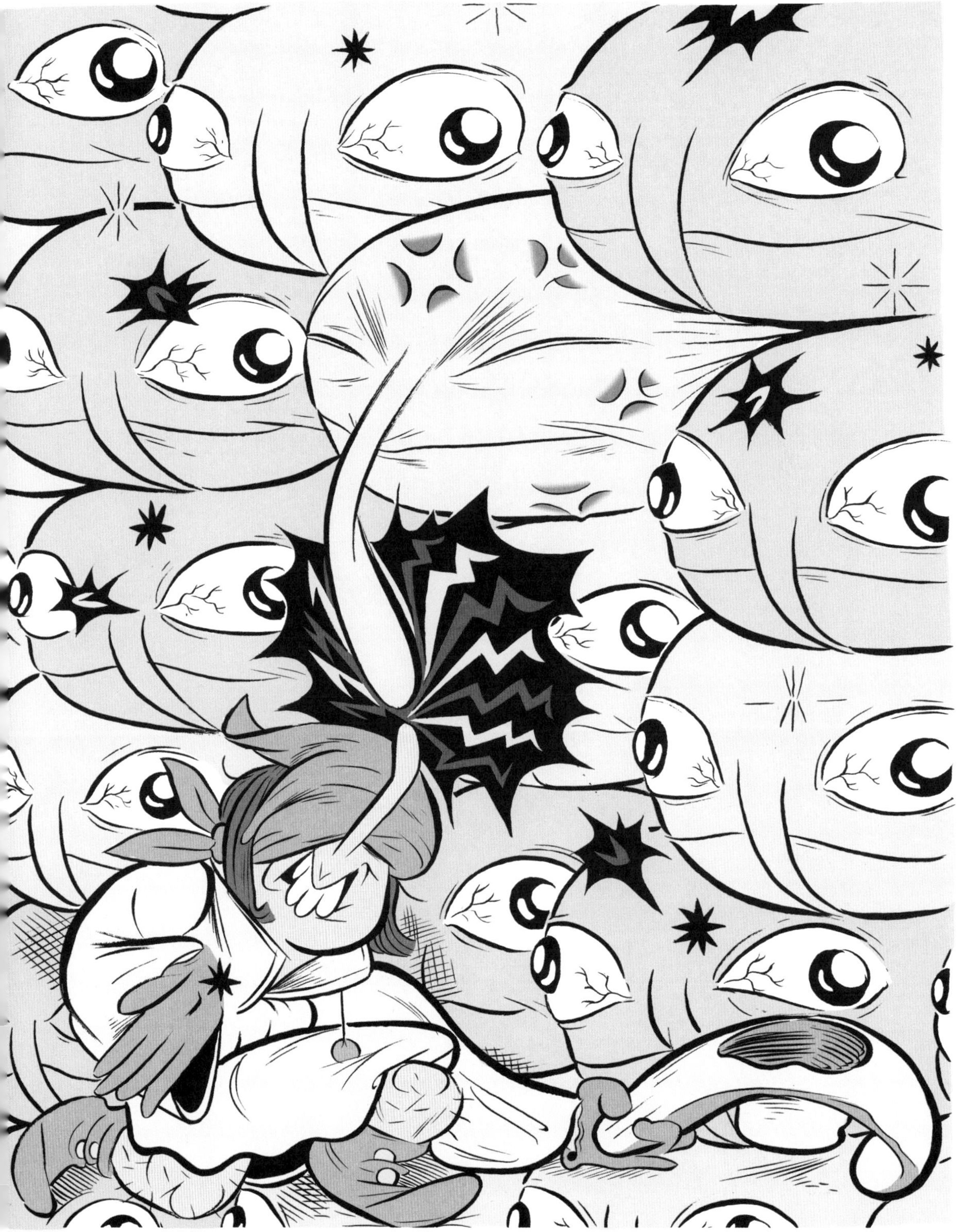

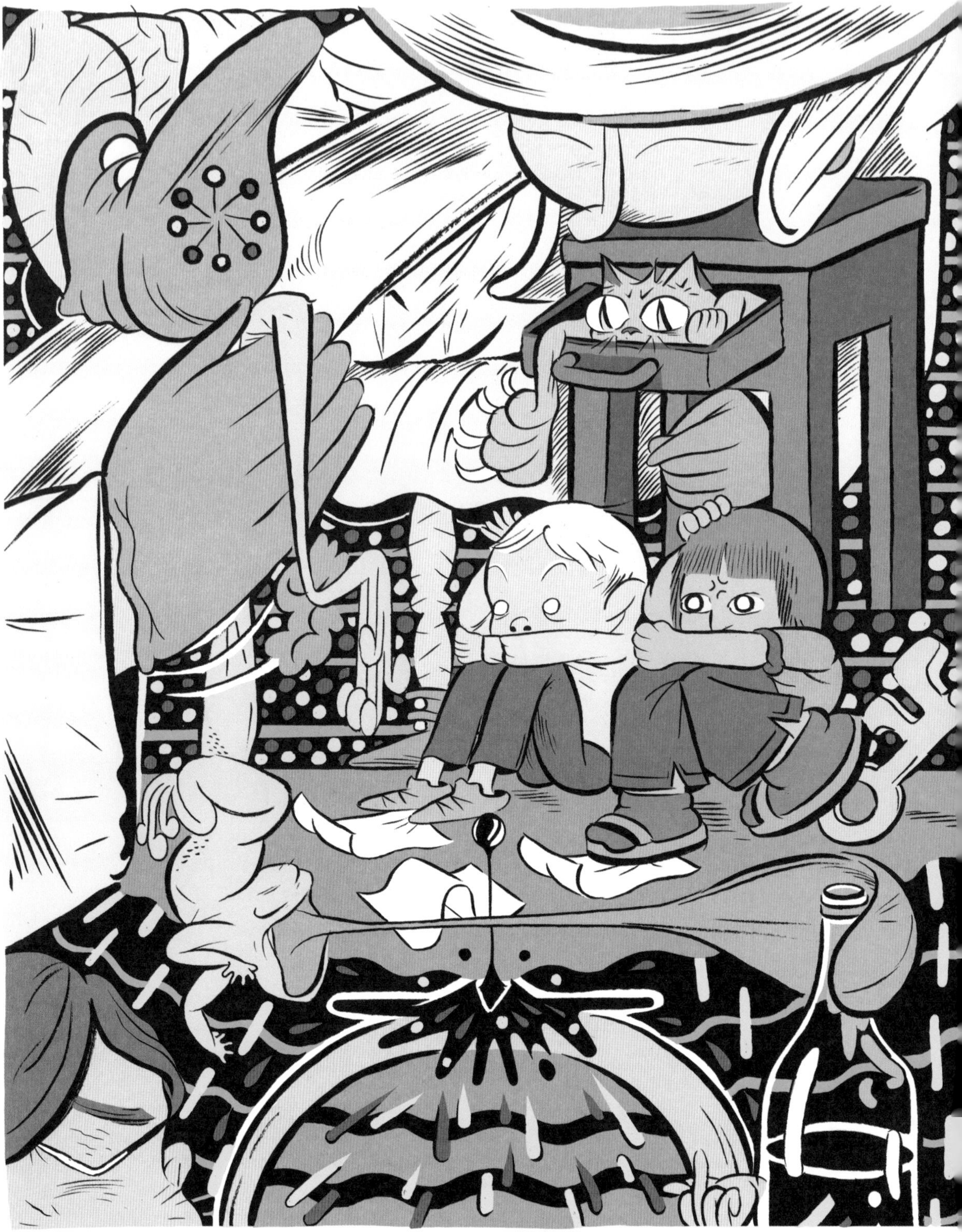

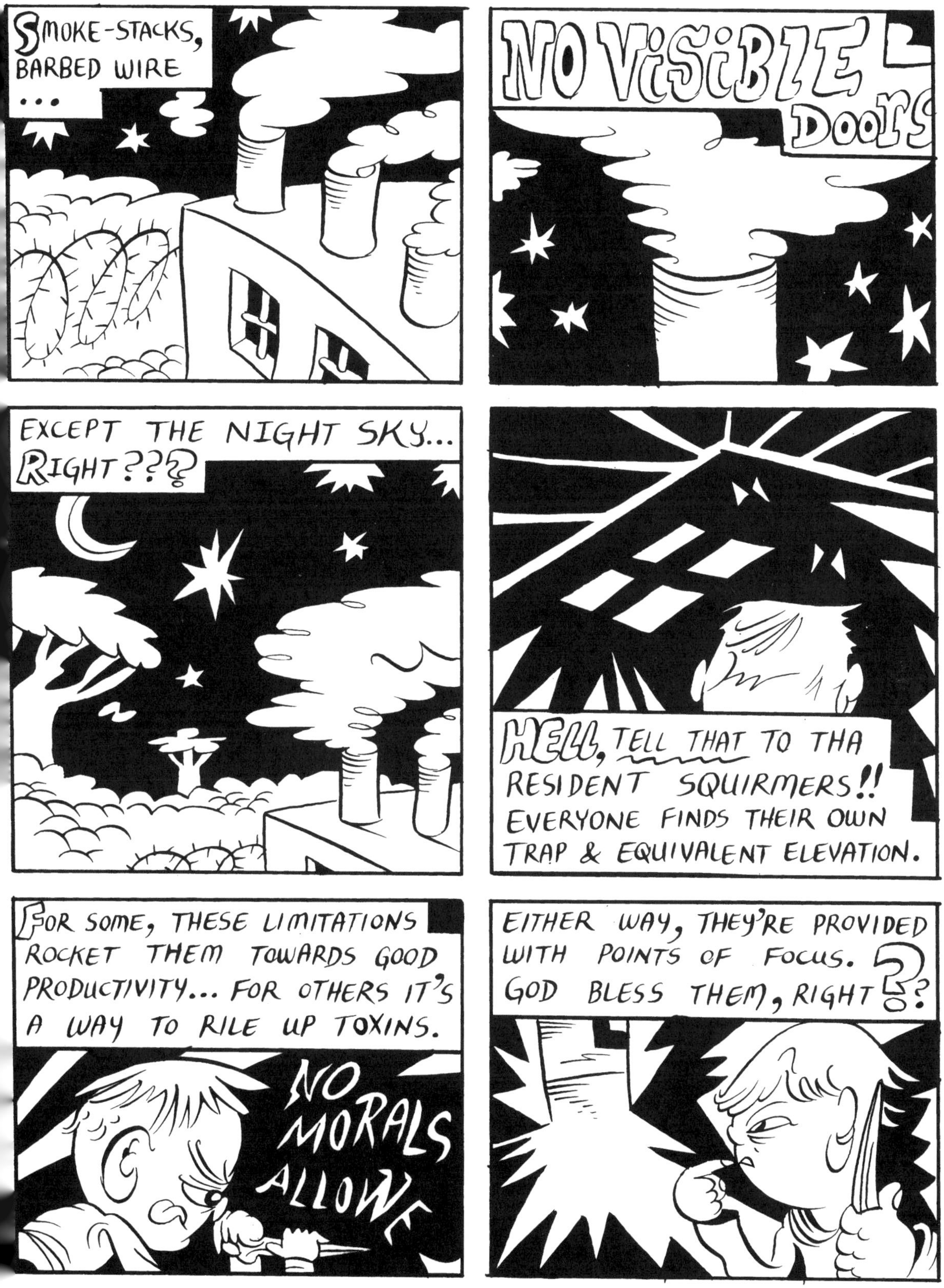
SMOKE-STACKS, BARBED WIRE ...
NO VISIBLE DOORS
EXCEPT THE NIGHT SKY... RIGHT???
HELL, TELL THAT TO THA RESIDENT SQUIRMERS!! EVERYONE FINDS THEIR OWN TRAP & EQUIVALENT ELEVATION.
FOR SOME, THESE LIMITATIONS ROCKET THEM TOWARDS GOOD PRODUCTIVITY... FOR OTHERS IT'S A WAY TO RILE UP TOXINS.
NO MORALS ALLOWE
EITHER WAY, THEY'RE PROVIDED WITH POINTS OF FOCUS. GOD BLESS THEM, RIGHT??

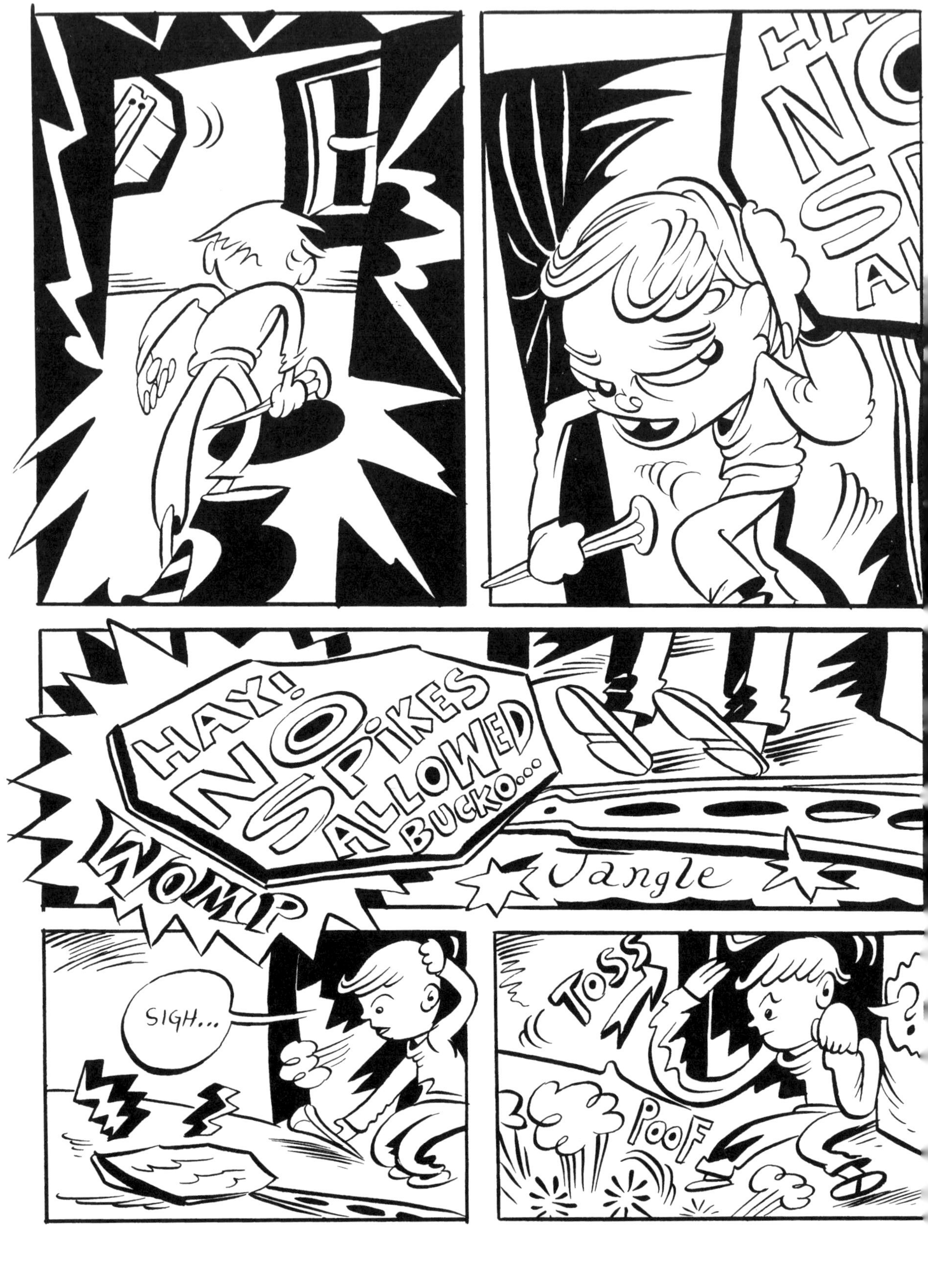
HAY! NO SPIKES ALLOWED BUCKO...
WOMP
Jangle
SIGH...
TOSS
POOF

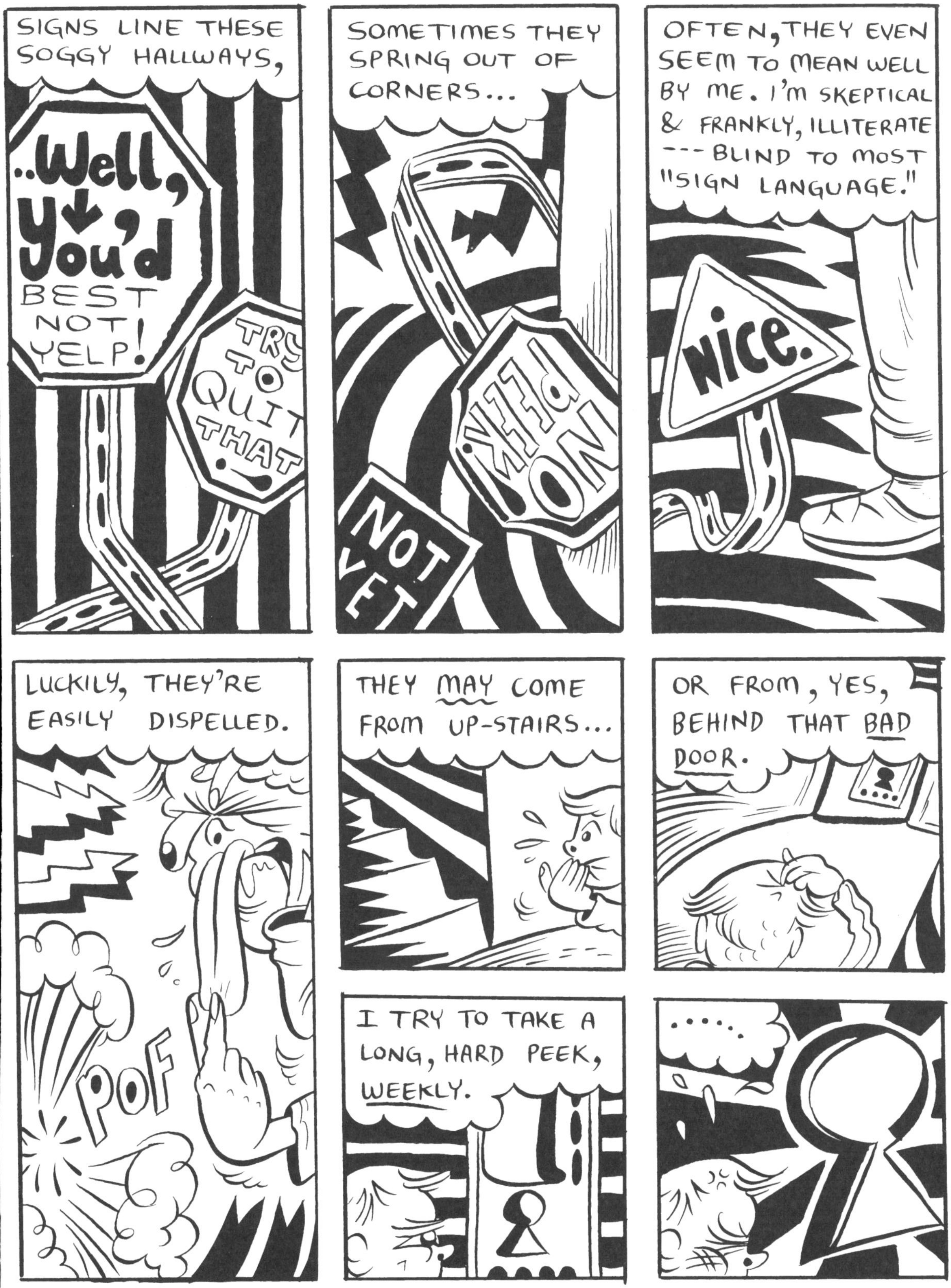
SIGNS LINE THESE SOGGY HALLWAYS,
..Well, y↓, you'd BEST NOT YELP!
TRY TO QUIT THAT
SOMETIMES THEY SPRING OUT OF CORNERS...
NO PEEK
NOT YET
OFTEN, THEY EVEN SEEM TO MEAN WELL BY ME. I'M SKEPTICAL & FRANKLY, ILLITERATE --- BLIND TO MOST "SIGN LANGUAGE."
NICE.
LUCKILY, THEY'RE EASILY DISPELLED.
POF
THEY MAY COME FROM UP-STAIRS...
OR FROM, YES, BEHIND THAT BAD DOOR.
I TRY TO TAKE A LONG, HARD PEEK, WEEKLY.
.....

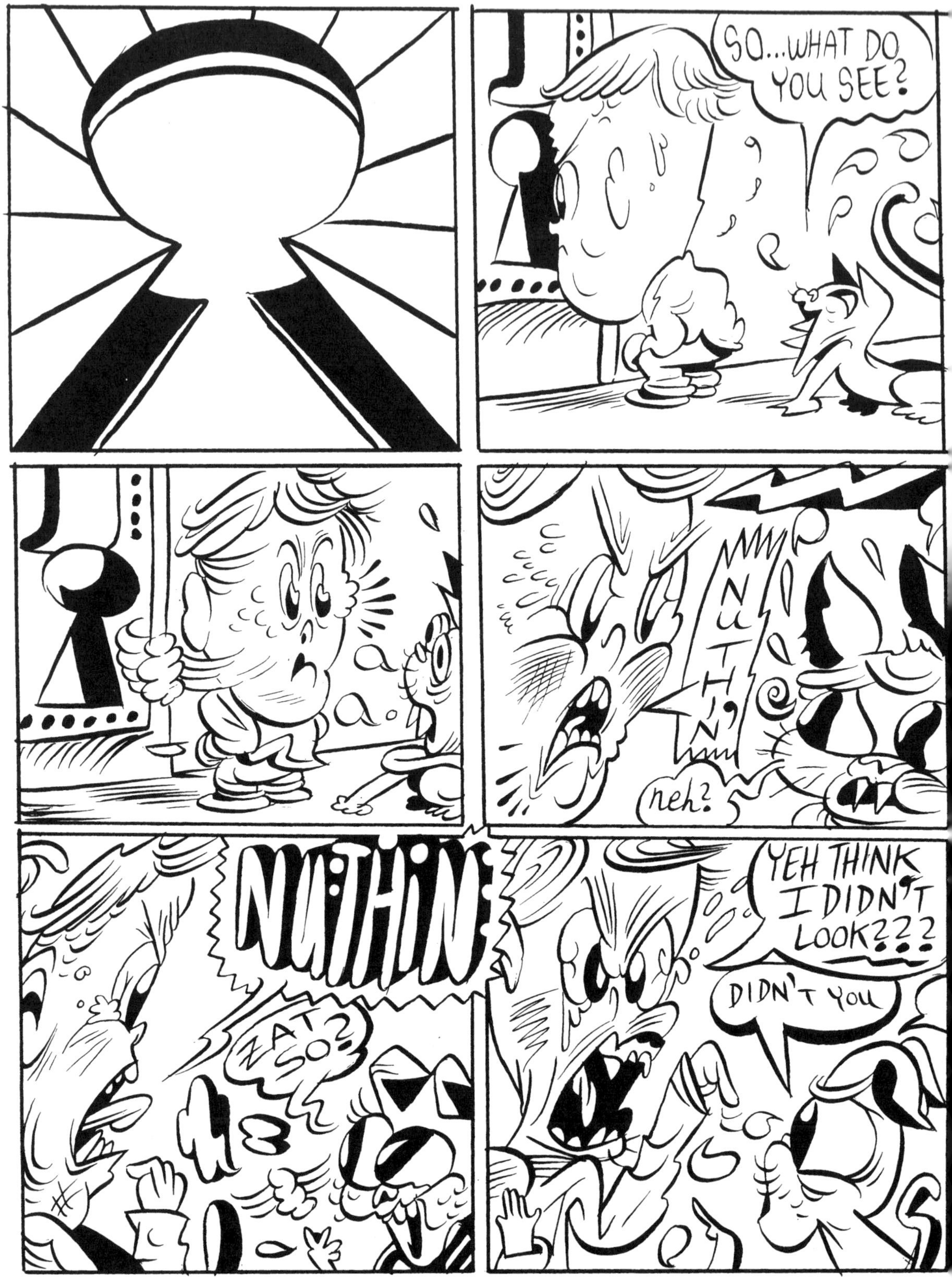
SO...WHAT DO YOU SEE?
NUTHIN
neh?
NUTHIN
ZAT SO?
YEH THINK I DIDN'T LOOK???
DIDN'T YOU

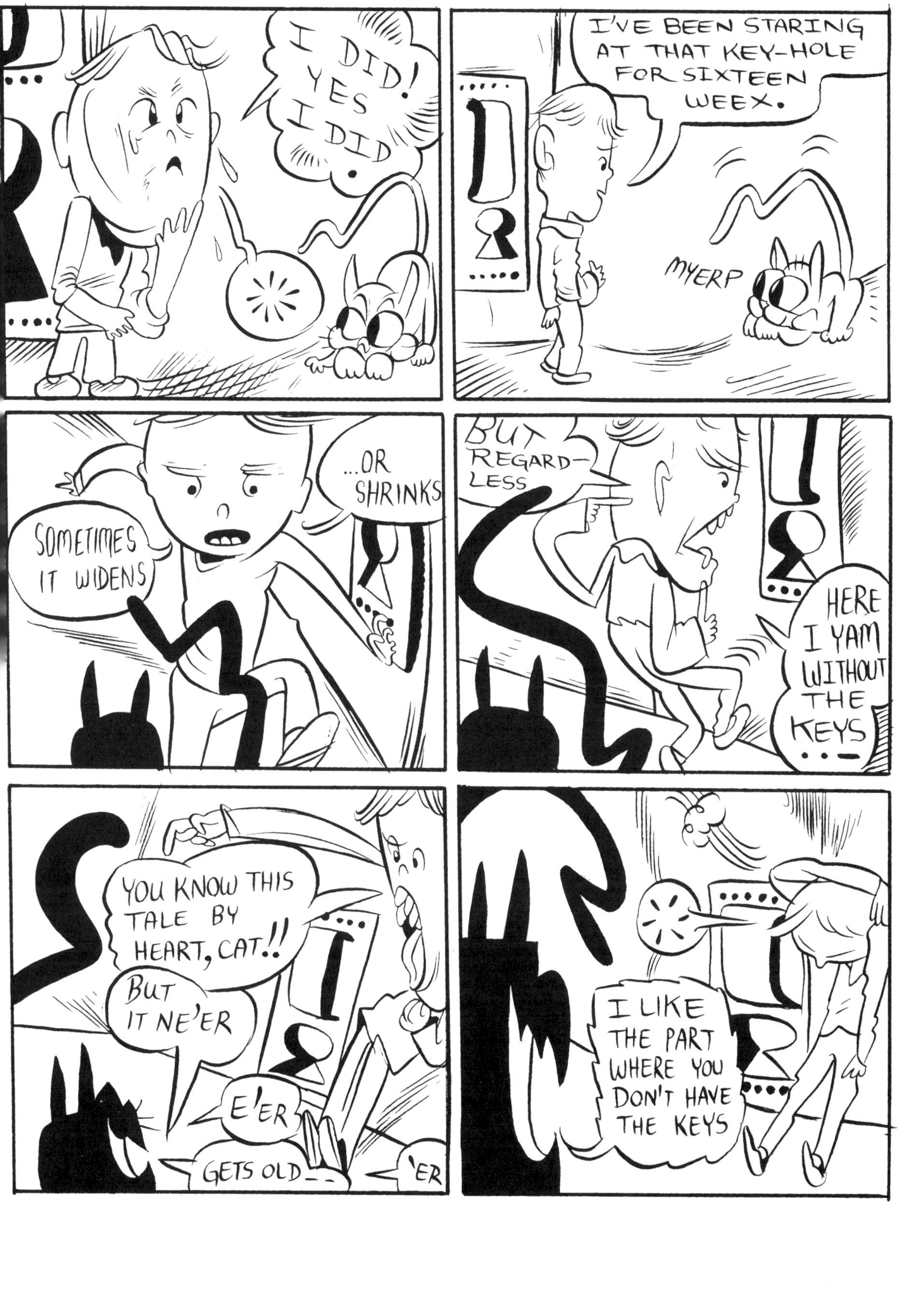
I DID! YES I DID
I'VE BEEN STARING AT THAT KEY-HOLE FOR SIXTEEN WEEX.
MYERP
SOMETIMES IT WIDENS
...OR SHRINKS
BUT REGARD-LESS
HERE I YAM WITHOUT THE KEYS
YOU KNOW THIS TALE BY HEART, CAT!!
BUT IT NE'ER
E'ER
GETS OLD
'ER
I LIKE THE PART WHERE YOU DON'T HAVE THE KEYS

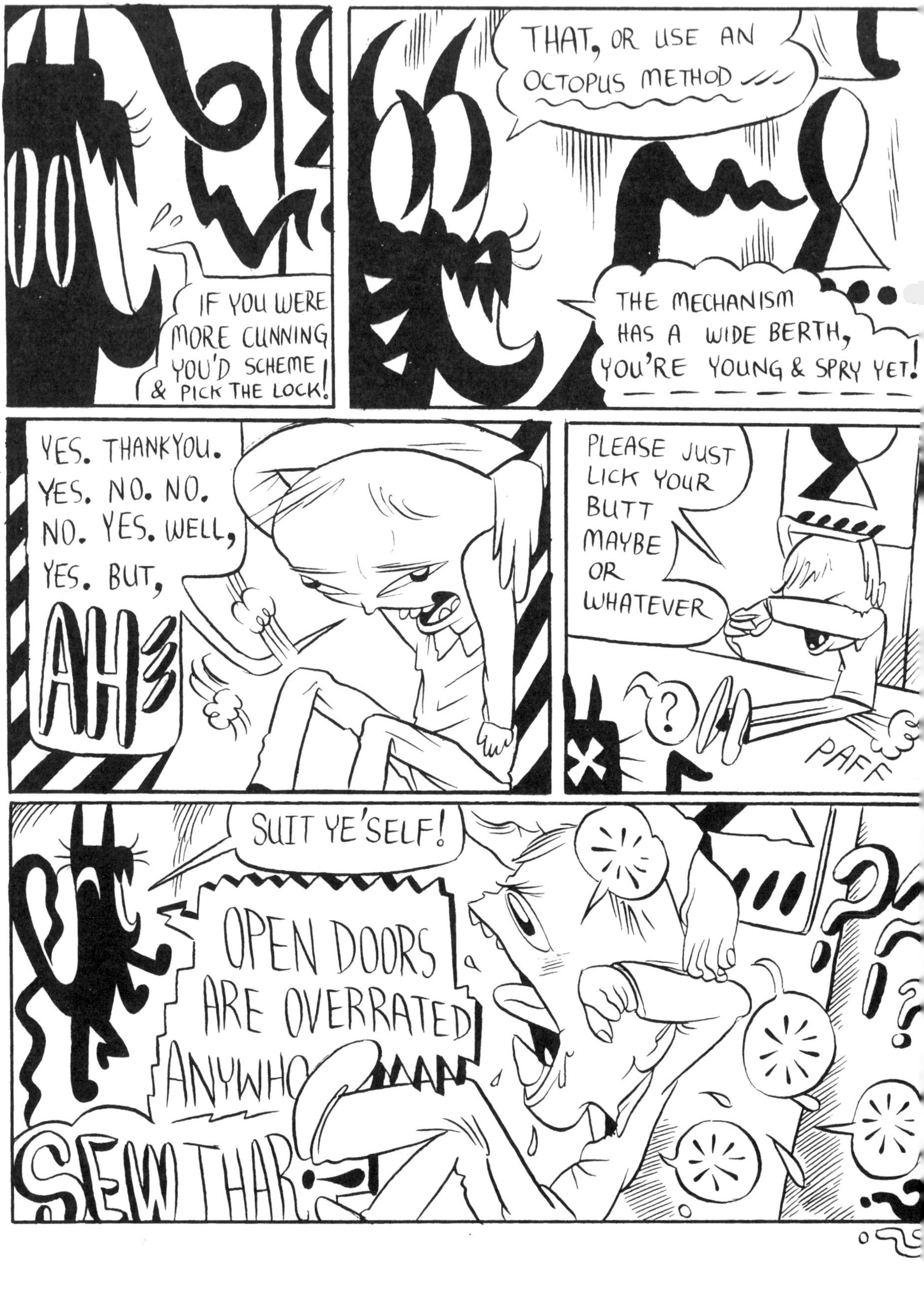

IF YOU WERE MORE CUNNING YOU'D SCHEME & PICK THE LOCK!
THAT, OR USE AN OCTOPUS METHOD
THE MECHANISM HAS A WIDE BERTH, YOU'RE YOUNG & SPRY YET!
YES. THANKYOU. YES. NO. NO. NO. YES. WELL, YES. BUT,
AH
PLEASE JUST LICK YOUR BUTT MAYBE OR WHATEVER
?
PAFF
SUIT YE'SELF!
OPEN DOORS ARE OVERRATED ANYWHO
SEW THAR

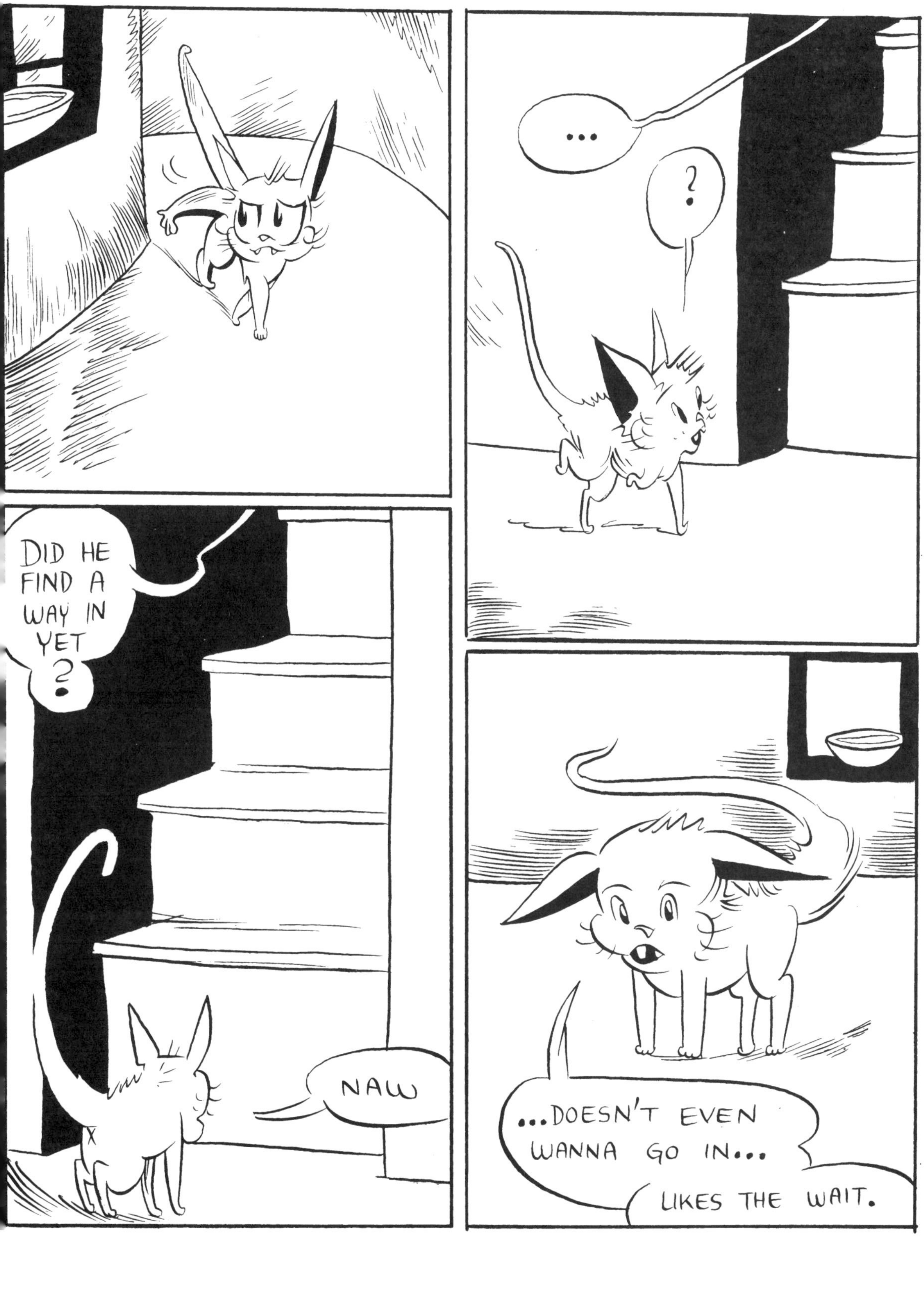
...
?
DID HE FIND A WAY IN YET ?
NAW
...DOESN'T EVEN WANNA GO IN...
LIKES THE WAIT.

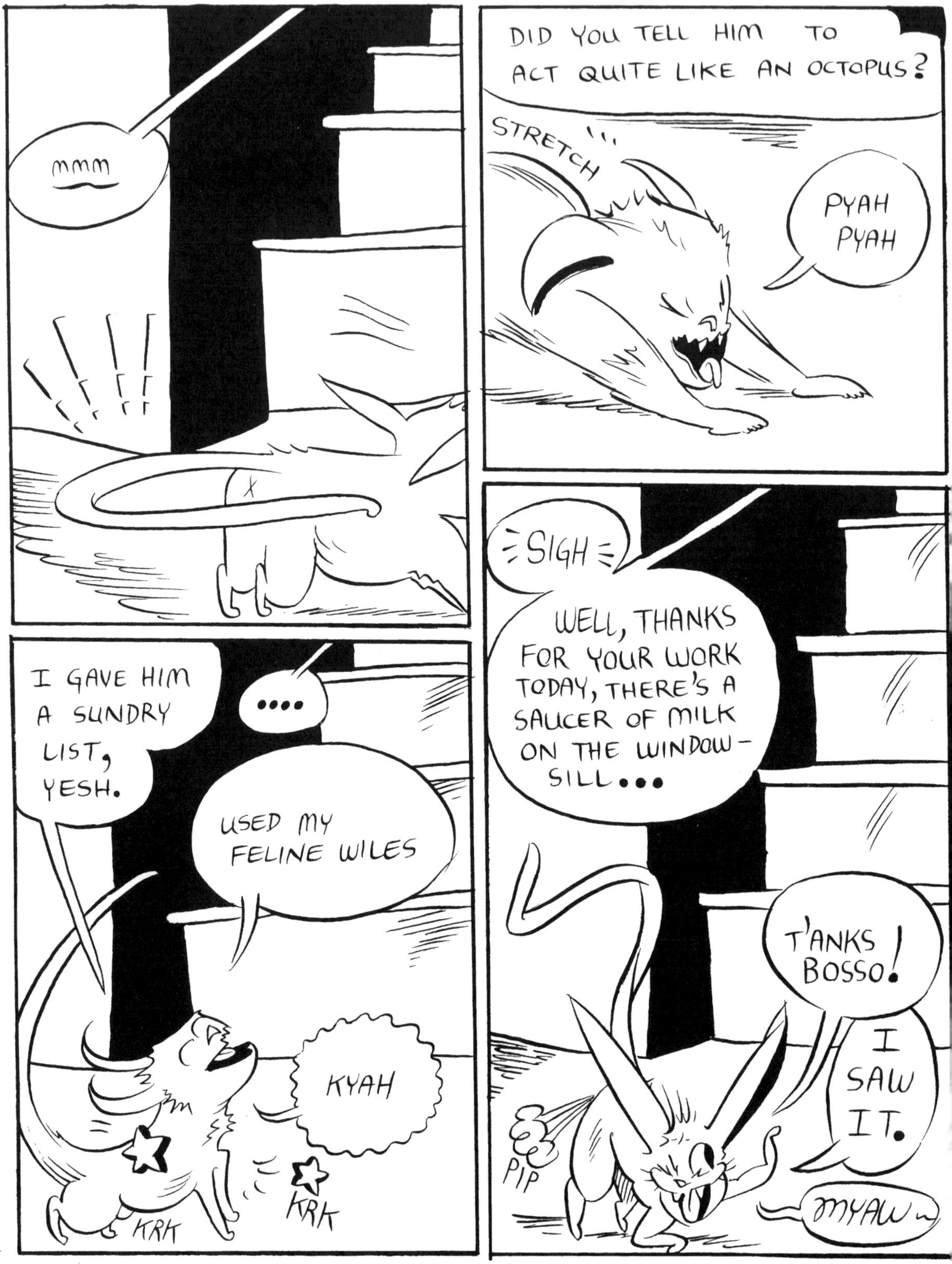
mmm
DID YOU TELL HIM TO ACT QUITE LIKE AN OCTOPUS?
STRETCH
PYAH PYAH
I GAVE HIM A SUNDRY LIST, YESH.
....
USED MY FELINE WILES
KYAH
KRK
KRK
SIGH
WELL, THANKS FOR YOUR WORK TODAY, THERE'S A SAUCER OF MILK ON THE WINDOW-SILL...
T'ANKS BOSSO!
I SAW IT.
PIP
MYAW

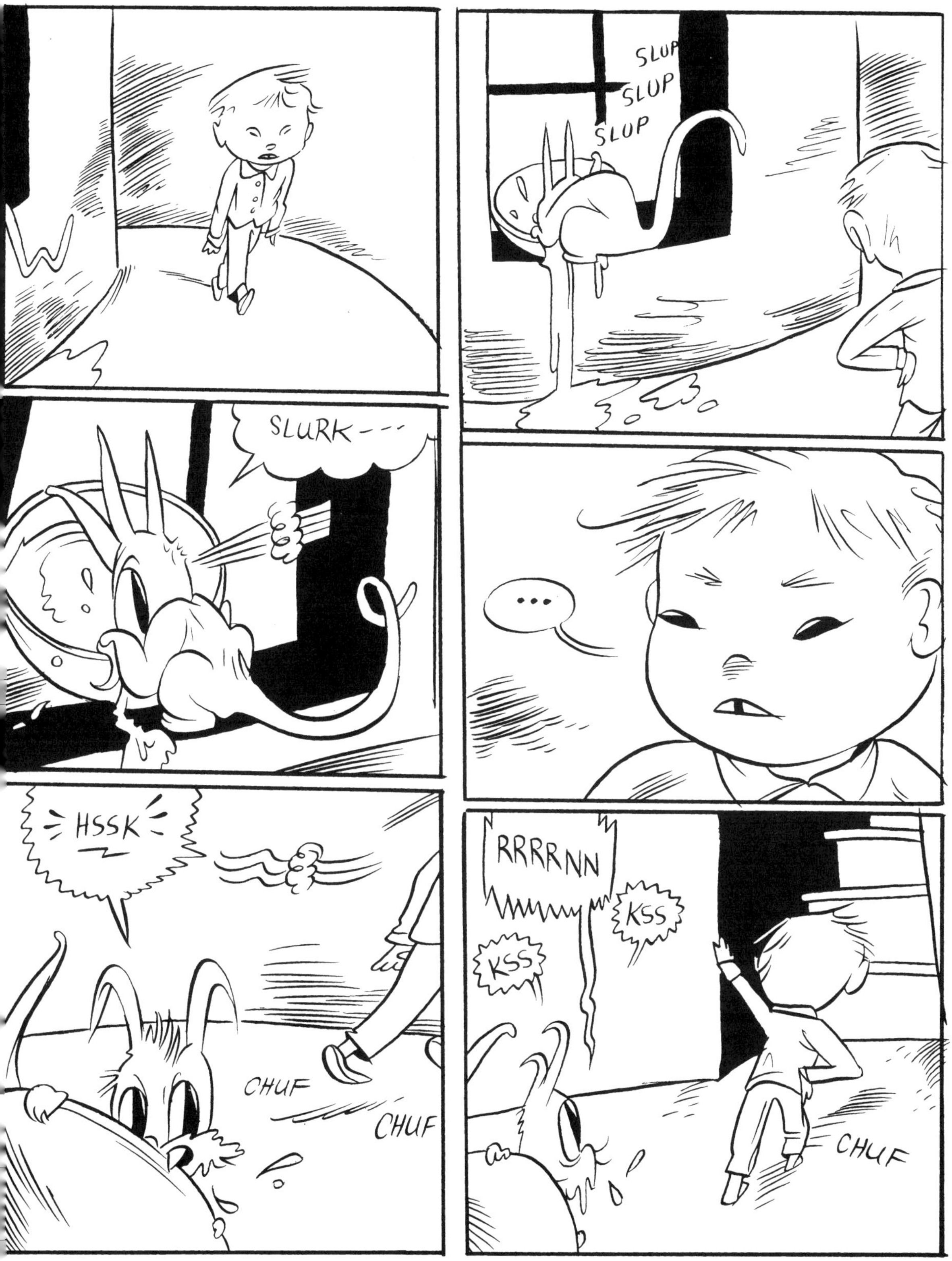
SLUP
SLUP
SLUP
SLURK---
...
HSSK
CHUF
CHUF
RRRRNN
KSS
KSS
CHUF

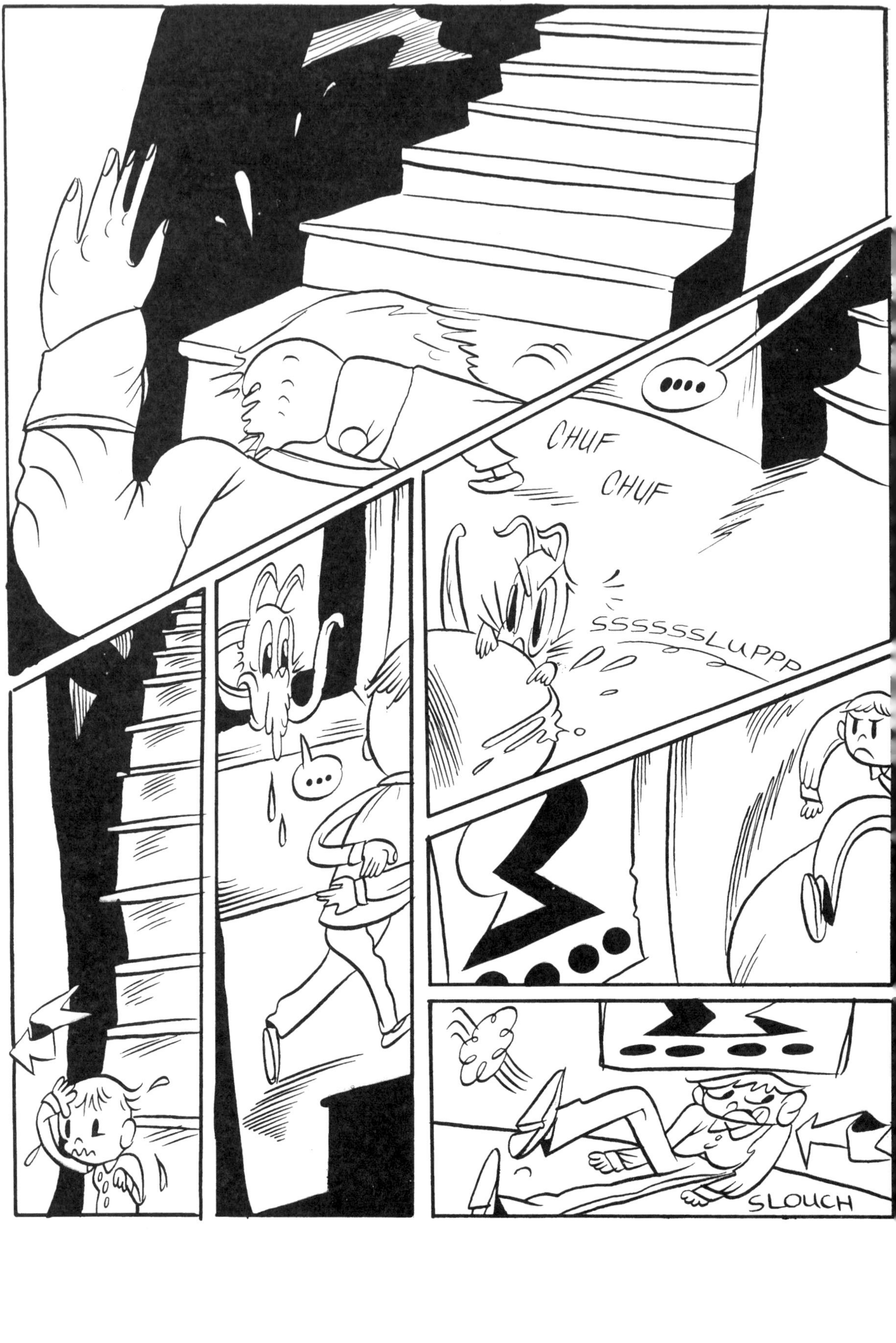
....
CHUF
CHUF
SSSSSSLUPPP
...
SLOUCH

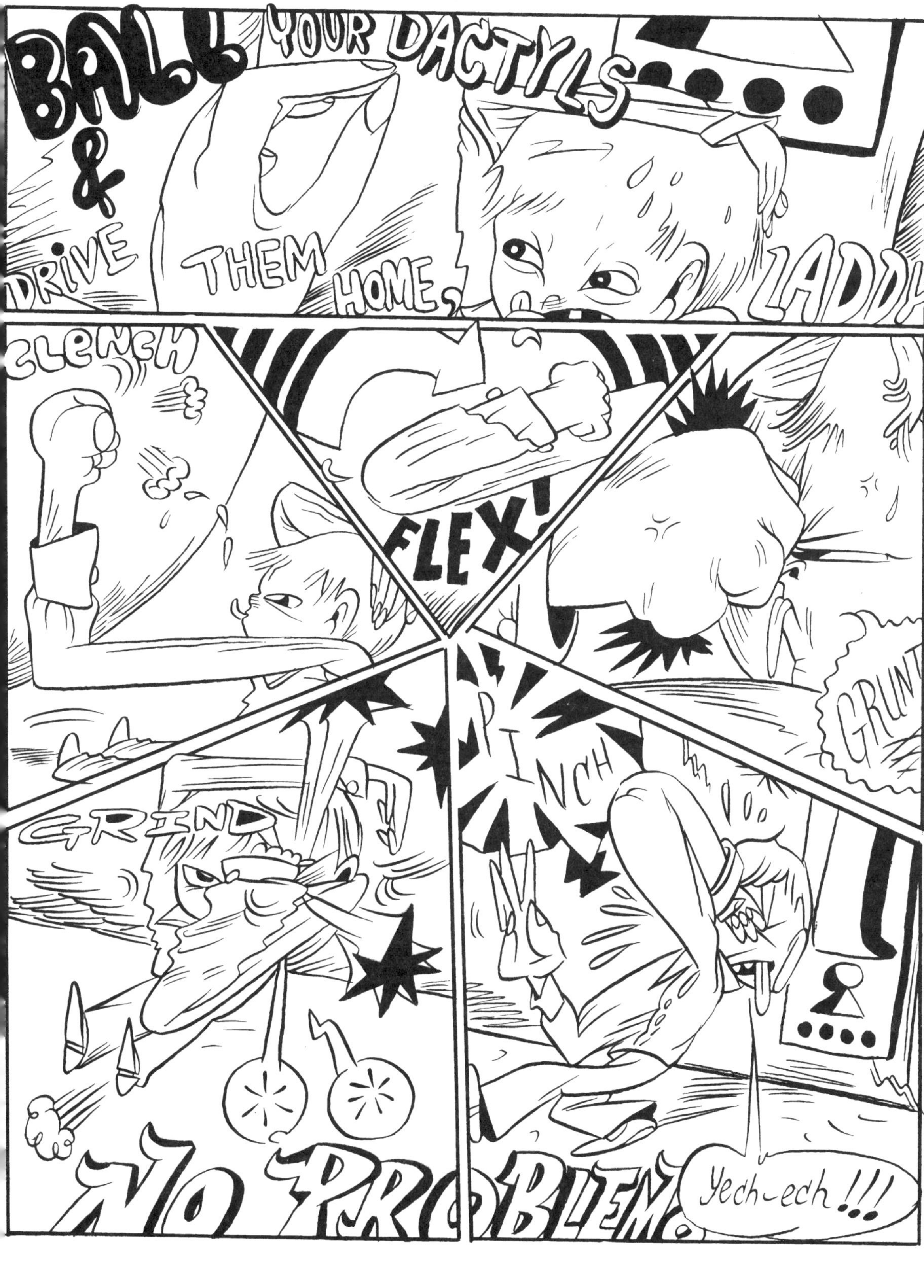
BALL YOUR DACTYLS....
& DRIVE THEM HOME, LADDY
CLENCH
FLEX!
GRUNT
GRIND
PINCH
NO PROBLEM.
Yech-ech!!!

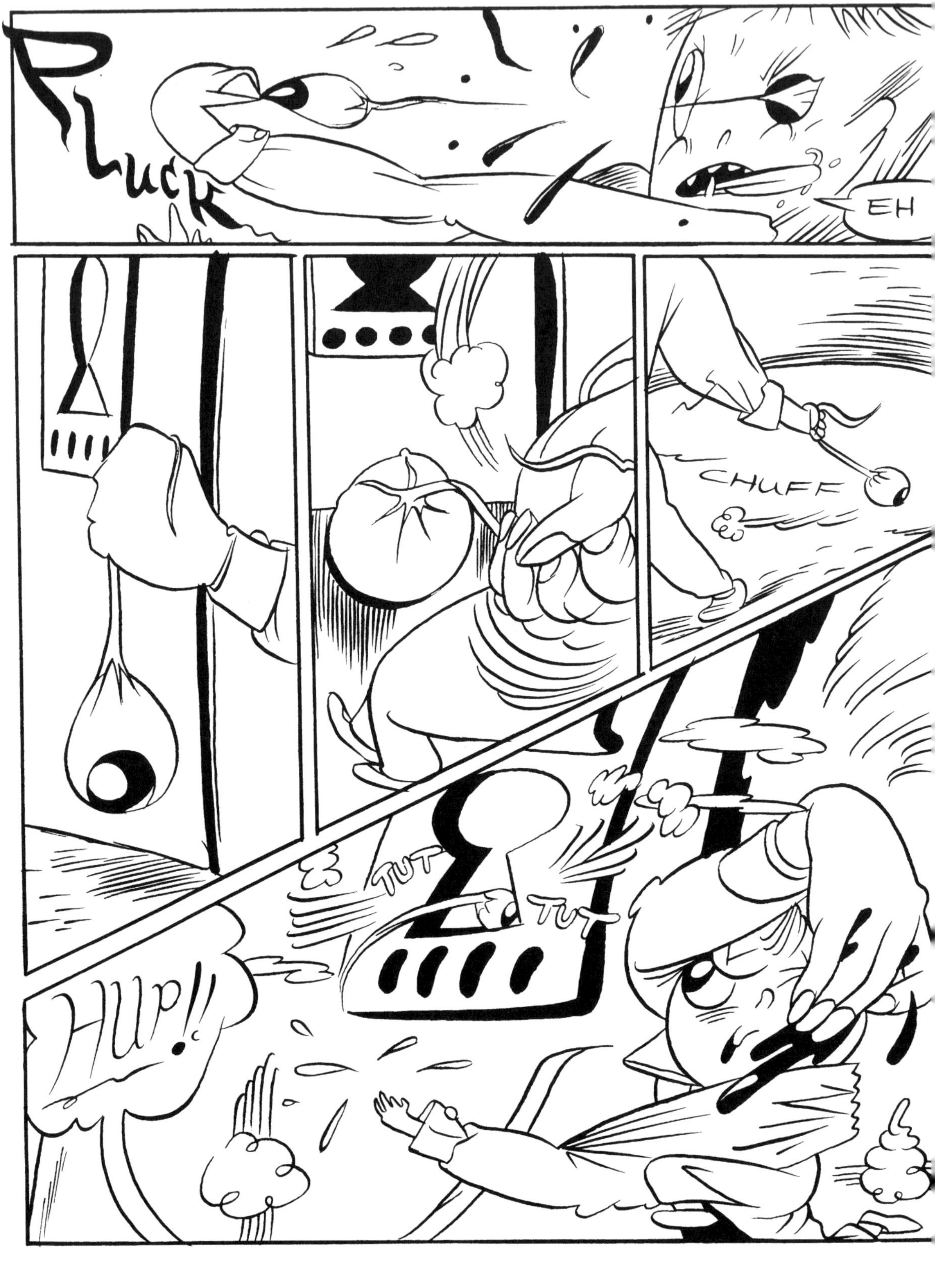
PLUCK
EH
CHUFF
TUT
TUT
HUP!!

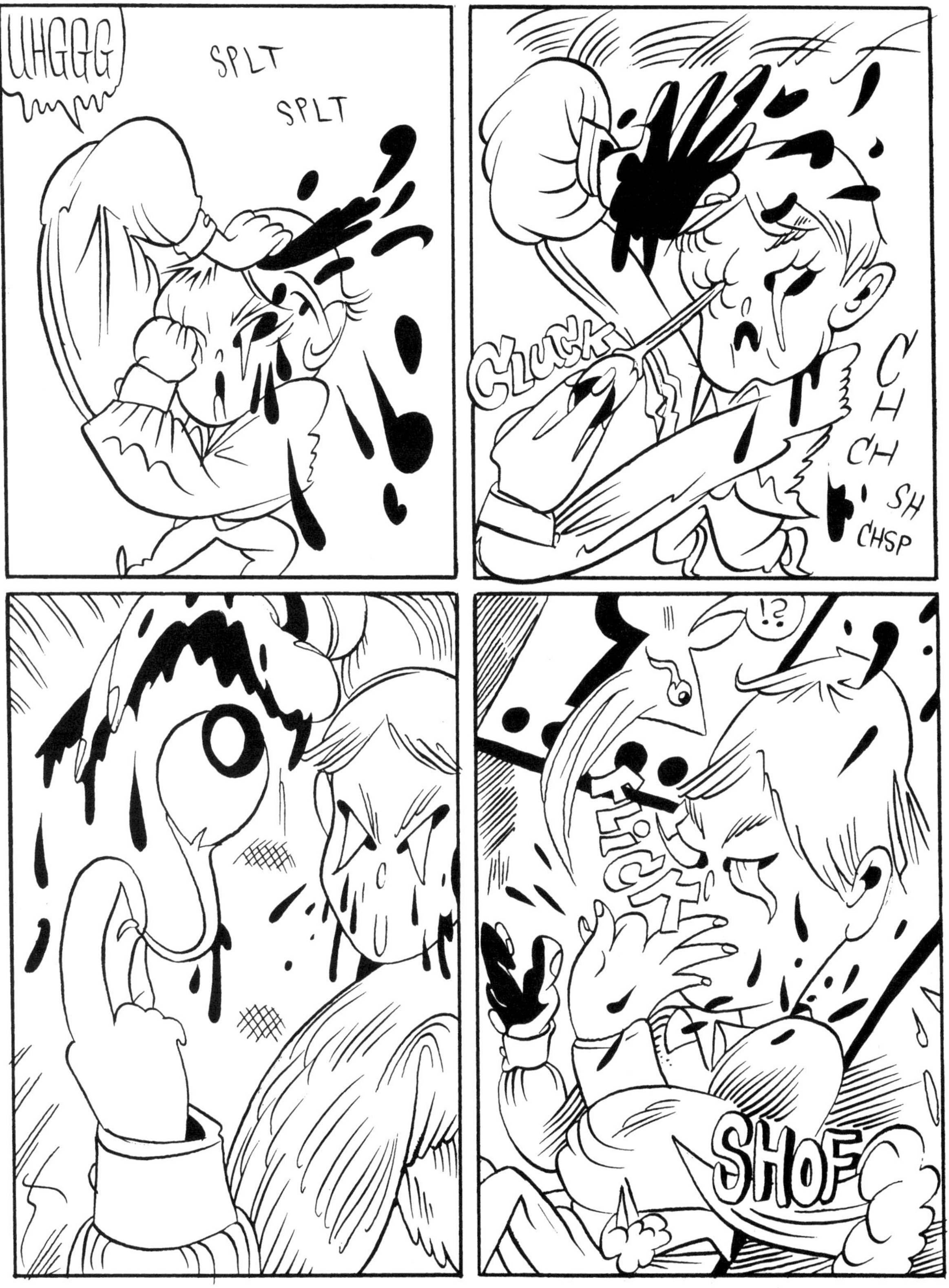
UHGGG
SPLT
SPLT
CLUCK
CH
CH
CH
SH
CHSP
!?
FLiCK
SHOF

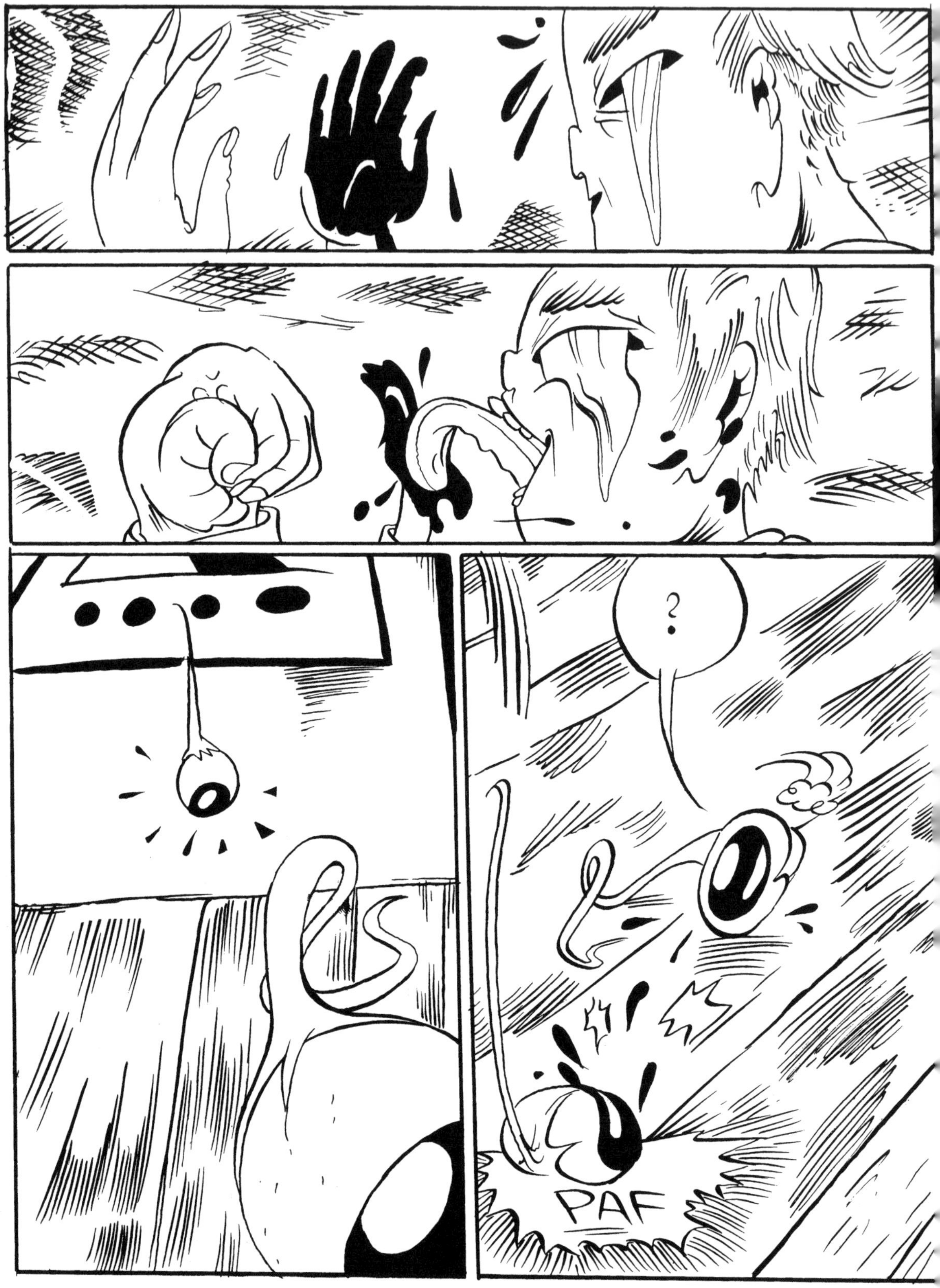
?
PAF

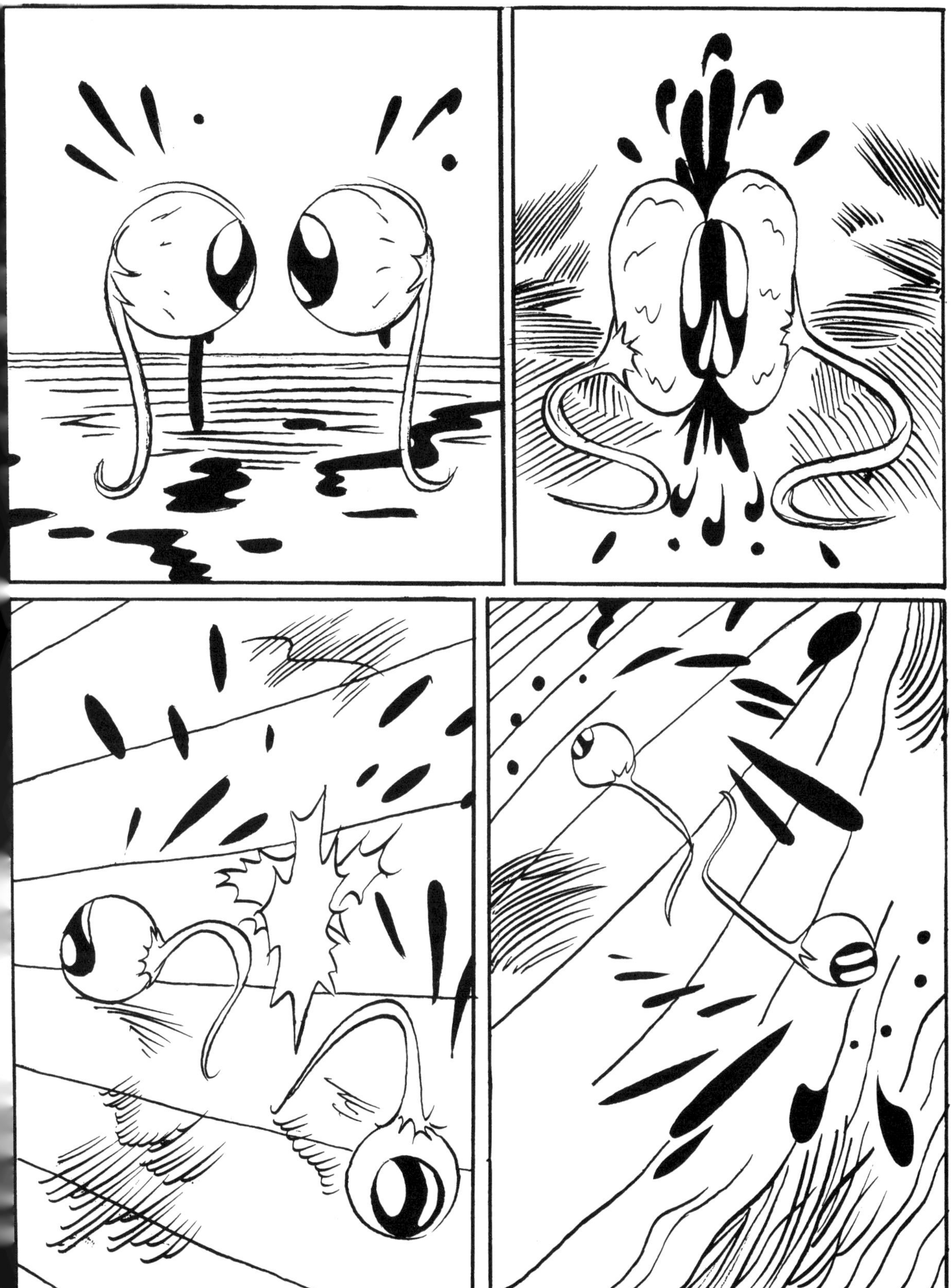

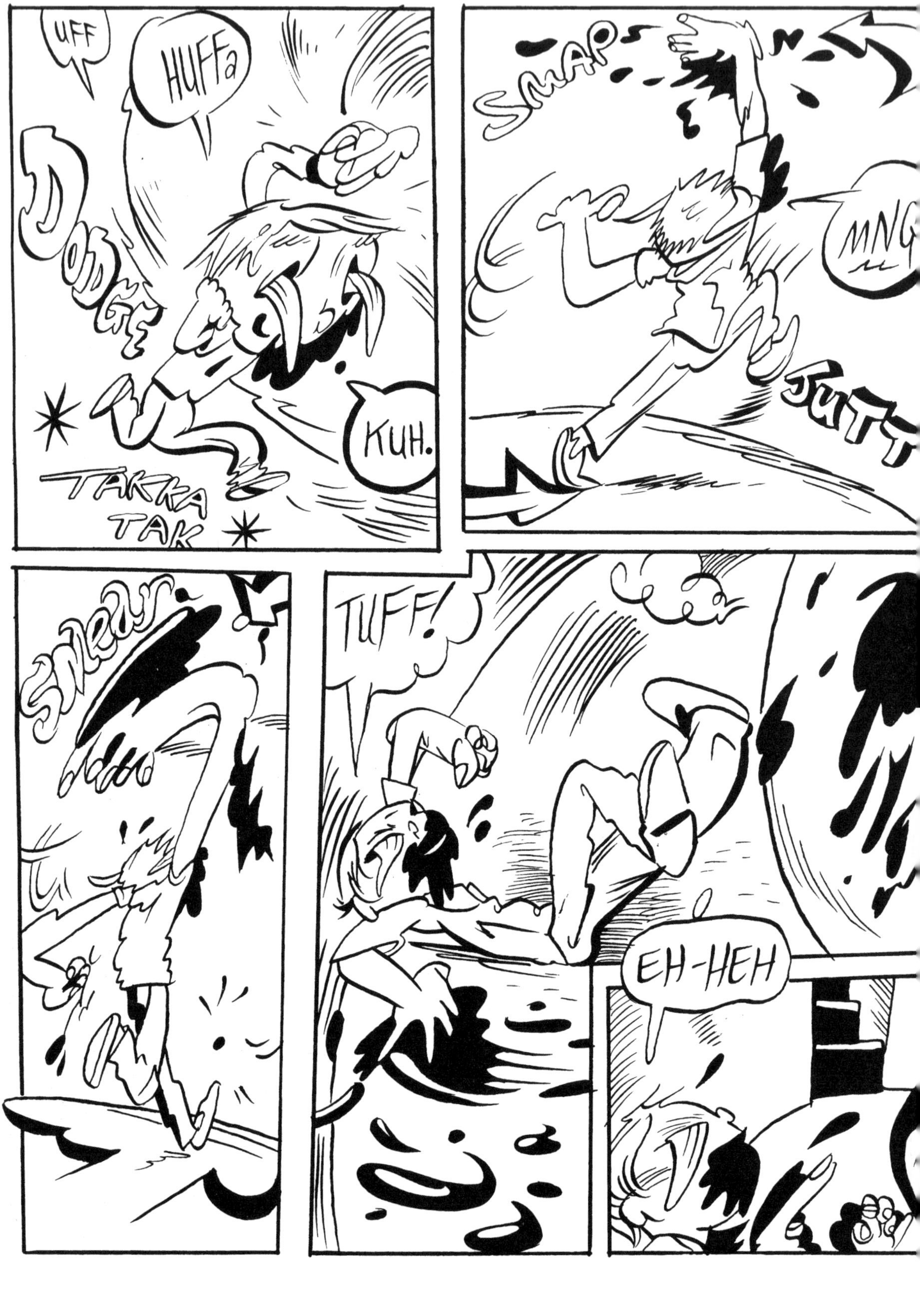
UFF
HUFFa
DODGE
KUH.
TAKKA TAK
SNAP
MNG
JUTT
TUFF!
EH-HEH

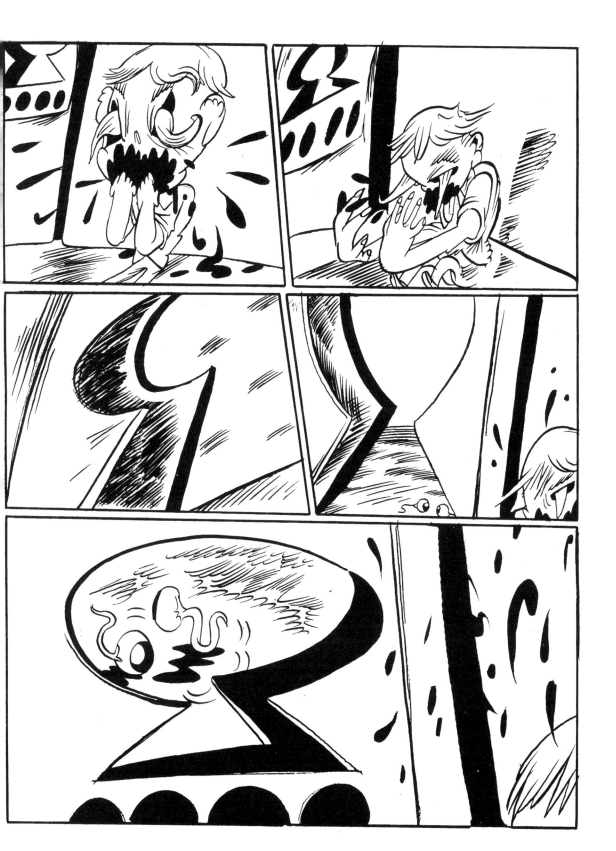

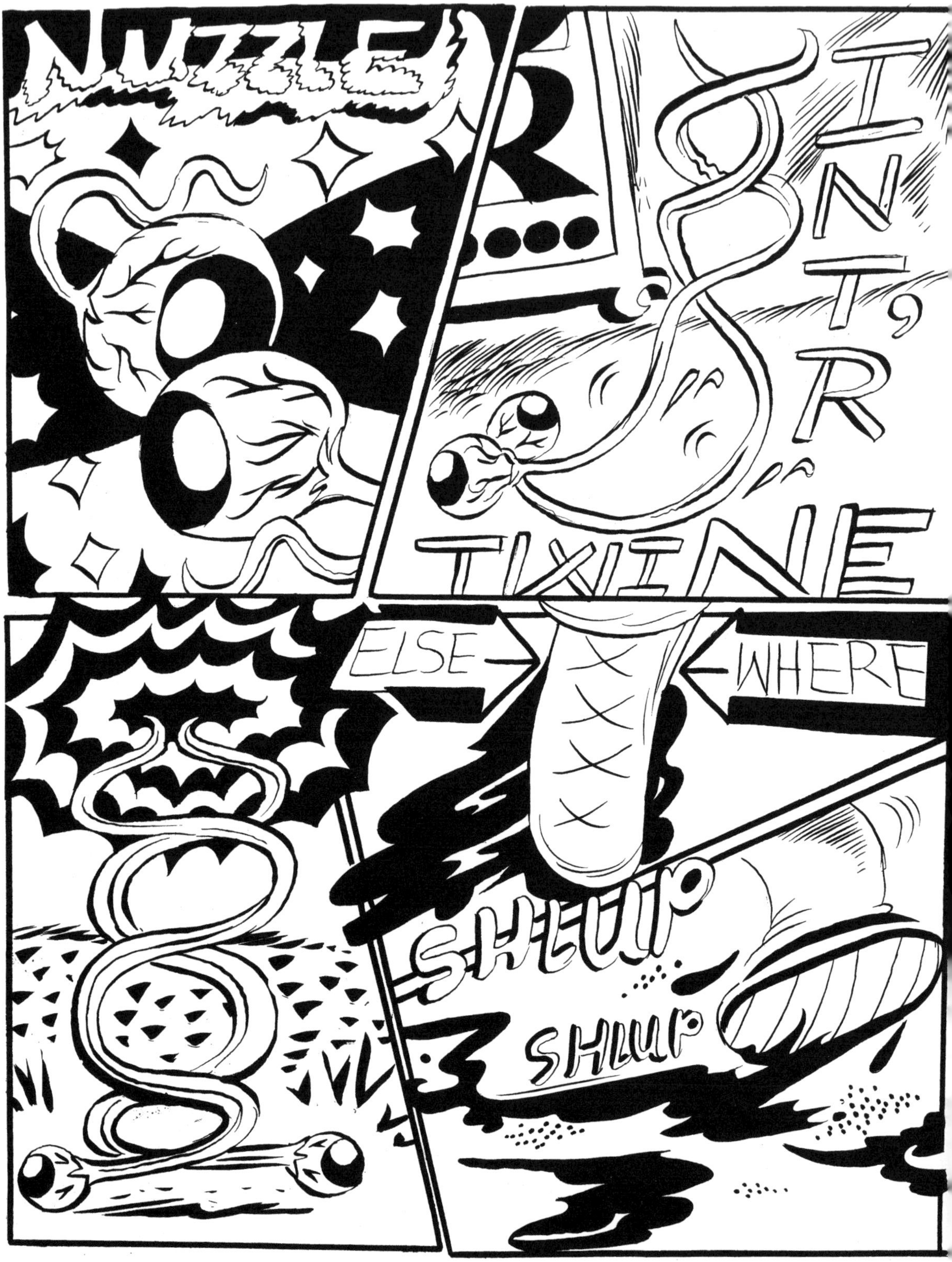
NUZZLE
R....
INTR
TIXINE
ELSE
WHERE
SHLUP
SHLUP

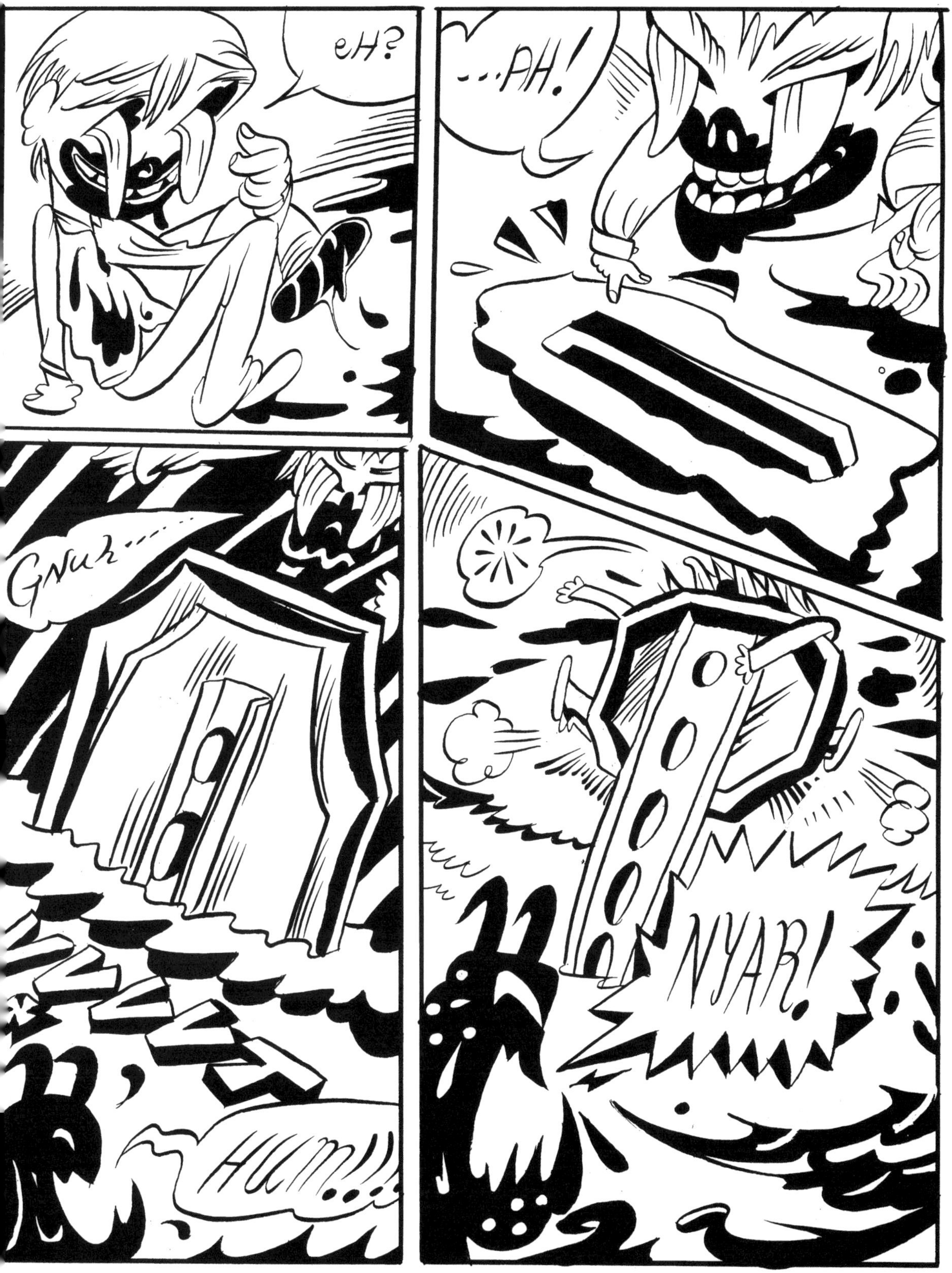
eH?
...AH!
GNuh......
HUM...
NYAR!

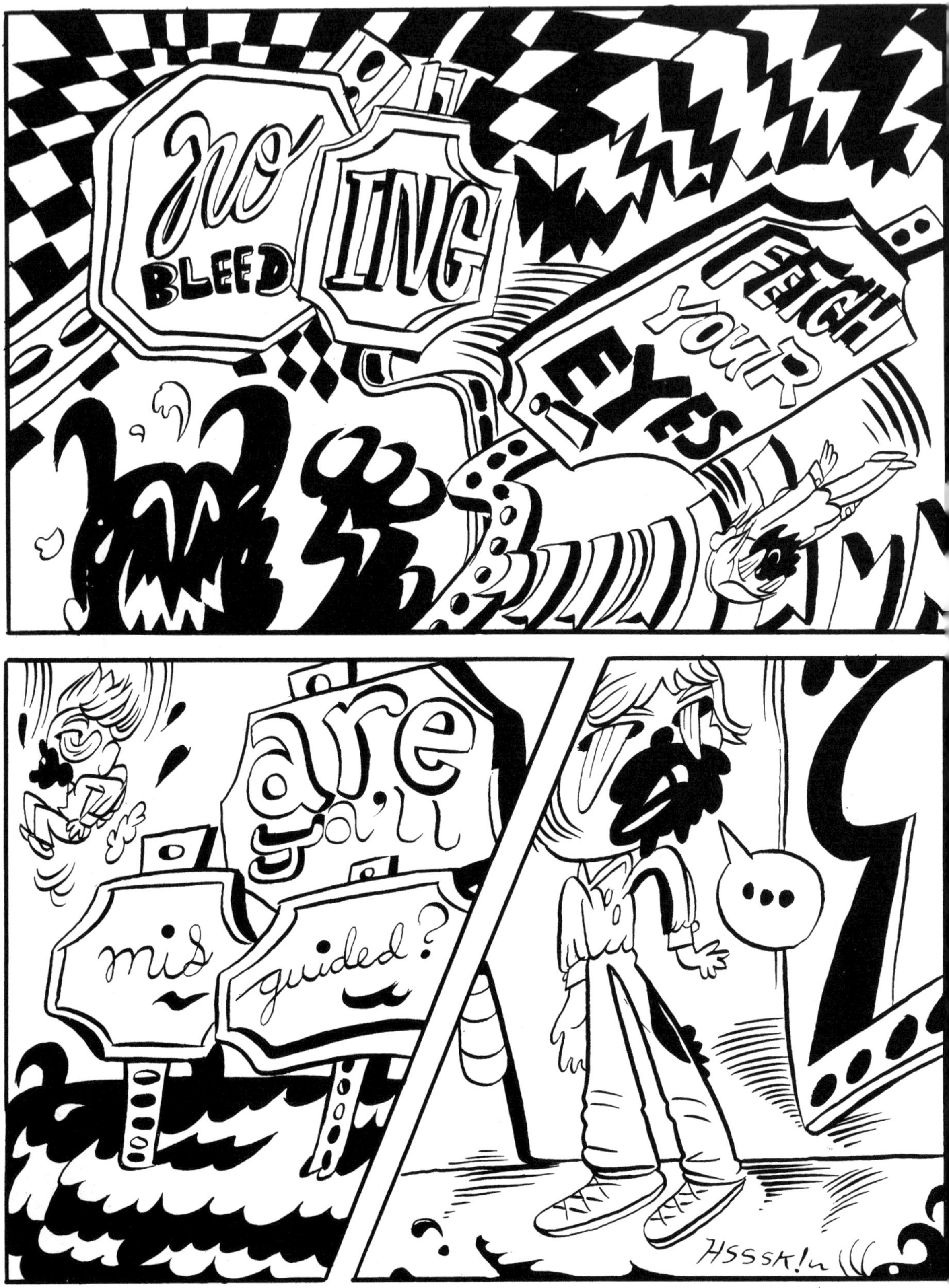
no
BLEED
ING
FETCH
YOUR
EYES
are
ya'll
mis
guided?
...
HSSSK!

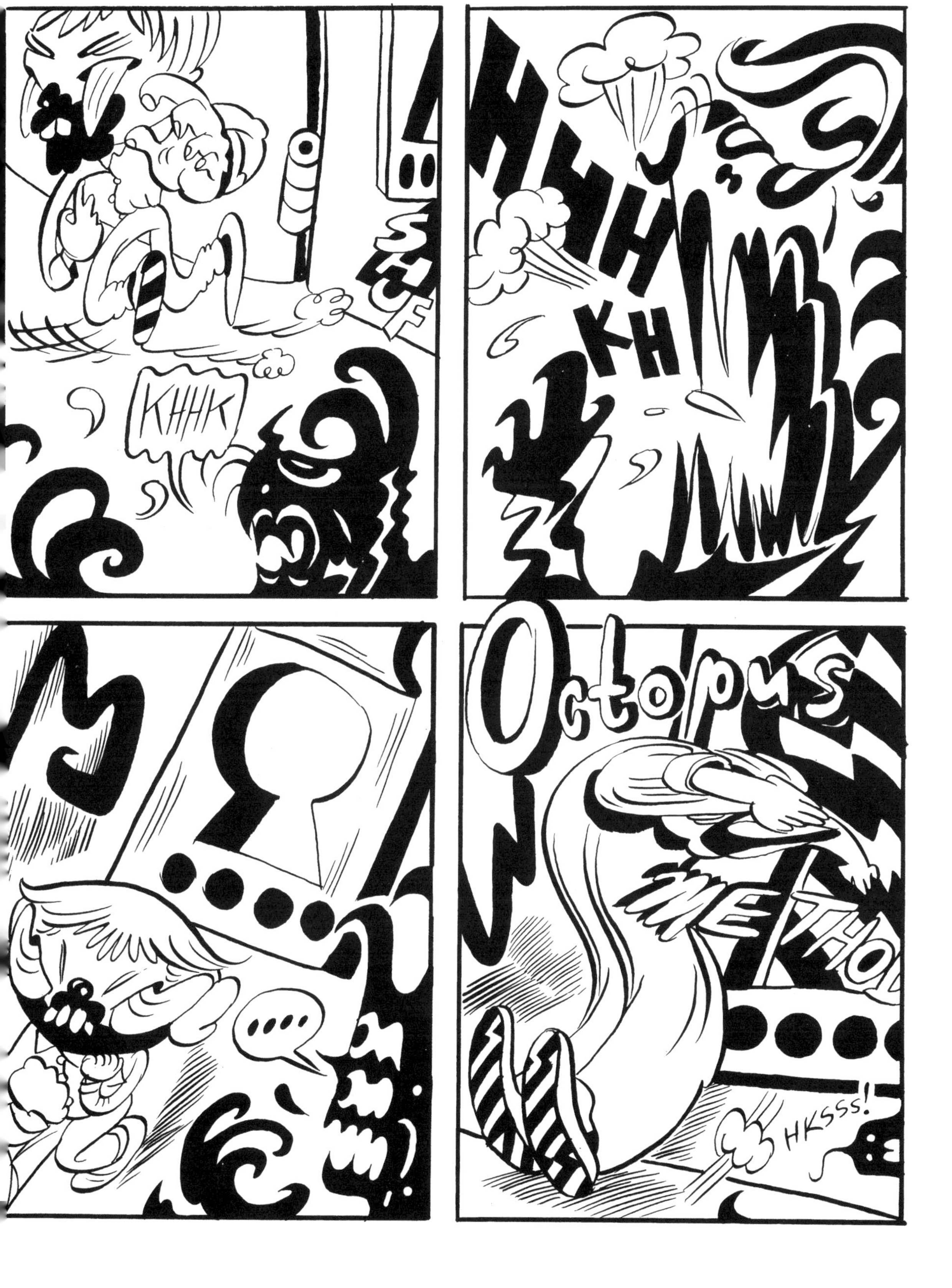
KHHK
KH
Octopus
HKSSS!

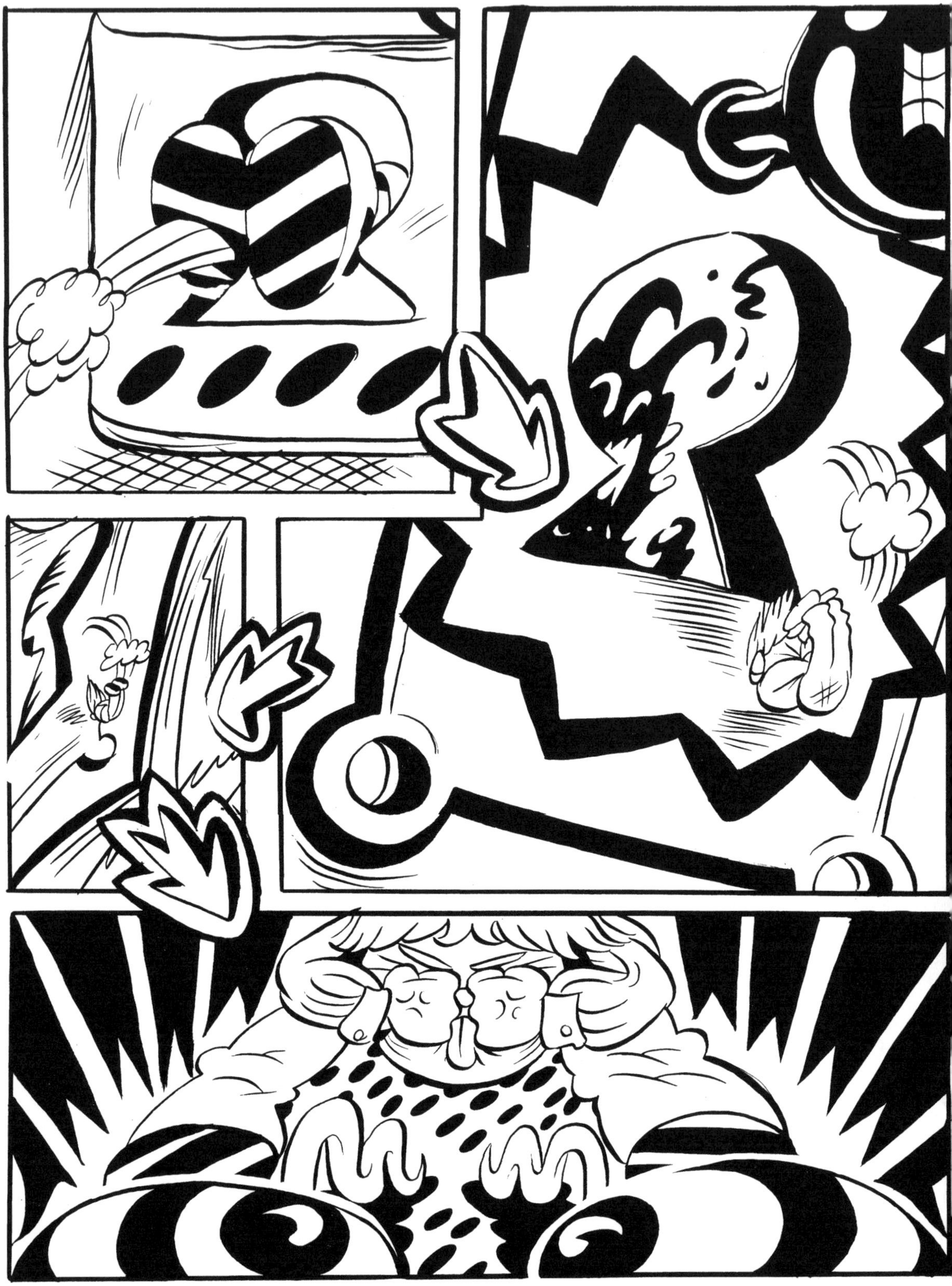

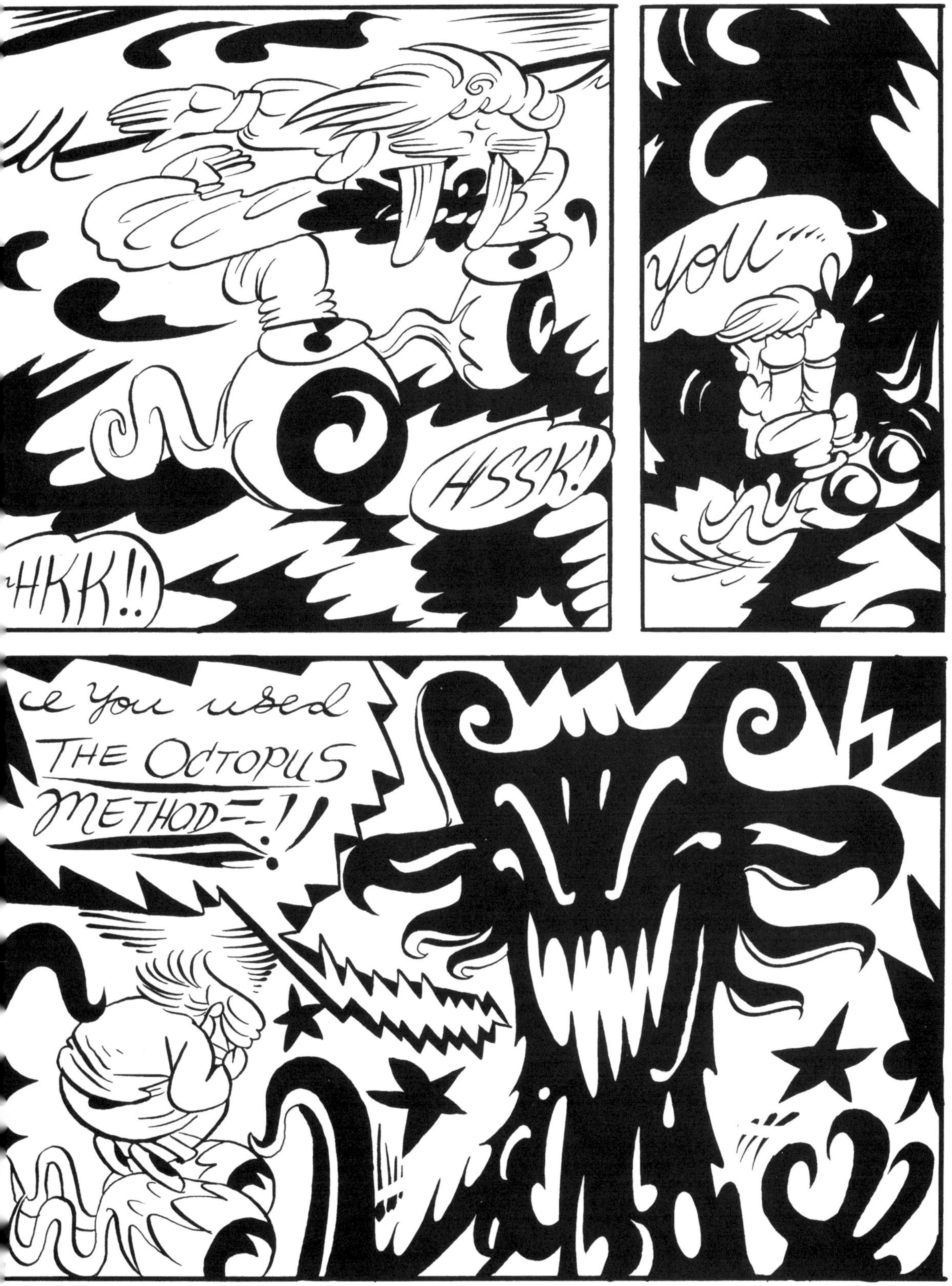
HSSK!
HKK!!
YOU
You used THE OCTOPUS METHOD--!!

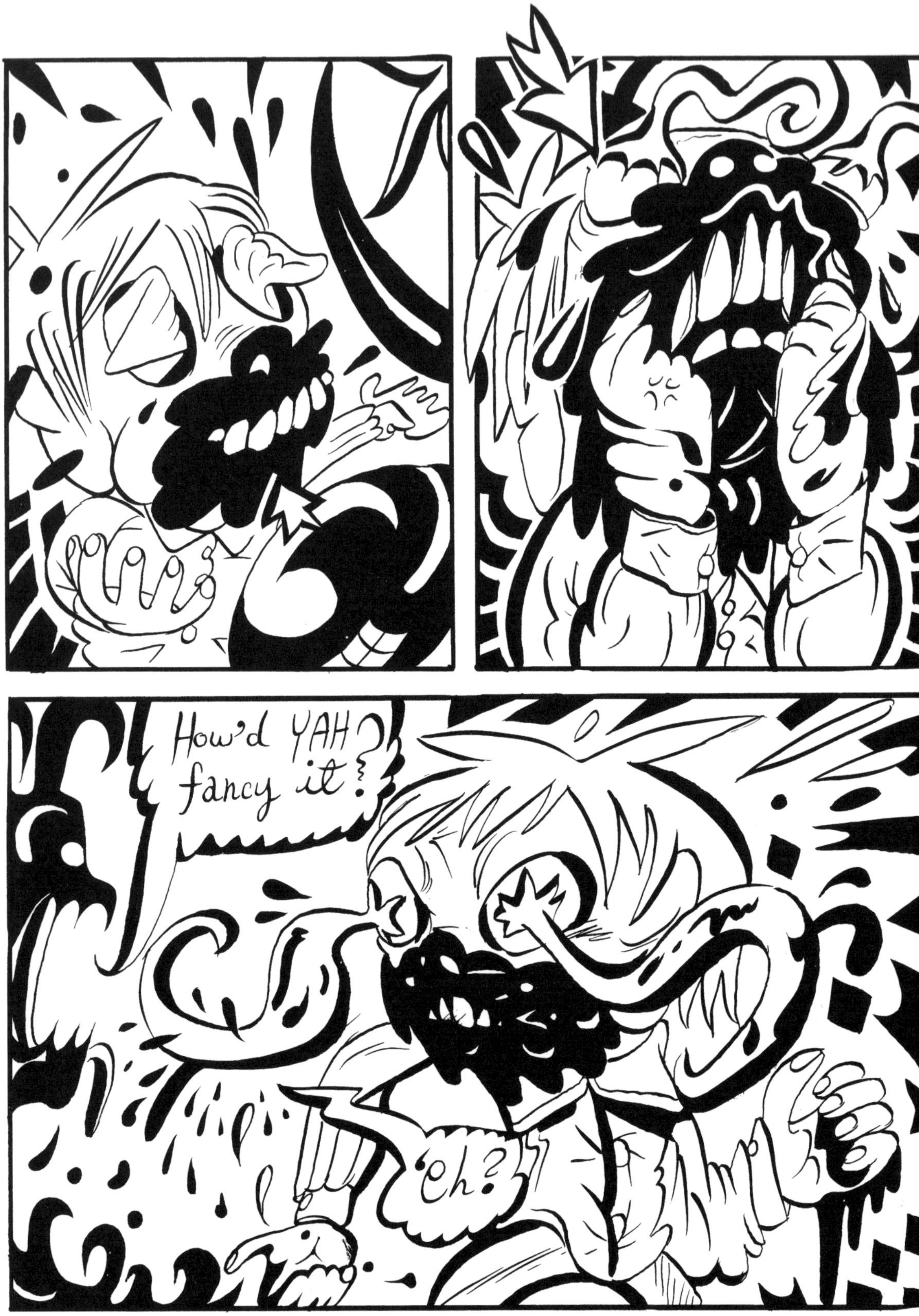
How'd YAH fancy it?
Eh?

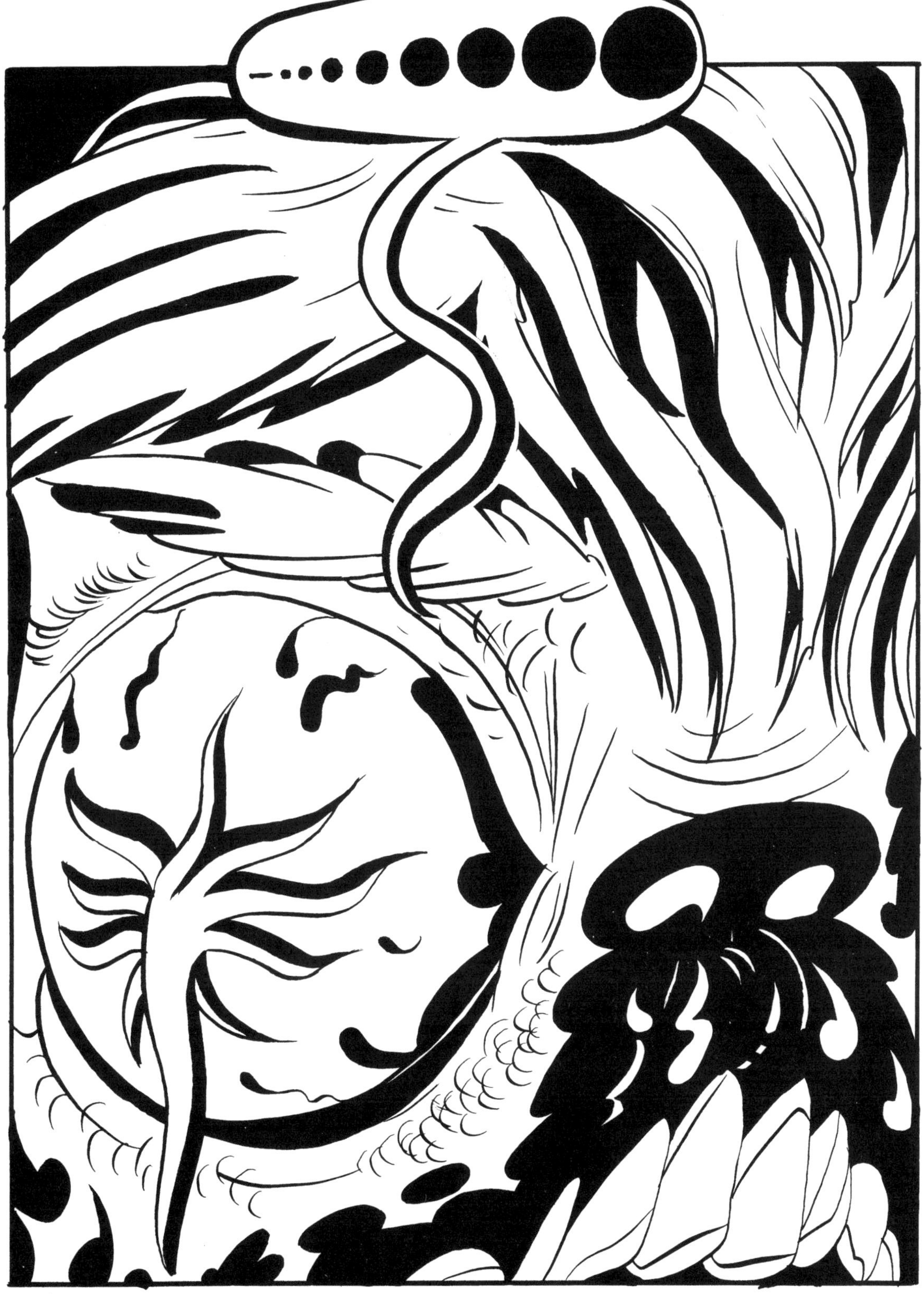

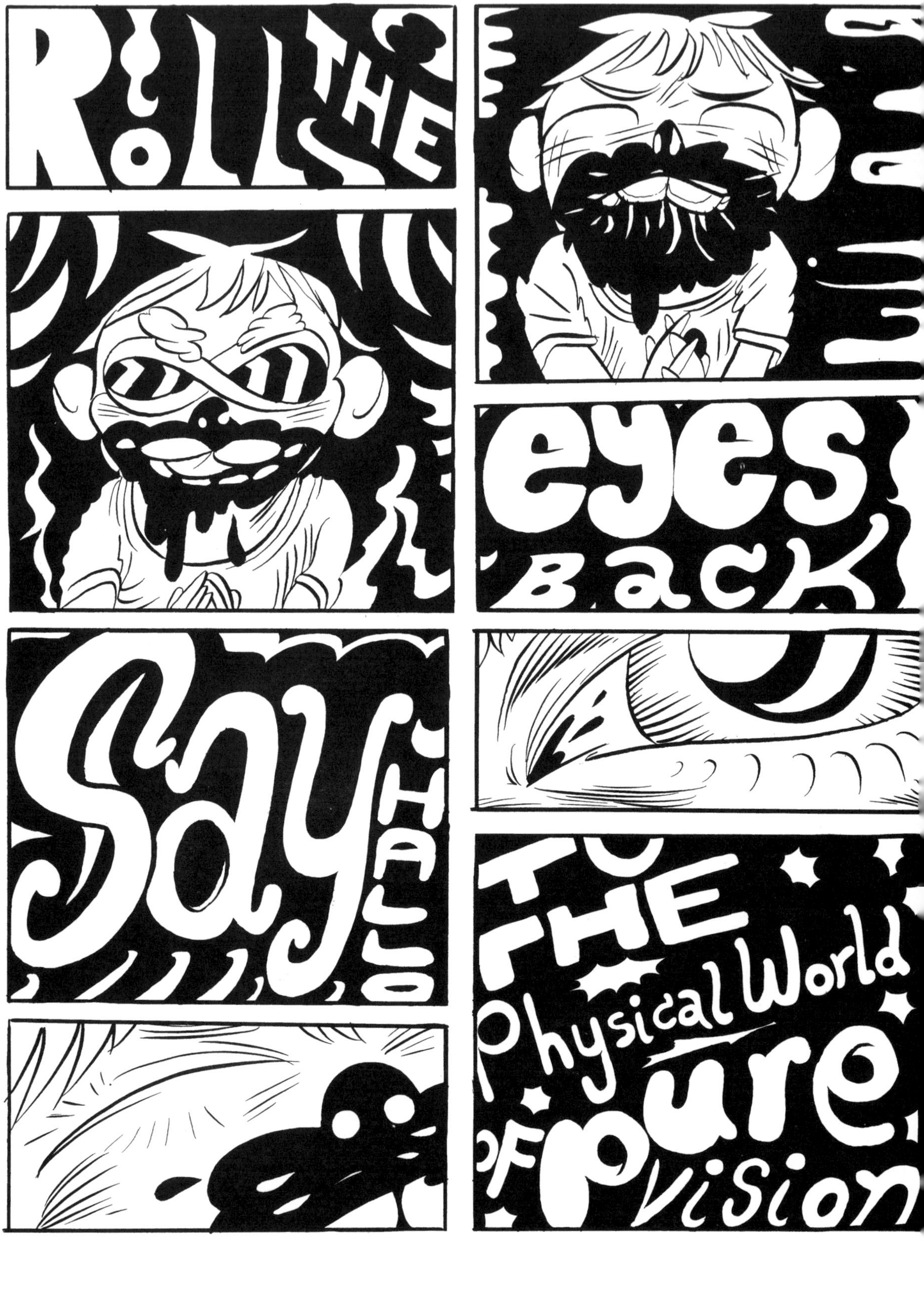

Roll the
eyes back
Say hallo
to the Physical World of pure vision

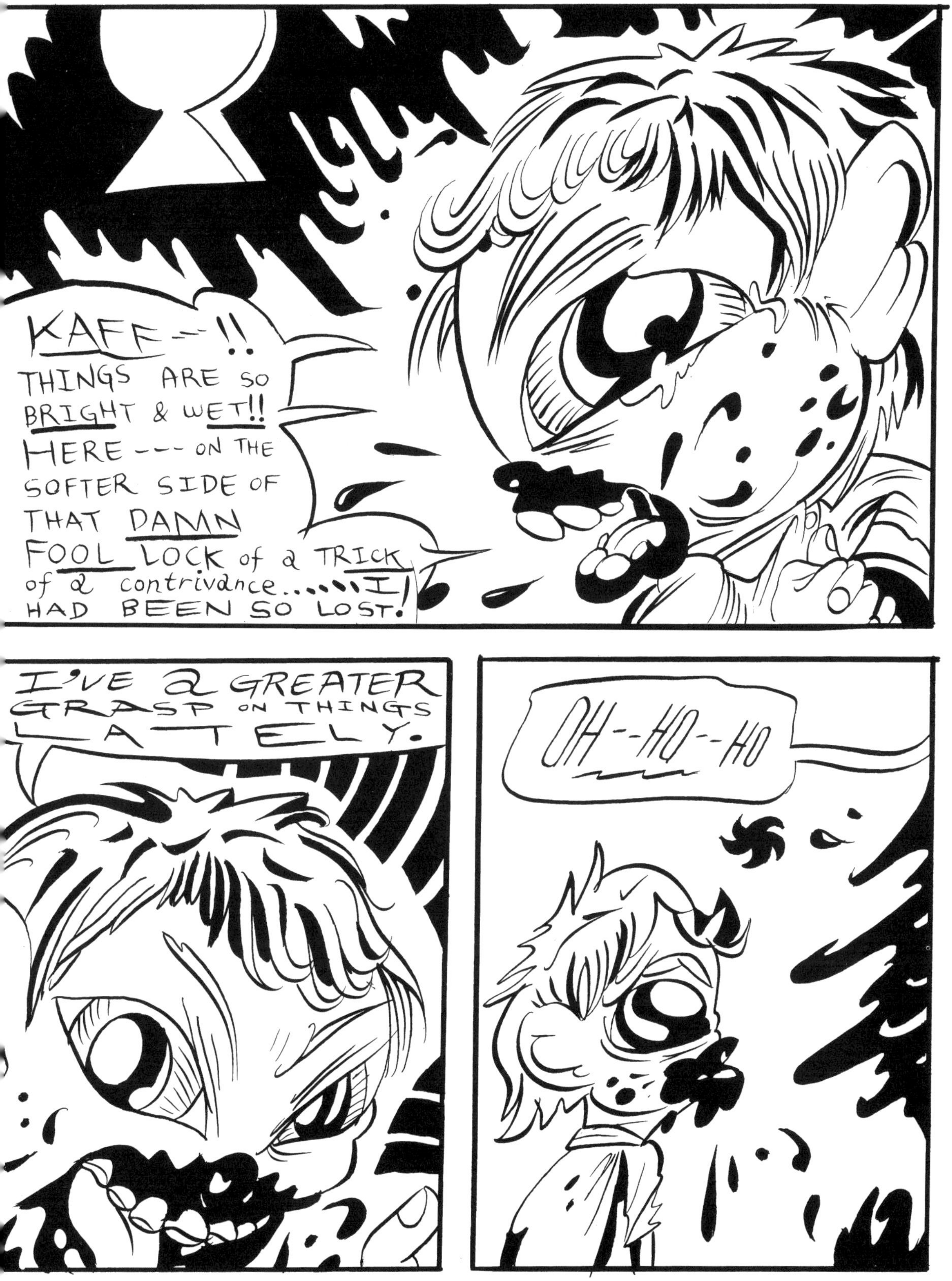
KAFF--!! THINGS ARE SO BRIGHT & WET!! HERE--- ON THE SOFTER SIDE OF THAT DAMN FOOL LOCK of a TRICK of a contrivance......I HAD BEEN SO LOST!
I'VE a GREATER GRASP ON THINGS LATELY.
OH--HO--HO

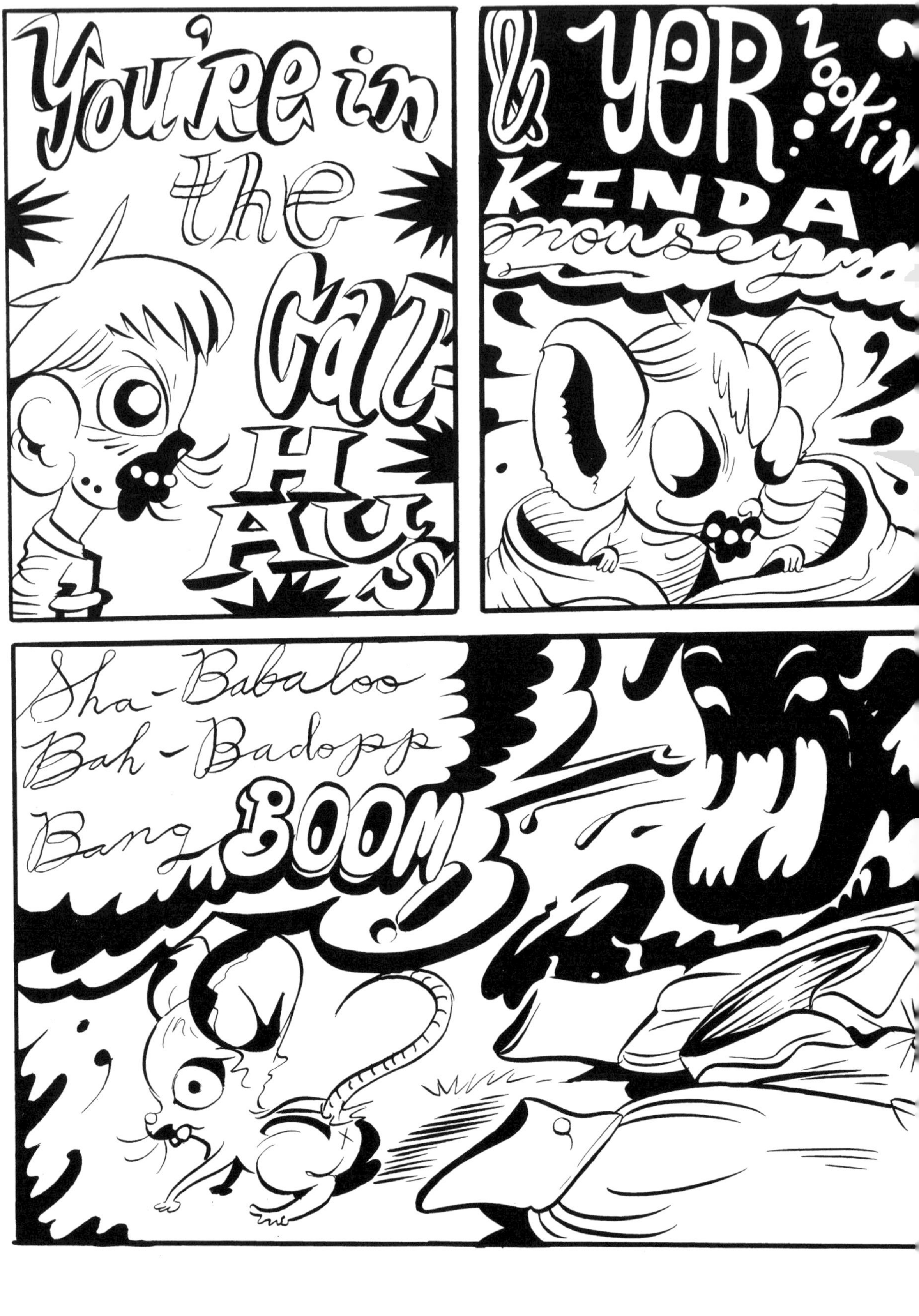
You're in the Cat-Haus
& yer lookin kinda mousey...
Sha-Babaloo Bah-Badopp Bang BOOM!

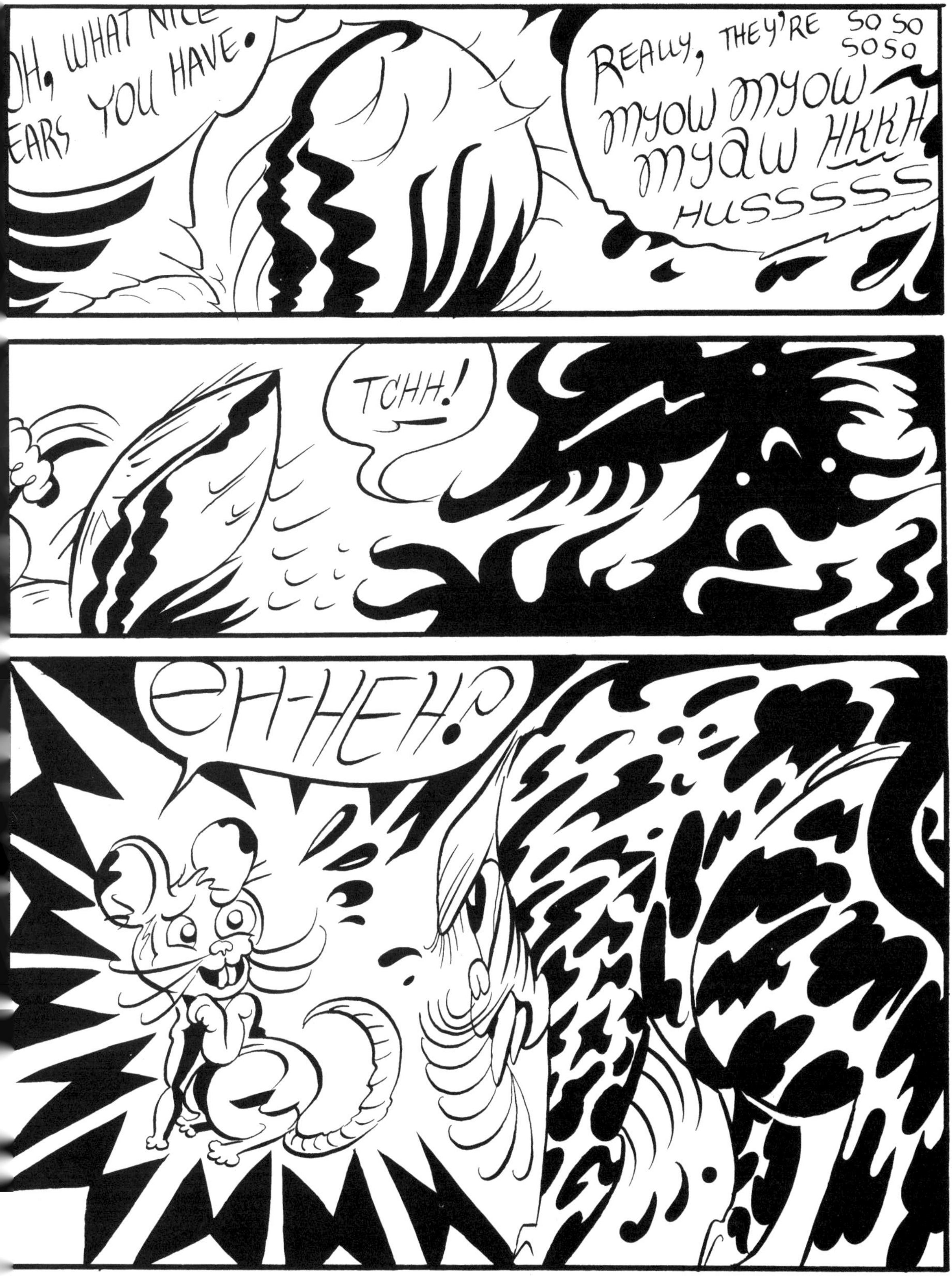
OH, WHAT NICE EARS YOU HAVE.
REALLY, THEY'RE SO SO SOSO
MYOW MYOW MYAW HKKH HUSSSSS
TCHH!
EH-HEH?

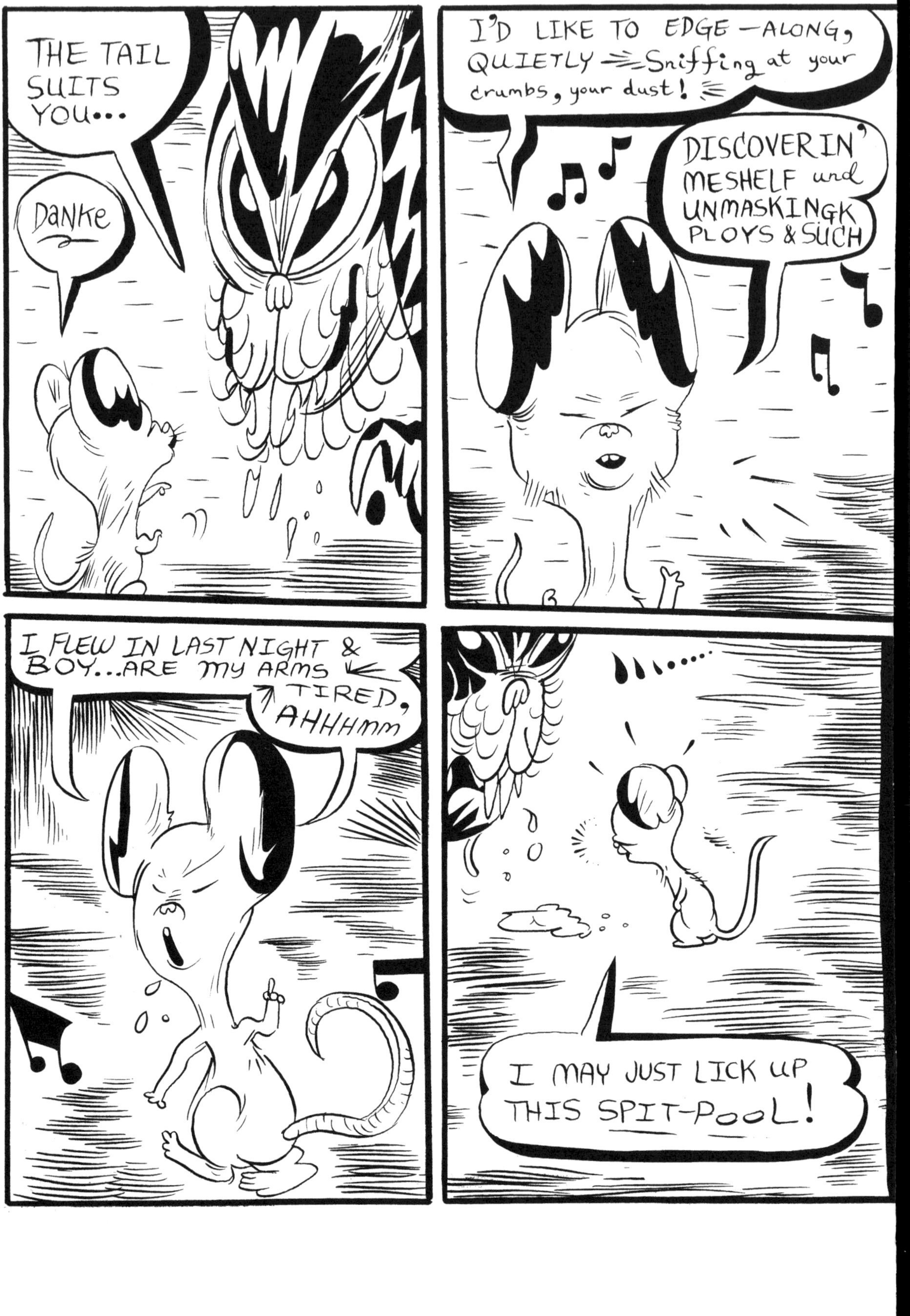
THE TAIL SUITS YOU...
Danke
I'D LIKE TO EDGE—ALONG, QUIETLY Sniffing at your crumbs, your dust!
DISCOVERIN' MESHELF und UNMASKINGK PLOYS & SUCH
I FLEW IN LAST NIGHT & BOY...ARE MY ARMS TIRED, AHHHmm
I MAY JUST LICK UP THIS SPIT-PooL!

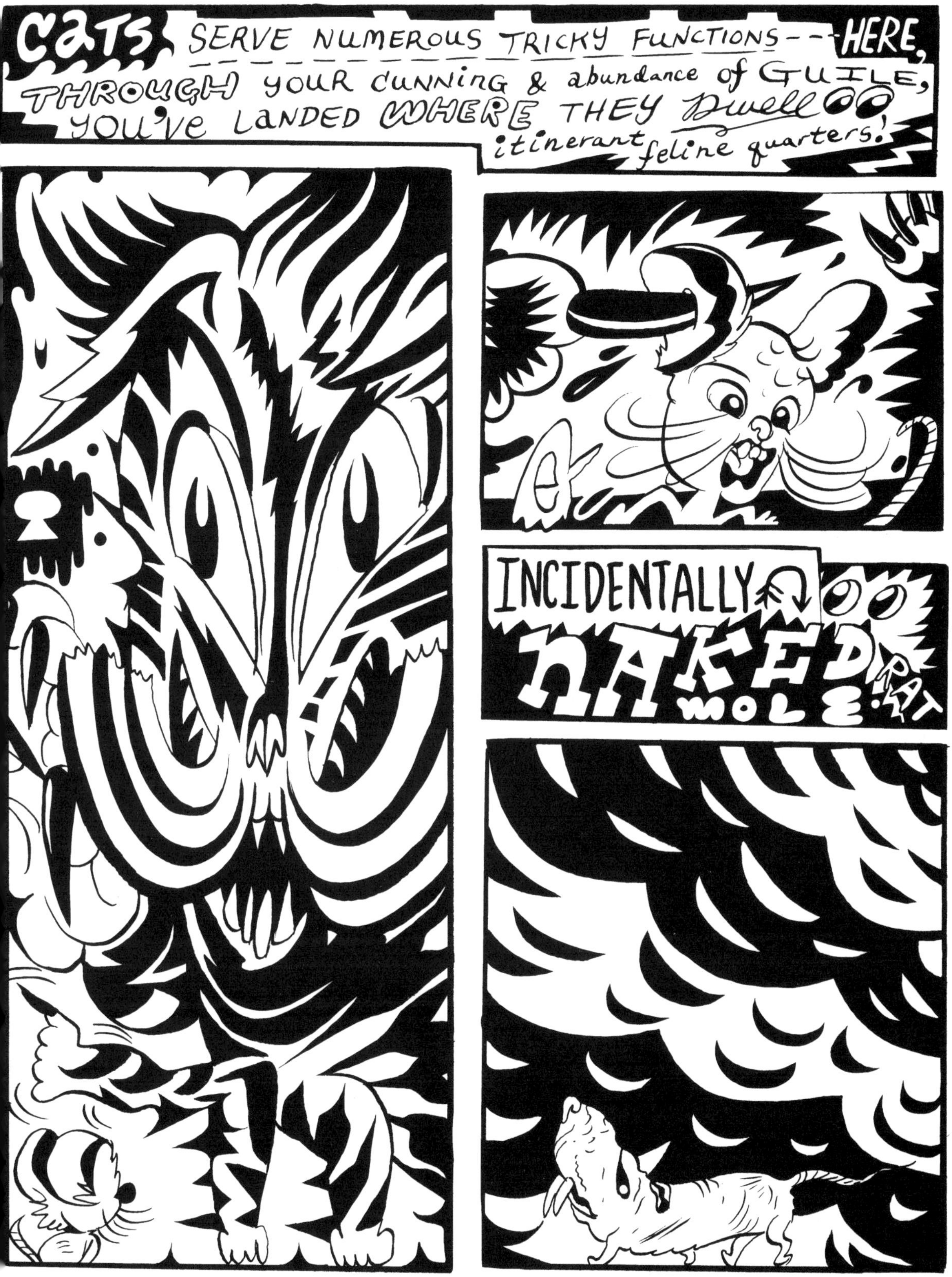
CATS SERVE NUMEROUS TRICKY FUNCTIONS---HERE, THROUGH YOUR CUNNING & abundance of GUILE, YOU'VE LANDED WHERE THEY Dwell
itinerant feline quarters!
INCIDENTALLY
NAKED MOLE RAT

THE N.M.R. IS FREE of the HALLS, FREE OF THE KEYS & H⊗LES to WHICH THEY'RE BEHOLDEN

HE SMELLS, HE LOCOMOTES, HE FINDS HIS LOCAL CLUMP & LATCHES ON →→→ Like: BAD GUM to a new shoe

HE DREAMS, THOUGH. DREAMS of THE RAW EDGE of the METAL SLOT, IT'S MIRROR IMAGE LESS THAN AN INCH AWAY, PARALLEL, FUNCTIONAL...

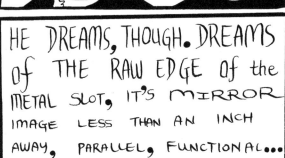

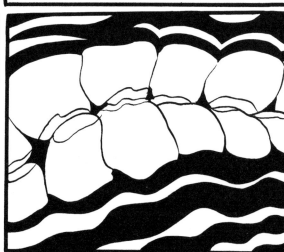

NEVER OPENING EYES VERY WIDELY, BUT WITH LIDS NOW TIGHT HIS TEETH ARE FREE TO TOUCH TIPS, GRIND down & flatten !!!

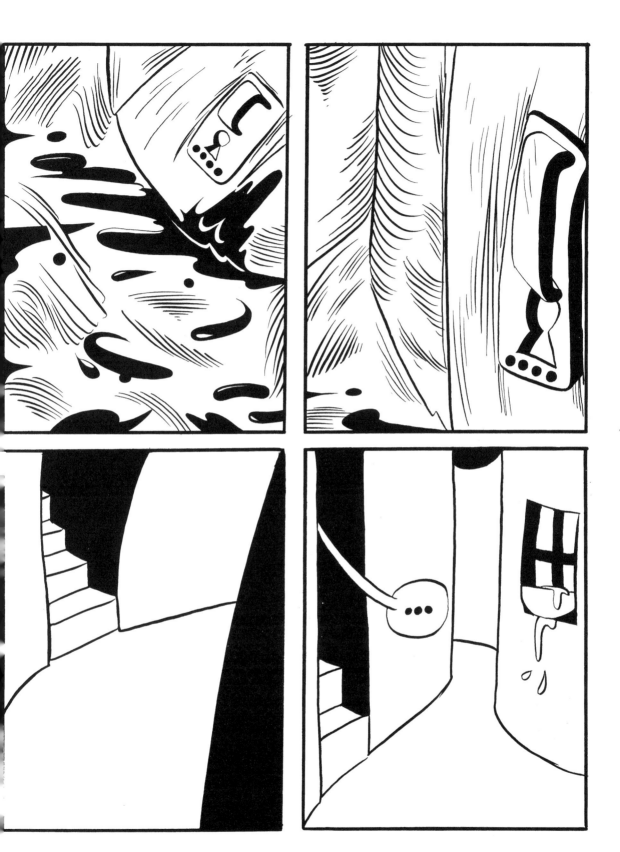

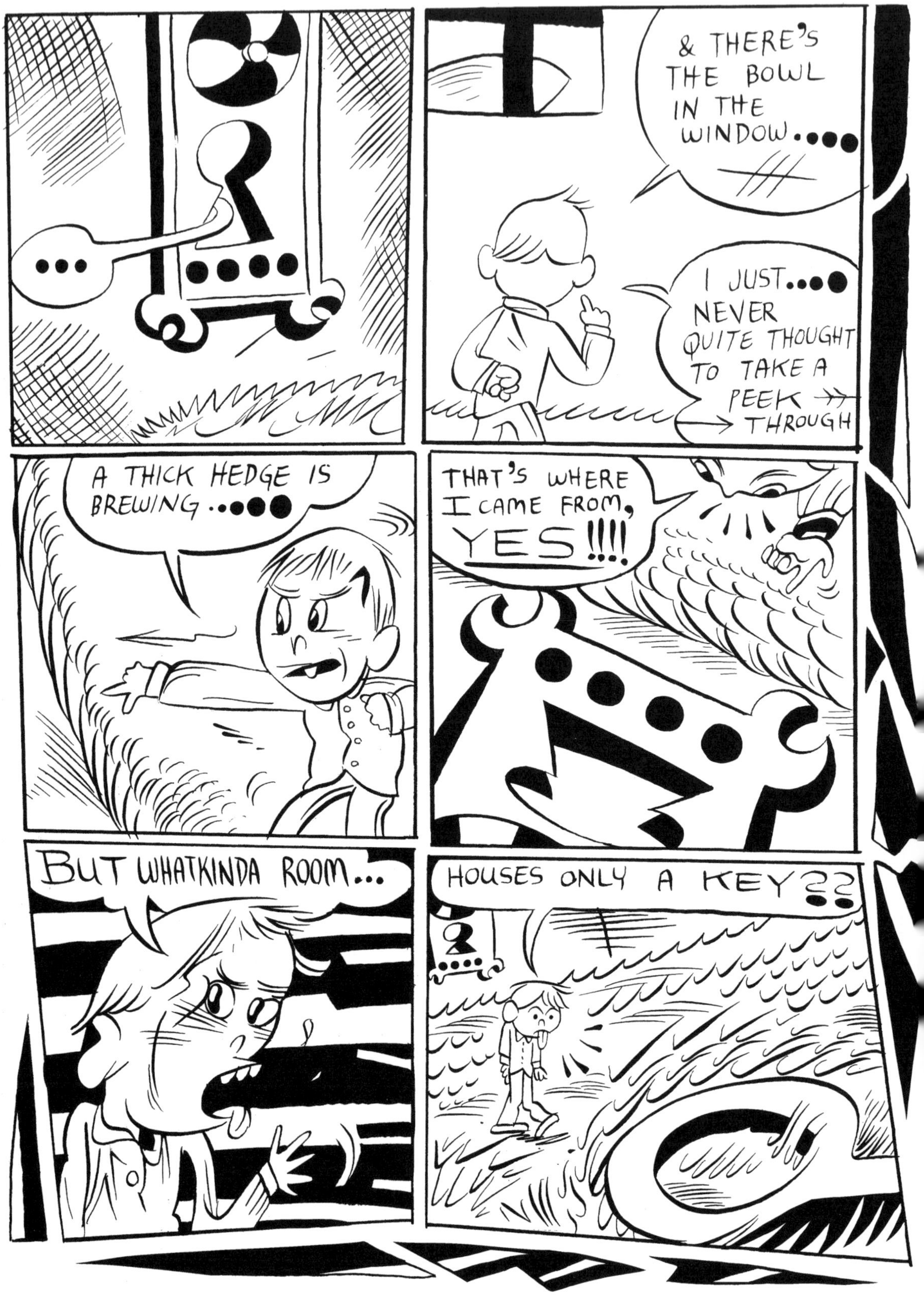
...
& THERE'S THE BOWL IN THE WINDOW....
I JUST.... NEVER QUITE THOUGHT TO TAKE A PEEK THROUGH
A THICK HEDGE IS BREWING....
THAT'S WHERE I CAME FROM, YES!!!!
BUT WHATKINDA ROOM...
HOUSES ONLY A KEY??

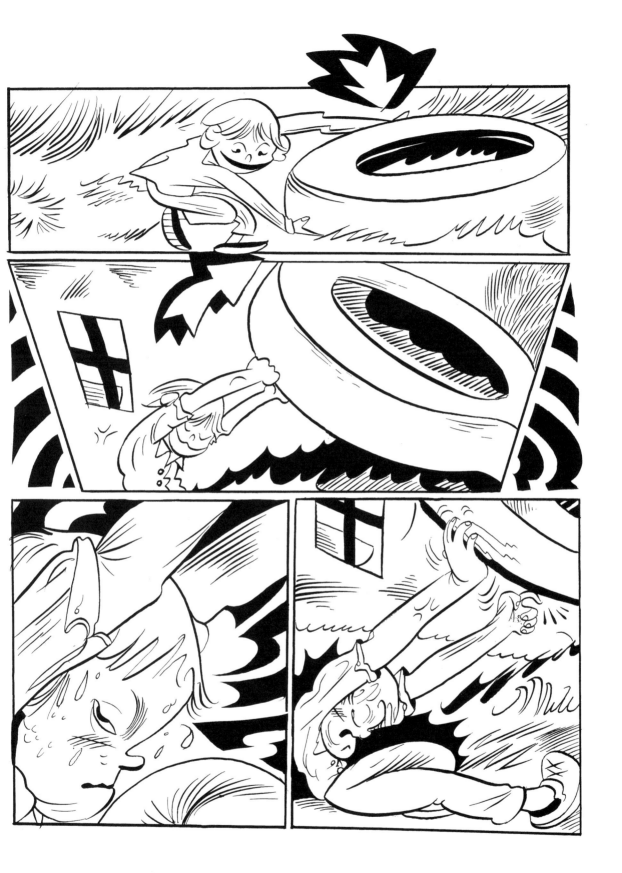

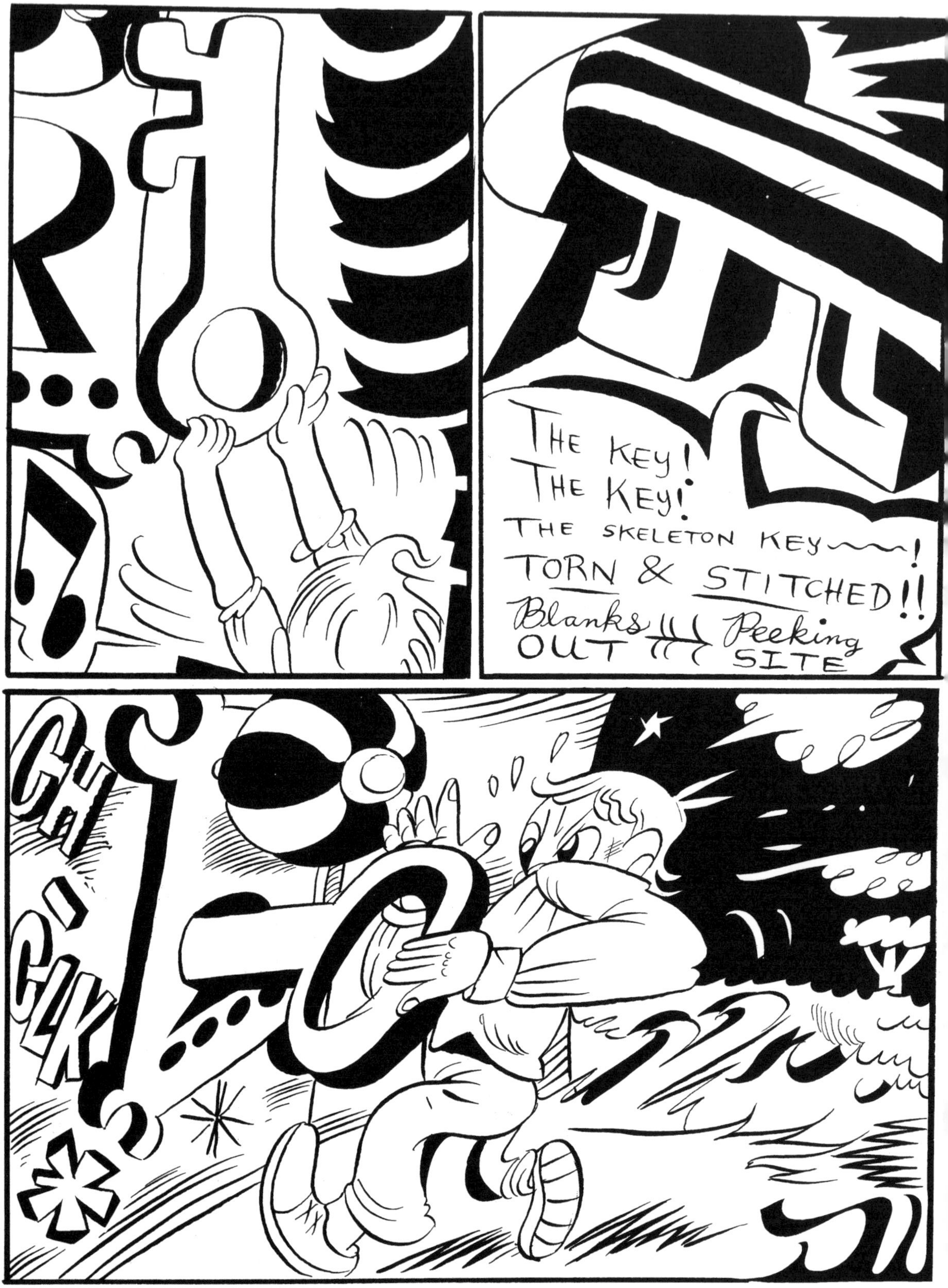
THE KEY!
THE KEY!
THE SKELETON KEY~~~!
TORN & STITCHED!!
Blanks OUT
Peeking SITE
CH-CLIK

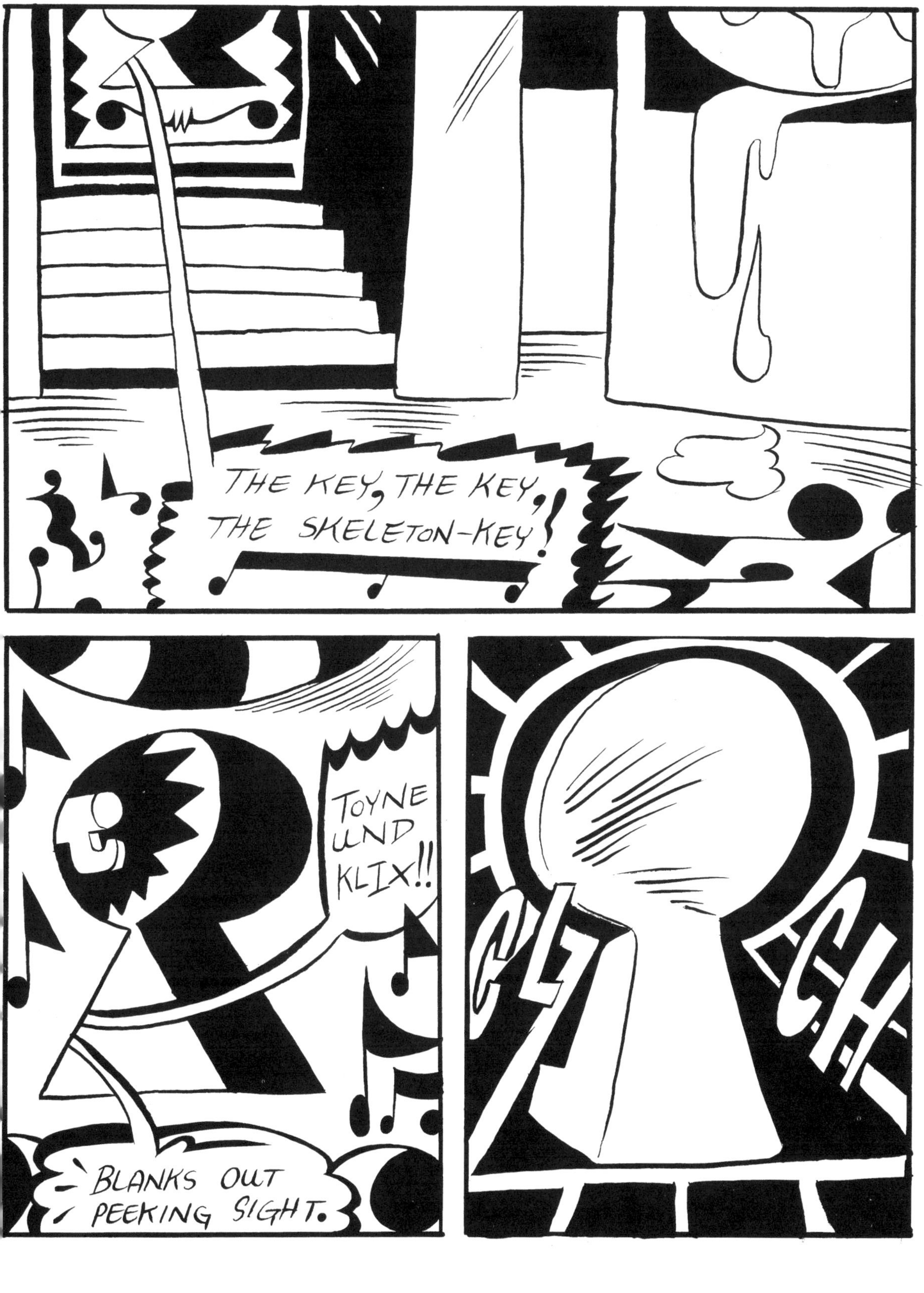
THE KEY, THE KEY, THE SKELETON-KEY!
TOYNE UND KLIX!!
BLANKS OUT PEEKING SIGHT.

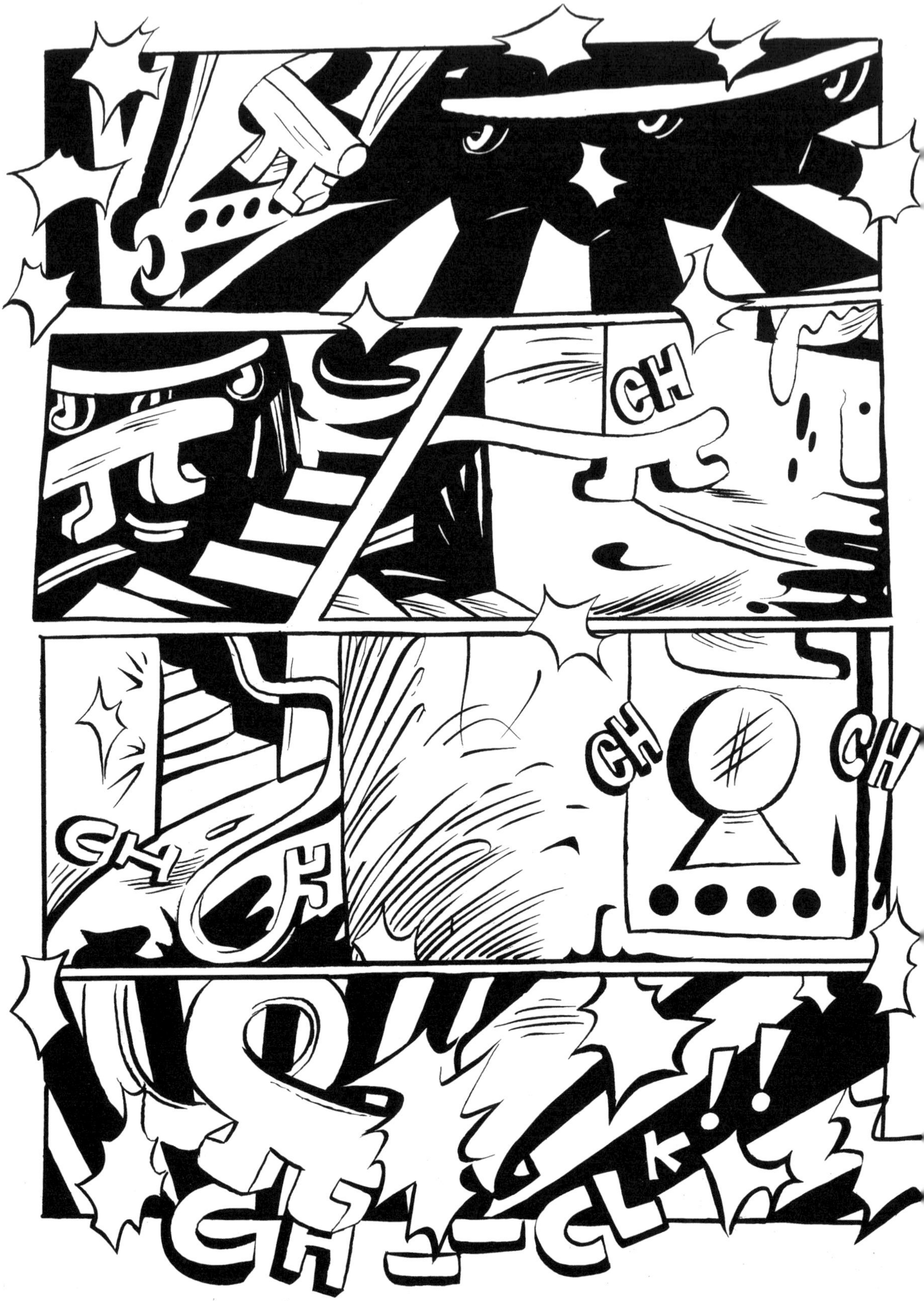
CH
CH
CH
CH
CH
CH
CHK-CLK!!

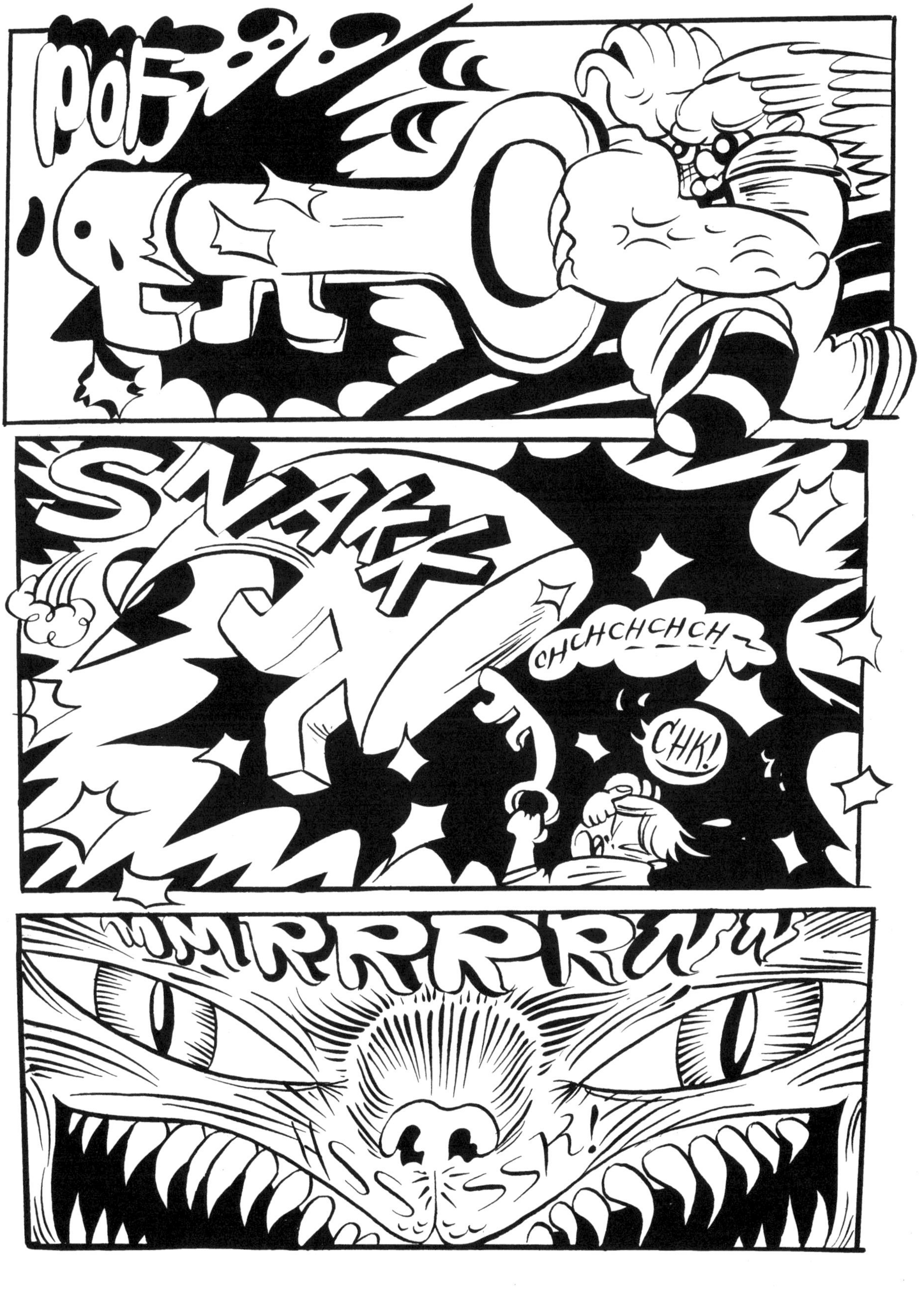
POF
SNAKK
CHCHCHCHCH
CHK!
MRRRRRW
HSSSSH!

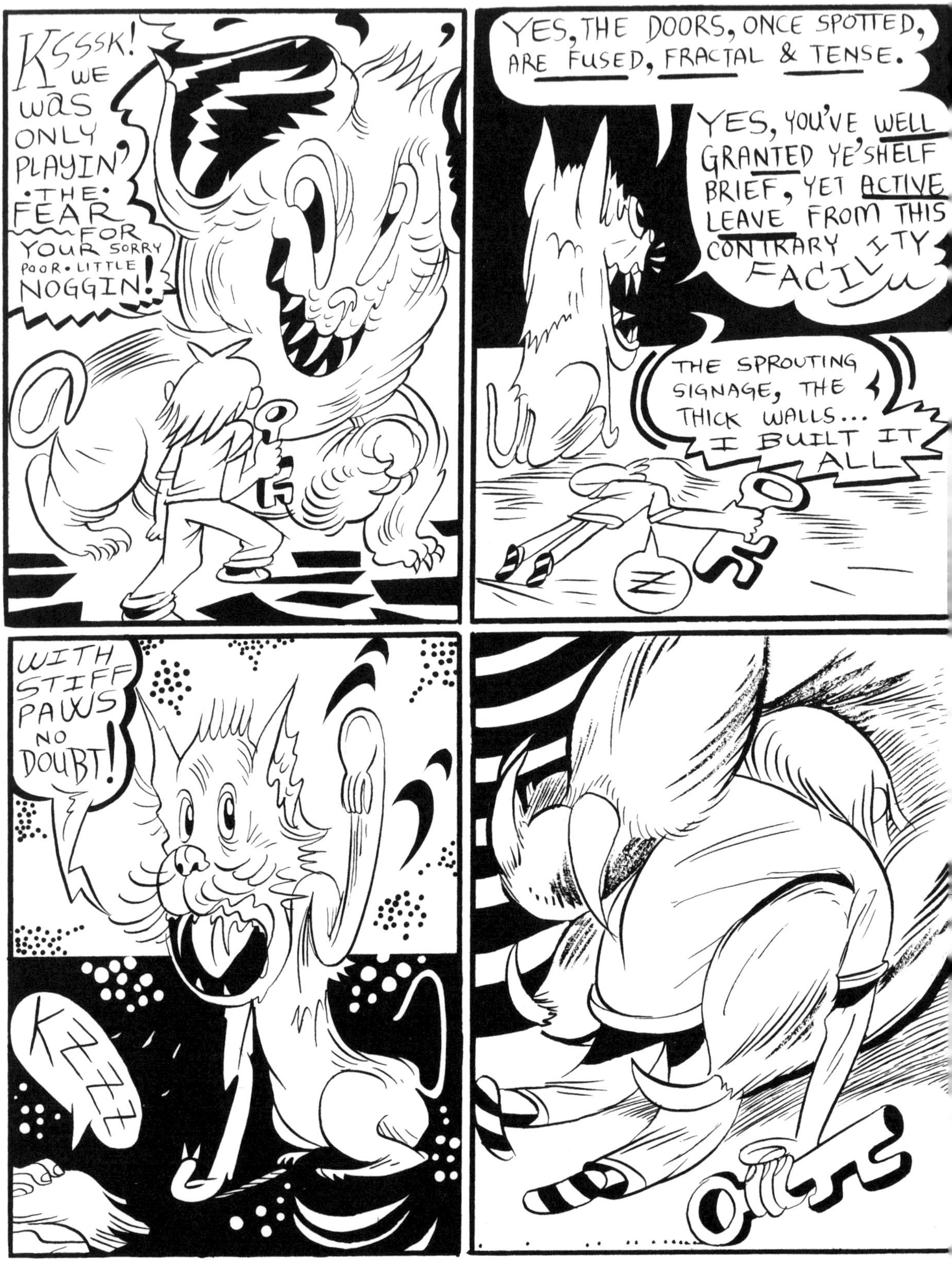
KSSSK! WE WAS ONLY PLAYIN' •THE• FEAR FOR YOUR SORRY POOR•LITTLE NOGGIN!
YES, THE DOORS, ONCE SPOTTED, ARE FUSED, FRACTAL & TENSE.
YES, YOU'VE WELL GRANTED YE'SHELF BRIEF, YET ACTIVE LEAVE FROM THIS CONTRARY FACILITY
THE SPROUTING SIGNAGE, THE THICK WALLS... I BUILT IT ALL
Z
WITH STIFF PAWS NO DOUBT!
KZZZ

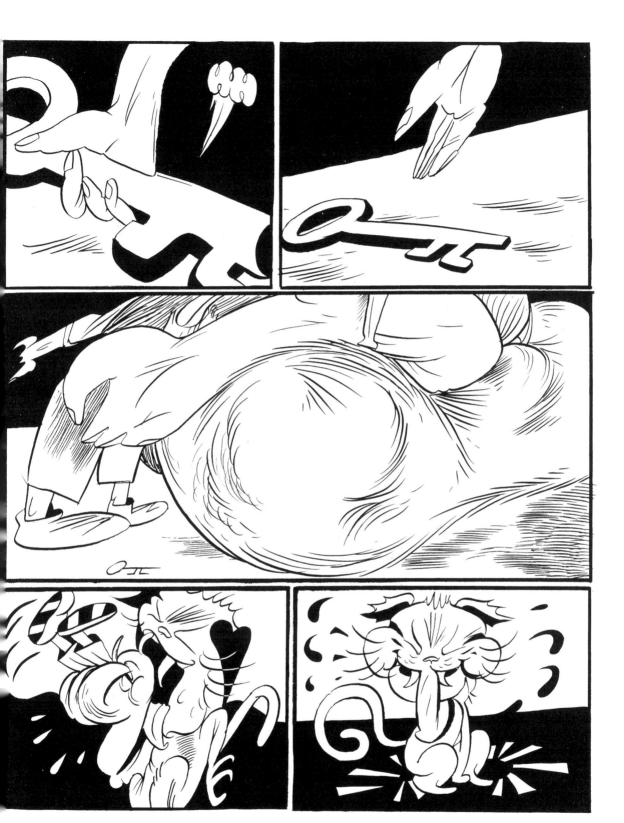

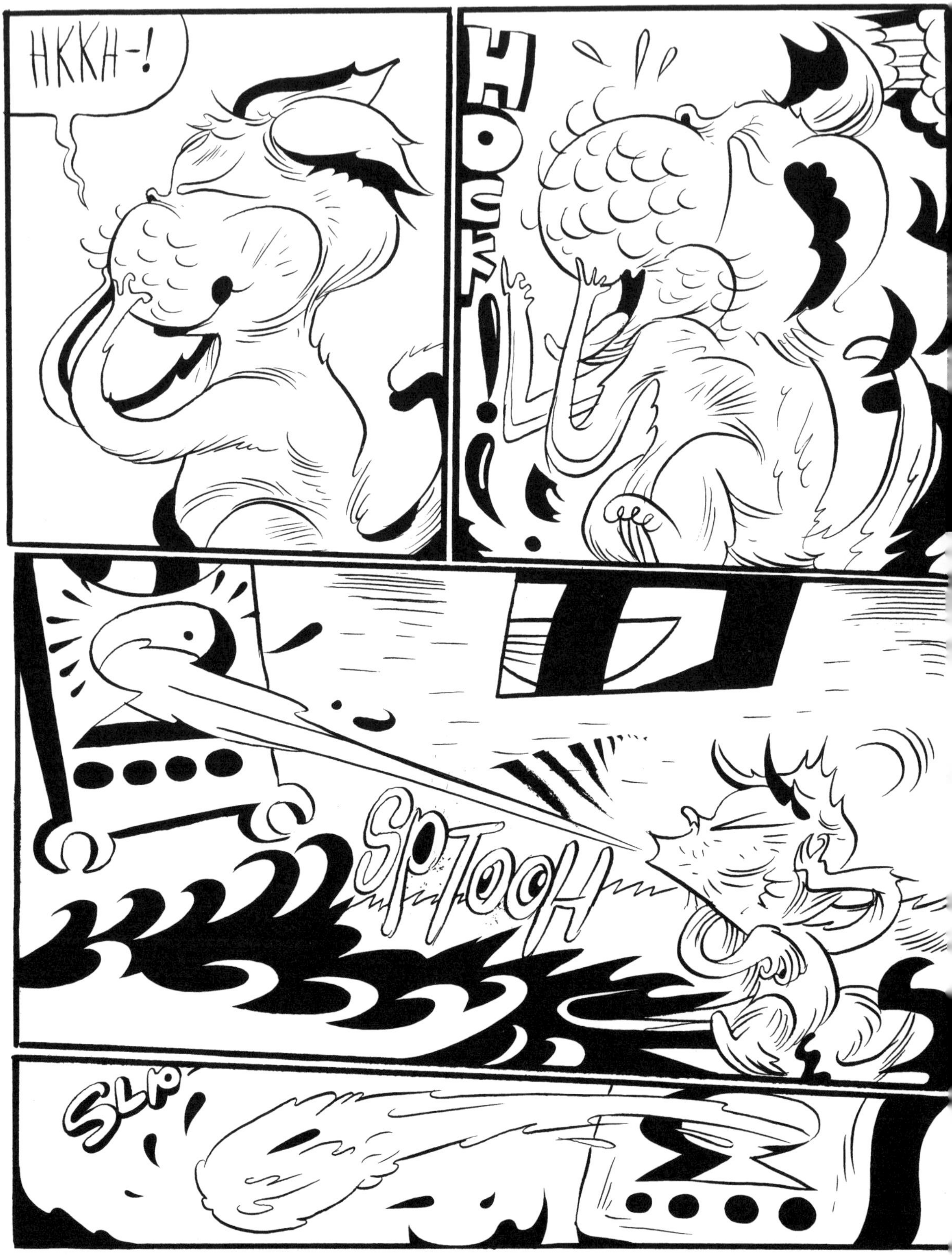
HKKH-!
HOCK!!
SPTOOH
SLP

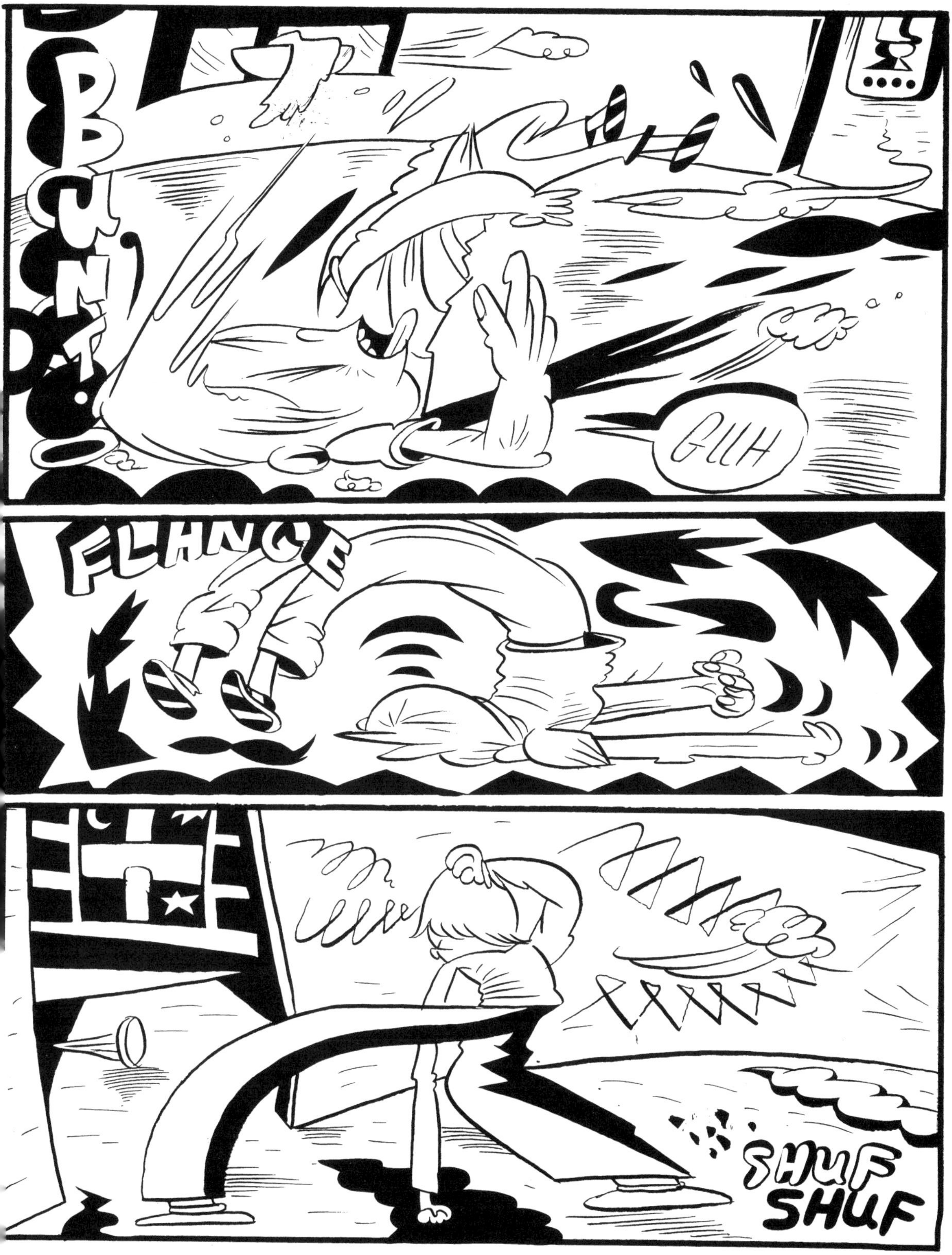
BUNT
GUH
FLHNGE
SHUF
SHUF

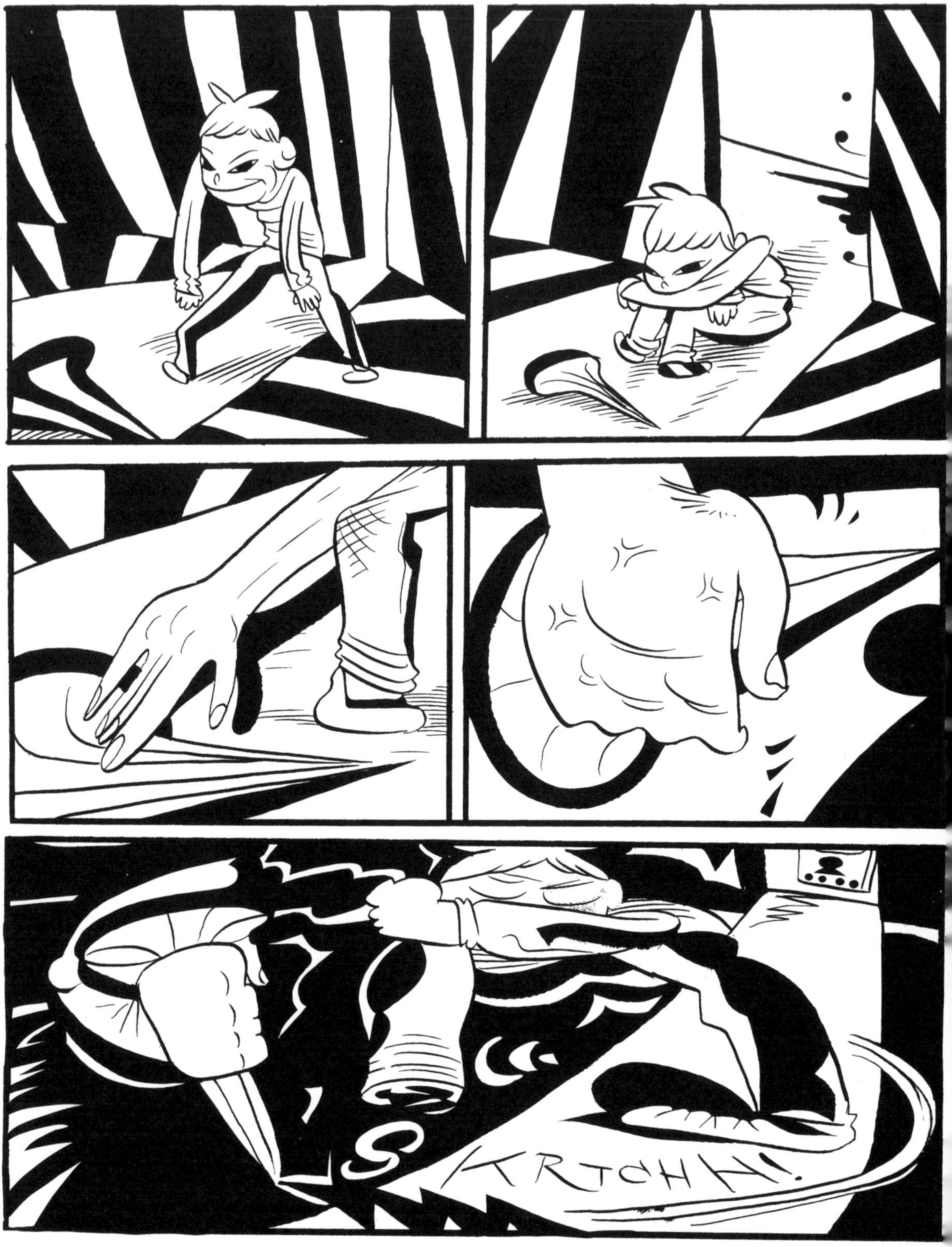
KRTCHH!

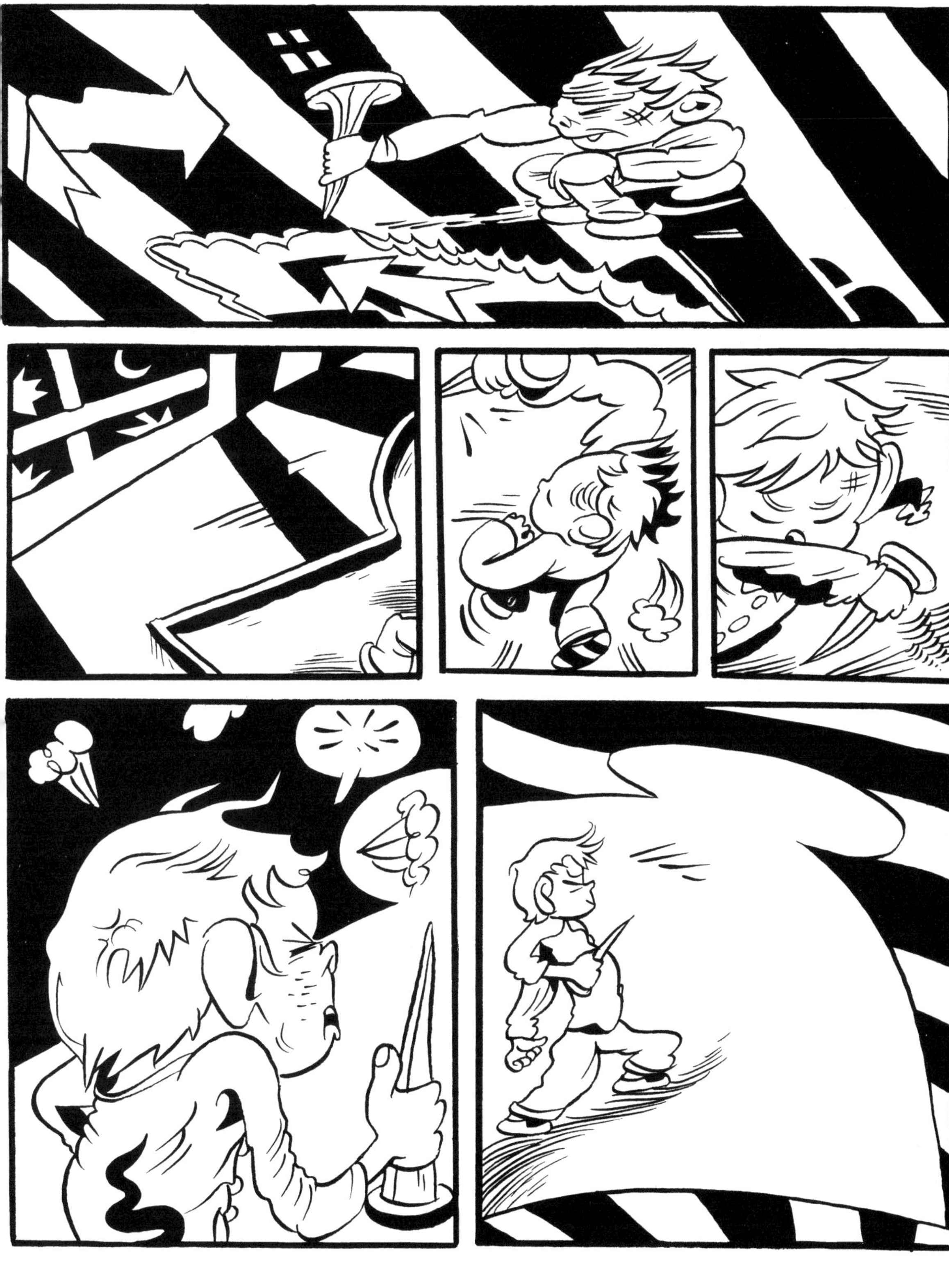

WHIPPE
KLANG
jangle

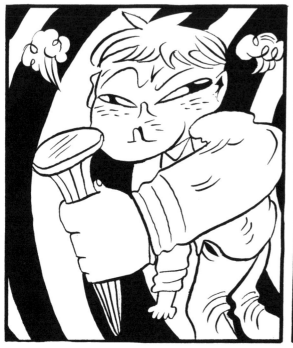

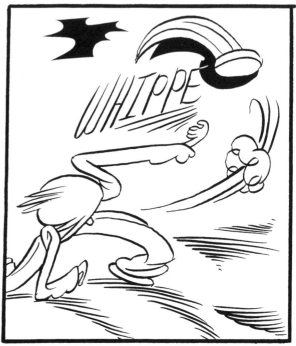

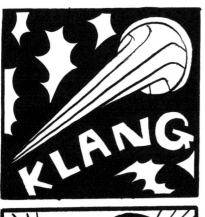

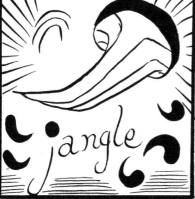

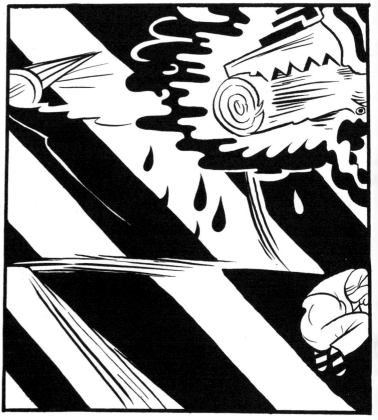

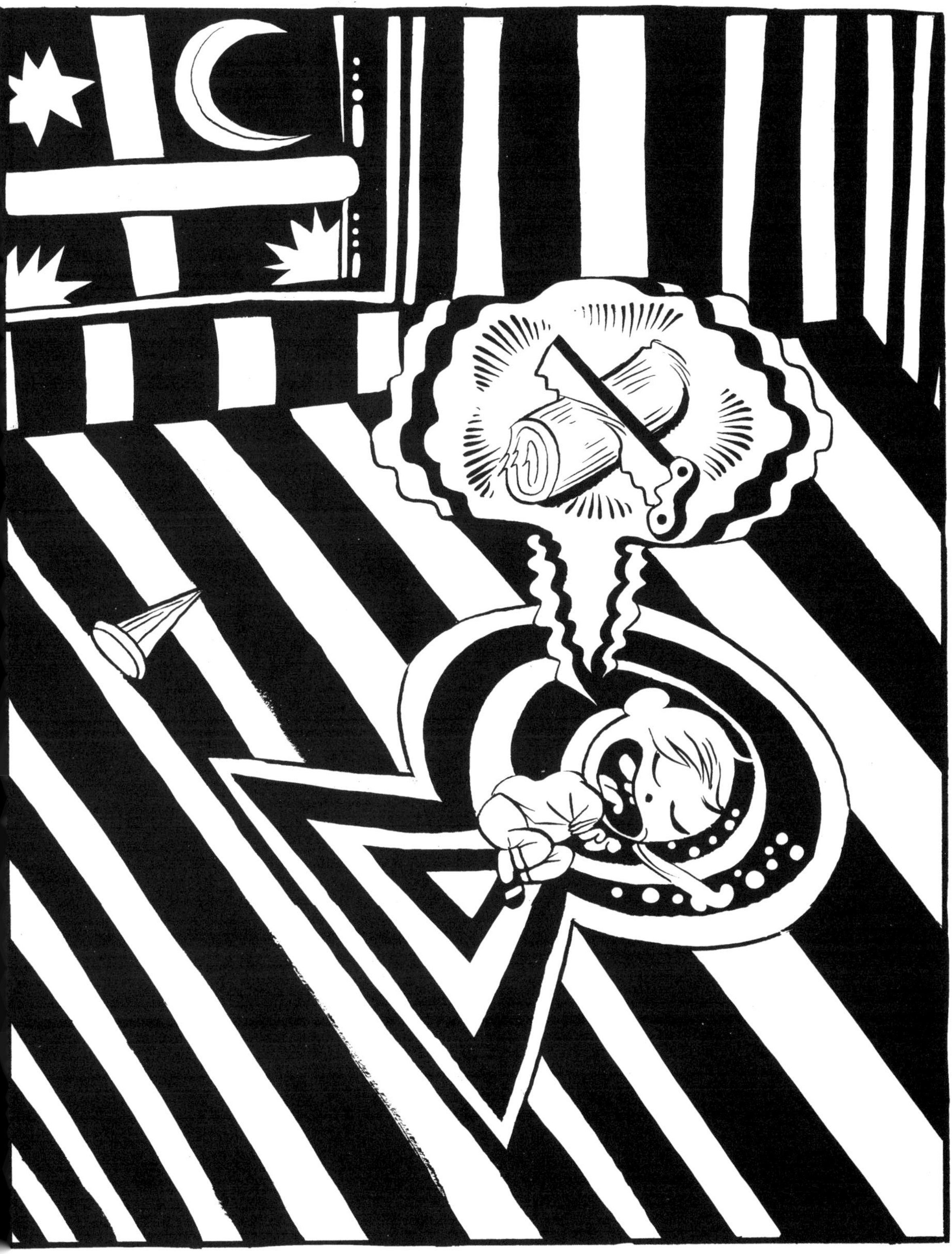

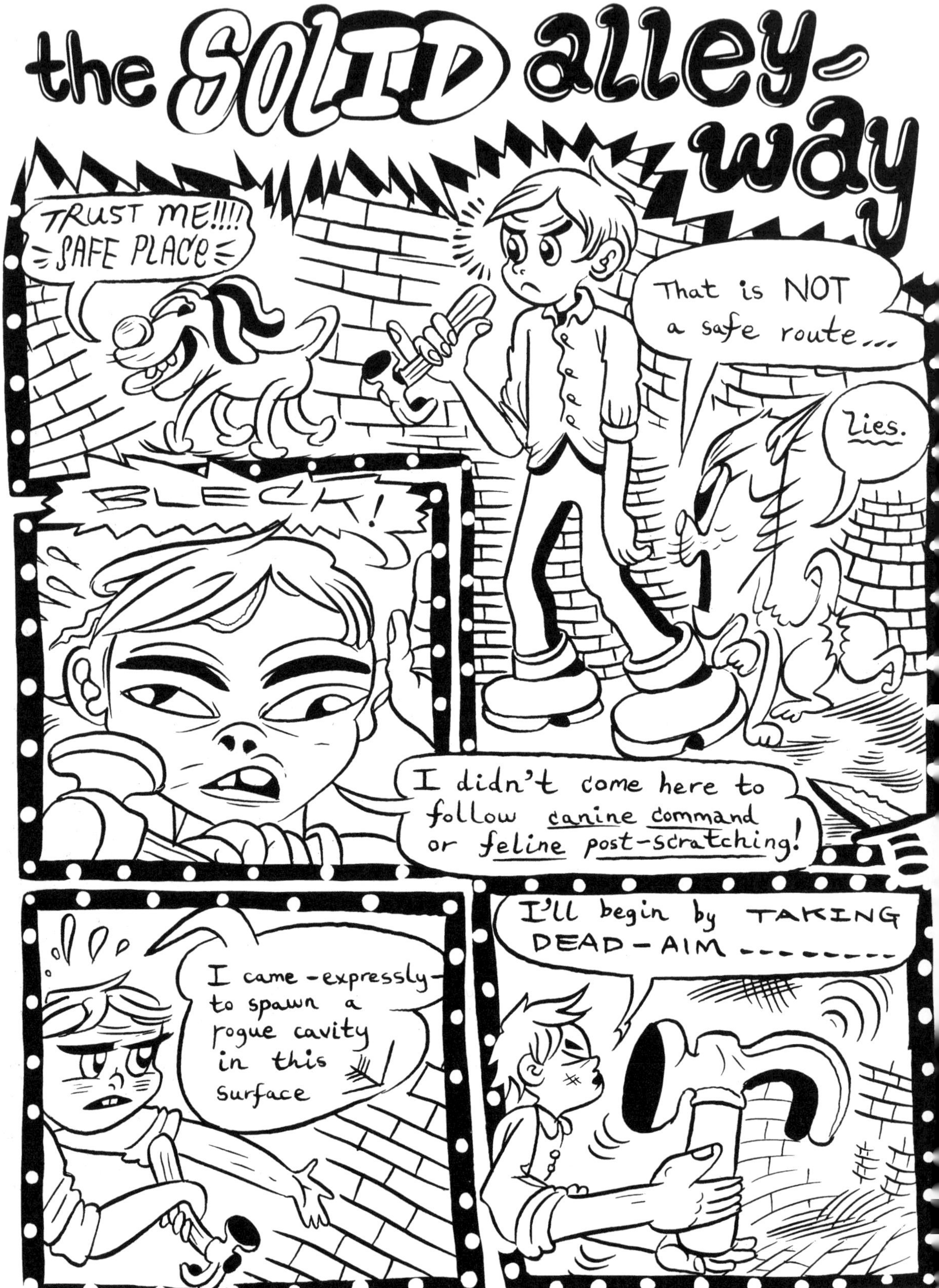
the SOLID alley-way
TRUST ME!!!! SAFE PLACE
That is NOT a safe route...
Lies.
BLECH!
I didn't come here to follow canine command or feline post-scratching!
I came -expressly- to spawn a rogue cavity in this surface
I'll begin by TAKING DEAD-AIM --------

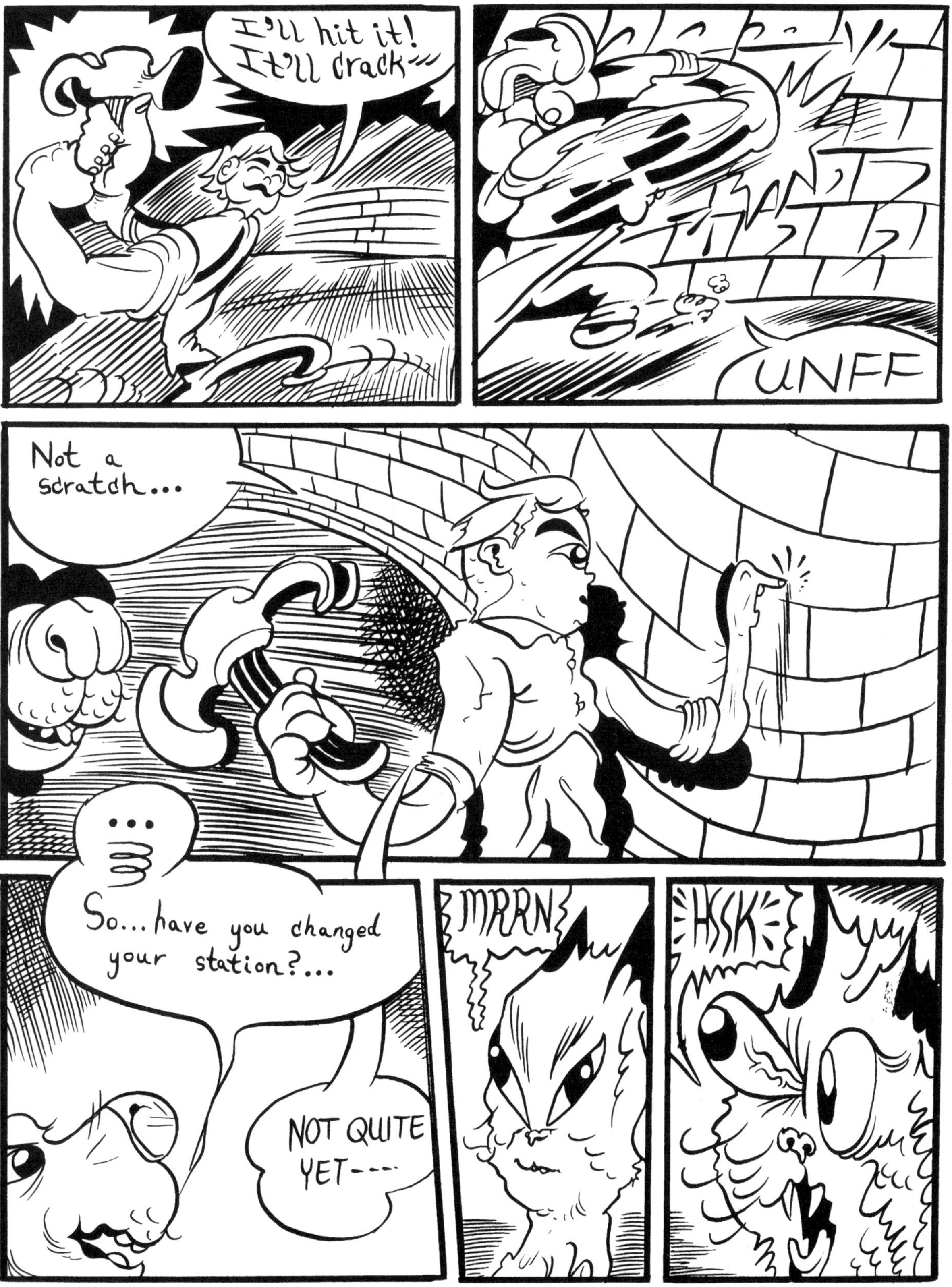
I'll hit it! It'll crack—
UNFF
Not a scratch...
...
So... have you changed your station?...
NOT QUITE YET---
MRRN
HSSK

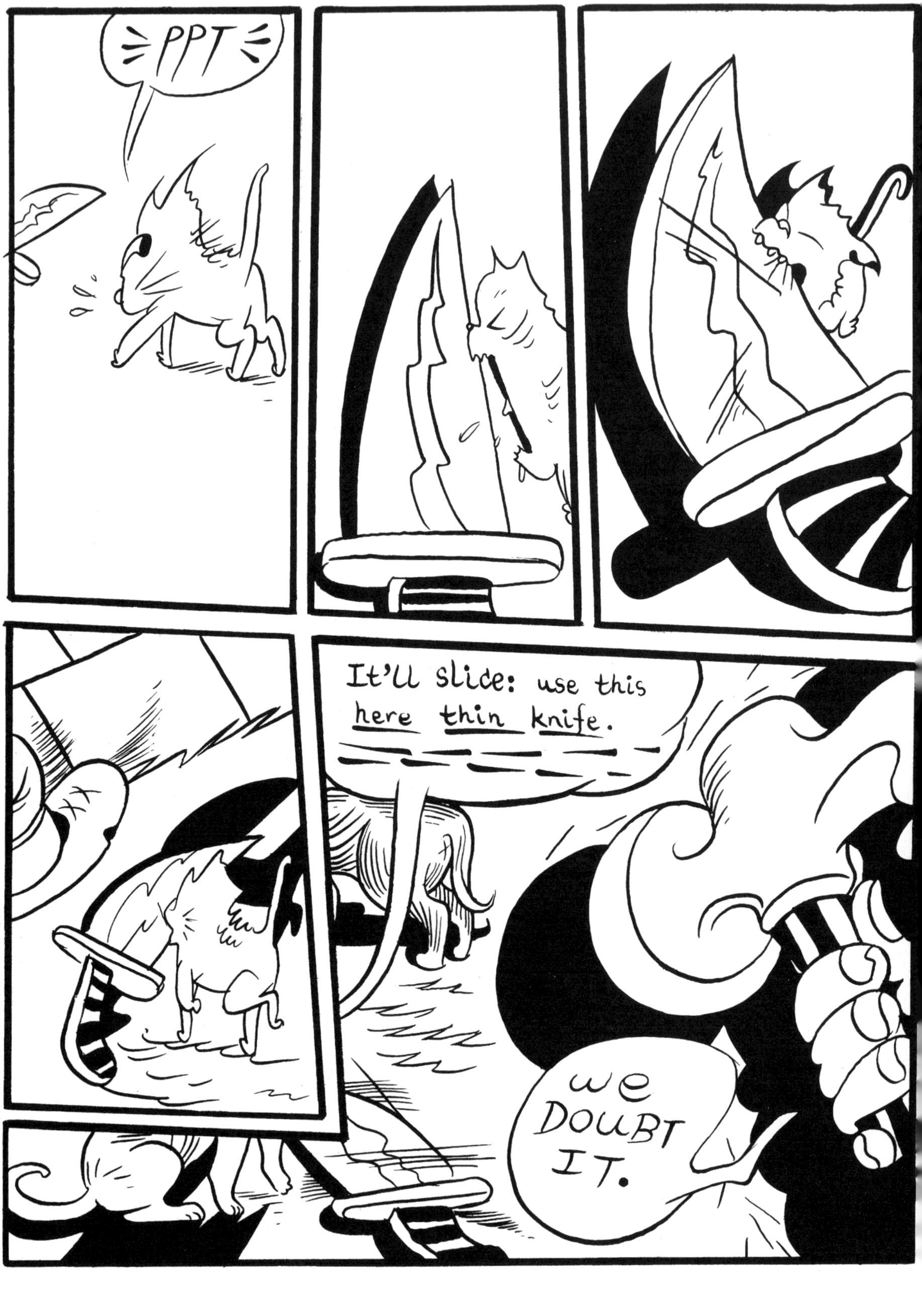
PPT
It'll slice: use this here thin knife.
WE DOUBT IT.

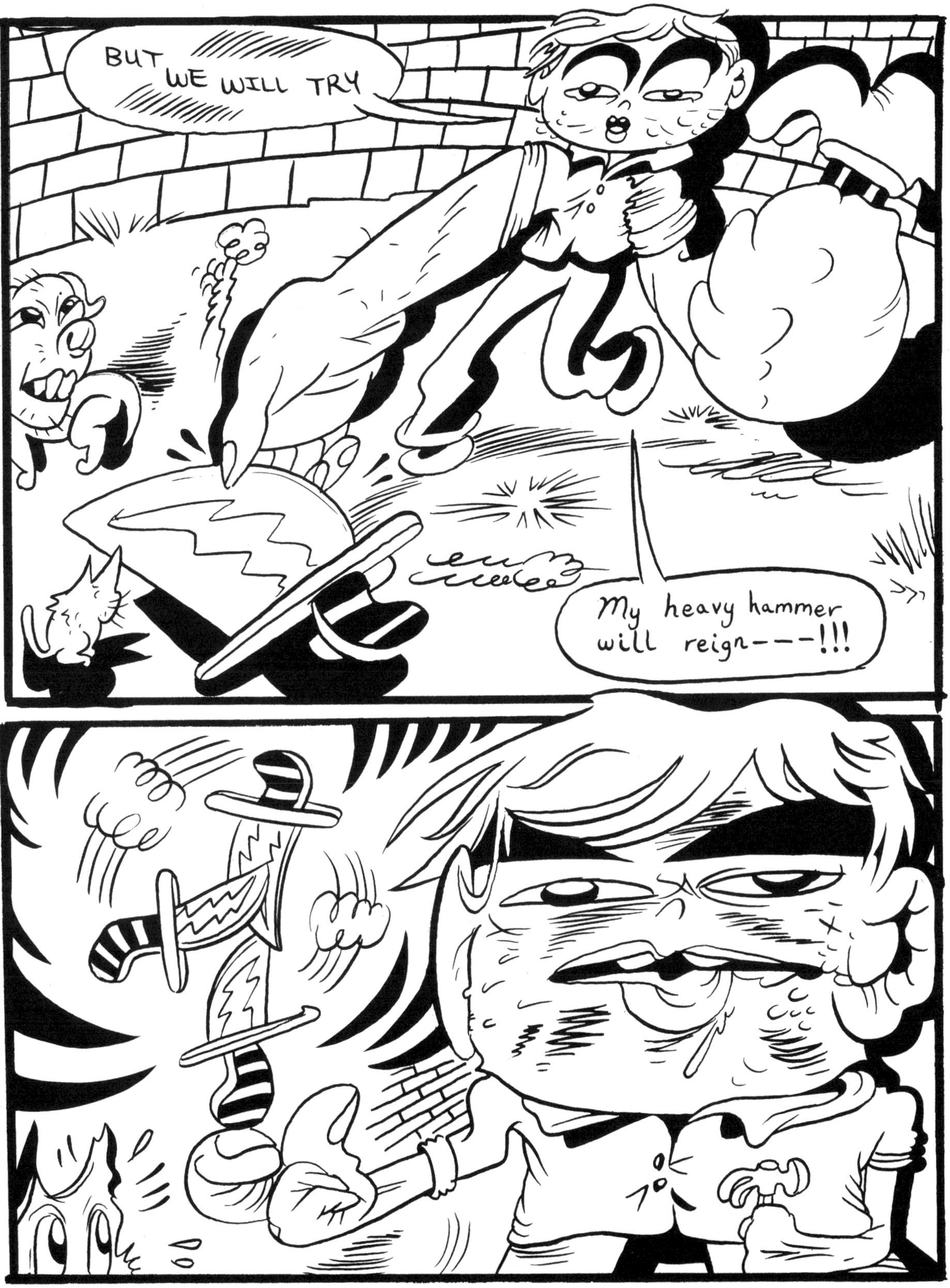
BUT WE WILL TRY
My heavy hammer will reign---!!!

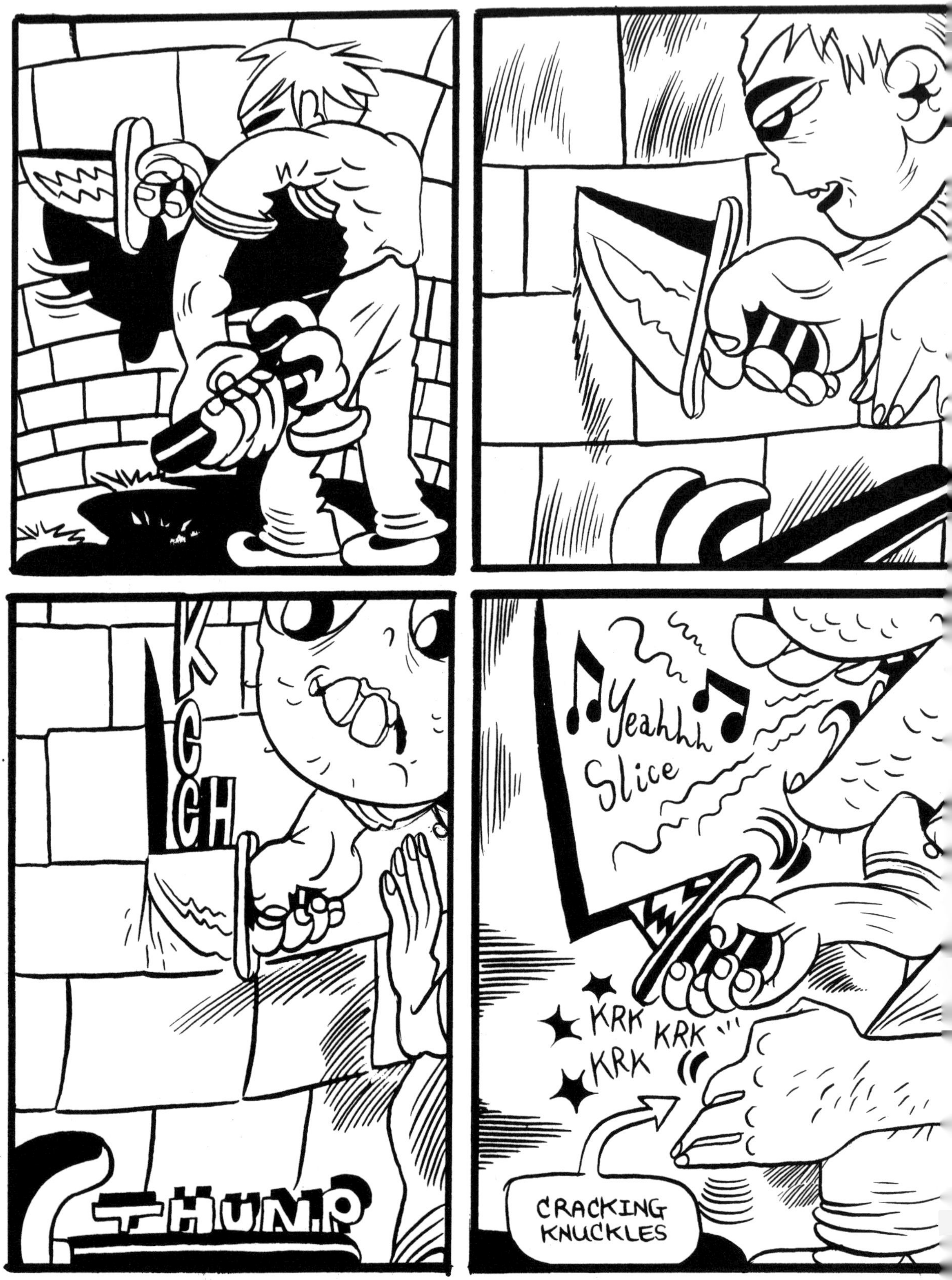
K
C
CH
THUMP
Yeahhh
Slice
KRK KRK
KRK
CRACKING
KNUCKLES

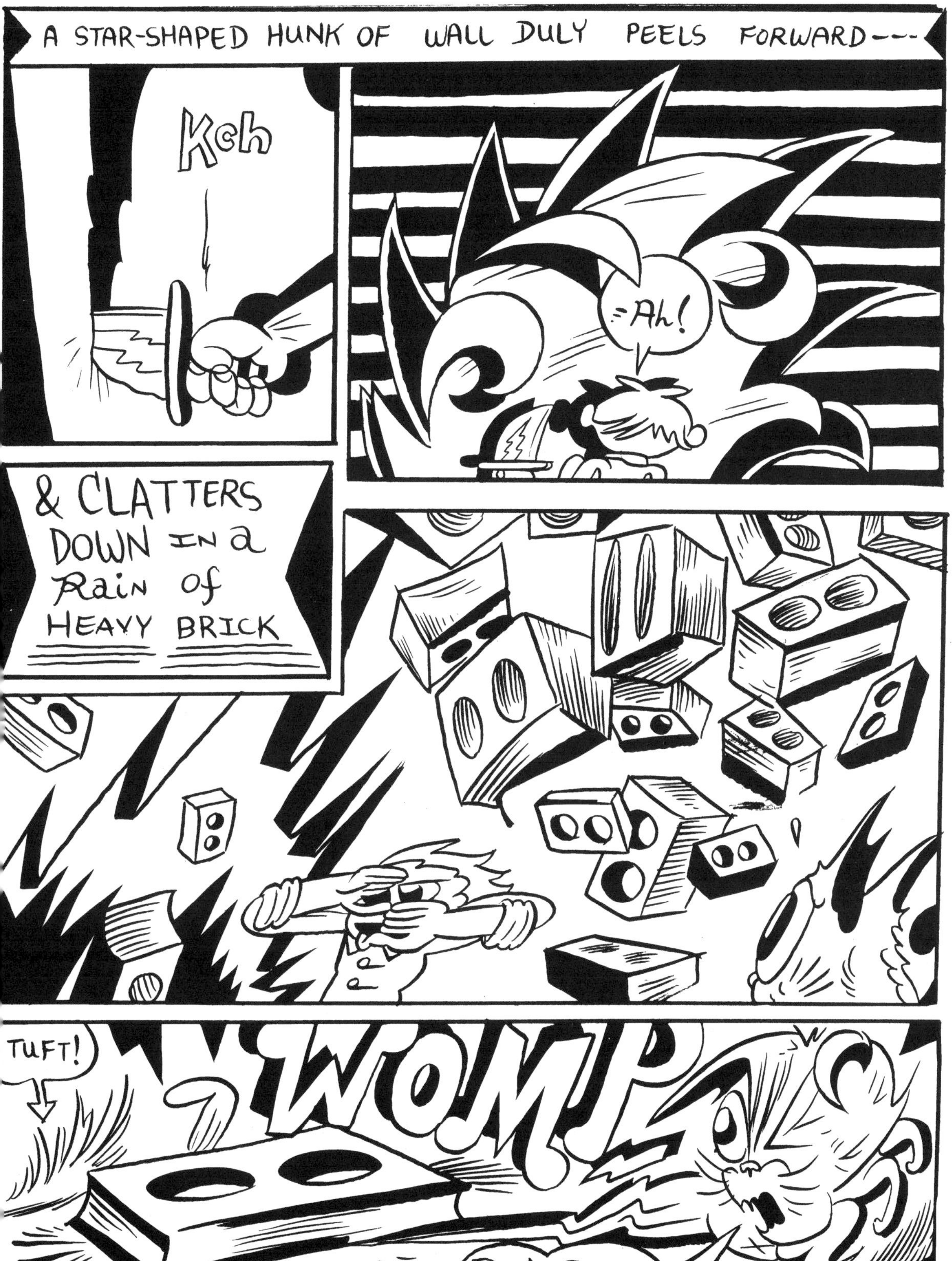
A STAR-SHAPED HUNK OF WALL DULY PEELS FORWARD---
Kch
Ah!
& CLATTERS DOWN IN a Rain of HEAVY BRICK
TUFT!
WOMP
RAOW

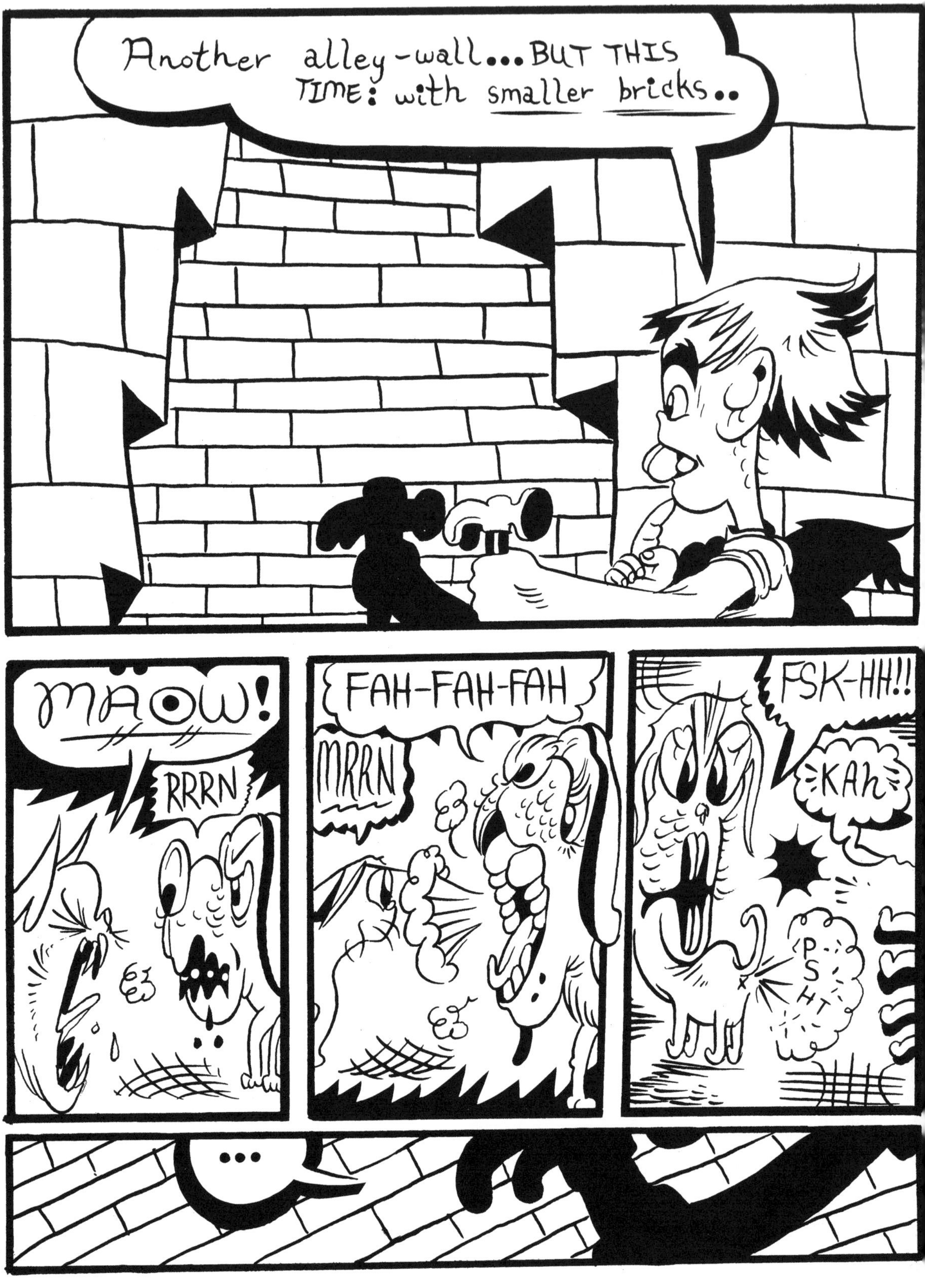
Another alley-wall... BUT THIS TIME: with smaller bricks..
MAOW!
RRRN
FAH-FAH-FAH
MRRN
FSK-HH!!
KAh
PSHT
...

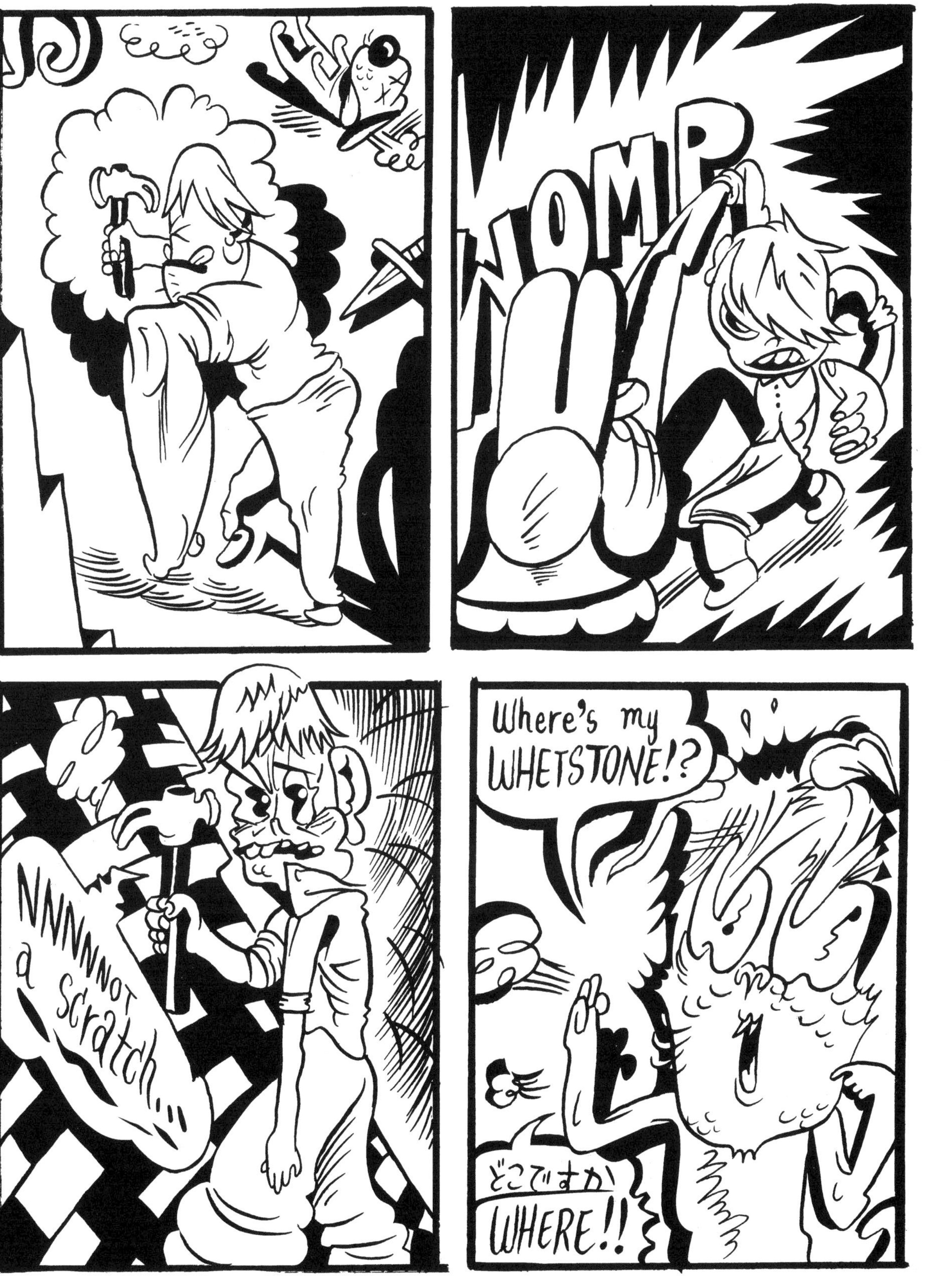
WOMP
NNNNNNOT a scratch...!
Where's my WHETSTONE!?
どこですか
WHERE!!

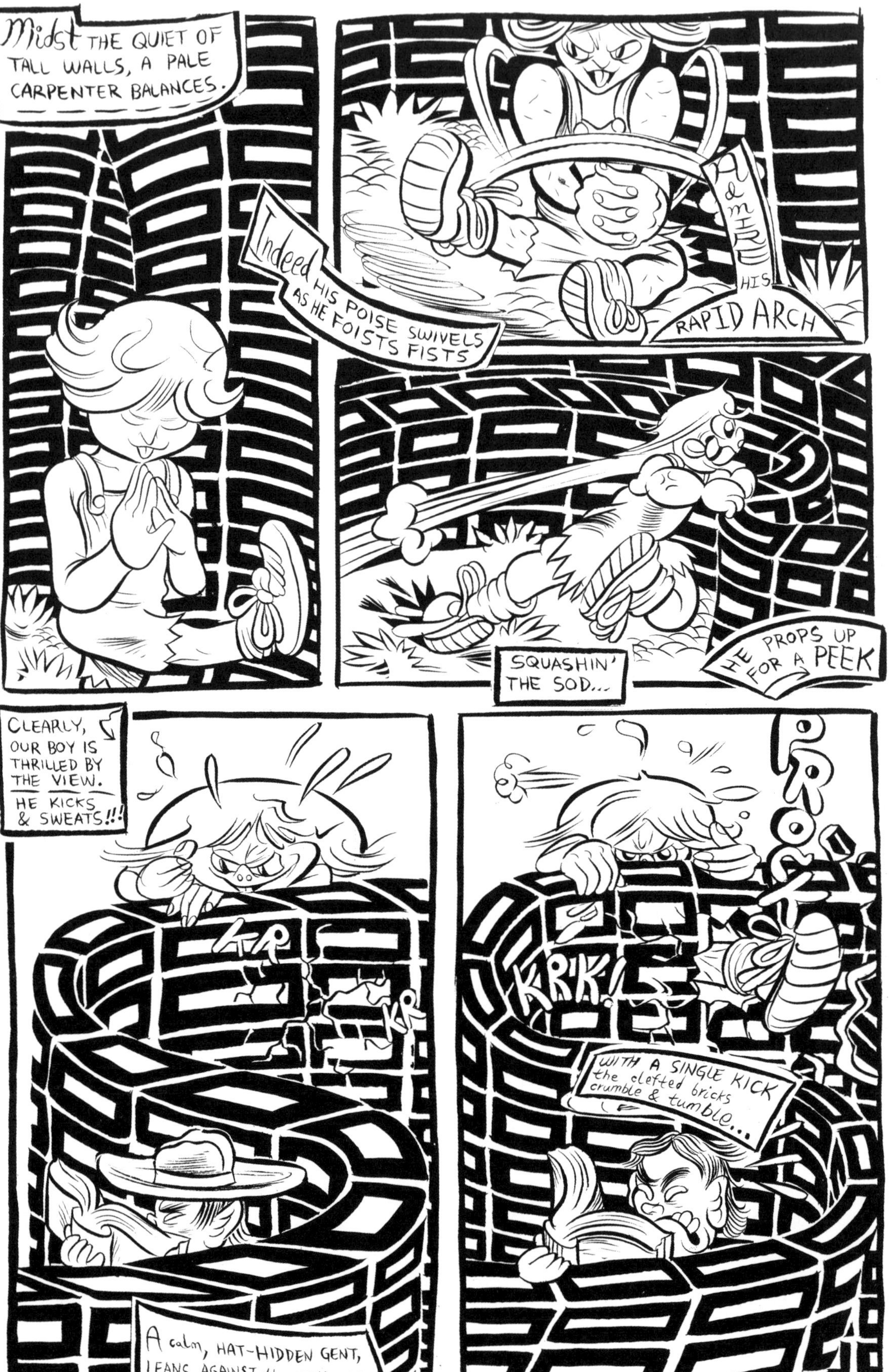
Midst THE QUIET OF TALL WALLS, A PALE CARPENTER BALANCES.
Indeed HIS POISE SWIVELS AS HE FOISTS FISTS
ADMIRE HIS RAPID ARCH
SQUASHIN' THE SOD...
HE PROPS UP FOR A PEEK
CLEARLY, OUR BOY IS THRILLED BY THE VIEW.
HE KICKS & SWEATS!!!
KR
KR
A calm, HAT-HIDDEN GENT, LEANS AGAINST the curve
PROCK
KRK!
WITH A SINGLE KICK the clefted bricks crumble & tumble...

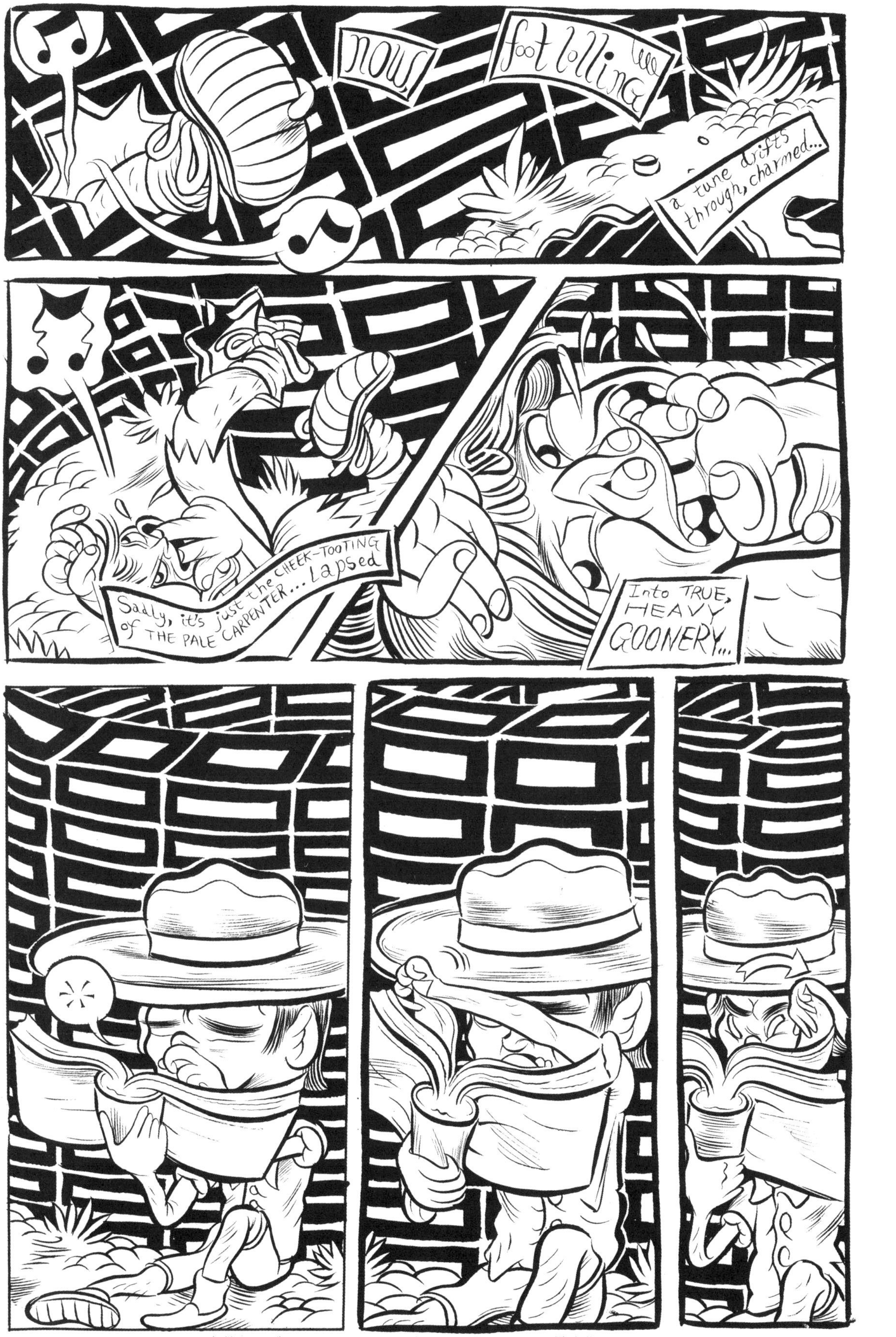
NOW!
foot lolling
a tune drifts through, charmed...
Sadly, it's just the CHEEK-TOOTING of THE PALE CARPENTER... Lapsed
Into TRUE, HEAVY GOONERY...

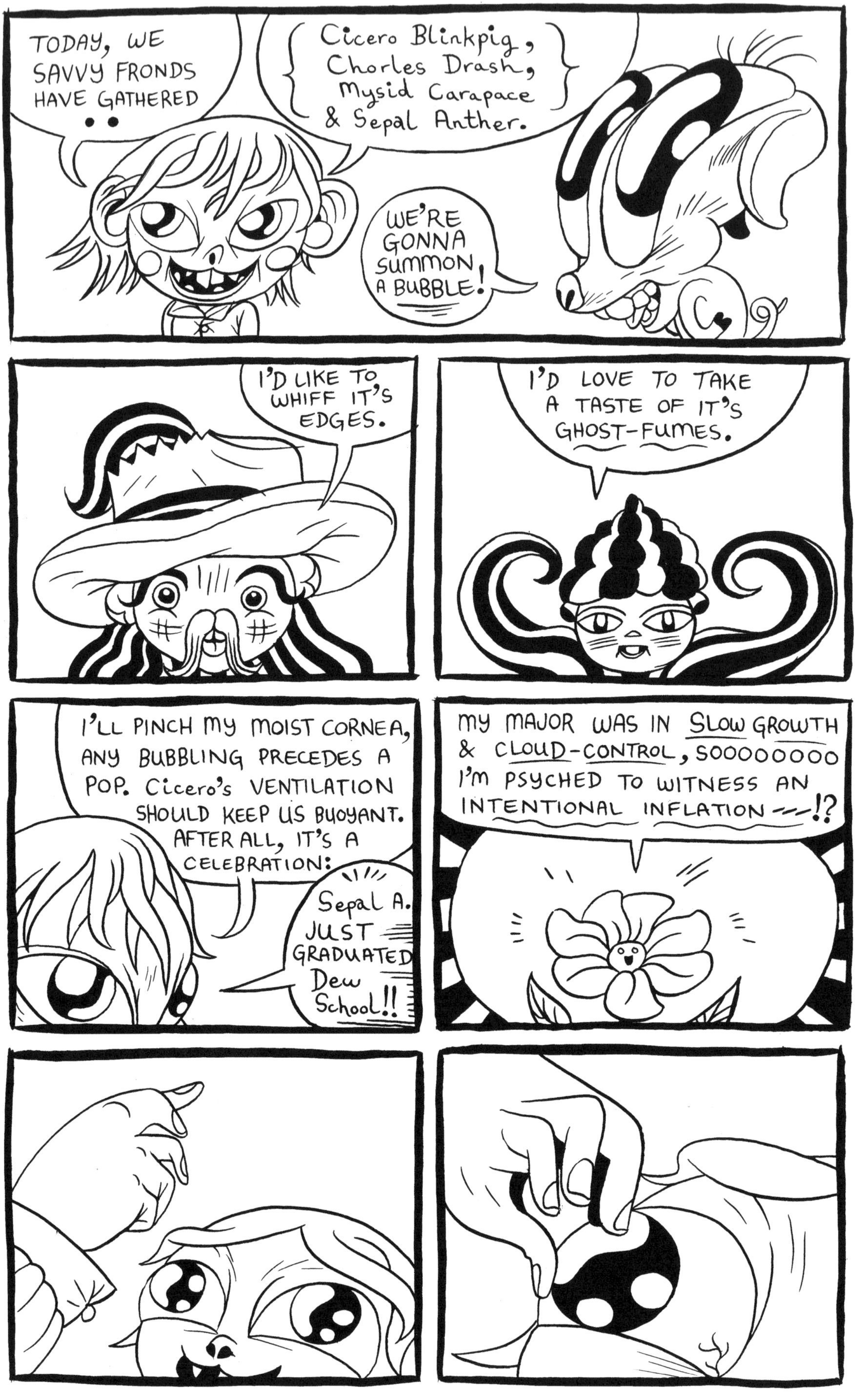
TODAY, WE SAVVY FRONDS HAVE GATHERED ..
{ Cicero Blinkpig, Chorles Drash, Mysid Carapace & Sepal Anther. }
WE'RE GONNA SUMMON A BUBBLE!
I'D LIKE TO WHIFF IT'S EDGES.
I'D LOVE TO TAKE A TASTE OF IT'S GHOST-FUMES.
I'LL PINCH MY MOIST CORNEA, ANY BUBBLING PRECEDES A POP. Cicero's VENTILATION SHOULD KEEP US BUOYANT. AFTER ALL, IT'S A CELEBRATION:
Sepal A. JUST GRADUATED Dew School!!
MY MAJOR WAS IN SLOW GROWTH & CLOUD-CONTROL, SOOOOOOOO I'M PSYCHED TO WITNESS AN INTENTIONAL INFLATION---!?

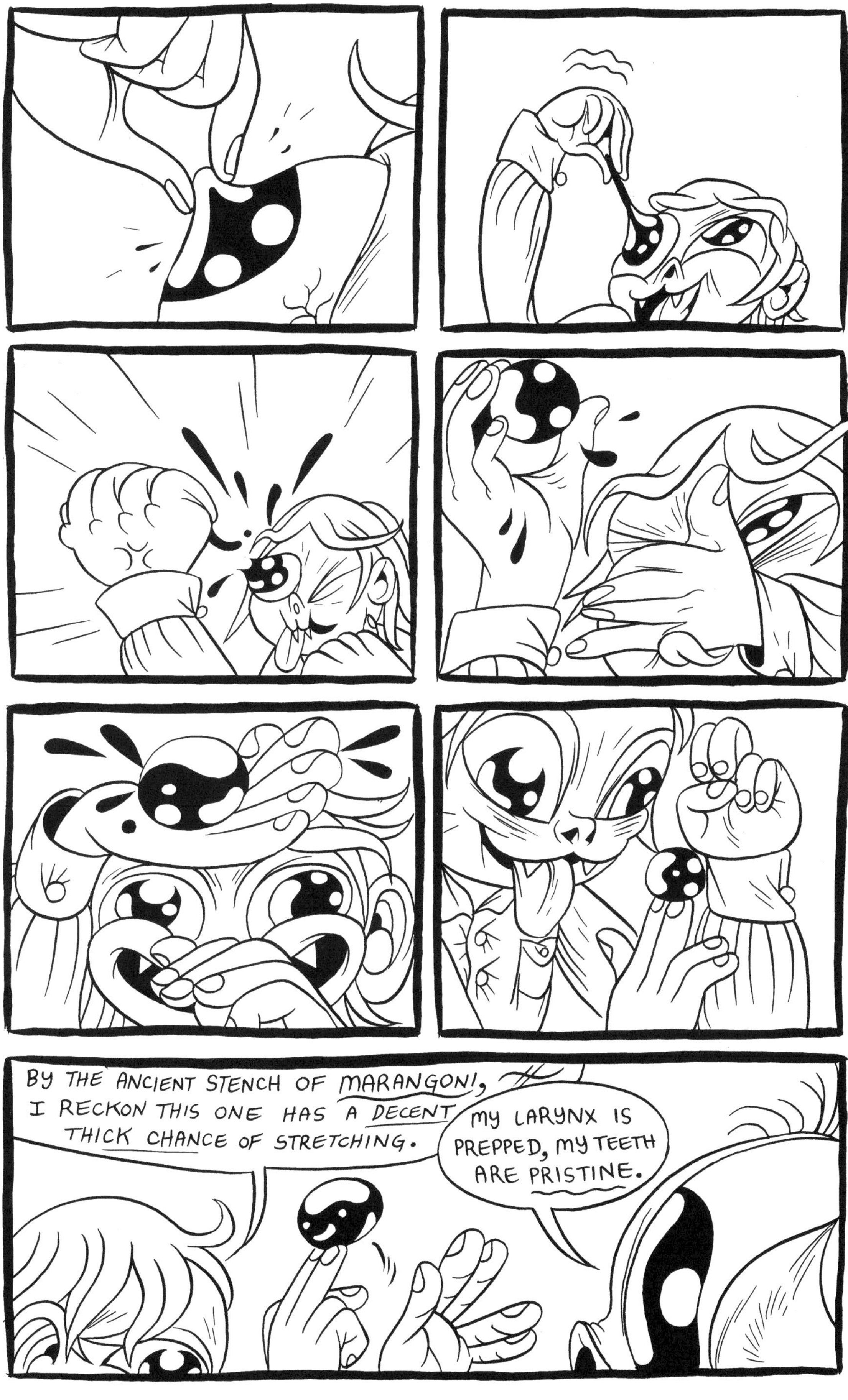
BY THE ANCIENT STENCH OF MARANGONI, I RECKON THIS ONE HAS A DECENT THICK CHANCE OF STRETCHING.
MY LARYNX IS PREPPED, MY TEETH ARE PRISTINE.

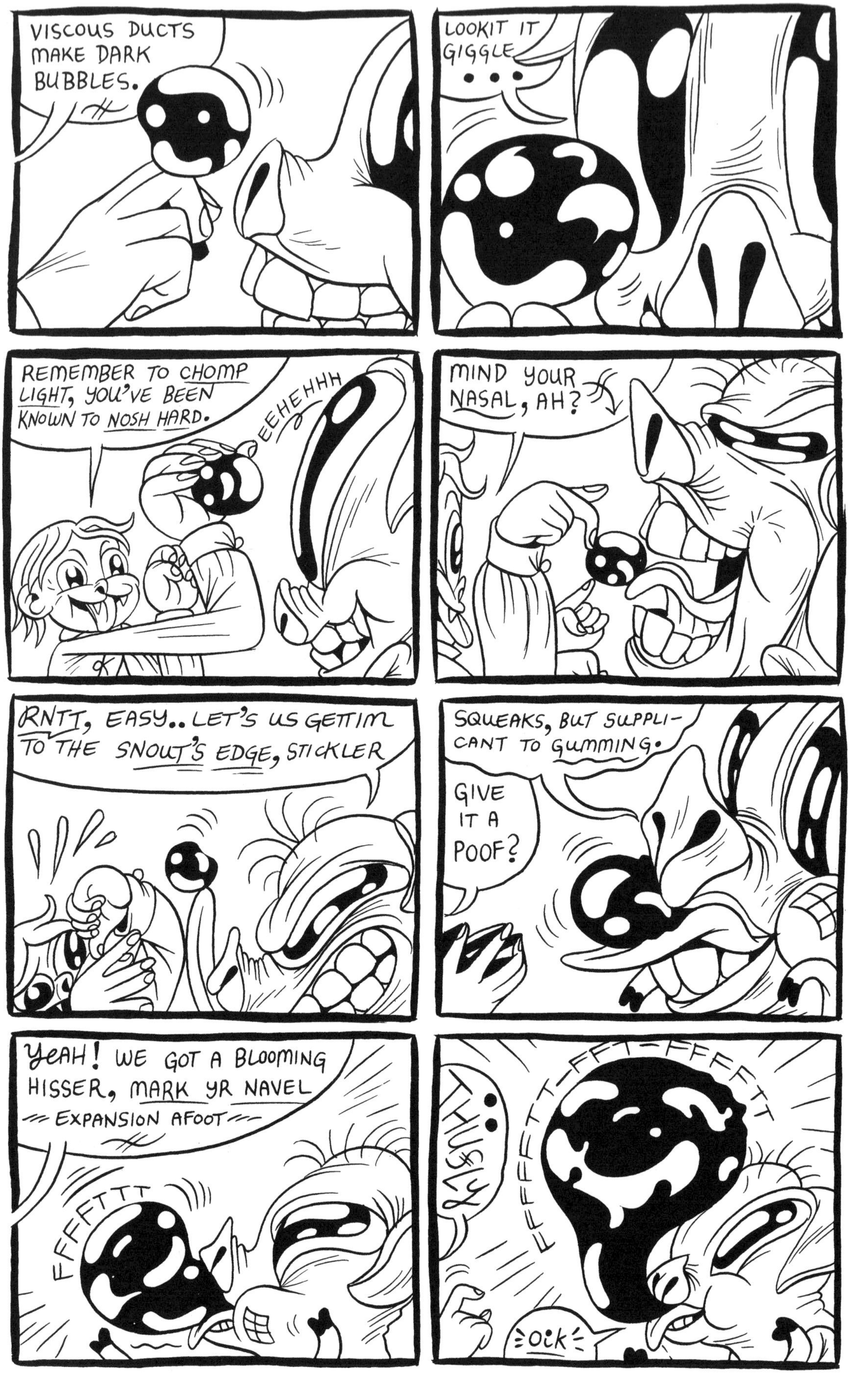
VISCOUS DUCTS MAKE DARK BUBBLES.
LOOKIT IT GIGGLE...
REMEMBER TO CHOMP LIGHT, YOU'VE BEEN KNOWN TO NOSH HARD.
EEHEHHH
MIND YOUR NASAL, AH?
RNTT, EASY.. LET'S US GETTIM TO THE SNOUT'S EDGE, STICKLER
SQUEAKS, BUT SUPPLI-CANT TO GUMMING.
GIVE IT A POOF?
YeAH! WE GOT A BLOOMING HISSER, MARK YR NAVEL
EXPANSION AFOOT
FFFFTTT
RASHUH!..
FFFFFTT-FFT-FFFFTT
OiK

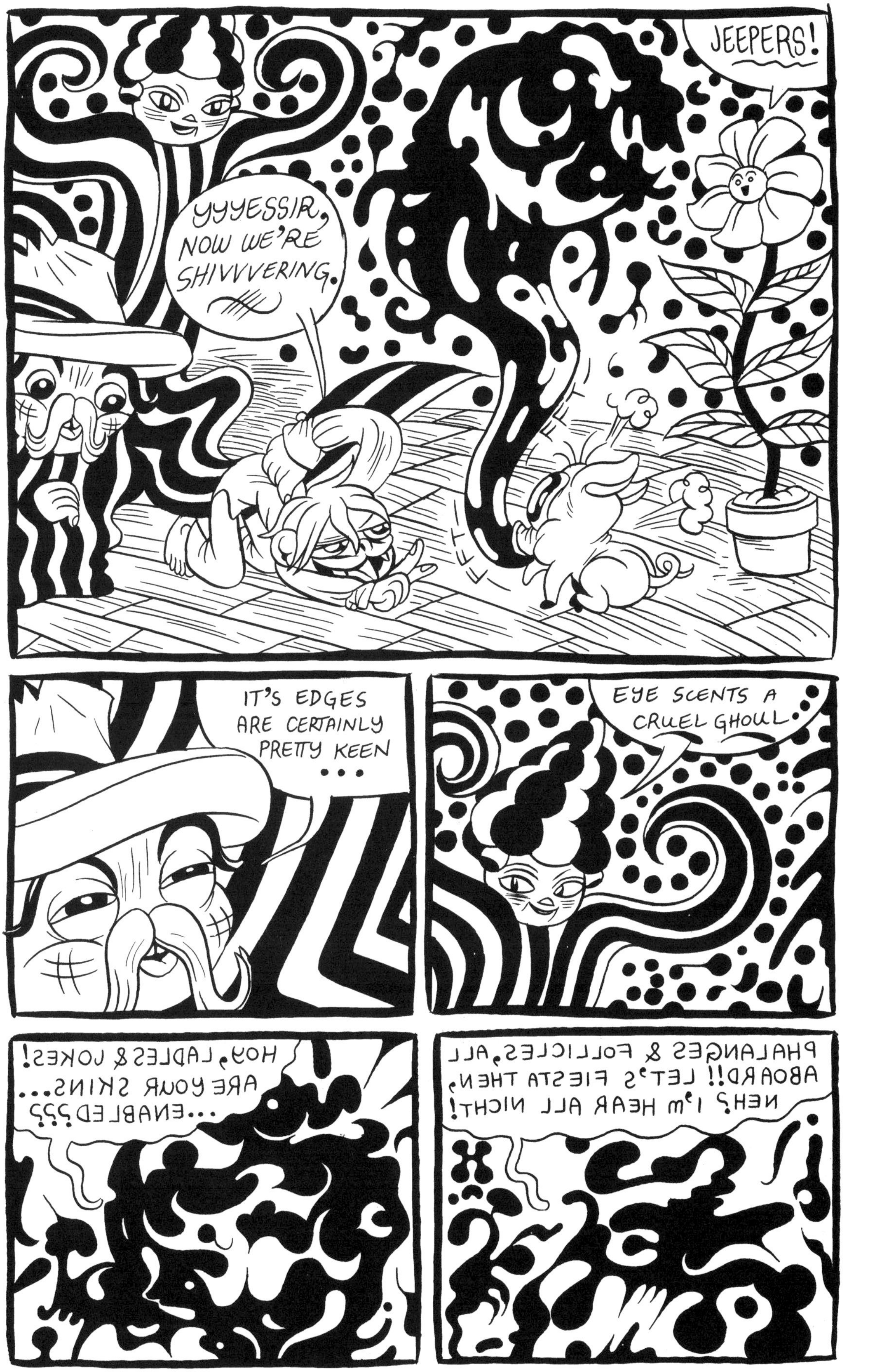

JEEPERS!
YYYESSIR, NOW WE'RE SHIVVVERING.
IT'S EDGES ARE CERTAINLY PRETTY KEEN ...
EYE SCENTS A CRUEL GHOUL.
HOY, LADLES & JOKES! ARE YOUR SKINS... ...ENABLED???
PHALANGES & FOLLICLES, ALL ABOARD!! LET'S FIESTA THEN, NEH? I'M HEAR ALL NIGHT!

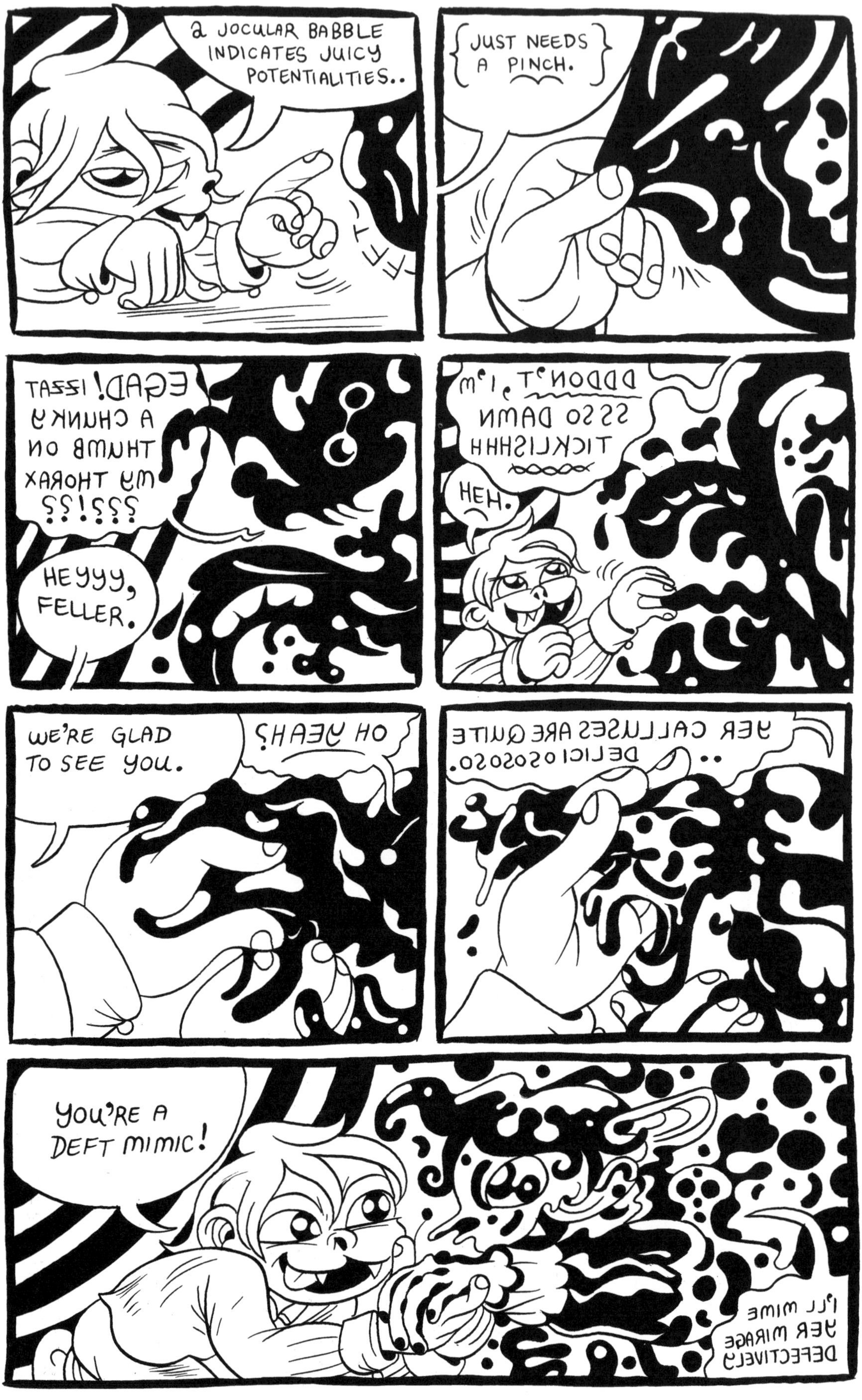
a JOCULAR BABBLE INDICATES JUICY POTENTIALITIES..
JUST NEEDS A PINCH.
EGAD! IZZAT A CHUNKY THUMB ON MY THORAX ???!???
HEYYY, FELLER.
DDDON'T, I'M SSSO DAMN TICKLISHHH
HEH.
WE'RE GLAD TO SEE YOU.
OH YEAH?
YER CALLUSES ARE QUITE ..DELICIOSOSOSO.
YOU'RE A DEFT MIMIC!
I'LL MIME YER MIRAGE DEFFECTIVELY

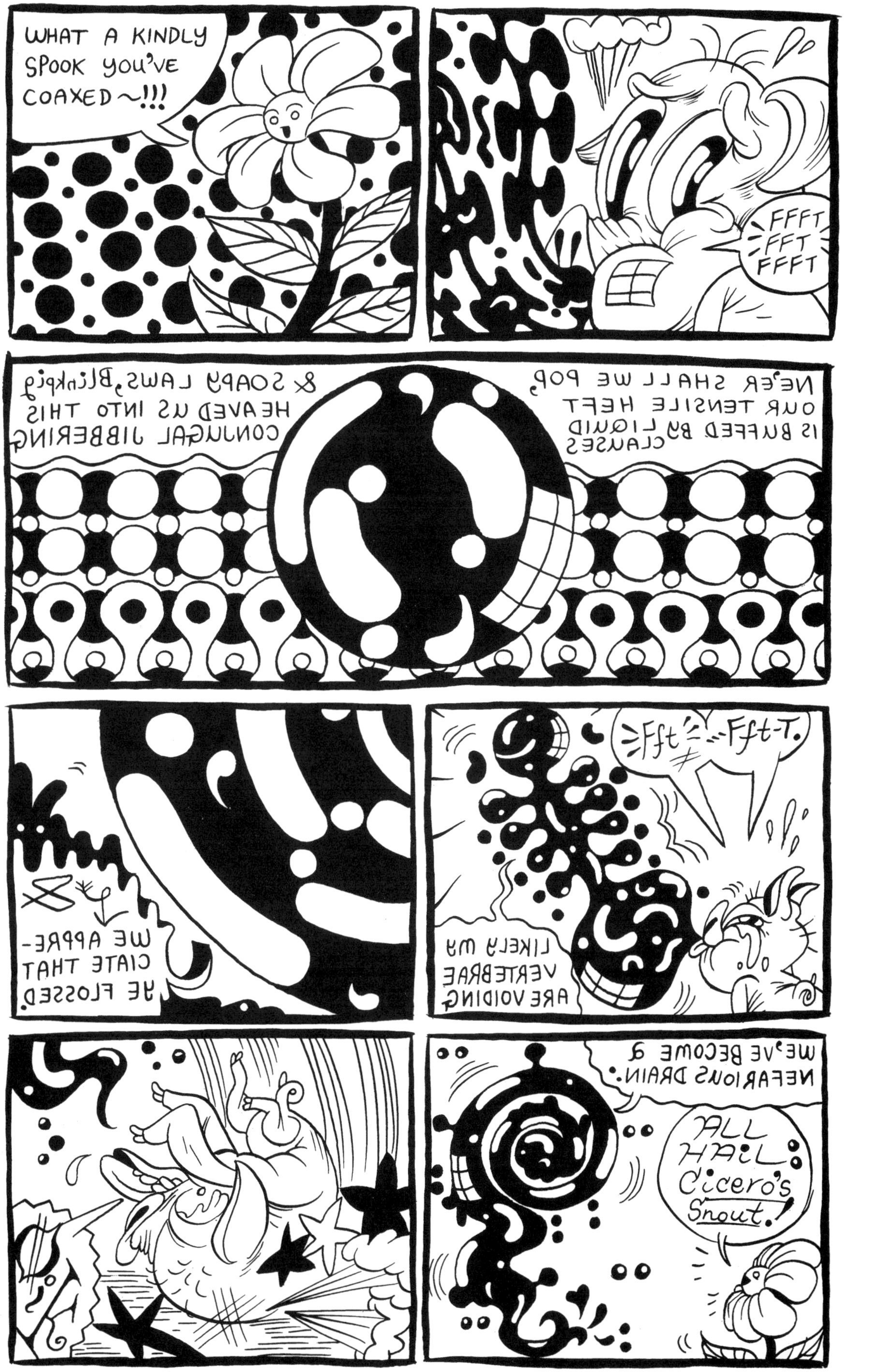

WHAT A KINDLY SPOOK YOU'VE COAXED~!!!
FFFT FFT FFFT
NE'ER SHALL WE POP, OUR TENSILE HEFT IS BUFFED BY LIQUID CLAUSES
& SOAPY LAWS, Blinkpig HEAVED US INTO THIS CONJUGAL JIBBERING
WE APPRE-CIATE THAT YE FLOSSED.
Fft -Fft-T.
LIKELY MY VERTEBRAE ARE VOIDING.
WE'VE BECOME A NEFARIOUS DRAIN.
ALL HAIL Cicero's Snout!

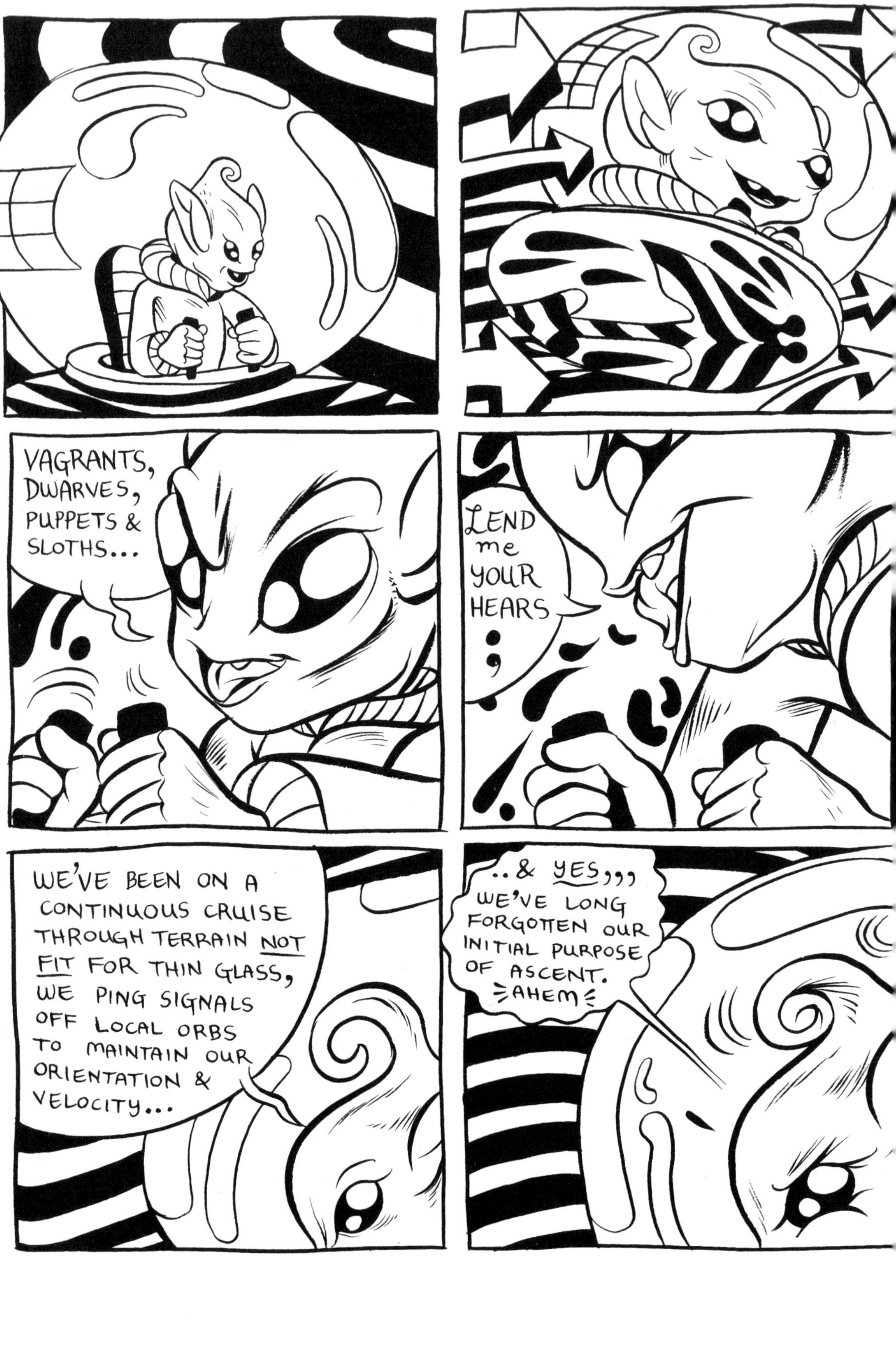
VAGRANTS, DWARVES, PUPPETS & SLOTHS...
LEND me YOUR HEARS ;
WE'VE BEEN ON A CONTINUOUS CRUISE THROUGH TERRAIN NOT FIT FOR THIN GLASS, WE PING SIGNALS OFF LOCAL ORBS TO MAINTAIN OUR ORIENTATION & VELOCITY...
..& YES,,, WE'VE LONG FORGOTTEN OUR INITIAL PURPOSE OF ASCENT.
AHEM

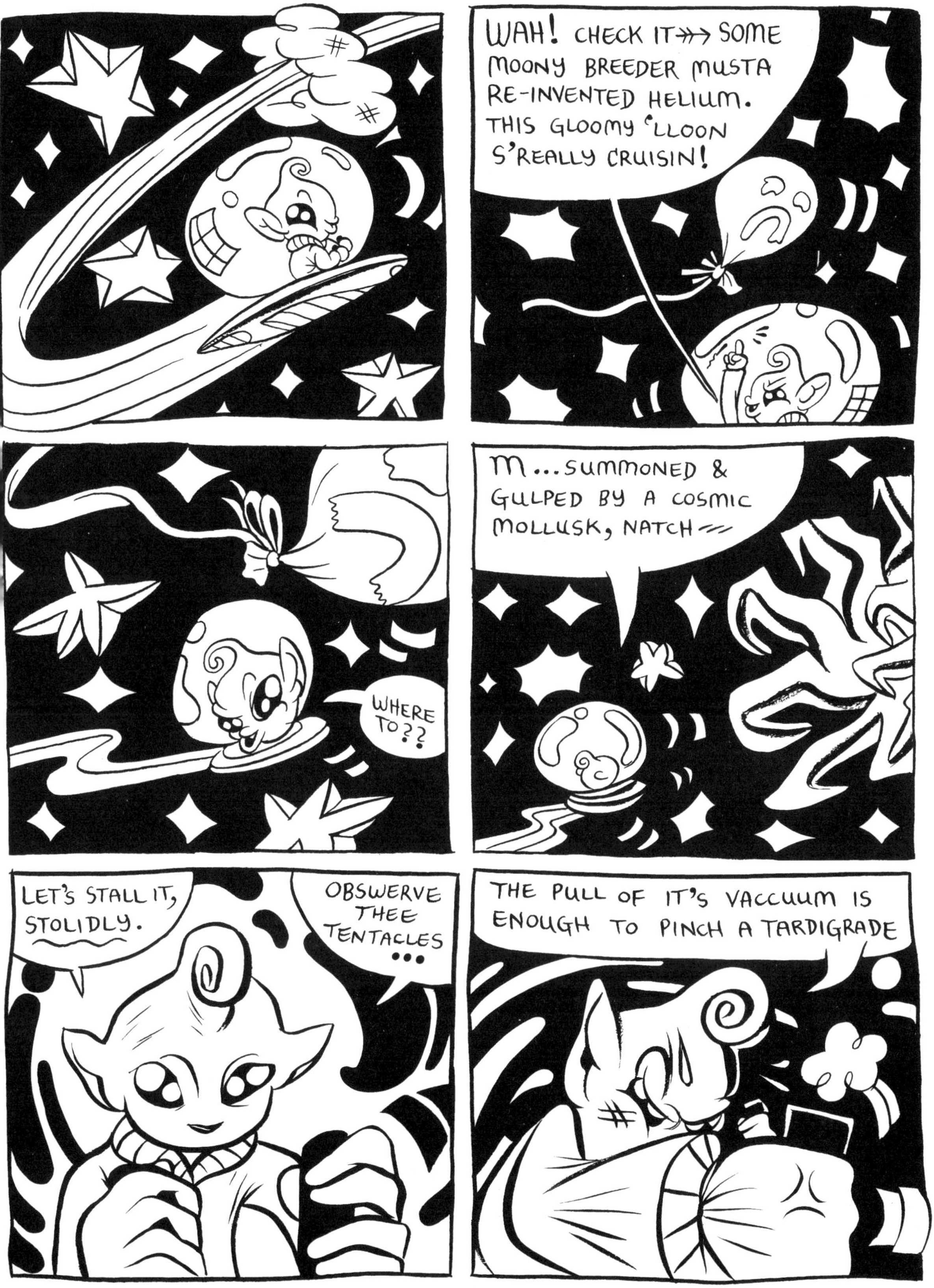
WAH! CHECK IT→→ SOME MOONY BREEDER MUSTA RE-INVENTED HELIUM. THIS GLOOMY 'LLOON S'REALLY CRUISIN!
WHERE TO??
M...SUMMONED & GULPED BY A COSMIC MOLLUSK, NATCH
LET'S STALL IT, STOLIDLY.
OBSWERVE THEE TENTACLES •••
THE PULL OF IT'S VACCUUM IS ENOUGH TO PINCH A TARDIGRADE

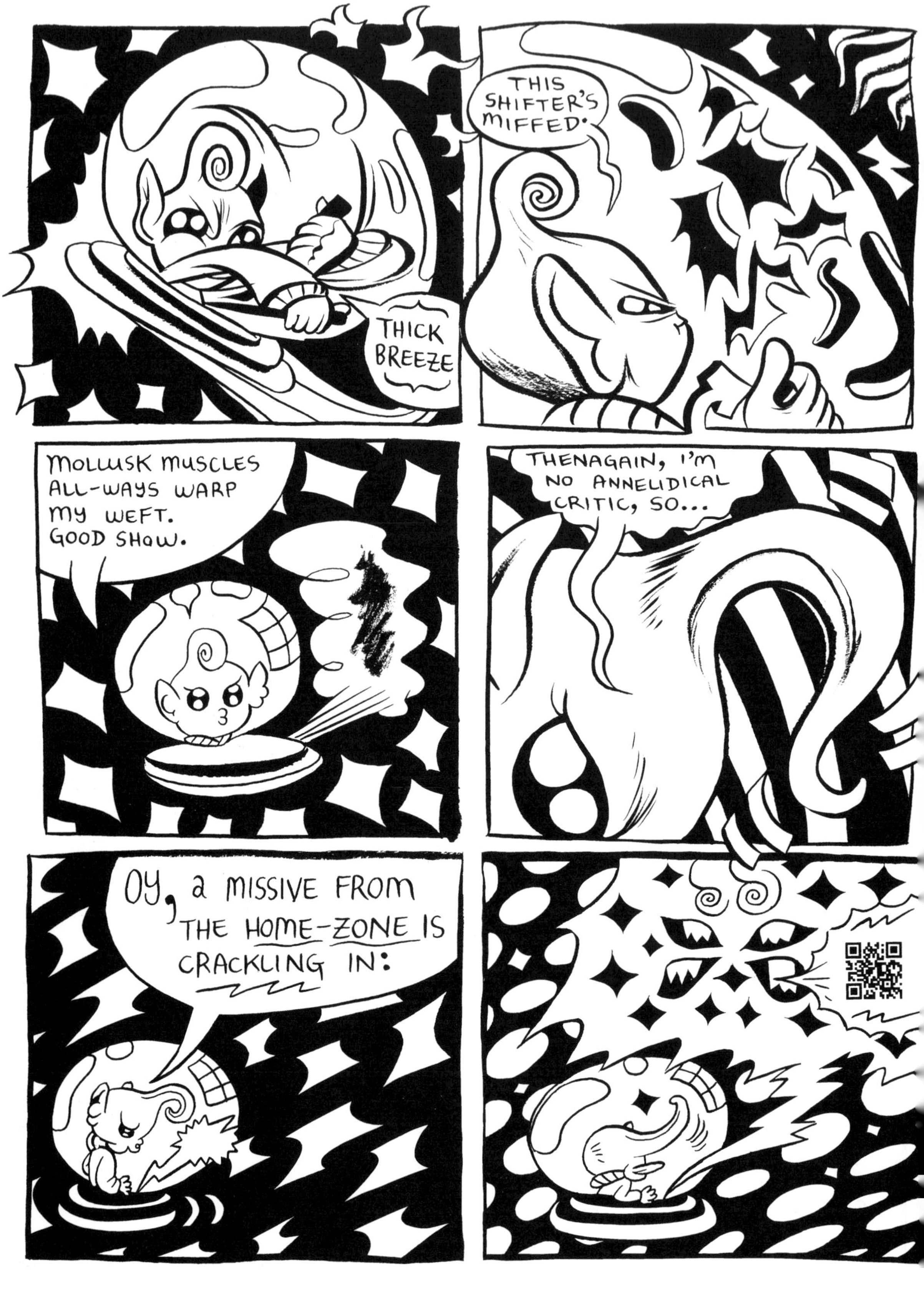
THICK BREEZE
THIS SHIFTER'S MIFFED.
MOLLUSK MUSCLES ALL-WAYS WARP MY WEFT. GOOD SHOW.
THENAGAIN, I'M NO ANNELIDICAL CRITIC, SO...
OY, a MISSIVE FROM THE HOME-ZONE IS CRACKLING IN:

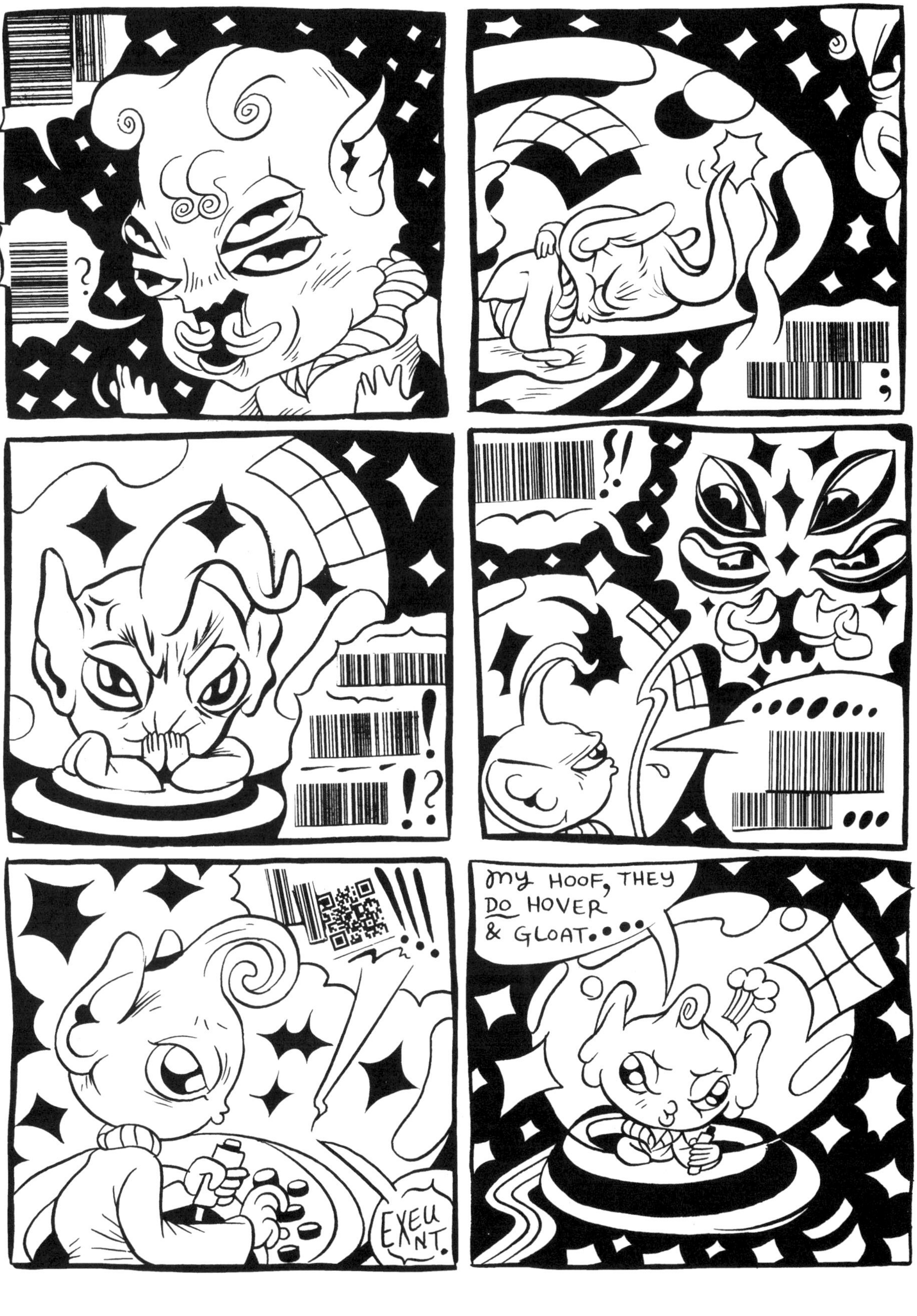
?
;
!?
!?
...
...
!!!
MY HOOF, THEY DO HOVER & GLOAT....
EXEUNT.

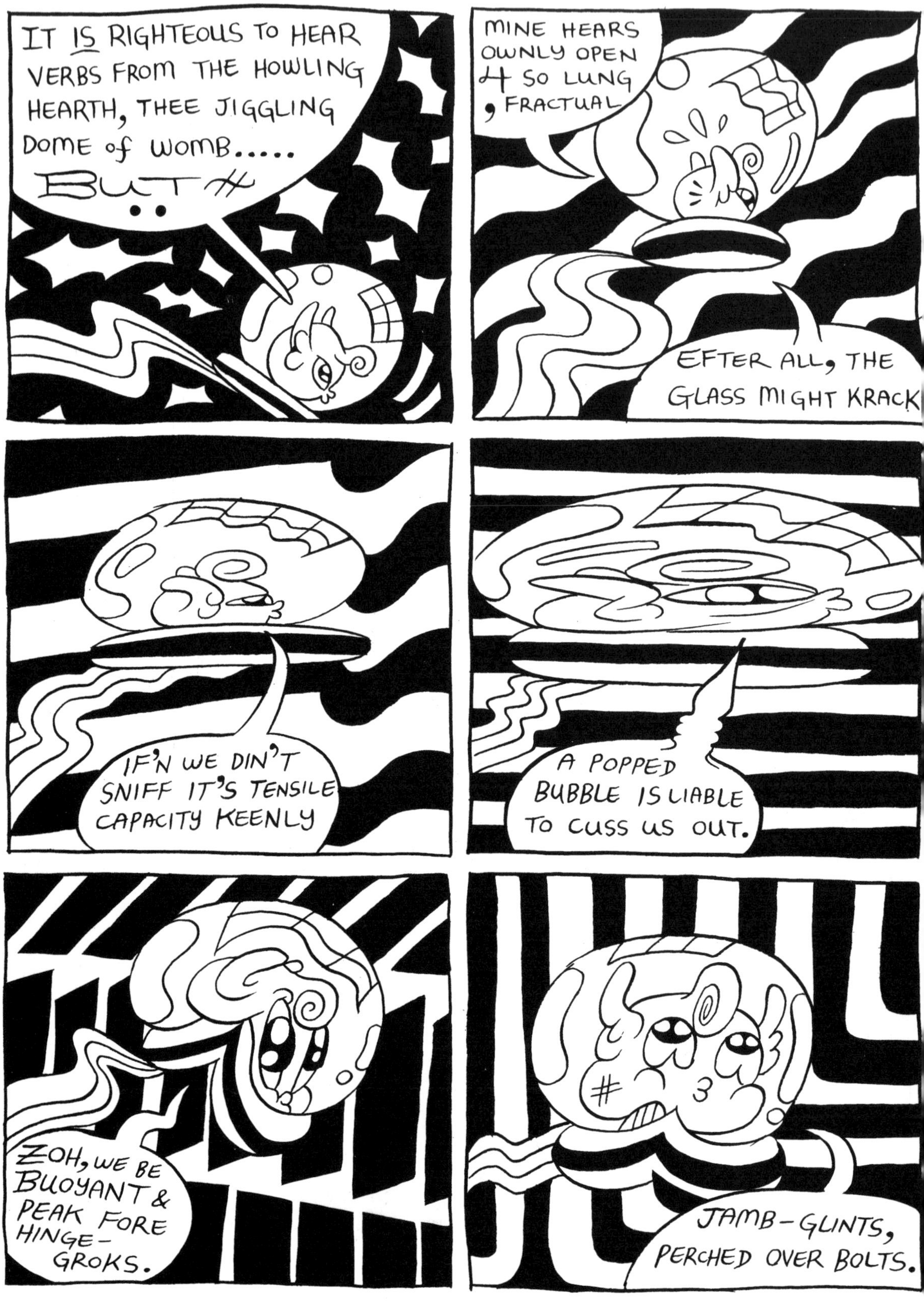
IT IS RIGHTEOUS TO HEAR VERBS FROM THE HOWLING HEARTH, THEE JIGGLING DOME of WOMB..... BUT #
MINE HEARS OWNLY OPEN 4 SO LUNG, FRACTUAL
EFTER ALL, THE GLASS MIGHT KRACK
IF'N WE DIN'T SNIFF IT'S TENSILE CAPACITY KEENLY
A POPPED BUBBLE IS LIABLE TO CUSS US OUT.
ZOH, WE BE BUOYANT & PEAK FORE HINGE-GROKS.
JAMB-GLINTS, PERCHED OVER BOLTS.

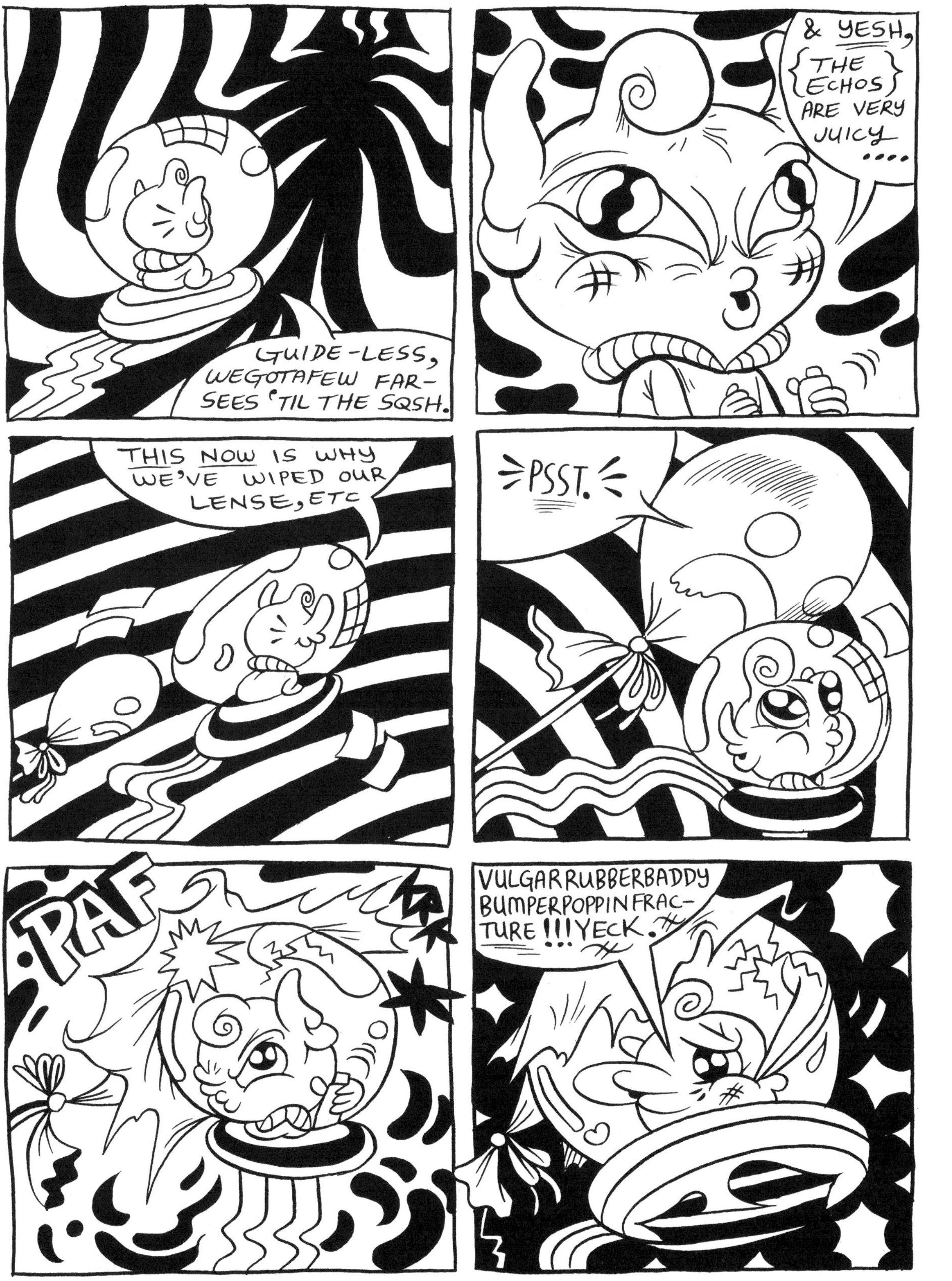
GUIDE-LESS, WEGOTAFEW FAR-SEES 'TIL THE SQSH.
& YESH, {THE ECHOS} ARE VERY JUICY....
THIS NOW IS WHY WE'VE WIPED OUR LENSE, ETC
PSST.
PAF
VULGARRUBBERBADDY BUMPERPOPPINFRAC-TURE!!! YECK.

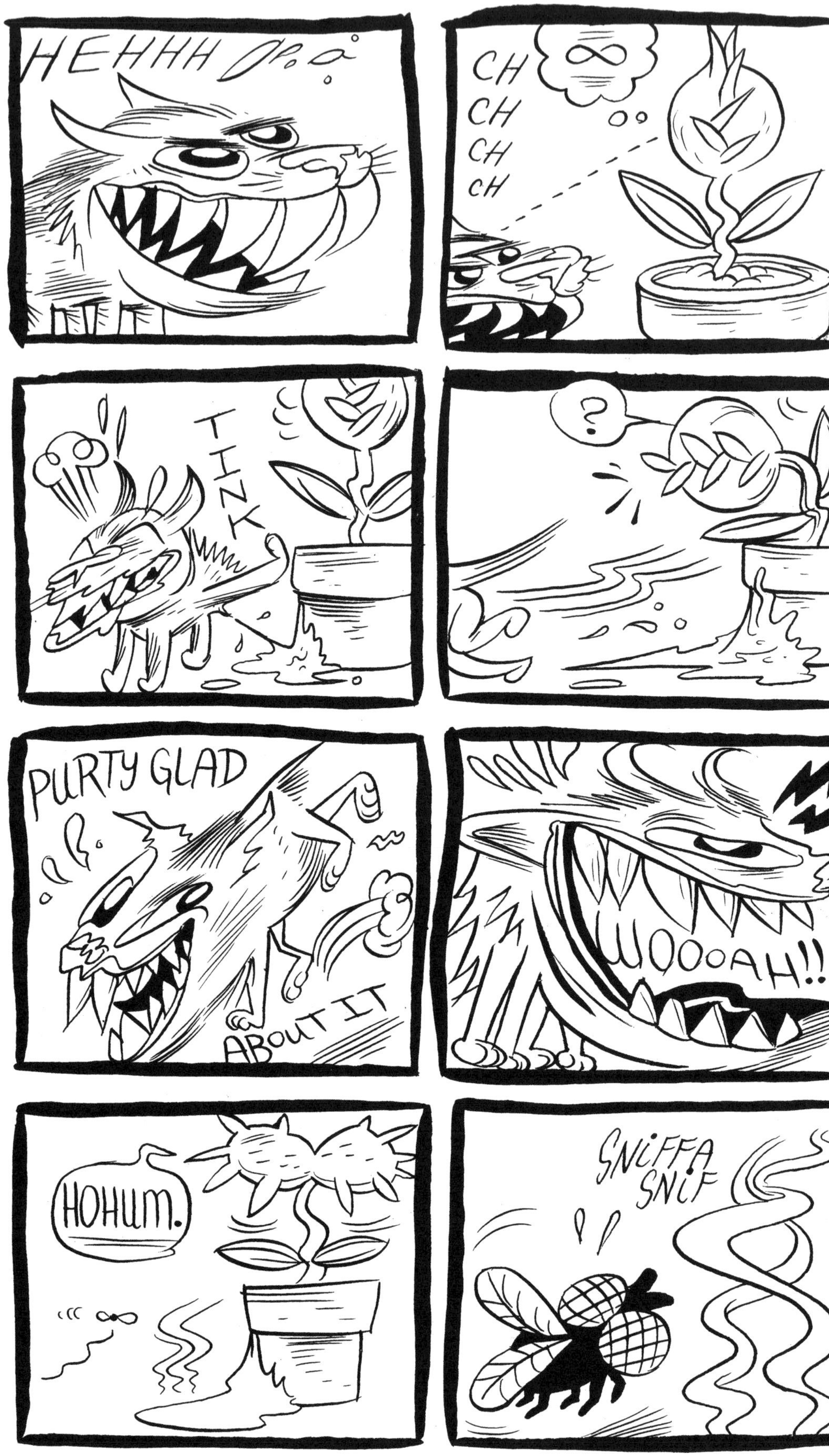
HEHHH
CH CH CH CH
TINK
?
PURTY GLAD
ABOUT IT
WOOOOAH!!
HOHUM.
SNIFFA SNIF

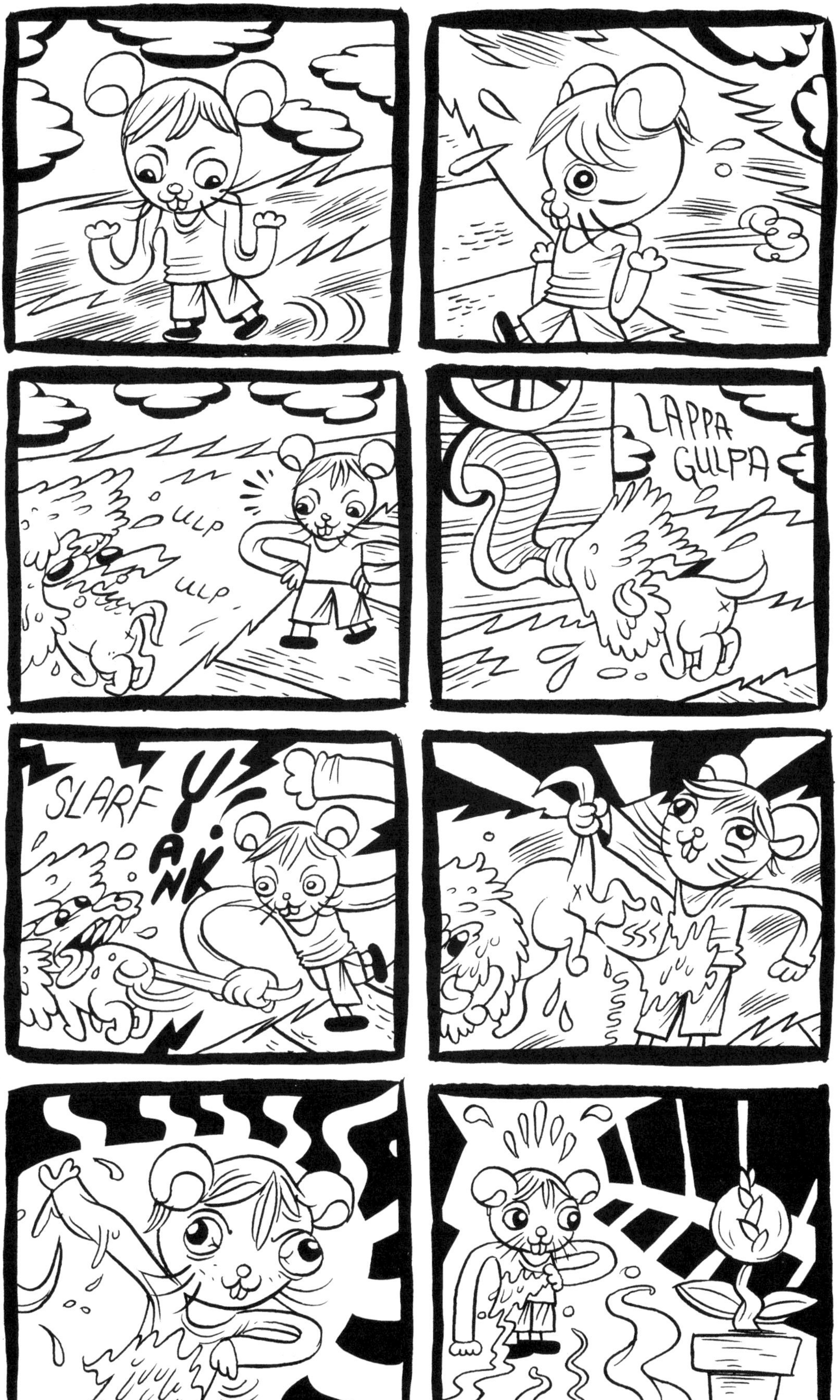

ULP
ULP
LAPPA
GULPA
SLARF
YANK
SSS

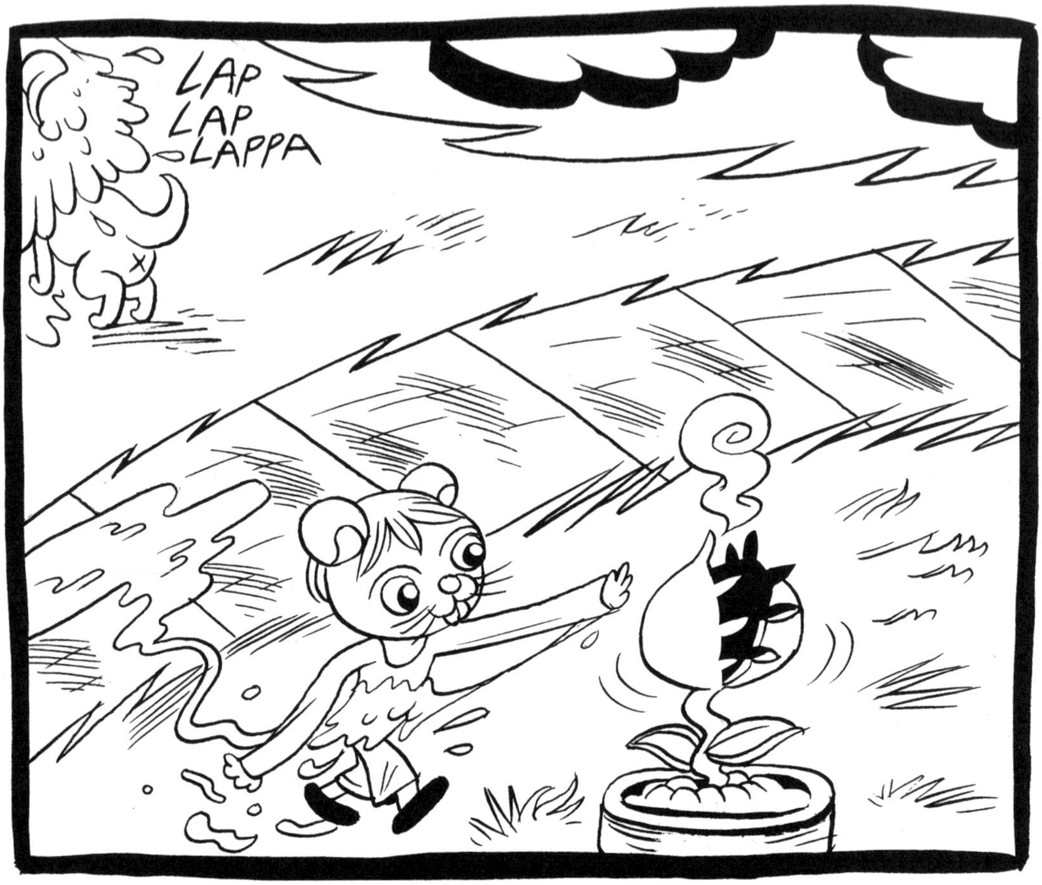
LAP
LAP
LAPPA
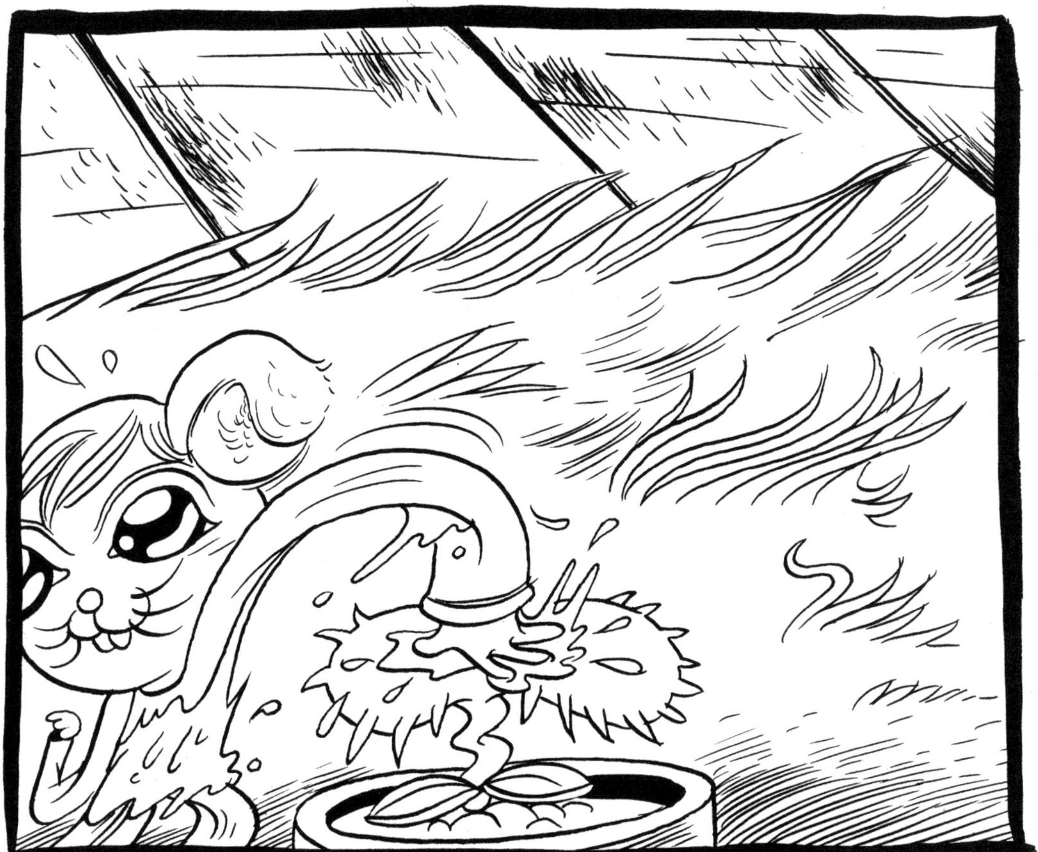

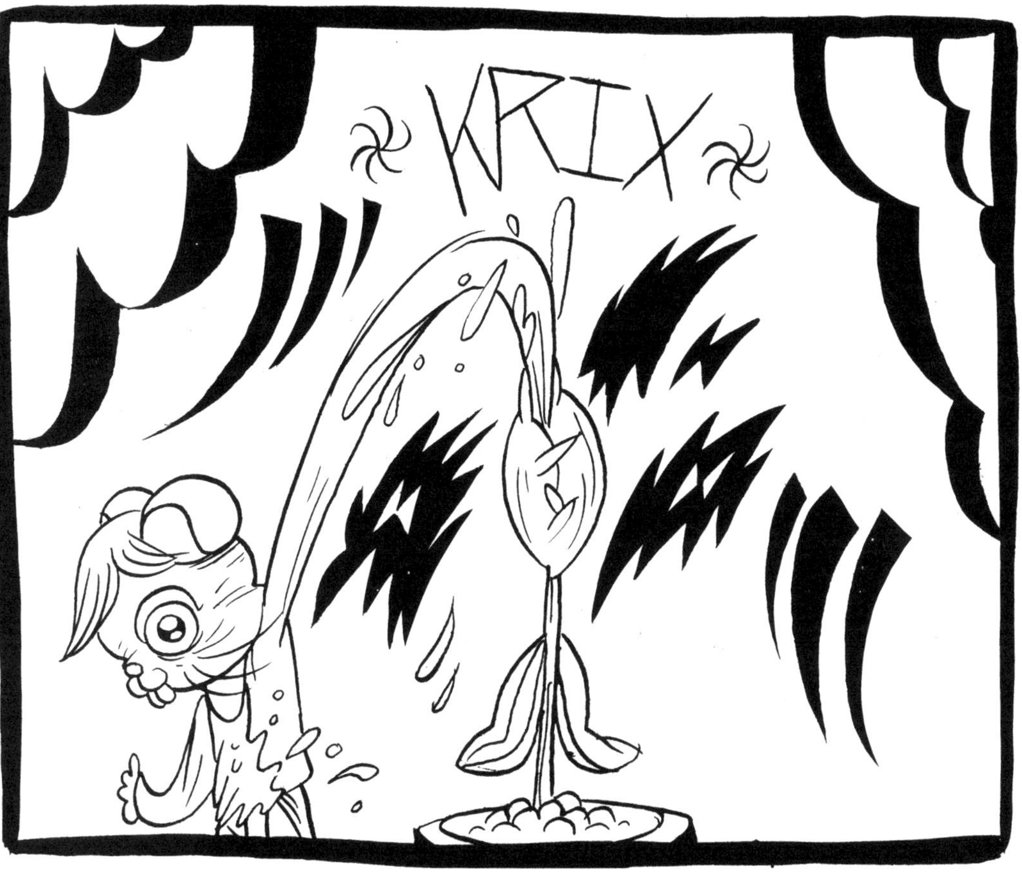
KRIX

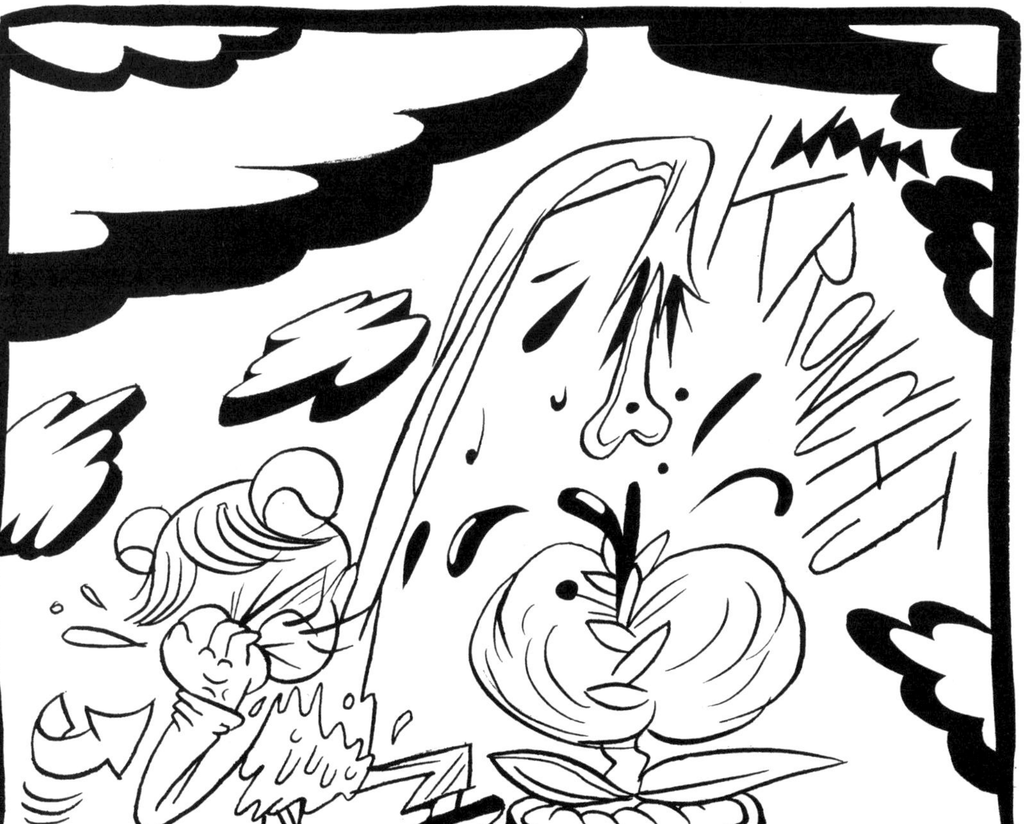

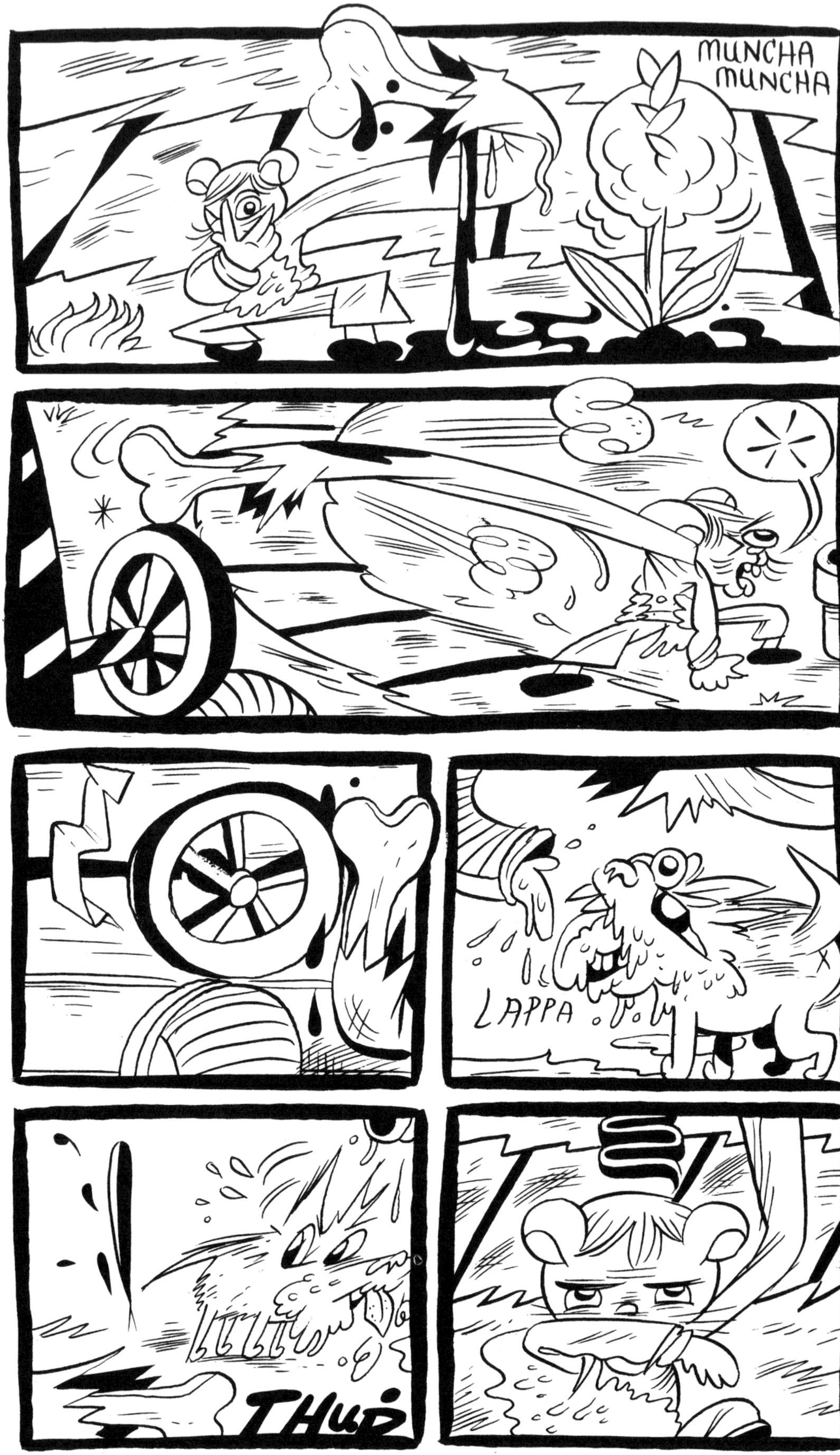
MUNCHA
MUNCHA
LAPPA
THUD

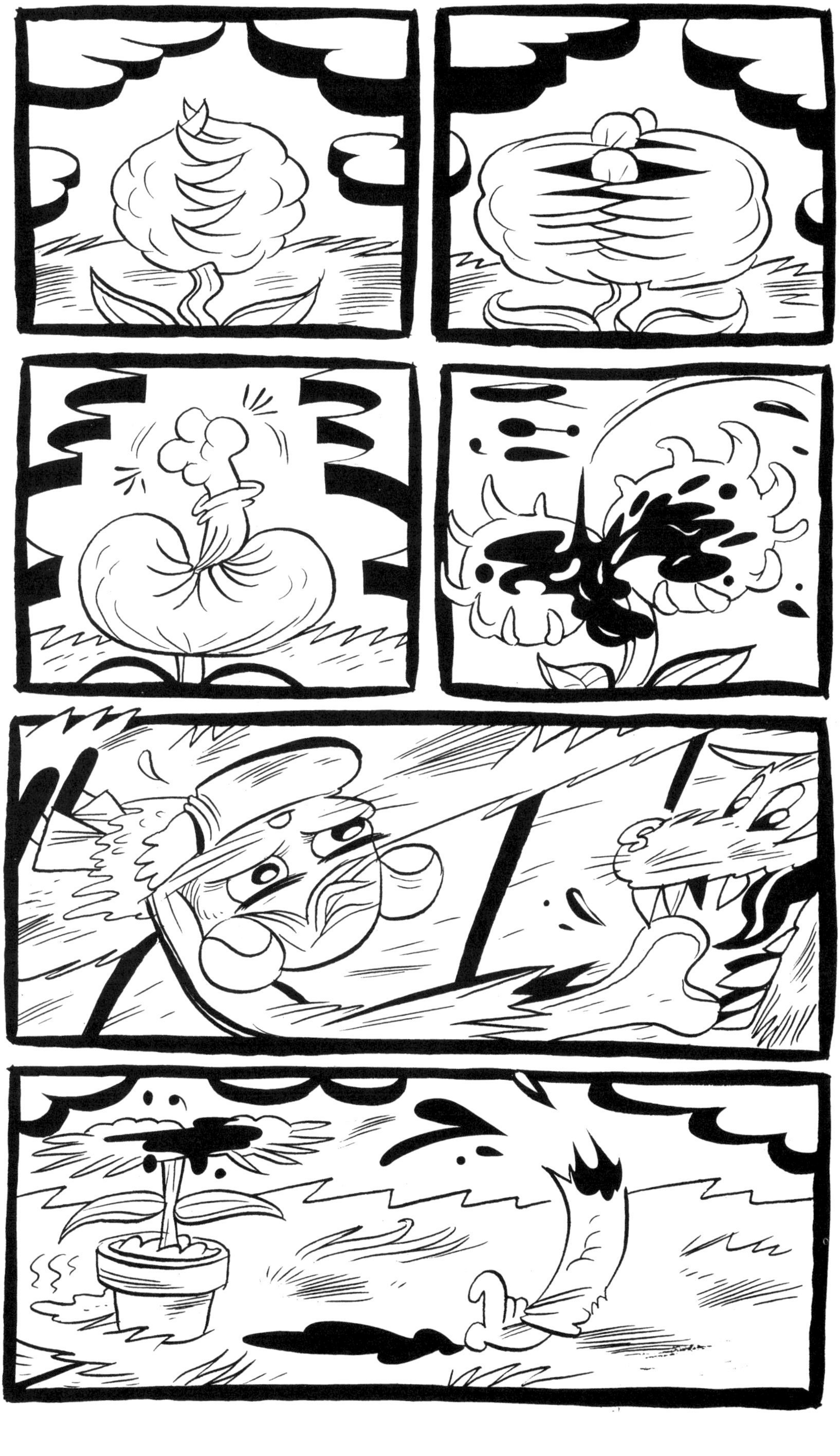

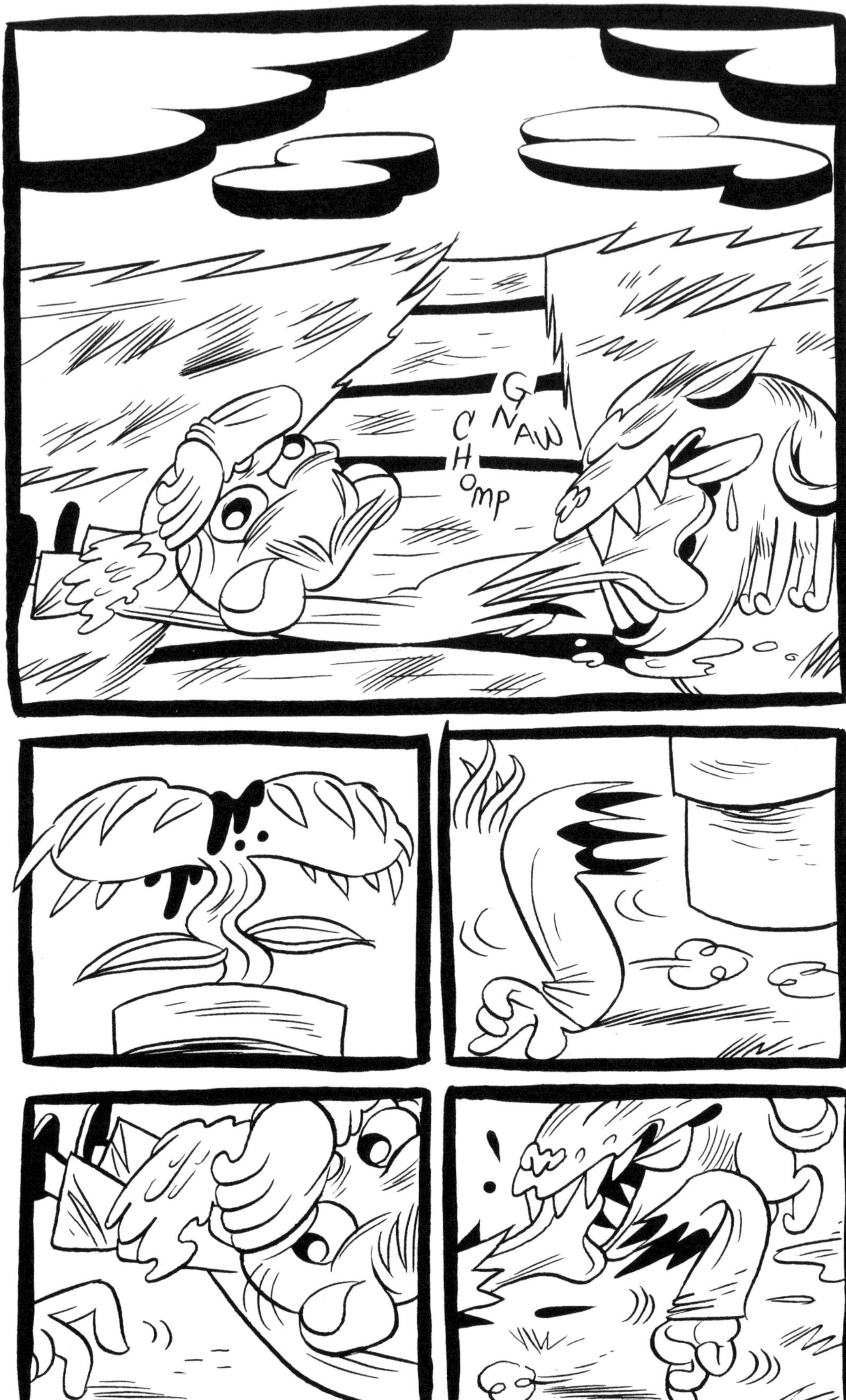
GNAW
CHOMP
!

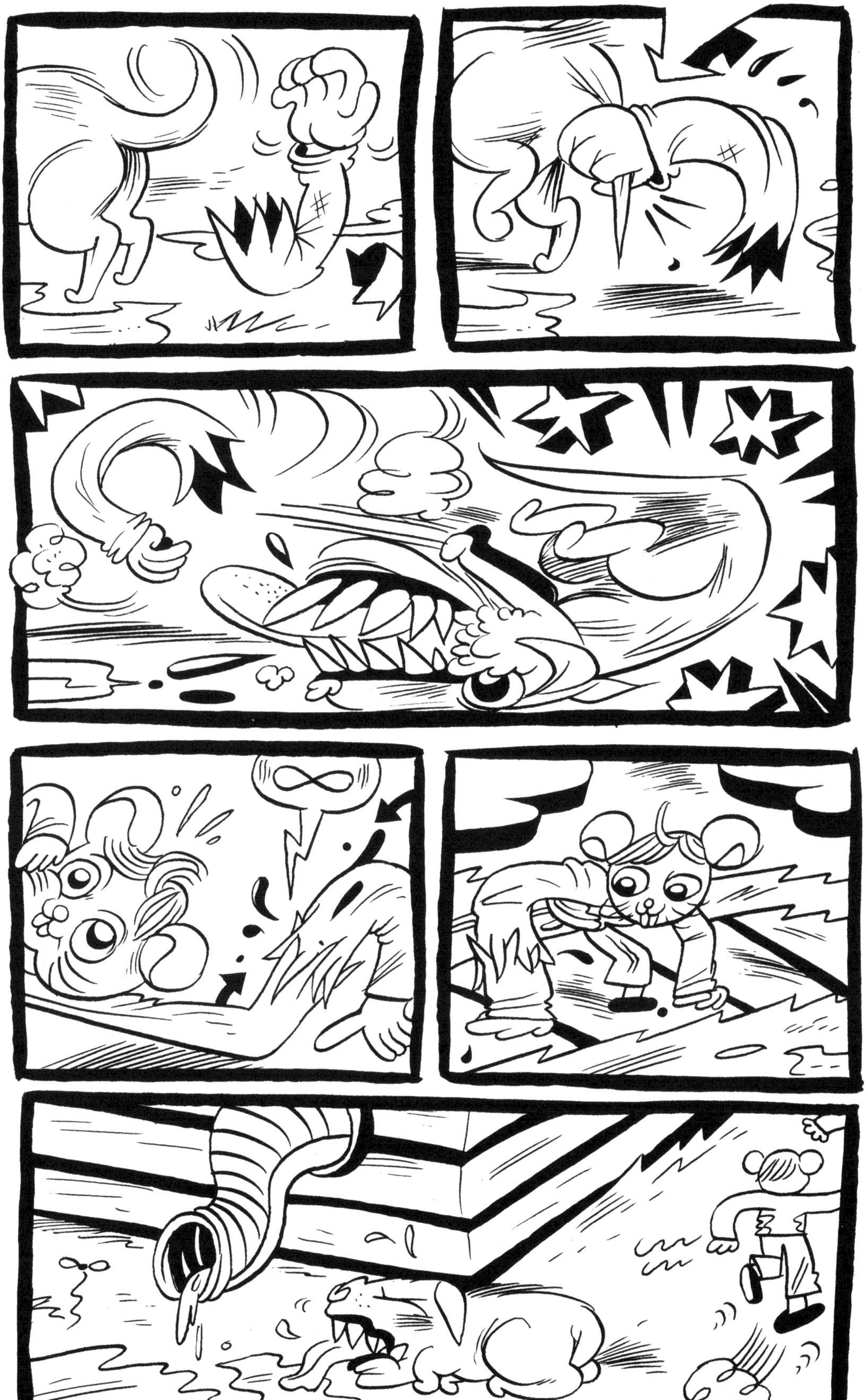
∞

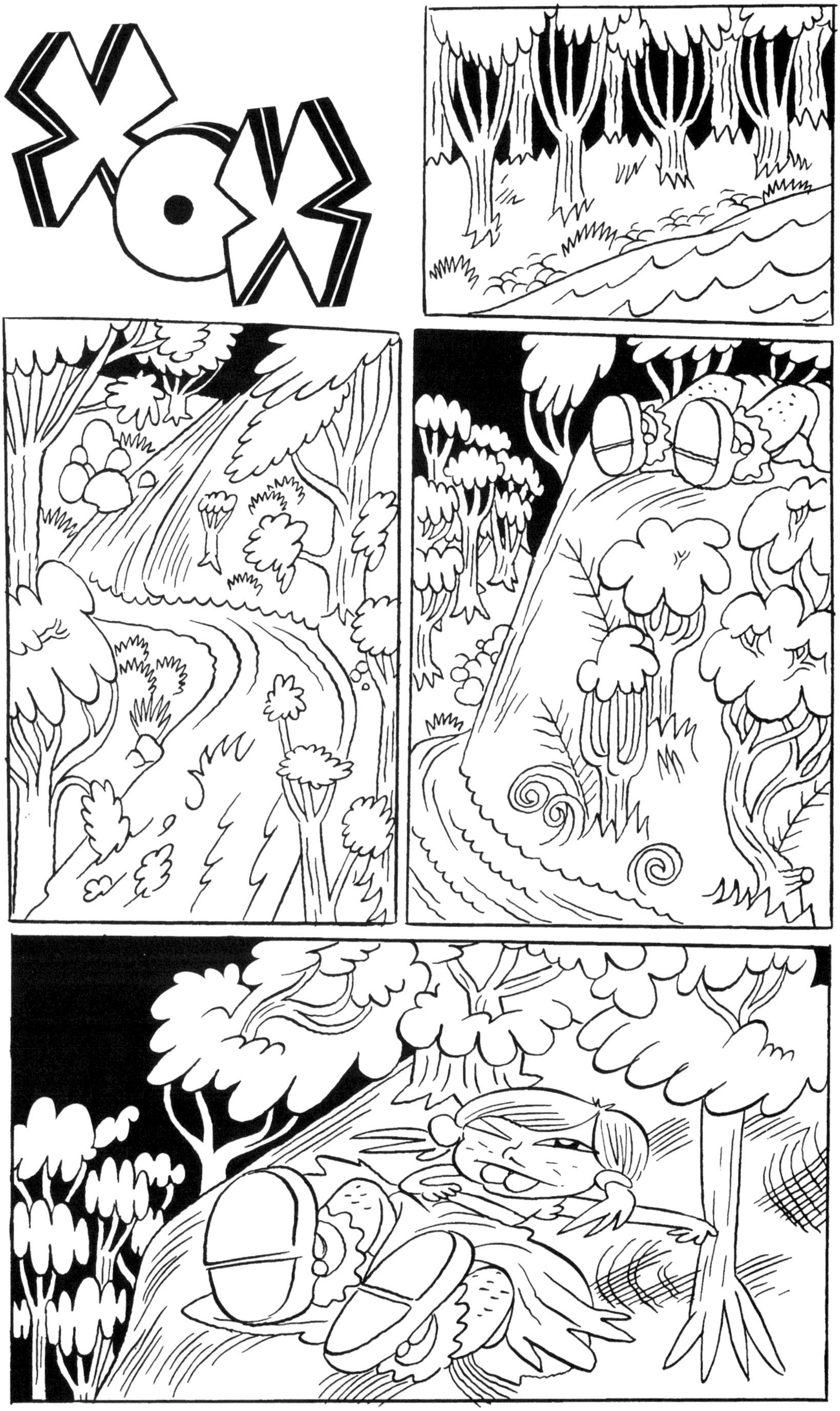

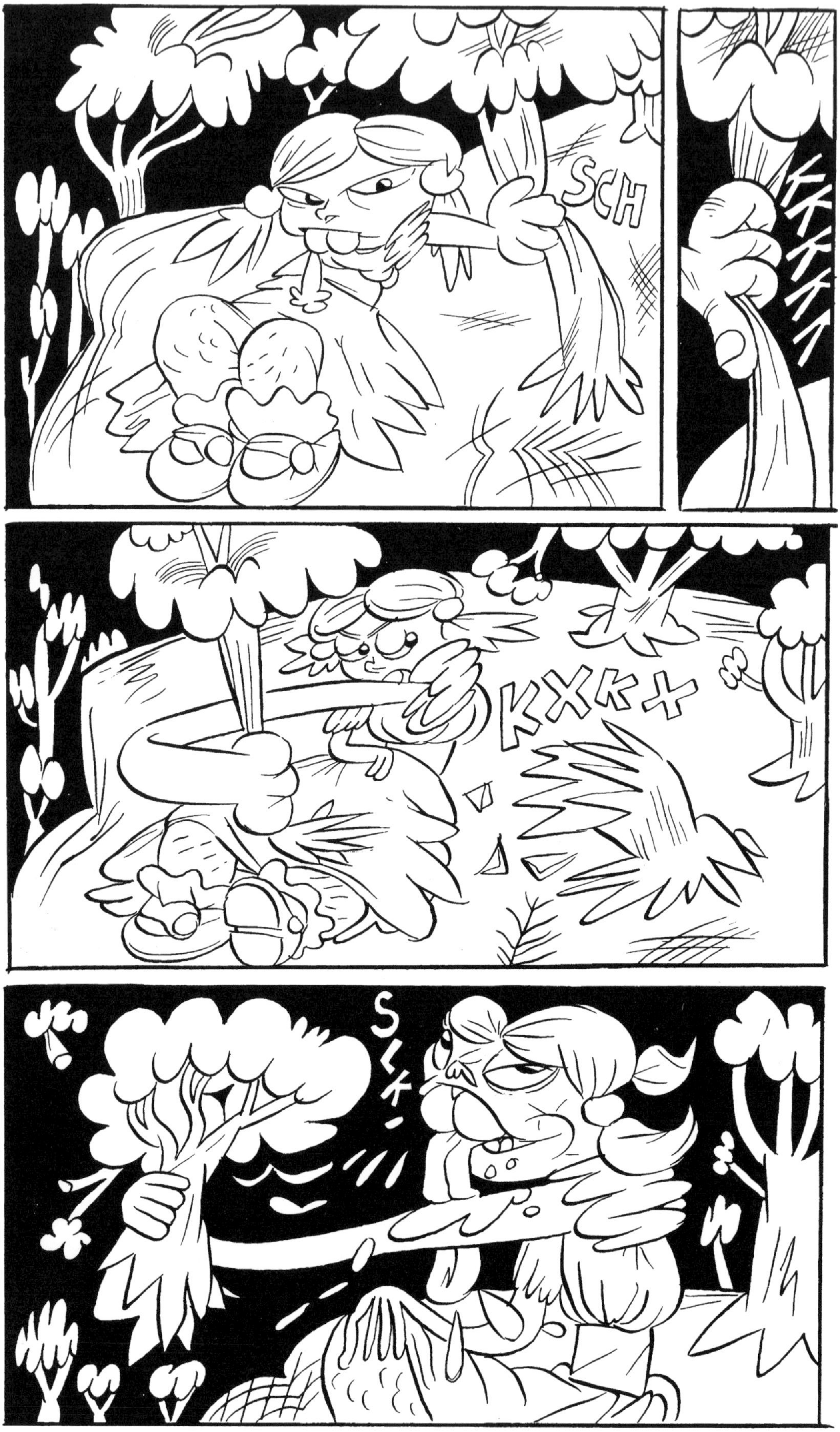
SCH
KKKKKK
KXKK+
SLK-

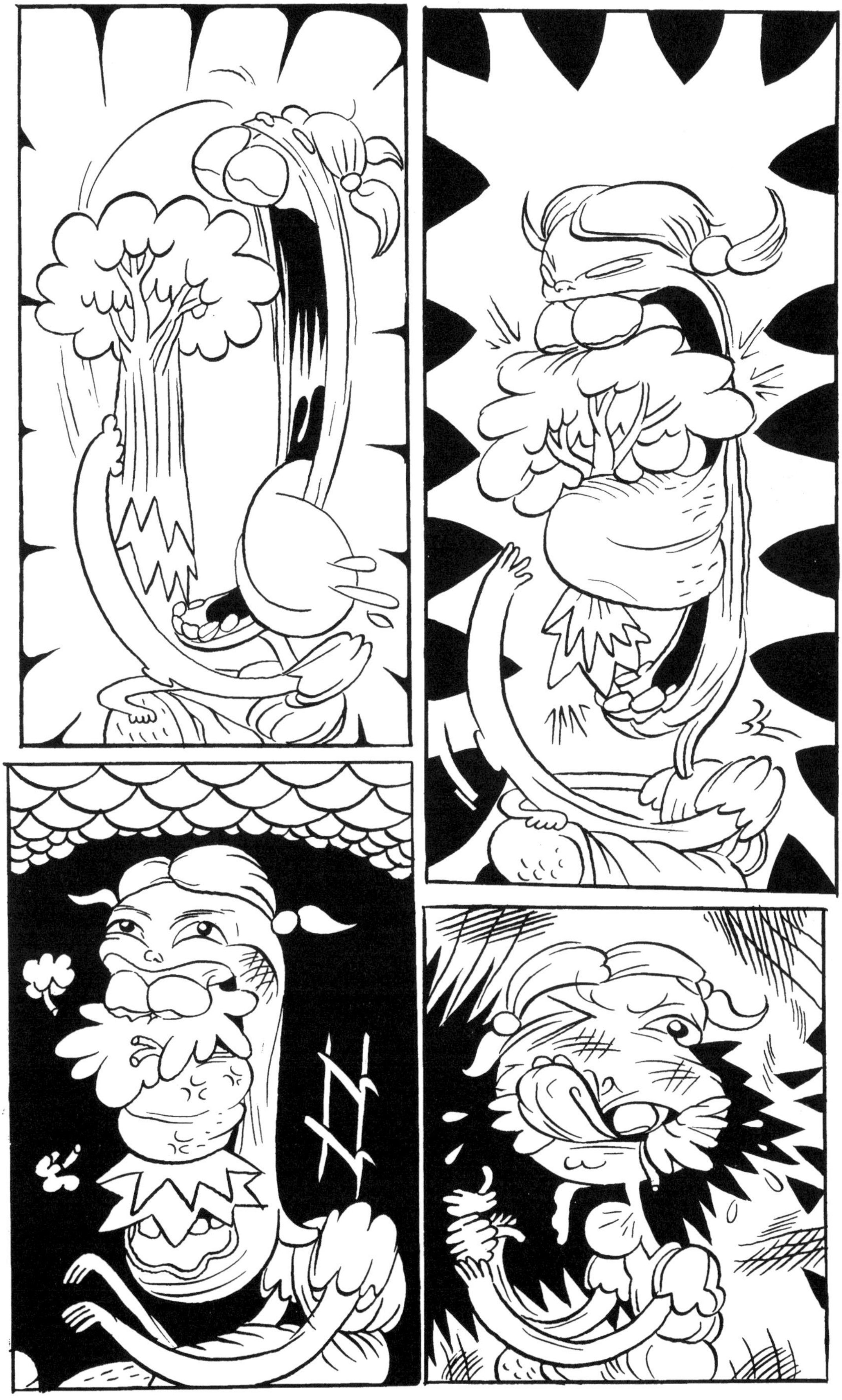

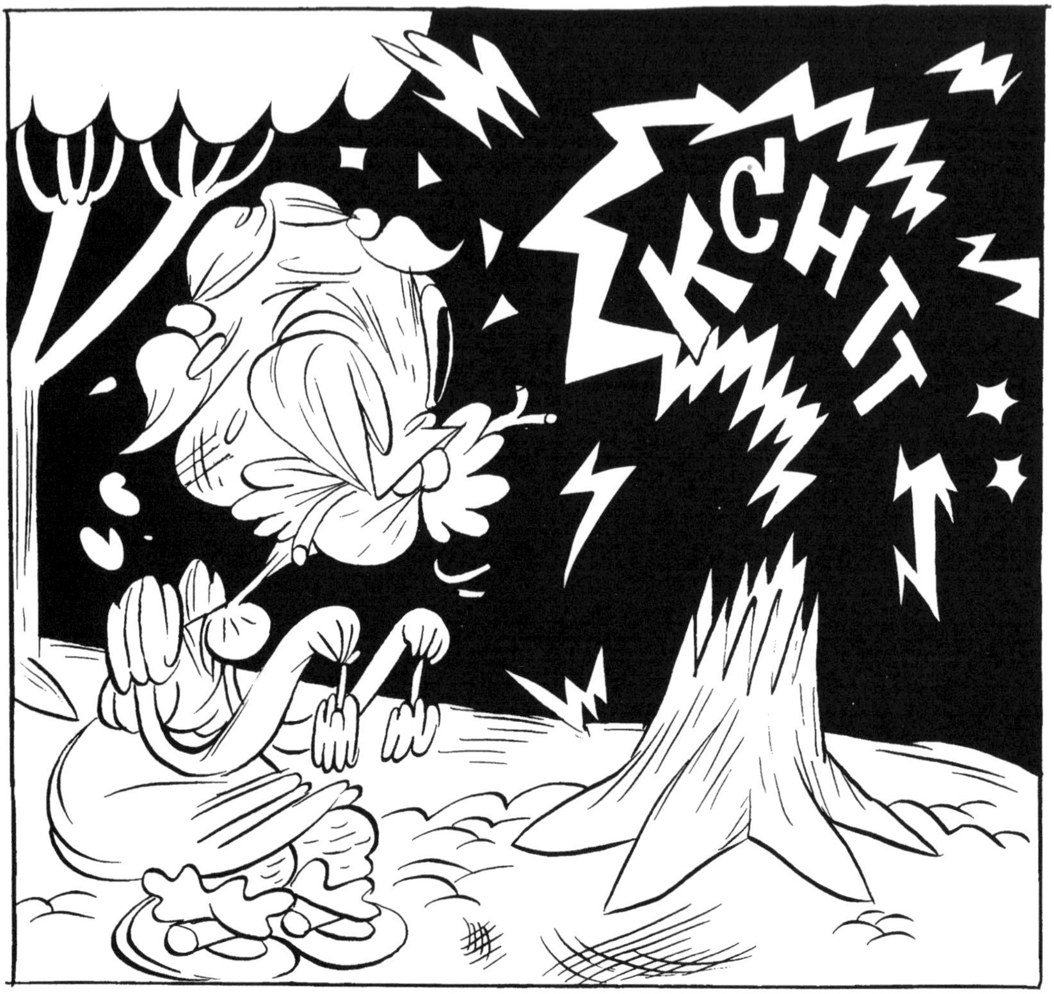
KCHTT

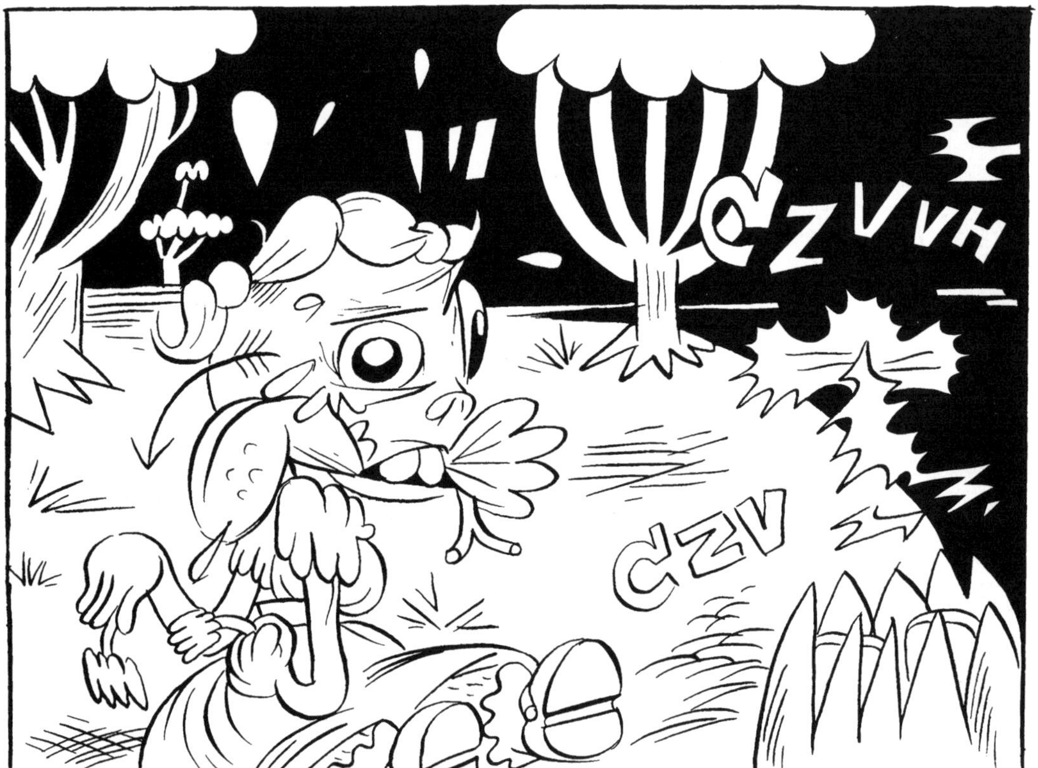
CZVVH
CZV

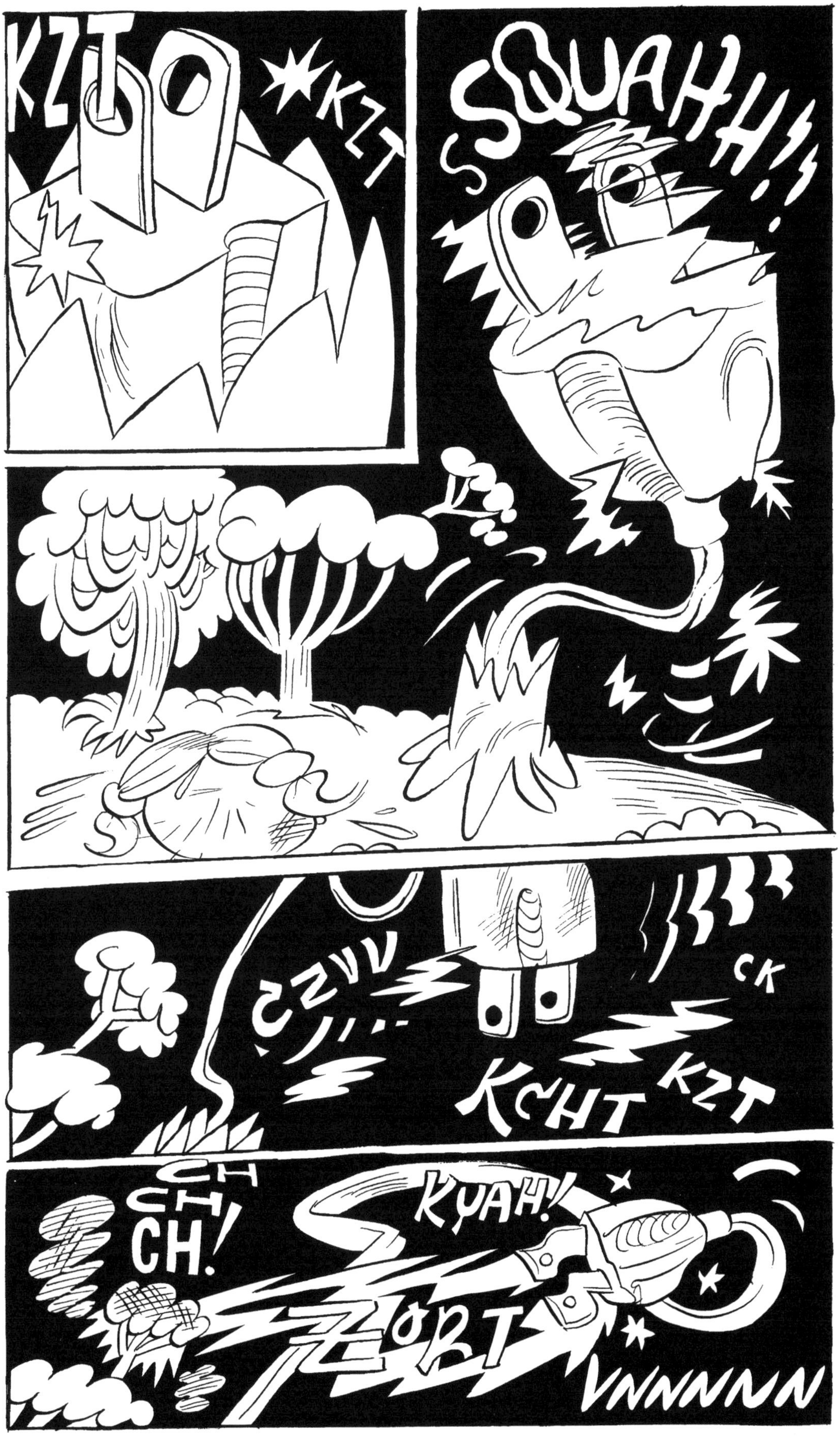
KZTO
KZT
SQUAHH!!
CZVV
CK
KCHT
KZT
CH
CH!
CH!
KYAH!
ZORT
VNNNNN

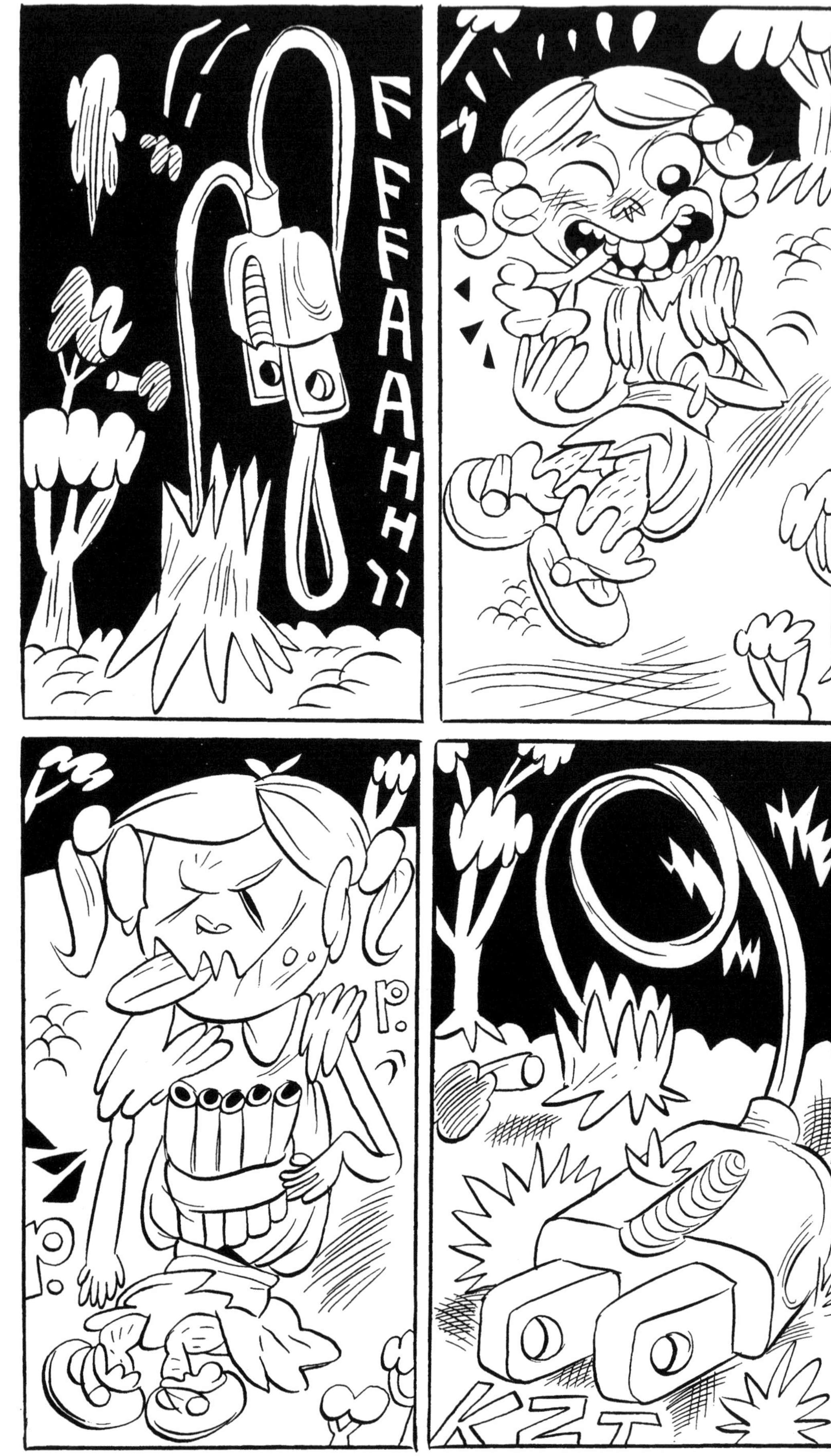
FFFAAHH"
p.
p.
KZT

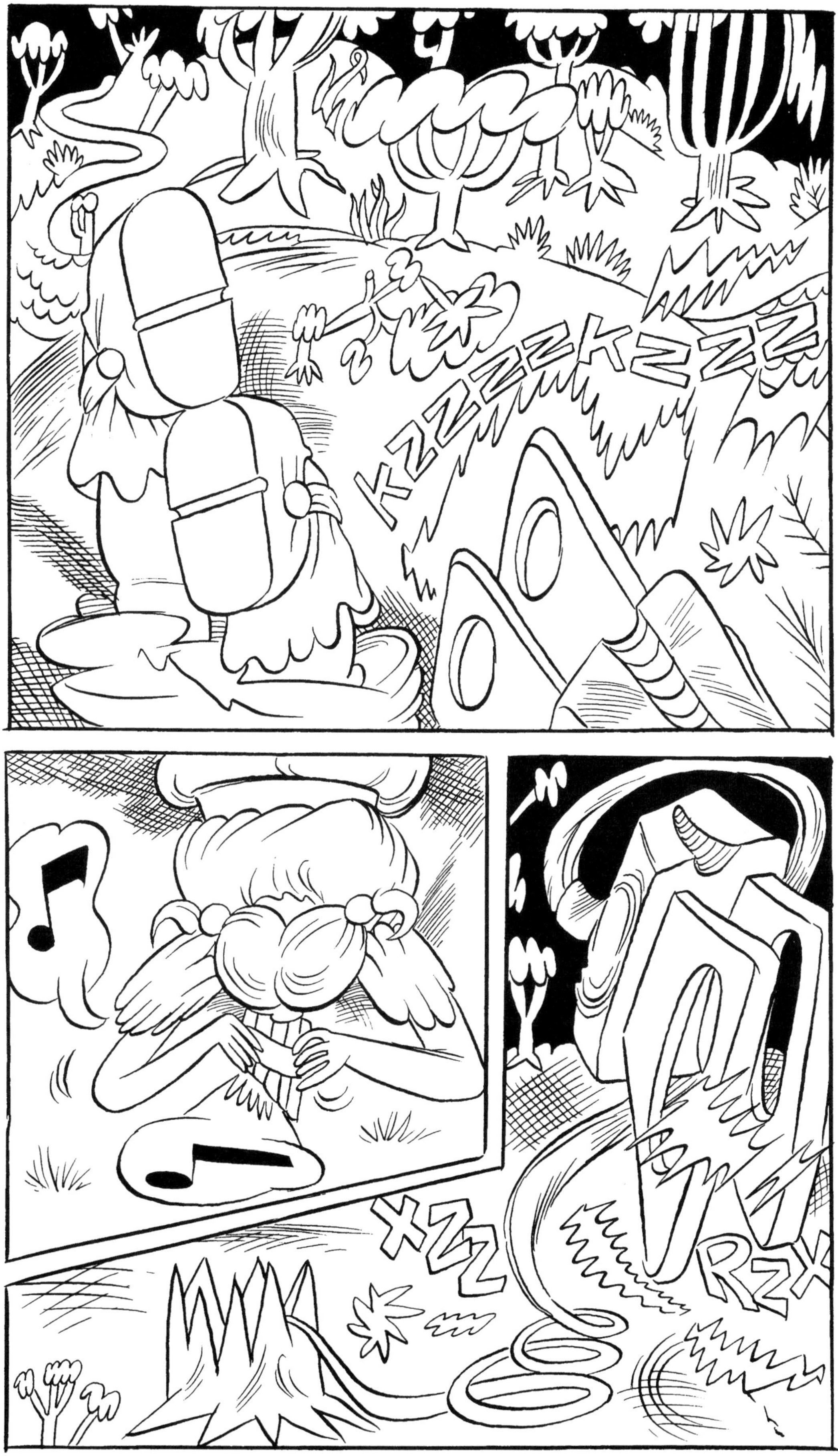
KZZZZKZZZ
XZZ
RZX

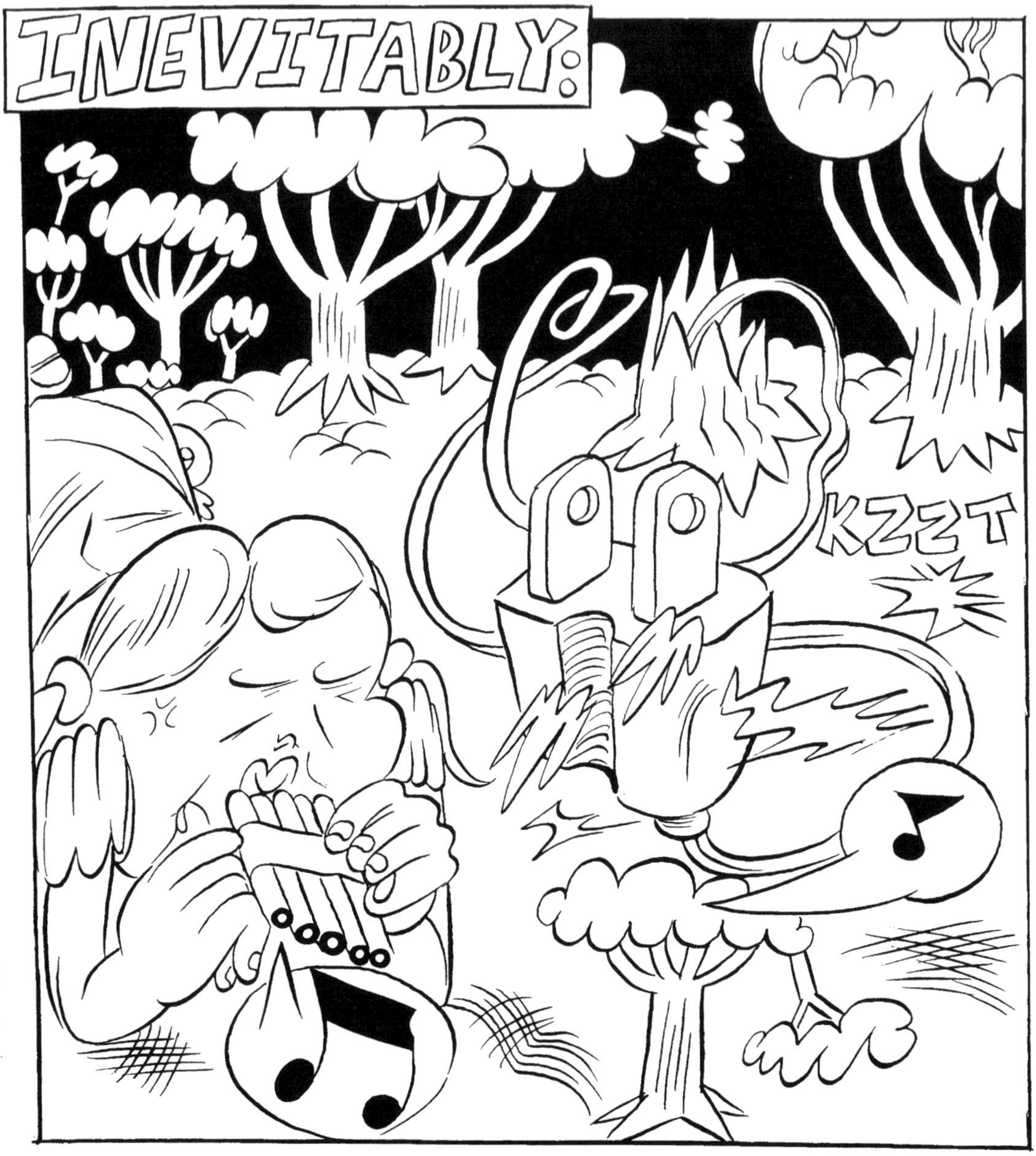
INEVITABLY:
KZZT

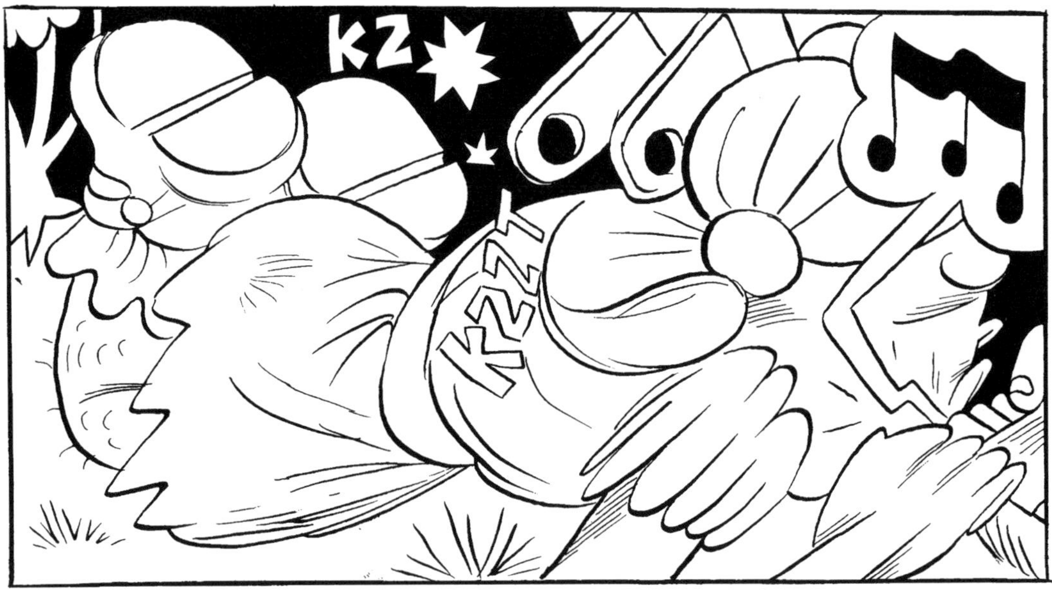
KZ
KZZT

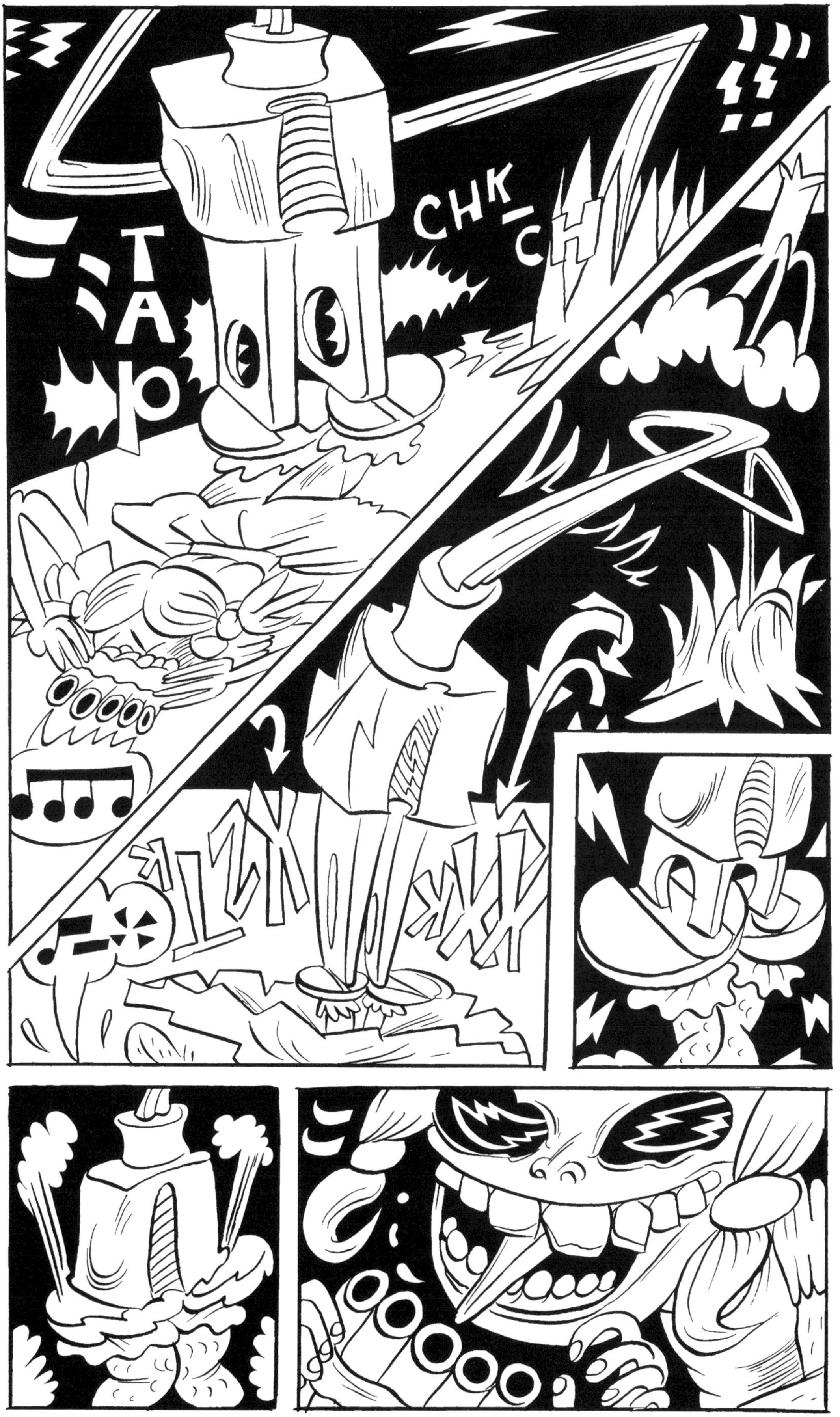

TAP
CHK-CH

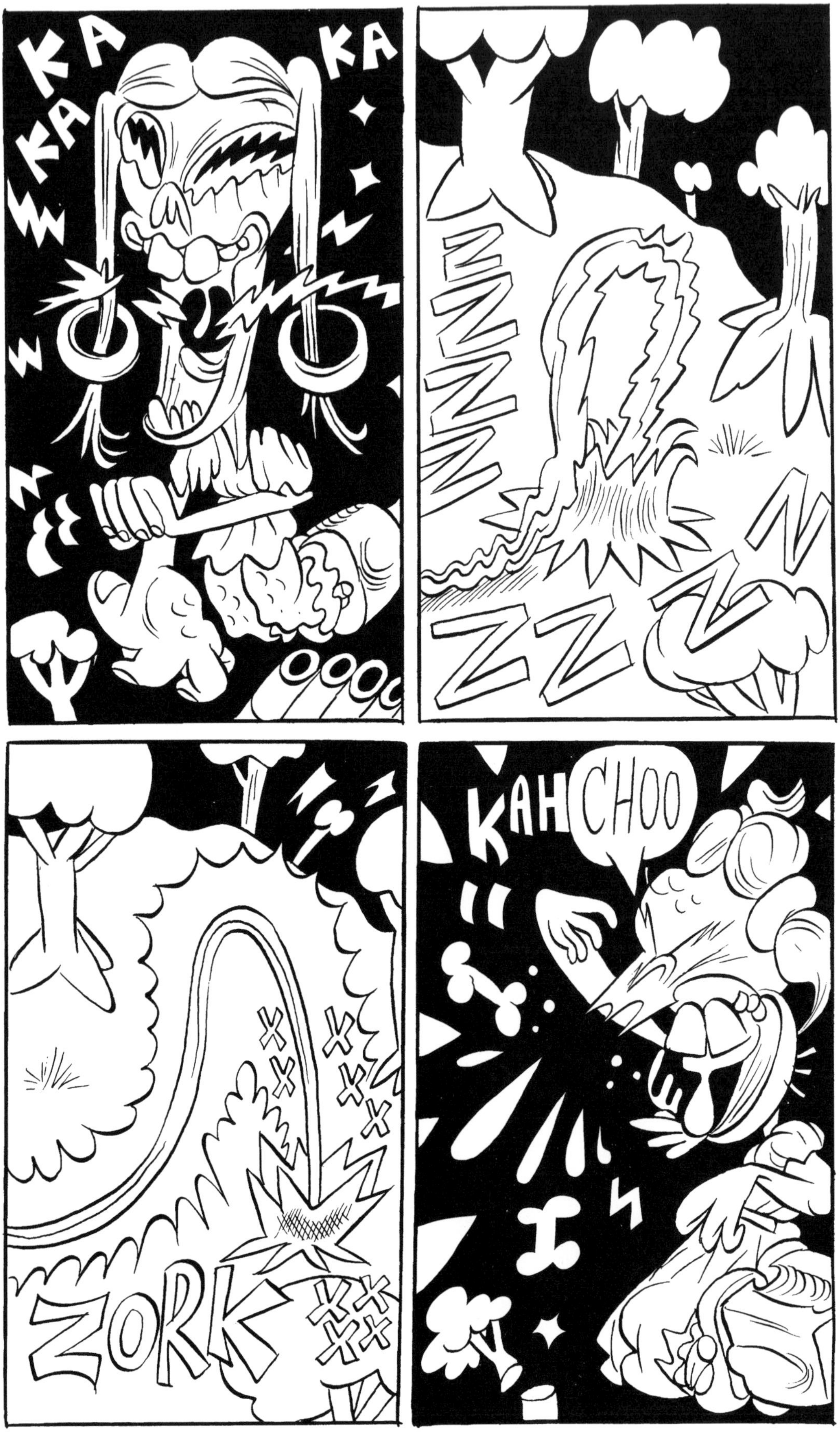
KA KA KA
KA
ZORK
KAH
CHOO

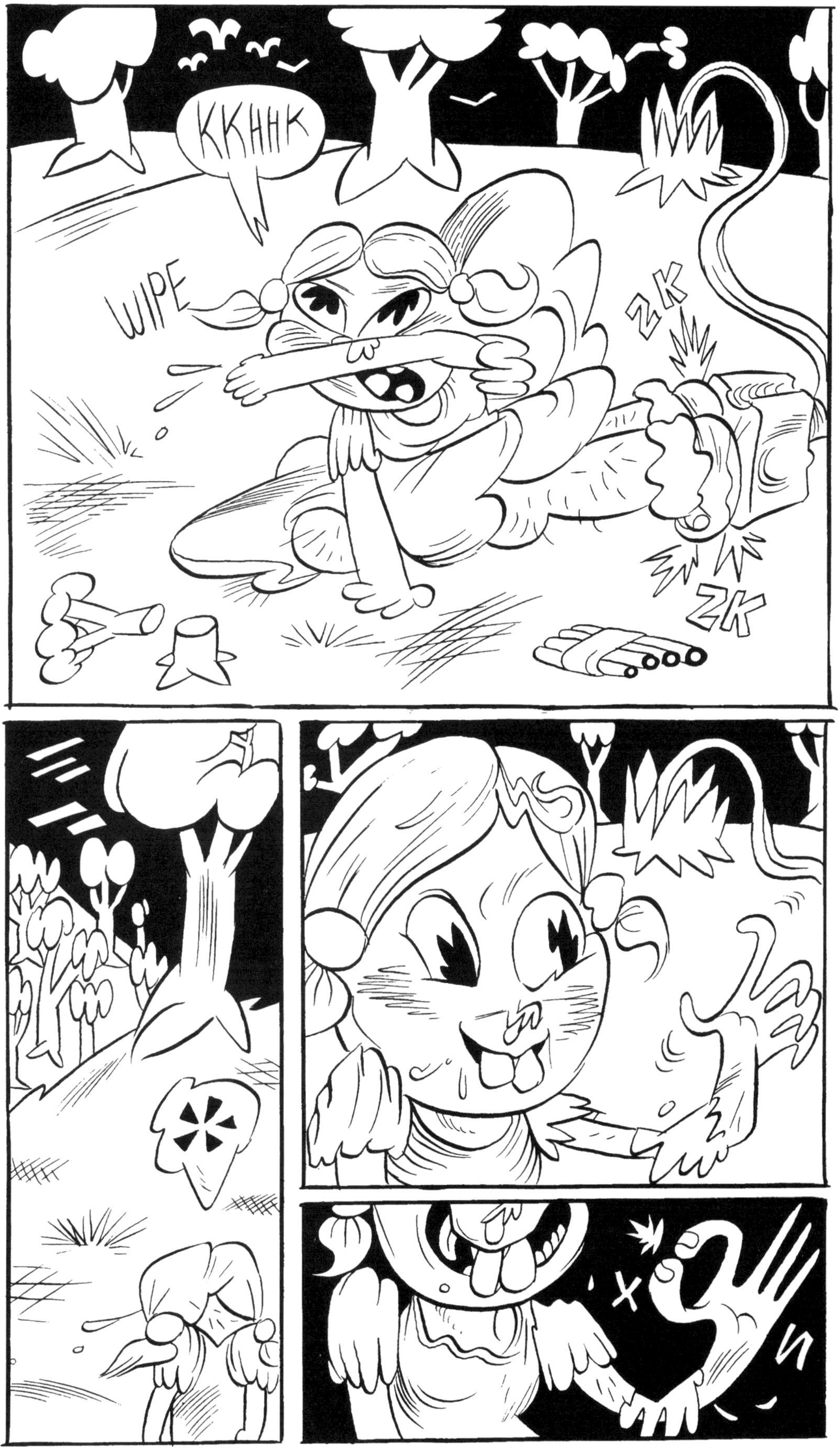
KKHHK
WIPE
ZK
ZK

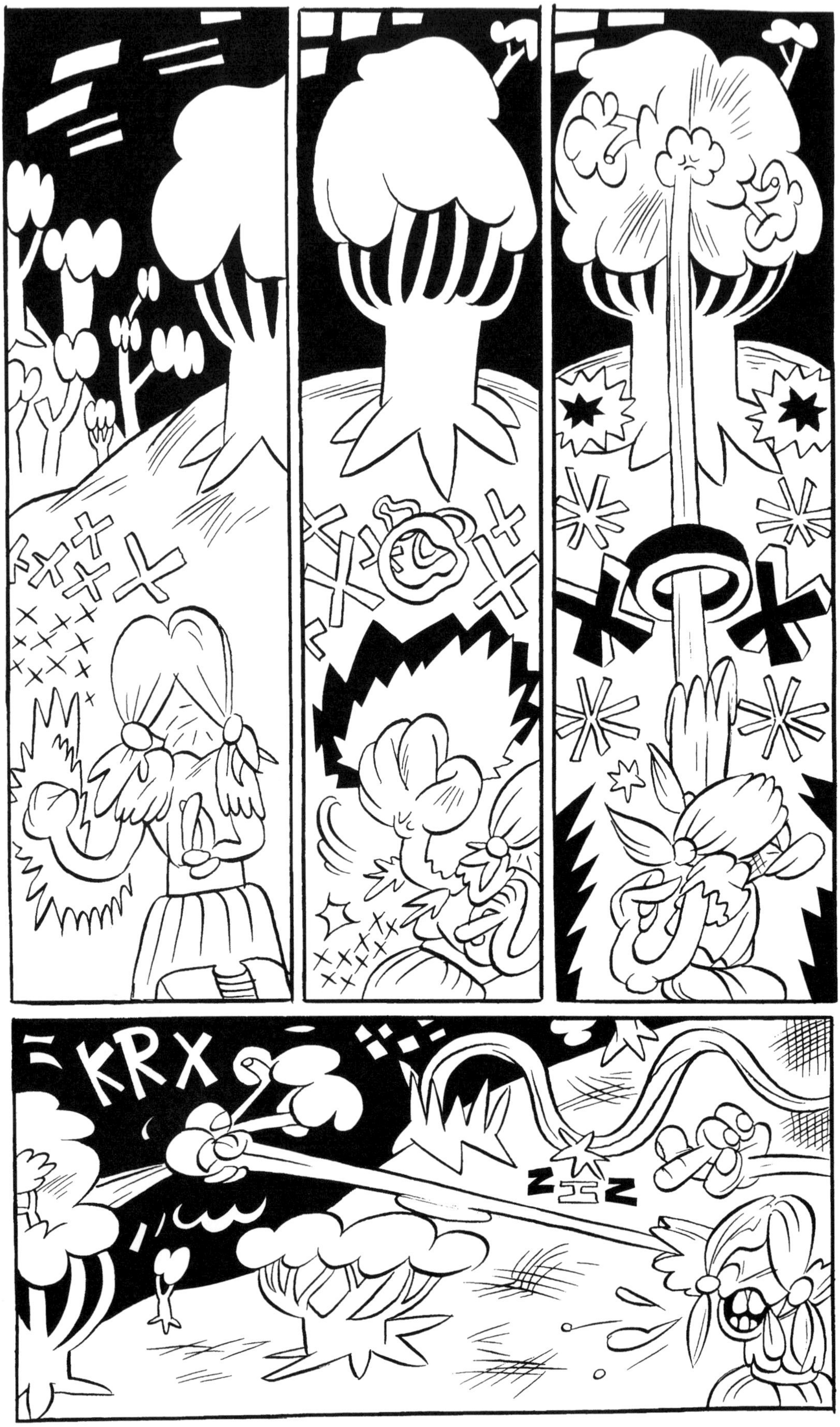
KRX
ZIZ

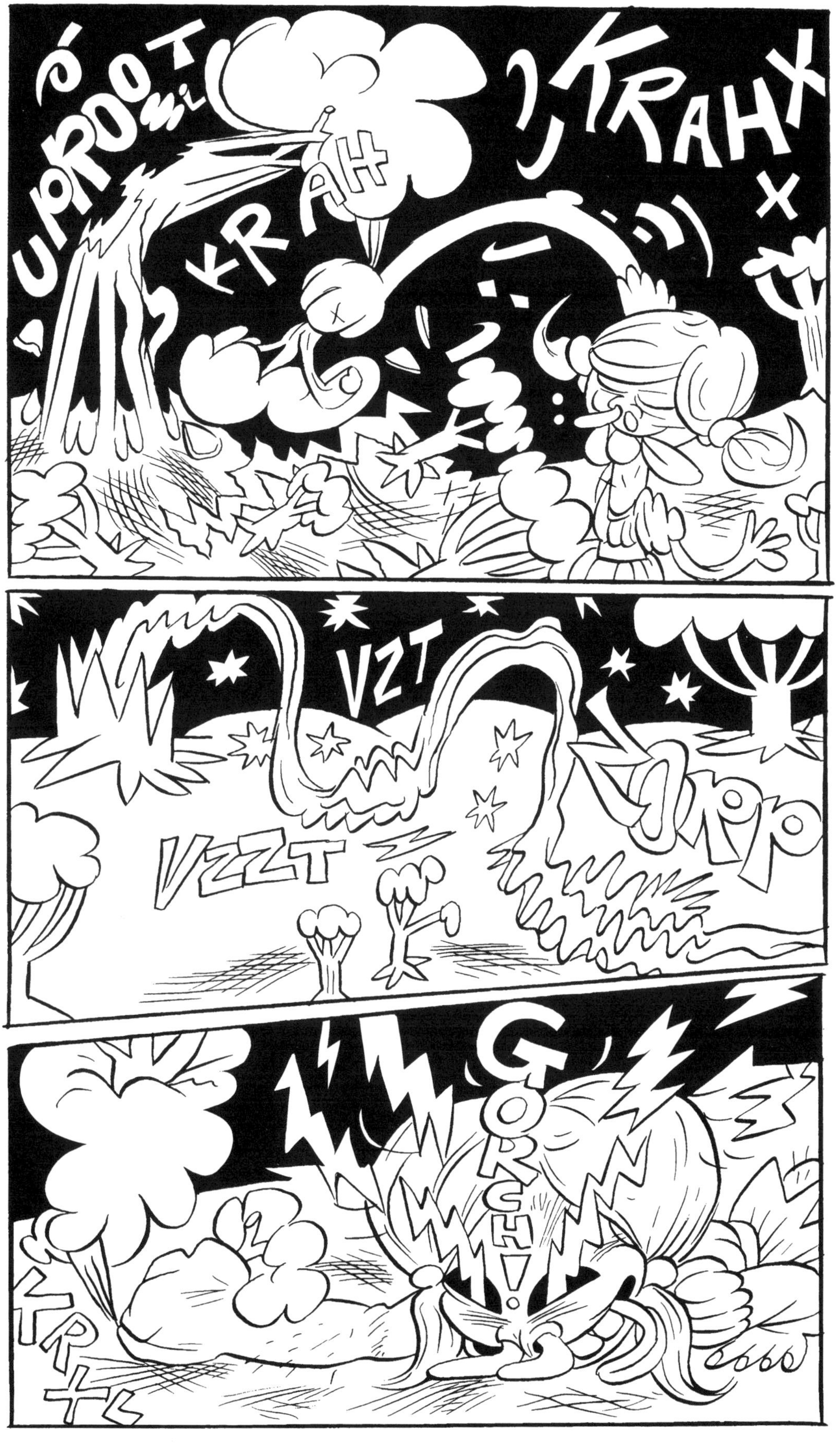
UPROOT
KRAH
KRAHX
VZT
VZZT
GORCH!
KRTL

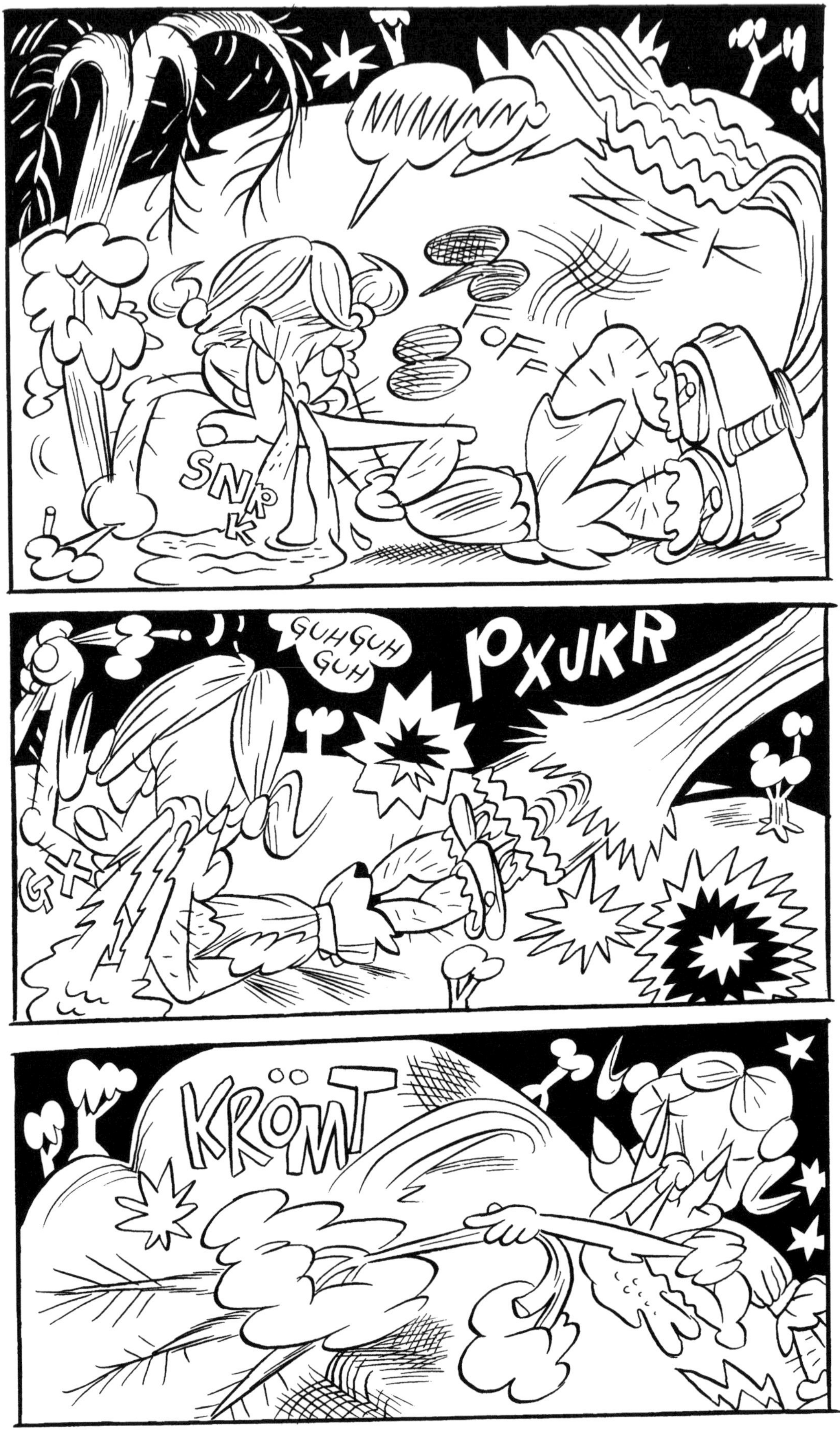
NNNNNNN
SNRK
OFF
GUH GUH GUH
PXUKR
GX
KRÖMT

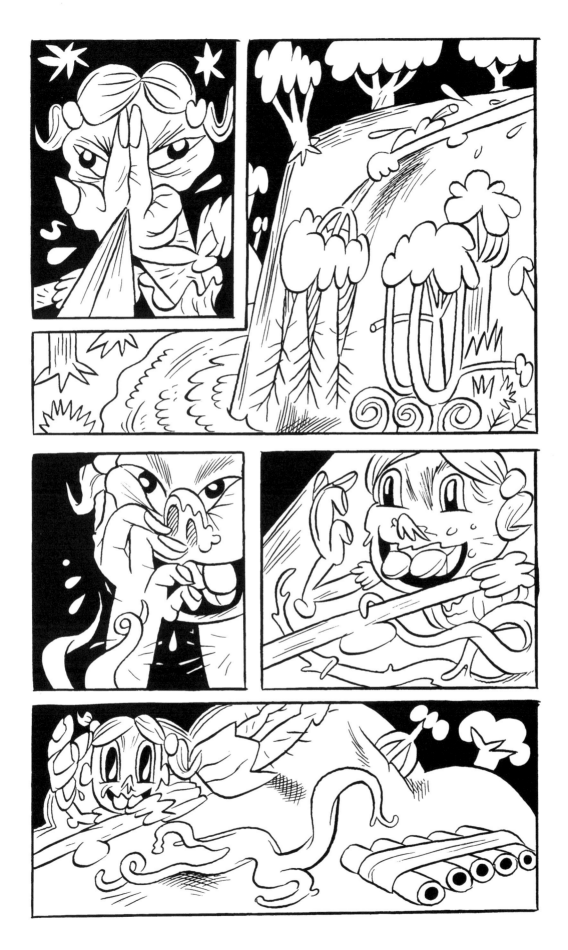

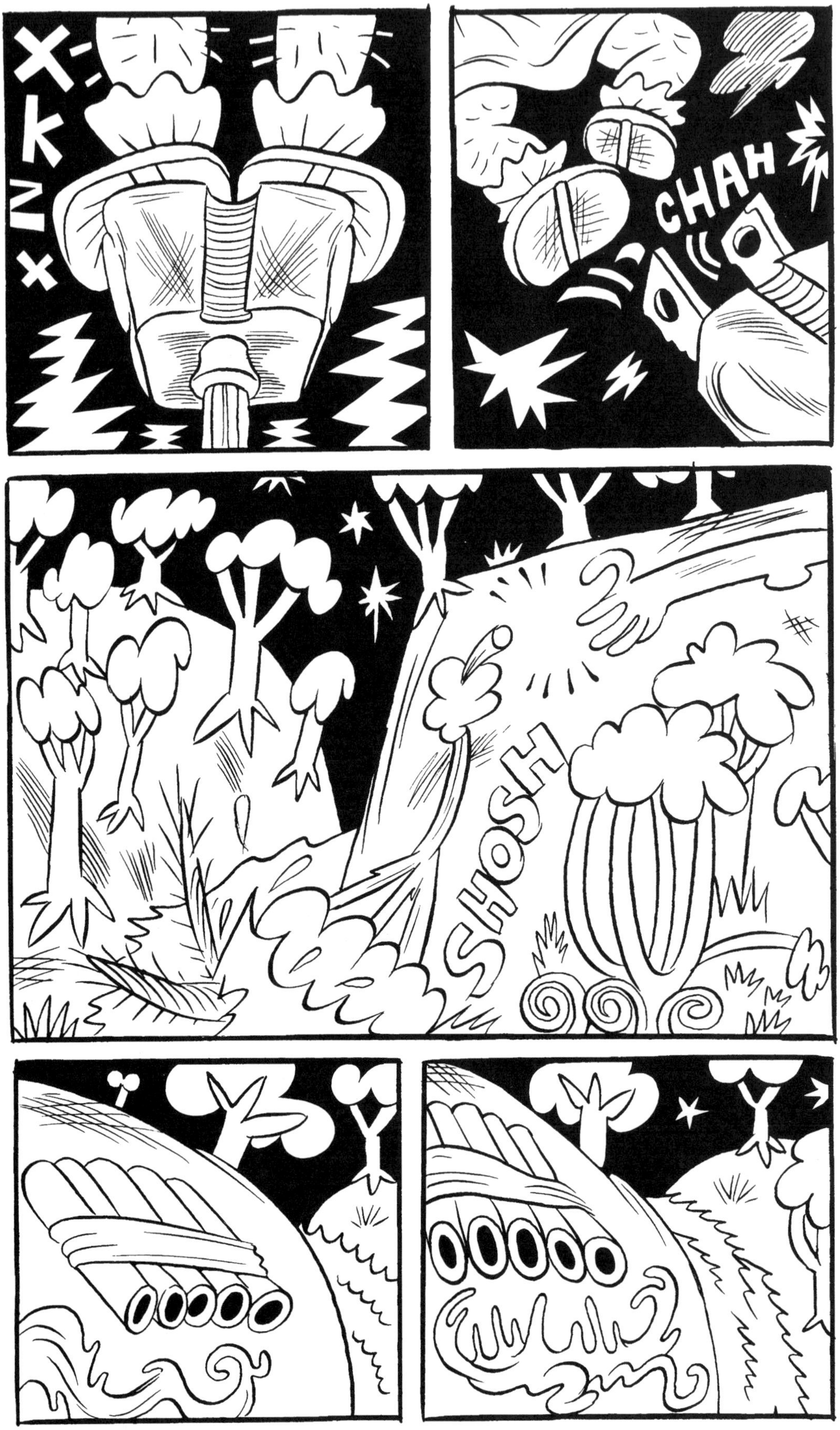
CHAH
SHOSH

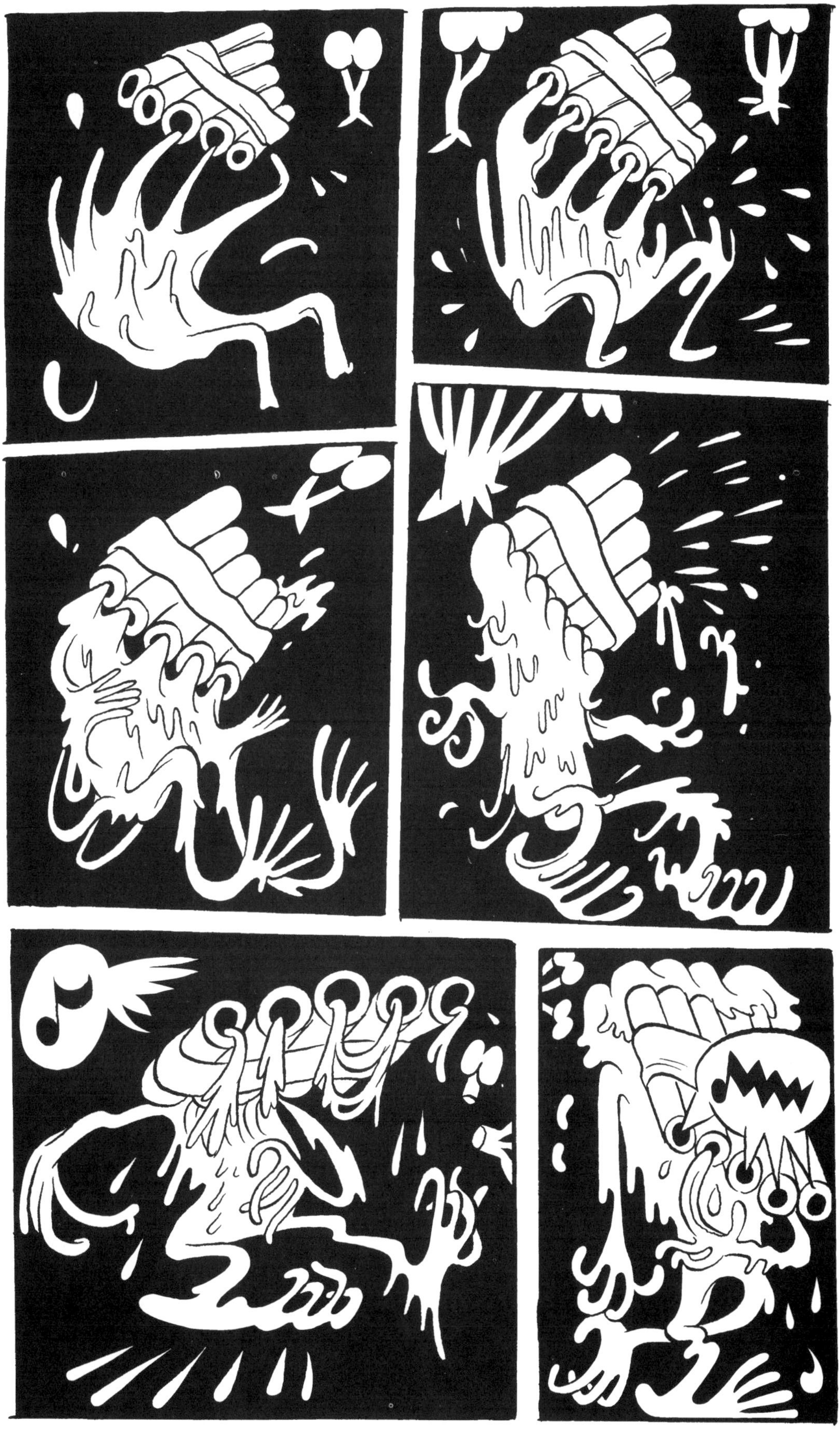

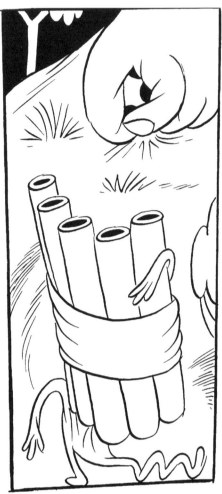

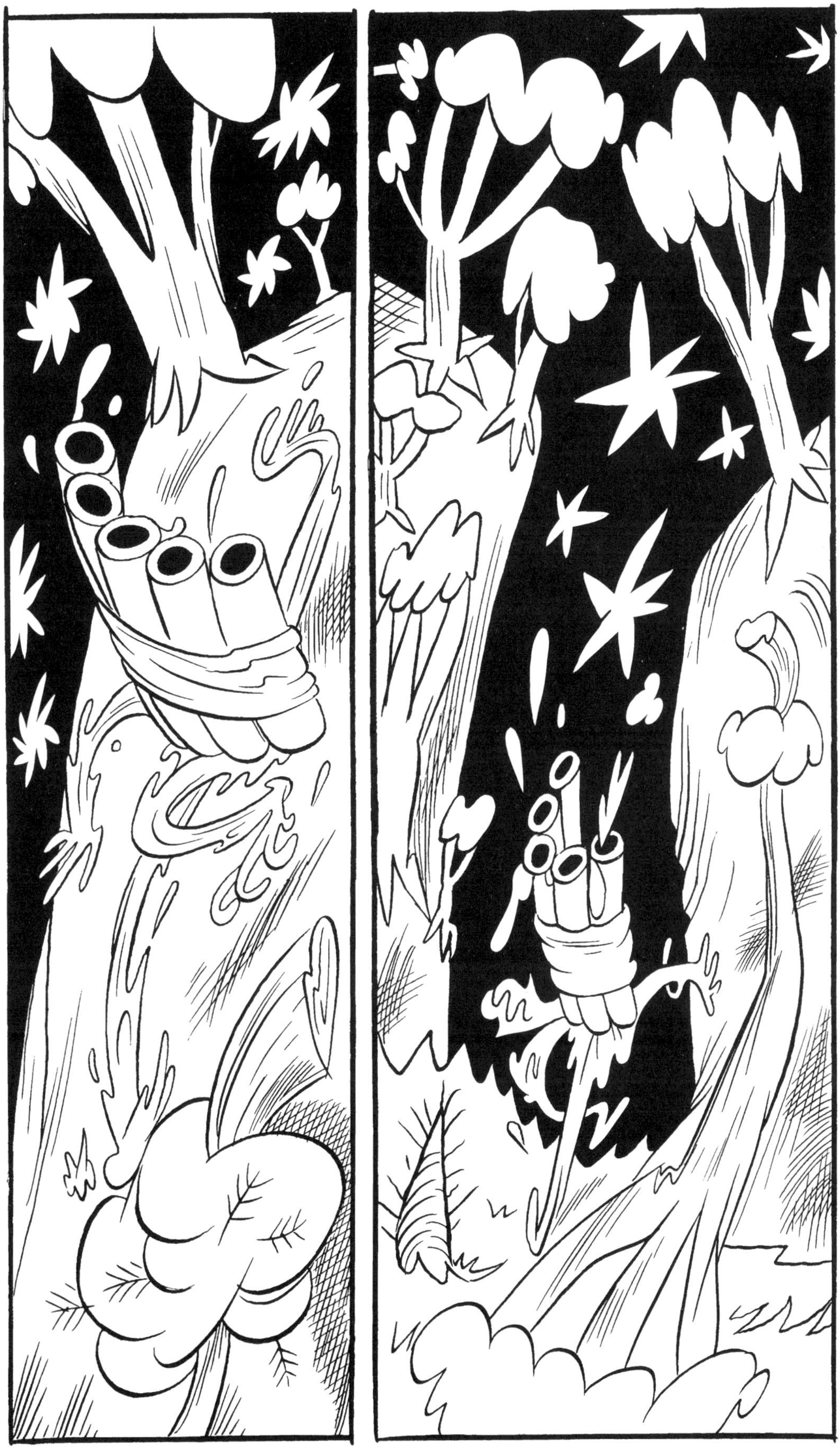

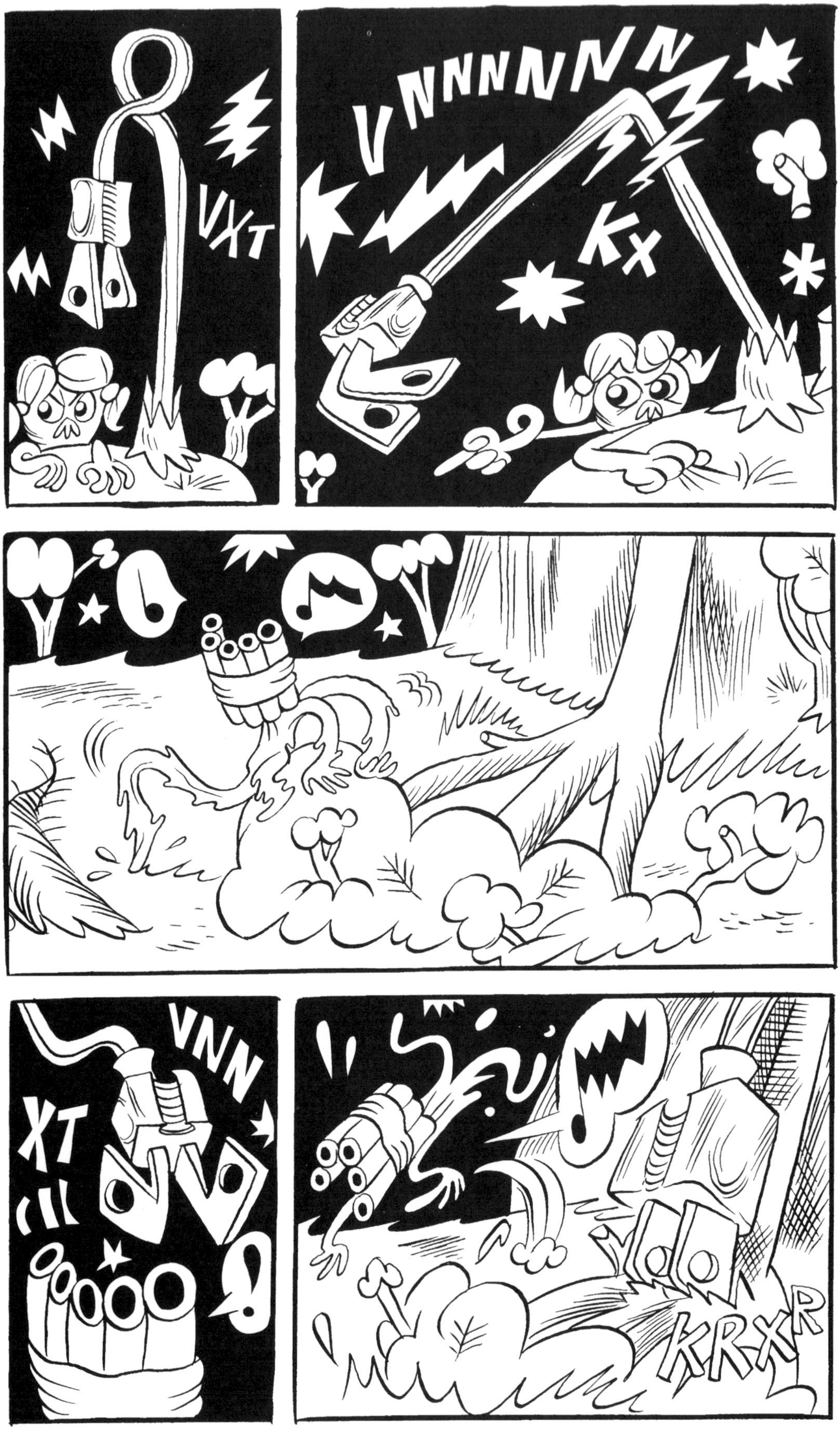
VXT
VNNNNNNN
KX
VNN
XT
KRXR

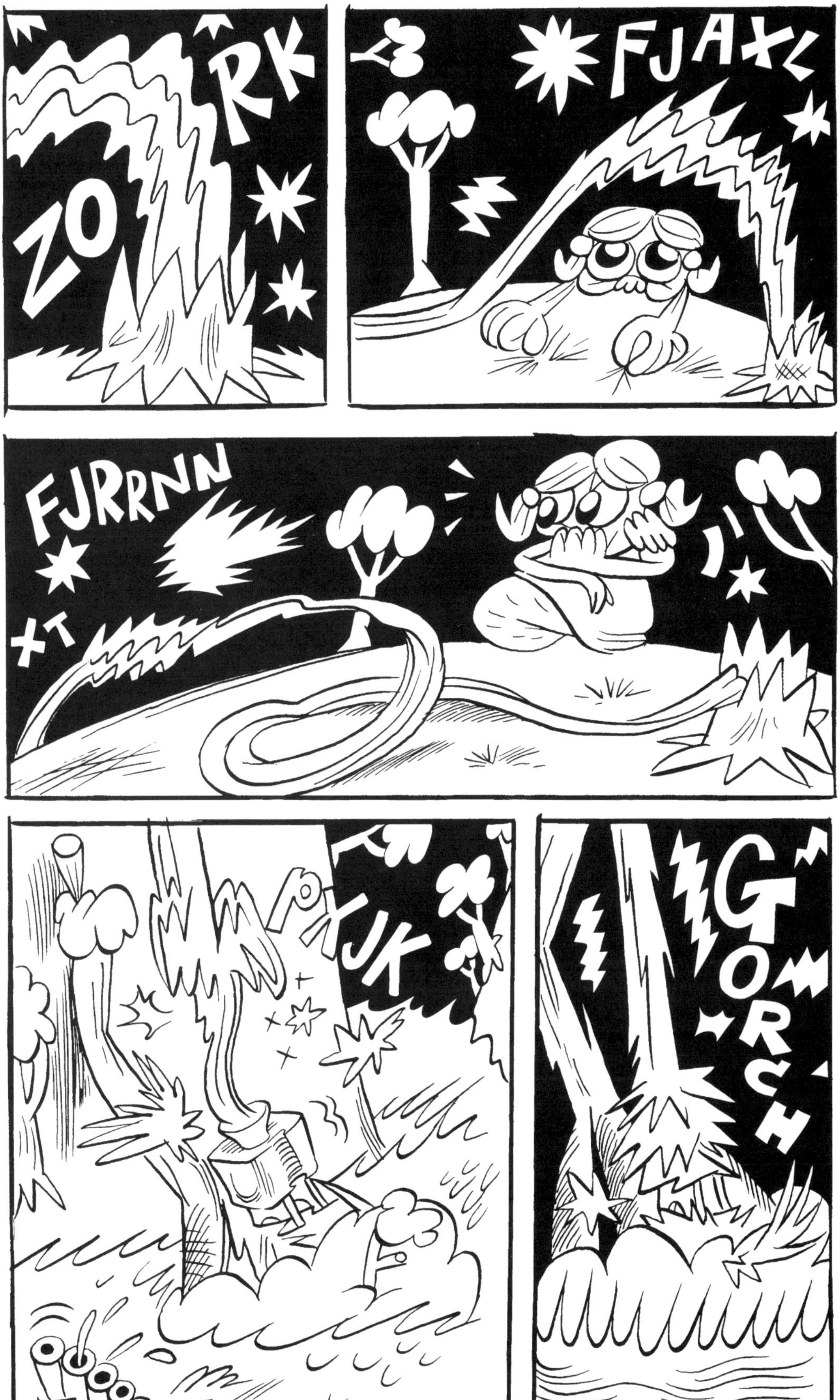
ZORK
FJRRNN
XT
GORCH

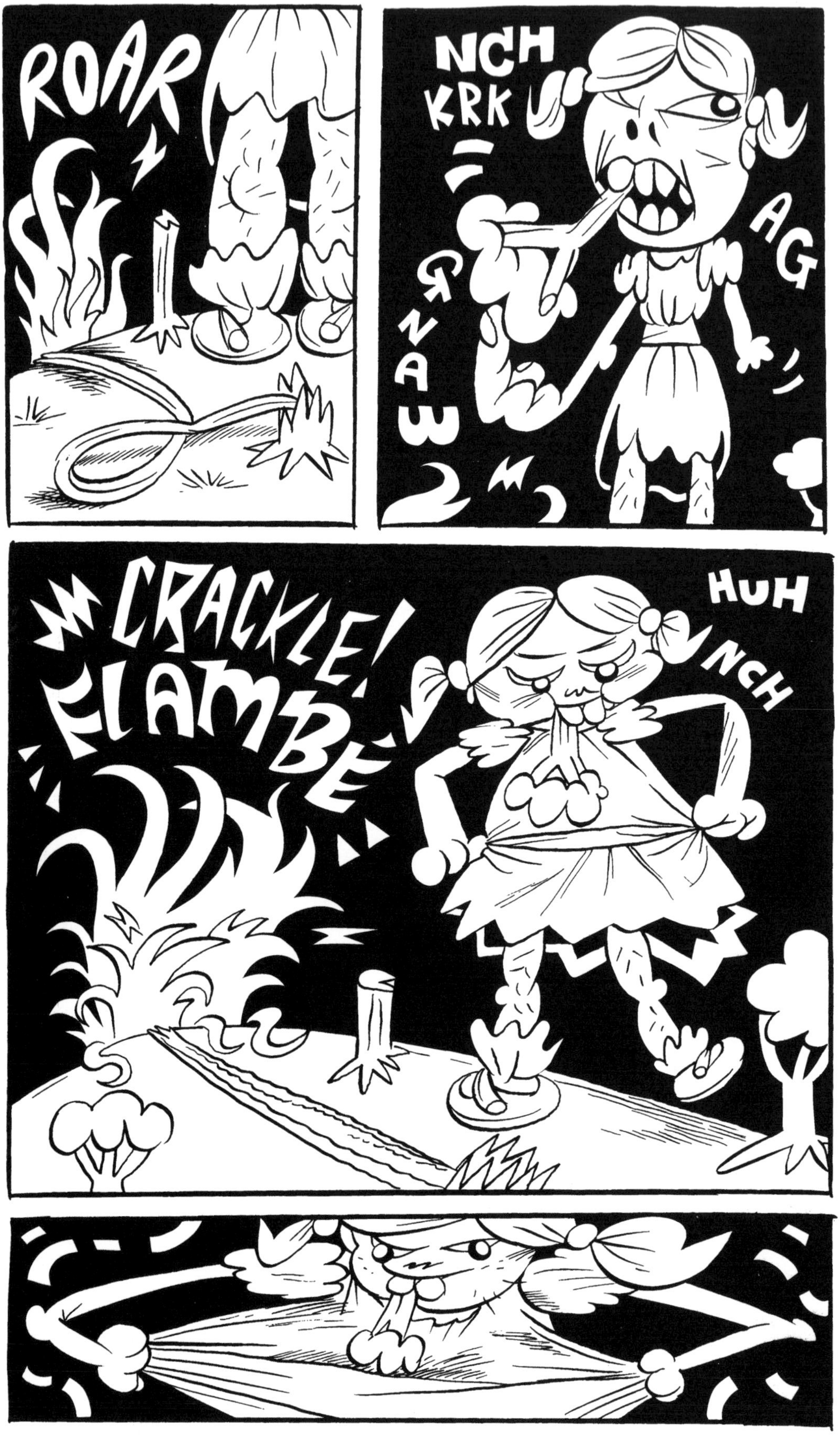
ROAR
NCH
KRK
GNAW
AG
CRACKLE!
FLAMBÉ
HUH
NCH

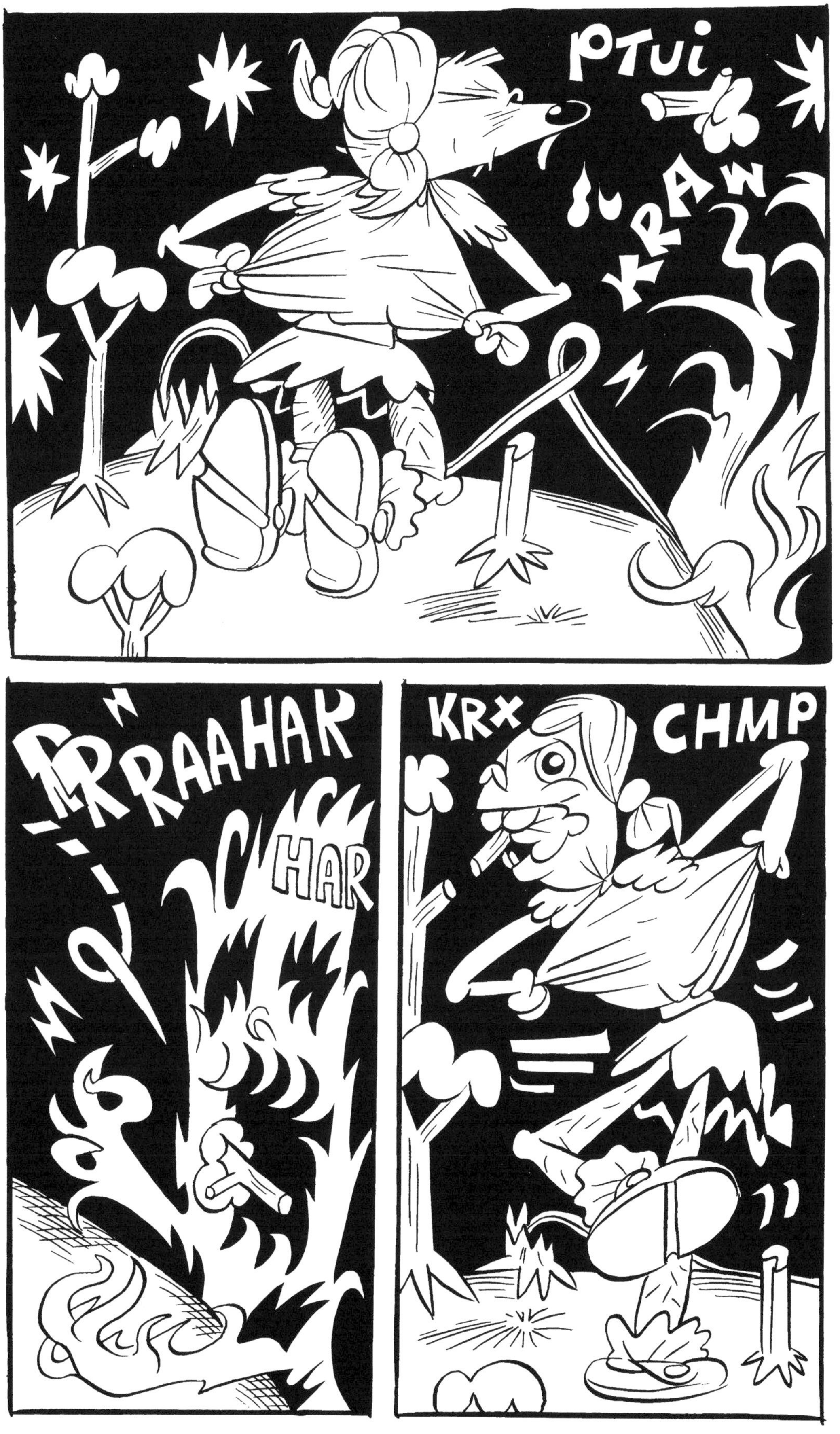
PTUI
KRAW
RAAHAR
HAR
KRX
CHMP

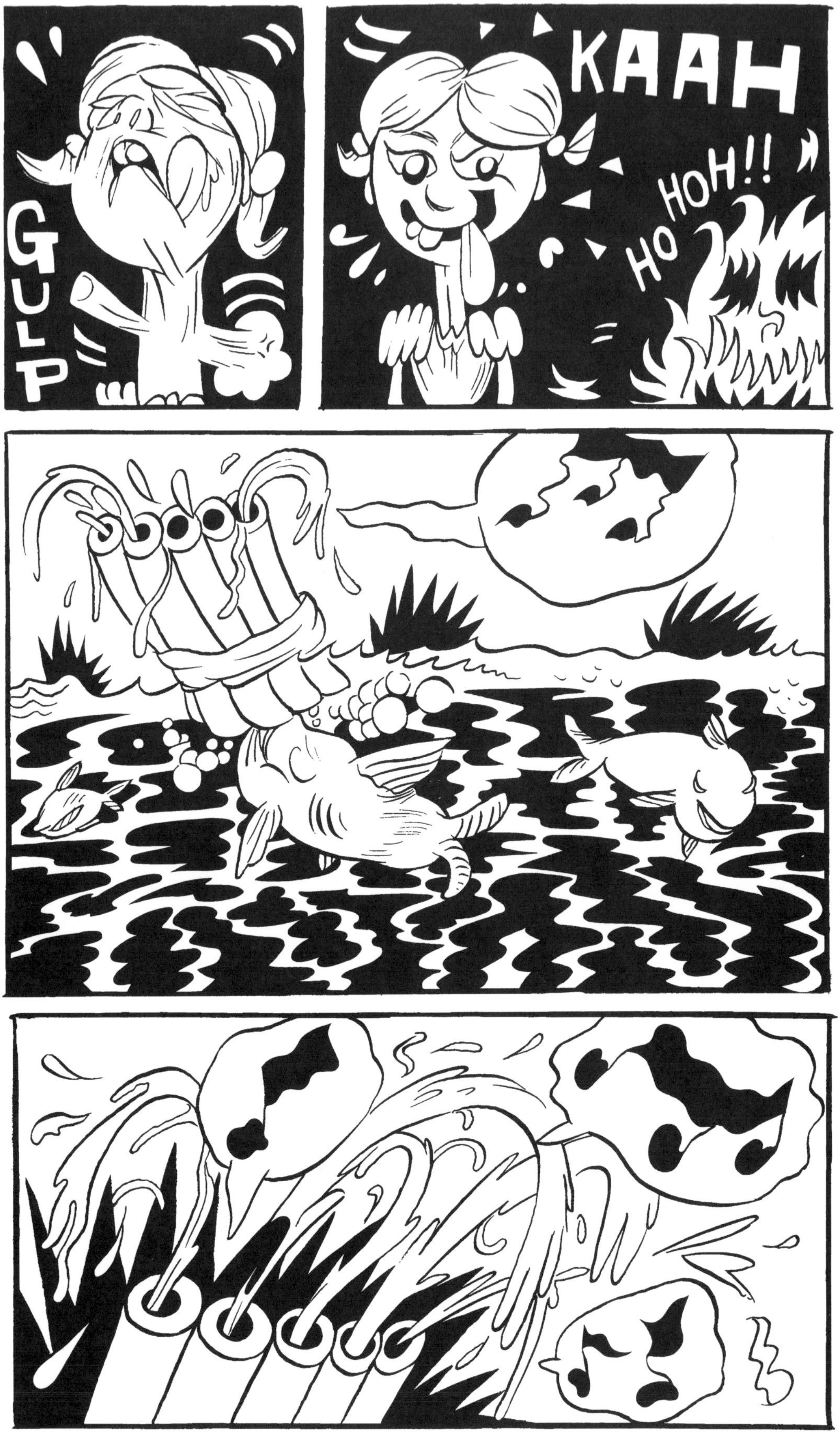
GULP
KAAH
HO HOH!!

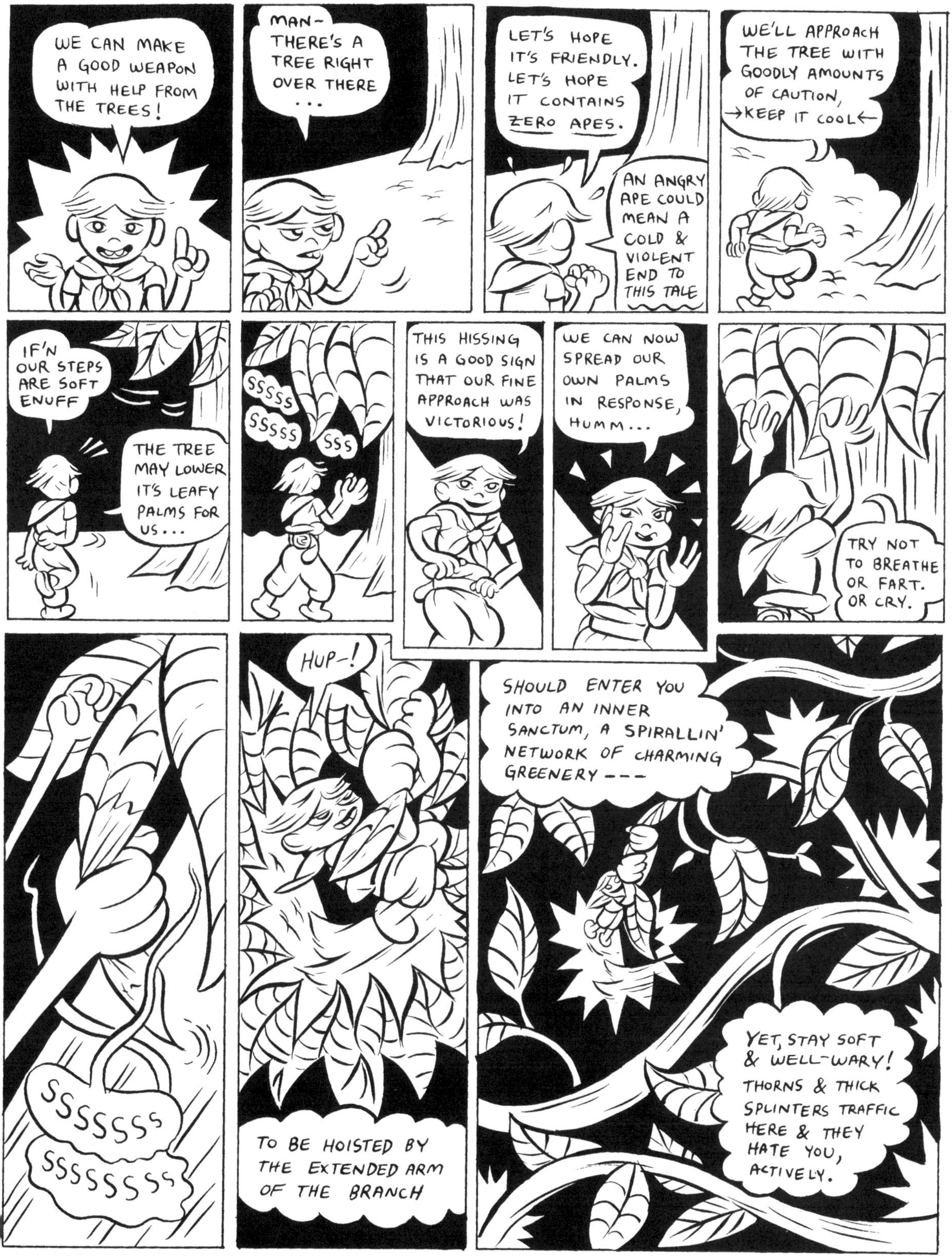
WE CAN MAKE A GOOD WEAPON WITH HELP FROM THE TREES!
MAN- THERE'S A TREE RIGHT OVER THERE ...
LET'S HOPE IT'S FRIENDLY. LET'S HOPE IT CONTAINS ZERO APES.
AN ANGRY APE COULD MEAN A COLD & VIOLENT END TO THIS TALE
WE'LL APPROACH THE TREE WITH GOODLY AMOUNTS OF CAUTION, →KEEP IT COOL←
IF'N OUR STEPS ARE SOFT ENUFF
THE TREE MAY LOWER IT'S LEAFY PALMS FOR US...
SSSSS
SSSSS
SSS
THIS HISSING IS A GOOD SIGN THAT OUR FINE APPROACH WAS VICTORIOUS!
WE CAN NOW SPREAD OUR OWN PALMS IN RESPONSE, HUMM...
TRY NOT TO BREATHE OR FART. OR CRY.
SSSSSSS
SSSSSSSSS
HUP-!
TO BE HOISTED BY THE EXTENDED ARM OF THE BRANCH
SHOULD ENTER YOU INTO AN INNER SANCTUM, A SPIRALLIN' NETWORK OF CHARMING GREENERY ---
YET, STAY SOFT & WELL-WARY! THORNS & THICK SPLINTERS TRAFFIC HERE & THEY HATE YOU, ACTIVELY.

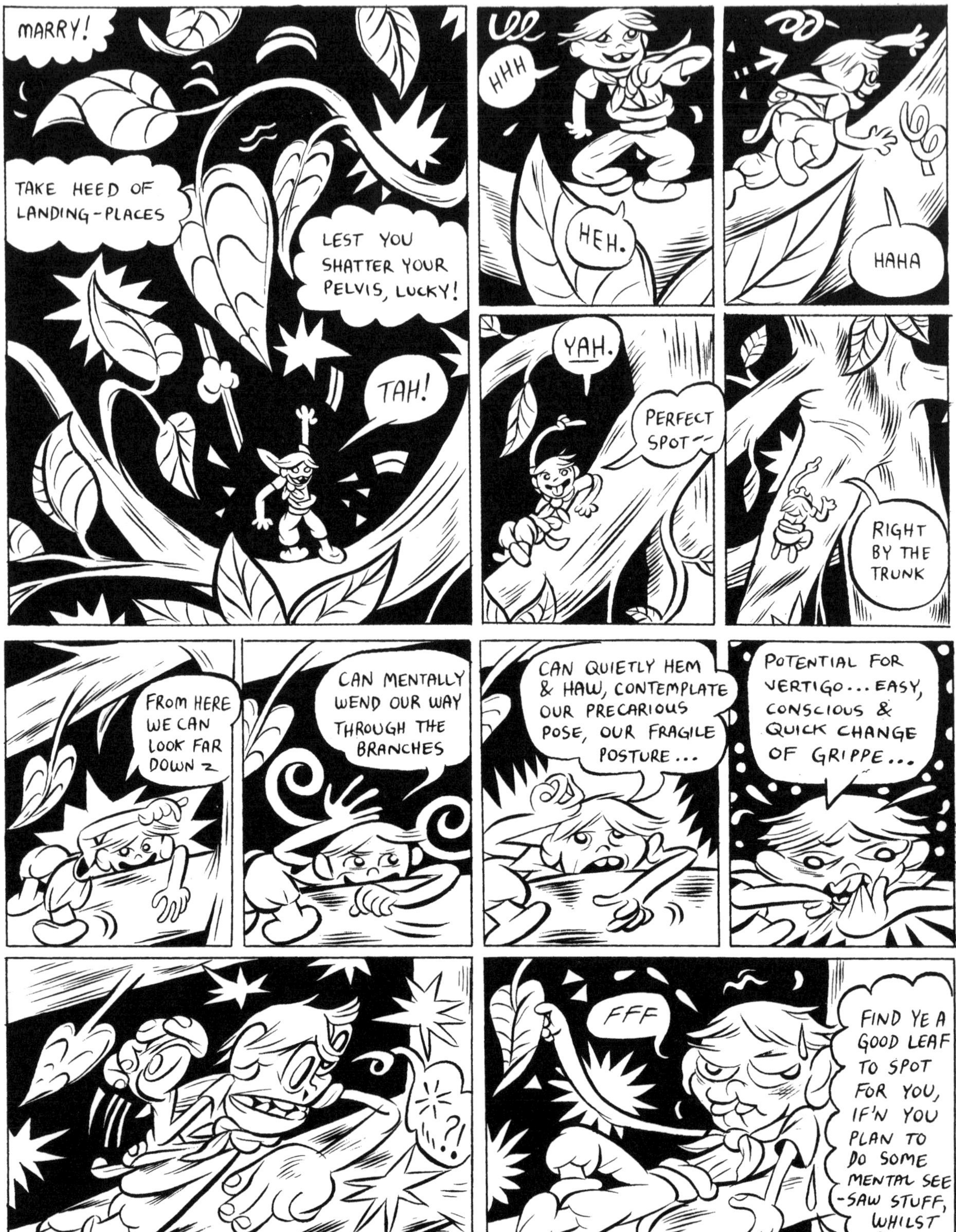
MARRY!
TAKE HEED OF LANDING-PLACES
LEST YOU SHATTER YOUR PELVIS, LUCKY!
TAH!
HHH
HEH.
HAHA
YAH.
PERFECT SPOT--
RIGHT BY THE TRUNK
FROM HERE WE CAN LOOK FAR DOWN--
CAN MENTALLY WEND OUR WAY THROUGH THE BRANCHES
CAN QUIETLY HEM & HAW, CONTEMPLATE OUR PRECARIOUS POSE, OUR FRAGILE POSTURE...
POTENTIAL FOR VERTIGO... EASY, CONSCIOUS & QUICK CHANGE OF GRIPPE...
!?!
FFF
FIND YE A GOOD LEAF TO SPOT FOR YOU, IF'N YOU PLAN TO DO SOME MENTAL SEE-SAW STUFF, WHILST ALOFT.

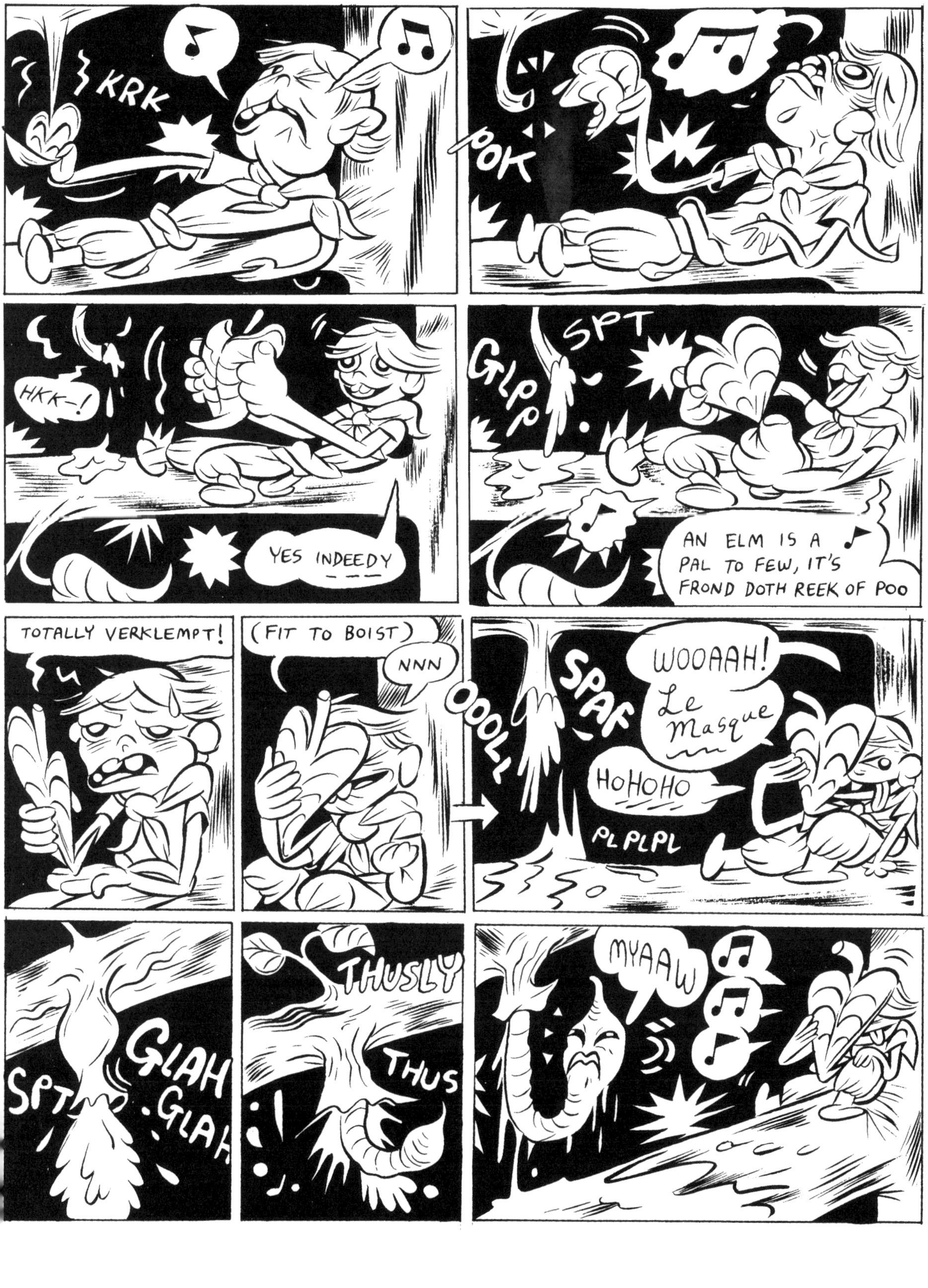
KRK
POK
HKK-!
YES INDEEDY
GLPP
SPT
AN ELM IS A PAL TO FEW, IT'S FROND DOTH REEK OF POO
TOTALLY VERKLEMPT!
(FIT TO BOIST)
NNN
OOOLL
SPAF
WOOAAH!
Le Masque
HOHOHO
PLPLPL
SPT
GLAH
GLAH
THUSLY
THUS
MYAAW

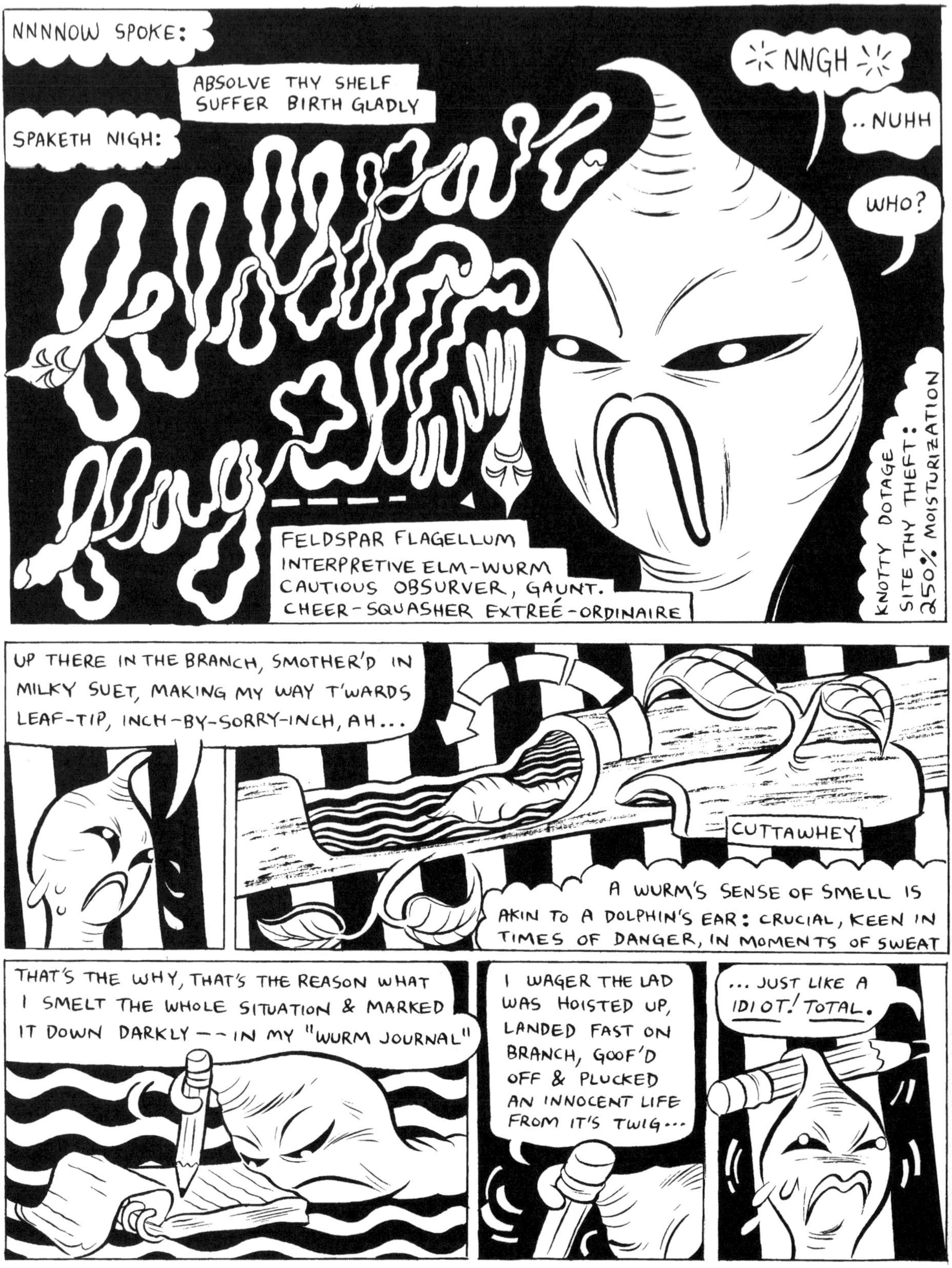
NNNNOW SPOKE:
ABSOLVE THY SHELF SUFFER BIRTH GLADLY
SPAKETH NIGH:
NNGH
..NUHH
WHO?
FELDSPAR FLAGELLUM
INTERPRETIVE ELM-WURM
CAUTIOUS OBSURVER, GAUNT.
CHEER-SQUASHER EXTREÉ-ORDINAIRE
KNOTTY DOTAGE
SITE THY THEFT:
250% MOISTURIZATION
UP THERE IN THE BRANCH, SMOTHER'D IN MILKY SUET, MAKING MY WAY T'WARDS LEAF-TIP, INCH-BY-SORRY-INCH, AH...
CUTTAWHEY
A WURM'S SENSE OF SMELL IS AKIN TO A DOLPHIN'S EAR: CRUCIAL, KEEN IN TIMES OF DANGER, IN MOMENTS OF SWEAT
THAT'S THE WHY, THAT'S THE REASON WHAT I SMELT THE WHOLE SITUATION & MARKED IT DOWN DARKLY -- IN MY "WURM JOURNAL"
I WAGER THE LAD WAS HOISTED UP, LANDED FAST ON BRANCH, GOOF'D OFF & PLUCKED AN INNOCENT LIFE FROM IT'S TWIG...
... JUST LIKE A IDIOT! TOTAL.

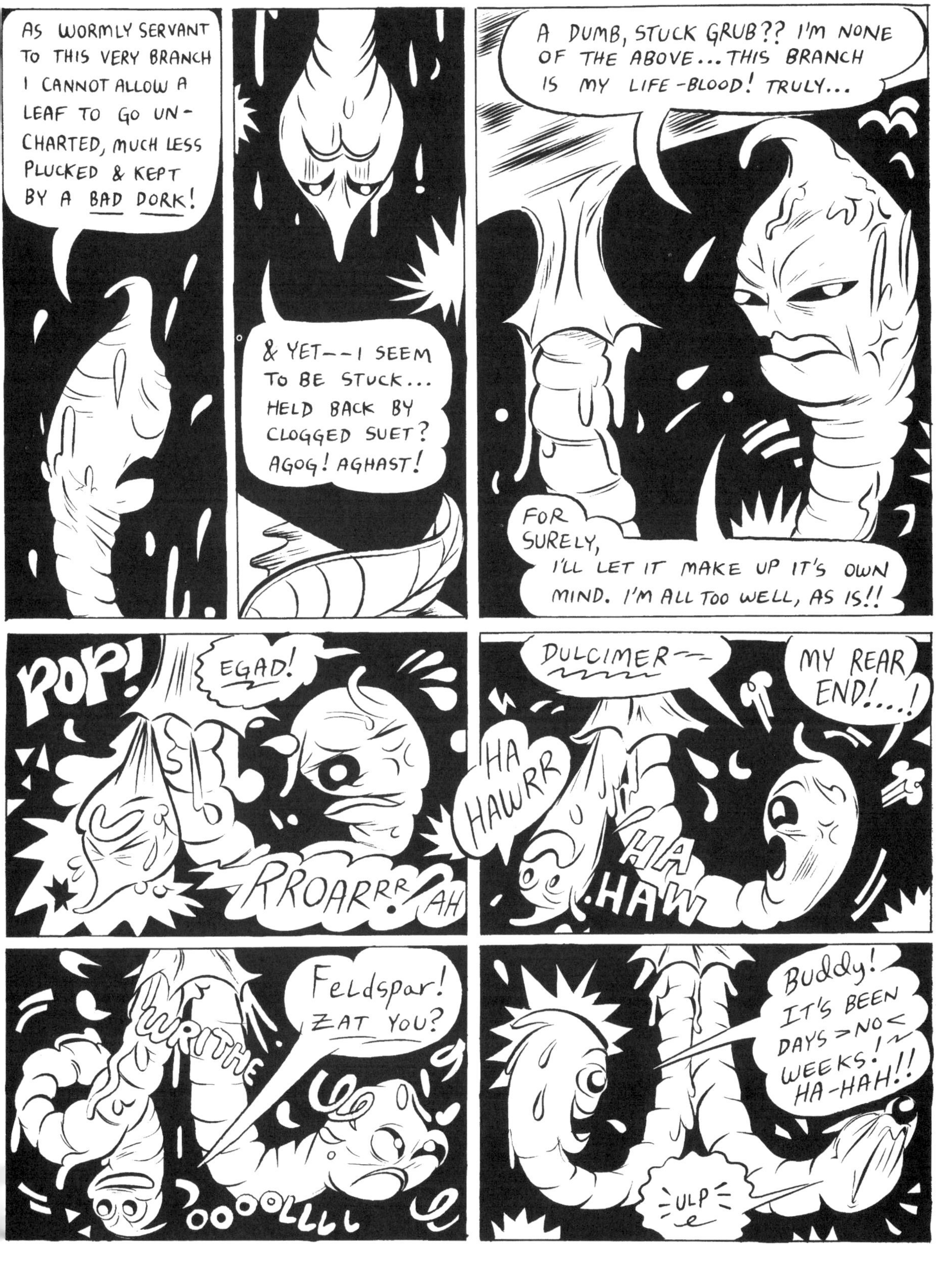

AS WORMLY SERVANT TO THIS VERY BRANCH I CANNOT ALLOW A LEAF TO GO UN-CHARTED, MUCH LESS PLUCKED & KEPT BY A BAD DORK!
& YET--I SEEM TO BE STUCK... HELD BACK BY CLOGGED SUET? AGOG! AGHAST!
A DUMB, STUCK GRUB?? I'M NONE OF THE ABOVE... THIS BRANCH IS MY LIFE-BLOOD! TRULY...
FOR SURELY, I'LL LET IT MAKE UP IT'S OWN MIND. I'M ALL TOO WELL, AS IS!!
POP!
EGAD!
RROARRR! AH
DULCIMER--
MY REAR END!...!
HA HAWRR
HA HAW
Feldspar! ZAT YOU?
WRITHE
OOOOLLLLL
Buddy! IT'S BEEN DAYS >NO< WEEKS! HA-HAH!!
ULP

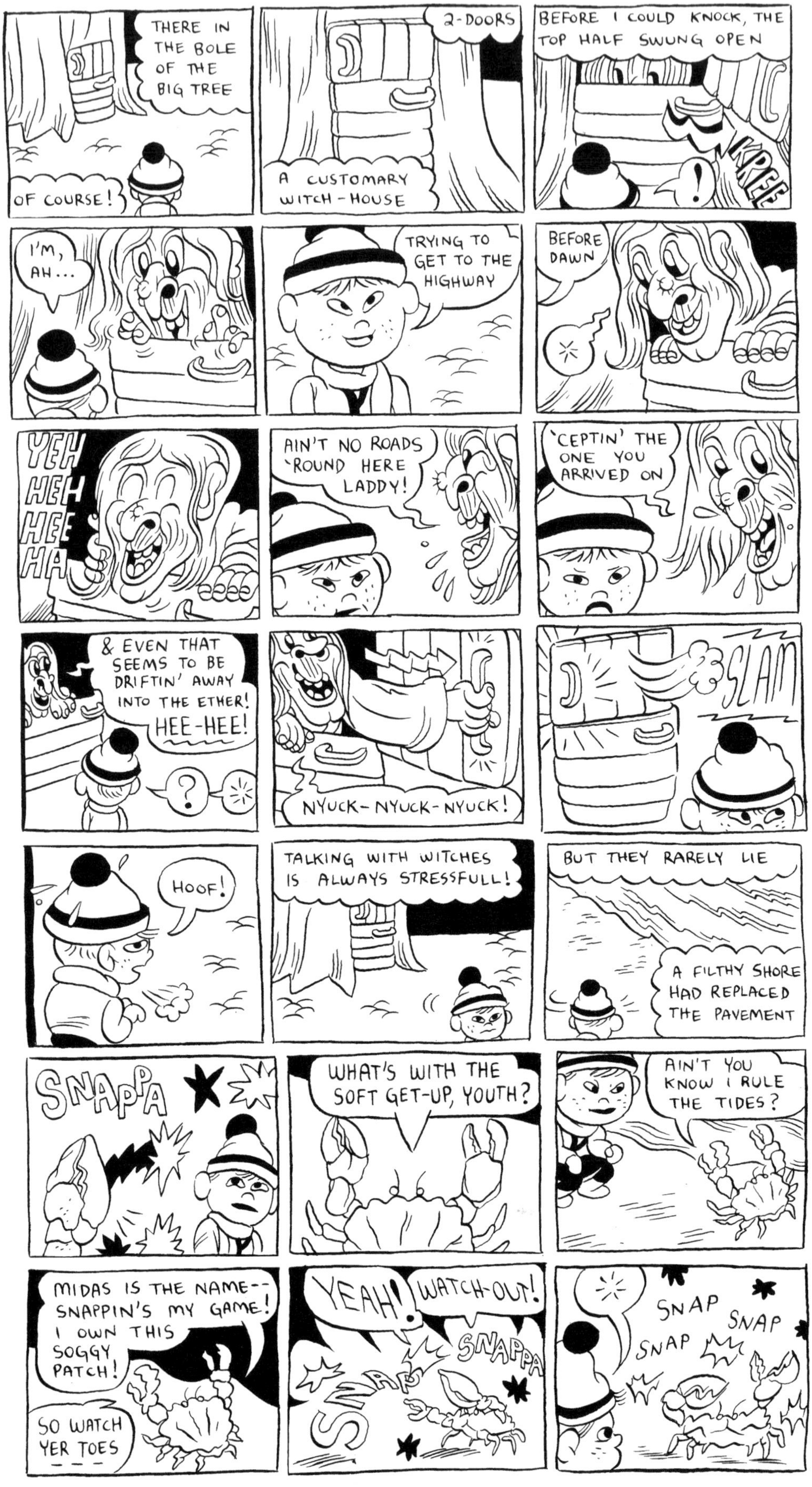
THERE IN THE BOLE OF THE BIG TREE
OF COURSE!
2-DOORS
A CUSTOMARY WITCH-HOUSE
BEFORE I COULD KNOCK, THE TOP HALF SWUNG OPEN
KREE
!
I'M, AH...
TRYING TO GET TO THE HIGHWAY
BEFORE DAWN
YEH HEH HEE HA
AIN'T NO ROADS 'ROUND HERE LADDY!
'CEPTIN' THE ONE YOU ARRIVED ON
& EVEN THAT SEEMS TO BE DRIFTIN' AWAY INTO THE ETHER! HEE-HEE!
?
NYUCK-NYUCK-NYUCK!
SLAM
HOOF!
TALKING WITH WITCHES IS ALWAYS STRESSFULL!
BUT THEY RARELY LIE
A FILTHY SHORE HAD REPLACED THE PAVEMENT
SNAPPA
WHAT'S WITH THE SOFT GET-UP, YOUTH?
AIN'T YOU KNOW I RULE THE TIDES?
MIDAS IS THE NAME-- SNAPPIN'S MY GAME! I OWN THIS SOGGY PATCH!
SO WATCH YER TOES ---
YEAH!
WATCH-OUT!
SNAPPA
SNAP
SNAP
SNAP
SNAP

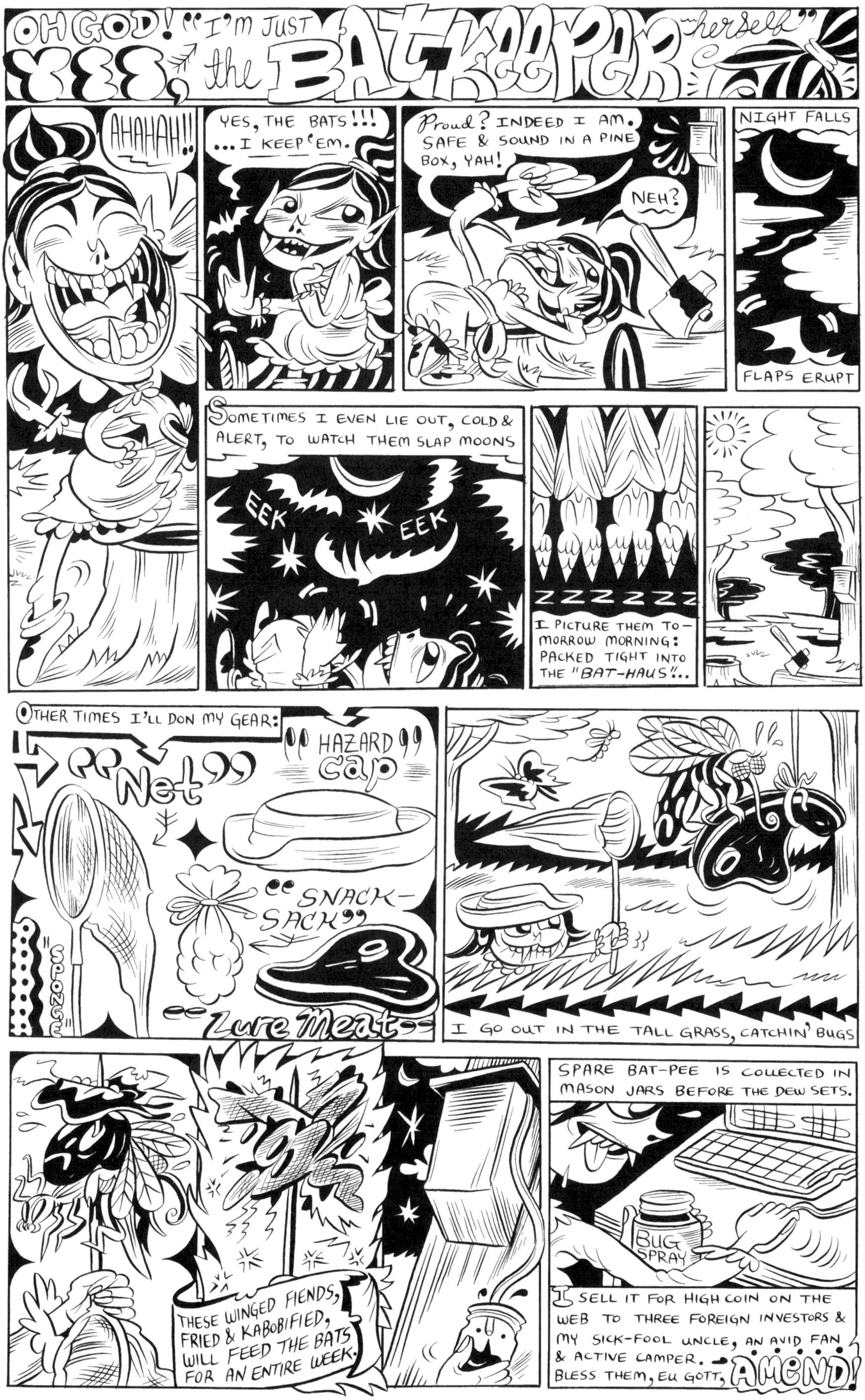

OH GOD! YES, "I'M JUST the BATKEEPER herself"
AHAHAH!!
YES, THE BATS!!! ...I KEEP 'EM.
Proud? INDEED I AM. SAFE & SOUND IN A PINE BOX, YAH!
NEH?
NIGHT FALLS
FLAPS ERUPT
SOMETIMES I EVEN LIE OUT, COLD & ALERT, TO WATCH THEM SLAP MOONS
EEK
EEK
ZZZZZZZ
I PICTURE THEM TO-MORROW MORNING: PACKED TIGHT INTO THE "BAT-HAUS"..
OTHER TIMES I'LL DON MY GEAR:
"Net"
"HAZARD cap"
"SNACK-SACK"
"SPONGE"
"Lure Meat"
I GO OUT IN THE TALL GRASS, CATCHIN' BUGS
THESE WINGED FIENDS, FRIED & KABOBIFIED, WILL FEED THE BATS FOR AN ENTIRE WEEK.
SPARE BAT-PEE IS COLLECTED IN MASON JARS BEFORE THE DEW SETS.
BUG SPRAY
I SELL IT FOR HIGH COIN ON THE WEB TO THREE FOREIGN INVESTORS & MY SICK-FOOL UNCLE, AN AVID FAN & ACTIVE CAMPER.
BLESS THEM, EU GOTT, AMEND!

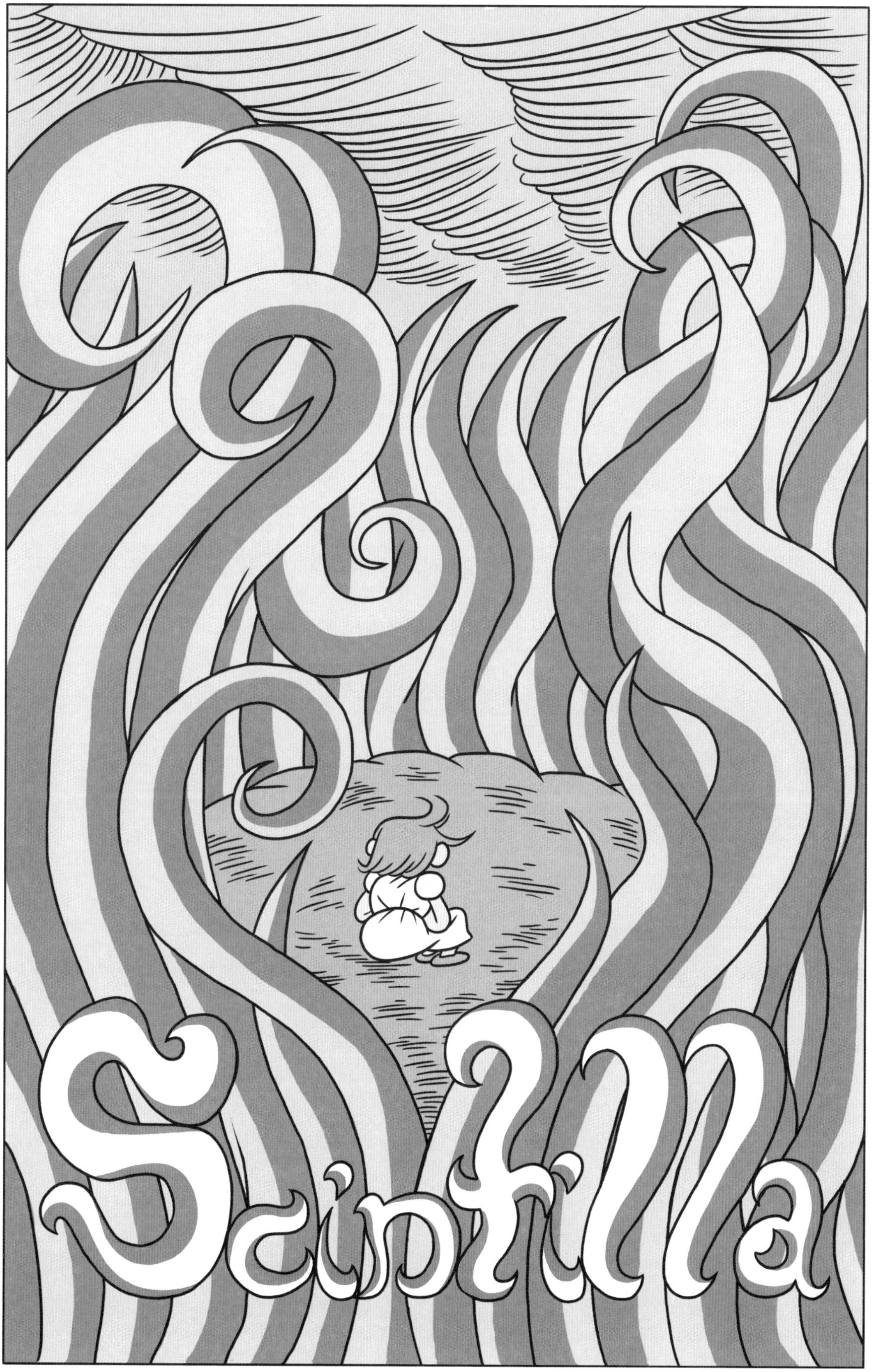
Scintilla

contents

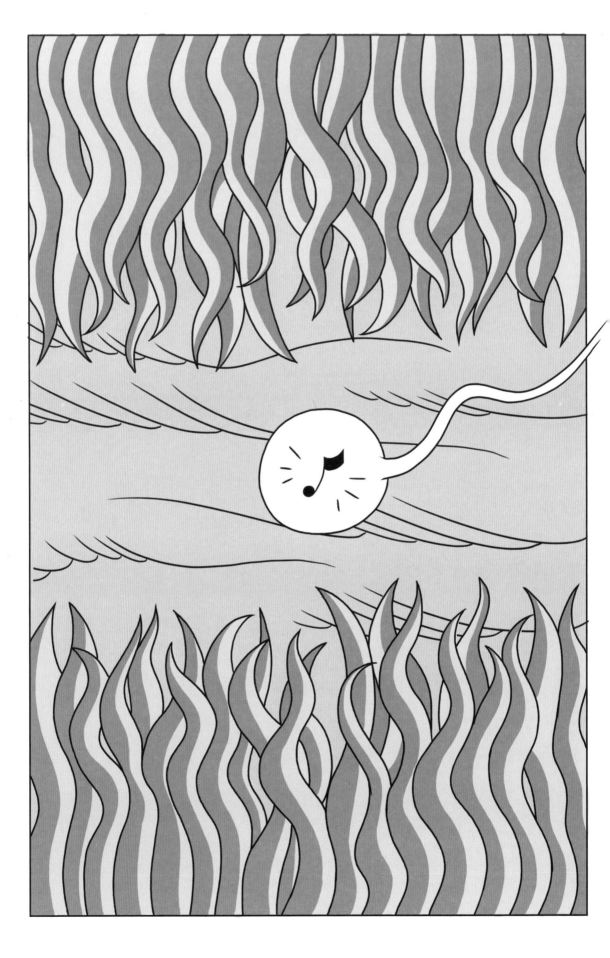

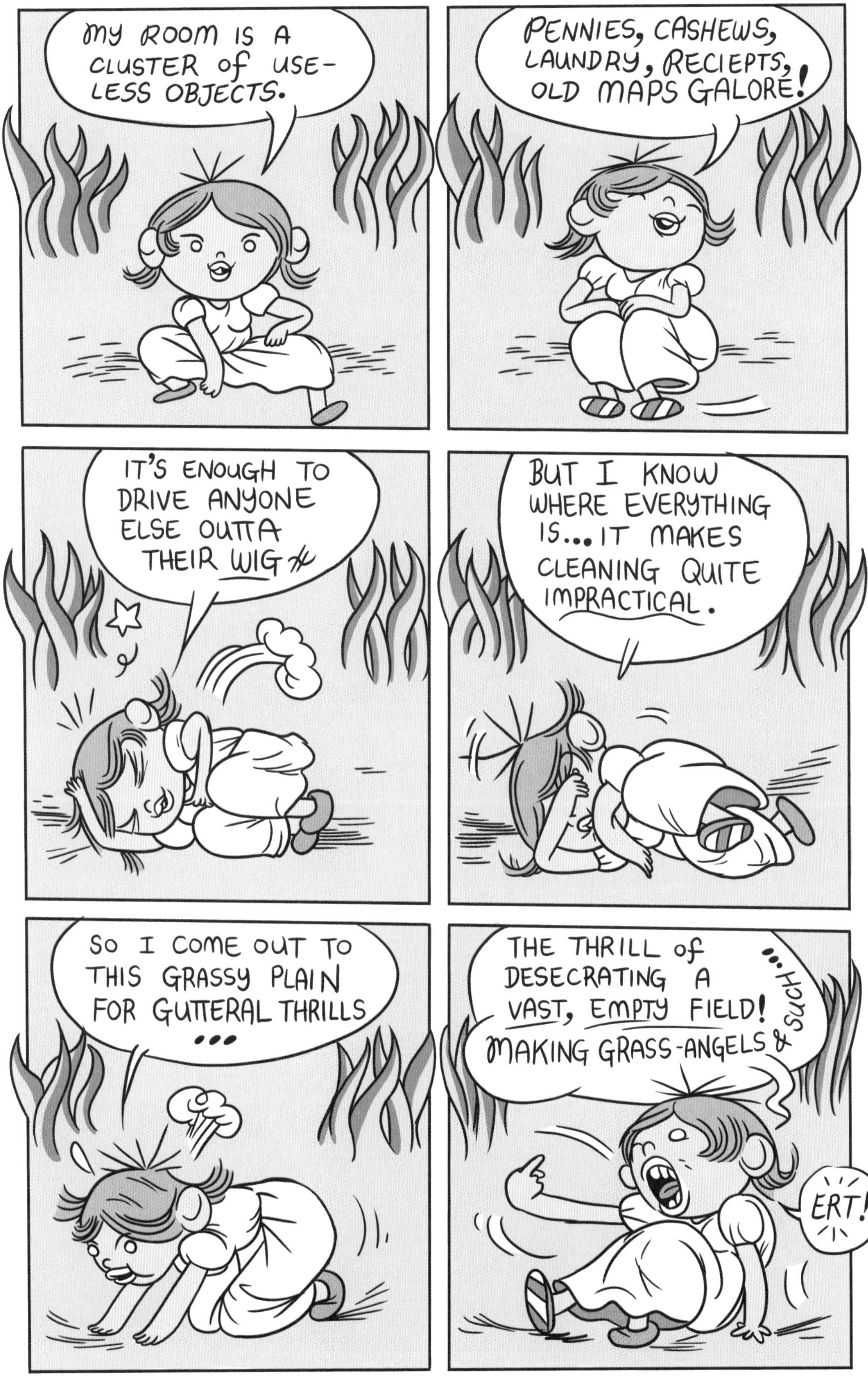
MY ROOM IS A CLUSTER OF USE-LESS OBJECTS.
PENNIES, CASHEWS, LAUNDRY, RECIEPTS, OLD MAPS GALORE!
IT'S ENOUGH TO DRIVE ANYONE ELSE OUTTA THEIR WIG
BUT I KNOW WHERE EVERYTHING IS... IT MAKES CLEANING QUITE IMPRACTICAL.
SO I COME OUT TO THIS GRASSY PLAIN FOR GUTTERAL THRILLS ...
THE THRILL OF DESECRATING A VAST, EMPTY FIELD! MAKING GRASS-ANGELS & SUCH...
ERT!

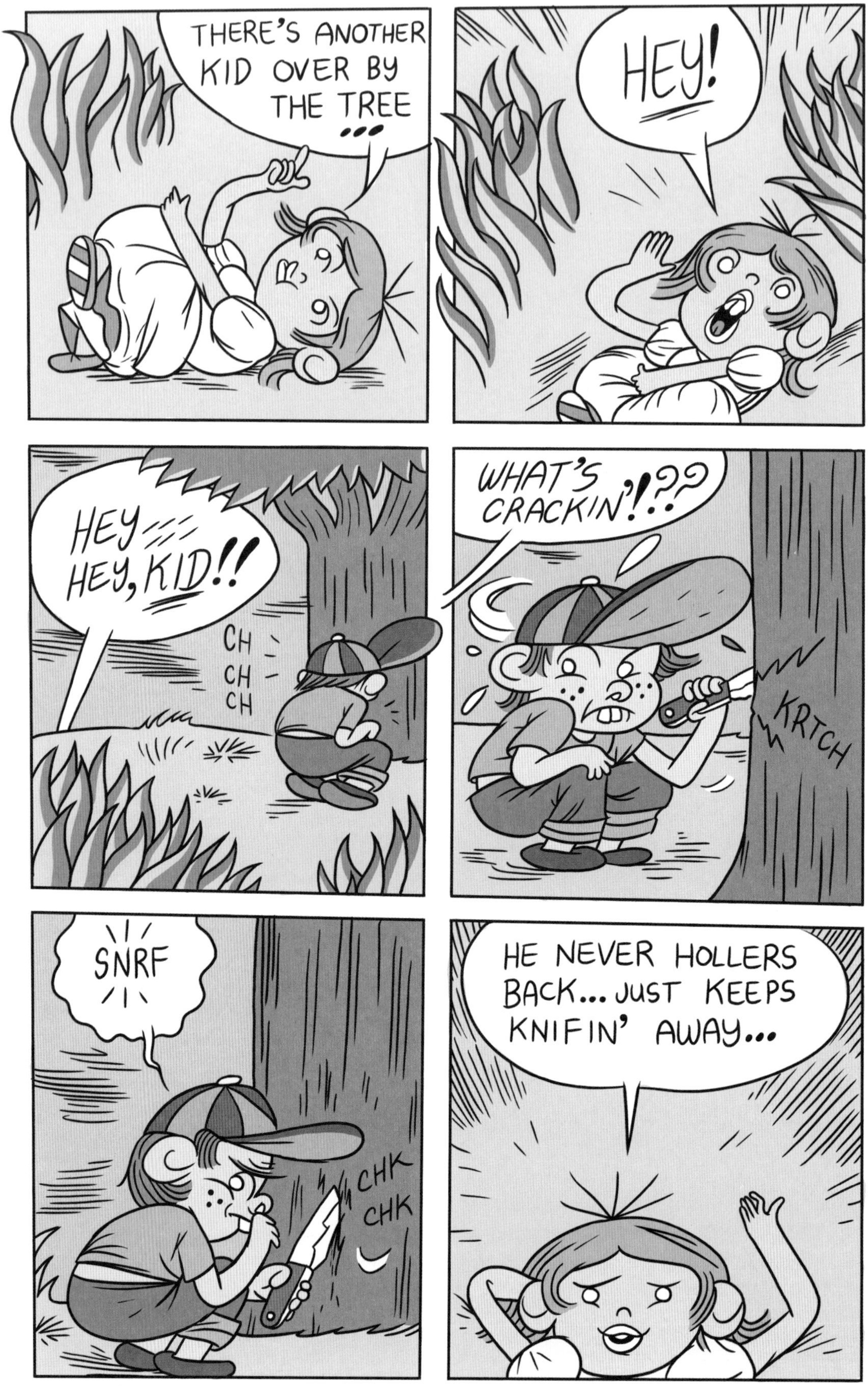
THERE'S ANOTHER KID OVER BY THE TREE ...
HEY!
HEY HEY, KID!!
CH CH CH
WHAT'S CRACKIN'!??
KRTCH
SNRF
CHK CHK
HE NEVER HOLLERS BACK... JUST KEEPS KNIFIN' AWAY...

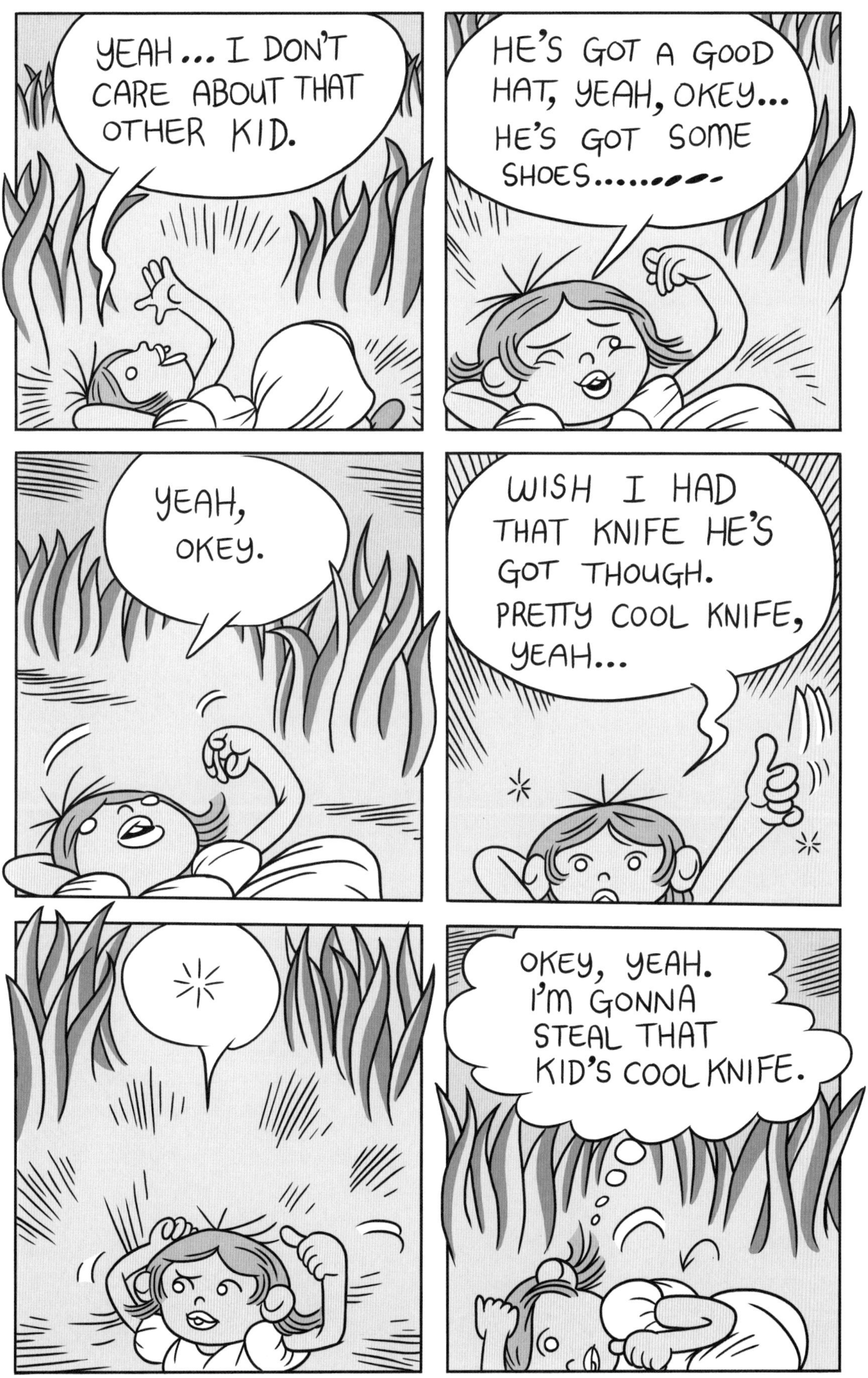
YEAH... I DON'T CARE ABOUT THAT OTHER KID.
HE'S GOT A GOOD HAT, YEAH, OKEY... HE'S GOT SOME SHOES.........
YEAH, OKEY.
WISH I HAD THAT KNIFE HE'S GOT THOUGH. PRETTY COOL KNIFE, YEAH...
OKEY, YEAH. I'M GONNA STEAL THAT KID'S COOL KNIFE.

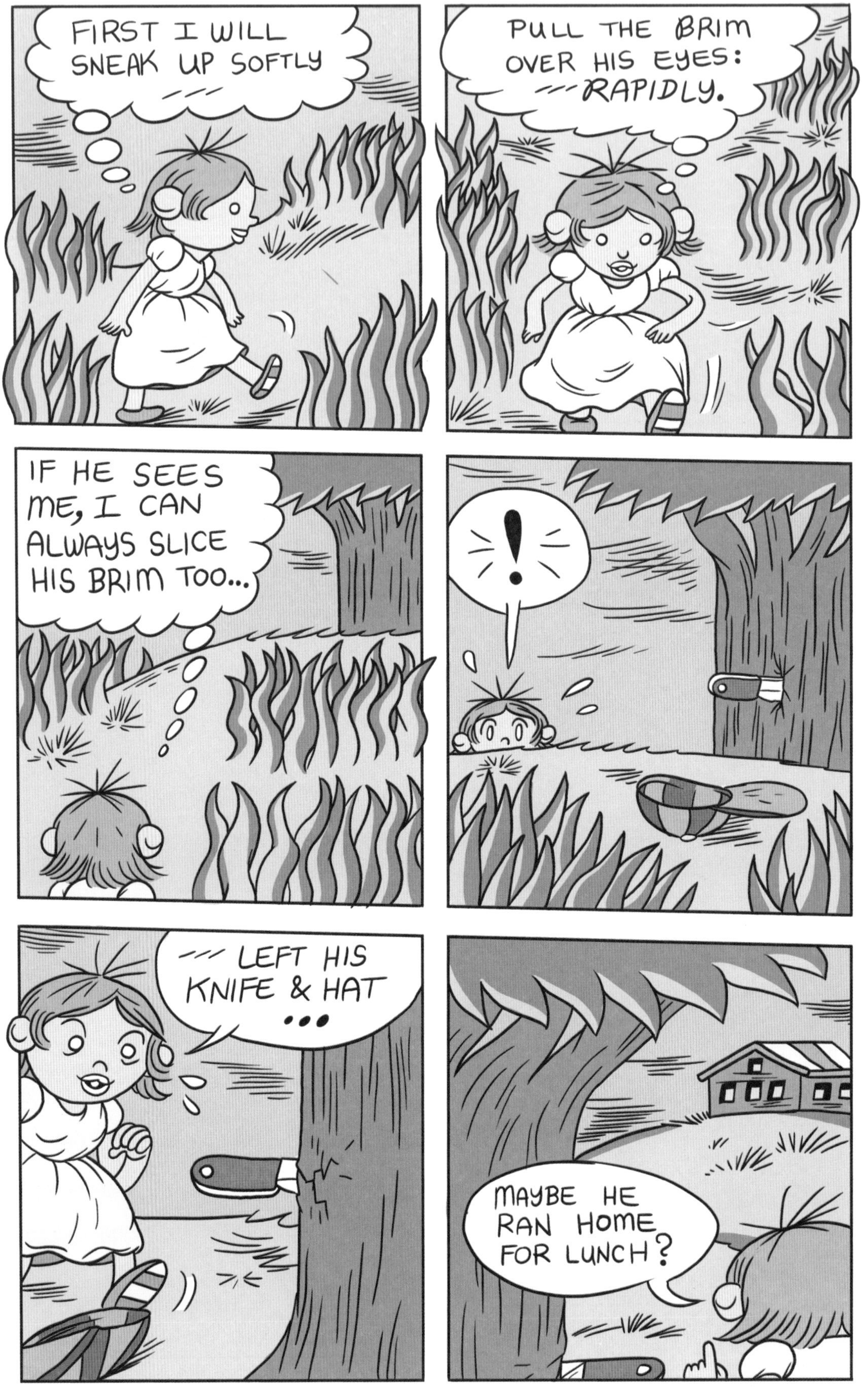
FIRST I WILL SNEAK UP SOFTLY ---
PULL THE BRIM OVER HIS EYES: --- RAPIDLY.
IF HE SEES ME, I CAN ALWAYS SLICE HIS BRIM TOO...
!
--- LEFT HIS KNIFE & HAT ...
MAYBE HE RAN HOME FOR LUNCH?

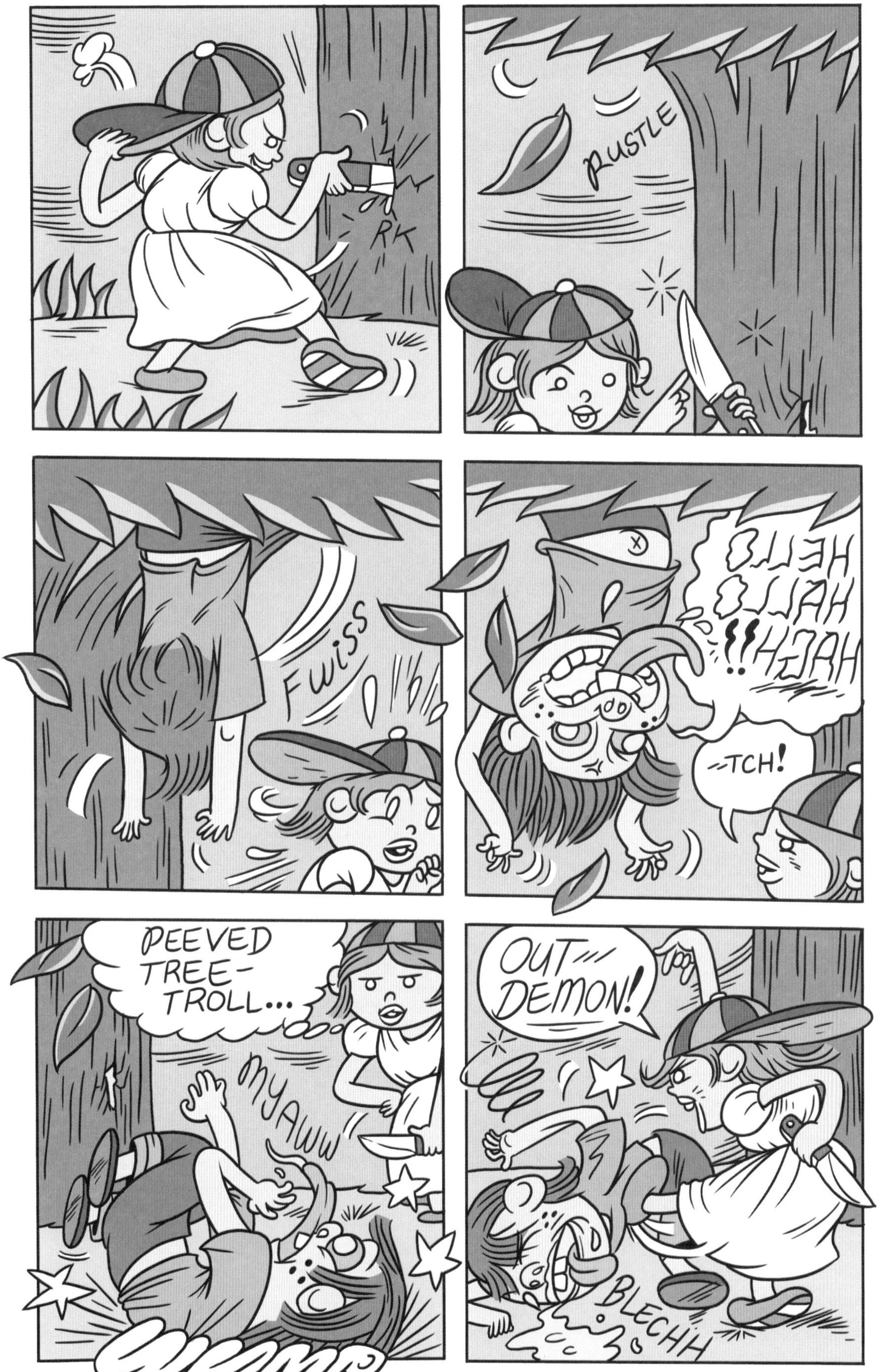
RK
RUSTLE
FWISS
HELLO HALLO HAHAH!!
-TCH!
PEEVED TREE-TROLL...
MYAWW
OUT DEMON!
BLECHH

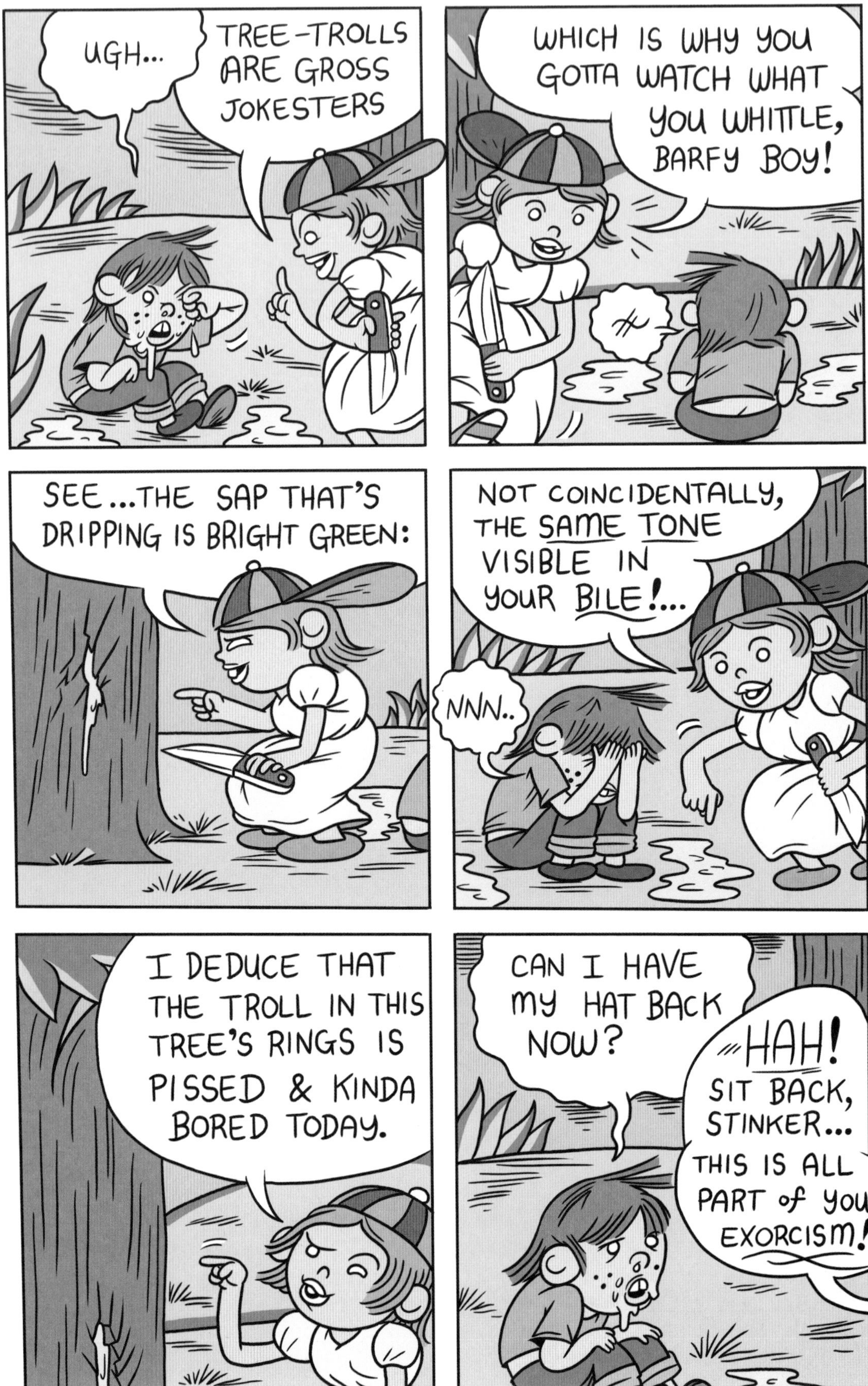
UGH...
TREE-TROLLS ARE GROSS JOKESTERS
WHICH IS WHY YOU GOTTA WATCH WHAT YOU WHITTLE, BARFY BOY!
SEE...THE SAP THAT'S DRIPPING IS BRIGHT GREEN:
NOT COINCIDENTALLY, THE SAME TONE VISIBLE IN YOUR BILE!...
NNN..
I DEDUCE THAT THE TROLL IN THIS TREE'S RINGS IS PISSED & KINDA BORED TODAY.
CAN I HAVE MY HAT BACK NOW?
HAH! SIT BACK, STINKER... THIS IS ALL PART of YOUR EXORCISM!

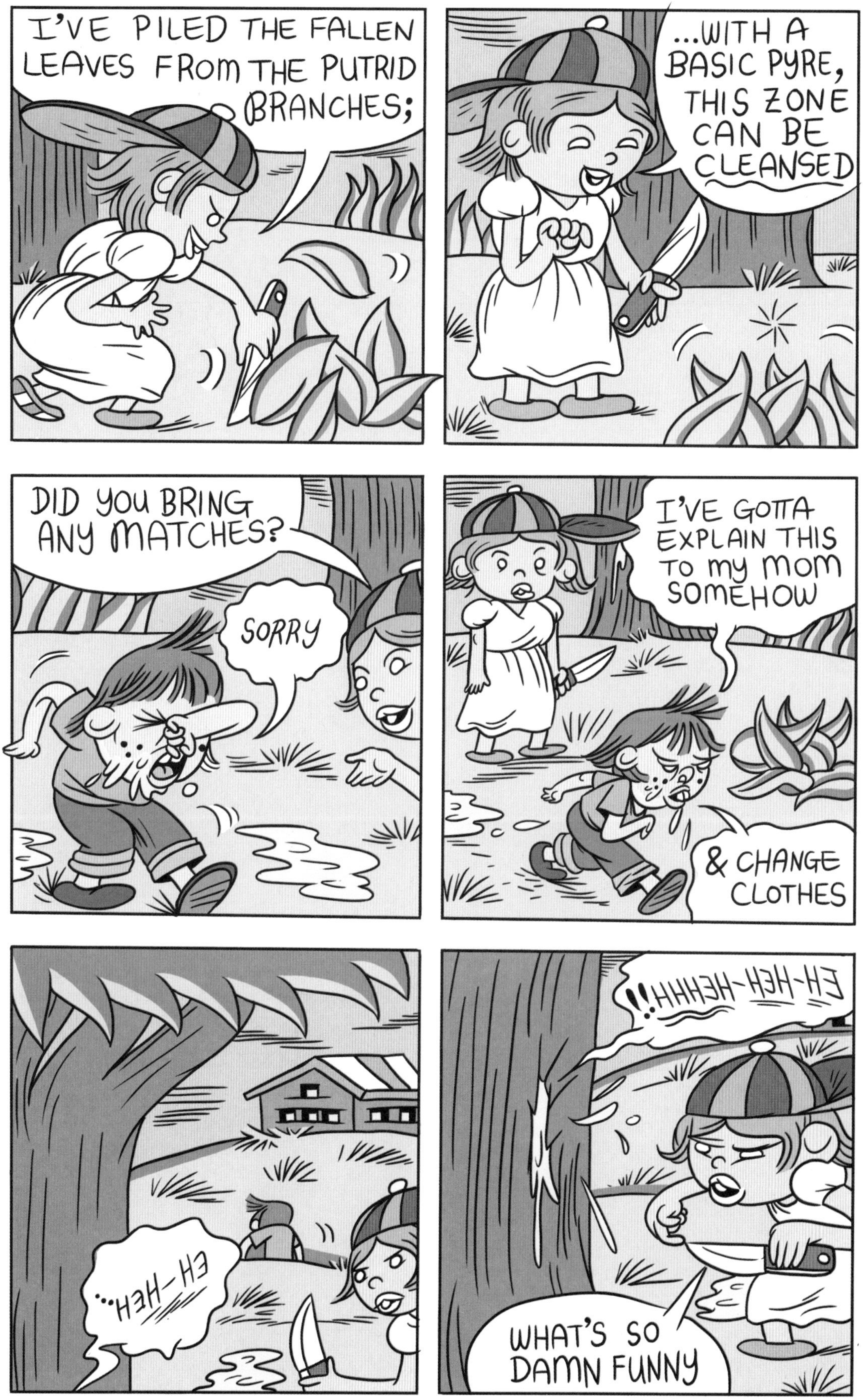
I'VE PILED THE FALLEN LEAVES FROM THE PUTRID BRANCHES;
...WITH A BASIC PYRE, THIS ZONE CAN BE CLEANSED
DID YOU BRING ANY MATCHES?
SORRY
I'VE GOTTA EXPLAIN THIS TO MY MOM SOMEHOW
& CHANGE CLOTHES
EH-HEH...
EH-HEH-HEHHH!!
WHAT'S SO DAMN FUNNY

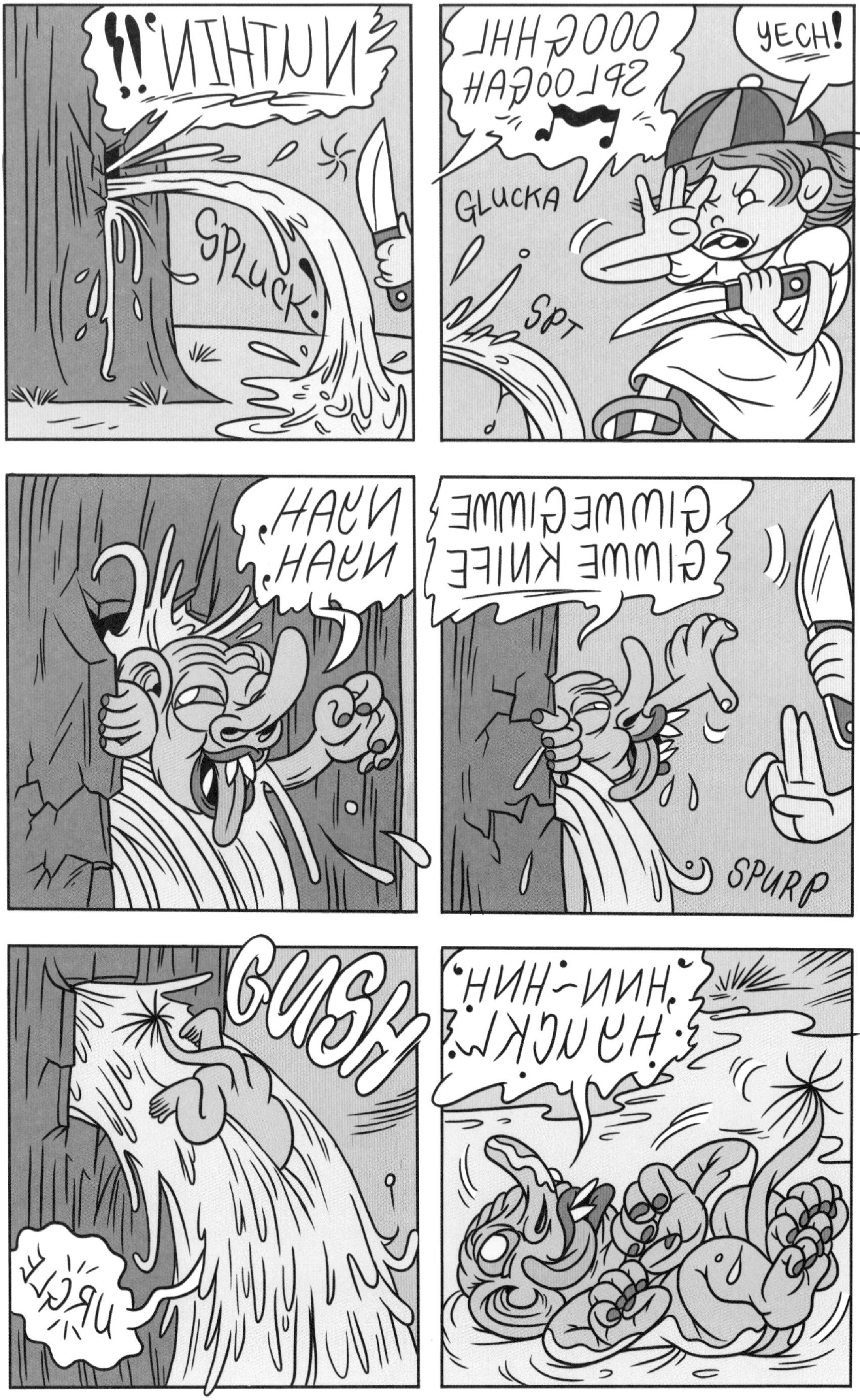
NUTHIN'!!
SPLUCK!
OOOGHHL SPLOOGAH
YECH!
GLUCKA
SPT
GIMMEGIMME GIMME KNIFE
SPURP
GUSH

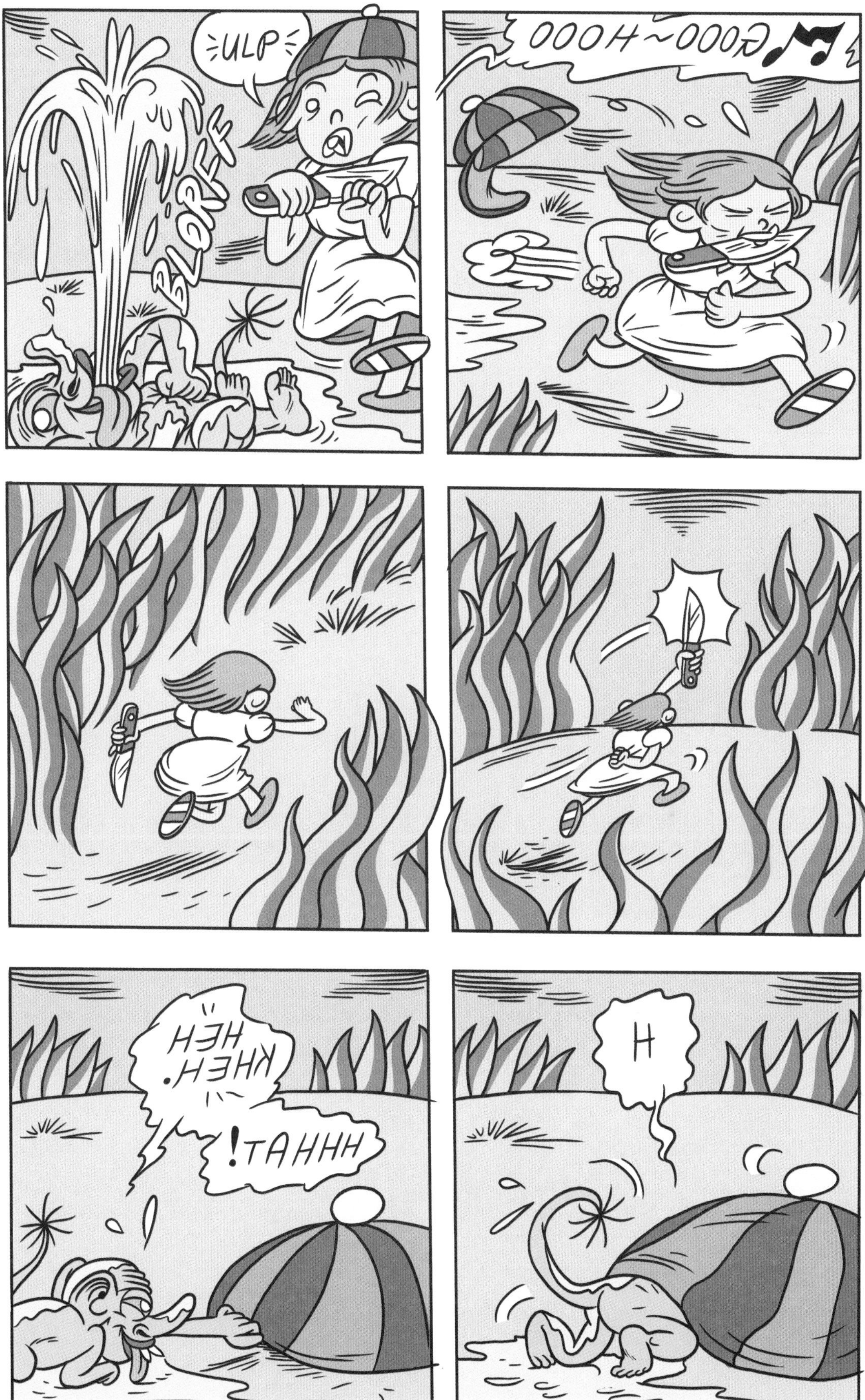
ULP
BLORFF
GOOO~HOOO
KHEH. HEH HEH
!TAHHH
H

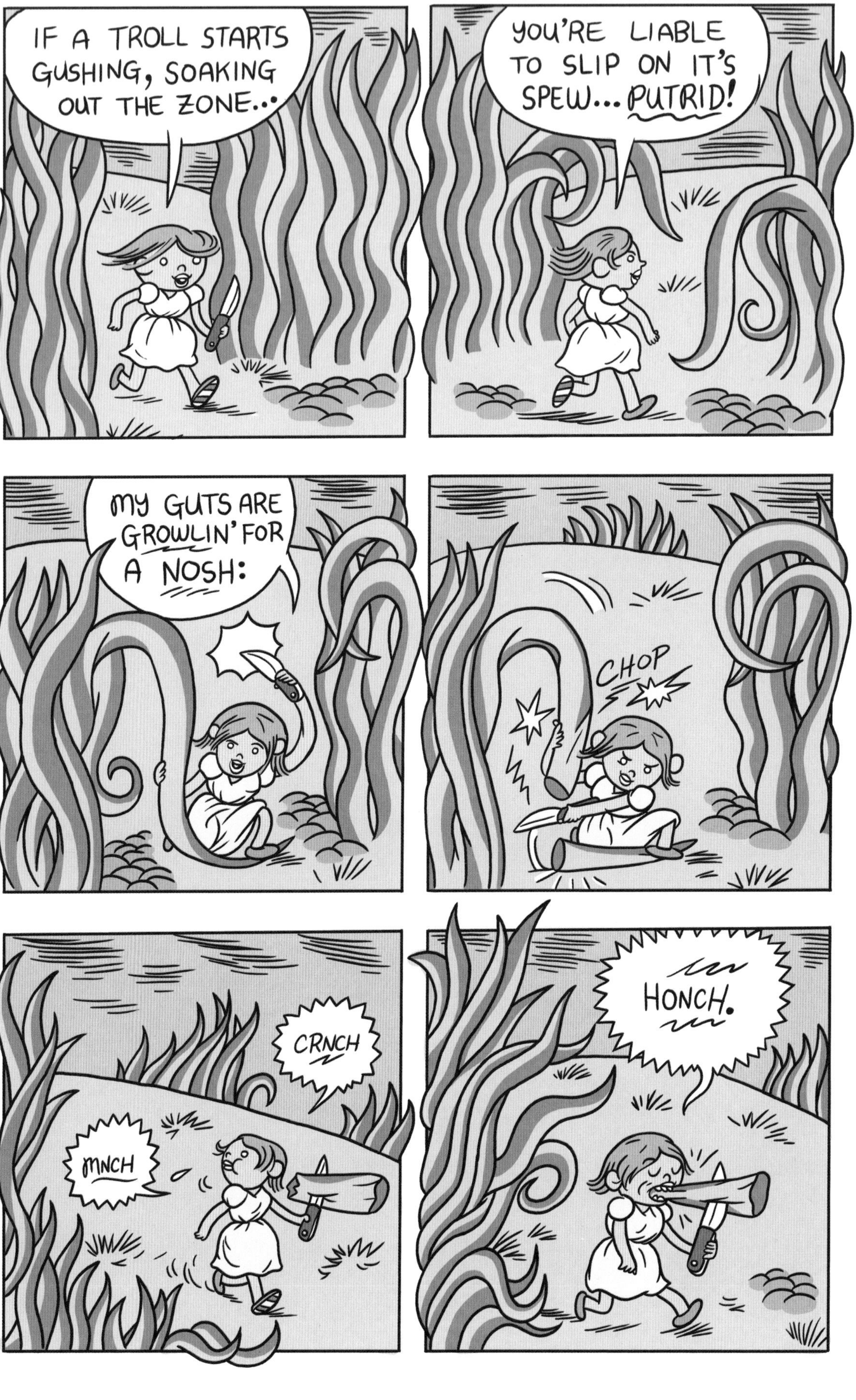
IF A TROLL STARTS GUSHING, SOAKING OUT THE ZONE..
YOU'RE LIABLE TO SLIP ON IT'S SPEW... PUTRID!
MY GUTS ARE GROWLIN' FOR A NOSH:
CHOP
CRNCH
MNCH
HONCH.

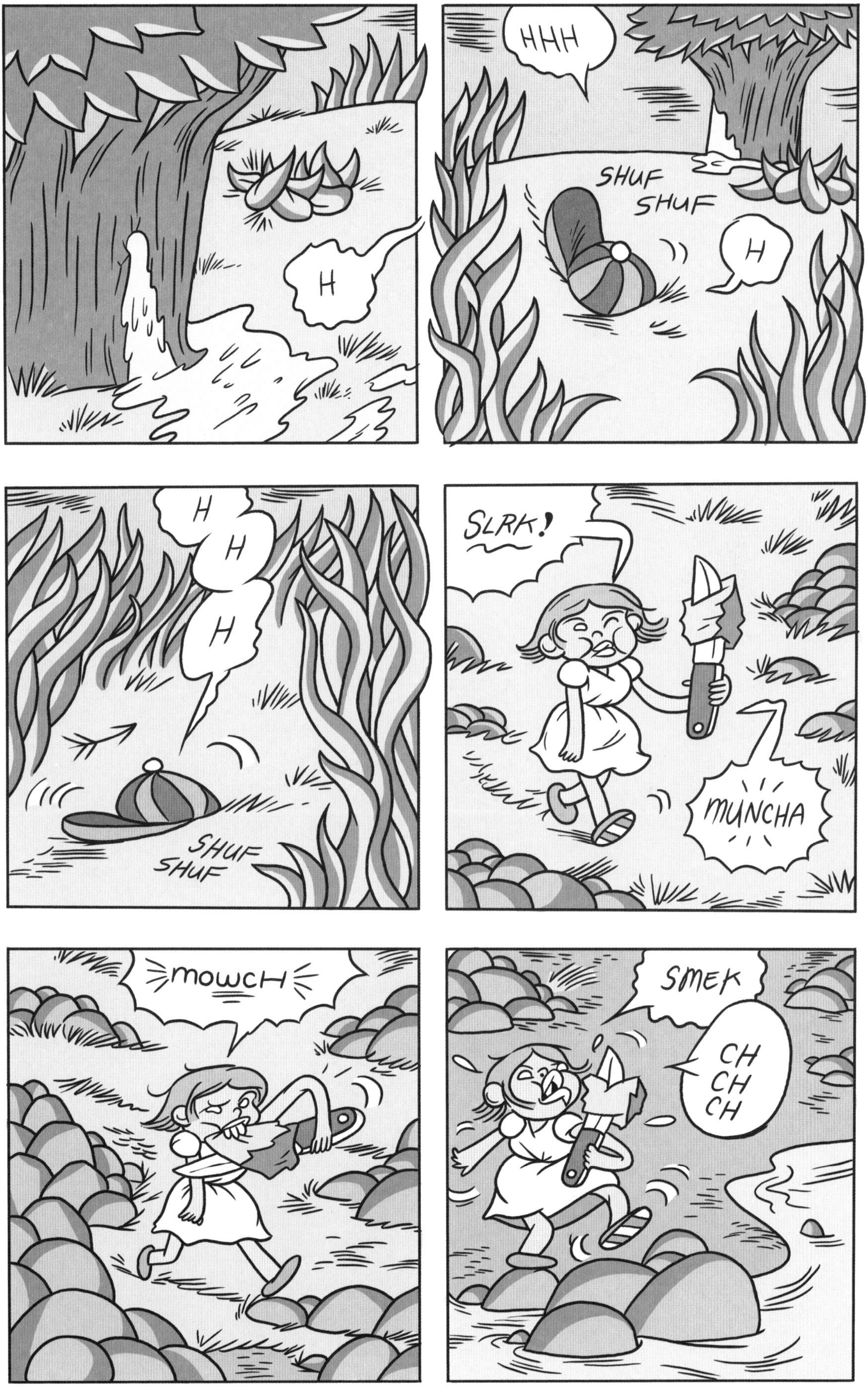
H
HHH
SHUF
SHUF
H
H
H
H
SHUF
SHUF
SLRK!
MUNCHA
MOWCH
SMEK
CH
CH
CH

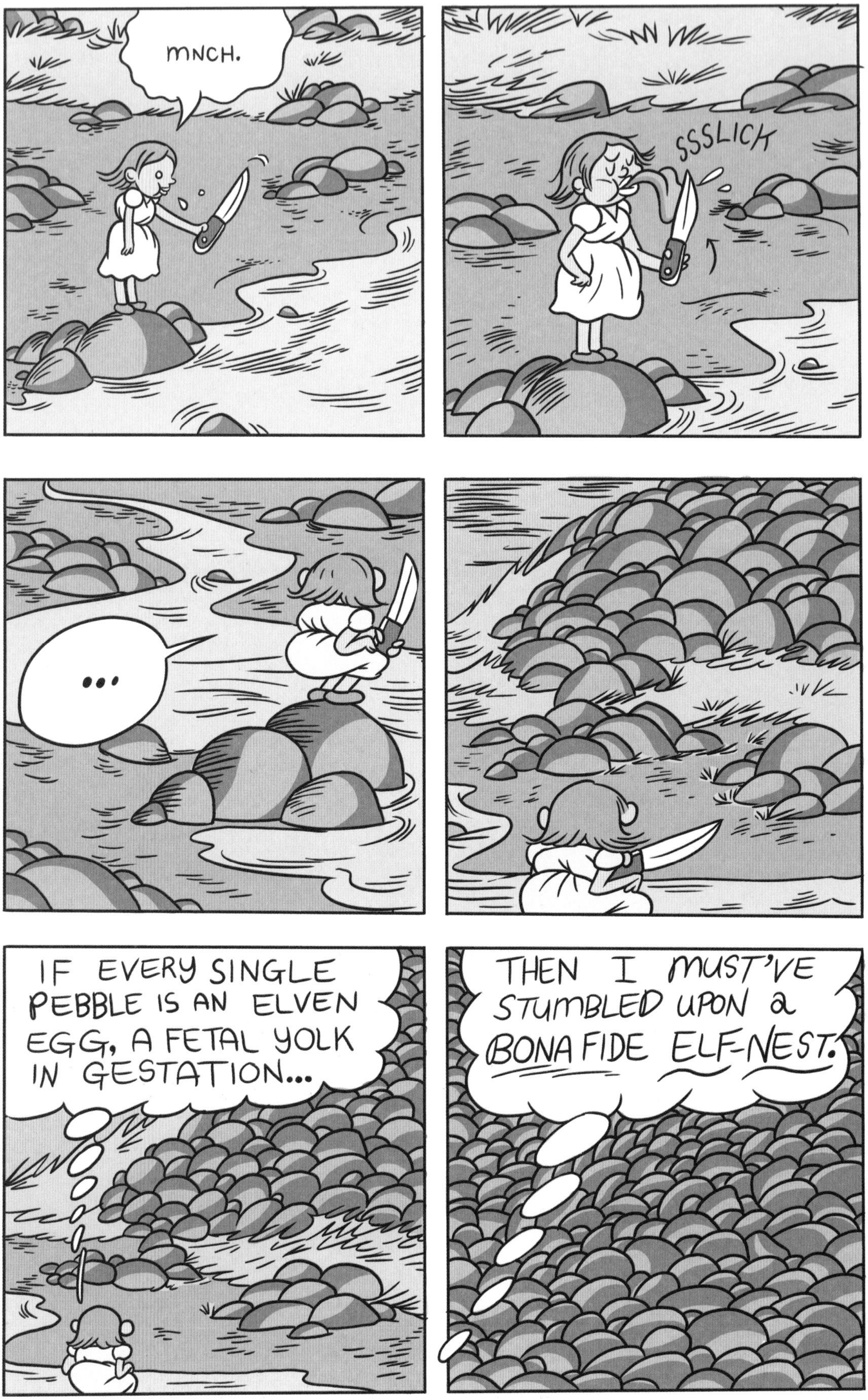
MNCH.
SSSLICK
...
IF EVERY SINGLE PEBBLE IS AN ELVEN EGG, A FETAL YOLK IN GESTATION...
THEN I MUST'VE STUMBLED UPON A BONA FIDE ELF-NEST.

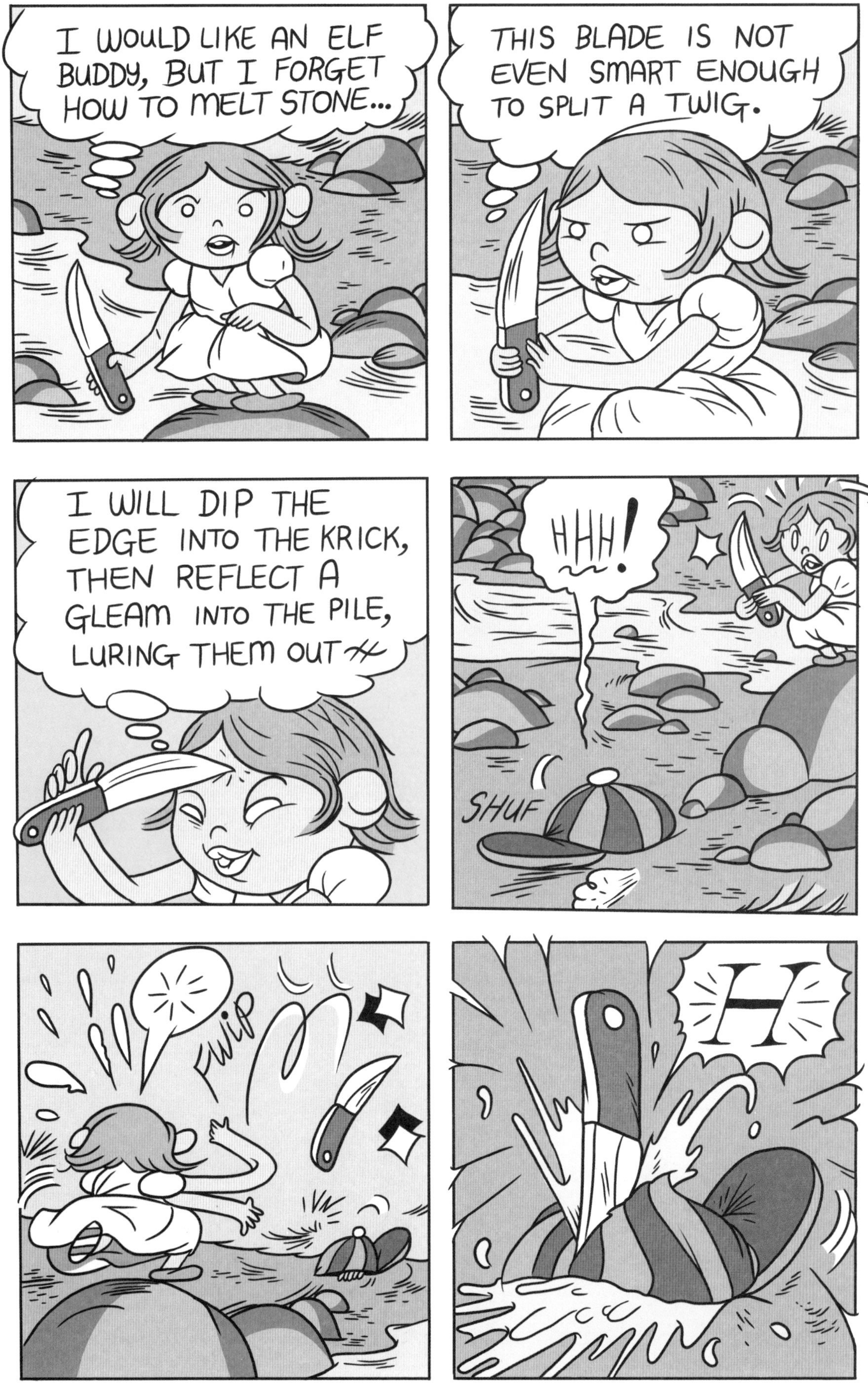
I WOULD LIKE AN ELF BUDDY, BUT I FORGET HOW TO MELT STONE...
THIS BLADE IS NOT EVEN SMART ENOUGH TO SPLIT A TWIG.
I WILL DIP THE EDGE INTO THE KRICK, THEN REFLECT A GLEAM INTO THE PILE, LURING THEM OUT
HHH!
SHUF
FWIP
H

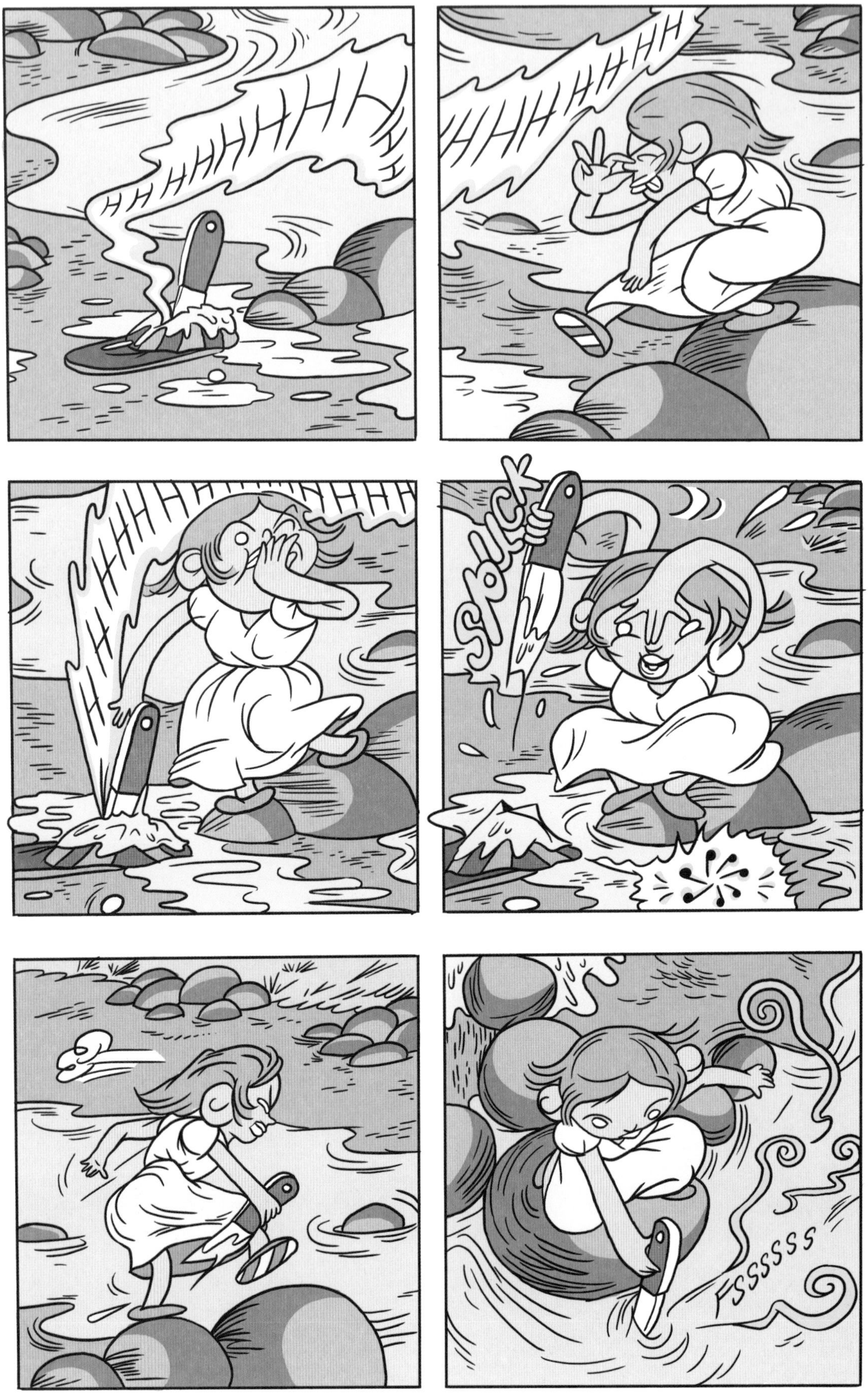
SPLUCK
FSSSSSS

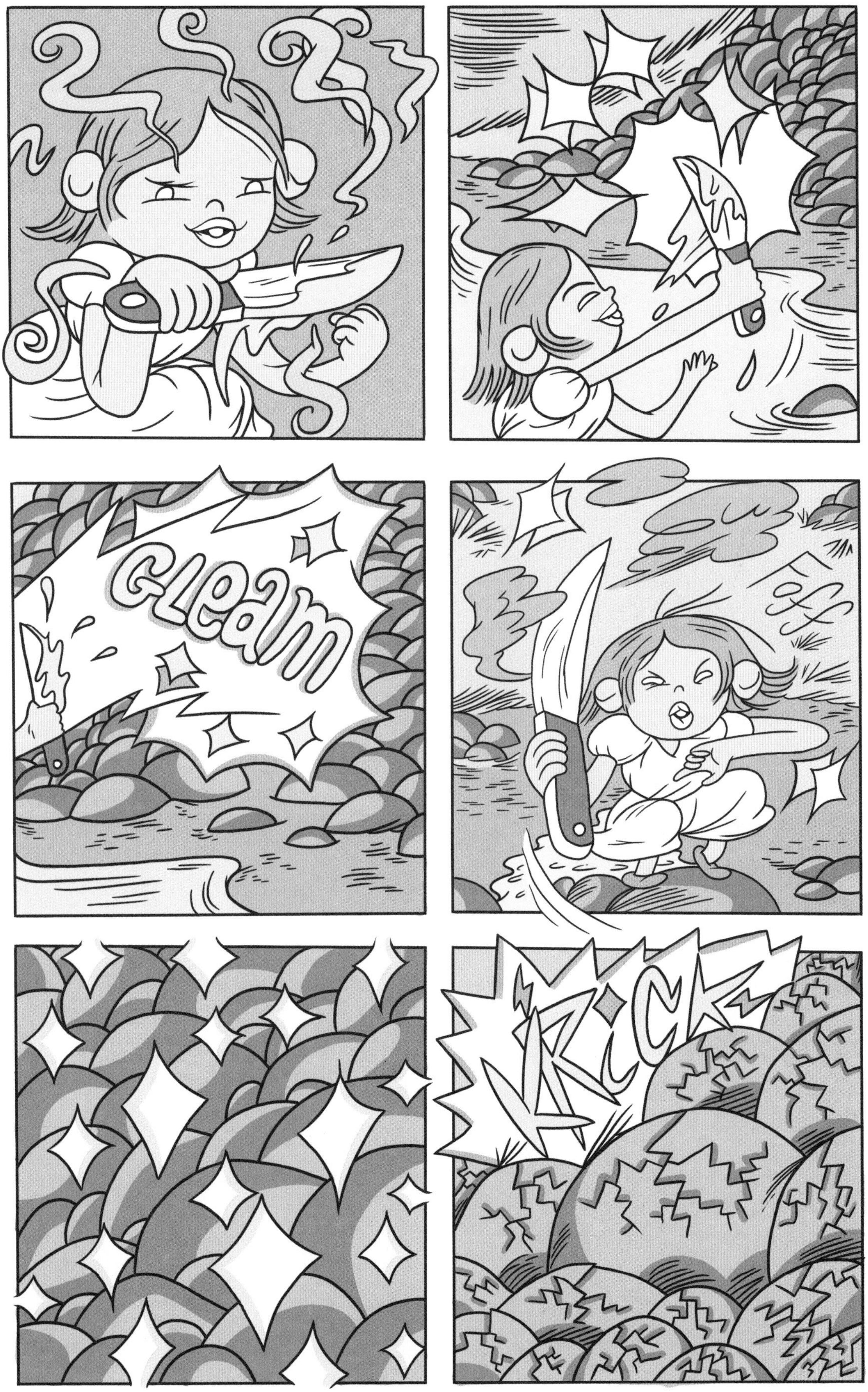
GLEAM
Foff
KRICK

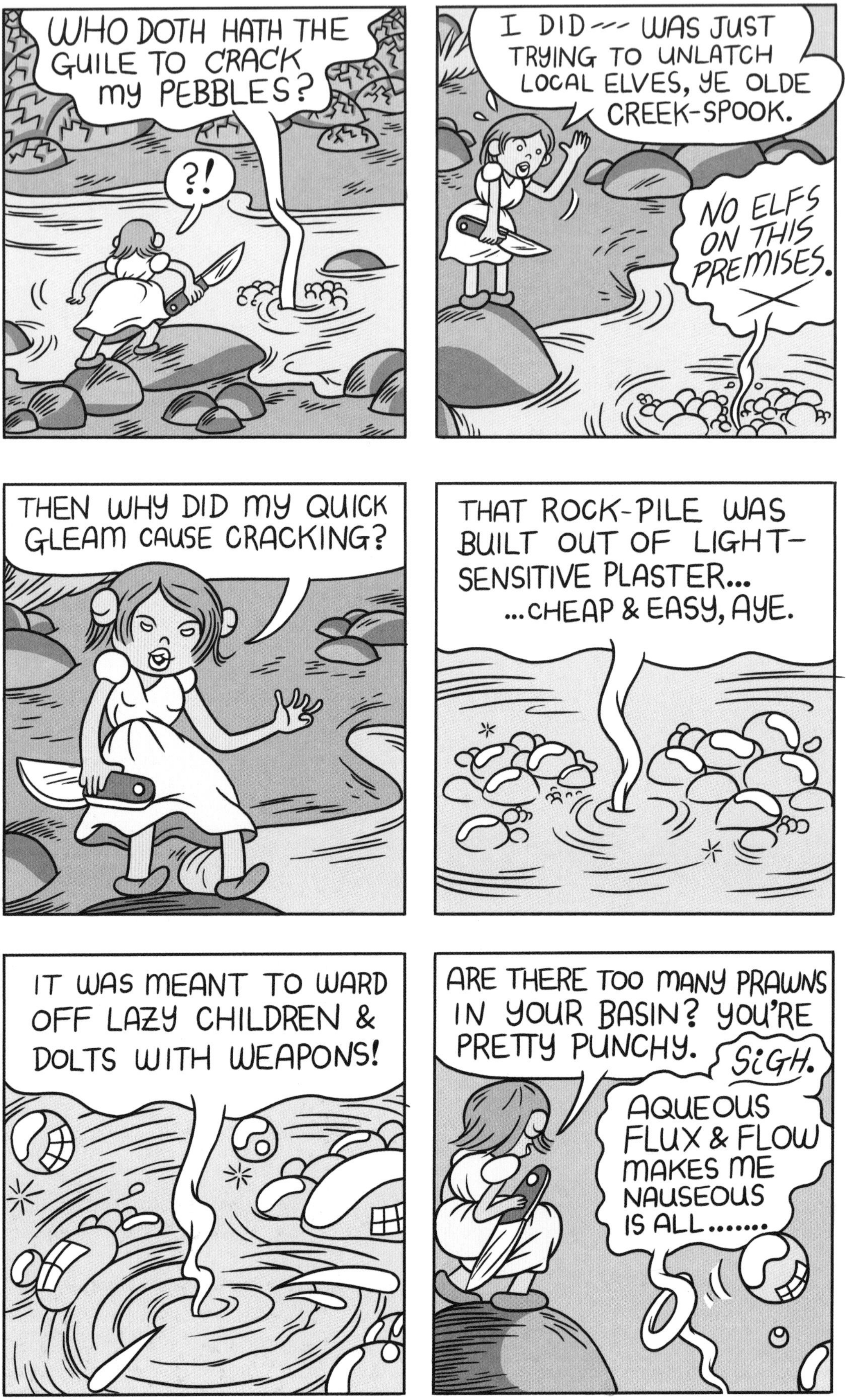
WHO DOTH HATH THE GUILE TO CRACK my PEBBLES?
?!
I DID--- WAS JUST TRYING TO UNLATCH LOCAL ELVES, YE OLDE CREEK-SPOOK.
NO ELFS ON THIS PREMISES.
THEN WHY DID MY QUICK GLEAM CAUSE CRACKING?
THAT ROCK-PILE WAS BUILT OUT OF LIGHT-SENSITIVE PLASTER...
...CHEAP & EASY, AYE.
IT WAS MEANT TO WARD OFF LAZY CHILDREN & DOLTS WITH WEAPONS!
ARE THERE TOO MANY PRAWNS IN YOUR BASIN? YOU'RE PRETTY PUNCHY.
SIGH.
AQUEOUS FLUX & FLOW MAKES ME NAUSEOUS IS ALL.......

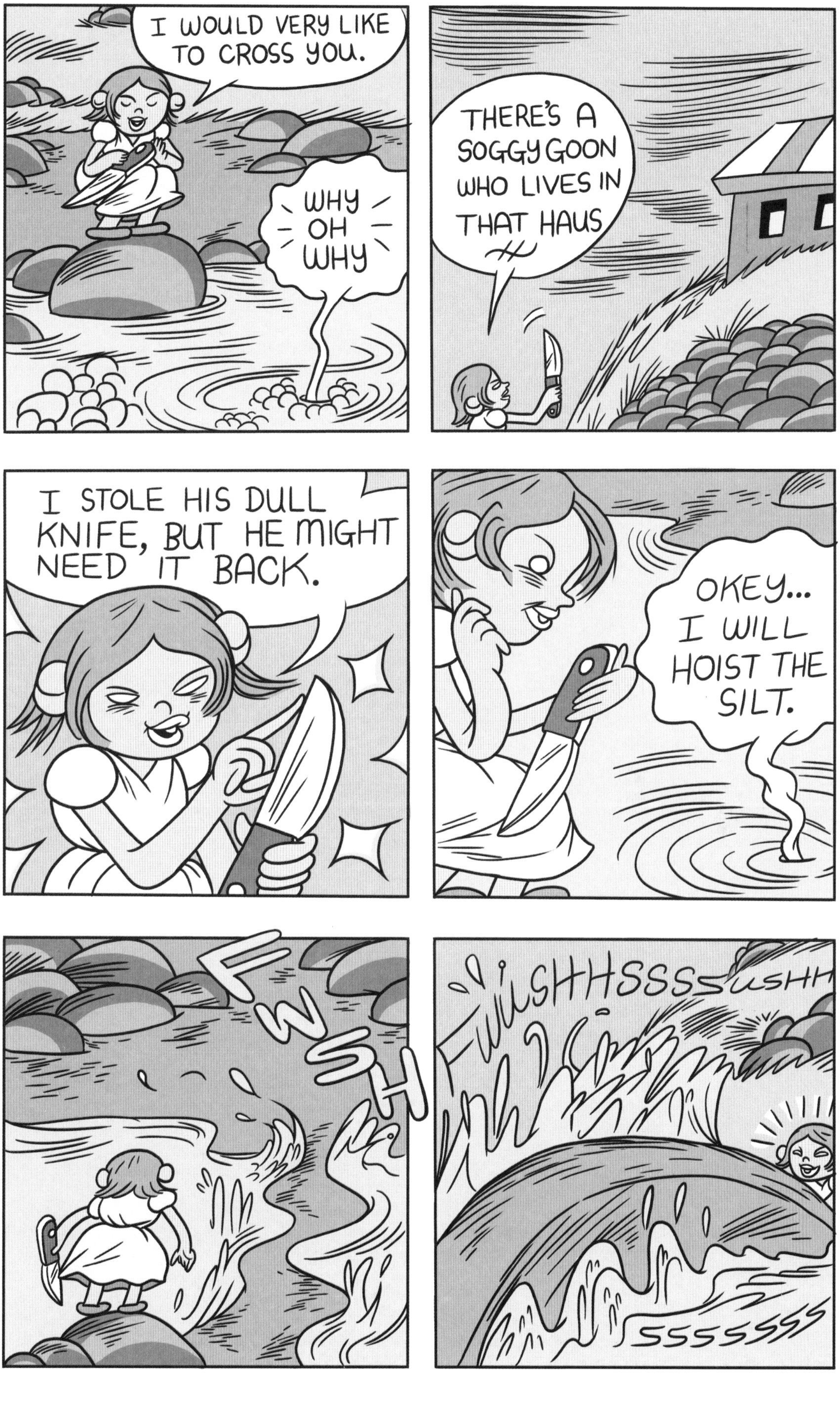
I WOULD VERY LIKE TO CROSS YOU.
WHY OH WHY
THERE'S A SOGGY GOON WHO LIVES IN THAT HAUS
I STOLE HIS DULL KNIFE, BUT HE MIGHT NEED IT BACK.
OKEY... I WILL HOIST THE SILT.
FWSH
FWUSHHSSSSushh
SSSSSSS

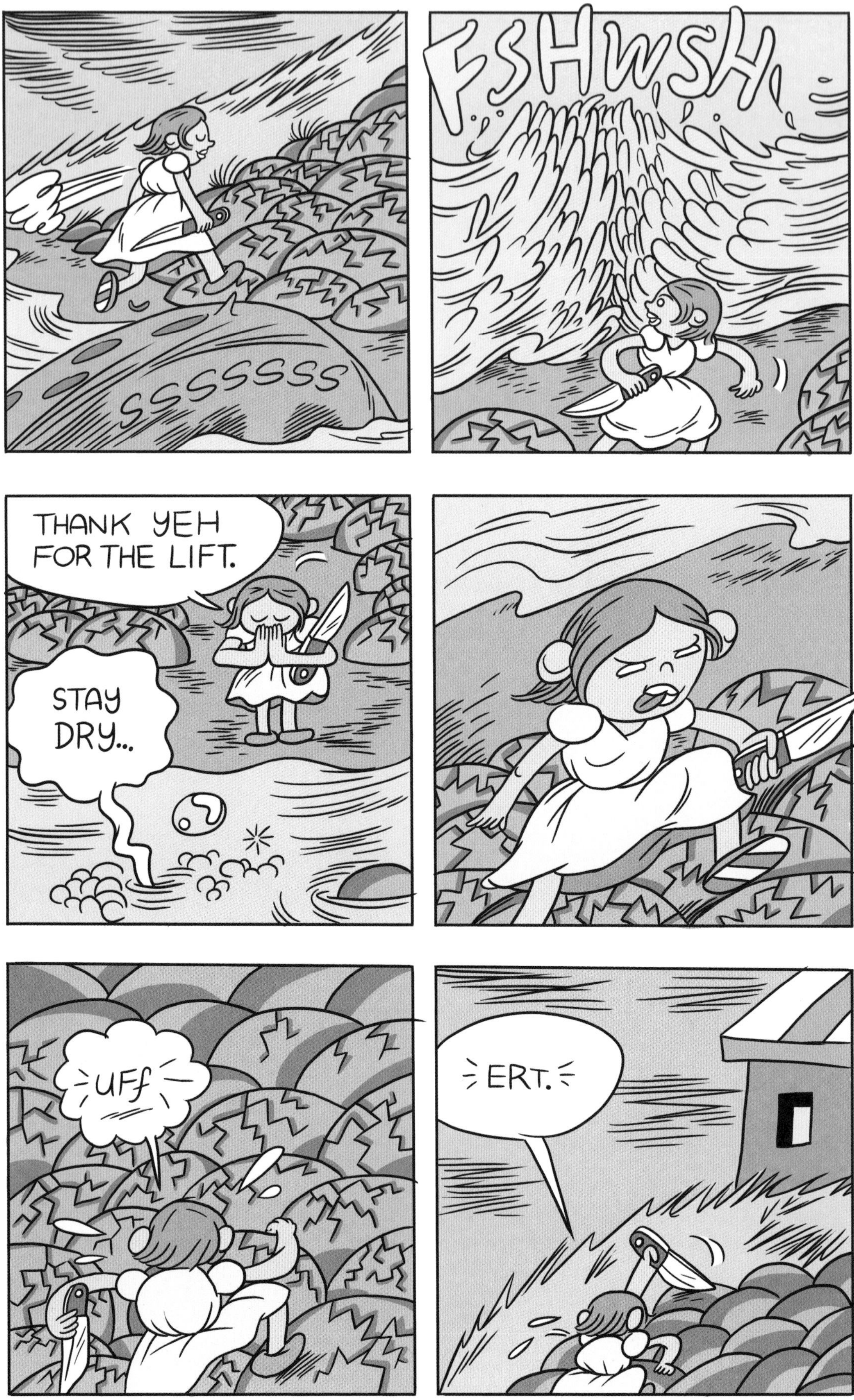
SSSSSSS
FSHWSH
THANK YEH FOR THE LIFT.
STAY DRY...
UFF
ERT.

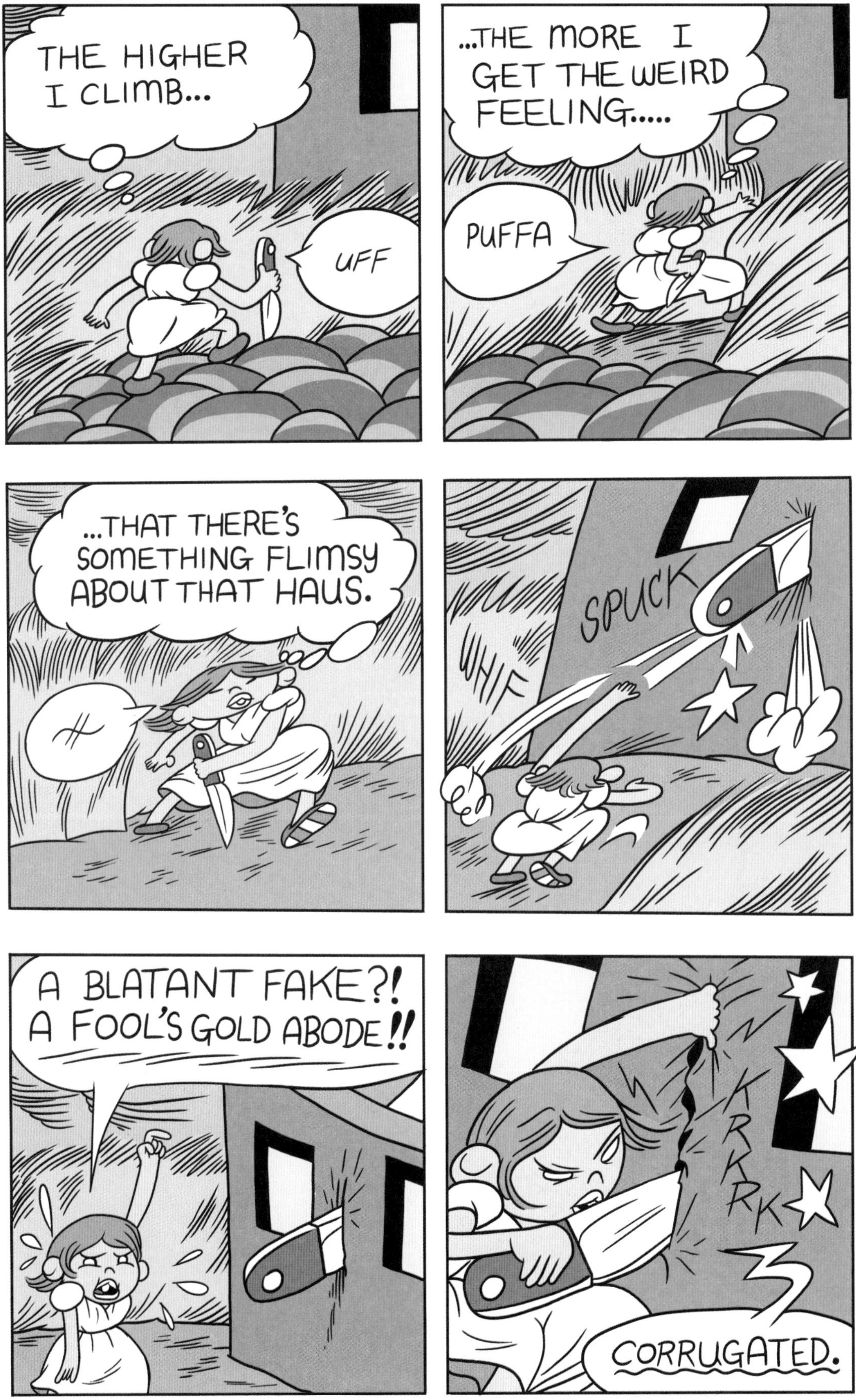
THE HIGHER I CLIMB...
UFF
...THE MORE I GET THE WEIRD FEELING.....
PUFFA
...THAT THERE'S SOMETHING FLIMSY ABOUT THAT HAUS.
SPUCK
WHIF
A BLATANT FAKE?! A FOOL'S GOLD ABODE!!
KRRKRK
CORRUGATED.

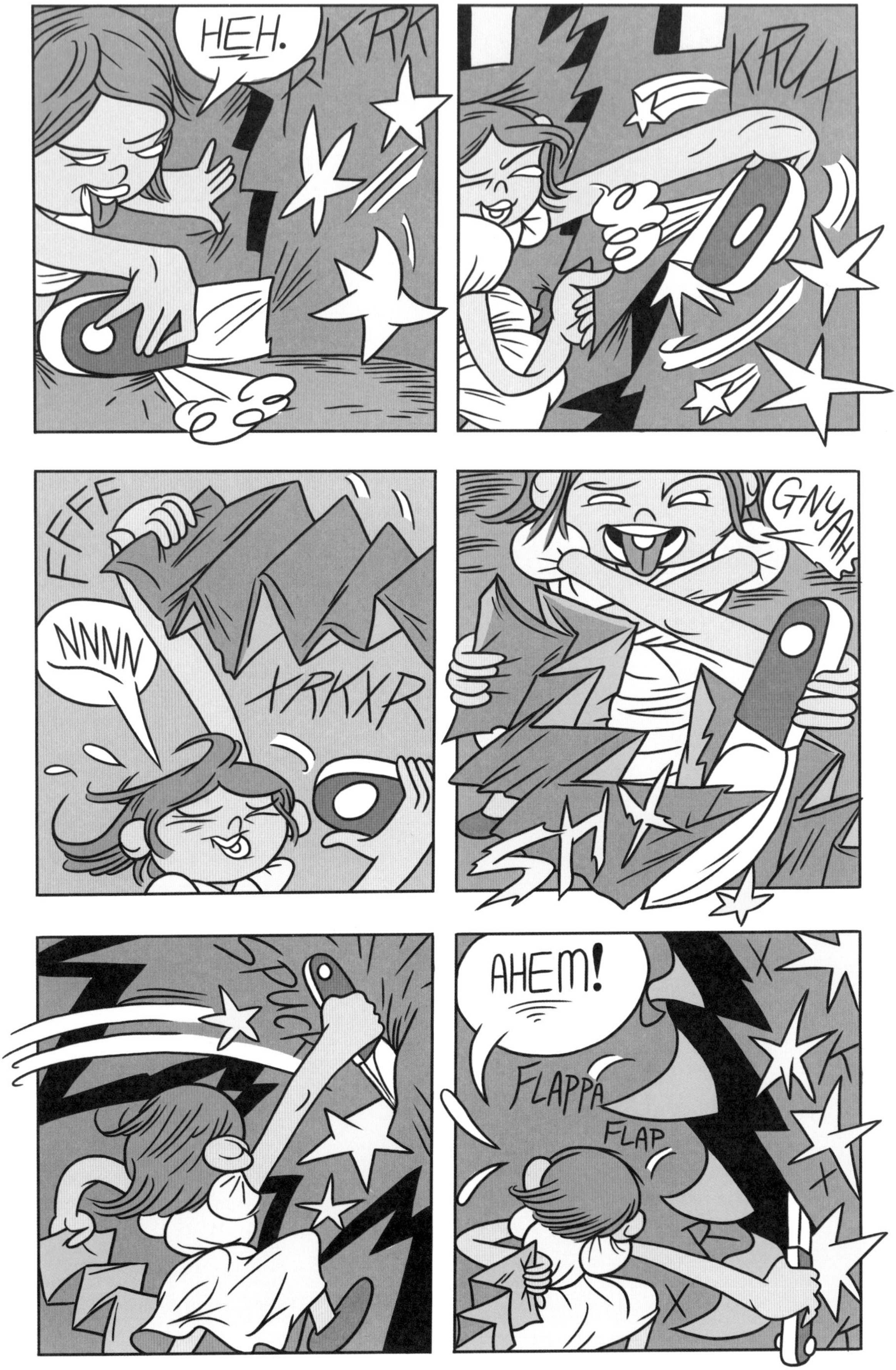
HEH.
KRK
KRUX
FFFF
NNNN
XRKXR
GNYAH
SPUCK
AHEM!
FLAPPA
FLAP

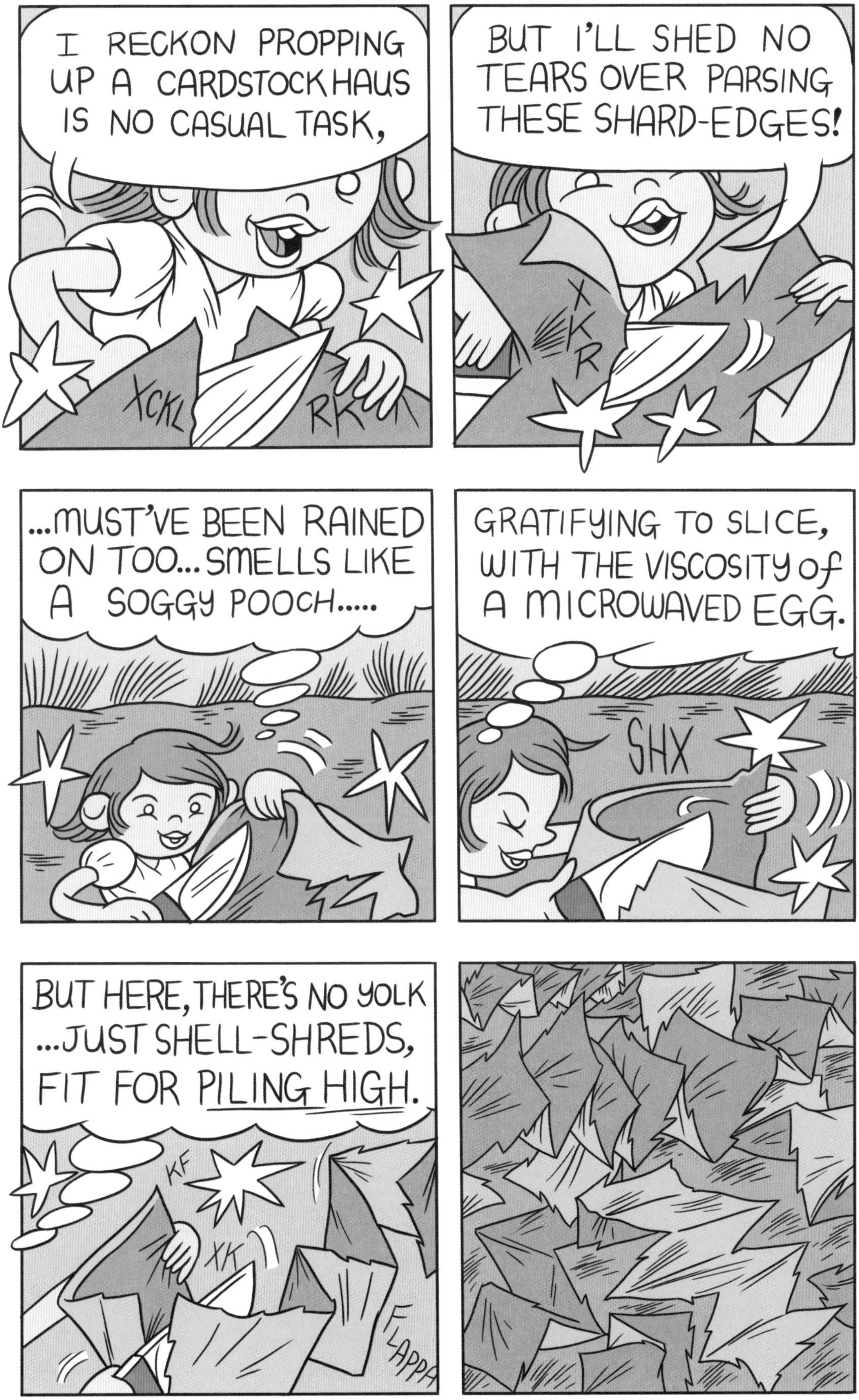
I RECKON PROPPING UP A CARDSTOCK HAUS IS NO CASUAL TASK,
XCKL
RK
BUT I'LL SHED NO TEARS OVER PARSING THESE SHARD-EDGES!
XKR
...MUST'VE BEEN RAINED ON TOO... SMELLS LIKE A SOGGY POOCH.....
GRATIFYING TO SLICE, WITH THE VISCOSITY of A MICROWAVED EGG.
SHX
BUT HERE, THERE'S NO YOLK ...JUST SHELL-SHREDS, FIT FOR PILING HIGH.
KF
XK
FLAPPA

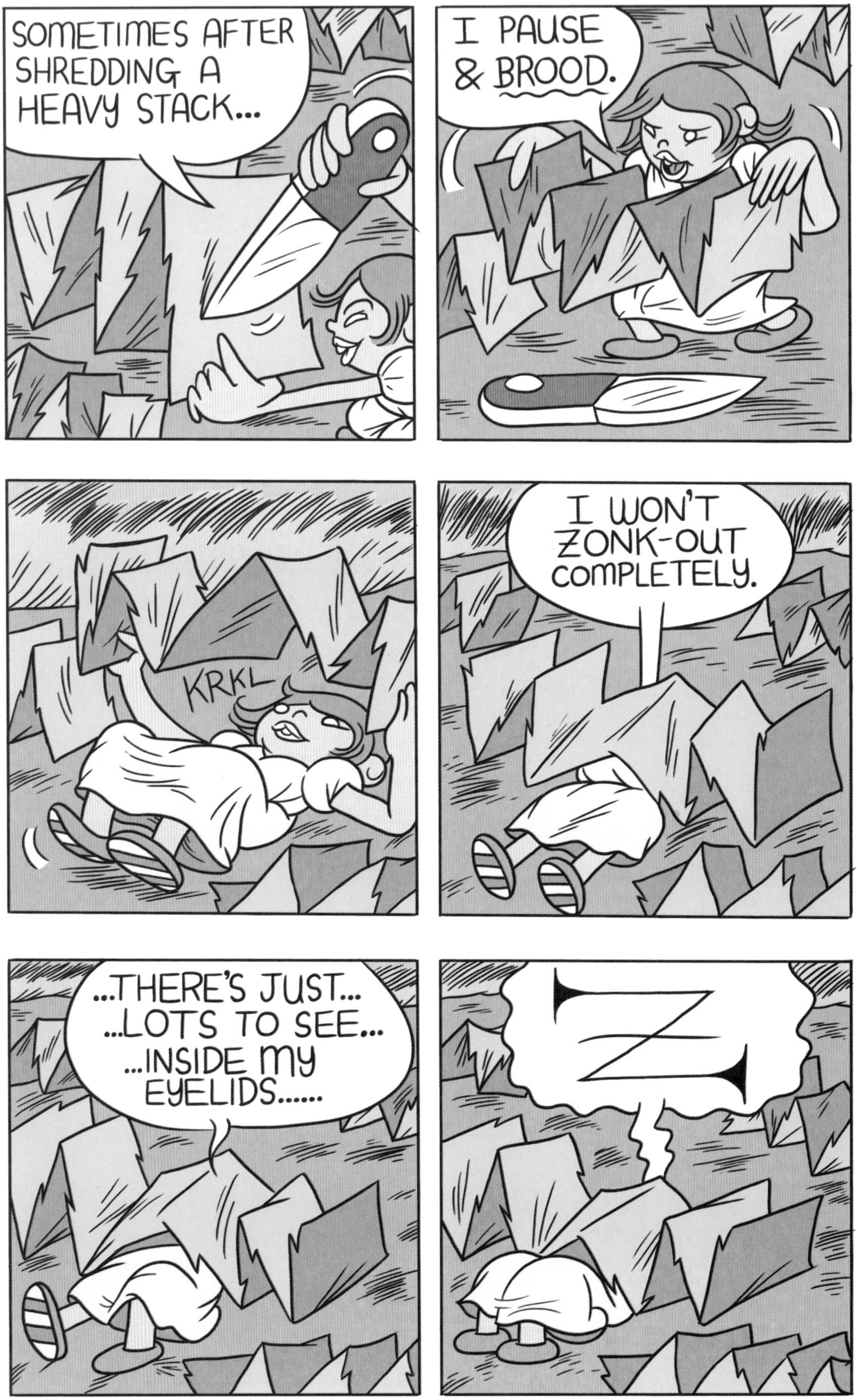
SOMETIMES AFTER SHREDDING A HEAVY STACK...
I PAUSE & BROOD.
KRKL
I WON'T ZONK-OUT COMPLETELY.
...THERE'S JUST... ...LOTS TO SEE... ...INSIDE MY EYELIDS......
Z

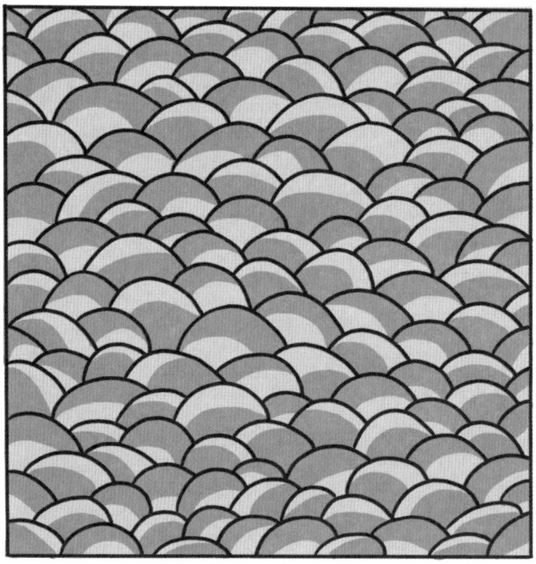
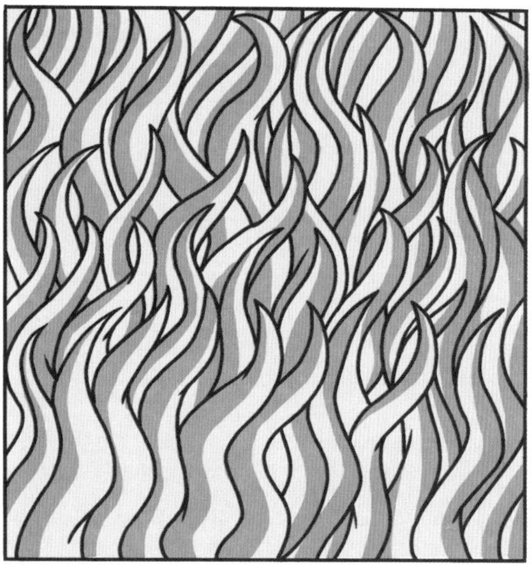
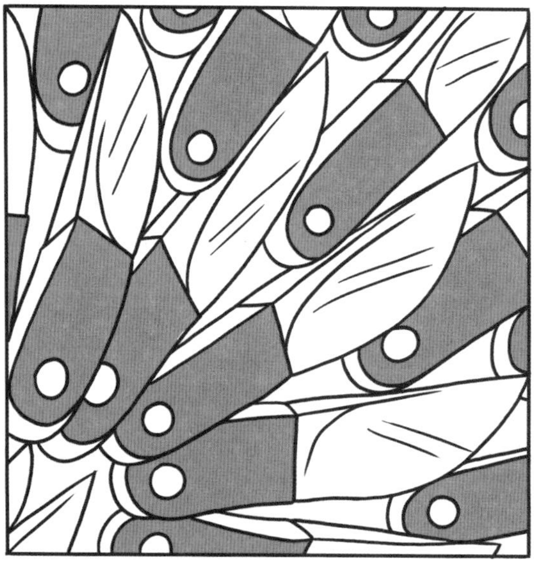
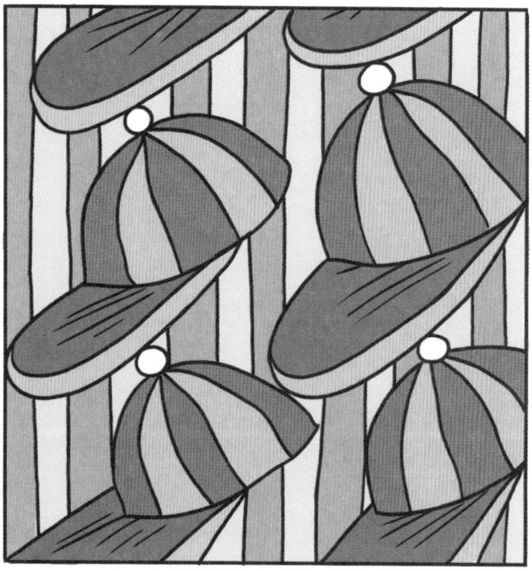
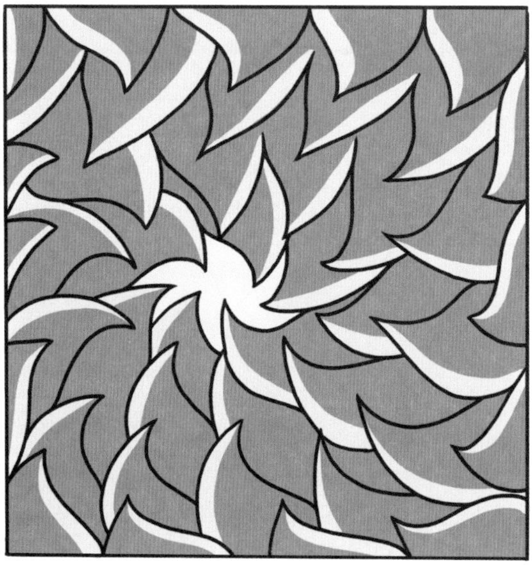
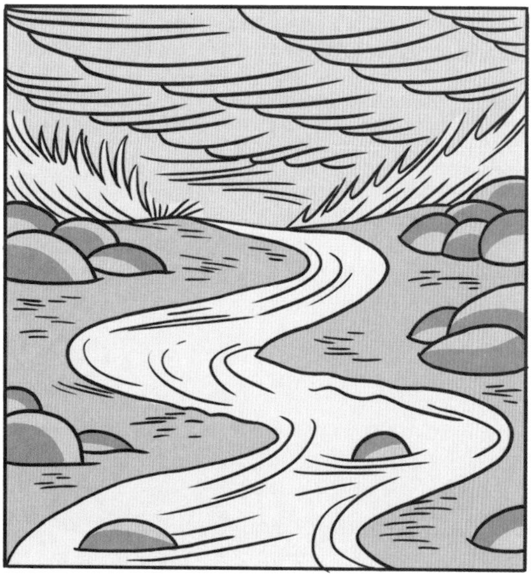

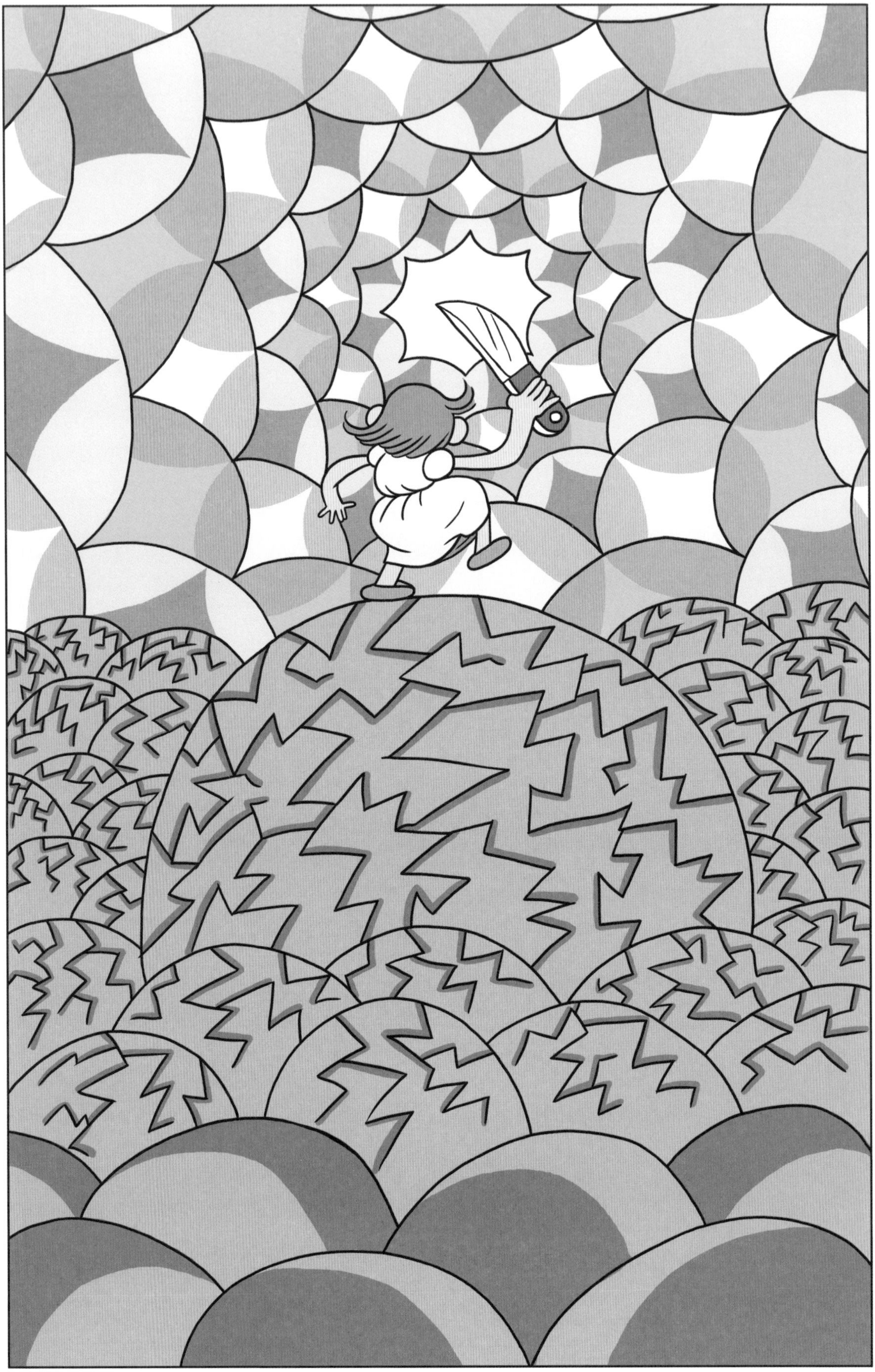

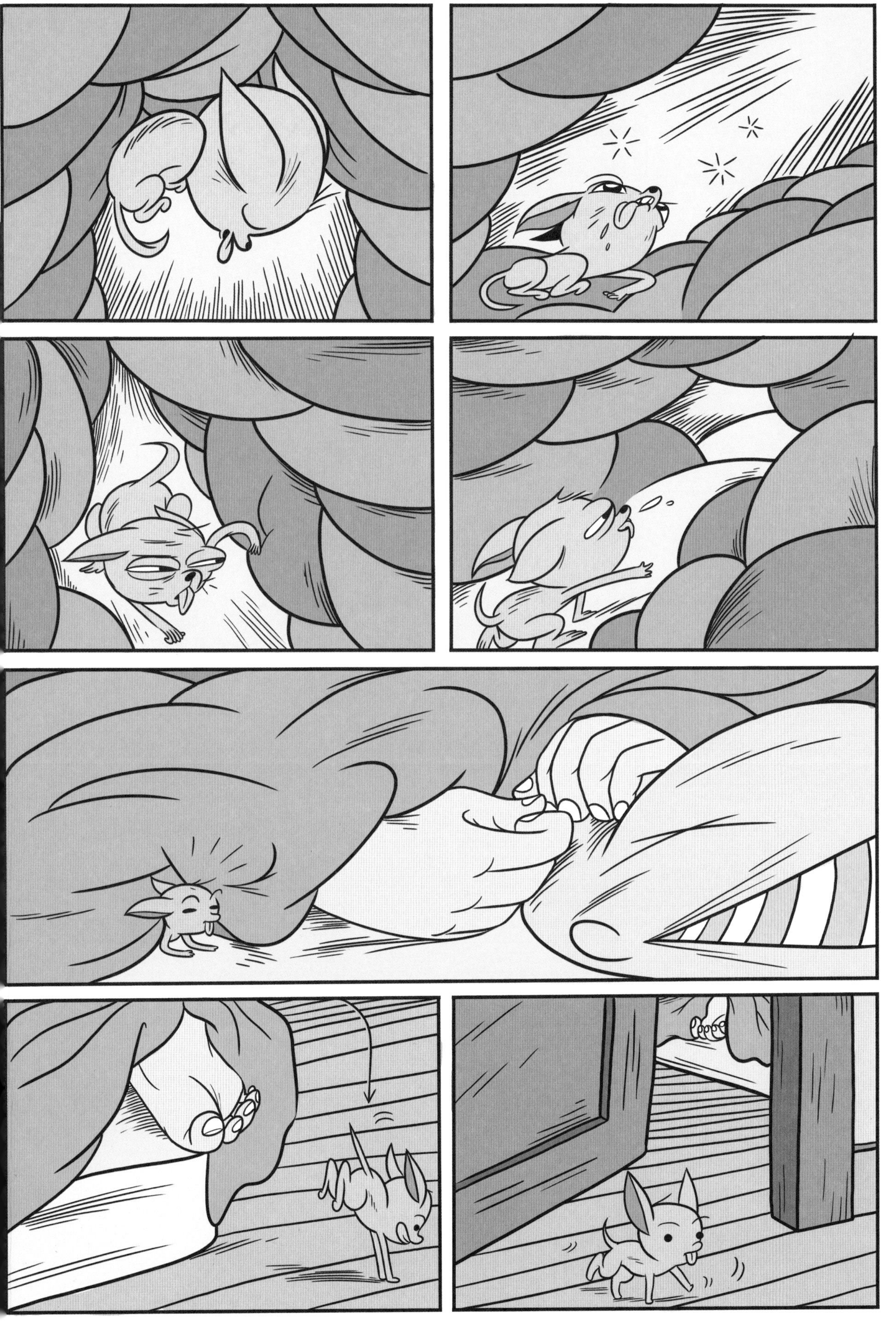

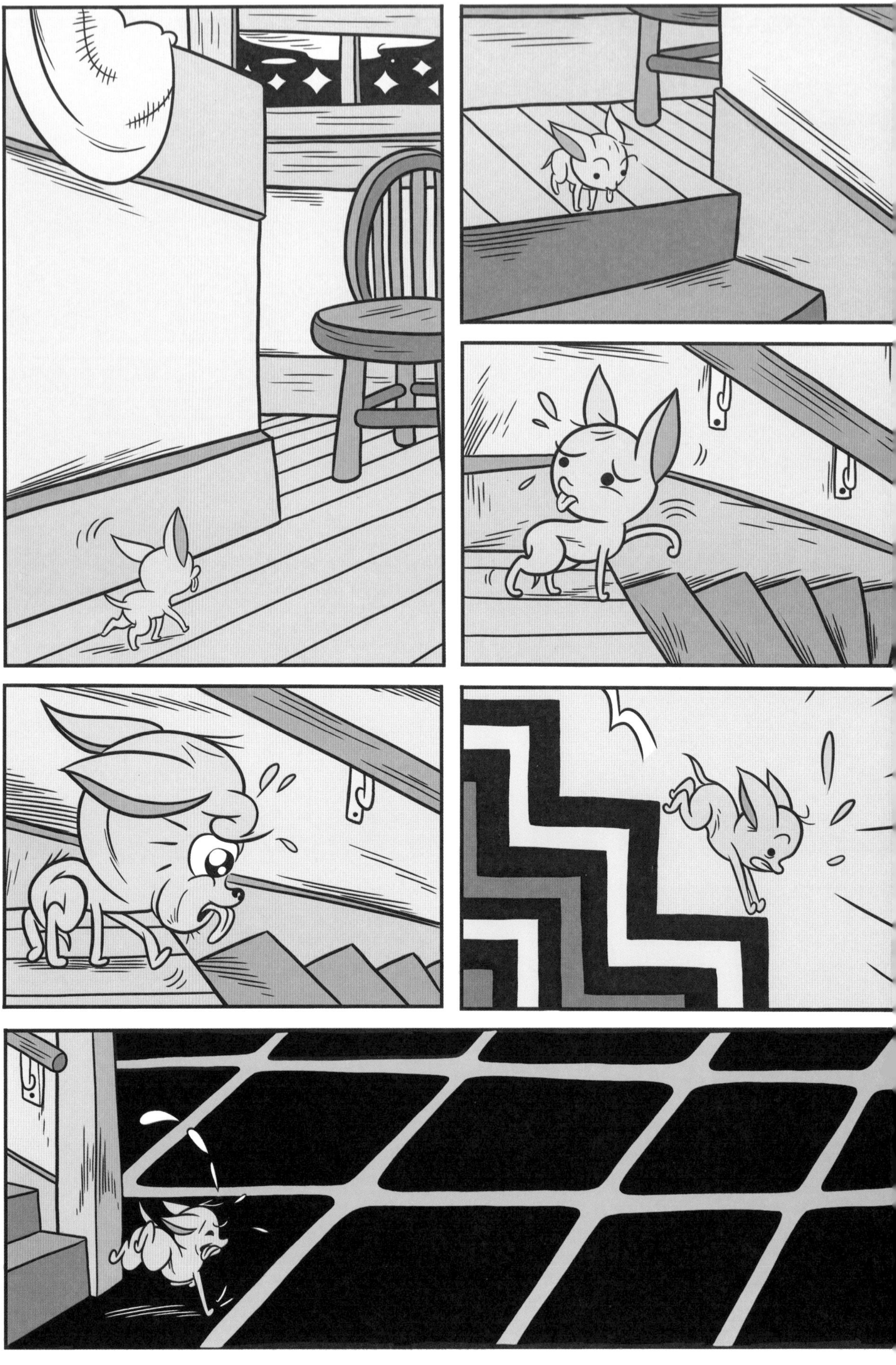

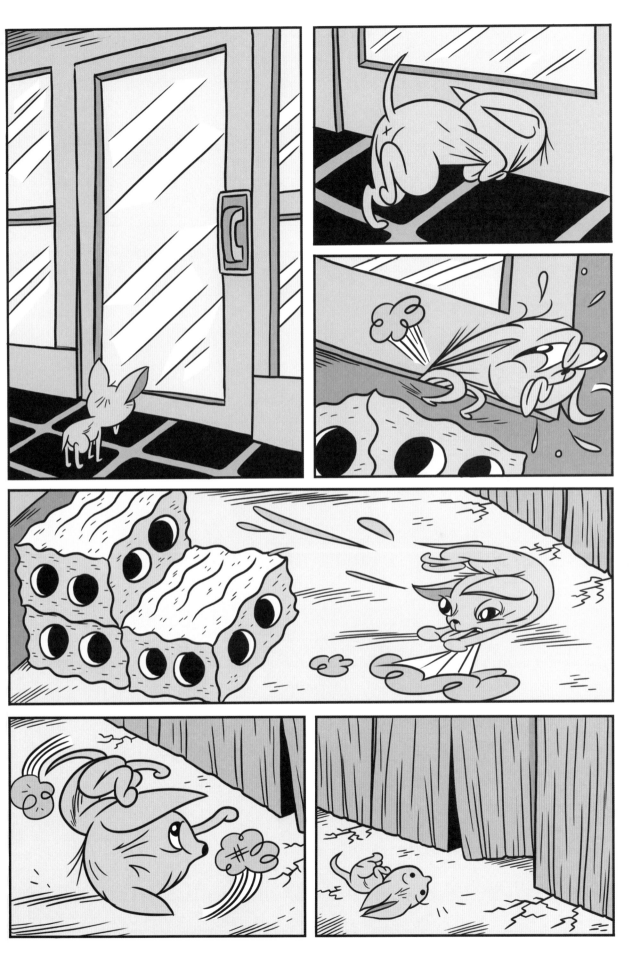

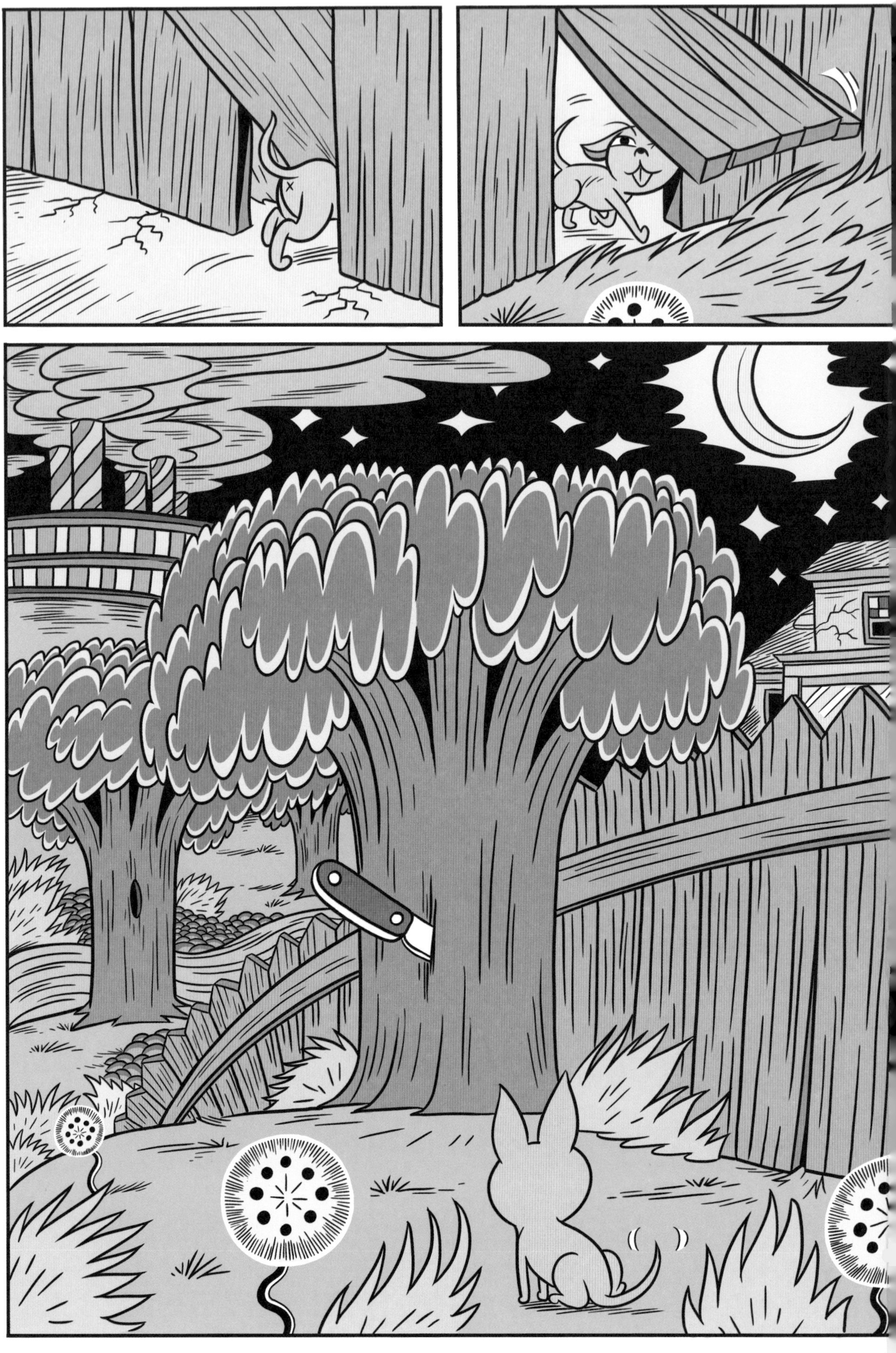

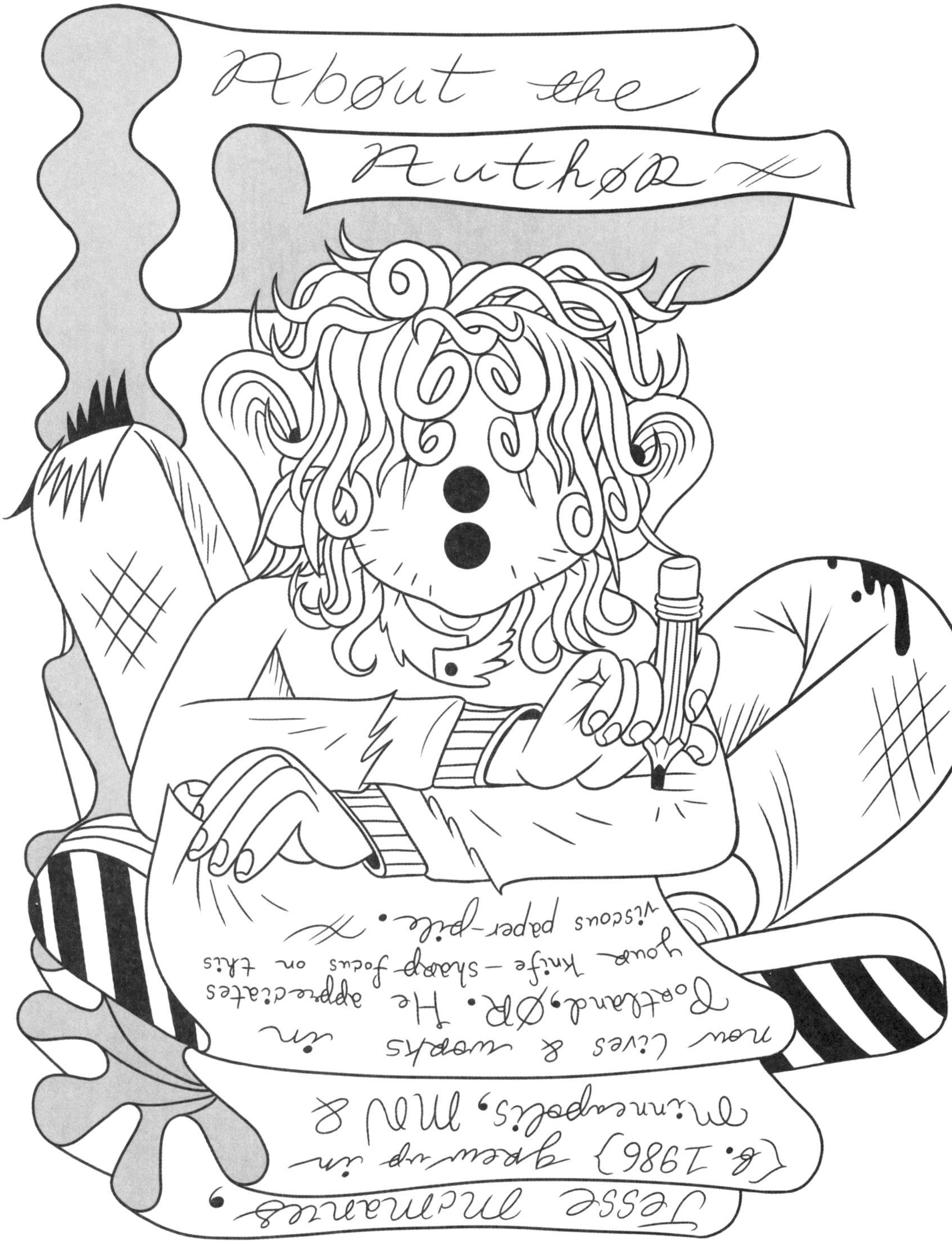
About the Author
Jesse McManus, (b. 1986) grew up in Minneapolis, MN &
now lives & works in Portland, OR. He appreciates
your knife-sharp focus on this
viscous paper-pile.

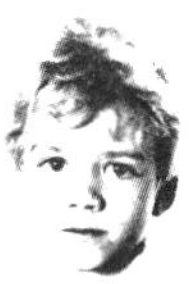

THIS BOOK IS DEDICATED TO my mom & DAD.
{R.I.P. TROWSER Ø1999→Ø2013} THANKS TO:
POOKA HAYSTACK, PANDREW STRONJ, MASON STRONJ,
AUSTIN E., JTM, J. OVERBY, MR. COLOSTOMY,
BENT IMAGE LAB, GRIDLORDS, SMOKE SIGNAL
& BIG BRAIN COMICS.

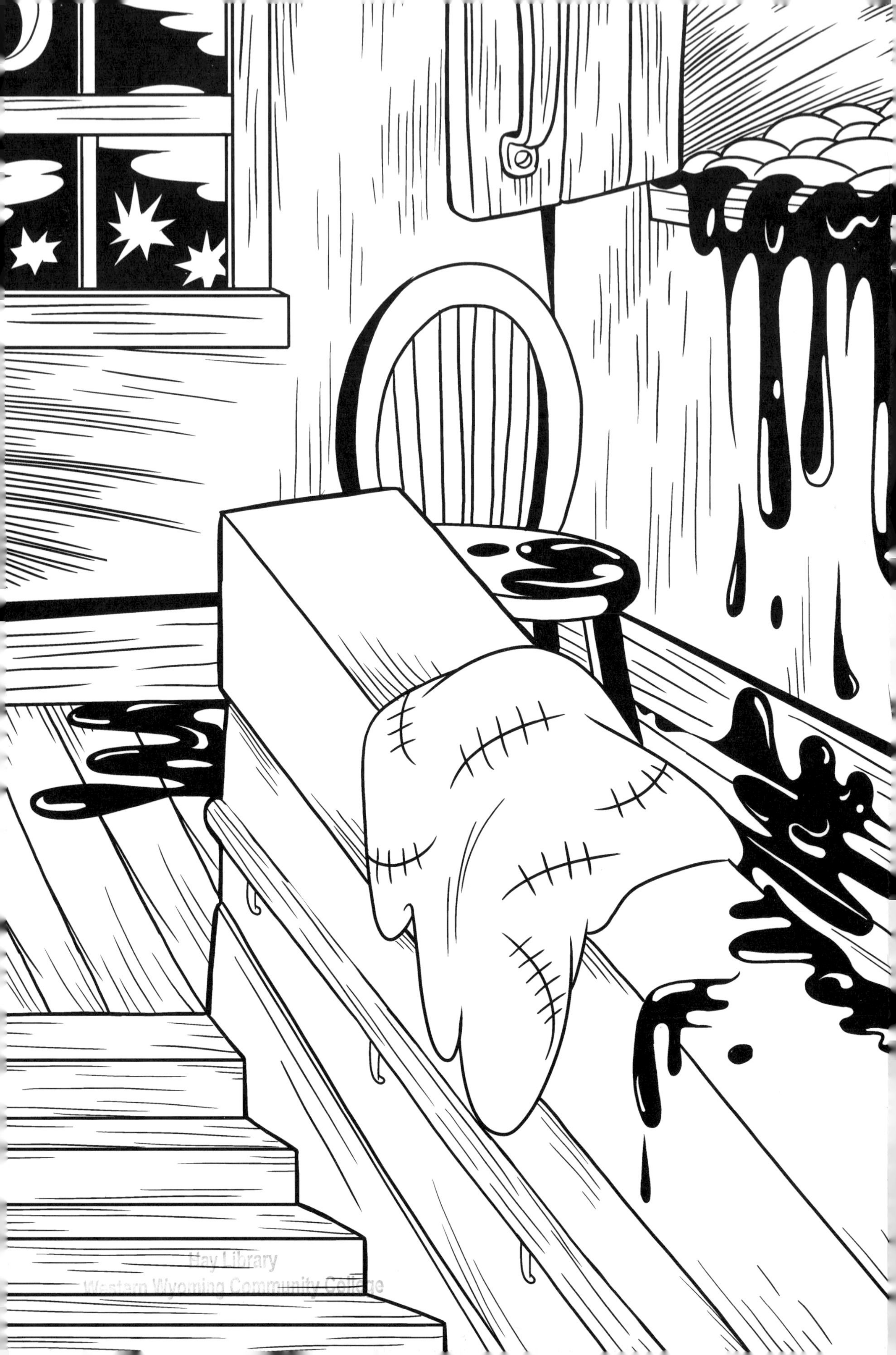